N.L. Terteling Library

Swisher Memorial Collection

THE COLLEGE *of* IDAHO

THE

T R U E

AND

AUTHENTIC HISTORY

OF

JENNY DORSET

Consisting of

A NARRATIVE BY A RETAINER,

Mr. Henry Hawthorne

Along with the History of Two Households,
that of Dorset and Smythe,
and How They Came to Their Great Battle
and How It Finally Ended, &tc.

AND

VARIOUS SONGS, JOURNAL EXCERPTS, AND

LETTERS SUCH AS SEEM PERTINENT

PRINTED FOR THE AUTHOR BY THOMAS AND
JOHN WRIGHT IN CHARLESTON, THE YEAR 1795

— *A Novel by* —

PHILIP LEE WILLIAMS

Published by
LONGSTREET PRESS, INC.
A subsidiary of Cox Newspapers,
A subsidiary of Cox Enterprises, Inc.
2140 Newmarket Parkway
Suite 122
Marietta, GA 30067

Printed in the United States of America

1st printing April 1997

Library of Congress Catalog Card Number: 96-79797

ISBN 1-56352-365-5

Book design by Jill Dible
Jacket design by Tonya Beach
Imaged by OGI, Forest Park, GA

Words and music for songs in *Jenny Dorset* composed by Philip Lee Williams

THIS BOOK IS FOR
Linda, Brandon and Megan

AND IN MEMORY OF MY GRANDPARENTS,
Arthur Samuel Williams (1891–1935)
and Isabel Jaynes Williams (1890–1947)

Lee Oliver Sisk (1898–1969)
and Lillie Mae Kirby Sisk (1898–1988)

CONTENTS.

BOOK I.

BOOK II.

BOOK III.

BOOK IV.

BOOK V.

BOOK VI.

BOOK VII.

AUTHOR'S PROLOGUE

I authorize, swear, commit my bond, Etc., that this History is true insofar as God gives us the knowledge of the True. I have changed no names, spared no feelings where it could not be avoided, and lived honestly through all the parts of this Story. To those who might gainsay me regarding particular dates and circumstances, I can only say that God, in the end, will sort Truth from Fiction, and that Time will serve me well, as I have served it.

Obediently, Etc.,
Henry Hawthorne

THIS

HISTORY

IS

DEDICATED

TO

GEN. GEORGE WASHINGTON

Lately President of These United States

IN HOPES THAT HE MAY LOOK WITH FAVOR

AS NEED BE UPON YR. HUMBLE SERVANT

Henry Hawthorne

THE

T R U E

AND

AUTHENTIC HISTORY

OF

JENNY DORSET

BOOK I.

— 1. —

CONTAINING OBSERVATIONS ON THE WORLD AND ON THE CHARACTER
OF TWO FAMILIES, SPECIFICALLY ONE JENNY DORSET.

Nature, I have learned in my long life, may be frugal or extravagant by turns, bestowing grace on one generation and grief on the next. For myself, Nature saw fit to honor me with modesty and manner and to punish me with such a great age that I have outlived even the most sprightly of my children. But no matter. The History you hold in your hands is in a sense the chronicle of this young country and its age. If we have not yet a Holinshed or Pliny, then perhaps you will forgive the audacity of one Henry Hawthorne, your humble servant.

This History, however, is not the story of my life and burdens, though I often find myself tangled in it. It regards the life of one Jenny Dorset, a woman who in her passions was undiscriminating; in her manner, unmanageable; and who gave her parents great joy and great sorrow.

The Reader may think from the above that I was in love with this lady. But she was much younger than I, and besides that, I was not of her class, she being the natural daughter of Adam Dorset and his wife, Lydia Foxe, both of fine families, and I being part of their household staff and the child of a poor mother and a father lost upon the sea. I never thought that I might rise beyond my birth and become part of that pleasant brood of landowners whose quarrels are mostly invented to stifle boredom. I have always been a fortunate man, however, and have moved with the pace of months, not hours, of tortoises, not hares.

This History, however, does not merely concern the misadventures of Jenny Dorset but the fate of two families, one born to wealth and another arriving late to it and therefore coveting it even more. I had the good fortune to serve the former, at the estate of Adam and Lydia Dorset. They lived twelvemile from Charles Town on a magnificent plantation which grew fatter each year with rice, indigo, and cotton. Both the Dorset and Foxe families brought money to the match, and so barely ten years after Mr. Dorset married Miss Foxe, their wealth was established. God graced the union with three sons, Abel, Isaac, and Matthew, before He gave the Dorsets a daughter they named Jenny. Of the three boys, Matthew was the kindest, given to idling his hours away studying farm animals, while Isaac was a thick-headed boy whose stubbornness would be his undoing. Abel was the eldest, and a boy whose seriousness at first masked a sour disposition and a tendency to be choleric even in the best of times. The dramatic change in his character was a happy turn both for the family and for the Province of South Carolina.

Within about half a mile of the Dorsets' mansion and vast holdings was another plantation. This house was built within great splendor, less because its owner was inclined toward that manner than because of the message it gave to the Dorsets. Charles Smythe had come from Virginia with nothing more than the shirt upon his back and managed, through clever buying and selling, to raise great holdings in Charles Town in a space of less than a decade. Where Mr. Dorset indulged in the pleasures of aristocracy, Mr. Smythe was suspicious of leisure. If Mr. Dorset built a hut for his hounds, Mr. Smythe built a house for his. Where Mr. Dorset raised fifty guests for his hunt, Mr. Smythe invited three hundred to his. Charles Smythe's wife was his greatest ornament, a pleasant and fetching woman born Ophelia Van Dyke to an educated but poor North Carolina family who worshipped only one thing beyond God: William Shakespeare. As Ophelia carried this passion with her after her marriage to Mr. Smythe, their three heirs were named, in succession, Hamlet, Iago, and Fortinbras. Mrs. Smythe never quite forgave her husband for the naming of Iago. As she had named Hamlet, she gave her husband the right to name the second child. Casually opening a volume beside her bed, he placed his finger with great misfortune on a scene from *Othello*, and thus poor Iago received his burden. (Even worse, due to his general lack of knowledge, Mr. Smythe pronounced the appellation "Eye-A-Go," and forced the rest of the house to do the same.)

And so, set against each other were two great fortunes and two families of varying circumstances. And yet all would agree that if there were a comet in that heaven of gentry life, it was Jenny Dorset. If she burned out rather too quickly for all who knew her, perhaps it was God's plan, lest the rest of Charles Town, perhaps even South Carolina and Georgia, burn with her.

— 2. —

MY OWN HISTORY AND HOW IT AFFECTS
OUR STORY OF JENNY DORSET.

If the history of Jenny Dorset requires a certain amount of tact and turning aside at crucial moments lest propriety be offended, my own story has less spice. But a few comments are perhaps in order so the Reader can judge me.

As I have said, my own father was lost at sea. That is how Mother always put it to me, and how I eagerly accepted it. A pall of familial tragedy slipped on my shoulders very early, and I wore it like a king's cloak. When other boys might speak of their fathers with fear or loathing, I would only pull myself upright, stare into the near distance and proclaim, "My father was lost at sea." The images positively thrilled me, to be honest. He died when I was but a weanling. I remember neither England, the ship, nor the man himself. Since Mother explained no further than her ready-made statement, I accepted that somehow my father had been swept overboard in a mischance of storm or other natural violence in the North Atlantic. I raised his stature to something heroic, as might befit a Perseus or Ulysses. Perhaps, if his legend be known, Dr. Arne or Mr. Handel might be induced, I thought, to compose a work about his exploits.

After a series of jobs in Charles Town, my mother was fortunate to find work for us with Mr. Adam Dorset when I was but seventeen and he twenty-two. It was therefore something of a shock when, in my twenty-first year, a traveler to the Dorset estate, which was called Longacre, had been on the very ship, the *Olive Branch*, which had brought us to Charles Town from London. I had by that time acquired the manners which have so often been described as elegant and would not have dared to speak directly to this visitor, a merchant with whom Mr. Dorset had some business. The man's name was Burke, and his physiognomy was as unpleasant as his name.

The night was, I believe, in January, for I remember a great fire in the hearth of the dining room. Mr. Dorset at this time was only twenty-six himself and had not yet married Miss Lydia Foxe nor begat Abel, Isaac, Matthew, or Jenny. Indeed, Miss Lydia Foxe, later the lady of the manor and my employer, was but fourteen that year as I reckon it. Adam Dorset had that lightness of spirit that all men have who have not yet entered the Holy State of matrimony, and he welcomed Burke with a suckling pig and a group of fiddlers. As I attended table, they roared with drink and laughter, speaking with great fine humor and indelicacy of the men and women of Charles Town. (Though now our town is properly called "Charleston," I can think of it in no other way than it was called in my youth.)

Only afterward, when nearly everyone had retired, did this Burke approach me as I was banking the fires for the night, and grin through rows of fine teeth that were small enough for a young child or a fur-bearing animal.

"You know what befell your papa?" he said. He had already made it known that he had travelled for years on the *Olive Branch*, so I assumed he knew the entire heroic truth of my father's fate.

"He was lost at sea," I said.

Mr. Burke at this point began to laugh peculiarly through his nose, so that he resembled nothing so much as a springtime stallion looking for his mare. He leaned drunkenly toward me and fell heavily to the floor. I helped him up, and he brushed himself off as well as he could. He looked very serious for a moment, and then, seeing me again, fell once more into a vast laughing fit.

"He drank above half a barrel of Portugee wine the last day of the voyage and fell into the harbor as we docked," said Burke, still snorting and laughing. "Captain, he said he never in twenty year on the sea seen a thing sink so fast."

"My father," I said with persistence and honor, "was lost at sea."

"Ask your mum," he said, and then he passed out headlong, landing with great effect on the cold floor. I dragged him to a divan and raised him to it because it was my job to do so.

A few days later, I confronted my mother with Burke's heinous charge, and she only shrugged and sighed.

"Well, dear, it *was* the sea," she said, and nothing more, which speaks well for her tact and poorly for my gullibility. After that, I was careful to give little weight to family legends and I was even more circumspect when it came to saying anything about myself.

But as Nature has allowed me this long life, I suppose She cannot mind me now unburdening what is (in truth) a sad but entertaining and instructive story. If I knew little about the truth of my father's passing, I found that no one else knew much more of their heritage or seemed to care much. The truth is that Men will live as they might, with one eye for the ladies and the other for the Devil, and whatever else may come can only be greeted with a sigh at best.

— 3. —

IN WHICH THE READER IS GIVEN CERTAIN WARNING ABOUT
THE CONTENT OF THIS HISTORY AND OFFERED THE CHANCE TO READ
SOMETHING ELSE, ERE HE BE OFFENDED.

Delicacy is the palette of one, like myself, who has served a great house. I was expected to anticipate company; accept blame; attend outrageous turns of Fortune as if they happened every day; and all the while never raise my voice, much less my hand. My dedication has been such that I have mastered all these arts and more.

And yet as God values honesty and forgives sinners, I cannot relate this history of Jenny Dorset without stepping across many bounds of propriety. Although I will spare the reader full knowledge of the marvelous variety of profanities that Adam Dorset possessed, I must lunge at his character with the lance of truth or I will miss him entirely. Just so with Jenny.

In her early childhood, she was quite the trouble of her mother's life. Early on, she picked up her father's tendency to exclaim about insignificant things.

I very well recall one evening in summer when Jenny was perhaps six, when Mr. Dorset and the family were outside on the great lawn playing at bowls, a game he took seriously and at which he was very poor. Abel, who was nine at the time, had repeatedly bested his father to the vast amusement of his wife and the other two boys. Jenny, seeing her father lose once more, began to wave her hands wildly over her head and shriek incoherently.

"You're the worst G—d—d player at bowls on this earth!" she cried.

The family became still. A moment later, Abel began to titter, and Mr. Dorset responded as most fathers would and backhanded him so hard the poor boy landed upon his head and began to weep. Isaac and Matthew, equally put out by their father's outburst, also began to cry, and they huddled to their mother as puppies do. Only Jenny remained back, rocking on her feet and regarding her father with what seemed great amusement.

"I'll have your mouth scoured with soap!" cried Mr. Dorset. He took a step toward her, and she took a step backward and began to laugh. How can I describe that laughter, even at her tender age? It was like snowflakes spread by angels, like the most beautiful melody ever scored, like the wrinkling of leaves by a warm spring wind. He took another step forward, she another step back, laughing more and more so that her entire frame shook. "Arrgh! You shan't run from me!"

"You can't catch me," she said, trying to take her breath back from her lovely laughter. The boys, sensing something terrible and yet marvelous, quit huddling around their mother, and Abel's tears were stanched.

"I'll take the measure of your vile language!" he said, and he began to chase after her. Believing his rights as father would give him the strength to catch Jenny, he began to chase her around the green, and Old Bob (of whom more later) and I hid our amusement but the other children did not. They began to openly cheer for Jenny's escape, to the great consternation of their father and the modest amusement of their mother.

"Stop or I'll thrash you!" Adam Dorset cried.

"You're G—d—d terrible at bowls!" Jenny cried, still running and still laughing.

"Waugh!" cried Mr. Dorset. His arms flew over his head as if he were catching on fire. "I'll kill the man taught you such filth!"

No matter how much he chased her, arms high over his head like a phantom of the fanciest tales, he could get no closer. Jenny, who in her sprightly childhood might have distanced him by a fair mile, stayed only just out of his grasp. At this point, I glanced over at Mrs. Dorset, and upon her face was a smile of light amusement as one often sees in women who find their mates roundly mastered. On and on, they chased, not unlike the ceaseless whirling of Paolo and Francesca.

Finally, gasping and holding his chest, face red as life can allow before it fades into an apoplexy, Mr. Dorset suddenly stopped running and watched with unabashed pleasure as Jenny flitted around the vast expanse of yard like a firefly. Indeed, I thought then that she might rise into the oaks surrounding that yard if she had only a mind to do it. She looked at her gasping father and laughed as angels do, and raised her arms over her head in mimic of his chase and danced and danced far into the gloaming and then back.

Later, Mr. Dorset held the girl on his lap and read her a story and acted as if the fine farce had never happened. We all might have taken a lesson then of Jenny's ability to act as she pleased and then be praised for it, good or ill, but we could no more censure her for long than God could ultimately censure Adam. As God let the first Father live (though out of Eden), Mr. Dorset sighed and wondered what hand of Glory was at work in his only daughter.

— 4. —

WE GO BACKWARD AND ESTABLISH OUR HISTORY BEFORE
THE BIRTH OF JENNY DORSET, INCLUDING AN EXPLANATION OF MR.
ADAM DORSET'S ODD PROCLIVITY FOR PERIODS OF RELIGIOUS FERVOR.

No man can say what traits bred in himself are passed to his children. Fathers often ascribe their best characteristics (if any) to their children. Mothers, ready to agree in part, ascribe their children's bad behavior to their fathers. I have observed that a powerful belief in goodness is a slippery parcel, and that those who grasp for it most, find it most eludes them. And so it was with Mr. Dorset, who (as I am told) from his earliest years went through cycles, as the moon does, of extreme debauchery on one hand and extreme piety on the other. I know that in my years of service to him, Mr. Dorset might come home from Town smelling of rum and Heaven knows what else one evening and the next morning implore all of us to join him on our knees in prayer.

As I have said, I came to his service early. I myself was born in 1725, and we came to him, Mother and I, in 1742, when I was seventeen. He was but a few years older than I, and yet he was already building his plantation, for if he had genius in anything, it was in raising pounds and pence.

Mother was a cook and house servant, and, at first, I helped tend the fine yard he was building, but soon he fancied me a house and body servant, a role I found suited my natural taciturnity. He bought me a fine suit, a powdered wig, and good cotton stockings.

Mr. Dorset was not meanly born. His father was one Parker Dorset, who was a silversmith. But the father died early of some fever or another, and the mother was unable to find another mate and so slipped from one house to the next as the silversmith's money was spent, until she had to take work briefly as a domestic. That bitter episode in Adam Dorset's life often came to the fore when he spoke of his youth, and he proclaimed that his own children would never have to endure such shame. (For her part, Adam's mother, after he had made his fortune and given her a fair share of it, took a packet to London and never returned and rarely wrote. She never saw her granddaughter, Jenny, which is just as well.)

Mr. Dorset much later sent to London for a portrait of his mother, but what came back was the image of a haughty woman who appears to have only barely escaped something terribly unpleasant. To me it proved that water is often thicker than blood and that gratitude has no sure port in the harbor of family.

I was twenty-four when Mr. Dorset married the fetching Miss Foxe and children began to grace their union. After the marriage, he became more settled because his wife demanded it, but before, when the plantation was rising and spreading, he was quite a rake, and the staff despaired lest he come to some unfortunate end in Charles Town or during one of his riotous hunts.

"Hawthorne, so you think we go to Heaven when we die?" he asked me one day when he was in the yard firing his piece at any animal which moved. This was a year or two before his marriage.

"The Bible guarantees us that reward, sir," I said.

"Bah!" he cried. "Waugh! Then where do slaves and Indians go?"

"I haven't the grasp of theology to know that, sir," I said.

"They go to Heaven?" he said, voice rising. "If they go to Heaven, then how could we live with ourselves? What if a slave goes to Heaven with an iron in his hand? He would smite the man who beat him upon this Earth, Hawthorne. Can you think of such a thing? Or dogs? What of dogs? I could not bear the thought of a Heaven without dogs! What does the Bible say of dogs?"

"I am not certain on that score."

"No one is certain! Then I shall peek into Heaven itself and find the answer for myself! A peek into Heaven, Hawthorne! Think on it!" With that, he fired his gun at the sky at a steep angle, toward nothing I saw that flew, unless it was far above the clouds and bore the shape of angels.

Some time after that, he left for town on a fine morning. It was a cold day with a rain coming on, and Mother was baking pies from the great pumpkins we had grown that summer. I recall that aroma as one recalls love from a distance, rich and lovely, yet sad, too, because it just escapes our reach. The day was quiet as I recall, except for the groans of a slave named John who badly cut a finger while beheading a chicken for our supper that evening.

The next day, a steady cold rain rinsed the countryside, the kind of day a house servant does not mind, for it portends fine fires and dinners and rum and looking out the broad windows over the plantation, down toward the swamps where the rice grew in season. Late in the morning, the front door opened just as I was wiping dust off the bannister of the magnificent staircase that rose to the second floor. It was Mr. Dorset, smelling of rum, clothing torn, eyes wild, staggering from point to point, mouth slack with fear.

"Hawthorne! Oh! Waugh!" he cried. He staggered through the hallway into the large comfortable sitting room and collapsed in a heavy leather chair near the fire, which I had urged to a fine height only minutes before.

"Sir, what in the world has happened?" I said. "Shall I send for a physic?"

"Yes!" he cried, leaping up and then falling to his knees before the blaze. "I mean no! Get on your knees with me, Hawthorne!" A few of the other servants, including my mother, were standing in the doorway staring in shock at Mr. Dorset, and for a moment I hesitated. I was looking at the others, when he grasped my sleeve and pulled me to the polished floor and made me kneel beside him. His eyes were round, eyebrows folded up so high they seemed part of his hair.

"A physic, Mr. Dorset?" My mother told Old Bob to go put on a kettle and brew some coffee.

"The Great Physic, Hawthorne!" he cried. He tented his fingers beneath his chin and began to sway back and forth. "I came up the road in the night, and halfway home, a light came from the heavens, and I fell off my horse, and God climbed into my chemise with me."

I tented my fingers with him and glanced at my mother, who had closed her eyes and was shaking her head. Molly McNew was fanning old Mrs. Wilson vigorously, and Molly's twin brother, Tom, was grinning like a dog let in from a storm.

"God was in your clothing, sir?"

"In my very chemise, and my trousers, too!"

Mrs. Wilson emitted a small but terrible cry. Tom McNew ran away, carrying a brief gale of laughter with him.

"In your trousers, too, sir?"

"It was the Light of Galilee, Hawthorne! Waugh! And I begged His pardon for being insensible with drink and fatigue and for losing seventy pounds and several pence, I forget how much, at cards. And He spoke to me in a great whisper, like the sigh of a wind in the night, and He said the world was ruined and that I should help make it a better place to live. Oh! I shall do that! Hawthorne, look at me."

He turned and grasped both my hands in his, which were wet and frozen with cold. His hands trembled. His mouth wobbled like the line of flight a butterfly takes. Mrs. Wilson, who was very stout and had poor nerves, was still making pitiful cries regarding Mr. Dorset's remark upon his trousers.

"I am looking, sir."

"Forgive me all the wrongs I have done you!"

"Sir, you have never done me a wrong in your life," I said, quite truthfully. Though he was sometimes passing strange, he never mistreated anyone, slave or servant, though he could be too merry when drunk.

"I have! I have done ill toward every living creature! I beg you to forgive me! I beg the squirrels and the birds and the deer to forgive me! Naaagh! I ask God to escape my clothing and see that I ask forgiveness for my multiple sins!"

With that, he leaped up and began to run toward the assembled servants in the doorway, I presume to ask their forgiveness, but the effect, considering his wild eyes and soaked clothing, was to frighten them insensibly, and Mrs. Wilson, heretofore merely in a swoon, fell heavily to the floor, though Tom McNew, who had returned, softened her collapse somewhat.

Fortunately for us all, Mr. Dorset took that opportunity to collapse as well. I carried him upstairs to his bed, undressed him, and put him in the covers, then got his fireplace going with a fine steady blaze before closing his door and coming back down.

"He's given Mrs. Wilson the vapors," said my mother, who was by the large fire in the sitting room. Tom McNew came giggling into the room.

"Did you shake God from his trousers?" he asked.

"He is asleep now," I said loyally. "I shall see to his health when he awakens."

Fortunately for us all, he did not awaken that day, but on the following morning, he came downstairs fit and hearty as if nothing had happened, and that evening, two ladies we had never seen before arrived to visit him, and one slept in a guest bedroom, and the other, apparently, slept in the room with Mr. Dorset. Mrs. Wilson the next day said God was going to strike Mr. Dorset dead, but I have come to find that God has a greater sense of the ridiculous than most give Him credit for.

— 5. —

WHEREIN THE CHARACTER OF MISS LYDIA FOXE DORSET,
THE MOTHER OF OUR JENNY, IS SOMEWHAT EXPLAINED,
OR EXPLAINED AS FAR AS WOMAN CAN BE.

No one who looked upon the lithe and lovely form of Jenny Dorset could doubt from where her beauty came. In her prime, long before the years and the worries of life came upon her, Mrs. Dorset was wondrously beautiful, though full of cares for her wayward brood and her uncontrollable husband.

Mr. Dorset met her at church in Charles Town during one of his periods of piety and good manners. He was impressed with her yellow hair, blue eyes, and good family, and she was impressed by his self-possession. Women believe ofttimes that a godly man is a good one, though they soon disabuse that notion, each in turn, for no man can be long godly with a beautiful woman, and no woman can be beautiful long with a godly man.

She soon came to the plantation, which he had never called anything, but began calling Longacre for the effect.

"Upon my word, Henry, how long since you and your mother came into my service at Longacre?" he asked. They were dining. Lydia had come with her brother William as an escort.

"Pardon, sir? Long what?" I said. He looked at me as if stricken. Lydia glanced at Mr. Dorset, and William was preoccupied only with his manners, which were dainty as a girl's.

"Longacre," he said, leaning forward and glaring at me. "Our plantation here. Hawthorne, what's come over you?"

"Ah, Longacre," I said. "My hearing is poor today. A fowling piece blew its pan this morning. Forgive me, sir."

"Dear, dear," said William Foxe.

"Bless your heart," said Lydia. Ready to seize the day with his godliness, Mr. Dorset held up his palm to me in a kind of blessing or anointment.

"Then I shall certainly pray that your full hearing be restored," he said.

The courtship went forward with great haste, because Lydia felt she had found a fair match, and Mr. Dorset was eager to solidify his position in the Province with a good marriage.

Serving a master and a manor well requires a balance of dedication and tact, so I could not forebear standing aside with Miss Lydia Foxe on one of her subsequent visits and hint that Mr. Dorset's godliness and piety were of a variety that came and went like the seasons.

"It is like the phases of the moon, Miss Foxe," I said. "Each day of the month, she shows a different face, an inconstancy that is not unlike the way men who believe in God approach their Maker. For at times, they will be out of sorts with Him for shaping this life for an end upon this Earth only when cares have finally been overcome."

"Oh you dear," she said. "You are as kind as Mr. Dorset. I hope you come to a reconciliation with God before your day to leave."

"Ma'am?" I said. At that point, Mr. Dorset came into the room and swept her away. Later I told my mother that at least I had tried. She was none too impressed.

For reasons I cannot understand, Mr. Dorset maintained his composure throughout the courtship, which lasted more than eight months, coming home in sad condition from town only once, bearing with him a bolt of calico cloth and a red-haired woman who called herself Antonia.

I went with him when he presented himself to Lydia Foxe's father, a grave and unpleasant man who had clearly asked after Mr. Dorset's reputation but was too mannerly to bring it up directly. While they talked, I stood in the entrance hall, wearing my powdered wig and a look of detachment, but I overheard the conversation, during which Mr. Dorset tried his best to be acquisitive and godly at the same time.

"Sir, I know from your holdings and transactions that you can financially care for my daughter's well-being," said Mr. Foxe, who was more than six feet tall and strong enough to make the shorter Mr. Dorset go white. "I am more concerned that she be treated well, that you will care for her in all the vagaries that life can bring toward you. Plus, as you know, she has always lived in town and may not be suited to live upon a plantation."

"She will be treated as a servant treats his queen," said Mr. Dorset with a grand flourish, "as a pilgrim treats his saint, as a man should treat his wife, with godly devotion and a kind and loving heart."

"Well, then," said Mr. Foxe. "And you will always attend to your character in her presence?"

"As I do in the presence of any man or woman," he said with more hope that proof. Unable to stifle a brief laugh, I covered it with a cough, and presently a tiny fat woman came shuttling out to me asking if I wished some tea. I did not.

The wedding was a grand affair, with a round of parties that exalted Mr. Dorset and exhausted the rest of us. Only once did Mr. Dorset come near to revealing his full nature, during a ball at our home, which he had now begun to call Longacre, the name by which it went from then on.

That particular ball was the culmination of a tumultuous day, which began with games and sport on the grounds, including a horse race, cockfighting (at which Mr. Dorset was particularly keen), and a grinning contest for old women. One particular woman, who served a plantation about twenty miles from Longacre, took the prize in grinning. She was near ninety, they said, and she could touch the tip of her nose with her bottom lip, an achievement that gave the men great merriment and horrified nearly all the women. Mr. Dorset, for his part, fell upon the ground holding his sides on watching her, to the shock of his intended, who huddled a bit closer to her brother William, who was dabbing his nose with a handkerchief.

Mr. Charles Smythe had only recently married Ophelia Van Dyke, and she was carrying their first child, who was to become Hamlet Smythe. She was indisposed but came anyway, and Mr. Smythe kept sourly commenting upon the marriage because he knew it would add wealth and standing to Mr. Dorset.

Mr. Dorset's indiscretion, however, was not his lack of manners during the grinning contest. Late in the afternoon, when the barbecue was nearly cooked on the spit out back and the fragrance of the beeves was nigh irresistible to the company, I went upstairs in the house to get a clean shirt for Mr. Dorset, who had soiled his during the cockfights. The house was peculiarly quiet, except for what sounded like a dog growling — an odd sound since Mr. Dorset's hounds, of which he was very proud, were never let loose to roam the yards until Jenny Dorset came along. I opened the door to the clothing closet and was not shocked to find Mr. Dorset kissing a woman named Mrs. Daulty, murmuring drunkenly while pushing his hand up along her exposed thigh. I cleared my throat as I came in, and she leaped up and ran from the closet, passing me so close I could smell her fragrance.

Mr. Dorset lay back, looking at first irritated and then somewhat grateful.

"You find in me a man with a weakness for the female sex," he said.

"I'm not the one from whom you should protect that secret," I said.

"You're an honorable man, Hawthorne," he cried, leaping up and clapping me on the back.

"That is my misfortune," I said.

"Waugh! That you should have come into my service! Fortuna! The turn of the great wheel! Brave Hawthorne!" he said. I made him change his shirt while he spoke of his wedding, of his bride-to-be, of the ball to come that evening.

"Be careful of Mr. Smythe, sir," I said. "He speaks ill of you."

"That blockhead!" he shouted. "Aye! I'll cut him to the quick, that pasty-faced monster! I've seen blobs hauled in the nets of the sea prettier than he is!"

At that, he began to laugh somewhat hysterically, and I only calmed him by grabbing his shoulders and shaking him very hard. After that rough handling, he regained his manners and went back down to the others. Mrs. Daulty later received singing lessons from one Signor Alvarez and moved to London, where her debut was greeted with some hostility.

For her part, Lydia did not appear to know of Mr. Dorset's dalliances, and she remained as lovely and chaste a bride as one could want. Unfortunately, she found out soon enough that if Woman's feet are constant, Man's feet are almost always made of clay.

— 6. —

THE SERVANTS OF THE SMYTHE AND DORSET FAMILIES EXPLAINED,
BOTH AS TO THEIR NAMES AND POSITIONS AND THEIR REASON
FOR BEING IN THIS HISTORY.

No good servant ever serves anyone better than himself. Unless he find satisfaction in the establishment and protection of manners and order, he cannot find pleasure in the security of assisting a person of means.

Because employment with the wealthy was much desired, those who captured the jobs tended to keep them for a long time, often until death. So it was with the service staff of Longacre. The eldest was Robert Burke, known to everyone as Old Bob. Born in about 1697, he was the very picture of elegance, or at least had been at some dim point in his past. By the time our history opens in 1753 with the birth of Jenny Dorset, Old Bob already possessed that astounding facility for becoming lost and disordered that he kept for the next twenty years and more.

He was unnaturally tall, perhaps near six feet, but thin as a razor. He was also moderately deaf and so walked around all day with one hand cupped to an ear lest a command escape him. He was always eager to please Mr. Dorset but rarely did, as he was slow as the movement of months in his actions. He was not unpleasant but neither was he inclined to think beyond his most immediate task. He was in later years inordinately forgetful as well. Once, during a dinner that Mr. Dorset was giving with some irritation for the entire Smythe clan, Old Bob was sent for more wine. When, after a time, he did not come back, Mr. Dorset himself leaped up and went after him. Ten minutes passed before he returned.

"The old fool's climbed one of the apple trees!" he cried. "Waugh! What comes into his mind?" Mr. Smythe might have just heard of victory on the battlefield so great was his triumph. Jenny, anyway, came to rely greatly on Old Bob, and her mother more than once was to say that Jenny's penchant for running away must have come from Old Bob.

The head of the household staff was Mrs. Emma Wilson, a dour and stout woman born about 1705, as I reckon, in Ireland. She never smiled, often wrung her hands in despair, and prayed fervently that God would take her to Heaven rather sooner than later. During her service there were times many of us wished God were more prompt on that score as well. She loved nothing more than giving orders, unless it was urging on Mr. Dorset's bouts of piety, of which she approved. She had gray hair the whole time I knew her, a thick nose with a small wen on the side, and a mouth no more than a thin and anxious line, which wobbled whenever she was preparing to lose her temper.

My mother and myself I have spoken of already.

The last members of Mr. Dorset's household staff were quite the most interesting and came to have a strange part in the drama of his life. Tom and Molly McNew were orphan twins that Mr. Dorset had taken when they were children in Charles Town. Fourteen years younger than myself, they were both red-haired and covered with freckles.

Mr. Smythe's staff was as imperious as their master, and possessed, in one of those odd coincidences which life often provides but books do not, its own set of twins, which Mrs. Smythe insisted on helping to name. They had been orphans. The twins she named Thomas and William, but out of gratitude when she came into the Smythe household, she renamed them Desdemona and Roderigo. They were the same age as Tom and Molly McNew, which in my humble estimation was a joke delivered to the plantations by a jolly and mirthful God.

Roderigo and Desdemona were among the happiest and least-principled people I ever saw. If Jenny Dorset were rather wild and full of spirit, Desdemona Smartt was like a leaf in a storm. She was never out of trouble, and often her brother was with her. Neither was as attractive as the red-haired McNew twins, but they were not unpleasant, either, being blond-haired and blue-eyed.

The head of the Smythe servants was one Diana Seton, altogether the most charming woman I ever knew in my life. Even more ancient than Old Bob, she was tall, regal, fair, and nearly bald, which she hid with a man's powdered wig. An apoplexy had rendered her left hand almost useless, but she would not complain. Her husband had been killed in a tavern when they were quite young, and her three children had all died of various misfortunes along the way, and yet she remained unbitter.

The final member of the Smythes' household staff was Herr Schlitz, who was in his early fifties at the birth of Jenny Dorset, an immigrant from Germany who had never (or so it was reputed throughout the area) smiled in his entire life. His command of the English language was weak at best. Once I said, "Herr Schlitz, I hope you have planned well for the Smythe ball next week," and he bowed at the waist and said, "Well for the times, people and town, pig things, Herr Hawthorne." I smiled at him, but of course he did not smile back. I do not think God could bear the presence of such a dour man, but I am probably wrong.

For myself, I married a wonderful woman named Anne Wells, and she bore me two daughters, but as I have resolved to speak as little as I may of my own circumstances in this History, and as discretion dictates I remove them from the sometimes sordid goings-on herein, we shall take our leave of my family for some time to come.

If the competition between the Smythes and the Dorsets was a river, the battle between their servants was the sea. In this they were encouraged by their employers, and these wars ranged from minor pleasantries such as cockfights to straightforward fistfights.

The intrigues almost never stopped during the time I served Mr. Dorset, which was nearly all my life. One by one, God plucked that company to Glory, or at least I hope that He did. One can only be charitable for others who were weak, for God loves one who forgives, if not forgets.

— 7. —

IN WHICH WE FINALLY ARRIVE AT THE BIRTH OF JENNY DORSET
AND DISCOVER MR. DORSET'S INDISPOSITION ON THAT NIGHT,
WHEN HE BECOMES A FATHER FOR THE FOURTH TIME AND RECEIVES
A WELL-DESERVED TONGUE-LASHING FROM MRS. WILSON.

The plantation grew heavy with its bounty as the years passed after the wedding of Adam Dorset and Lydia Foxe. Abel was born in 1750, a very difficult birth which greatly taxed Mrs. Dorset. Isaac came in 1751, and Matthew in 1752. If Mrs. Dorset had chosen to care for the children herself, she might have been too exhausted to bear another child and the world would have been deprived of the life of Jenny Dorset. By then, however, Mr. Dorset was so wealthy that he hired more household servants to help care for the children, who were brought at opportune times to their mother and father for brief audiences so as not to vex them overly.

As the time came for Mrs. Dorset's confinement with Jenny Dorset, her husband was in a fine mood for he had just written an ode which he planned to send to the *Gazette* for publication.

"Waugh, listen to what I have received from the Muse this morning in my library!" he cried one morning, flying into the sitting room like an unbridled horse.

"The Muse," muttered Mrs. Wilson with disgust. Old Bob, attending Mrs. Dorset in a lounging chair near the fire, said, "Shoes? You need shoes?"

"No, Bob, indeed not!" cried Mr. Dorset. By the wildness of his eyes and the waving of his arms, I could tell he had been up all night writing and allowing himself frequent refreshment. Mrs. Dorset seemed briefly to be heading toward tears then recomposed herself.

"Not so loud, if you please," said Mrs. Wilson, in the unhappy way she said everything.

"I have written an ode upon the coming birth of my daughter," said Mr. Dorset.

"You're cold?" cried Old Bob, cupping his ear and trying to be helpful. I shook my head gently, but all it did was confuse Old Bob further.

"You don't *know* it's a daughter," said Mrs. Wilson. "Only God in His wisdom will send which He chooses. You should be more careful in your demands of the Almighty."

"Bah!" he cried. He knelt before his ill-looking wife and unsteadily lowered his head in a sorry imitation of some gallant thing he'd read in a book. Then he stood, held out the octavo sheet of paper upon which he had been scribbling all night, and began to read in a loud, wavering voice that made even Old Bob jump.

> *Muse hath thou seen'st worthy to send*
> *Another child from the Kingdom of Childs*
> *To this country and its various wilds*
> *Where land starts and sea doth end.*

He paused and waited for us to praise him. Mrs. Wilson entirely ignored him, and Old Bob, hand cupped around his ear, stood very near him, smiling, irritating Mr. Dorset, as a poor critic's praise will annoy the best of poets, which Mr. Dorset certainly was not.

"Go on, dear," said Mrs. Dorset with more loyalty than taste. His eyes lit up, and he cleared his throat once more.

For God hath in His great and humble mercy
Brought us to this land which is quite warm
Through the fair day and through the storm
From the Island that men call Jersey.

"Jersey?" said Mrs. Wilson. "You're from no such place. Nor any of your kin. The only person we know from Jersey is that woman in Town who was arrested for running that tavern where perversions were practiced!"

"Diversions!" said Old Bob. "Well and good!"

Mr. Dorset looked at her with grave irritation, and his bibulousness began to display itself in earnest, with weavings and muttered imprecations. Mrs. Dorset again bade him continue. Old Bob looked transported, as if Mr. Milton himself had landed in our midst.

And so to us he grants a sort of boon,
A female girl child to brighten our lodgings
Whilst I do my thinkings and my codgings
In the proper circuit of the palest moon.

Here Mrs. Wilson burst into laughter, and I smiled myself, despite my resolve to humor Mr. Dorset. Mrs. Dorset suddenly gave up a great groan from her couch, and held her stomach, and for a moment, we all thought the baby was imminent, but she finally sighed and leaned back. Mrs. Wilson wiped her forehead. Outside, one of the field servants screamed at something then did not do it again.

"Sir, please continue with your ode," I said. His eyes were glowing now like old coals, lids drooping down.

A female child with golden black hair
And a cape of goodness her shoulders hold.
A small girl into whose coming I foretold
While coming up a set of stairs.

Her name shall be Jenny, with all that guile
Which women are bound to us men by.
She will make the very wind sigh
For such a welcome and satisfying style.

She will be my bonny and busy lass
She will dip the stars down to what hath been.
She will delight the company of all men
With her plangent wit, her maidly sass.

"My word, that is the most ridiculous ode ever written in the Province of South Carolina," said Mrs. Wilson. "Surely you could find something better to do with your time than write such things."

"Ah, well done!" cried Old Bob, starting to applaud. As all those in the arts will grasp the smallest compliment to believe, and dismiss the greatest bulk of their critics, Mr. Dorset suddenly came alive once more.

"Brave Bob!" he cried. "Who knows more of these arts than anyone else in the province! Then you shall receive the glory of hearing my ode in full!"

"A bull?" said Bob. He turned to me, confused and leaning with his cupped ear. "The master's bought a new bull?" Mrs. Dorset began to laugh then groaned loudly, and Mrs. Wilson beneath her breath rebuked Mr. Dorset for his insensitivity toward his wife. Not that any of it mattered. Like a storm blowing in from the harbor, Mr. Dorset was determined then to continue with his ode, and so he did.

My Jenny will be the fair and brightest Dorset
Whose hand ever set foot upon the shore.
She will bring us ultimate glories and more
With form so pure she'll wear no corset.

Mrs. Wilson gave out a small, strangled sound but did not interrupt Mr. Dorset again lest his recitation take longer than its impending natural course. He went on for some time, with allusions to Furies, the King, the Cherokee Indians, our late war with the Yamasees, Spaniards, and varied Muses, Greek heroes, and historical incidents that I am quite certain he invented.

Like Oximander at the Battle of the Ten Forks,
You will raise in us a greatness to come,
You will learn your words and sums,
And men shall bring you figs and porks!

Like the few and like the very callous many
You will excel in all the greatest arts,
E'er to be seen in these parts,
My perfect and dispensable Jenny!

"Dispensable?" cried Mrs. Wilson. "Why on earth would you say such a thing about your own child?" Mrs. Dorset looked suddenly quite uncomfortable and held her painful, child-swollen stomach with one hand and rubbed her forehead with the other.

"Because I love her?" said Mr. Dorset, suddenly dizzy from his efforts.

"If you love her, she's on no account dispensable!" said an angry Mrs. Wilson. Just then, Mrs. Dorset, brought to that time by God that all must endure if the world is not to grow bare of men, screamed aloud most piercingly. Everyone ran to her except Old Bob, who, staring out the window, commented that someone must be slaughtering a hog for dinner.

We took Mrs. Dorset upstairs, or at least Mrs. Wilson and I did, for Old Bob never turned back to the room, instead spying to see if bacon were perhaps in order. Mr. Dorset, exhausted by his labors, collapsed into a chair, laughed quite loudly once, then fell asleep.

— 8. —

GOD, SEEING THAT MRS. DORSET HAS HAD HER FAIR NUMBER
OF SONS, LOOKS UPON THE GREAT TALLYSHEET OF HEAVEN AND
DEIGNS THAT THE DORSETS SHALL HAVE A DAUGHTER.

Only two hours after her confinement that morning, Lydia Dorset gave birth to her daughter Jenny on the couch which had seen the birth of her other three children. I stayed downstairs to attend Mr. Dorset, but he was quite insensate with fatigue from his literary labors and from a considerable amount of French wine, of a vintage which he believed was the handmaiden of his Muse.

Abel, Isaac, and Matthew Dorset were still babes then, of course, and so they were kept away from Mr. and Mrs. Dorset for most of the time, as befit a man with great wealth and no patience for small children.

I sat in a chair near the heavily snoring Mr. Dorset, awaiting any instructions he might make should he awake. Mrs. Wilson, arms red from heated water and fatigue, came into the room, looked at the Master, and made a sour face.

"Should Mr. Dorset awake during any part of the day, inform him that he has a daughter," she said.

"Upon my word, he was right!" I said. "Fancy that."

"He doth vex me," she said. She stood quite near him and watched at him thrashing about in sleep, groaning, speaking, and unfortunately emitting impolite bodily noises. He suddenly laughed, then coughed, then fell asleep once more. I thought Mrs. Wilson might actually kick the man, and I quickly weighed such an action and found it appropriate and would not have censured her if she had. Instead, she went back upstairs, muttering all the while. I sat with Mr. Dorset.

I have found that stillness is a great virtue that no men and few women can bear. I have often felt my soul restored by a fine stretch of immobility. If I feel anger or sadness or confusion over the injustices of this life, I can but sit quietly for an hour, and a calmness descends over me unlike sleep yet just as refreshing. I was so involved when Mr. Dorset suddenly sat up on his bed, belched loudly, and stared wildly around the room.

"God wot!" he cried. "I've invented an orange indigo!"

"Sir?"

"I've dreamed an orange indigo! Think of its value, Hawthorne! A new dye of orange indigo shipped into Europe by the ton, and only I able to grow it!"

"Sir, there is no orange indigo," I said.

"Oh," he said, quite disappointed. "Then it was but a dream."

"Dreams have their counterparts in this life," I said. "Perhaps you shall discover it one day."

He discovered the shuffled papers of his poem on the floor and scooped them all up out of order and stood before me.

"I have composed an ode," he said, as if he had no memory of his earlier recitation. "Shall I give you the honor of hearing it first?"

"Sir, your wife has borne you a daughter as you slept," I said gently. He dropped the sheets, and they fell gently, as a tree's leaves will blow away and then down with the winds of autumn.

"My wife has borne me a daughter?" he asked.

"I believe she and the child are both is good health," I said. "Upstairs."

He paused for perhaps ten seconds, during which he appeared to think of many things, upon which I shall not speculate. His face registered joy and grief; confusion and certainty; courage and cowardice, all in their turn. Where only a few minutes before I had been loyal but sad for his rude manners, I now saw something else, a man understanding the full magnificence of childbirth and knowing that he will never in his life feel that way again.

"Waugh! A daughter!" he screamed. "Waugh!"

He took off running through the room then out of it and up the stairs, where from the commotion I realized he had been intercepted by Mrs. Wilson. She shouted at him, and he began to laugh, which angered her more. But he could no more be held back from that room than the tides could be stopped from rising in Charles Town harbor.

— 9. —

BEING A LETTER FROM MR. CHARLES SMYTHE,
CONGRATULATING MR. DORSET ON THE BIRTH OF
JENNY DORSET ON THE TWENTY-FIRST OF JULY
IN THE YEAR OF OUR LORD 1753.

Foxhaven
August 3, 1753

My dear Dorset,

Allow me to be the first to congratulate you on the arrival of your child, which I am sure is only the latest of many your wife shall bear. Mrs. Smythe and our children, Hamlet and Iago, join with me in wishing for them better than their brothers have had, at least in material wants. For myself, our manor house has proper facilities for the rearing of children, and I am sure that some day yours will as well. I should be glad to offer you a loan at a suitable rate or help you raise the money through horse races, &tc., if you so choose.

I have talked to Mr. Timothy at the GAZETTE about which ode he shall print for the celebration of the summer solstice, and he, alas, has chosen mine over yours. I know how this must disappoint you, but if you keep your quill to the paper, some day you will master your rhymes much better, I am sure.

My son, Hamlet, who is now four years old, has written his entire alphabet. When your boys are pressing ten, I am sure Hamlet will be keen to teach it to them.

Again, our congratulations on the daughter. Though she will be of little help to you on a plantation, she will I am sure be an ornament for your old age.

Cordially yours,
Charles Smythe, Esq.

As Mr. Dorset kept drafts of all his letters, I am able to reproduce here his reply. It set a standard which the Smythe-Dorset correspondence lived up to during the ensuing years.

Just as our Province battled the French, the Indians, and then the British, so Mr. Smythe and Mr. Dorset battled for some years hence.

Longacre
August 4, 1753

Dear Mr. Smythe,

Your charming letter arrived last evening by your servant William Robichaux, and I am vexed to tell you how much it pleased me that you took notice of the fact that my fertility has now exceeded your own twofold. Were you a bull on my plantation, I would sell you for meat to the Huguenots, as you seem to have little capacity for that human husbandry which only the best-suited among us may achieve. I, at least, congratulate you in turn on the two children you have thus far been able to father. If there is ever another, I shall rejoice with you in that unlikely feat.

I regret greatly to hear that your latest ship, which you expressly caused to be built at your design, has sunk fivemile out of the harbor. 'Tis a great pity, surely, and I can only pray that next time such a vessel might have more of God's luck on its side and perhaps a keel as well.

I suspect my daughter indeed shall be an ornament for my old age, as I intend to have an old age. I have read in the GENTLEMAN'S QUARTERLY that men with choleric dispositions (such as you must in all fairness admit you possess) almost always live shorter lives than their calmer, more self-possessed brothers. However, I promise you that I shall look in upon your widow often, and that if any of your plantation yet remains after the sale to pay debts, taxes, &tc., then I shall most humbly help in any way I might.

Your devoted serv't,
Adam Dorset, Esq.

— 10. —

AMID THE GENERAL CELEBRATING OF JENNY DORSET'S BIRTH,
OLD BOB WANDERS AWAY, AND MR. DORSET ASKS ME TO JOIN HIM
WITH A PARTY OF HIS FRIENDS TO RIDE OUT TO A HUNT IN HOPES THAT
WE MAY BAG DEER AND OLD BOB AT THE SAME TIME.

As I have mentioned before, Old Bob was subject to fits of wandering, just as Our Lord wandered in the Wilderness for forty days and nights. No one knew why this affliction was visited upon Old Bob, but one day he would be absent from the work of the house, and, upon noticing, a person might say warily, "Has anyone seen Old Bob?" The staff at that point would sigh, and hope for an hour or so that he might totter in from the woods where he sometimes went to commune with the natural world and see to the health of Mr. Dorset's cattle, sheep, and pigs, which wandered freely but never too far, a quality the Reader will notice in several characters of this History. For myself, I thought Old Bob's bodily compass was subject to turns, as a sail pulls a ship about in a freshening wind. For days, his compass would point steadily south, and then, upon awakening, he would find its poles reversed, and he would head off by foot or horse.

By noon upon a certain day in early September, we had ascertained that Old Bob was nowhere to be found, and Mr. Dorset, restless from his wife's need for tenderness after the birth of her child (for most men will flee tenderness as if it has a snout and cruel fangs), sent for his friends and had them rounded about Longacre in less than two hours' time. Were I the fabled Bard himself, I could not describe the color of a hunt mounted by Mr. Dorset. His pack of hounds, which was the sorriest lot of hunting dogs in the Province, would be held at leash's end by the trainers, straining and barking joyously. Without exception, when Mr. Dorset gave the command for their release, whether on a fox hunt or merely for the joy of chasing what game might have strayed near the house, they scattered in a hundred directions, each following a scent the others appeared not to take. Mr. Dorset would swing about wildly in his saddle cursing and roaring at them, shouting at the trainers, cursing all Dogkind. He would then ride forth on the hunt, and sometimes, by chance or the design of a Merry God, a few of the dogs might cross his path, most often chasing each other rather than a stag or hare.

This particular day, as he left the infant Jenny crying in her nursemaid's arms, he seemed more attuned to the hunt than I had seen him in months. More than two dozen men had assembled, bearing the names of many good families, some of whom had already attained wealth, others of whom would do so shortly. They often brought their servants with them to fetch a flask of rum or pluck a rabbit from the brush, since they were forbidden to bring their own dogs and Mr. Dorset's pack would usually tear apart the hare in a matter of seconds if they knew a lucky shot had been made.

The day was sunny and warm but not hot, and a mild breeze ruffled the leaves. The dogs strained and yelped, and Mr. Dorset sat high in his fine saddle, Lord of the manor and blessed with a surfeit of friends. Only one person's presence among them caused Mr. Dorset's eye to go askance: Mr. Charles Smythe. Even though Mr. Smythe and Mr. Dorset could barely seem to stand each other, the imagined civilities of English life gave each a code of conduct which forbade open displays of crude anger. (In those halcyon days, long before the Revolution, each of the plantation owners from Charles Town to the up-country outdid himself in trying to be English, from the formal gardens to the minor pleasantries of horse races and grinning contests. The presence of mannered servants such as myself has faded in this new country, and I am sorry for that. Revolutions do not encourage displays of finer manners.)

"So the old man has lost himself again," said Mr. Smythe with a smirk.

"It is his nature, sir," said Mr. Dorset. "And it is my nature as a Christian man to go after him. I must set an example for my four children, and that means I have to work twice as hard as you do, dear Smythe."

The hounds were making such a terrible racket that Mrs. Wilson came shuttling from the house to the great lawn out back and shouted at Mr. Dorset that the children needed their naps and to get these beasts away from them. Mr. Dorset held his hand over his eyes in defeat, and Mr. Smythe laughed as a man will when he takes advantage of another.

"What was Old Bob wearing?" asked Thomas Mole, who sidled his horse near Mr. Dorset. This Mole had a plantation not three miles from Longacre, and he was new to wealth and so wasted it in even more inventive ways than Mr. Smythe or Mr. Dorset. Though he was perhaps the ugliest man I have ever seen, a torpid, ungainly fellow with the shape of a snail without its shell and the same vigor, his money had allowed him to marry a lovely girl and bring to this earth two children, both of whom resembled their father in the most appalling way.

"It need not matter!" cried Mr. Dorset. "My animals shall scent him, and we will have him back directly and then we can attend the hunt!"

"Indeed," sniffed Mr. Smythe.

I held my counsel. A good servant always does. But looking back now nearly half a century later, I can see that Old Bob's wandering that particular day was a clear warning from God about the character of Jenny Dorset. None there, unfortunately, was farsighted enough to know it.

Mr. Dorset raised himself in his saddle as if to survey his property. He seemed pleased. Everyone was as eager to leave as the dogs, except Thomas Mole, whose nose had begun to bleed, an unfortunate curse that always afflicted him in moments of great stress.

"Away the hounds!" cried Mr. Dorset. Each trainer, holding four dogs, leaned down and untied them. In less than thirty seconds, they scattered each in a different direction. "Waugh! Aaggh! G—d—d beasts! Come back here! Now back to this hunt now!" He rode to one of the trainers and began to berate him with his riding crop. "It is your failure yet again!" Mr. Smythe was holding his horse in check, for it was stamping and excited, as all were that were standing by the dogs.

"Mayhap they've found Old Bob already!" shouted Mr. Smythe above the din.

"Curses upon all those animals!" shouted Mr. Dorset. He thereupon took a new swing with his crop at the trainer and fell cleanly from his saddle onto the lawn. I climbed down and helped fetch him up, but he was in no mood for assistance, and he swung at me with his riding crop. I dodged the blow, but he lost his balance once more and fell to the earth.

"A stag!" cried a man called William Mulberry. I turned and to my amazement saw a fine but winded buck standing near one of the barns, having apparently been flushed accidentally from its hiding place by the scattering hounds. (By then, their barks had almost evaporated in the distance.)

"Stand aside!" called Mr. Mulberry, and he raised his piece and somehow managed to shoot Thomas Mole in the buttock. Mole fell from his horse, which ran away with the deer, step for step, until they'd both disappeared into the woods. We attended Mr. Mole, though none of the men wanted to get very close.

"See after him, Mulberry," said Mr. Dorset. "Your piece felled him."

"I am dying!" cried Mr. Mole, though that seemed to stretch the point somewhat, as only a small amount of blood darkened his fundament.

"I'm not touching that," said Mulberry with a shiver. "I cannot say where it hath been of late."

"Call for a reverend to speak words over me, and inform my beautiful wife of my death in battle," said Mr. Mole, who was starting to assume that heroic pose which men will take for no reason in times of disorder.

"See to him, Mulberry!" cried Mr. Dorset, reaching down to Mr. Mole's buttock and then bringing his hand back as a woman might upon seeing a spider.

"Appears a flesh wound," said Mr. Mulberry. At that point, one of the hounds made its way through the now-dismounted company and paused before Mr. Mole and indicated by point that it had found its quarry, an act which drew Mr. Dorset's rage. He kicked the poor beast, which yelped and disappeared back into the distance with his fellow hounds.

"I expire now," said Thomas Mole weakly.

"It's no longer bleeding," said Mr. Smythe.

"I could make a poultice," said Old Bob.

"By all means then, Bob, make a poultice," said Mr. Dorset, eager to shed the responsibility. He stared for a moment more at the felled Mole, then turned and placed his hand over his forehead. "Old Bob! Where have you been? We had come to hunt for you!" Mr. Smythe fell to the sweet grass, holding his sides and laughing, and Mr. Dorset required all of his patience not to strike the prone gentleman.

"Bless me, I can't say," said Old Bob, puzzled. "Unless I was summoned by His Majesty." The men laughed heartily. Mr. Dorset handed his horse to a groom, and went inside with Old Bob to announce his discovery to the others. The hunting party began to drift away, and I helped Mr. Mole remount, though it cause him no small amount of grief.

The last of the dogs reappeared at Longacre some days later.

— 11. —

HOW JENNY DORSET GROWS,
AND ADVICE THAT HER MOTHER GIVES TO ME REGARDING
THE SUFFERING OF WOMEN UPON THIS EARTH,
ALONG WITH DIANA SETON'S VISIT TO INFORM THE DORSETS
OF MRS. SMYTHE'S DILEMMA AFTER THE BIRTH OF
HER FINAL SON, FORTINBRAS.

God loves outward appearances. He gives us to think the sea will always be calm and beautiful, then sends a violent storm as we sleep. He designs a river to be level and navigable through much of its course, and then turns it into a maelstrom. Just so, he allowed Jenny Dorset's first two years to be placid, even docile, leading the family to presume that her own course would be straight and calm for a long life, designed as they believed God gave it to women, learning domestic arts and bringing forth the next generation to remember the previous ones with love and respect.

Indeed, the other children were at times so loud that Mr. Dorset would clap his hands over his ears, cry aloud, and run off to his library to work on an ode or songs for a masque he was sure would bring him fame in London. Isaac in particular was a noisy child, once setting fire to the stables after having taken a flaming stick from a blaze built to dispose of some old bedclothes. His father beat him mercilessly on discovering the act, then slipped into another religious conversion, in which he lingered for not more than two days before he was again released.

Abel was always a serious child, and he was already beginning that life for which he was to become wellknown in the Province. Matthew was kind and gentle with his new sister, being only a year older and thinking her some kind of doll or small animal which was oftentimes a pleasure to play with.

The first year of her life was a fine one for us at Longacre, though much was going on in the Province. Our difficulties with the Cherokee Indians had already begun, and we at their behest built a site called Fort Prince George some 250 miles from Charles Town, in the foothills of the mountains at an Indian town called Keowee. In my youth, we had seen many Indians about Charles Town — Creeks, Chickasaws, a few Yamasees, Etc. — but by 1750 we saw few any more except those come for the trade or to be exhibited by the selfsame kinds of men who would trade in slaves. I have not yet spoken of that pernicious institution, but there were altogether more men of color from Africa and elsewhere brought to South Carolina as slaves than there were white people. At times, their eruptions would send all the planters fleeing with their families back to Town, but not so often by the time of Jenny Dorset's childhood. Mr. Dorset and Mr. Smythe, by virtue of the land that must be worked, each had several score slaves, and, as a Christian man myself, I could never countenance such a thing, though I must admit in this History that no master ever treated a slave more kindly than Mr. Dorset.

Jenny Dorset, as I have recounted, was bright-eyed and beautiful, with yellow hair and her mother's rich blue eyes. Even before her six-months birthday, she was laughing and beguiling her father, who often went to town for one of his club meetings or to see music or plays, and would bring her back ribbons or other playthings of delight.

One afternoon, when the nurse had left Jenny to Mrs. Dorset by the fire in the sitting room, I came in to ask if she had need of me. She did not, but bade me sit in a chair near the fire. A cold rain streaked the windows. It was in February in the year of 1755. Mrs. Dorset was still tired after the exertions of childbirth, and I knew, with the certainty of unspoken things, that she would bear no more children for her health would not permit it, and her husband was at least that loving and sensible.

"Mr. Hawthorne, do you know what God hath given woman to endure upon this earth?" she said softly. In that afternoon light, with the house quiet (Mr. Dorset was in town arranging some business or another), she was very beautiful, and I cannot but admit that in another day or time, in another position of life, I could have admired her more than I was allowed by fate.

"A great deal certainly in this house," I said cautiously. She laughed, and Jenny, who was playing with a ball of thread, laughed with her and then went back to her playing.

"He gives a woman the suffering of childbirth and unfaithful men," she said. "He gives her no voice in the world she inhabits and then expects her to grow in dignity and attendance each year. He expects her to bear indignities with silence, darkness with light."

"Ma'am," I nodded.

"But for her, there should be some other thing," she said. "A new place in this world." She glanced at her quiet daughter, and I could see the justice in what she said and the little likelihood of it at the same time. "She should be at least granted her due as the one who keeps her family together against all ills. I mean you no disrespect, but if families relied solely on men for their nurture, we might as well all shift as savages in the western mountains."

"Ma'am," I said.

"I have not thought so far as to worry about my sons, for they shall grow into their father's wealth and become good fathers in their own right, but what of a young girl in this Province, here so close to the frontier? Will she gain that gentility I was denied for having the misfortune to be born so early in its history instead of in a fine English manor house?"

"No one can say," I said.

"Then the world may go as it will, and come what may as it will, but I can only hope that my girl will grow with the breeding she has been vouchsafed, and with the quiet strength a woman must have to endure these bitter days."

I have often thought back upon that rainy afternoon, because I am certain that in no wise could she have given a less accurate description of the life Jenny Dorset would come to lead.

She appeared pleased that she had shared her sentiments with a person of the offensive sex and had picked up Jenny and was playing with her upon her lap when Old Bob came into the sitting room, wearing his best servant's dress, except for his stockings, which were drooped down around his ankles, exposing his legs, which were thin as a chicken's. Mrs. Dorset, who might have been shocked, placed her long lovely fingers over her smile to hide it, as a woman of taste and breeding should.

"Miss Diana Seton, of the Smythes, to see Mrs. Dorset," he said stiffly.

"Show her in, please," said Mrs. Dorset. Old Bob cupped his hand over his ear and leaned closer.

"Glowing men?" he said.

"Show her in!" I said more loudly, and he smiled at both of us and bowed and went for her. Mrs. Dorset gestured for me to take her daughter, which I gladly did. Though it was unusual for a man to help care for children in those days, I often sported with them, for I found their idle lack of guile and intrigues to be a strong tonic against the constant plotting of the Dorsets and Smythes. Presently, Old Bob came back into the room, pleased at being able to help, and bowed low and showed in the imperious and unpleasant Diana Seton from the Smythe staff. She was that year about sixty, I imagine, but she might have been as aged as the Bible recounts Methuselah, as her face was creased from religious fasting and a life of keen observations on the misery of herself and others. She wore a visiting dress of black, which made her deep-set brown eyes seem to glow like little coals.

"Ah, the little one," she said, glaring at Jenny, whom I held in my arms near the fire. Jenny made a cooing noise and kicked me in the chest. "How nice. Mrs. Dorset, may we speak in confidence?"

"Mr. Henry Hawthorne is caring for Jenny and is a man of sensitive feelings," said Mrs. Dorset. "I count entirely upon his discretion and manners."

"Well then," she said. "But it is a matter of delicacy from Mrs. Smythe upon which I must speak."

"Please do so," said Mrs. Dorset.

"It is a problem of nature," said Diana Seton. "Neither our wet nurse nor Mrs. Smythe has enough nurture to sustain the new little one, Fortinbras."

"Fortinbras?" said Mrs. Dorset. "The new boy is named Fortinbras?" Once again, Mrs. Dorset hid her smile as a lady must, but Diana Seton could only grimace and nod, as if the very fact of the name gave her a pain between the eyes.

"Yes," said Mrs. Seton, "and now she has sent me to ask if your wet nurse could help us in this time of trial and in the sustenance of the poor child, lest this problem cause his nurture to fail."

"So you are asking if we can give this gift to the little child?" asked Mrs. Dorset. "I am sure that Mr. Dorset will have no objection. Our wet nurse is an ample woman. Kindly bring the child here for a time, and we shall feed it well."

"Mr. Smythe has instructed me to purchase her from you for a price you shall set," she said.

"Purchase her?" said Mrs. Seton. "Indeed not. I am sure that Mr. Dorset will have no objection to having little Fortinbras with us for a time."

Afternoon turned into evening, and when Mr. Dorset came in late from his business in town, I told him of our impending company.

"Waugh! That b—s—d under my roof?" he cried. "Is it my fault that God has dried up the women of that miserly man's home? It's retribution for his ungodly ways and for the squandering of his sense and wealth! I'd liefer sell them a cow to nurse the puking little babe than give them the loan of my nurse for one minute of one day!"

Of course, he lost that battle, as he was to lose so many more battles in the coming years, but for many years he held a secret hope for failure against Fortinbras Smythe, though, as it turned out, he need not have wished it so greatly, for the Smythe children failed quite well on their own. As I recall, however, it was the last favor that a Smythe asked of a Dorset until a very sad episode many years later, and, in that sense, it is parcel of this History.

When Fortinbras left us after three months to return home, Mr. Dorset made a fine fit of wanting to burn all the bedclothes he had slept upon, and only the loud rebuke of Mrs. Wilson made him turn away from those plans.

— 12. —

SEVERAL YEARS PASS, AND JENNY DORSET, NOW SIX YEARS OLD,
BECOMES INVOLVED IN THE DISCUSSIONS OVER WAR
WITH THE FRENCH, AMONG OTHER THINGS.

By the year 1759, when Jenny had turned six and her brothers, Abel, Isaac, and Matthew, were respectively nine, eight, and seven, the Province had found itself well at war with the French and their Indian allies. Just who those allies might be at any one moment was a matter of grave confusion, and even the Cherokee, who had been allies of the Crown for some years, were poised to turn against us. There was great talk in our area of mounting a Provincial troop to go and bring the Cherokee back into order, though most of these men could in truth not hit a barn from twenty paces with their muskets. As many of them had great wealth, they were blessed with idleness, and men when idle come to believe many fanciful things, not the least of which is that they possess courage. Many were genuinely brave during our Revolution later, but just as many were not, and no man can know his courage until it is tested.

For his part, Mr. Dorset had come that year to think of himself as a mixture of Julius Caesar, Hannibal, William Shakespeare, and the eminent composer Dr. Arne. He would fly into the field at a moment's notice to look for game, firing at anything which moved and more often than not winding up looking for his wayward pack of dogs. He would then come home, exhausted, and struggle mightily to write yet another of his odes or masques, most of which he unfortunately caused to have published in one form or another. (Sensing that Mr. Dorset was gaining through his literary endeavors, Mr. Smythe also began to pen verse, which was, if anything, more wretched than Mr. Dorset's.) When the French war came, however, Mr. Dorset wanted to show his patriotism by forming his own regiment from the Province, and when Mr. Smythe heard of it, he was possessed to form his own in the selfsame manner. The result was two small armies of about seventy-five men each, which began to meet at the houses and drill and practice firing under the leadership of two of the least capable commanders in the history of the Province.

Our troop was called Dorset's Regulars, though there was nothing regular about us. After several weeks of meeting and listening to orders from Mr. Dorset, the most exciting thing which had happened was the explosion of a fowling piece in the hands of one Gaston Roux, who lost one finger and most of his esprit de corps. I had discovered that I was a steady shot, but the only thing we fired toward was straw images of Frenchmen that Mr. Dorset had made Mrs. Wilson and Old Bob sew for us. We heard that Mr. Smythe's men, which he called the South Carolina Provincial Volunteers, had accidentally killed several cows of disputed ownership, and that our justice of the peace (for that was our only legal recourse in the backcountry in those years) was studying the situation with gravity.

The boys of the Dorset household looked upon the proceedings with some confusion. Abel, being the eldest and wanting to please his father, wore a costume sewn for him by his mother to resemble an Austrian cavalry officer's tunic. Isaac had no idea what was happening, though he ran about with a wooden play musket screaming "Fench! Fench!" in a particularly piercing voice. The docile and quiet Matthew was more pleased to play at the spinet (or against it) and look at the commotion from the great windows of the house at Longacre.

The only Dorset child who was entirely taken by the proceedings was Jenny. By this time, she was perhaps the most beautiful child ever born in South Carolina. The first day she saw the men outside drilling, I was inside attending Mrs. Dorset, who was having ladies from the area over for a tea and wanted me to help move some furniture. Jenny was dressed in certain flounces and ruffles, articles of clothing whose proper names I regret to say I never knew. Outside, there was much shouting and cursing at the imaginary French and their Indians (much of it coming from Mr. Dorset) along with considerable firing and marching in very poor formations. Jenny could not take her pretty eyes from the commotion before her, even though her mother begged her to come back and help Matthew with his fingering of a new piece by Mr. Handel.

"The French are such that we should kill them all," said Jenny, turning to me. Her face was red, as if she had gone into a fury. "Waugh! Death to all the scurvy Frenchmen!"

Mrs. Dorset, who was standing nearby watching Old Bob move a chair apparently into the fireplace, turned sharply.

"Jenny Dorset! What talk! You must never talk like that, for it is not as a lady should speak!" she cried.

"A lady must speak her mind," said Jenny. "I have been told such by my father."

"Your father would not know a lady from a lamb," said Mrs. Dorset in a rare flash of temper. "Now please be a lady and see how your brother plays the spinet."

"I must hate the French, for my father does," said Jenny.

"Hate is the coin of idle minds, Jenny Dorset!" said her mother. "God in his wisdom has made woman to support man, not to fight wars or to hate. Of hatred there is enough in this world already. Hatred is the child of envy, and envy is the child of greed, and greed is the child of sin."

"If a Frenchman comes here, I shall shoot him dead," said Jenny, holding her skirt and making a perfect curtsey, as her sometime tutor in manners, Mr. Osborne, had shown her. She continued her turn as if part of a minuet, smiling beautifully. Even her mother was struck dumb by the incongruity of the sight. "I shall shoot him dead, shoot him dead, if a

Frenchman comes, I shall shoot him dead." She sang it softly.

"Mind your tongue," said her mother in a soft, distracted voice, as if to say, *My goodness, what goes on in that child's head?*

"My father says, my father says," she sang and turned, "my father says the French are low villains."

"Jenny!" said Mrs. Dorset.

"What say you, Mr. Hawthorne?" Jenny sang, dancing near me. "Are the French low villains?"

"There are men for good or evil among all races," I said instructively. Instead of taking the lesson, she laughed brightly, turned on her heel and ran across the room into the front hall, opened the door, and dashed into the bright sunshine. Mrs. Dorset was worried.

"Get her!" she cried. "The army is out there!"

I ran for Jenny, though in my heart I knew she could have suffered little from Dorset's Regulars, since they could not have hit her had they been aiming at twenty paces. This, as I recall, was the first instance of Jenny Dorset's wandering spirit taking hold of the house, and, as she hardly noticed Old Bob, I don't see how it could be blamed on him. Mrs. Dorset would often blame Jenny's infelicities on her husband, but that is the case with most wives, and most often, unfortunately, the truth. Still, Mrs. Dorset was hardly bound by her marriage oath to simple obedience and support, and, often by ways that shall be shown later, managed to have her way at Longacre, to the consternation of Mr. Dorset, who always quite foolishly believed himself in control.

The day was sharp, with only a few twirls of fleecy clouds overhead, and a bit of smoke near the army, a few of whom had fired their pieces into the air, I believe, for effect. Jenny was on the lawn, running, turning, like a flower blown in a gale. She held her arms up, and in that moment I daresay I never saw a thing more completely alive in this world. She sang and shouted, and I got close enough once to hear that it was yet about the French, but she easily eluded capture, for even though I was only thirty-four years old at the time, her feet were light as an angel's wings and mine of more earthbound stuff. I was doing poorly when I looked up to see that Mrs. Wilson and Old Bob had joined in the chase. Mrs. Wilson's face was frighteningly red, and she merely shouted the child's name over and over. Old Bob ran in small circles with the slowness of the setting sun, not quite getting anywhere or wanting to. Finally, our chase captured the attention of the army and its commander, and Mr. Dorset joined in the chase until we had cornered Jenny against the house. She was laughing so hard she could not gather her breath, and none of us could breathe from the exertion. Mrs. Wilson was choking and wheezing in a most shocking manner. Old Bob got to us a few moments later.

"Come inside with you, child," said Mrs. Wilson. "There's guns about."

"Gums?" said Old Bob. "Her gums worn out?" He cupped his ear.

Mr. Dorset came flying up and tripped over the sword hanging at his side and fell headlong into an exotic bush he had caused to be planted at the site. He extricated himself with the greatest profanity, Mrs. Wilson all the while exclaiming that God would punish the man for speaking so vulgarly in the hearing of a child. Old Bob, satisfied that we had found Jenny, walked off. Sensing that something was afoot, the hounds in their quarters behind the house began to bark violently. Thinking the chaos was part of their drilling, the Regulars also broke formation and rushed the house with great shouting and a few shots. Jenny had never seemed more happy or beautiful.

"Arrgh! Upon my word, this is the d—d—st happenstance!" cried Mr. Dorset. "Jenny, are you alright? From what do you run, child?"

"I run to kill the French, Papa," she said in a voice more childish than the one with which she normally spoke.

"Good then!" he cried. "For the French are low villains and should all be shot and hung from the nearest trees!"

I looked up and saw Mrs. Dorset watching the proceedings from the window with an expression of gravest distaste. Then an odd turn took us. For a moment, perhaps not more than half a minute, everyone converged on the spot where Jenny stood against the house, and utter silence took hold, as if in the presence of some holy icon or at the beginning of a Crusade. (For I have read that the wanderings of Richard the Lion-Heart began with just such piety and ended in great and wanton bloodshed, as was the custom of that time, and, it seemed, ours.) The sun danced through the leaves of the trees. The day was still and perfect, and a wind came upon us, with such light and utter perfection that I believe we all knew we had been selected for a rare gift of Nature, a pool of pleasure that seemed to form around the small body of a lovely child.

However, perfection lasts but briefly on this earth. And when we do find it in the flesh, we chase it down until it troubles us no more, for Human Beings can no more bear too much Goodness than they can bear too much Evil. That battle in our hearts between God and the Evil One was ordained to keep us in balance, though some go so far one way or another they never find the way back.

Just so, Jenny Dorset herself broke the spell. She shrieked something that included a word about the French, raised her arm as the Maid of Orleans did in various depictions of her valor, and ran off around the house.

"Come back here!" cried Mrs. Wilson, who, sensing the futility, chose the moment to fall faint to her seat in the grass. Mr. Dorset looked at her and said *waugh* very softly, and then set out for Jenny. With the instinct of birds scattered by a shot, all of us followed him, ignoring the plight of Mrs. Wilson, who it must be said looked peaceful in the grass, as if she had succumbed to the sweetest sleep.

And so the entire troop of Dorset's Regulars came around the house, only to see that Jenny was heading, arms up and screaming, straight for the large cornfield that separated in summer part of the distance between the Smythe and Dorset properties, that field belonging half to each.

"There she goes!" cried Mr. Dorset.

"Yes!" the troop mumbled. And I sensed for the first time that they were following him and had somehow come to believe that this was a military operation. I felt the spirit of the event myself. We had not reached the field when we saw Old Bob by the dog pens, opening the door, to the astonishment of the dogs' handlers, who had risen from a spell of idleness themselves and could not understand what Old Bob might be about. With a great barking of utter joy, the dogs spilled from the pens' gate and came running toward us.

"Hie! Hie!" cried Mr. Dorset. The two dozen hounds came at a leap toward us, reached us, went straight past us around the house and disappeared with their barking into the distance in the opposite direction from which Jenny had gone. Only one dog remained, and he had run to the back door, whimpering with such pitiful urgency that Matthew Dorset, up from the spinet, let the dog inside. Mr. Dorset put his hand over his head, uttered an unspeakable oath, and then turned toward the cornfield and shouted his daughter's name. The others took it up, and soon the world seemed to resound with that double syllable: *Jen-ny! Jen-ny!*

The army of Mr. Smythe was drilling that same day around Mr. Smythe's house in the distance. As I have said, they were, if anything, even worse than Mr. Dorset's gang, for, Mr. Dorset's wealth being older, he attracted an older and therefore less wayward crowd. It was only when we had gone a hundred yards into the cornfield in search of Jenny that I realized what might occur if we pressed onward. Foolish man! I chastised myself.

Halfway into the corn, we stopped and listened. Jenny was not far ahead, and she suddenly appeared between the sharp green cornstalks. Her eyes drew all the light from the sky. Sun danced in the silk of her hair. So many men attending her whims had obviously given her great joy, and she raised her hands, shouted, turned, and disappeared into the corn.

"Hie! Hie!" cried Mr. Dorset, and with his arm he waved his men onward. We moved, and I was brought into the military spirit of it. Suddenly there was a great rustling to our right, and, as none of us had the presence of mind or in truth the time to stop our dash, we could not stop when Mr. Dorset's hounds came flying across in front of us, heading at cross angles to the direction Jenny had taken. Half of us, including myself, were tripped up and fell over the dogs, and such a lot of cursing would have scored the ears of a gentle child, had she been near us, which she was not. Before we could all rise, the dogs and their barking had once more disappeared.

Now, as we moved onward, it was clear that Jenny was running toward the Smythe house, and before long we heard a commotion in front of us. By that time, Mr. Dorset was lost entirely to the moment, his face red, his manner poorly controlled. I do think he had somewhat forgotten about Jenny. I myself had not, and so was startled to see her pass us on the right, laughing and running back toward the Dorset house. I tried to tell Mr. Dorset, but by then our motion was too great, and could not have been stopped anyway. And so we burst from the cornfield to the rear of Mr. Smythe's troop, which was marching only two hundred yards away on the grass near his great house.

"Waugh! Jenny!" cried Mr. Dorset, suddenly remembering where he was, but by then it was too late, and his Regulars kept moving toward the opposition, determined to take the field. For his part, Mr. Smythe, appearing to believe he had exposed his rear, so to speak, turned and waved his men toward the Regulars. Mr. Dorset's dogs suddenly burst from the corn and ran past us once more, tongues lolling out, apparently grinning, chasing shadows and exulting in the exercise.

Now, it should be noted that these men knew each other, all living in the same area but with loyalties to one of two great houses. And so when it appeared we were attacking, Mr. Smythe's troop assumed it must be a test of some kind. Everyone resolved not to fire a weapon, except into the air, which nearly all of them did. When we came to them, all threw down their muskets and began to grapple as wrestlers will, shouting and screaming. I cannot guess what the sight must have been from the lofty mount of the windows of the Smythe house, but once I glanced high up and saw Ophelia Van Dyke Smythe looking out the curtain in great confusion. I took it in my head to hail her and explain the strange nature of this combat, but just then a man hit me in the side of my head, and I fell to the grass and tried for some time to clear the whirling stars from my mind. (Mr. Dorset much later asked if I had been one of his casualties upon the field of battle, and he was overjoyed when I admitted I was.)

The men slugged each other without mercy, screaming about French and Indians and Prussians. Occasionally, a more learned man among them would shout of some historical battle of import, such as Marathon or Hastings, and another invoked the Muse for strength just as he was sent sprawling down the green.

For His part, God shaped the battle as a master plans a game of chess. I have always thought that the King of Heaven smiled that fair afternoon at the pleasant stupidity of the sight. He gave one side the advantage and then the other, and finally managed to pair off Mr. Smythe and Mr. Dorset themselves in a fight that was clearly designed to make a Moral Point. As I was dizzy from my wounds and unable for a time to stand, I saw them standing face to face, fighting as if the winner might inherit all the land thereabouts. I have never owned a parcel of land and cannot imagine why great wars are fought over it, but I saw in their eyes a determination to hold the field.

"Attack me from the rear, Dorset!" cried Mr. Smythe. "'Tis a cowardly thing to do!" Mr. Smythe took a great swing and missed. Mr. Dorset laughed darkly.

"Your lack of vigilance, sir, is superseded only by your lack of intelligence!" cried Mr. Dorset, who took a swing back and lightly clipped Mr. Smythe. Nearby, the dogs had reemerged from the cornfield and come among the men, playing with them, tripping them, barking furiously.

"I shall burn your land, your house, your country to the ground!" screamed Mr. Smythe.

"Waugh! With that army, you could not burn a sack of chestnuts!" said Mr. Dorset. Then a curious thing happened. Both turned to look at their armies, only to find they had ceased the battle entirely and were sitting about taking out pipes, smoking, and lolling about to no purpose.

Messrs. Dorset and Smythe, having realized that the battle had ended inconclusively, decided, with the unspoken agreement by which men often avoid bloodshed, to retire from the field. As was common in those days, each bowed deeply to the other, less as a matter of respect than a matter of inviolable form.

Mr. Dorset helped me up, and when we walked back toward the cornfield his men straggled behind us, and soon we were back safe on the grounds of Longacre. Many of Mr. Dorset's slaves were standing about very perplexed at the action, though none was more perplexed than the army itself. I could only thank God that we had not engaged Frenchmen or Indians, either of which would have reduced us to a handful of begging stragglers within minutes.

"Mr. Dorset, sir," I said. "Your daughter, Jenny?"

"Aaaugh! I had forgotten we had gone for her!" he cried. He turned suddenly, but she was standing only twenty feet away, smiling beautifully. Her mother was right behind her, along with Old Bob, Mrs. Wilson, and the McNew twins. I had another seizure of fatigue and sat upon the grass.

"Such a sight as this!" cried Mrs. Wilson. "A disgrace."

"We have taken the field and saved the day!" said Mr. Dorset to his wife. She glanced at him coldly.

"You are the greatest fool I have ever seen upon this earth," she said.

"And a low villain!" said Jenny Dorset.

Mr. Dorset could only grumble and turn away from his family to his men, who were all heading home. Clearly, neither found much to praise in what Mr. Dorset considered a great victory.

— 13. —
MR. DORSET COMPOSES A SONG COMMEMORATING THE
EVENTS OF THE DAY AND HIRES MR. LIGHTSEY,
A CELEBRATED CASTRATO, TO PERFORM IT AT A GREAT BANQUET
HE THROWS A WEEK FOLLOWING THE EVENT.
THE ENTIRE SMYTHE FAMILY IS PRESENT,
AS GOOD FORM DICTATES.

I fear that thus far in this History I have spoken more about her family than about Jenny Dorset herself, but that is best how we speak of our childhoods, by recalling less how we were than how the events of the day shaped us. As the wind will sculpt clouds and blow them away or cause them to swell and pour out their rain, just so our families, if we are lucky enough to have one, and the events of town or day.

The night of Mr. Dorset's great banquet, his daughter Jenny at age six was already the center of everyone's attention and heart, so beautiful and so wise beyond her years that she was treated with the greatest deference. (The children often came to such parties, and that night even the miserable trio of Smythe brats was about with their nurses.)

"Now, we shall have the event all have waited for!" cried Mr. Dorset as they sipped rum and talked. "Mr. Lightsey, if you please!"

Mr. Lightsey's voice was so high and so clear, and came across them all with such force that no one could doubt the quality of the music or the words. Mrs. Dorset fanned herself, and Isaac Dorset began to weep. Mr. Smythe, though he had far less talent than Mr. Dorset, could not restrain his victorious smile. Even Mr. Lightsey seemed mildly appalled by what he inflicted upon the assembly. Jenny was laughing, though not at the song, of which she certainly understood little. She laughed because she sensed in them an embarrassed merriment, something completely wrong, and so unspoken. Tact would become even less one of Jenny Dorset's virtues as the years passed.

Only Mr. Dorset continued to believe that his song was a triumph. His innocent cheer was poignant to me, and I felt sorry for him as no one else there did. Mrs. Wilson, lingering in the corner awaiting an order, seemed oblivious to the awkwardness and maintained her usual sour demeanor. Mrs. Smythe had brought along Herr Schlitz, and he was nearly as deaf as Old Bob; despite a repeated request from Mrs. Smythe for some kind of assistance, he only rocked on his feet and smiled, as if he heard a pleasant sound far in the distance or held close to him a pleasing memory.

"I daresay, they'll be singing that in London in a fortnight!" cried Mr. Dorset. "Mr. Handel himself will feel the heat of my success at his heels!"

At that assertion, Mr. Smythe, who was trying with poor luck to restrain himself, began to laugh in his peculiar braying manner, not unlike the sound a donkey makes when excited beyond its capacity for silence. At first, Mr. Dorset believed he was agreeing, but soon it was clear that Mr. Smythe was mocking my Master, and in a most grievous way. Old Bob, watching Mr. Smythe, could not restrain his own laughter, and so began to giggle himself, followed by Jenny Dorset, whose high-pitched and very sweet laugh pierced the air. Soon the others were all laughing but for Fortinbras Smythe, who was only five at the time. He began to cry. Mr. Dorset seemed befuddled by the sounds. He turned and glanced at Mr. Lightsey, and that odd fellow took it as a sign that he should once again commit music, and so "Victory at Longacre" (reproduced in full here) began all over again to the delight, consternation, and ultimately irritation of them all. Poor Mr. Dorset, still not quite understanding he was being mocked, mouthed the words as Mr. Lightsey sang. Fortinbras Smythe put his hands upon his ears and gave out with a piercing wail that should have distracted Mr. Lightsey and his harpsichordist at the very least but which, by an odd coincidence, appeared to be part of the song itself.

Finally, Time allowed the song to end once more, and Mr. Smythe began to applaud the performance, with tears of laughter pouring down his unmannered cheeks. Finally, Mr. Dorset understood that he was the object of some derision, and he ceased parading his struggles with the Muse before us. It must be said he never let his lack of talent stand between himself and his Muse, and to the end of his days he kept composing and scribbling perforce as if he were blessed with a rare gift.

"That must have been some battle, upon my word," said Mr. Smythe. "Were you present for it, or did you just read about it in the *Gentlemen's Quarterly?*"

"I was present, and were it not for the cowardly desertions from the other side, we would have had an ever greater victory," said Mr. Dorset.

"Ah," said Mr. Smythe. "Then you weren't present for it! I was, and upon my word, I never saw such a misbegotten attack or such a rout. The offending group, and I dare not use the word *troop* for fear of offending common sense, as I recall retreated in dishonor through a cornfield and fell upon the grass out of breath."

"Hail, vic-torious ar-my," sang Old Bob suddenly, painfully off key. Everyone turned to him, and for a moment I thought Mr. Dorset would rebuke him in front of the company, and he might have but for a commotion outside on the green, where Molly and Tom McNew had become involved in a furious fight with Roderigo and Desdemona Smartt. Their screams and curses, and the novelty of two sets of twins going after each other, roused the women to the vapors and Messrs. Smythe and Dorset to a state of great and jolly excitement. They ran from the room to watch the proceedings. Old Bob kept singing.

"Shall I be paid, then?" asked Mr. Lightsey in his high, sharp voice.

Mrs. Dorset buried her face in her hands and shook her head. Sad to

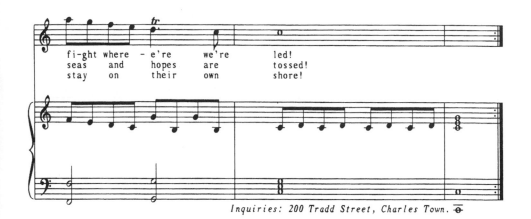

fi-ght where – e're we're led!
seas and hopes are tossed!
stay on their own shore!

Inquiries: 200 Tradd Street, Charles Town.

say, she was in that position for some years at Longacre. Jenny leaped up, and I followed her out the door. The twins were beating each other with fine spirit, though I was surprised to see that the boys were fighting the girls, pulling hair, biting, screaming, uttering curses as bad as any sailor on the wharf at Charles Town. For their part, the men were watching with great laughing, and though such now seems rude and unnecessary to me, I can only report it in this History as it happened. Jenny Dorset watched the proceedings with pleasure, then disappeared around the house. She was gone for some hours but returned before dark.

— 14. —
MR. DORSET SUFFERS ANOTHER BOUT WITH PIETY
AND RAISES FUNDS FOR A CHURCH, CAUSES IT TO BE BUILT,
AND THEN GOES ON A TRIP TO ENGLAND,
WHERE HE LOSES HIS RELIGION COMPLETELY FOR SOME TIME.

Not long after Mr. Lightsey sang "Victory at Longacre," Mr. Dorset had a vision. He had been in Charles Town attending to the further distribution of his music (such as it was) when he failed to return home at the appointed hour. Mrs. Dorset, who loved the man with a fidelity that spoke better for her than it did for him, was quite worried, though she said nothing until the next morning.

"Hawthorne, go into town, would you, and inquire about my husband's whereabouts," said Mrs. Dorset. Her worry was so genuine, her devotion so touching, that if she had asked me sail to the Indies in search of him, I likely would have done it.

Jenny stood close to her mother that morning and looked entirely calm, with a shy smile, as if she knew for certain that her father was fine. I patted her on the head, nodded to Mrs. Dorset, and had a groom saddle my horse for the ride into town. It was, I believe, late summer then. The heat was heavy. The Dorsets often visited Charles Town in the hottest months, for it was cooler than the inland areas by its relation to the sea. But the Town was also subject to waves of disease, such as yellow fever and small pox, and so the city was often good or bad, depending on the air, the heat, the rain, and other factors. Mr. Dorset escaped to town often, not only to worry over his business but to attend his literary and musical affairs, mostly pushing his poor products on an unwilling populace. I have found, however, that poor men will praise the poor products of rich men, in hopes that wealth will somehow stick to them as tar sticks to a stone. As Charles Town had in those years equal numbers of the very poor and the very wealthy, the tolerance for the products such as Mr. Dorset's was amazing.

I rode the distance to town without incident. (Once on that same journey a few years after, I was chased for some miles by a pack of wild dogs intent on consuming me and my horse.) I knew that Mr. Dorset frequented several taverns, and so I visited them one by one, inquiring as to his presence. Each one said, to my astonishment, that he had passed time there in the past two days but was no longer present. Finally I came to Raper's Tavern, a low, smoky place that was busy, even though it was early in the afternoon, with an assortment of sailors, frontiersmen, and town folk of sometimes gentler manners that did not last long in that company. I made my way through the tavern, barely avoiding a full mug of rum which one man threw at another while calling him a stinking woman, which I suppose was meant as a vile curse, though it sounded rather funny to me.

I looked about in the gloom, and was about to leave when I saw Mr. Dorset sitting at a table in a corner with what I believe was a Cherokee Indian and a rough man from the backcountry. They were all drinking from full mugs, and Mr. Dorset moved unsteadily from side to side, tears coursing down his unshaven cheeks. Every few seconds, the Indian would lean over and touch a spot between Mr. Dorset's eyes and speak a few words. The frontiersman laughed each time, and each time, Mr. Dorset wept more profusely. Had I given in to Nature's urgings, I would have turned on my heel at that point and left, for my misgivings of the scene were great. But, as I was a poor man whose coin was struck in such denominations as loyalty and honesty, I could not turn away. I approached.

"Waugh! Hawthorne!" cried Mr. Dorset. He began to cry harder and harder.

"Sir, Mrs. Dorset and your children worry about you," I said.

"And I worry for them!" he cried. The Indian reached over and touched the spot between his eyes again, and Mr. Dorset's weeping became stentorian, to the delight of nearby men, who cursed and called him a coward and threw things toward him, including a small plug of tobacco, a shard of crockery, a shilling, and a crumpled sheet from the *South Carolina Gazette*. Mr. Dorset paid none of it any attention.

"Sir, this is unseemly," I said.

"His God's done crawled in his ears and spoke in musical tones," said the frontiersman, who was so drunk he could barely talk.

"Musical tones!" cried Mr. Dorset.

"Sir," I urged.

"And his God's done told him to make a journey," said the man. The Indian reached toward Mr. Dorset again, then made a small, fluttering sound, and slid under the table and did not move. The frontiersman looked down at his companion and shrugged.

"A journey," said Mr. Dorset. "Waugh, Hawthorne! My poor wife! My poor, poor children!"

At that point, he began to sing a hymn of some familiarity but changed by his condition so that it was somehow new and almost touching, as a child might sing upon first believing in the grace of Our Lord. He then slouched over and fell under the table with the Indian. The frontiersman looked down and shrugged and kept sipping his rum. He would surely have sat all day with his companions beneath the table, but I retrieved Mr. Dorset amid a hail of insults and small objects from those who sat nearby. I dragged him out the door after inquiring about his bill and instructing the proprietor where to forward the request for payment. I got Mr. Dorset into the sun, wiped his face with water from a trough, and slapped at him, but he only moaned and sang a few words from hymn tunes, so I had to tie him to his horse, which I found behind the tavern, face down and arms around the creature's neck. But as that horse had seen such indignities before, it walked beneath its awkward burden as I led it back to Longacre.

Mrs. Dorset, that kind and forbearing woman, was so pleased to see her husband that she forgave him his loss of manner and control, put him to bed, and ordered quiet so that he would awaken somewhat refreshed from the abuse he had given himself in Charles Town.

When he awoke late the next afternoon, he was in such a state of prolonged suffering from his adventure that he only moaned and cried for some time, holding his head and cursing rum, lawyers, the French, Woman, and whatever else came to his thinking. Finally, he slept once more, and this time soundly, so that everyone was pleased for the quiet, even Old Bob, who could hardly hear the commotion anyway.

When he awoke on the third day from his drinking (a Biblical number which did not escape him), Mr. Dorset had once again succumbed to piety. Never had I seen a man more miserable for his sins, both major and minor. Had he but lived a century before, I do not doubt he would have asked me to whip him to drive out the demons. As it was, he prayed for hours on end with bouts of weeping and prostration that terrified the boys. For her part, Jenny Dorset found it amazing and wonderful, and she watched her father as he wandered around the house, beating his breast and asking that God strike him dead if he ever acted as such a sinner again. The misery such begging caused the house was in no small amount due to the certainty that sooner than not, Mr. Dorset would sin again and sooner than not, God would tire of his remarks and gather him home.

Mr. Smythe came by to witness the transformation for himself, and to the horror of the servants, Mr. Dorset took it upon himself to wash Mr. Smythe's feet as Our Lord had done to show humility.

"Oh tosh, Dorset, see here, that's not necessary," said Mr. Smythe, alarmed at the thought of the act, which though it would give him an advantage socially over Mr. Dorset might also be seen as participation with a madman.

"I shall do this, for thou art tired and dust-covered," said Mr. Dorset. "What I shall do to these my brethren, ye shall do it back unto me."

He bade me gather a basin of water for him from the well, which I did, though harried at every step by Mrs. Wilson who assured me that it was a blasphemy and we would all burn in hell for it. As the bursting pheasant will distract an idle dog, so a rock thrown through a window by Tom McNew took her away from her vigilance against the act. And so I carried the basin of water into the parlor. Mr. Smythe had been then backed into a corner, and was telling Mr. Dorset with some heat to leave his shoes and stockings alone, as he did not wish his feet to be washed. Mr. Dorset was equally convinced that he must wash the feet of his neighbor, and began to chase him around the room.

"You are taken of the Devil!" cried Mr. Smythe. "I shall write it to the *Gazette* so people shall not come hereabouts and be abused by your hospitality!"

"I am your servant and cannot do less than you command me, as Our Lord did what the world commanded of Him so he could suffer for His flesh," said Mr. Dorset, looking at the ceiling.

"Bah!" cried Mr. Smythe. "Wash your *own* feet!" And with that he charged out the door, mounted his fine horse and rode home. (Mr. Smythe's poem upon the occasion was called "Ode on the Mad Washing of Feet," and Mr. Timothy printed it in the *Gazette*. The first stanza went thus:

At a hall in the wild that he calleth Longacre
A man with his God he hath wrestled.
He hath neither diamond nor nacre,
And his heart hath he crushed with a pestle.

From that point, the poem got progressively worse, ending with a plea to God to shelter us all from madmen. As he was in a period of forgiving everyone everything, Mr. Dorset forgave Mr. Smythe, until the following year when, having escaped his bout with piety, he challenged his rival to a duel, of which more later.)

Mr. Dorset's religion could not be contained long by his house, his family, or the neighbors. Our area had grown so that we could nearly but not quite be called a town, and Mr. Dorset believed that he could make a difference in the spiritual health of the place if he erected a church house, and so he spent a lavish amount of money on a church about half a mile from Longacre, somewhat between it and the Smythe property. He imported fine masons from England and France, and hired an Italian named Mocatello to paint scenes from the Holy Scriptures on the walls and ceilings. We only found out later that this Mocatello had been chased from his native land as incompetent, and indeed his angels looked more like strumpets than part of the Heavenly Host.

Mr. Dorset had taken as much care in hiring the masons as he had in selecting his artist, so barely a fortnight after we held our first meeting there, superintended by a dour parson from Town, the walls began to droop and sag so that anyone entering the church had equal chances of meeting His Maker in the spirit or the flesh.

It was at this time that my Master decided that he must make a pilgrimage to holy sites in the Mother Country. Of course, Mrs. Dorset was very upset, as she had never seen her husband's religious inclinations last so long. Each of us in our nature is given certain balances for good or ill, and most of us find a safe harbor between each and rest there for our lives. Mr. Dorset, alas, was always in one or the other but rarely in equipoise between them.

It was not enough that he go to England. He decided one Sunday morning while kneeling in prayer that his daughter Jenny should accompany him.

"Not if God Himself should strike me dead!" cried Mrs. Dorset upon being told.

"The very idea," said Mrs. Wilson. "Taking that child over the sea."

"Wild bees?" said Old Bob, hand cupped on his ear.

"God has instructed it," said Mr. Dorset quietly, fingers tented as if in prayer. An argument ensued, mostly from Mrs. Dorset, for her husband would not raise his voice or dispute hotly for he felt it unworthy of a good Christian man. Jenny came in about halfway through the argument, and after fifteen minutes more understood the fulcrum of the dispute and cast her lot firmly with her father.

"I shall go to England with him," she said.

"When cows fly!" shouted Mrs. Dorset, who was becoming disordered by the discussion.

"I would be glad to go and keep her in my care," I said. "And Mr. Dorset as well."

I shall never forget the look upon Mrs. Dorset's face at that moment: resignation, fear, a small amount of hope, perhaps, and a deep sadness. As we stood in the steep tension of the moment, Abel, Isaac, and Matthew came into the room, all crying and arguing violently about who owned a small toy. Mrs. Wilson went to them and took it away, handed it to Old Bob, and herded the boys out of the room. Mrs. Dorset sat in a chair, crossed herself, and wept silently. Old Bob sat on the floor and began to play with the toy.

"I shall instruct Mrs. Keane [for that was the name of her nurse] to begin to pack for the trip," said Jenny. She turned in a lovely whirl and left the room as an actress might exit the stage. Mr. Dorset went back to praying. Mrs. Dorset stopped crying and looked vacantly around the room. Old Bob laughed out loud at the pleasure of playing with the toy.

And so we came to the harbor in Charles Town not a fortnight later, laden with dozens of bags. Word of Mr. Dorset's pilgrimage had spread among his acquaintances, most of whom thought it very funny. A large number of his Regulars came, along with an assortment of drinking companions from various taverns, many of whom had been indulging themselves for some hours before our boarding. Mrs. Wilson, Old Bob, and the McNew twins were there, but Mrs. Dorset had stayed at Longacre with the three boys, all of whom had been thrown into fits of howling when they found God had told their father Jenny might go to England and that they could not. Abel particularly felt himself godly and knew for certain that Jenny, who indulged in occasional blasphemies and lies, was not. Abel was so distraught that his fingers became frozen in a way that did not allow him to perform on the spinet. Also present was Mr. Charles Smythe, who had come for the send-off, along with his servants, Herr Schlitz, Diana Seton, and that house's twins, Desdemona and Roderigo Smartt. Mr. Smythe appeared to have visited a tavern himself. His joy at the impending absence of Mr. Dorset was so great that he was jolly, even boisterous.

"The *Catherine*," he said, as if trying to remember. "A poor ride if I say so myself. You'll be lucky, Dorset, to arrive with your limbs whole."

"As God desires," said Mr. Dorset piously.

"Oh, right," said Mr. Smythe. He turned and whispered something to a man I did not know, and they both laughed uproariously. I was offended, but Jenny, dressed warmly and standing next to me, smiled with them, arching one eyebrow as she was apt to do if she felt some mischief was abroad in which she might partake. "Then, I presume if I do not see you again in this life, I may see you in the next."

"If I am worthy," said Mr. Dorset. One of the Regulars, at that point, came up behind Mr. Dorset and became quite sick from drinking too much rum. Jenny screamed and danced out of the way.

"Ah, the poor man speaks for each of us on your departure," said Mr. Smythe, and the company dissolved in laughter, and even I smiled, for it was clever, a much more clever comment than he usually made. The sick fellow pulled himself together and staggered off.

"Perhaps I shall find the strength to do good upon my return," said Mr. Dorset.

"It would be no small relief," said Mr. Smythe.

The day was cool and damp, and the ship *Catherine*, at bay before us, seemed a fragile bond to hold us upon the bosom of the ocean. But we boarded anyway, and soon a fair wind took us out of the harbor and out into the deep blue of the Gulf Stream.

— 15. —

THE SHIP ENCOUNTERS A TERRIBLE STORM DURING WHICH MR. DORSET'S FAITH IS SORELY TESTED, AND I BECOME MUCH BETTER FRIENDS WITH JENNY DORSET THAN I EXPECTED.

The *Catherine*, in her heyday, had been a decent enough vessel, carrying passengers and cargo from England to the Indies and Charles Town and thence in return. By the time of our voyage, however, she was an unstable old tub with a tendency to roll about even in the mildest swells. As soon as we had shipped past the sight of land, Mr. Dorset took violently ill in our tiny, cramped cabin and went on deck to hug the rail and stare balefully out to sea. After assuring myself that Jenny was safe (and indeed I never saw anyone less affected by seasickness), I joined him. The men of the crew were sympathetic with the several passengers who were ill as the vessel listed and rolled. The captain, one Seamus O'Toole, was a blunt man with one eye which constantly flickered like the coals of a dying fire. I kept expecting it to stop its restless movement, but it never did. He would check on the health of passengers, scanning them with that flickering eyelid, looking up and down, and, when assured they were not near death, he would nod sharply once and be off to chastise the men, who, though decent enough, always seemed failures in his eyes.

"Hawthorne, upon my word I think God hath taken a turn against me," he said as he leaned over the rail and was sick. He stood back up, appearing the color of aged copper, a green-yellow that made him look like an old statue or a widow. "I cannot think of the return voyage with anything but horror."

"Sir," I said.

"My daughter," he said. "She is ill?"

"She is healthy as anyone on the ship, sir," I said. "She seems fairly taken with the idea of the sea."

"Hmmm. Hawthorne, may I inquire something of you?"

"Sir?"

"My daughter, Jenny. Is there anything about her that you might describe as, well, unusual?" he asked. He clutched his stomach and closed his eyes for a moment, and out of pity I held my answer until the spasm passed.

"She is strong," I said, not knowing what else might be proper.

"Strong," he said weakly. "And from whom would she have gotten that characteristic?" I found the remark so innocent and yet so telling that I erupted in a great laugh, which I covered with a coughing fit. With his Christian uprightness, Mr. Dorset put his arm around me, thinking I had been taken ill by the motion of the boat. I righted myself in short order.

"I beg your pardon, sir," I said. "I am fine now. Certainly Jenny received her sense of strength from her parents."

The weather was not terribly foul, but the wind, which was to starboard, would not leave the vessel be, and we suddenly shifted so violently that both Mr. Dorset and myself were thrown onto the planks, where his piety was sorely tested for a brief moment.

"G—d—n this stinking stack of splinters!" cried Mr. Dorset as I helped him back to his feet. "Curse it to burn in eternal h—l!"

Soon, he regained his composure and begged my forgiveness for his blasphemy. I told him that I was in no wise his moral superior and that God would judge us each in turn on the full intent of our lives, not one moment of indisposition. He was so pleased by the thought that he immediately began to work on an ode to the sea. He walked away from me, declaiming and speaking in rough meter. A few of the sailors moved out of his way, taking with them looks of worry.

I went below decks once more and found Jenny Dorset in the lamplit cabin, singing and writing in a small book. She was untidy, and she had spilled ink on the floor and her clothing, and the delicate fingers of her right hand were stained black with the fluid. The ink pot itself slid a few inches away from her and back as the boat moved. She hummed idly to herself. I listened before I came to her proper and was amused to hear that it was "Victory at Longacre," which sounded much better without the words.

"Where is my father?" she asked. "Upon deck muling and puking like a babe in its nursemaid's arms?"

Even under those conditions, her voice was like a fine wine, her eyes bright with mischief, her attitude one of sure victory. I sat beside her, and she turned the bound pages upon which she had been writing and showed me that it was a journal she had begun. As I now have the journal in my possession, as I noted earlier, I shall quote from it occasionally, though not for the present, for those amazing sentiments that came to fill it did not really start until our return voyage. For now, she only described the sea and the cabin and the captain's nictitating eye in the language of a child.

"Well done," I said. "Your penmanship is remarkable for someone only seven years of age." She capped the ink bottle and set the pen and book aside. then she turned and sat before me.

"Hawthorne, tell me," she said. She leaned forward, not unlike one of the conspirators who slew Julius Caesar, less in an act of intimacy than in one seeking an advantage.

"Yes, miss?" I said.

"I have spoken to Tom McNew, and he told me that my father is a great fool because he does not know there is no God," she said. "You may speak with me. Is there a God?"

Had she asked if there were a sun, I would not have been more taken by surprise. She picked at her fingernail as if unconcerned, but I could tell that the answer was important to her, and I tried to summon the good grace with which I had been endowed by Nature, tried to order my words carefully so that the effect would be salutary. Unfortunately, I paused a few moments too long, for Mr. Dorset burst into the cabin just as I was about to speak of our Duty and the sufferings of Our Lord.

"Waugh!" he cried. "I have the first quatrain for a great poem about our ordeal at sea."

He arighted himself, looked in the mid-distance as he did when reciting, as if keeping his eyes on Inspiration herself. Jenny, who might have been disappointed to have missed the wisdom of my counsel, was instead delighted, and clapped as she always did when her father was about to deliver himself of his appalling verse. On this occasion, he did not disappoint. He held his seasickness in check and spoke in a loud voice:

> The heaving sea hath made its larger life from God,
> Hath given of its gulleys, puffs, and cods!
> The heaving sea shall hold us to her cheek,
> For a few days or a few weeks!
> The heaving sea. . . .

Just as his self-possession had cheered him, so now the thought of that "heaving sea" began to turn him green once more. He spoke the word *heave* two or three times in trying to start his poem again, but each time his throat clenched shut, and he looked about the cabin with a fear for his stomach that he could not master.

"Sir?" I said finally.

"*Finis*," he whispered, and he bolted out and headed for the stairs and the deck, groaning and making other sounds which in earlier times might have led a priest to call for a formal ritual to cast out spirits. Jenny looked where he had fled and smiled, then clapped once more, and turned back to me.

"A God?" she asked.

"I doubt it not," I said. I tried to summon more, to say what I felt a good father would, but in truth the sorry scene, the thought of the "heaving" ship, and my own sudden distress at having left my mother and the firm land all came to overwhelm me with sadness, and I desisted.

"Poor Hawthorne," whispered Jenny Dorset. "Poor old boy."

I was so taken by this reversal of roles that I decided to counsel Jenny further, though not in matters of faith, and so it may be possible that her later character was somehow molded by my words, though I believe I charged her to lead an upright life. I also with great likelihood gave to her a distrust for those in charge, a skepticism for the received wisdom of the world, and a touch of my own peculiar amazement at life and its vagaries. During the remainder of the voyage, which was unpleasant but hardly unsafe, Jenny and I spoke of many things, and she gave me her confidence, showed me her sadness at times as I showed her the order of the stars upon deck at night. Had she been my own child I do not think I could have cared more for her or felt more tenderly toward her future.

Mr. Dorset did not complete his poem, instead growing less religious with each passing day. He spoke only for a day or two about his religious pilgrimage, and, toward the end of the voyage, I had to shield Jenny from his dalliance with the wife of a wool merchant from Kent. When we arrived in London, I cared for Jenny without help for three days while Mr. Dorset drank and whored his way from one side of the vast Metropolis to another. The *Catherine* was not due for a return trip for several weeks, but by the time Mr. Dorset had spent all that human capital which we may spend in a short time upon the pleasures of the flesh without succumbing completely, I had to fetch him and book passage back myself on another ship called *The Dove*. True to its name, its pace was limpid and flying, and the trip back was much less heaving than the one over. For three days, Mr. Dorset slept in his dissolution, to the mild amusement of his daughter, who tenderly cared for him both out of duty and curiosity. He mumbled bits of his poetry when he came about and asked when we might be arriving in London. He spoke of God one moment and someone named Harriet the next. I was for a time appalled until Jenny gave me a glance that revealed her understanding of what had transpired. After that, I did not try again to shield her against the world.

"I could think of the sound of angels," she said one warm evening as we walked the deck and looked at God's mass of brilliant stars. She held my hand, as a child often will, for the reassurance and the consolation. "It should be nothing at all like my father's music but more like the singing of a thousand harps. I should one day like to be an angel, Hawthorne."

"You shall certainly be an angel," I said. She laughed, and in that laughter was the sound of a thousand harps.

For his part, Mr. Dorset made up fantastic stories of his pilgrimage when we returned to Longacre, including various miracles and invented cathedrals. Neither Jenny nor I ever contradicted him, and as such were his conspirators. Needless to say, his piety had evaporated completely by the time our heaving ship reached home.

— 16. —
MR. DORSET, RESTORED TO HIS FORMER STATE OF MIND
AND TEMPERAMENT, RECEIVES A LETTER OF WELCOME FROM
MR. SMYTHE AND REPLIES IN TURN.

Foxhaven
September 9, 1759

My dear Dorset,

It is with no small surprise that we welcome you back to the provinces from your all-too-brief sojourn in London. I have received word from authoritative sources that your pilgrimage was in every way as successful as the church you caused to be built in this vicinity some time ago.

In your absence, I have continued to drill my army, and lately they have been conscripted to attend next spring with a large group which will be heading to punish the Cherokee Indians for their deceits. I understand that your Regulars, which have gained such fame through your amazing composition "Victory at Longacre," have been dissolved, though a few continue to fight private battles when vexed or sober.

I have done my utmost to stanch the despicable rumours which have circulated hereabouts concerning your character from certain quarters in Charles Town. When Mr. Samuel Veazey averred that you were a "religion-sotted old fool," I told him that I believed your inebriation with the spirit genuine. When Mr. Lyttelton said that certain women were supposed to be readying suits against you for breach of promise or for failure as promised to support their bastards, I told them that you, as an honest man, had always supported your bastards.

Believe me, sir, I took no pleasure in saying that some other gentleman must have been guilty of running naked into Tradd Street on a certain night a few months past, waving his arms and crying, "Waugh! the bloody trollop has robbed me!" I said that my dear friend Mr. Dorset would never have used the word "trollop," being more familiar both with the word and the person of "whore."

I assure you that we are pleased that you and your daughter have returned from your small trip, and I also say that if you are attacked by Indians,

French, or any of the varied women in Town who appear to confuse you with another "Adam Dorset," my men will take pleasure in defending your house and your honor, should either be standing some months hence.

Cordially yours,
Charles Smythe, Esq.

To which Mr. Dorset replied, with uncharacteristic lack of restraint:

Longacre
September 10, 1759

Dear Smythe,

Only my standing as a gentleman restrains me from coming over to your hovel and thrashing you within a shilling of your life. I have seen dogs foaming at a tavern's door with more sense or manners than you possess.

I will not answer your accusations, for as a gentleman I must not. I feel duty bound, however, to say a few things which may give you pause.

First, sir, you are ugly. You are ugly as an old woman who in her superannuation hath sprouted a field of hair upon her nose. You are as ugly as the arse of your poor starved horse, which sometimes strays into my crops to escape the starvation your cheapness forces upon it.

Second, you are a coward. If you were put in charge of all troops of His Majesty in the Provinces I do not doubt but that in a fortnight we should be conquered by the Portugees.

Third, you insult the memory of the Bard of Avon by hanging upon your sniveling brood names from his glorious productions. Had your offspring the blood of anyone but you, I would worry that the names be despoilt for good. Having your intelligence and drive, however, I am sure they will take the names into well-deserved oblivion.

Fourth, I spit on you.

And sixth, should you ever utter such blasphemies upon the streets of Charles Town, I will have you driven into the sea where you can accompany your fleet of ships which now so nobly plow the bottom of the bay.

Your devoted serv't,
Adam Dorset, Esq.

— 17. —

THE EXCHANGE OF LETTERS, FAR FROM CLEARING THE AIR
BETWEEN THE TWO MEN, LEADS TO A DUEL FOUGHT ON THE GROUNDS
OF LONGACRE, AND AN UNEXPECTED ENDING TO IT.

Mr. Smythe demanded satisfaction for the insult, which Mr. Dorset was pleased to give him. Both households were thrown into a fearful uproar. Instead of sparing his children's tender emotions should he not survive the duel, Mr. Dorset trumpeted loud and far his superiority as a marksman and refused to practice with his pistols, though we heard constant gunfire from Foxhaven, where it was said Mr. Smythe had hired a shooting master late from Paris who had tutored the Marquis de Savon in his successful match with Mr. Timothy Slate of London. At all hours could be heard the firing of guns and corrections to an unsteady hand at Foxhaven. For his part, Mr. Dorset took the odd step of giving his training into the hands of rum from Jamaica and to his inkwell, from which poured a torrent of verse and music even worse than anything he had inflicted on us before. Fortunately, he did not publish any of it, as he was keeping quiet to prevent authorities from intervening in the duel. (Later, after the fight had ended, I quietly gathered all these works and burnt them in the fireplace, an act for which the literary leaders of this country now owe me a debt of gratitude.) Mrs. Dorset went about wringing her hands and weeping, imploring Mr. Dorset to think of his four little children and the inevitable poverty to which they would descend if he should be killed. His belief in his superiority to anything a Smythe might do, however, kept Mr. Dorset from considering such a thing. He would only laugh heartily, shake his head, and, if seized by an eruption from the Muse, head for his desk to add yet another stanza to the narrative of his bravery. Jenny, not so surprisingly, became overexcited by the entire prospect. She caused a fine gown to be sewn so she could wear it on the appointed day. For her part, Mrs. Dorset ordered black.

As the day neared, I cautiously reminded Mr. Dorset that he had not yet chosen a second in the duel and that the rules and his honor said he should do so. He said nothing about it until that evening when the Dorset family was assembled at table. He was roaring with good spirits among the fragrance of a goose and other delicious victuals, though the boys and Mrs. Dorset were all somber. Jenny smiled beautifully and hummed the tune from "Victory at Longacre."

"Now then," said Mr. Dorset. "As to this matter on Tuesday next. I have given the matter of my second a great deal of thought. I could have Isaac Bolcombe, who is a fair man and a good shot. Or I could have John Johnson, the tailor, who is steadfast for me and would be here in an instant should I call. But that would admit to the fool Smythe that I believe his threat genuine, that I require the help of men known for their cunning and strength with arms. No! I shall not give him that satisfaction." Here, Mr. Dorset took a great draught of rum, belched loudly, devoured a leg from the hen, and then wiped his greasy hand on his trousers, to the great distress of Mrs. Dorset and of his son Matthew, whose fine manners were revolted by the sight. "No, I shall not give him that satisfaction. I shall select as second someone here from this very house!"

My heart fell, for I was the youngest of his most-trusted staff, and it was not unknown that I could handle a gun myself, having acquired a reputation as a good hunter over the past few years.

"Ridiculous," said Mrs. Dorset bravely.

"Waugh! Not so! For I fear no man, and certainly I fear no greasy groundhog like Smythe!" cried Mr. Dorset. Jenny clapped wildly. "I shall take as my second . . ." He looked about the room, and, as Fortune would have it in her infinite mirth, Old Bob was enmeshed in a curtain, trying without success to tie it off for the evening. Mr. Dorset cried and pointed.

"Oh no," said Mrs. Wilson.

"Oh yes!" cried Mr. Dorset. "I select as my second Old Bob!"

"Second?" cried Old Bob when he saw Mr. Dorset shout toward him. "Not above a minute to tie it off, but a second? The fastest hands an angel has cannot do it in a second." He then fell down, ensnared in the cloth, pulling it from the frame. The entire sight was calculated to give humor to us, but no one laughed but Mr. Dorset and his daughter, for the rest of us knew that a gun in the hands of Old Bob was frightening indeed.

The appointed day came. Mr. Smythe arrived at Longacre, dressed in blue silks and the latest finery. His second was Pierre Theoroux, perhaps the best shot in Town, a ruthless man who loved blood as a pilgrim loves God. Altogether, they looked confident and sure of their mission. When Mr. Dorset came from the house, he was wearing half-soiled linens, holding the pistol box in one hand and a glass of wine in the other, being trailed by Old Bob, who was, at Mr. Dorset's direction, reading from his epic poem about the duel. Somehow, Old Bob had injured his left foot and walked with an extreme limp, so that every word of the poem which came when the lame foot was put down became swallowed up in a sort of hiccough. The effect was such that, despite the gravity of the situation, I fell against a tree in laughter.

They came to the shooting ground, and the formalities commenced. I stood nearby and watched as the men took their weapons and listened to the instructions. As they listened, an amazing thing happened. Mr. Dorset, who now looked as vulnerable as a child, had neglected to completely tuck in his chemise, and Mr. Smythe, no longer able to bear his disorder, reached to stuff it back. When he did so, Mr. Dorset raised his arms automatically, as a child will when attended by its mother. Suddenly, both men, touched by the unexpected tenderness of the scene, got tears in their eyes. I believe to this day that they realized that Life was a far more interesting game than Death, and that if they endlessly insulted each other there was in those taunts a kind of affection, not unlike that which attends certain marriages.

Old Bob, however, misreading the moment, threw his arms over his head and cried aloud.

"He robbeth my Master!" cried Old Bob. The poor fellow then reached for the pistol, and, wheeling to fire, shot the small finger of his own left hand off. Mr. Dorset, seeing the mistake, cried loudly, and Mrs. Dorset, hidden inside, heard her husband's cry and, assuming he had been mortally wounded, began to scream. For their part, both Mr. Dorset and Mr. Smythe began to attend to Old Bob, who fell in a swoon and began to address God intimately. They stanched the flow of blood. The reader with a more delicate constitution might turn here to the next part of this History, for what happened next is shocking, though not without humor.

Upon the firing of the gun, Mr. Dorset's pack of hounds broke from their lodgings and came in a howling, barking mass toward us, sniffing the ground. I espied that poor Bob's unfortunate finger was lying in a small pool of blood just as one of the dogs did, and that dog gathered it and held it between his lips as a man does a cigar, whereupon he was attacked violently by twenty other dogs. It took three grooms an hour to get the dogs back up, and we saw no sign again of Old Bob's small finger.

Mr. Dorset and Mr. Smythe carried him from the field inside, and when Mrs. Dorset found what had happened, she fell about her husband's feet crying and praying and ignoring Old Bob, who suffered from a mild delirium and believed for a time that he was once again entangled in the curtains. I never saw two men work together with greater dispatch or understanding of each other than Mr. Smythe and Mr. Dorset. They bandaged Old Bob, put him to bed raving about fabrics, then retired to the sitting room for a mug of hot rum.

For some time after that, I was convinced that the men might truly become friends, but their fight was too much fun to stop, and soon they were back at it. For his part, Old Bob wore his disfigurement like a medal, for he believed the finger lost on a day he had saved his Master from robbery.

— 18. —
AN APOLOGIA FROM THE AUTHOR FOR HIS MULTIPLE FAILURES
AND FOR NOT MAKING CLEAR SOME OF THE IMPORTANT PERSONAGES
WHO WILL PEOPLE LATER PARTS OF THIS HISTORY.

I have no skills comparable to our Great Authors and have therefore brought into this world so far a misshapen narrative which gives only a glimpse of the Dorset and Smythe families in periods of great uneasiness. I have not shown Mr. Dorset on days when he attended his farms and helped enlarge his fortunes and thereby provide for his family, servants, and slaves. I have not described Mr. Smythe's tenderness when his son Iago was very ill in the mid-1750s. Nor have I described as well I should the others in our story.

Ophelia Van Dyke Smythe, for example, committed many good works in her life, helping provide for the poor and unfortunate. Lydia Foxe Dorset also cared for many people and managed to survive life with Mr. Dorset for some years. I have spoken little of my own mother's role with the Dorset family, less because of its importance (she was a valued member of the staff) than from a desire to protect her Sacred Memory and its Privacy. Likewise I have not spoken of the fact that in 1758 I was wed and that my wife gave me four fine children, two of which survived their infancy.

I have spoken even less well of the McNew twins at Longacre and the Smartt twins at Foxhaven. I have described all of these people, however, in relation to how they came into the story of Jenny Dorset, and, until some time later, they were more stage hands than actors in the drama.

Therefore do I apologize and ask the reader's indulgence. Amazing facts regarding all these people shall be revealed in time.

— 19. —
JENNY DORSET LEAVES A MESSAGE TO HER PARENTS
IN THE SPRING OF 1761 THAT REVEALS SHE HAS GONE TO THE
CHEROKEE COUNTRY WITH A FAMILY NAMED GROAT, WHICH PASSED
LONGACRE AND STAYED FOR A TIME TO REST THEIR HORSES.

During the winter of 1759–60, the Province of South Carolina was engaged in a war with the French, about whom I can say nothing so ill that it expresses my distaste for their entire race, and their Indian allies. As I have said, the Cherokees had been our friends before, but the French, making the same kind of promises their men habitually make their women before abandoning them, had turned the Cherokees from us to the path of war. It was therefore unlikely that a family of wanderers named Groat appeared one night in late winter at Longacre, carrying only the most meager rations on their horses. They were lost. Though the road from Charles Town to Ninety-Six and then Fort Prince George was well known by then, the man had by a natural arrogance gone from it, looking for a shorter way. He was a short, red-faced fellow with heavy, thick fingers and a German accent. He appeared at our door asking for food and directions and leave to stay in our barns for a few days of rest, all of which Mr. Dorset granted, as he often did strangers in those days. Mr. Groat had the look of violence about him, eyes darting one way and then another as if expecting a bullet to come his direction any moment. He rode with his wife, who was pale and blonde and utterly silent. Whatever he told her to do, she did without response, her eyes always to the ground. I was shocked, having become accustomed to the women of Longacre, who preferred arguing to eating on most occasions. With Mr. and Mrs. Groat were two small children, a boy and a girl, both as blond and paleskinned as their mother and just as frightened. They huddled near their mother as chicks do to a hen. I resolved to ask indulgences for them, but Mr. Dorset was busy designing a topiary garden with hedges to be in the shape of fanciful animals of his own invention and could not be bothered. I got some blankets from the house for them, and they stayed between the Dorset family and the slaves. Because of his pride, Mr. Groat insisted on working for their board and food, and he helped our sawyer fell some trees and cut them into lengths for the stove. Mrs. Groat worked with many others in preparing the land for our house garden and herb patch. The children worked at laundry, never smiling or complaining. Our sawyer, one Sisk, told Mrs. Dorset one day that Mr.

Groat worried him because he often lost his temper and struck and cursed the wood as he chopped it. I held back from them. Only Jenny Dorset seemed so intrigued by the children that she could not stay away.

One evening, after the Groats had been with us for about a week, Jenny came to me in the dining room. The family had completed its meal, and I was polishing the table, a job I always found most agreeable at the end of a long day, for it was useful and the wood always responded with a high gloss. Jenny sat in her father's chair at the end of the table, something he expressly forbade anyone else to do. The boys always obeyed him in that regard, though Jenny rarely did. I told her good evening and asked if her nurse had not called her to be readied for bed. She shrugged and looked down, wanting to say something yet not quite ready. I continued my work, and the table responded, throwing off my own satisfied reflection.

"Mr. Hawthorne," she said finally. "Do you think the Groats shall survive among the wild Indians?"

"I couldn't say," I responded. "I might say, though, that as pride goeth before a fall, arrogance doth also. You have read that, I am sure. Mr. Groat seems too sure that he is right about everything."

"Yes," she said. "But do we not need men who believe in victory?"

"That is true, but only victory of a kind," I explained. "Not the victory of Pyrrhus or others which have caused the victory to lose as much as the vanquished. The best kinds of victories are those in which reason and right triumph together. I daresay Mr. Groat may have strength on his side but I doubt his reason."

She was deep in thought, and I was proud that I was able to add something to her education. I was an autodidact and so was more pleased with my learning than those educated by greater masters. I looked at her solemn face and thought that she was persuaded by my grasp of logic. I submitted to the sin of pride.

"You're wrong, of course," she blurted. "As all adults are. The best victories are those for which no possible gain can be had. The victories of the heart, Mr. Hawthorne. If Mr. Groat were right and reasoned well, too, we should have made him King of America. As we believe him mad, we send him to the barns and then on his way to the Indians with only his bravery to hold him. I am certain of this."

I was so startled by the wisdom coming from a child not yet eight years old that I stood before her, holding my oiled rag and unable to say a word. If such thought seems impossible to you from one so young, I can only say that Jenny Dorset matured young in some ways and never matured at all in others. I was very nearly dumbfounded.

"As you say, Jenny," I said, bowing. (I was particularly vain of my ability to bow with elegance that was not quite deference and certainly not submission. We often speak more with unspoken gestures than all the words our esteemed Authors can scribble.)

"That's all, Mr. Hawthorne," she said, nodding. She leaped up and was gone, leaving in her place the sprightly memory of her honest inquiry. For my part, I tried to finish my work polishing the table, but it was futile, for I had seen a clarity and shine in Jenny that I would never see in a table, and so my work that evening was spoilt.

I thought very little of the incident until it became evidence for a startling turn of events. The next day, I was cleaning the fireplaces, a task which I decidedly did not enjoy, when Mr. Dorset came running into the sitting room with his usual excitement.

"Hawthorne!" he cried. "Come to the library and see the drawings for my topiary garden! Waugh! It will be a wonder of the age!"

"Sir," I nodded. If Mr. Dorset was always in competition with Mr. Smythe, their respective libraries were not close in quality or number. I had seen Mr. Smythe's library the year before, and it consisted of several uncut sets of standard tomes, nothing of real interest and obviously unread. Mr. Dorset, on the other hand, had nearly a thousand volumes, one of the largest collections in South Carolina, and he had read many of them, often writing ill-tempered comments about the Authors in the margins or making notes to have his overseer buy certain provisions during the planting season. Mr. Dorset had the facility of turning everything in his life into a miscellany that held his own scattered but interesting world. I went into the library with him, and he had several large sheets of thick, cream-colored paper on his desk, each covered with drawings worthy of a child no older than Isaac Dorset or perhaps Iago Smythe. The drawings were of topiary designs, each of an impossible beast of Mr. Dorset's own design.

"Now, Hawthorne," he said. "Here is the ring-necked monkey-dog. And next is the tiger-butterfly, and here is the deer-cat. Waugh! Have you ever seen anything like this?"

"Upon my word not," I admitted.

He was no doubt preparing to lecture me on each species when Mrs. Wilson, trailed by a madly weeping Lydia Dorset, burst into the room.

"Not now!" cried Mr. Dorset. "I am wrestling with the Muse!"

"Gone!" cried Mrs. Dorset, and she started to swoon, and fell, but only when she was close enough to a sofa to land squarely on it.

"Gone!" cried Mrs. Wilson. The sensitive Matthew Dorset came into the room and said the same word; he fell to his knees and began to weep in utter silence. I glanced through the window, thinking I might see something, but all I espied was Old Bob chasing a chicken.

"Who in the world is gone?" said Mr. Dorset, reluctantly putting his drawings down and leaning to his wife.

"Jenny," she gasped. "Gone with the Groats."

"Aaahhhh! Fie!" cried Mr. Dorset. He leaped up so suddenly that Mrs. Dorset, who had been holding him for balance, fell from the sofa to the floor, where she was unnoticed by her husband. Mrs. Wilson and I helped her back up. "Gone with the Groats? Gone with the Groats? I shall assemble the Regulars! Kidnapped my daughter!"

"They didn't kidnap her," screamed Mrs. Dorset. "And for God's sake don't call your Regulars. Here! Oh! It's too terrible!" She gestured for Mrs. Wilson, who held a small piece of paper in her hand. Mrs. Wilson gave it to Mr. Dorset, who read it slowly.

"Waugh! Run off with Groats to live among the Indians?" he cried. He read the note once more. "Run off with Groats to live among the Indians?" He read the note a third time. "What is this? That she spoke with Mr. Hawthorne and he said Mr. Groat was a brave man? Wha'?"

"Sir, I did not say that exactly," I said.

"But you spoke with her about this Groat?" he asked. I suddenly felt as if I were a conspirator when in truth I was innocent.

"I listened to her speak of them," I said.

"Then you shall no longer be a part of this household staff!" he cried. "I banish you to the wilderness, even to the Smythe household! You shall wander in the desert for forty years!"

"The desert, sir?" I said unwisely. "We live closer to swamps."

"Fie on't!" he screamed. "Out! Out d—d Hawthorne!"

I was downcast at being so accused, but, rather than fight accusations from which I could not adequately defend myself, owning to the vagueness of Jenny's letter, I felt it better to take my leave, and so I bowed and went into the yard to get some fresh air before deciding what to do next. I had been out there for no more than fifteen minutes when Mr. Dorset came flying out the door, arms over his head and calling my name. At the distance of all these years, I can say that I was not surprised, for it was in keeping with his character that he wanted back sooner than later what he threw away.

"Forgive me!" he cried. "I know you cannot have thrown in with Groats! Hawthorne, what shall I do now?"

I realized of a sudden how much Jenny meant to him, for he fell distracted to his knees and began to weep like a child, his frame shuddering. I could hear Mrs. Dorset screaming from inside the house and Mrs. Wilson trying to comfort her. I knelt beside my Master and comforted him as I could. "I have failed her! Given her too little love and security! For she hath rebuked me and thrown in with Groats!"

"We must go and get her back," I said gently.

"Get her back!" he screamed. "From the wild Indians and French? From the clutches of the Groats?"

"The best victories, sir, are the victories of the heart," I said.

The words had a tonic effect on him. He stood, brushed the grass and varied insects from his clothing, and looked at me with new respect.

"It's true, isn't it?" he asked. "It's true that the best victories are the victories of the heart? For what am I if I cannot see my darling Jenny each evening? What is my heart if I do not have the full complement of my children to comfort me in my old age? Who shall view the fantastic animals in my topiary garden then? Who shall bring me grandsons to dandle on my knee and to speak of the great wars with that miserable fool Smythe? Who shall bring the generation which will hold against his miserable offspring? Oh, Hawthorne, we must go after her, after the Groats, and into whatever hostile country we find! We must take courage and find Jenny even should we forfeit our lives in the pursuit! We must not worry about the torture at the hands of the Indians! We must not worry that we might have even our entrails pulled out and hung about our necks!"

He paused for a moment, and the meaning of his words sunk into his ears, and he clamped his hand over his mouth to keep himself from being sick. I patted his back, and after a few moments he regained a portion of his composure. Just then, Old Bob came around the house, still chasing the chicken, which eluded him with the ease a fox could escape an elephant. We both watched, our small dramatic scene interrupted, until Old Bob and the chicken disappeared around the house.

"I shall go with you to bring her back," I said.

"Brave Hawthorne!" he cried. "Brave Dorset!" He then took three steps back toward the house and collapsed into a faint. I took him into the house, and at first Mrs. Dorset thought him dead and was even more hysterical, but then he came around, and she flailed him with her tongue worse than Xanthippe ever did old Socrates. Finally, worn out, she left, trailing Mrs. Wilson with her.

As the day was passing, and we had no provisions together, we resolved to leave at first light the following day. Servants were sent to Town to buy materials, and Mr. Dorset arranged for about twenty men to come with him, including myself. Had we all known then that this was but the first of many excursions Jenny Dorset would make in her life, we might have allowed a few days to pass before we set out for her. But we could not have known then that Jenny would become such a character in the lives of so many in the Province or that she would have a role in the Revolution against Great Britain some years thereafter. We only knew that she had thrown in with Groats and headed for Indian country.

We made our farewells to the women of Longacre early the next morning. Mrs. Dorset was too shaken to come down. For his part, Mr. Dorset, though worried for his daughter, seemed to think he was no less than Hannibal preparing to conquer the Alps. He was in boisterous good spirits and would have remained so had not Mr. Charles Smythe come riding up just as our wagons were preparing to leave.

"Oh my God," said Mr. Dorset when he saw his rival dismounting.

"No, just Charles Smythe of Foxhaven," said Mr. Smythe wryly, "though you may think of me thus if it pleases you."

"I am off," said Mr. Dorset. "I cannot speak with you now."

"Please a moment," said Mr. Smythe.

They walked to one side, and then a miracle occurred. They spoke earnestly and quietly, and after a few moments I saw that the morning sun sparkled with the tears on both men's cheeks. They clasped arms. Although Mr. Dorset refused to say of what they had spoken, I knew it was about the love of children, about the brief transit of life and our place in it. And I knew that whatever battles might come in the future between them (and there were many), they would never be able to erase that moment when they embraced.

I must at this point beg the gentle reader's pardon, for, having come to the end of the first book of this History, I fear I have described less about Jenny Dorset than about her father, but that is proper, in that each of us is the product of those early years. I cannot think what life I might have led if my father had not been lost at sea or my mother had not come to Longacre. I can only say it is what Nature intended.

As Mr. Charles Smythe rode back to Foxhaven, we set out to find Jenny Dorset, her father and I leading the way.

BOOK II.

— 1. —

My religious sentiments have come upon me slowly and steadily over the
years, unlike those of Mr. Dorset, which flung themselves at him riotously and unexpectedly. I must admit that I have never suffered an epiphany
or had a vision that could not be explained by rum or fatigue. I do not
believe this means God loves me less but that He has allowed my character to parallel my age, growing as a tree grows. Each year, I flatter myself
that I have grown another ring of consideration and thoughtfulness.
Patience may be the best virtue I ever possessed, certainly not one which
causes much good in the world but a good quality nonetheless. Therefore
I can say with the blessings of long thought that I believe the expeditions
of the Crown against the Cherokee Indians were immoral.

Of the two great fights we took to them, one was already aborning that
late winter of 1760 when we set out in search of Jenny Dorset. Under the
command of Col. Archibald Montgomery, twelve companies of Highlanders had been brought down from the North where they were fighting the French, about whom age has not given me any reason to speak
well. In early April, these troops landed in Charles Town and a little more
than two weeks later set out up-country to fight the Cherokees. We left
a few days before them so that they were in our rear, so to speak, though
we knew they were coming. As it turned out, the force did little harm but
to a few of the lower Cherokee villages, and another force a year later finished the job.

The Cherokees had killed settlers and others along the frontier, but the soldiers and others had killed as many Indians, and I saw that in no wise was one the moral superior of the other. For his part, Mr. Dorset was concerned about his daughter's well-being, but he was even more excited by what he continually referred to as the "Dorset Expedition." After only two days' journey, he had convinced himself that he was a great visionary, an explorer who would open parts of the land to the Province. He seemed to enjoy the hard conditions of sleeping beneath the stars, which I had done but little in my life and did not like at all.

I have not told of a small incident that occurred at Longacre just as we were to leave. Mr. Dorset had arranged to have a groom bring ten of his dogs with us for hunting, and though I felt this a ludicrous decision, considering how untrained the mongrels were, I said nothing. When the dogs came dashing around the house, past our train, and off into the woods, we were amazed to see right behind them Old Bob, eyes red from weeping, speaking with great supplication to his Master. Mr. Dorset, who always enjoyed such displays of loyalty, was touched, even though he kept turning to curse the dogs.

"What is the problem, Bob?" he cried. Two of the dogs were fighting furiously near the horses and bothered them so that a teamster had leaped down with a whip and was chasing dogflesh about without much effect. Bob scratched his cheek with the stub where his little finger had been, then began to weep. From behind his back, he produced a bedroll. He fell to his knees.

"Please do not leave me here," he moaned. "How can I serve you if I am so many miles from you then?"

"Brave Bob!" cried Mr. Dorset. He put his hand into the air as I had seen in certain paintings of military leaders. "I salute your loyalty!" Just then, Mr. Dorset's horse, an unreliable nag called Henry, reared up, dumping him on a dog which had run back among the wagons. The dog, aggrieved by such a blow, bit Mr. Dorset on the leg, causing him to curse in a wild manner and lash out at the poor animal, which fortunately disappeared once more.

"Who can handle your dogs but I?" said Old Bob.

"You have never handled the dogs," I said.

"Then I could surely learn," cried Old Bob.

"Learn, he could!" shouted Mr. Dorset. He limped to Bob and clasped his arms about him. Old Bob went briefly back into the house to bid his farewells, and then joined us on his own horse, which was by far the worst beast of burden I ever saw, a sway-backed mare called Hadrian, the least-favorable name ever given to a horse.

And so the Dorset Expedition set out. We had to cross some country to get to the main road which led north, and this was uneventful except for the sighting of an alligator. Our lead teamster, a stupid and arrogant fellow named Watrous, took a shot at it, and his musket blew up, giving him slight facial burns which caused him pain and made the rest of us suffer his ill temper for days. We headed up toward Ninety-Six, which was a frontier outpost perhaps 175 miles from Charles Town. On the third night, a tremendous thunderstorm came over us, and we sat beneath our oiled tenting, very tired and alone.

"Hawthorne, what would make a child of that age run away with Groats?" asked Mr. Dorset. Lightning crashed near us, causing the dogs (several of which had found their way with us and were eating as they could from rodents and such) to howl piteously. "Would you say that she is having so bad a life at Longacre that she would go off with such poor specimens of the human race?"

"I cannot say that I understand much of the human race," I admitted. "But perhaps, having seen such a voyage as she did, she wants now to see new and more amazing things."

"Waugh! Amazing things?" he cried. "More amazing than Longacre? What could more be more amazing than such a vast holding carved from the very virgin wilderness? What could impress more than one man growing to become an important writer and composer in this desert?"

"Swamp," I said.

"Oh, right," he said, waving the example away.

He was beginning to launch another thought, perhaps even a speech, when Watrous ducked under our awning, dripping with water and wearing a scowl. He came in and squatted, and I never before saw a person of so few redeeming qualities, almost more animal than man.

"Waterhorse?" said Mr. Dorset, who was never good with names.

"Watrous, sir," he said. "Sir, I beg to inform you that Tomlinson in the far rear has turned his wagon around and headed back toward Charles Town." Just then, another thunderclap struck, but it was nothing compared to the fury of Mr. Dorset. Poets with better command of the tongue than I might have said he "exploded," but that word is lacking, too, in describing the rage which was unleashed. Mr. Dorset roared like

a bull, and burst from beneath the oiled cloth and into the rain, where
Watrous and I followed him. He uttered every profane vowel he could
summon, and thrashed about, waving his arms, which we would see only
in the occasional flashes of lightning. Certainly he looked the madman,
and Watrous and a few others held back, though I had seen it before and
merely stayed out of Mr. Dorset's reach. Old Bob, who had apparently
been sleeping, wandered out in his nightgown, accompanied by a dog he
had named Flipsy, a small white mongrel which had taken a liking to him.
His own poor horse, Hadrian, was tied nearby, quietly munching grass
and staring balefully at the small fire which remained against the rain.

"Bah! Fie!" cried Mr. Dorset. "Saddle Henry for me, Waterhouse! I
shall fetch Trombleman to a lesson or cut his heart out, one or the other!"

"Rain," said Bob, amazed.

"It's Watrous," the teamster said darkly. "And you should forget Tomlinson. Him riding in the dark even on the road will come to no good.
You would never make way, and going for him in the morning won't
hardly get no daughter back to you, meaning no disrespect."

"Then I shall send someone to kill him on the road!" screamed Mr.
Dorset. "A thief he is, taking my provisions! I will hire me a highwayman
to track him down and throttle him! Death to Trombleman!"

Mr. Dorset then struck a pose such as might be seen on a medallion
or in public statuary, standing that way so long that the effect of a pose
was too obvious to deny. Old Bob told us that he was getting wet, and he
went back inside, as I did. Mr. Dorset quickly followed suit, damning
Mr. Tomlinson to eternal perdition and swearing revenge. (As it turned
out, the man disappeared with the provisions and to my knowledge was
never seen again.)

We turned the lamps low and fell asleep to a tremendous rainstorm.
When I awoke the following morning, I found Mr. Dorset in a state of
such anxiety that I feared a party of Indians might have found us. He was
walking around our campsite waving his arms high, then higher, making
grand and odd gestures.

"Hawthorne!" he cried when he saw me. "I shall be famous throughout the entire world for this!"

"Sir?" I said.

"For 'The Departure of Trombleman'!" he shouted. "Listen now to the
first two stanzas and tell if you have ever heard anything more perfect on
this earth." The camp was stirring, and Watrous and several other rough

men were about, making bizarre noises and coughing from an over-indulgence in spirits the evening before. I leaned against a tree. Old Bob's horse was still eating grass and looking bored. Mr. Dorset cleared his throat.

> *Now the dying embers of the fire had been spent*
> *When we found that Trombleman had went*
> *Forth in steal with our manifold provisions!*
> *Such a dastard act that all the divisions*
> *Of hell could not scarce hold or detain!*
>
> *And I, the leader of this expedition,*
> *Summoned up the ghosts from perdition*
> *To pursue Trombleman with their furies*
> *Past the reach of justices or of juries!*
> *Through the lands of the insane!*

Mr. Dorset was wild with inspiration. He came to me, smiling with such exhaustion and belief in his genius that I could not speak ill of his appalling talent.

"What of that?" he said.

"I am amazed," I said honestly.

"Oh, Hawthorne! Brave critic!" he cried.

— 2. —

THE FIRST OF WHAT WILL BE MANY INSTALLMENTS FROM
THE JOURNALS OF JENNY DORSET, DESCRIBING HER DEPARTURE WITH
THE GROATS, HER ILL-TREATMENT AT THE HANDS OF MR. GROAT,
AND HER SUBSEQUENT DETERMINATION TO SETTLE HER SCORES,
ALONG WITH COMMENTS FROM THE AUTHOR.

Because Jenny Dorset's journal has become my sole property, and because the Maker will shortly lay me down to eternal rest, I shall share it, even should critics doubt its proper place in this History. For one thing, Jenny often did not date entries, calling them only by the day of the week, which was often as far ahead as she thought or planned. I have been able, however, to put these journals in their proper order through comparing their contents with my memory. I believe the Reader will value honesty as much as privacy and so forgive my breach of the trust she showed in what were meant to be private papers. The only good thing I can say about the Groats was that they allowed her to bring quill, ink, and her journal, though not from indulging her fancies. I learned some years later that it was because none of the Groats could read or write, and, owning to Jenny's tender years, they wished her to practice should the talent become useful. None had the least idea what she was writing.

THURSDAY — *I will go with the Groats before light in the morning. Oh, adventures! I shall become a story myself to be written in the* GAZETTE. *Mr. Groat seems a decent man. He works hard. Mrs. Groat does not speak. The boy, Andrew, is a vile, thick-lipped monster, waugh! But the girl, whose name is Lucinda, is very sad for all. I shall take my leave of the house without speaking to anyone. Today one of father's dogs bit the justice of the peace as he came around. An unpleasant scene.*

FRIDAY — *I am gone from home without family now or friend! What adventures await me as a settler in the Indian country? I do not know. Mr. Groat beats the horses fearfully. Once Lucinda began to cry at his ill treatment of the beasts, and he came back from his own horse to the wagon and beat her as well. Mrs. Groat did not try to stop it. I was made to work very hard. I do not like it.*

SATURDAY — *A terrible rainstorm. A group of soldiers bearing papers stopped us and demanded to know our destination and cargo, and asked if we had ever heard of a man named Groat or his wife and children, and Mrs. Groat and the children whispered no. As you can see, I have the three children, said Mr. Groat. They let us go. What has he done?*

SUNDAY — *For reasons I cannot say, Mr. Groat was kind as we rested for a day. He affected a little dance, and sang an Irish song. He went away to look for signs. I played with Lucinda, who will answer no questions about anything. I saw Andrew with his trousers down in a Private Act and was curious about his system but could not ask. I presume it is like horses.*

MONDAY— *We are not going to Ninety-Six but instead passing it to the east to avoid men. Mr. Groat once more is very foul and angry. Once when Andrew asked the name of a tree after Mr. Groat had given us an order of silence, his*

*father beat the poor boy. As Andrew could not cry out, he swallowed his tears.
I never saw such cruelty. Mr. Groat is a vile, low creature, and I hope he dies.*

TUESDAY— *I wonder at how Mother is handling this absence. I miss her and
the house fearfully now, even Father and the servants, but I cannot say if they
notice my absence. Today we saw our first Indian, far away across a small
creek. He was grazing his horse and simply looking around. The sky was full
of clouds that were puffed up into white and gray pads by God. I heard birds
that never lived near us.*

WEDNESDAY — *Mr. Groat works me fearfully hard. I haul water and fire-
wood. Mrs. Groat says not a word. He beat poor Andrew so badly today the
boy wept. I have come to live with wicked people and should have stayed at
home. I am not unhappy. I will get revenge on him. I will find him asleep
and sell him to mean Indians. I will watch him pay.*

— 3. —

WATROUS AND SEVERAL OTHERS REVEAL THEIR TRUE NATURE,
AND MR. DORSET, OLD BOB, AND I ARE LEFT TO NAVIGATE UP THE
ROAD IN SEARCH OF HIS DAUGHTER WITH MEAGER RATIONS AND
NO CLEAR IDEA OF WHAT WE ARE DOING.

The fourth night out, we camped beside a large stream, which had
pools full of fish. We affected rods and lines, and Old Bob caught a
large sunfish, but it barbed his hands as he took it from the hook, so he
dropped it back into the water. We had plenty of food, however, on the
wagons, and I knew that we could easily make it to Ninety-Six where
more provisions could be had. One by one, Mr. Dorset's Regulars had
made their excuses and dropped away to ride down the road back
toward Charles Town, until only myself, Old Bob, Watrous, and five
teamsters were left in the expedition. Mr. Dorset somehow felt this
could only bring him more glory and so bade each one farewell in turn.
All the dogs had turned back or abandoned us except for Flipsy, the
hound which seemed to think that Old Bob was a God in human disguise and hung near him to the amusement of Mr. Dorset, who said it
was the son Bob never had. This day we ate well, and as the evening was
dry and pleasantly warm, we made a large fire before which Mr. Dorset
recited from his poetry and sang from his numerous songs, including

one called "There Was a Man Called Smythe," a bawdy piece about our neighbor, who would be coming up-country with his volunteers short-ly, accompanying Montgomery's Highlanders. We drank well, Mr. Dorset particularly. Old Bob, who persisted in maintaining his habits from Longacre, again put on his nightgown and cap and lay on his bedroll beneath an elm tree. Soon, Mr. Dorset fell asleep from too much rum and Art, and I turned myself in as well.

Sometime in the night, Watrous raised an alarm. I heard him shout something about Indians and then fire, and I stood to find the woods alight with flame. Watrous shouted for us to go down near the creek as the Indians had set fire to the woods. I had trouble awakening Old Bob because of his deafness and Mr. Dorset because he was drunk. I did res-urrect them, however, and we fled, Mr. Dorset calling all the while for troops and for his horse. Flipsy barked madly, and Old Bob's horse, Hadrian, came with us, walked into the stream, and sat down to watch the spectacle. Soon, the fire began to abate, and I felt it curious that the other men had not joined us after they had moved the wagons from the fire's path or come with us to defend ourselves against Indians. We wait-ed for some time until it was clear that the wagons were gone and so were the teamsters.

We crept back up the hill, except for Hadrian, who thrashed about in the water as if he were a duck. When we reached the campsite, we found the woods fire burned out and the wagons gone.

"Brave Waterhouse to save the wagons!" cried Mr. Dorset. "Do you see Indians there?" The campfire still burned brightly. We saw nothing and heard nothing but the wagons disappearing back down the road. I under-stood the situation too well and did not want to reveal it to Mr. Dorset, but I knew I must.

"Sir, they have taken the wagons and left us here," I said quietly. "It was not Indians. It was the teamsters robbed us." Mr. Dorset grabbed his chest and staggered backward a few feet, making inarticulate sounds and curses. Old Bob knelt before the fire to play with his dog.

"Waugh! Bah! Fie!" gargled Mr. Dorset. "Villains! Quick, my horse!"

I looked about and saw no horses, only Hadrian, who was whinnying and splashing down in the creek. I told Mr. Dorset they must have dri-ven off all the horses but for Old Bob's nag, who was bathing at the moment. He ran about waving his arms and calling down heaven on Watrous, whom he still called Waterhouse, begging that God would strike both him and Trombleman dead for being despicable b—t—ds, Etc. After a time, even the sounds of the wagons disappeared, and we were left alone. The teamsters had at least off-loaded a few provisions so we would not starve. Soon, Old Bob fell asleep with his dog, taking little notice of the events. Mr. Dorset's drunkenness came back over him, and he, too, went back to sleep. I built the fire back up and was left alone with the sounds of Hadrian as he slapped and snorted in the water.

The morning brought a surprise. Instead of stealing our horses, they had merely driven them away so that we found them standing not far off. This should have given us hope, but Mr. Dorset felt so vile that his anger was directed at everything, including myself, Bob, the King, and all leaders of the Province of South Carolina. Old Bob asked if he could continue to wear his nightgown as we travelled, but I gently said it was impractical, and so he changed back. As we prepared to leave, the dog Flipsy took it in her head that Mr. Dorset was bothering Old Bob (which was true, though Old Bob did not notice) and so bit my Master on the ankle. I thought Mr. Dorset might shoot the animal, but instead he merely made a few remarks about the contemptability of all dogflesh and rubbed his ankle as we set out up the road. The remainder of the Dorset Expedition now included a deaf old man on a swaybacked horse, a house servant who had never undertaken such a journey in the wild, and a would-be poet who, while wanting his daughter back, was ill-suited to anything but parlor fires. If we now knew our limitations better, there was a certain nobility in refusing to relent in the face of sure failure. God surely would have a plan for those who would not stop, despite various and repeated warnings along those lines.

— 4. —

We arrive safely at Ninety-Six and find that Mr. Groat
is a Great Villain being sought by the Province of Virginia
for beating a man to death and stealing from him a ham.
Alarmed, we secure a guide named Stearne and
press on toward Fort Prince George.

Ninety-Six at that time was nothing more than a large and sprawling fort, though growing with rough houses and something of a permanent populace. While I fancied Longacre to be in the country, it was in no way anything like Ninety-Six, which was the last outpost between the

Province of South Carolina and the Cherokee Country. Now this Cherokee land was divided into three areas, being the Lower, Middle, and
Overhills towns. The depredations of which we had heard afflicted all
three, which was why Colonel Montgomery and his force were heading
up the road behind us. We might have waited for that army and sought
passage with them, which would have made good sense. That, in the
main, was why the Dorset Expedition chose to press on.

The town seemed secure against attack and teemed with men and
friendly Indians. (I pointed out to a gentleman I met that you could not
any more tell a good Indian on sight than you could a good white man,
and he was so aggrieved I thought he would hit me, but he merely
stormed off.) Our journey up the trail had been rather uneventful but for
the time the dog Flipsy ran off, and Old Bob went after her and rode into
a hornet's nest which dangled from a tree limb. His stings were painful
but inconsequential, and the dog wandered back to camp. For his part,
Mr. Dorset speculated that if Old Bob's horse had been less swaybacked,
the collision might have been averted anyway. We were passed by parties
going the same direction but more quickly, and those retreating down the
trail, all of which warned us about Indian problems. Mr. Dorset asked
each group about the Groats and Jenny, but none of them had heard of
such. Mr. Dorset despaired of his daughter's health, though we were to
find out later that she was sorely trying Mr. Groat by this time.

Ninety-Six was colorful, with very rough characters who dressed in
worn deerskin and looked for provocations rather constantly. Fights were
common. We were able to lodge briefly in a small house, whose owner,
one Isham Snavel, extorted a fine premium from Mr. Dorset for us. Still,
the rest was excellent, and I daresay I never slept better. The next morning, upon Mr. Dorset's request, we went around town, each of us, to
inquire about Mr. Groat. The town was not big, but so many people con-
gregated thereabouts that it took a time to speak with them. Old Bob and
his dog went in one direction, Mr. Dorset in a second, and I in a third.
After several hours, I felt with certainty that the Groats had not come
through Ninety-Six because no one I met had heard of such a man at all.
I was about to give up when I mentioned the name to a man whose bearing gave me to think he was of some importance in the town.

"Groat?" he cried. "Well enough I know that villain!"

"Villain?" I inquired.

"Aye, villain," he said. "In Virginia way, he killed Tom Nearn, beat him about the head and stole the ham in his curing house," he said. "Been chased down the coast all the way, has Groat."

"How do you know this?" I asked.

"Because of my relation to the deceased!" he cried. His voice sounded so wounded that I was sure Mr. Nearn was a brother. "Tom Nearn was a good man. He married the widow of my cousin Samuel Soler!"

"Then I understand your grief," I said.

"Ah, I never liked Sam," he said with a shrug.

"Why then would he have given his real name to us when we had no reason to know him from anyone?" I asked.

"Pride!" the man cried. "Pride! A man has nothing but a name he will guard and raise it even if he be a fool or a robber. You would not believe what men assign their names to. In Charles Town I have seen in the *Gazette* such verse that would embarrass a hog, and yet names are affixed to it! Pride, sir!"

I was too familiar with that circumstance to inquire further and so I bowed, and we departed each other. When I got back to Mr. Dorset and reported what I had learned, he howled, cursed, and said that he knew all the time that Groat must be a villain. I omitted, out of tact, the part of the story about verse in the *Gazette*. We could find no one who had actually seen the Groats, however, and so we determined to get a guide to help us. (The dog Flipsy came back by noon, but Old Bob not until an hour after that, having become lost for a time.) I wanted to spend another night with Mr. Snavel, but that was decided against because of the rate and because Mr. Dorset felt (probably with some justification) that when the troops arrived they would forbid anyone else going toward the Indian country. And so we secured the help of a very foul and squint-eyed man named Stearne, who said he could take us around in safety among the settlers to see if the Groats were among them.

Before we left with this man, however, we had an afternoon and an evening to pass. Early in that same afternoon, Mr. Dorset has a brief spell of religion and cried and tore at his breast and swore that the entire folly of Jenny's disappearance was his fault. He begged God for forgiveness, then asked my forgiveness (which I refused, since he had done me no ill), then Old Bob's (who misunderstood and thought it was a curse of some kind), and finally disappeared during the evening hours, comparing himself to John the Baptist. He would be setting forth in the wilderness. While searching for Jenny, he could cry, "Prepare ye the way of the Lord!"

Unfortunately and quite typically, he descended from his good intentions and did not return to our room that evening. The following morning, after a search that brought me acute embarrassments, I found him lying with a black-haired woman, of whom I shall only say that her work and her pleasure were one and the same. I resurrected Mr. Dorset from the situation and recompensed the woman for her labors. The room they occupied was so dirty and smelt so badly of rum and tobacco that I took Mr. Dorset to a nearby creek and bathed him as well as I could before dragging him back to our leased room. Stearne was waiting on his horse, and he cast an unpleasant eye on Mr. Dorset, as did several other more upstanding citizens of Ninety-Six.

I settled our bill, and we came outside just as riders from Montgomery's Expedition came into town, saying the troop was but a day away. The populace went into a frenzy of joy. Sensing that his opportunity could be closing, Mr. Dorset righted himself, gathered Stearne, Old Bob, and the dog Flipsy, and we set out.

We did not get out of Ninety-Six, however, without one more shameful incident. The dog Flipsy had taken it into his head to attempt a forceful seduction of every woman he saw in the street. As we rode away, he dashed up to an unsmiling but comely lass and proceeded to attack her leg as if he found it the most attractive mate on earth. Old Bob, misunderstanding, thought it somehow charming. Mr. Dorset, even in his condition, summoned great disgust.

"Waugh! Villain!" he cried. He reached for whatever he could find to throw at the dog and came up only with a chunk of dried meat. Sadly, his intentions were better than his aim, for he hit the woman square in the head with the meat, which was as hard as a stone, being in need of water-softening. Flipsy's attentions to the woman had roused other dogs, who had come over to see how his amours fared. The woman, being knocked flat by the meat, lay insensible, but the dogs smelled the dried ration and fell into the most frightening fight, some of it taking place over the fallen body of the woman herself. Flipsy, having sensed that his attentions would be unsuccessful, escaped from the screeching pile of dogs. Men and women appeared from everywhere, but Mr. Dorset calmly rode out of town, and Old Bob, Stearne, and I followed, along with the dog, which seemed quite pleased by the chaos that boiled in his wake. We heard dogs barking and growling for some time as we headed north.

For his part, Mr. Dorset fared surprisingly well that day, and Stearne, sensing that in some way Mr. Dorset was as low as himself, appeared to hail him as a brother.

— 5. —

STEARNE DECIDES THAT WE SHOULD STOP AT FORT PRINCE GEORGE.
WE DO, AND FIND THE GARRISON HAS LONG BEEN IN A STATE OF SIEGE.
THEY TELL US THAT ONLY FOOLS WOULD VENTURE OUT BEFORE
MONTGOMERY ARRIVES. MR. DORSET TAKES THIS INTELLIGENCE
TO HEART, AND WE LEAVE THE NEXT DAY.

By this time, I was becoming somewhat accustomed to sleeping out of doors. Almost anything, I came to see, was better that Ninety-Six, which was infested with fleas, lice, and women as bad as the men. Though this Stearne had been recommended to us by someone whose name I have forgotten, he soon proved himself to be rather worthless. He insisted that we head for Fort Prince George, which was ninety-six miles up the road (as the name of the previous town implied). We could have gone that way ourselves, and I told him so, and he offered to let us go on without him, but, as Mr. Dorset had already paid half his fee, it seemed to make little sense. And so we rode along, seeing an occasional Indian or soldier. Once I shot an enormous turkey and was still indulging my sense of pride when our dog took the bird into a small cave where we could not approach, and ate the entire thing, including many of the feathers. It caught up with us some time later but was sick for many miles. Mr. Dorset lectured the dog severely on the wages of sin.

The first night, little happened that brought any trepidation upon us. We were fortunate in that Mr. Dorset was too enfeebled by the ride and his condition to share any new verse. Stearne as he slept made a repeated series of quite horrible noises, but soon they seemed merely to be another part of the landscape. The second night, Mr. Dorset, Old Bob, and I were arguing over the comparative virtues of weather. I had spoken in a friendly way of rain, though Mr. Dorset was inclined toward heat. Old Bob, not hearing our discourse well, said he preferred claret. Mr. Dorset was preparing to rebuke Old Bob when Stearne, who was off to one side, shouted something I could not understand. Suddenly, our campsite was filled with Indians who were shouting and waving their arms. If their intention was to frighten us, I must report with some embarrassment that they succeeded. Old Bob cried out and fainted. Mr. Dorset got his gun, but he had neither ball nor powder so was reduced to swinging it over his head like a club. Stearne rode off and hid. The dog Flipsy ran away as well. I alone saw what happened next. They did not mean to harm us but only wanted our horses. Fearing (I supposed) that more of us might be about, they managed to get only one horse — Old Bob's Hadrian.

After they had taken it away, we managed to bring ourselves back to order. Mr. Dorset cursed for a long time, and Old Bob came around from his swoon. Stearne lied that he'd tried to chase them. We sat for some time around the fire, fearing another attack. We were half asleep when an Indian came riding into the light, holding Old Bob's sway-backed nag by its bridle. The Indian delivered himself of a long, bitter speech then threw the bridle down and rode off. I did not have to know that tongue to understand that the horse had been found unsuitable and the raid a failure.

The third night was enlivened by a large snake, which Flipsy brought live by the fire as a gift, we supposed, for Old Bob. The serpent was vexed beyond its tolerance, and struck at everything near, including the fire. The dog found this very funny and barked and jumped back and forth until he tired of the game and broke the snake into several parts.

Fort Prince George lay in a sylvan valley next to a river named Keowee. A Cherokee village of that same name was beyond the river, though few Indians seemed about. We had read in the *Gazette* of the murder earlier in the year of the fort's commander, one Richard Coytmore, and to be honest I entered the valley with some trepidation. Fortunately, we were not molested, but neither were we welcomed to the fort, which bulged with settlers who had come in due to worries of the marauding Cherokees. Many of the garrison there made fun of us for traveling alone in such a time, and more than one told me personally that Stearne was a great liar who could not guide us anywhere. This was proved true when he disappeared our first night there and never showed back up. Mr. Dorset immediately began sketching in his mind a masque to be called "The Treachery of Stearne."

When, the next day, Mr. Dorset informed the garrison officers that we would press on looking for Jenny and the Groats (as no one there had seen or heard from them), they said we could kill ourselves if we wished, but it would be easier to drink poison than ride into the hills to be tortured by the Indians. I agreed, as did Old Bob. The dog Flipsy completely refused to travel farther, being happy at the fort and possessing no loyalty, even to

Bob. Our worries notwithstanding, Mr. Dorset bought a few supplies from the sutler and bade us join him as we rode north on the eastern side of the river.

I prayed to God to take care of my loved ones at Longacre.

— 6. —

ANOTHER SECTION FROM JENNY DORSET'S JOURNAL,
INDICATING THAT WE WERE CLOSER THAN WE KNEW TO HER
AND THAT SHE DEEPLY REGRETS THROWING IN WITH GROATS.

SUNDAY — *Oh! For the days at Longacre. How I miss them! Mr. Groat is a horrid monster. This morning, he made me write a message he was to transport to Fort Prince George, saying he was an advance from a troop and needed kegs of flour, &tc. Instead of such a thing, I wrote several verses from the Book of Genesis, and when he showed it to them, they laughed so hard that he flew into a terrible rage. When he got home, he chased me for some time but was unable to catch me. Instead, he beat Mrs. Groat.*

MONDAY — *Mrs. Groat seems somehow changed. Her visage, always showing no emotion before now, has become more determined. She looked at me once in a very telling way, as if to say something. I can guess. Mr. Groat has demanded we build a house. He is cutting logs and making us fit and shape them. He caught me when I was unawares and beat me badly, but I did not cry. I saw a bear today and prayed to God that it would eat Mr. Groat.*

TUESDAY — *I am sick.*

WEDNESDAY — *I have become well once more. An Indian came by to visit us, and I thought he might take our hair, but he only wanted some sugar, which Mr. Groat gave him. I also gave him Mr. Groat's pistol. He doesn't know that yet. I have decided that I will run away when Mr. Groat's attention is elsewhere. What fun it is to write what I wish in here. Right now, I am telling him that I write of how pleased I am to have gone with him to this country. He is a villain and a fool.*

THURSDAY — *He has said he will go away for a few days to hunt. During that time, I will leave and go back to the fort.*

— 7. —

WE LEAVE FORT PRINCE GEORGE AND COME TO THE GROATS' POOR
HOUSE, ONLY TO DISCOVER THAT JENNY HAS RUN AWAY. THE RETURN OF
MR. GROAT AND UNPLEASANT CONSEQUENCES.

The day we left the fort was very miserable, with a cold rain and heavy
clouds on the shoulders of the steep hills around us. I began to think
about service and what a good servant owed a master, and I concluded
that this went far beyond that pledge. I could not, however, abandon Mr.
Dorset in his search because of my fondness for Jenny and because he
sometimes needed tending.

There were in that country a number of Cherokee villages, including
Estatoe, Conasatchee, Toxaway, and others whose names will not come
to me now. We had a map drawn for us at the fort by one David Gordon, who was on his way to join Montgomery's force as it neared us.
Unfortunately, none of us read maps well, especially Old Bob, who at one
point claimed that if we went east we would arrive in Paris.

"Faugh! Would that it were true," said Mr. Dorset. "Then I would
trash those French within an inch of their lives."

"Why, sir?" asked Old Bob.

"On principle," said Mr. Dorset.

We did not learn until some time later how foolish it was to be about
in that country at the time. Raiding parties had killed a number of settlers, few of which were still out. As always, some men believed they were
invulnerable. Those who are most subject to this malady are always the
ones worst shocked by grievous turns of events. I therefore braced myself
for trouble.

We intended to use Mr. Gordon's map to stay clear of the Indian villages in our search for the Groats. As usual, however, we misconstrued
certain markers and rode directly to the edge of Estatoe, a Cherokee town
of about two hundred lodges. When we realized what had happened, Mr.
Dorset and I turned and began to move away as quietly as possible. (I
silently thanked God that Mr. Dorset did not see fit to compose an ode
on seeing his first Indian town.) Old Bob, breathtaken by the village, and
not hearing our retreat, lifted himself high from the swayed back of
Hadrian, and remarked in a clear voice, "Look, sir, it's a wad of them
Indians!" At the sound of his voice, I turned and glanced over my shoulder and saw that several Indians had spied Old Bob and were running for

their horses to make a pursuit, screaming hideously. Old Bob, somehow thinking it was part of a pageant, much like those our horseraces or grinning contests included, began to clap.

"Get the fool away!" cried Mr. Dorset. I normally would have fled as Mr. Dorset did, but his command was a thing I was accustomed to obeying, so I kicked my horse, rode to Bob, and took his horse by the bridle, turning him toward me. When he saw the alarm in my eyes, Old Bob did not need to be told we were in grave danger.

Unfortunately, his horse, Hadrian, also espied the danger and began to run and buck wildly about, tossing Old Bob up and down until the beast found its feet, saw the dust left by Mr. Dorset, and went in that direction. I followed. The full chase was shortly engaged by the Cherokees, who I must admit were marvelous riders. If their goal with their screaming and waving was to frighten us, they succeeded well, at least in my case. We rode as hard as we could for nearly three-quarters of an hour before the Estatoe Indians felt we had had enough. Finally, realizing we were no longer pursued, we slowed, stopped, and found water for the horses and ourselves.

"I suspect there was a slight misreading of the map," said Mr. Dorset, wheezing and holding his chest.

"That was my conclusion as well," I said.

"No harm done," he said. "A good ride's all, eh, Hawthorne?"

"A good ride," I said.

At that point, he took out the map, turned it several directions trying to make sense of it, and then threw it on the ground. I agreed that it was useless now, yet I did not feel lost or even downcast. The land was so lovely, the water so sweet, that a kind of peace descended on me, and I knew then that certain authors were right to say that being pursued and not caught was the best physic on this Earth.

That night was one of the most memorable of my life. We camped on a hill slope near the creek in a place where a fire of some nature had cleared the trees so that the Heavens were spread out before us in their vast glory. I have often recalled that night at times when my faith has weakened, for I cannot accept that the stars would thus arrange themselves without the help of a Guiding Maker who loved the patterns He was creating. We saw several meteors, and the night was deeply still but for insect sounds. I have never spent a more tranquil, unclouded night in my life nor ever hope to.

"This world is a most strange place," said Mr. Dorset. His usual energy was subdued, and Old Bob fell asleep early. Even our horses sensed no threat and dozed by the trees where we had tied them. "I have lost my daughter and may not regain her and somehow feel I am to blame. And yet God here is granting us his boon, Hawthorne, a balm, as if this were Gilead. I grant I don't know what to make of it."

"Perhaps that we have tried to live well and this night is a reward for that act," I said quietly.

"Ah," he said. "I have been a fool, my friend. A fool and a fool and a fool. I have tried to set my life forth against this world as a balance, larger than God intended. I find such pleasures in the flesh that I lose my way from God, and I find such pleasures in God that I always take the wrong passage in His presence and wind up back at the flesh."

"So do we all," I said.

"Eh? But not as far as I do."

"Your pilgrimage is of a greater level than most of us can see," I said. "You are not satisfied with serving. You must be the pivot or the fulcrum of the action."

"I fear my daughter has the same disorder," he said mournfully.

"I fear you are right," I said.

What use would more words have served on that night of glory? We let the fire die away to a glow of embers, and I sat for a long time looking at the stars before I slept. The next morning, we mounted again and began to ride, only to discover to our great surprise that we were near a small, crude house. Two children were working very hard cutting wood outside it. We recognized them immediately as the Groatlings. Mr. Dorset drew his breath in sharply and grabbed the reins of Hadrian so Old Bob wouldn't wander off or toward the house as we conspired.

"Waugh! To have come directly to this!" cried Mr. Dorset. "Praise! Praise be to God! Let us raise our heads high and thank our Maker!"

"Might I suggest this is the wrong time?" I whispered. "Perhaps we can thank God in our hearts?"

"Eh?" said Mr. Dorset. "Well spoken, Hawthorne. God loves a cheerful worker, and there's work to be done."

"Get my gun?" said Old Bob. He was already trying to withdraw it from his saddle, and I dissuaded him only with great effort. Mr. Dorset said we would do this as civilized men should and ride straight to the house. And so we did, coming down a long wooded slope. The children saw us only when we were upon them, and they dropped their axes and ran straightly and silently for the house. Presently, Mrs. Groat appeared holding a gun at her shoulder and swinging it among us, not being able to tell from sight who our leader might be. The more she looked, the more confused she became, for Old Bob was the eldest and might have been the wisest; Mr. Dorset was the best fed and could have been the wealthiest; I was the least assertive and might have been in charge through a modest strength. Alas, only the second was true, and it had no bearing whatever on leadership.

"Stand there, or I'll shoot ye!" she said. Her voice was wavering.

"I am Adam Dorset of Longacre," said Mr. Dorset in the same voice he used to declaim his odes. "You have my daughter, Jenny, you Groats, and I shall relieve you of her on this occasion."

"My husband will be here soon," she said. She thumbed the hammer back and pointed it at Mr. Dorset, who seemed finally to be in charge because he had spoken.

"I would deliver myself of the same message to him," said Mr. Dorset. He looked around the area for his daughter, as I did, and caught no sight of her. "But you know I am in the right and I would not resort to the law."

"The law?" she said. She began to laugh as if she were mad, showing she had lost several teeth. Her pale blonde looks changed monstrously when she laughed, and I saw what a great fee living on this frontier had wrought from her. The children huddled behind her, though expressionless and silent. "There is no law here. Not for no woman nor no man. You can kill who you will here or beat who you will or starve who you will and nobody, not God, will do a thing about it. You can curse God and live for it. You can work until your fingers bleed, and still there is no law."

I knew instantly that she spoke of her vile husband. I felt shame and shock.

"I only want my daughter," said Mr. Dorset. His voice had changed, its hard edge softening somewhat.

"And I would give you the brat back were she here!" screamed Mrs. Groat. "Never upon my life have I seen such a thing, what with her mouth and her stubborn ways."

"Sounds like her," I whispered to Mr. Dorset. He raised one eyebrow at me and shrugged.

"Where would she have gone?" asked Mr. Dorset. The woman began to cackle again. It was clear that she was quite mad, and I did not doubt that God had made her so to survive such an ordeal.

"Sold her to them Indians," she said in a voice that was almost singing. Then she did something strange: she threw her gun on the ground where it discharged, frightening Old Bob's mount, which began to spin in circles. Old Bob managed to hold on only by good luck, and the horse Hadrian finally snorted and came to a stop. Mrs. Groat was crying furiously now, down on her hands and knees, digging in the earth for no reason I could see. Her children were just as silent and unmoved.

"Which Indians, by God?" asked Mr. Dorset in a loud, angry voice.

"To the Indians!" she said, looking up from her digging. Mr. Dorset repeated his question, to which Mrs. Groat said only a single word: "Toxaway."

"Toxaway," said Mr. Dorset. "We shall go there, then."

I felt very bad about leaving the Groatlings with their deranged mother and vile father, but in this world a man cannot save every creature worthy of salvation or even try, for he would then have no life to live himself. Such sacrifices may be common among saints, but certainly not among mere men such as myself or merer men such as Adam Dorset.

— 8. —

WE RIDE IN THE DIRECTION WE THINK THE CHEROKEE VILLAGE
OF TOXAWAY MIGHT BE. AN AMAZING CONFRONTATION WITH
AN INDIAN WHO DELIVERS HIMSELF OF A LONG SPEECH
INCLUDING THE WORD *DORSET*, AND APPEARS TO BE
VERY ANGRY WITH US. BRIGANDS DEMAND OUR MONEY.

As we no longer had Mr. David Gordon's map, we pressed forward in a direction in which we hoped the village of Toxaway might be. Mr. Dorset was more downcast than I had seen him, for he could not help but wonder how well the Indians might be treating Jenny. None of us was particularly inspiring as a hunter, and, because we had lost our dog Flipsy along the way, I was beginning to worry that our worst enemy might be starvation. For though game was not scarce in those hills, nor fish missing from the streams, we might watch them swim or run past us for days without being able to take one properly.

The longer we rode that day, the more we realized that we had no proper idea where we might be. We saw the land in its wild state, and that frontier of the Province held me in awe. I felt more strongly than ever that the hand of Providence was at work. We also passed on one occasion the skeleton of a man and the rotting remains of his clothes, which showed him to be a white man. As Christian men, we could not pass without offering the wretched man a proper burial, so we scraped away at a hillside in the crunching web of roots for more than an hour before we had a hole deep enough in which to lay the bones. Due to our lack of experience with skeletons, however, we did not know that it would fall to pieces when moved, and so we soon had leg and arm bones in several different places. Old Bob picked up the skull and looked at it closely.

"Upon my word, an Irishman!" he said. Mr. Dorset looked at me with a mixture of delight and disgust, raising one eyebrow.

"Bob, how, pray tell, can you tell it was an Irishman?" asked Mr. Dorset.

"Set of the jaw, sir," he said. "Your Irishman holds his mouth open thus from drink."

We looked at the skull and realized that the jaw and its teeth, in fact, were still on the ground. Mr. Dorset made a kind of choked sound and slapped his forehead as he was apt to do whenever something vexed him greatly.

"Bob, you are the most unusual specimen of humankind ever seen in this Province!" said Mr. Dorset.

"I am?" said Old Bob. He smiled vaguely and handed me the skull. He wandered off a few paces to consider the honor just bestowed on him by his Master, and I took the head and its wayward jaw and put them together in the grave and covered them up. Mr. Dorset stood piously at the graveside with his hands crossed.

"Now we shall have a few words for this departed brother," he said. Old Bob came back over, still looking as if he had suddenly been granted wealth or a papal indulgence. "Oh Lord, we beseech Thee to look after this the spirit of a lost soul here in the wild country of your Province of South Carolina. We beg your pardon for any sins this man may have committed or any lewd women he might have consorted with during his life, women of red hair and bounteous figures." At this point, Mr. Dorset had distracted himself so much that he ceased delivering the eulogy and stared at nothing I could see with a pleasant smile on his face.

"Sir?" I prompted him.

"Yes," he said. He cleared his throat. "Well, we beseech your blessings and ask that you should at least consider the soul of this man to enter in your presence even if you find him to be a fool or an insufferable villain."

"A villain?" said Old Bob, cupping his ear. "This Irishman was a villain?"

"If he *should* have been," said Mr. Dorset. "How in the name of God could I tell what he was? He's nothing but bones now, Bob! He could have been John the Baptist for all I know!"

"Ah," said Old Bob. "Then he lays a place before us in the wilderness."

Mr. Dorset was about to remonstrate once more when the logic of the words, their precision and indelible truth stopped him. This man clearly possessed an accidental knowledge that stood him well in many circumstances.

"Well spoken, Bob," said Mr. Dorset. He looked back down at the small mound of earth. "Amen."

"To the emerald isle of Erin," said Old Bob sadly.

We rode on that day, and a thunderstorm of frightening proportions came rising over the hills toward us, hurling bolts of lightning and fierce thunder. Mr. Dorset was more scared of storms than any grown man I have ever known, relating them, I believed, to a bad episode upon the ocean once. Our horses did not like the cracks of heaven, either, and so became difficult to handle. We therefore rode into a copse where a natural cave was broken from the rocky hillside. Old Bob and I hobbled the horses, and we all went into the cave and squatted down to await the end of the storm. At each thunder crack, Mr. Dorset would emit a *waugh* or a *fie on't*, while Old Bob, with his defective hearing, seemed to think the sounds were coming from behind us down in the cave itself. For my part, I held my counsel, but I felt at that moment a great sense of loss and of being lost that I cannot now describe. I thought of Longacre and the lovely grounds and the order of the house. I thought of Charles Town and of fine food that I so enjoyed serving Mr. Dorset and his guests. I even thought of the three Dorset sons and how bereft they would be if their father did not return from this search for their sister.

I was beginning, in truth, to brood, when two amazing things happened at the same time. First, the storm abated so suddenly that the sun came out, spreading jewels of water from the leaves and earth in a dazzling display of Nature's delight. I was so taken by the spectacle that I did not see the Indian until he was almost in front of us. He had been riding past, I gathered, had seen our hobbled horses, and come up to the cave. When he saw us, he dismounted and came toward us. Our weapons, such as they were, remained in the bags on the horses, so we were unarmed except for a large knife I carried.

"Waugh!" cried Mr. Dorset as he backed into Old Bob.

"Waugh!" the Indian said in return. (If the Reader finds it unlikely that the Indian repeated the same syllable of surprise or disapproval, I can only apologize that I am reporting the facts as they occurred in this History.) We thought he would shoot us, for he carried a gun, but, instead, he began to deliver a very angry speech, in which he sometimes spat upon the ground, waved his arms, and shook his fists. He seemed very angry, and I had such little experience with those people that I did not know what to say to the man to calm him. When he paused for a moment, Old Bob spoke for us.

"Irish?" asked Old Bob. "Then we buried your comrade well."

Mr. Dorset and I looked with deep alarm at Bob, who was pleased with himself. The Indian, taken off guard by Old Bob's speech, began once more to shout and wave his arms, pointing at us, the earth, the sky, our horses, the trees. He was very worked up. He spat once more, and in a clear voice uttered two more syllables that were perfectly clear: *Dor-set*.

"Eh?" said Mr. Dorset, sotto voce, to me. "Hawthorne, did he say what I thought he said?"

"Yes, sir," I said. "Upon my word, he did."

"Dorset!" cried the Indian. Then he spat once more and came right up to us and seemed to curse us roundly. I held my knife but did not draw it, because for all I knew several of his band were nearby. That close, I could see that he was a young man, magnificently dressed and painted, with black eyes and thin lips. He growled at us. Old Bob began to sing an ancient Irish melody very softly, and the Indian's eyes seemed to roll into his head slightly in a gesture of disbelief in our stupidity, a gesture repeated, to my surprise, by Mr. Dorset. The Indian shook his head, as if, having been offered a poor horse for sale, he had left in disgust. We came out of the cave and looked around the damp earth, but the Indian was clearly gone now, and we could take a breath after his verbal assault.

"Aye, God, he has met my daughter!" cried Mr. Dorset. "Then she be well!"

"I made the same assumption," I said.

We unhobbled the horses and slowly rode onward, still not knowing where we were going but looking for signs nonetheless. Mr. Dorset told Old Bob that the man who spoke to us was a Cherokee Indian, not an Irishman, and that he should hold his tongue around people he did not know. Old Bob said that your Irishman changed his spots like a leopard and could not be trusted to look the same way twice. He also said that another storm was imminent because his foot hurt. We were glad to find, an hour later, that his anatomical weathervane had failed him.

We came to a creek which tumbled joyously with foamy water from the storm and decided to follow it, thinking it would take us to a river and thence to an Indian village where we might ask about Jenny. We were slowly making our way through the woods when he heard the sounds of horse hoofs behind us. We turned in time to see five riders, rough white men who closed on us quickly, then surrounded us. Their leader, a dark-skinned fellow with greasy hair, rode up to us with an unpleasant sneer on his face. I had been robbed once on my way to Charles Town, though all I had was a guinea and my horse, which was so poor they let me keep her. I was still unprepared to find that our gravest threat in this wild land would come from white men.

"Now then," said the man. "Where on earth might ye be going? Don't ye know there's a war about with the Cherokee?"

"Sir, I am Adam Dorset of Longacre," said Mr. Dorset imperially.

"Is that a fact?" said the man. "Well, d—d if that means a thing to me. What does mean something to me is any money you might be carrying and your guns."

"Curses from h—l!" cried Mr. Dorset. "Brigands!"

The men began to laugh. Old Bob, thinking something humorous had been spoken that he could not hear, affected to laugh along with them. Mr. Dorset slapped his forehead as he often did when confronted by something beyond his bearing. Finally, the leader rode up close to Mr. Dorset.

"Brigands," he said. "We wasn't never nothing so fine, but I will relieve your party of guns, powder, ball, and any money you might have," he said. "In fair exchange for not killing you and allowing you to keep the horses, such as they be."

"I had rather suffer the pains of death than be disgraced by such as your kind," said Mr. Dorset, whereupon the man lifted his gun and pointed it at Mr. Dorset's stomach and quit smiling. Sensing the man's resolve and that disgrace in itself was perhaps not so bad, Mr. Dorset quickly withdrew his purse and threw it to the man, along with his riflery materials. The other men took the same from myself and Old Bob.

"Now then, squire, don't take it so hard," said the lead brigand. "Better men than yourself have been separated from their goods in this country."

"I deny it," said Mr. Dorset bravely. "I deny that entirely."

The men laughed at us, kicked their horses, and left us sitting on a hilltop in wild country, owning nothing but two knives with which to defend ourselves.

— 9. —

We stumble into a village where we are captured
and find to our astonishment that Jenny Dorset is being held
or, rather, she is holding them. A conjuror gives her back to
us along with a bitter speech that seems to reflect on the
character of the girl. We make our escape.

We rode on that morning, not knowing where we were going but hearing occasional gunfire and worrying that soon we should be overtaken by men of one race or another who would want to separate us either from what was left of our possessions or our hair. I have learned that the greatest enemies of any man are often the ones he least suspects. By that time in our sojourn, I felt everyone was our enemy, and I had succumbed to bitterness.

As I recall, Old Bob was holding forth on the creatures of the sea. It was late in the afternoon, and Bob had averred that whales could indeed be a lost tribe of Israel as mentioned in the Bible, a claim that caused Mr. Dorset to slap his forehead once more. Old Bob then wondered aloud if, when Jesus fed the multitude with but a few fishes, the Scriptures meant that fishes also were another tribe of Israel.

"Bob, in the name of G–d, that would make the multitude eaters of human flesh!" cried Mr. Dorset.

At that moment, we were riding down a wooded slope and were startled to find ourselves at the edge of a large Cherokee village. In its center was an enormous townhouse, surrounded by log huts of a standard design. Dozens of children and women were about, as well as several dogs. I was going to exclaim on our accidental misfortune when we were suddenly surrounded by Indians on horseback who took the bridles of our horses, and, amid great shouting, pulled us into the village. Old Bob's Hadrian, which with its sway back could not walk well, went the entire distance sidewise, which caused Old Bob to hold on with the gravest concentration lest he fall off.

"Waugh!" cried Mr. Dorset. "*Indian* brigands!"

The Indians got us to the townhouse and motioned for us to get from our mounts, which we did, as they had guns, bows, and other weapons all trained upon us. I was near despairing when a familiar sound suddenly erupted from one of the huts near the townhouse. Jenny Dorset came storming out of it, yelling at an Indian and wagging her finger. She wore Indian clothing and looked healthier than I had ever seen her at Longacre.

"You are a low villain, and I curse you to death!" she cried.

Mr. Dorset, on seeing his daughter, uttered a cry at once so full of surprise and yet love that my eyes filled with tears. Old Bob could only point at Jenny and make odd sounds far back in his throat. The Indian toward whom Jenny was shouting took her by the arm and dragged her to us.

"Jenny, child, we have come to save you!" cried Mr. Dorset. She looked at the three of us and our sorry mounts and began to laugh, though she did seem pleased we had arrived for a visit. The Indian holding her arm came close to Mr. Dorset since he spoke and said the word *Dorset* quite clearly, as the other one had. When Mr. Dorset nodded, the Indian thrust Jenny toward her father and began to make a terrible speech, full of arm waving, shouts, and grunts. Mr. Dorset held his daughter and stroked her hair, and she did then melt somewhat and hug him and place her head upon his chest. Being her father's daughter, she could not let it go, however, and interrupted the Indian's speech by walking over and kicking him in the leg. Other Indians began to howl and hoot and make threatening gestures toward us. The assaulted one hopped around on one leg and cursed us roundly. From his dress, which included shell rattles and a gorget hung round his neck, I deduced he was a conjuror, as I had read in the *Gazette* that such men dressed that way in the Cherokee land. When he finished hopping, he came right up in Mr. Dorset's face and told him more terrible things about Jenny, who seemed by her demeanor to confirm the conjuror's words. Finally, half exhausted, he held a rattle over her head and began to chant some kind of formula. Then he shook the rattle toward the village, and I understood that he was trying to ward off her influence from further infecting the town. Then he came to us and pointed down the trail which left the village, heading, as I took it, due south. Then he spat upon the ground, uttered with contempt the name *Dorset* again, and bade us leave his presence. A woman came from behind him and shrieked a few syllables at Jenny and then hit the conjuror with her hand and went sulking toward her lodge.

"Hie, then!" cried Mr. Dorset. He mounted and took Jenny up behind him on the horse. She held only the small book I later found was her diary, quill stuck inside. A few Indians were marveling at Old Bob's horse, wondering, I took it, how it could walk and yet have such a swayed back. The conjuror angrily ran them away, reminding them, I think, to be angry with us. We rode off, and I kept looking over my shoulder thinking they might give us an arrow in the back, but no such thing happened. A few hundred yards from town, Mr. Dorset broke into a loud rendition of "Victory at Longacre," but he quit when his daughter threatened to return to the Indians unless he ceased his infernal noises. I marveled, all the way back to Fort Prince George, that we were not abducted or shot at, but I later discovered that Jenny had learned a few words of Cherokee and put what she called a curse on them should any harm come to her or anyone who came after her. They were only too glad when we showed up.

— 10. —
A SECTION FROM JENNY DORSET'S DIARY
WRITTEN WHILE SHE WAS A CAPTIVE AT THE CHEROKEE INDIAN VILLAGE
OF TOXAWAY, WRITTEN IN AN INK MADE FROM WATER AND SOOT.

FRIDAY — *I might as well live with Groats as with these villains. A man whose name is spoken all back in his throat took me. He thought to make me work, and I spit on him. He was about to hit me but I began to sing one of Father's songs. They believed me possessed of spirits.*

SATURDAY — *I would not work today. They are starving me, but I will not starve. I will sit here and sing more and more. I am stronger than they.*

SUNDAY — *They could not bear the singing and so told me through signs that I need not work. They gave me food and asked only that I sing no more. Then I declaimed a poem of my own making in the model of one of Father's odes. This seemed to upset them, and so I kept it up most of the day. The man whose name is far back in his throat holds his hands over his ears and threatens me.*

MONDAY — *A terrible rainstorm. Poor Groat children. Such a man their father was. Should I ever have the chance, I will put a knife in his back and say to the children, You are free now, go ye in peace from him. I would give a guinea to the widow Groat.*

TUESDAY — *They tried to make me work again, as the other children do. I sang Father's song A WOMAN IS A LOUDISH THING, and they once more shut me alone in a little log house and made signs against me. They are Indian Groats!*

— 11. —

WE ARRIVE BACK AT THE FORT TO FIND THAT MONTGOMERY'S TROOPS
ARE NEAR AND PLAN TO ATTACK THE INDIAN VILLAGES, SO, WITHOUT
WAITING, WE SET OUT SOUTH TOWARD HOME. ON THE WAY, WE PASS
THE ARMY AND DISCOVER THAT MR. CHARLES SMYTHE AND HIS
VOLUNTEERS ARE WITH THE ARMY. WE SPEND A NIGHT THERE.

Fort Prince George was fairly in a state of frenzy, as Indians were still taking an occasional shot at the garrison. How we managed to come through I cannot imagine, unless word of Jenny Dorset's curse had preceded us. We walked through the gates and came inside, where a young soldier who was very nearly unstrung with fatigue and fear waved his arms about and told us that we were all soon going to meet our Maker.

"Baker?" cried Old Bob, cupping his ear. He turned, smiling to Mr. Dorset. "They have brought a baker. Loaves for the guests, I s'pose."

Jenny applauded Bob's pleasant ignorance, but Mr. Dorset merely slapped his forehead. The young soldier again told us we were all going to meet our Maker soon and that we should confess any sins. Right after that, another soldier came past flipping a shilling and singing. We made inquiries of him, and he said the army was about, and that if we did not want to engage in war, we might remain in the fort or escape south as rapidly as we might. Considering that we all had suffered enough in that country, Mr. Dorset decided we should leave and tried to use his good name as a barter to obtain a gun, powder, and ball. The officer to whom Mr. Dorset spoke said the name Dorset didn't mean any more to him that a pig's name, and he would be a great fool to give up a piece on a man's name anyway.

"Waugh! Then you are a low villain!" cried Mr. Dorset. The officer shrugged, and it was clear then that we might as well leave, and so we did. I half thought we might be shot as we left, but the Indians on the hills around the fort seemed content to drop occasional shots into the fort and left us alone. We rode for some miles in silence. There was little event until Old Bob rode into a low-hanging tree limb and knocked himself off Hadrian. For a time we thought he had died, but then he came around and told us he had seen stars and angels. He then deigned to thank God for the vision, but when he got up to his knees for prayer he uttered a groaning sound and fell over once more, and it took a considerable amount of water and rubbing his arms to awaken him again.

After riding nearly all day, we came to an amazing sight: an enormous army which had camped for the evening on some hills near a river. We knew that it must be Montgomery, and we also knew that we must eat, so we rode slowly, looking for someone to furnish us with sustenance. Imagine our astonishment when someone called to us!

"Dorset! Look here!" cried a familiar voice. It was Mr. Charles Smythe, who camped with his volunteers. (They did not look better trained than before, unfortunately, and several of them were inspecting their guns with great suspicion or curiosity.)

"Smythe!" cried Mr. Dorset. For a brief moment, they were honestly glad to see each other, and as we dismounted I saw Mr. Smythe clasp Mr. Dorset to him and then hug Jenny, who tried to wriggle away.

"She is in fine health, then?" asked Mr. Smythe. He tousled Jenny's hair, which vexed her so badly she broke away and walked several yards and stared morosely at the river.

"The best, as I have rescued her myself!" said Mr. Dorset, stretching both his height and the truth. "I have navigated this rough land and lived among the Indians, Smythe! I don't doubt it is already the matter of legend hereabouts!"

"Legend?" said Mr. Smythe. He began to laugh a little. Old Bob came and asked if we were staying, and, as Mr. Smythe nodded, Bob tied off the horses with help from Jenny, who had been talking to one of Smythe's volunteers.

"Legend, yes?" said Mr. Dorset, confused. "What would you gainsay such a name for a man who endured hardships, traveled vast distances, saw his very life threatened to rescue his daughter from the clutches of foul Groats and Indians?"

"Lucky, I would say!" exclaimed Mr. Smythe. He thought it a great joke, and several of his fools who stood nearby (for a wealthy man always has his fools and his seers) began to laugh and slapped their stomachs.

"Luck is a trollop who has never encamped with Adam Dorset, Esquire!" cried Mr. Dorset. "Hawthorne, tell them of my bravery!"

"As you say, sir," I muttered. He waited for me to say more, but I felt in that sentence I had confirmed what he said, even though I had seen little particular bravery on the journey, though a considerable resolve. When it was clear that I had given my entire speech, the unfortunate effect was to make the men laugh ever harder.

"Fie on you, Smythe!" cried Mr. Dorset. "If luck showed her face in this country it was to keep you alive without falling on your gun and shooting yourself in the foot or fundament!" Mr. Smythe's eyes went suddenly bright and yet somewhat comfortable, as if he had been confirmed in a suspicion.

"You are a great liar," said Mr. Smythe.

"And you are a great fool!" cried Mr. Dorset.

Having greeted each other thusly, they fell to wrestling in the grass, shouting and cursing at each other but doing little real harm. Two of the men finally pulled them apart, and we encamped with some of the Highlanders that night, who were very rough but completely captivated by Jenny, who danced and sang for them. After the fires began to die and we were rolling into our blankets, I watched Jenny for a long time.

"What is it, then, you would ask, Hawthorne?" she said.

"Only that it is a miracle that someone of such beauty would also have such brass," I said. That may sound uncomplimentary, but the sincerity with which I delivered it apparently touched her. She smiled beautifully at me, that smile which would slay the hearts of many men in South Carolina in the coming years.

"Then you should remind me when I am of age that I should marry you," she said. With that, she turned away, and soon slept peacefully.

— 12. —

WE RETURN SAFELY TO LONGACRE. WE LEARN THAT IN OUR ABSENCE THE MCNEW TWINS HAVE WREAKED HAVOC UPON THE HOUSE AND GROUNDS. MR. DORSET COMPOSES AN ODE UPON THE CHEROKEE INDIANS WHICH IS UNFORTUNATELY PRINTED IN FULL IN THE *GAZETTE*.

Soon after we rode down the road back toward home, we heard from other travelers that the army under Montgomery had inflicted serious losses on the Cherokees, burning a number of their villages. All proclaimed it a great victory. War is a fickle mistress, however, and within a few weeks the troops were to be stopped in the mountains, where they retreated and rushed back to Charles Town, doing very little real harm to the Indians. Jenny, for her part, was mostly quiet on the way home, and I do think she was pleased to be heading there. As she was out of ink, she could not write in her journal, which made her cross. Only once did she wander off, and then to chase a wild pig, which came grunting into our campsite one morning as we prepared to leave. She came running back and told us she had seen the French army in the woods being led by a giant riding an elephant. None of us paid her any mind but Old Bob, who was briefly alarmed until he realized that it was yet again fancy, not fact.

We were received with heroic feasting and celebration at Longacre, and Jenny's brothers, Abel, Isaac, and Matthew, even seemed glad to see her. Mr. Dorset gave a ball to thank the Almighty for Jenny's safe return and invited the people from far and wide, including the Smythe family, which did not include Mr. Charles Smythe, he being on the expedition to punish the Cherokees at the moment. For her part, Mrs. Lydia Dorset was overcome with relief at having us all back, and she was so affectionate toward her children one and all that each person commented in turn of her loving nature. The great party would have been even greater but for an incident involving the Smythe boys.

As I have said, Hamlet Smythe was serious and dour, without much to say. Iago was full of the same mischief that God put into Jenny Dorset, but poor Fortinbras was regrettably no more than an idiot. At this time, their ages were eleven, nine, and six respectively. Mr. Dorset was delivering himself of an endless and tiresome speech dealing with the Crown's political mistakes in handling the French and their Indians, when Fortinbras made a quiet braying noise — like the sound of a donkey from some distance away. A few moments later, he did it once more, this time louder. Just as Mr. Dorset had wound himself into a whirlwind of condemnation of all armies and very nearly all men, Fortinbras began to bray extremely loudly. Most of the men laughed at the sight while the women felt a pity for the sad creature.

"Muffle that brat!" cried Mr. Dorset finally, a phrase which offended Mrs. Ophelia Van Dyke Smythe greatly. No matter how much she tried, however, she could not accomplish the task of stopping the braying of Fortinbras, and soon the entire room was in an uproar. Jenny, sensing that this was a chance to join the fun, began to make the lowing sounds a cow makes in the evening. Mrs. Dorset tried without success to stop her noises. The McNew twins, Molly and Tom (who were then in their ninth year), at that point began to cackle as a hen does upon laying her egg. Not to be outdone, the Smartt twins, Desdemona and Roderigo, who had been brought along by the Smythe servants, fell to the floor and made the sound of hogs. Mr. Dorset shouted for order and stamped his feet, but the more he did so, the worse the din became, so that soon it appeared we were in the midst of a lively barnyard. Just then, Fortinbras Smythe stood and screamed at the height of his voice that he was a donkey, and then he became ill in a most appalling manner.

"Fie!" screamed Mr. Dorset. "We should have never allowed Smythes in this house! They're no better than Groats!"

There ended the party to celebrate Jenny's return home, for Mrs. Smythe and her servants collected their children and servants and departed for Foxhaven, the unfortunate Fortinbras reeling sickly all the way out the door. The other guests, sensing the disorder would not soon be restored, also left one by one, and then Mrs. Dorset fell into a fit of crying and retired upstairs, accompanied by Mrs. Wilson and the three Dorset boys. Soon, the only ones in the sitting room were Mr. Dorset, Jenny, Old Bob, and myself. He slumped in a chair and was inconsolable. For her part, Jenny could not stop imagining herself a cow and kept swaying up to her father and making cattle sounds. He looked dejectedly into the fire.

From the corner of my eye, I espied Old Bob, elbows bending in and out, moving around the room in the posture of a chicken.

If the gathering to welcome Jenny home was less than a success (though she enjoyed it enormously), the subsequent problems with the McNew twins threw the house further into disorder. Mr. Dorset had become quite dour after the end of our journey to the wilderness, and I was afraid he would be seized again by Piety, but he mostly attended to his business ventures and the plantation, and I attended to my duties in the house.

Perhaps I have failed in describing the McNew twins in detail, but they looked a good deal more like the Smythe family than the Dorsets, though as orphans they should have looked like neither, of course. They were taken in a moment of sentiment, but, by the time they were eight years old, their purchase was regretted. Both were of slender frame with hay-colored hair and a speckled complexion, blue eyes, and high cheekbones. Neither was quite attractive or quite ugly, but both were lazy and disobedient. They had the same standing as I did, part of the servant staff, but as children they were indulged, and when they failed in their duties, someone was always there to forgive them. Mrs. Wilson had helped rear them, along with a woman I have not mentioned heretofore, a certain Jane Holding, who had lost her own children through fevers and who came from Charles Town to help. Neither twin, however, was inclined to maternal affections, and soon they grew somewhat wild.

We found on our return that the McNews had been making a terrible mess of things in our absence, releasing the dogs in the night, breaking windows and glassware, bending the tableware past use, and generally causing a fury among the staff. Mrs. Dorset had lashed Jane Holding with a violent fit of temper, and she had packed her bags and left, which showed how little suited she was for motherhood anyway.

Jenny, upon hearing of the rampage by the McNews, whom she had theretofore mostly ignored, began to take an interest in them, particularly in Molly. She and Tom were two years older than Jenny and thus had the advantage of knowing more methods of mischief, which Jenny respected. They began to engage in minor conspiracies, once tying a bell to the tail of a wandering but wild cat and letting it loose in the dining room when Mr. Dorset was entertaining M. Ledoux, a merchant from Nice who was interested in buying indigo from us. The effect was even more dramatic than anything the gang might have imagined, for the cat so frightened Mrs. Wilson as she entered with a tray of tea that she dumped it largely into the lap of the very stout and humorless M. Ledoux. He jumped to his feet cursing in French and caught his cuff in the tablecloth, thereby removing about half the dishes to the floor. The McNews were looking through the window, but Jenny was at table with the family. Her look of utter joy was so contagious that I nearly caught it before I realized its impropriety and managed to help clean up the wreckage.

On another occasion, the McNews, hearing that our area had secured a parson in hopes of having a church better than the one Mr. Dorset had caused to be built (by then it had entirely collapsed and was being used to stable cattle), laid plans to trick the Good Man. Jenny was in the thick of this, and I saw their scheming on the day before Parson Jincks' arrival and worried, but in my position I could do nothing about it. This Jincks, in truth, was an overbearing gentleman whose religion had more noblesse than oblige, and whose enormously fat frame was already the subject of whisperings in the kitchen. The morning of his arrival, Mrs. Dorset came to me somewhat worried that we might not have a chair large enough for the man. I assured her that Mr. Dorset had discussed the same with me and we had arranged a certain Venetian piece at table which would hold the man. This same chair, sad to report, had been worked upon by Jenny and the McNews. They had sawn one of the legs almost entirely through so that when the Good Man, who was in truth far fatter than anything I might have imagined, sat upon it, he instantly fell to the floor in a red-faced heap. He lay on his back, rolling to and fro but apparently unable to rise without help, and so Mr. Dorset, Old Bob, and I helped him, and only with the greatest exertion did we manage to get him upright once more. At that moment, we heard the sound of the front door opening, and to my great astonishment the dog Flipsy, whom we had left in Ninety-Six, came charging into the dining room. He came straight for Mr. Jincks' leg and leaped upon it and began to love it, as if it were an ardent suitor.

"Waugh!" cried Mr. Dorset. He kicked at the dog but in the act kicked the Good Man's leg from beneath him and sent him heavily to the floor again. Mrs. Dorset took the opportunity to faint. Jenny Dorset laughed so hard that no sound escaped her lovely lips. Her small frame shook silently for some time, and through the window I espied the bright faces of the McNews. Later, I asked Jenny why she was being such a bad girl and she lectured me.

"Mr. Hawthorne, those who are good are sad and bored and those who are bad are happy and excited," she said. "Those who are rich are afraid to lose their money, while those who are poor have another drink and do not worry of it. What would you have me be, happy or sad?"

Her logic and clearheadedness for someone of such a tender age astonished me greatly; I could only admit that she had a point, to which she said only, "I know it," and disappeared, trailing a new scent her indulgent father had bought for her in town.

One morning not long after the disaster with Mr. Jincks, I was cleaning the silverware when Mr. Dorset came storming into the room completely disordered, holding a sheaf of papers in one hand and a quill in the other. I knew from his demeanor that he had been writing verse, and, though I tried to summon my spirit of loyalty, my heart sank.

"Hawthorne!" he cried. "By the gods, I have uttered a masterpiece!" He walked back and forth in front of me, looking over the papers with amazement and thanks for the bounty of his talent.

"Let me congratulate you, sir," I said. He stopped in front of me.

"Yes!" he said. "Yes, congratulate me, Hawthorne, for I shall become famous now. A hundred years hence they will speak my name with reverence and raise up statuary of me. For God hath chosen me to be His vessel. Why, Hawthorne? Why do you think God hath chosen me to be His vessel?"

"I could not say, sir," I admitted.

"No," he said, looking away. I could see from the stains on his sleeves that he had also been drinking wine. "I could not say either. That is the mystery. Why is one man chosen for greatness and another consigned to be a Smythe? Ah! Why is one woman born a princess and another a whore, Hawthorne?"

"I could not say."

"Nor I," he said. "Hawthorne?" He came too close and held on to my sleeve. "Shall I grant you the honor of first hearing this 'Ode on the Rescue of Miss Jenny Dorset'?"

"I am perhaps unworthy of the honor."

"'Tis likely true of any mortal man!" he cried. "But I shall grant you this gift as may be!"

He cleared his throat, but it did not seem to suit him, so he went for a glass of wine, which he brought with him, drained in one swallow, and set upon the table. Now, he was ready.

> *When rosy Phoebes in his morning coat,*
> *Hath brought among us people named Groat,*
> *When Father Helios came about to spurn,*
> *I saw young Jenny Dorset start to yearn*
>
> *For the great hills where the Indians live*
> *And fulsome flowers beg to often give*
> *Their bounty to a field of wheat or oat.*
> *Thence was fled from here the family Groat!*

He paused here for effect as our dramatists do upon the stage, and, though I could in no wise hide my amusement at his literary ineptitude, I disguised the smile as well as I could, turning it perhaps into bemusement rather than mockery. He easily believed I was amazed by his verse (which, in itself, was entirely true). He continued in this vein for some twenty minutes or so, but I will spare the Reader the discomfort of seeing so fine a man as Mr. Dorset show his failures with such eagerness. When the ode was published in the *South Carolina Gazette* a few weeks after that, it was the subject of such general derision that one troupe of young and waggish men in Town turned it into a musical play, but changed certain passages so they took place in a tavern. Mr. Dorset at first thought he was being honored, but, upon being informed this was not so, he rode to Town with the intention of thrashing the upstarts who were mocking him. Instead, he stayed for four days, drinking rum and apparently enjoying the entertainment. I rescued him from a French woman whose reputation stood up about as often as she did.

— 13. —
JENNY GROWS. SHE AND I BECOME GREATER CONFIDANTS,
AND HER BROTHERS BEGIN TO DIVERGE IN WAYS NOT WHOLLY
UNDERSTOOD OR APPRECIATED BY THEIR PARENTS.

Months passed, then a year, then another year. Our war with the Cherokee Indians came to an end the following spring when an expedition under Col. James Grant did what Montgomery had failed to do. Grant's army chased the Indians far into the hills, burning their crops and towns, leaving them quite destitute. The Province and Crown, seeing that the Cherokees were utterly defeated, decided with the compassion known to men of power to punish them even further. Mr. Charles Smythe's group of volunteers had returned from the Montgomery expedition claiming to have been at the vanguard of the drive into the mountains, but later we found most of them had been sick with measles and remained near Fort Prince George, where one was arrested for stealing a chicken.

Our relations with the Mother Country in the early 1760s had not yet soured as they soon would under Mad George, and so it was a fine time for a young family to grow into greater prosperity on a plantation. For my part, my wife and I began to have a family of our own, which diverted me somewhat from the most earnest service I might render Mr. Dorset. During this time, however, Jenny Dorset began to grow and blossom, becoming each day the most beautiful young woman imaginable, which was her father's delight and her mother's worry. For men will admire a beautiful woman far more often than another of her own sex, though why that should be I have never properly understood.

Jenny, in 1765, was twelve years old. She was slender and graceful. When visitors came, they could not take their eyes from her any more than I could. Though she had controlled her more urgent impulses to wander (at least for now), she had maintained her attractively mischievous temperament, and her collusion with the McNew twins had become so close that she seemed more their sibling than that of Abel, Isaac, and Matthew. The boys had become separate in their ways as well, with Abel as the eldest (he was fifteen) being serious and reserved and planning to take over the plantation. Isaac was interested only in games, and poor Matthew was interested only, as it appeared, in the intricacies of animal husbandry. Abel was so much his father's son that he would become pious when that sentiment strangled his father as it often did. When Adam Dorset would wench and drink, Abel would copy it in a minor way, being stubborn and unpleasant or, indeed, drinking too much wine at table.

"Hawthorne, may I ask you about God?' Jenny said one day. As I recall, it was winter, for a fire merrily crackled in the hearth. We were the only ones in the room.

"I could tell you little about that," I said. "I am mostly educated by my own hand."

"Is not such an education the more valued for being hard won?" she asked.

"There are men who would say that," I said. "But I do not know if it is true." In those days, young girls were educated poorly if at all, and the sons of wealthy men often went to England for study. True to his unpredictable inclinations, Mr. Dorset had refused this course, instead bringing to Longacre an excellent though dour tutor named Mr. Billing Snave. He instructed the boys faithfully and occasionally he taught Jenny, though her parents were both more concerned that she learn domestic arts.

"Tell me," she said, then paused for a pleasant moment. "Do you believe that we are placed by God upon this earth to suffer or to please and be pleased?"

"Some enjoy their suffering more than their pleasures, I will grant you that," I said, and she burst into bright laughter. "But I would say I think God would not create our race only to abandon us to baser instincts."

"What are baser instincts?" she asked.

"Greed, cowardice, any of the sins written in your Bible," I said, though not very convincingly.

"The Bible says *everything* is a sin," she said. "And the Reverend Jincks says that our reward is in the next life and that in this one we should not expect happiness to find us as a bird finds its nest after a flight."

"I cannot think the Almighty would begrudge us happiness," I said. "But it is hard won if it exists at all, and, like the Reverend Jincks' bird, it always lifts out of your grasp if you move toward it."

She walked around the room, testing steps for a new dance that her instructor had taught her that week. Her graceful movement on the polished floor was so elegant, so pleasant of line and form, that I realized God was in a way speaking through her, as He spoke through everyone, to point out a strength or weakness on the long journey toward Heaven.

"I believe we are made to enjoy this life," she said, stopping in front of me. "I believe that God in His mercy will forgive each of us our sins, but I cannot say I think suffering makes anyone more pure. Can you say that, sir?"

"I cannot," I said.

From that day, Jenny began to come to me with many questions about Life and the World, and, though I answered them as I could, she was thinking far beyond me already. And yet Jenny was never quite ready for philosophies or her father's religious trances. Just when I thought she might be turning toward a more mature demeanor, she and the McNew twins would find some new incalculable mischief to enter. Perhaps one example might suffice.

One evening at table, Isaac announced that he was sure that rats generated themselves from rags and such in corners and were not properly born as other animals. Mrs. Dorset was horrified by his lack of manners and became almost sick at the thought.

"Isaac, confine your thoughts to loftier subjects," she said, dabbing the corners of her pretty mouth with a linen napkin. "What has your Mr.

Snave taught you this week regarding the mathematics?"

"Rats!" cried Jenny. She spoke very slowly. "Large, thick, hairy rats with tiny feet and yellow teeth!"

"Fie on rats!" said Mr. Dorset. "I was bit by rats once in bed in Town!"

"What bed in Town?" asked Mrs. Dorset with some alarm.

"They grow from filth and rags and oiled papers," said Isaac with the prim and proper enunciation taught him by his tutor. Matthew, who had been thinking of some other thing, brightened.

"Oiled papers," he said. "Fancy that."

"Dirty rats with great long nasty toenails," said Jenny, making the shape of claws with her fingers.

"Jenny!" said her mother. "Stop this now!"

"A rat will make off with your clothes and your powder!" said Mr. Dorset. "It will eat anything in the room. I shouldn't be surprised to find a rat in my hair on awakening."

That comment was too much for Mrs. Dorset, who placed her hand over her mouth and left the table and went to her room upstairs to recuperate. The talk turned to other things, but I could see that familiar spark in Jenny's eyes and awaited for another development, which came only a few days after. She and the McNews, I found out later, captured a rat in the horse barns and put it into a small box. Early in the morning, when Mr. and Mrs. Dorset were still abed, she stole into their room and opened the box next to her father's head then made her escape quietly. The hour was early but I was already awake assisting Mrs. Wilson with preparations for the morning meal, when we both heard a loud shout upstairs, followed by a gunshot.

I ran through the house and up the stairs. I would not dared have gone in my Master's bedroom, but the door was open, and Mr. Dorset stood there in his nightclothes, holding his gun and breathing quite hard. Through the open door I could see Mrs. Dorset sitting in bed and holding the covers to her face. The doors to the children's rooms were open. Abel, Isaac, and Matthew shared a room, and they were looking sleepy and frightened. Jenny looked pleased beyond measure.

"Waugh! Just as I said! I am a prophet in his own country, for a foul rat hath walked in my hair!" said Mr. Dorset. "And now it lies dead in its vile tracks!"

The boys tumbled into the room and exclaimed over the blood. Mrs. Dorset pulled the covers over her head and began to cry, and

Jenny surveyed the scene as a general might the field of a successful battle. I raised one eyebrow as I looked at her, and she merely lifted her finger and placed it to her lips, thereby including me in the conspiracy.

For their part, Isaac and Matthew had no idea that the rat might have been placed in the bed, but Abel, the eldest and least forgiving, certainly did. He began to quiz the staff, including the McNew twins, but none of them had seen a thing, and I would not betray Jenny. It was in his capacity as self-appointed Grand Inquisitor that Abel came to me one afternoon in my quarters. I was not needed at the moment and so was reading a book on flowers and hedges that Mr. Dorset had ordered during his fit for topiary. Abel, dressed immaculately as he always was, stood before me as a master, so I stood and bowed and asked how I might help him. He told me to seat myself once more, which I did, and then he began to walk back and forth in front of me with a serious face, hands held tightly at his back.

"Mr. Hawthorne, be good enough to explain to me what you may know of this rat incident," he said. His voice was taut and restrained, as tutors often teach their students to use in addressing them.

"Sir?"

"The rat incident, Hawthorne," he said, stopping in front of me and tapping the toe of his shoe. "Surely in your position you have heard the true story of how it developed, for I do not believe that this rat merely walked alone in my father's hair. The coincidence is too extreme."

"But why worry over such a minor occurrence?" I protested. "No one was harmed but the rat, and its life was interrupted only briefly from what it might have possessed anyway."

"Faugh!" he cried. "Then you refuse to acknowledge that you know about it?"

"Of my own accord I know nothing," I said, which was entirely true, since all I had seen was a wink from Jenny.

Abel left me almost in tears of frustration, and he never would bring to justice the felon who brought the low villainous rat into the house, though he continued to harbor suspicions and glared at everyone for days until his fury subsided. Isaac for his part worked at certain games with his knife and at bowls, while Matthew frequently visited the stables. Jenny watched the unfolding scenes of family life with great humor and disbelief.

— 14. —

MR. DORSET SUFFERS ANOTHER FIT OF PIETY. WE ALL ATTEND
SERVICES AT ST. MICHAEL'S CHURCH IN CHARLES TOWN, FROM WHENCE
JENNY DORSET ESCAPES DURING A PARTICULARLY LONG SERMON AND
LEADS US ON AN EXTENDED TOUR IN HER SEARCH.

If Nature gave Mr. Dorset a changeable life, he gave Jenny one of perfect
consistency. No matter how serious her father became about this life, she
never thought much of her own character and whether it might lead to
grief from others. She was born to absorb the world on her own terms,
which to my mind is a thing to be admired, though often she did unad-
mirable things. Not long after the rat incident, I was in the house talking
quietly with Mrs. Dorset about the French. I was saying that I felt the
French were low villains, an opinion in harmony with her husband's, as
I have said. She, on the other hand, believed the French had been misled
by their leaders and was speaking with some eloquence about French
cloth and manners when Mr. Dorset burst into the room, his clothes in
great disarray. His hair was aloft, as if it were catching flame. And his eyes
had turned round and large. He waved his hands in small circles near his
face. Mrs. Dorset, with admirable loyalty at a time when loyalty might
not have been the best virtue to display, stood and touched his arm to
inquire the reason for his appearance.

"By the . . ." he began and then stopped. "By the . . ."

"By the what, dear?" she asked. He continued to wave his hands near his
face. Abel had come into the room with his tutor, Mr. Billing Snave, and
both were shocked at Mr. Dorset's actions, or at least Mr. Snave was, Abel
having seen it before but not wanting to see it now. "By the what, dear?"

We all waited until his hands stopped moving. He looked around the
room with fear approaching devotion or hysteria, two characteristics
often confused for each other. Finally, he spread his arms as wide as
Moses must have on asking the Red Sea to part, and he explained.

"God hath appeared to me as an angel in the form of a hedge," he said.

"Beg pardon?" said Mr. Snave. "Did he say a hedge?"

"Aye, a hedge!" cried Mr. Dorset, and once more he began to make
small circles near his face with those swimming hands. "And he told me
that I was a man overcome with evil! As I am!"

"Adam," said Mrs. Dorset quietly. Jenny came into the room holding
a stick that she was brandishing like a saber. "Please control yourself."

"And he told me that as a man overcome with evil, I may never be able to swim forth to Heaven if I do not mend my ways!" he said. Tears came down his cheeks. Jenny looked entirely merry at the sight. He swam again and moaned and groaned. "And I am evil for so many things, including the woman from Italy with the pleasing smile!"

"What?" cried Mrs. Dorset. Realizing that his rapture had taken him into dangerous territories, Mr. Dorset did the only thing he could: he fainted on the floor. Jenny immediately leaped upon him and began to pound his face and beg him to awaken. Old Bob, having wandered in, took it into his head that Jenny had killed her father, and snatched her away and began to tell her that even being a female of the species, she would hang from a gallows for such a crime. I rescued her, and Mrs. Dorset, also looking for a proper reaction, fainted and fell headlong on her husband. Mr. Snave registered his distaste by walking to the window, opening it, and being quite sick and making terrible noises for several minutes.

All recovered happily, but Mr. Dorset continued to insist that God had spoken to him from a hedge, and so once more his piety spread through the house. Abel was thrilled and began to walk everywhere with a Testament like the Reverend Jincks, and Isaac made up a game in which the loser had to receive one of the plagues of Egypt. No one would play with him but the McNew twins. Matthew continued to visit the stables.

The building of St. Michael's Church had begun in 1752, the year of our Great Hurricane (and the year Mr. Charles Smythe's first ship sank in the harbor). By 1760, the pews were installed, and this lovely structure with its spires was home church for many wealthy merchants and landowners thereabouts. It was less usual for us of the servant class to visit it, but Mr. Dorset insisted that we all go *en masse*, even Old Bob, who could rarely hear anything spoken in a church because his hearing was getting worse. This was also the new church of the Smythe family, principally because it was the best place to be seen, but, unlike Mr. Dorset, Mr. Smythe did not bring his servants, Herr Schlitz, Diana Seton, Sylvia Smartt, or her twins, Roderigo and Desdemona. They were consigned to work on an enormous meal that the Smythes would share later on Sunday. This lack of egalitarian spirit caused Mr. Dorset to write a letter to Mr. Smythe.

Longacre
September 9, 1765

My Dear Mr. Smythe,
    God's richest blessing upon you! I have seen that you are not allowing your servants to attend service with your family at St. Michael's Church. Think, sir, how much of the spirit they are thus missing. For God loves a cheerful giver, and we should give as we can to those who take as they must.
    I ask that you think hard on this request and that you face the wisdom of it in your heart.

Your humble serv't, &c.,
Adam Dorset

To which Mr. Smythe characteristically replied:

Foxhaven
September 10, 1765

Dear Dorset,
    Of all the fools I have suffered in my life, you are the greatest. Nothing I have done would invite the smallest amount of censure from you, nor will I stand for it.
    You are a foul, whoring, disgraceful wretch who could not give me advice on breeding my hogs.

Your serv't and friend,
Charles Smythe, Esq.

True to his newfound religion, Mr. Dorset forgave Mr. Smythe for the insults, though he would later have his revenge. At any rate, we were attending church at St. Michael's and were suffering through a sermon by a clergyman fresh from England. His voice was deep and round, and he was proud, even vain, of it, and so he had rewarded our attendance by speaking for some two hours on the burning bush and why we were all unworthy and would surly roast in Hell with festering sores and putrid flesh for eternity. I sat behind the Dorset family with my wife and children, and across the way we could see the Smythes, who were all concentrating on the message but Fortinbras, who was making faces to himself as an old toothless woman will make in a grinning contest. Mr. Dorset sat still with his hands folded beneath his chin, and Abel did the same, while Isaac counted his fingers over and over, and Matthew stared with an open mouth at nothing I could see. Only Jenny's eyes were lively and looking. She kept glancing around the church, marking each thing she found humorous with a piercing glance, and after a time, having no more interest in the burning bush or Moses' sandals, I began to watch Jenny, and I believe there was as much a message from God in her smile as in the burning bush that day.

When the sermon finally ended, and we were dismissed, Mr. Dorset went up front to congratulate the minister. As he did so, Jenny broke away from her mother and dashed down the aisle, spilling on her way one Mrs. Isham Bolt, a superannuated lady who was famous in Charles Town for never having smiled. Mr. Bolt, long dead, was but a stationer, but Mrs. Bolt was left money from her father, being his only child to survive. This day Mrs. Bolt was so finely dressed that she could scarcely walk, and when Jenny bumped her, she tumbled to the floor, crying all the while that she was dying. Several men, including myself, helped her, and when she realized that she was not to achieve Heaven, she began to beg anyone within the sound of her voice to catch the little urchin and whip it soundly then starve or drown it. I felt that was unchristian, but like the others I feared her wrath more than God's at the moment. Still, I did not divulge Jenny's identity, and Mrs. Dorset, having seen it all, merely went quickly after her daughter. Abel had gone with his father to be obsequious to the minister, Isaac was speaking with the too-proper Hamlet Smythe (who was sixteen that year), and young Matthew was still in his pew, alone and staring. I managed to help Mrs. Bolt upright once more.

"Who was that brat?" she cried. "A guinea for her name!"

Those attending her were silent until a familiar voice spoke up, clearly and almost formally.

"Jenny Dorset," said Mr. Charles Smythe. "As God is my witness, that was Jenny Dorset."

As I did not want to stay longer and hear Mrs. Bolt denounce my employer's family, I made my way out of the church into a pleasant early afternoon. The sun was shining, and the streets no muddier than usual, as we had enjoyed a storm the day previously. I ran into the street and looked both directions, and only for a moment believed I caught sight of

Jenny's blue dress as she disappeared around a corner several blocks away.

"By my life, it's 'enry Hawthorne," a voice said. I turned to see Tom Braught, an unfortunate old man who had visited Longacre several times in the service of his master, a cooper named Jones who sold pots and pans to the Dorsets. This Braught had many years before been married and even had two children, but they died of yellow fever, and, in a subsequent epidemic, smallpox so disfigured Tom that his cheeks sank and his long, yellowed teeth fell out, all but the two most prominent in front, both of which seemed inclined to permanence. His hair was thin but oiled flat, and so he presented a most distressing picture, though he was kind and direct in his dealings. Sad to tell, he was called "Weasel" by everyone, and rather than taking it for disgrace, he felt it conveyed a kind of affection and encouraged everyone to use it. What a sorry thing it is to be too little loved in this world.

"Weasel," I said. "My charge, Miss Jenny Dorset, has fled from the church."

"I was in there, 'enry, and I can't says I blame her," he said. Then he laughed, showing off his yellowed fangs, and I felt an involuntary shudder, as one does on seeing a long-lost friend come back fat or otherwise changed.

"I must be after her," I said. I pointed down the street toward the docks, where she had run.

"May I have the honor to escort you in pursuit of her?" he asked.

"You may," I said.

I had that year turned forty and so was not fit for such exertions, but I knew enough of Jenny to believe that I must hurry after her or find her on a ship bound for Antigua or Naples. I managed to run without too much pain, but Weasel gasped and wheezed through his teeth and kept having to stop briefly to expectorate every twenty paces or so. The Town was calm but busy that Sunday afternoon. As always, many ships were in the harbor, bearing slaves, spices, books, cloth, and other items for sale. We got to the aforementioned corner and saw Jenny running off down the street. She was now so far away that calling for her or continuing to run would have been pointless, so I reluctantly walked back toward St. Michael's.

"She is fleet, then, 'enry?" said Weasel.

"In all ways," I admitted.

The Dorsets were in front of the church, looking about in alarm. My wife and daughters saw me coming up the street with Weasel and waited expectantly for my report.

"Sir, I'm afraid Jenny has run off in yonder direction," I said, turning and pointing.

"She is fleet," said Weasel.

"Then she should be left to her own devices," said Abel coldly. "For if the honor of being a Dorset is such that she would insult us, she should leave hence."

"Where is Matthew?" asked Mrs. Lydia Dorset.

"He's still in there," said Isaac, pointing back inside with his thumb. "He's not moved. Nobody told him he could move."

"I forgive her," said Mr. Dorset. He tented his fingers and looked up into the milky blue sky and moved slightly back and forth. "Waugh! I forgive her this insult to our name and pray that she be all right."

"Mr. Dorset!" screeched Mrs. Bolt. She waddled as a duck does toward him, waving her arm threateningly. Mrs. Dorset rolled her eyes and sent Isaac back inside to fetch Matthew. Mrs. Bolt's face was crimson, and the folds of flesh at her neck were most uncomplimentary to her character.

"She is fleet," said Weasel helpfully.

"Fleet!" she cried. "You insult me, sir! I will have you dismissed from me or shot!"

"Gentle lady. . . ." said Weasel. Fortunately, she turned to Mr. Dorset and began to hurl insults at him regarding Jenny, wishing upon him a number of curses never before uttered on the portals of that fine church.

"How can you say after all that it was my Jenny knocked you down?" asked Mr. Dorset.

"I have the word of a gentleman," she said. "Mr. Charles Smythe of Foxhaven, who would never tell a lie!"

"Faugh! Aaaah! Oooh!" cried Mr. Dorset angrily, clutching his chest. "Foul Smythe! I'll tear the b—t—d limb from limb and feed his filthy feet to the dogs!" We turned at the same time and saw the English clergyman, who had come forth in grandeur from the church and stared, appalled at Mr. Dorset. Old Bob, wishing to make a contribution, touched the sleeve of the Holy Man's tunic and pointed.

"Sir, I give you my Master, Mr. Adam Dorset, Esquire, of Longacre," said Old Bob. The clergyman sniffed as if he had smelt something disagreeable.

"Quite," he said. He swept past us and down the street with several attendants or sycophants, and Mr. Dorset was left to rail further at Mr. Smythe for compromising his position with his religious acquaintances. Mrs. Bolt harrumphed for a moment or two longer and then turned to leave. She took one step and fell headlong into the muddy street, where she kicked and wallowed like a fitful child or perhaps a happy pig. From there she shouted for some time, before a family named Gomes helped her up and took her away as she bawled and shouted. Isaac and Matthew emerged and joined their family. The day had not been a success.

"Hawthorne," said Mr. Dorset, pulling me aside and whispering, "remind me later that I am to get a fowling piece and shoot Mr. Charles Smythe in the buttocks."

"Yes, sir," I said.

We agreed that we must look for Jenny. Mr. Dorset sent the family home, all but Abel and Old Bob. My own wife kissed me goodbye and took our girls off. Mr. Dorset said that he knew people all over town, and that they would help us find Jenny. As I was to find out later, that would not be quite as easy as we had at first suspected.

— 15. —

JENNY DORSET'S ADVENTURE IN CHARLES TOWN, AS EXPLAINED
FROM HER POINT OF VIEW, INCLUDING HER CONVERSATIONS
WITH PIRATES, HER CAPTURE BY THEM, AND THE CLEVER WAY
IN WHICH SHE ESCAPED THEM.

Some years later, Jenny told me in detail about her escape from St. Michael's that day, and she wrote as well about it in her journal. As I had the story from her own lips, I think better of that version than the one from her diary. For in writing, the closer we get to Truth the better the writing be, as all learned men agree. That is why our Bible is most esteemed and why novels are least admired, for one represents the entire Truth and the other an entire Falsity. I myself have always forsworn the reading of novels and have confined myself to history and philosophy, which I believe has given me the ability to write of Jenny Dorset.

That morning in church, Jenny had, like her father, had something of a vision. Perhaps her own mind spoke thus to her, but it was a voice anyway. Few men or women ever hear the voice of reason or conscience if it can be avoided, so I was amazed that she recognized it at all. She felt suddenly and strongly that she must escape from the church, which she said was suffocating her with its pretensions. The very great Hypocrisy of those assembled made her ill, and she was determined to run from it. When she left the church, she did not at first intend to run away, but when she emerged alone before the rest of the congregation and the streets stretched away, she felt a great urge to move out, to see life as it teemed there in Charles Town.

And so she ran. After three quarters of an hour, she was alone and had, she suspected, lost anyone who might be coming after her. And so she walked slowly, looking in windows on streets she had never before visited. Most were closed for the holy day, but a few that sold marine implements were open, and she saw through the windows bolts of rope, lamps, and many barrels full of nails and such. She was peering into the window of such a business when a man stopped at her shoulder.

"Looking to outfit your vessel, Miss?" he asked. She was shocked that someone would speak to her, but not so shocked she would run off.

"Nothing I should do would be your business in any way," she said.

"You alone here, Miss?" he asked.

"My father is in there with his gun and coming this way now," she said. The man looked once at the shop and then turned and moved quickly away, and Jenny took the time to congratulate herself before she walked on down the streets toward the harbor. She was going nowhere in particular and wanted only to escape the family and church, both of which she found intolerably stuffy and unforgiving. She was not afraid.

She walked down a street, turned into an alley, and soon found herself outside a tavern door where a number of cats were eating scraps and drinking soured cream from a dish set there by a woman who plied several trades within. Jenny had knelt to speak with these animals when the door from the tavern burst open, and this woman, whose name Jenny never ascertained, came out cursing a man who had given her too little money for one of her services. Jenny only noticed her fine red hair and remembered her as the Red-Haired Woman.

"Now, what's a well-bred young Miss like yourself doing out here?" asked the Red-Haired Woman.

"Escaping from my family, which are intolerably stuffy and unforgiving," said Jenny.

The Red-Haired Woman began to laugh with her hands on her hips, roaring in a way that no lady, ever seen by Jenny, had done. She had less than a full complement of teeth and was thick in areas where Nature planned for her to be thin, and thin where she might be stout. Her face was somewhat scarred and flung with freckling, as they call it. Her nose kept running, and, without ceasing her raucous laughter, she would lift her skirts to wipe her nose, revealing her undergarments and not caring who saw them. Jenny, quite taken by the woman's lack of propriety and honest actions, laughed then, too, and the cats scattered briefly from their scraps but then came back.

"Then you should come inside and escape farther from them," said the Red-Haired Woman. "What is your name, child?"

"Dorset," she said. "Jenny Dorset."

"Dorset!" cried the Red-Haired Woman. "*There's* a name I know well enough." Even though, as I have said, Jenny told me all this years later, she missed the ironies of the situation, and delicacy forbids me from commenting any further on it here. And so Jenny went into the tavern where the Red-Haired Woman worked taking mugs of rum to the rough men who came from ships and God alone knows where else. As her father had protected her against such incivilities, Jenny was stunned by the low ceiling, the smoke which choked the room from dozens of clay pipes, and the foul stench of unwashed men and their trollops. She could only watch as one fight broke out, then another, spreading as a plague will, until the owner and several of his men pushed the drunken brawlers outside. Such a house was no place for a lady such as Miss Jenny Dorset, and the thought of it still gives me pain, though it surely gave her little but pleasure.

"Get her out of here!" cried the owner, one Samuel Daudet, to the Red-Haired Woman. "Somebody'll come shooting to get that back."

"She's escaping away from her family who are . . . what was it, deary?" asked the Red-Haired Woman.

"Intolerably stuffy and unforgiving," said Jenny.

"In— what do ye say?" asked the owner. Jenny repeated it, and the owner was to respond, but another fight erupted from two very short men who were standing on a table, and he was summoned to stop it. Jenny had never seen such excitement, and she began to swing her arms as a fighter will, crying for one man to land a punch, then the other. (I can picture the scene myself, and can well imagine all the faces in the room slowly turning toward her flushed and beautiful face.)

"I'll give you ten guineas for the girl," said a dirty man who sat nearby. He reached out and touched the hem of Jenny's dress, and she naturally recoiled.

"Ten guineas wouldn't buy you five minutes with the lowest whore in town," said the Red-Haired Woman, and his fellows began to laugh and berate him, which started yet another brawl. The woman, however, seemed changed, and Jenny could tell that she had begun to think of selling

her. Suddenly the men began to crowd around her, pawing as a cat will
when you dangle a scrap over its head. Jenny backed away to the wall,
sensing for the first time the danger in which she found herself. The Red-
Haired Woman was already seeing her fortune disappear in the mob.

"A hundred guineas for this girl!" she screamed, scratching herself once
more. At that, Jenny broke free from the men, fell to her knees and
scrambled between the ample legs of the Red-Haired Woman, and
escaped out the door. Over her shoulder, she saw the men all leap on the
woman in pursuit, knocking her to the floor where she began to shriek
and scream and curse. Jenny got back into the alley next to the tavern,
and her arrival so startled the cats that they began to howl and screech
and grow fluffed with fear. She ran as fast as she might, and soon the men
tumbled into the alley and began to kick the cats out of the way, creating
a great spitting and growling that could be heard for some distance.
Jenny, being naturally fleet, ran down the street and soon eluded the tav-
erners, who, being drunk, were in no shape to follow her and soon failed
in the chase, only to begin fighting again among themselves.

After a quarter of an hour, Jenny knew that she was no longer pursued
by them, and she laughed over their stupidity and failed entirely to see
the danger that surrounded her. She was walking slowly in the edge of the
street, when a fine carriage stopped next to her. Driven by a groom, the
passenger was an elderly man of some standing and wealth, and he immediately inquired of Jenny why such a young girl would be out alone on
the streets. Jenny told him that she was to set sail soon for London, where
she was to sing for Mr. Handel himself. The gentleman told her that this
would be a fine thing except that Mr. Handel had died some six years
before, and that to his knowledge no ship was leaving until two days
thence for London. Jenny insisted that Mr. Handel was still alive and that
she was debarking that very day, and the man asked again if she was sure.
Perhaps she might actually be headed for France to serenade the King?

"The French!" she cried. "I would never sing for such low villains and
scoundrels!" The man was so shocked by this language that he ordered his
driver on, and Jenny clapped her hands and laughed as she imagined the
Red-Haired Woman might. She walked on, singing, as she recalled, "Victory at Longacre" or another one of her father's effusions. The day was
pleasant, and though she kept looking back to see if her father or myself
were in pursuit, she saw nothing familiar, and with each step became
more confident in her independence.

It was in her mood of sweet defiance that she came upon a small child who had been left to its devices while its parent was within a house enjoying some historical vice of which we are all aware. This child was a boy of about eight years, a rough lad throwing stones at a parked horse to watch it stamp its hindquarters.

"Stop that this instant!" cried Jenny. "Why would you torture a beast like that?"

"You attend to your business, and I shall tend to mine," the urchin said. "And I shall throw a stone at you if you are not fast."

"Do, and I will thrash you," said Jenny. The boy began to laugh, for he was an unwashed child who was accustomed to the discomforts of the street, and Jenny was dressed in finery fit for St. Michael's Church. "Do you doubt that I can thrash you?"

"I doubt that you could thrash a mouse," the boy said. Jenny, true to the spirit with which Nature endowed her, leapt upon the poor boy and began to pommel him about the face and ears, tearing her dress and soiling her face in the process. Just at that point, a man from the open window two floors above, improperly dressed to display himself to the street, shouted down to ask what in the bloody blazes was going on.

"I'm thrashing your bloody mouse!" cried Jenny, smacking the child once more on the head. The man uttered a curse and began to dress rapidly, which was a signal for Jenny to withdraw. For the boy's part, he had become so stunned and unsure of how to fight a girl that he stood and stared at her as she delivered her penultimate blow then the last. He was starting to smile when she leaned forward and kissed him on the cheek, the first boy, she told me, upon whom she had ever bestowed such a favor. The boy then smiled wholly and was entreating her not to leave when the father, roaring from rum and amorous disappointment, burst from the front door of the house.

"You will come to me for a thrashing!" he cried. In his haste, however, he had not secured his trousers properly, and they fell somewhere above his knees, and he stumbled and fell heavily to the mud. His son, reluctant to see Jenny flee, went to help his father up but did not take his eyes off Jenny, who could not take her eyes off him until she disappeared around a corner.

By this time, she was having a fine day, and none of us was closer to finding her, though we were crying her name and roaming the streets where we had seen her go. She passed carriages heading home from church services, and men lying drunk and groaning in the gutter. She saw

ladies dressed in silken finery and women whose only distinguishing fea-
ture was their utter coarseness and lack of refinement. She saw a black
slave who was creeping forth, apparently having escaped from his master,
speaking in the African Tongue with great fear. She heard music from a
spinet that sounded finer than anything her father had written at Longacre.
She passed a bookseller and saw great volumes through the window and
wondered who could write such a thing, and why.

We are accustomed to hearing the word *drunk* with approbation, but
on that Sunday afternoon, Jenny Dorset was truly drunk with the dazzling
splendor of a world from which she had largely been shielded, and she was
intoxicated beyond resistance. The more she drank of that nectar, the farther she strayed, until she found herself near the great wall of the harbor
itself and looking at the bay and thence to sea. She could not resist thinking of her adventure on the seas from some time before, and she thought
of the sea as a highway and wondered where that road might lead.

She was pondering all this so intently that she did not hear a man
coming from behind her until he had picked her up around the waist
and was carrying her off. She cried out and kicked as hard as she might,
but the man, whom she could not see but could unfortunately smell,
held her tightly.

"My father is a great man, and he shall come to lay you low!" she cried.
This intelligence threw the man into such a fit of laughter that he nearly
dropped Jenny, but he managed to bring her down the dock and thence
to a small boat, upon which were six or seven more men. They were
preparing to cast off.

"Fresh cargo," the man said, and he pushed Jenny into the boat amid
a burst of laughter. By this time, Jenny had finally grown afraid, which as
I told her years later was a tribute to her growing maturity. She seated
herself between them, a group of men dressed in bits and sashes of col-
ored cloth. They wore fierce mustaches, and their eyes had the predatory
gleam of a hawk as it dives into the field toward a mouse. Each had a pistol or small sharp sword in his sash, and two of the men began to row
locked oars vigorously. Within five minutes, they were far out into the
Charles Town bay, heading for a small ship anchored a distance away.
Jenny at that point rued her foolishness and was sorry that she had not
told any of us goodbye, for she was sure they intended to use her ill and
decided to drown herself first.

As she stood to offer herself to the deep, however, one of the men grabbed her and tied her arms and legs and then secured the rope around the plank seats so that she could not move. If she could not escape by drowning herself, she would at least die, she thought, with her honor intact, and so she began to curse them. She used every phrase or word she had ever heard from her father's lips during his tirades at Longacre, including several normally reserved for the French or Mr. Charles Smythe. The men were unmoved, though irritated by her loud arguments against them. She called them scurvy villains without brains, courtesy, or courage. She said they were no better than pigs in their clothing and demeanor.

One particularly vile pirate made to strike her, but when Jenny did not back away or flinch, he withdrew his hand and stared at her suspiciously. The ship they took her to was, of course, not a pirate vessel, as no pirates actually docked in the harbor. Instead it was a brig flying the flag of some Carribean kingdom or another, a transport to the pirates' actual ship, which was in port some miles down the coast on the sea islands of the colony of Georgia.

Jenny was hauled on to the ship and immediately looked carefully over by the assembled men. One man knelt to lift her skirt to inspect her leg. Jenny was in no wise ladylike, so she waited until the man was holding her ankle before kicking him as hard as she might in the face. The man, a roundish fellow with an earring in his drooping ear, withdrew a long knife and threatened Jenny. She was protected by the others, however, and soon a brawl broke out over her. Several of the assembled men drew cuts of varying lengths and depths. In the midst of it all, buoyed with an inspiration perhaps from God, Jenny began to shriek.

"Leppe aleppe quintus fulgus brokam!" she screamed. The company grew somewhat silent and worried. "Blalllah mallah ning-ning faciae crepusculum!"

The fighting stopped entirely, except for two men who continued to kick and punch each other to little effect. The men discussed Jenny. Seeing that she had so far saved her virtue and her life, she began to scream the same sentences or something like them, this time even louder, and with rolling eyes and waving arms. The pirates moved to starboard away from her, where fierce arguments continued about what her demeanor meant. Seeing that her act was giving her space, she began to speak in other tongues that she did not know, and spat while doing so and moved in a kind of hopping circle. Then, with nostrils flaring and eyes wide, she stepped toward them and began to sing "Victory at Longacre" with such force and conviction that one of the men backed to the rail and fell overboard into the sea.

After a brief conference, two men came to Jenny, lifted her up and carried her back down into the launch, and rowed her back toward Charles Town, arguing all the while. Each time the argument would stop, Jenny would begin to sing in a very slow voice of the hideous terrors of the deep ocean. By the time they got back to the dock, the men carried her gently up, unbound her, and ran for their boat and rowed away from her forever.

At this point in her adventure, Jenny Dorset might have sat down for a time or at least considered how lucky she was, but her Nature did not include such thoughts, and so, as she reported to me, she began to skip back down the streets toward where she had been before. She was thinking of little when she came around the corner, only to see, not ten paces away, the gentleman who had been in the window with his trousers down a few hours past.

"Ho! Girl!" the man cried. "I have words with you!"

Jenny crossed the street and ran as fast as she could, but the man was nearly as fleet as she, and it took several blocks before she was able to elude him. She was breathing hard, and laughing, leaning on a barrel in an alley, when she realized God, in His circular nature, had brought her back to the tavern from whence her problems had begun that morning. She was thinking of walking back toward St. Michael's when the Red-Haired Woman suddenly came out of the door to empty a pail of water into the street.

"You!" the woman cried.

Jenny leapt up once more and began to run, but her speed was not necessary, as the Red-Haired Woman had no breath from indulging too long in various vices. Soon, Jenny was in the clear and was walking along, singing and humming, when she turned yet another corner and found herself right in front of myself, the Weasel, and Old Bob.

"Jenny!" I cried. "Where on earth have you been?"

"Merely walking on this fine Sabbath, Mr. Hawthorne," she said. Her soiled and torn garments made such an assertion unlikely at best.

"Fine cabbage?" said Old Bob, cupping his ear.

The family was so relieved to see her that not one of them chastised her or made much of her state of repair. (In truth, her father would have forgiven her had he known the truth, as he always did.) We rode in a stately way back toward Longacre, and Jenny talked the entire way, to the disgust of her eldest brother Abel, whose sense of piety and propriety were equally offended.

Once we stopped to cross a stream, and Jenny stood in the carriage and began to declaim an ode of her own making (though no worse, I must admit, than that of her father) about Charles Town and red-haired women and pirates and churches. None of them could make much of it, nor could I until some years later when I learned the truth. I can recall only one quartrain of the ode, and for what reasons I cannot imagine:

> *Every man in time becomes a beast*
> *As every beast in time becomes a man.*
> *The world is the ablest banquet feast*
> *And I am here to speak the truth!*

"Well spoken, brave daughter!" said Mr. Dorset. I could tell from their eyes, however, that no one else shared his opinion.

— 16. —

MR. DORSET DECIDES TO PUT OLD ENMITIES BEHIND HIM
AND ACCEPTS ON BEHALF OF HIS FAMILY AN INVITATION BY
MR. CHARLES SMYTHE TO SEE THE LAUNCHING OF HIS NEW TRADE
VESSEL, *THE PEARL*. THE UNPLEASANT CONSEQUENCES OF THAT EVENT.

Jenny Dorset, for her part, was idle and penitent for some eight or nine hours after she returned from the pirates, before assuming her normal ways. Old Bob had taken it into his head that Jenny had been ransomed from the French, and he acted out his wrath upon the savages by fighting an imaginary swordsman with the fireplace poker. His technique, however, was as awkward as anything about him, and upon one great thrust he managed to destroy a fine vase from the Orient that Mrs. Lydia Dorset greatly prized. She banished Bob to his quarters, where he sat with folded hands and downcast face until no one could stand it any longer, and he was summoned back to his service. Mr. Dorset's piety began to slip that very day, though it hung around Abel as a fragrance from a certain kind of woman lingers in the air long after she has gone. That evening at dinner, Jenny prayed to God for more than nine minutes as the supper cooled on their plates, and Mr. Dorset, who was ravenous, was only partially pleased at his daughter's reverence. The next day, however, Jenny and the McNew twins conspired to empty an egg of its yolk and refill it with a particularly noisome caterpillar, so that when Mrs. Wilson broke it for the Master's breakfast, she fell into a screaming fit, followed by an attack of the vapors. I did not find out about the trick until some time later. We each assumed that Mrs. Wilson merely had fallen prey to one of those moods common to women and which men cannot understand (though none ever tried hard to do so, I admit).

The family was dining one evening. The weather was warm and clear, and the house felt healthy and pleasant. The table was larded with fresh hens and several others fine dishes prepared by Mrs. Wilson, who had by then recovered. Mr. Dorset had been in his library the entire day working on an ode of unwieldy proportions, sipping wine all the while, and by evening his tongue was stained pink and his fingers black from the ink. He tried to straighten himself up for the meal but only managed to leave himself even further disordered, with ink smudges around his mouth and a thick tongue from the fruit of the vine. The family mostly ignored him, all but Mrs. Dorset, who stared at him with a mildly predatory gleam, as if she had gained an advantage, and Abel, who was clearly appalled at his father's condition. After grace had been spoken, Abel kept his head down for another minute or so, no doubt begging forgiveness for his father. Matthew began to eat noisily even before Adam Dorset had pronounced the Amen. No one could do much about Matthew.

"Aye, God, to be in bondage all day with that whore of a Muse!" cried Mr. Dorset, slapping his stomach.

"Mr. Dorset!" cried his wife, Lydia. "Children are present!" I hung back near the fireplace as always, awaiting their pleasure.

"Then children are present!" he shouted. "I cannot but descry what the Muse bids me do, for I am a great artist."

"You are a great fool," said Lydia softly but earnestly. "And great fools make those around them suffer the more for their foolishness."

"Who told you such blather?" he said. "Was it that fool preacher at St. Michael's?"

Mrs. Dorset's smile was twisted and slightly ironic.

"It's from your poem about the Carthaginians," she said. He seemed distracted for a moment, remembering, then a look of purest pleasure crossed his face as a cloud passes away before the face of the sun.

"Oh," he said. "Of course." He waved his fork around in small circles.

He cleared his throat. "A memorable effort, eh, Lyddie?"

"Memorable?" she said.

They ate quietly for a time, all but Matthew, whose manners were appalling and would take no correction. Mr. Dorset ate silently before he noticed a small envelope next to his plate.

"What's this, then?" he asked.

"Came this afternoon from the Smythes," said Jenny. "Mother said you weren't to be disturbed, that you were . . . what was it? Oh. That you were in the bookroom deluding yourself."

"Waugh!" he cried. "Woman, you will be the death of me!" His attention, however, shifted to the envelope. He opened it and read out loud.

MR. CHARLES SMYTHE, ESQ.
INVITES YOU AND YOUR FAMILY
TO THE LAUNCHING OF HIS SHIP
THE PEARL
ON TUESDAY NEXT IN TOWN AT
2:00 IN THE AFTERNOON

Mr. Dorset snorted a laugh, then considered it once more.

"Well, perhaps this is the chance we have to bury the enmity between these two great houses after all," he said. "For why should the best and strongest — by that I mean us, of course — not be willing to give a helping hand to a family trying to improve its fortunes? Is that not the Christian thing to do, Lyddie? I have always thought I was marked in a way for greatness, but I never knew in which direction my genius lay."

"Pudding?" asked Old Bob, who had tottered into the room with a tray full of small bowls that were tilting dangerously.

"Grab that!" cried Mrs. Dorset, but it was too late, for Nature had given Bob a new plane of vision, one that did not allow the carrying of plates or trays in a level manner. He dumped the pudding over Isaac's shoulder, where it landed on the table. Glassware broke, and a great smear of pudding coated the oak. Mrs. Wilson came up from the kitchen and chastised poor Bob while summoning several of the other servants to help clean up. I pitched in as well, and it took nearly a quarter of an hour before order was restored.

"Now," said Mr. Dorset. "Of what were we speaking?"

"Your genius," said Jenny.

"I wanted pudding," said Isaac sadly. Mrs. Dorset comforted him.

"Ah!" said Mr. Dorset. "My genius! Well, then perhaps I may have a genius for forgiveness!"

No one at table took that assertion with any seriousness, least of all myself, but we pretended it was so, and it was but a gentle delusion, the kind which holds all families together. Later that evening, I found Old Bob and comforted him for his mishap with the pudding, but his spirits were very low. I told him that I thought he was a fine servant and added much to the house of Dorset.

"I wear a corset?" he said in great confusion. I only patted his hand. That small measure of affection seemed to comfort him once more until his natural state of forgetfulness returned, a state we should all greatly desire in our own old age.

And so it came to pass that on the following week, the family and varied servants gathered, dressed in our finery, and left Longacre by carriage and horse for Charles Town, where we were to see Mr. Charles Smythe's new ship, *The Pearl*, dedicated and launched. I was under no belief that it would be a grand occasion. The day, however, was magnificent, kissed by God, as it were, with a mild offshore breeze and warm clear skies. Because of Mr. Smythe's standing in Town, many of the best men and women had come for the ceremony. *The Pearl* itself was a three-masted schooner, built for a modest cargo and speed, and from all outward appearances a fine vessel. It sat proudly in its slip with sails down but flags up and flying. Upon its bow was the carving of a woman that some said was Ophelia Van Dyke Smythe, though I had to admit that the wooden version had differing proportions from the real lady.

Among the annointed that day were Squire Burleigh Dunlap and his insufferable son, Tradd. Squire Dunlap was a lender of money and purveyor of goods and services. He was enormously fat and thoroughly detestable. His son seemed to have inherited his father's coarser traits while at the same time assuming some of the finer manners and interests of his mother. Tradd, for instance, wrote odes for the *Gazette* as Mr. Dorset did, and at times they were almost as bad as those penned by the Man of Longacre. Tradd also composed for the spinet and gave lessons upon it to the young ladies of Town. In his manner he was overly refined, like a dog whose breeding is so precise that it has neither strength nor stamina for the hunt. In his course of actions, he was unfortunately like his father.

Others were there, but soon it was clear that Mr. Dorset's friends came around his family and Mr. Smythe's circle clustered toward him at the edge of the ship. The dock was merry, and drunken sailors, women with poor reputation, merchants, and farmers all enjoyed the celebration, which was fueled by free rum and slices from several steers which had been cooked for the occasion starting the afternoon before.

The vessel herself looked fine and yet at the same time fragile. One might think of a large sea bird whose wings can carry it over the greatest waves and winds and yet fall prey to a boy with a stone if it sits upon a dock post. No one seemed to notice a certain creaking in the prow, a bending of boards along the sides in places where they should have been solid as stone. I held my counsel and stood with my wife and children and Old Bob.

Mr. Smythe at length mounted a small platform which he had caused to be erected not far from the slip, and I admit that it was touching how well his wife and children believed in him from the looks upon their faces. Hamlet looked smug and confident; Iago was oily and distracted, but his glance returned anon to his father; Fortinbras stared straight at his father but kept making cooing noises as a pigeon will make, and I was certain (as were many others) that poor Fortinbras Smythe would never amount to more than an idiot.

Mr. Smythe had been careful to surround himself with certain clergymen and officers of the Province, so that no one could mistake his importance or the importance of Commerce to Charles Town. He held his hands firmly behind his back and cleared his throat and began to give his speech.

"Gentleman, ladies, our friends of the Church, and of the State, I welcome you on behalf of myself and my family today to one of the signal events in the history of the Province of South Carolina, the launching of *The Pearl,* which I named with my wife in mind," he said. He gestured toward her.

"If he's to name it after her, he ought to've named it *The Swine,*" whispered Mr. Dorset rather too loudly. Mrs. Dorset elbowed him in the ribs, and he looked back toward the speaker. There was a smattering of applause for Mrs. Smythe, who curtseyed.

"I claim this as a signal event, for it represents an even greater expansion for our trade and for the goods it can bring us," said Mr. Smythe. "Better goods!"

"Aye, let it bring us some better women!" cried a drunk reeling on the dock, and the laughter took a moment to subside, to the great annoyance of Mr. Smythe. His consort stared at the man with great viciousness, and Mrs. Dorset, noticing Mrs. Smythe, smiled unctuously. For her part, Jenny had a stone in her hand and was looking with keen eyes at a scrofulous cat which was trotting by with a fish head in its mouth. I caught her eye and shook my head, and she reluctantly dropped the stone with a sigh.

"Better goods!" shouted Mr. Smythe again. At this point, the aroma from the roasting steers and the other food began to overwhelm the crowd, and eyes turned toward the feast. "And a legacy for me to leave the Town that I love so well. For it is in time of trial that a man shows his worth, and this new vessel shall help each of the merchants of the town import and export better than before! God grant me the wisdom to use this bounty wisely and well."

"God grant me a pint!" cried another man. Only the fact that a clergyman rose to speak quieted the crowd. One man tried to steal a piece of meat from the steer, only to be hit on the hand by a black man wielding a sharp stick. Old Bob was delighted and made a few feints, thrusts, and parries to show his enthusiasm.

The clergyman was fresh from Scotland, and with the dour tone and speech of those native to that land, he began to shame us all before God as sinners and foul, evil fellows, one and all, and said that lest we repent of these sins (which he enumerated at some length) we would surely burn forever in the fires of Hell. He ended by adding, almost as an afterthought, "Oh, and God bless this boat, Amen." Mr. Smythe was not pleased. I looked around for Jenny and saw her a hundred feet away trying to entice the cat, which had dropped its fish head and was sniffing around the cooking meat. She had the stone once more, held tightly in her small hand behind her back. I was too far away to do a thing, and I must admit that her demeanor, her energy, her eagerness for the adventure were admirable. Next came an official from Town, a famous personage whose name now escapes me. No one else I consulted for this History could recall who it might be, either. Nonetheless, he was a man of some standing, and he spoke with waving arms of the need for more trading vessels and of the lies told by the French and their Indians Etc. In all, a dreary performance.

Finally, several men with large hammers and axes began to cut the ropes which held *The Pearl* to her moorings, and suddenly, with a great moan and a creak, she slid from the slip and went completely down into the sea. The crew began raising her sails, and a small band started to play some of Mr. Handel's music to celebrate. Men who had been drinking rum raised their glasses or bottles in tribute, and Mr. Smythe's face was bright with joy. The ship took on a small roll as it moved out into the harbor, and within thirty seconds she had begun to roll in a wide arc, throwing men from the decks into the water. Some on the docks were screaming, and others were screaming with laughter.

"By God!" shouted Mr. Dorset, rubbing his hands gleefully. "By God!"

"Do something!" shouted Mr. Smythe. Mrs. Smythe began to fan herself vigorously. But no one could do anything, and within a few moments the ship had rolled completely over, emitted a gurgling burp, and sunk. Small boats quickly rowed to the site and rescued most of the men, who were swimming and cursing. Several men of the Town who had backed Mr. Smythe in his latest venture were now arguing with him. In his frustration, Mr. Smythe hit one square on the nose, and the poor man fell down without moving. At that point, a great geyser erupted from the wreck, making a sound that was indelicate at best and rude at worst. Mr. Dorset, who had until now somewhat restrained himself, fell to the dock laughing painfully and holding his sides. His wife, too familiar with such scenes, gathered Abel and Isaac and turned to look for Jenny, only to see her sitting near the food, sharing a greasy strip of meat with the cat, which was sitting on the lap of her pretty gown and eating from her hand.

"Waugh!" cried Mrs. Dorset.

Unable to stop laughing or enjoying the scene, Mr. Dorset got up and headed for Mr. Smythe. I sensed trouble and bade Old Bob to go with Mrs. Dorset, and I followed my Master. Several people were attending the knocked-down investor, and Mr. Smythe, red-faced and clenching his fists, looked as if he wanted to kill the first man who said a word to him. As was the case so many times, that man was his neighbor, Mr. Adam Dorset.

"Behold the mighty sea!" roared Mr. Dorset, pointing to the dead flat calm of Charles Town Bay. "See how she consumeth even the greatest of vessels!"

"Hold your tongue if you don't want it ripped out!" shouted Mr. Smythe. "I intend to kill that coward of a builder, and I don't mind if I kill you, too!"

The clergyman and the politician left together, sharing a bottle and

heading for the food. The docks were suddenly teeming with the fortunate and the less fortunate, all of whom were sharing in the food and
drink. Mr. Smythe was enraged.

"Away from that, you fools!" he screamed. "Away!" But he might have
been shouting at the ocean to subside. I looked up in time to see Mrs.
Dorset chasing Jenny, who was now being followed by the cat. Fights
began to break out over food and drink and, perhaps, women. The wreck
blew up a gust of water once more from its hold.

"She blows!" said Mr. Dorset. His humor, which I must admit made
me smile, was lost entirely on Mr. Smythe, who found a nearby stick of
wood and, having had enough, announced that he would kill Mr. Adam
Dorset. Jenny arrived upon the scene at precisely that moment.

"Ever seen a finer day, Hawthorne?" she shouted above the noise.

"Perhaps, Miss," I said. Mr. Smythe and Mr. Dorset began to circle
each other. "Or perhaps not."

"Perhaps not!" she said. The cat then stretched up with its claws on her
skirts, and she kicked it about five yards. The cat did not seem to mind
and came running back. It followed Jenny, who finally moved off toward
her mother and brothers.

Mr. Smythe swung his club repeatedly at Mr. Dorset, but the former
was in no danger of causing pain, and the latter was in no danger of suffering it. By this time a general brawl had broken out on the docks, most
of the food had been stolen by low-life sorts, and all the gentility had
abandoned the scene. The entire soaked crew of *The Pearl* finally got back
to shore. Mr. Dorset and Mr. Smythe continued to circle each other as
mad dogs will before the fight begins. These crewmen were quite vexed
by the sinking of the ship and stood before Mr. Smythe asking for an
accounting. As the men circled for a fight, however, strange things began
to happen in the sea. Chests, flasks, ropes, spars, and other parts of the
ship began to rise in a gurgling series, each shooting to a different height,
giving pleasure to the drunks along the shore.

"She blows!" cried Mr. Dorset once more.

"My eye teeth," said one of the unfortunate crewmen, more fascinated at the spectacle than angered at Mr. Smythe.

"Compose an ode on the death of your person!" shouted Mr. Smythe
as he swung again at Mr. Dorset. "For I mean to bash your brains until
the dogs eat them!"

"You fight like you make ships," said Mr. Dorset, who was fairly winded by now. Fortunately, Mr. Smythe had lost his own wind, and neither man had the strength to chase the other. At some length, they fell upon the thick planking and merely stared at each other, at first with bitterness, then somewhat with civility. In the meantime, a pack of very thin dogs had appeared and was trying to steal what was left of the food from the servants. Men threw rum bottles and rocks at the dogs to little effect. I was amused by the spectacle until I saw that two of the dogs had cornered Old Bob near an off-loaded supply of goods in large boxes. Bob fenced the dogs with his cane but was in danger of losing ungallantly, as one of the mongrels had pulled his trousers half down. A nearby woman screamed at the sight and fled. I dashed to Bob and tried to kick the dogs away.

"And lo, the lion will lie down with the lamb," said Bob weakly. He fell to his seat, and I took his cane and finally managed to chase the dogs away. As I did so, I noticed that the men had faded away when the food and drink vanished, and even the crew of *The Pearl* was walking off, soaked and muttering. The harbor was littered with the remains of the ship, and, those remains being now salvage, men in small boats were out eagerly hauling them up. A large sea bird landed near Mr. Smythe and looked at him.

I walked back to the adversaries and stared with some pity at them both. Neither had much to say, and I might have taken my Master back home then, except that Jenny Dorset appeared from where I could not guess. Her cat had left, which was just as well, but Jenny was smiling so beautifully that even in her soiled dress, I could not take my eyes from her.

"I have written an ode on the proceedings," she said in a clear voice. Someone had overturned a small box, and she climbed upon it, put her hands behind her back, and cleared her throat. She looked up at the sky as if it might give her inspiration or strength. Then her gaze leveled out at the two sorry men before her.

> *Let us then praise* The Pearl,
> *Gone down to the sea for all,*
> *She was a tub made for squirrels*
> *Not for ladies nor for balls.*

Mr. Smythe laughed in spite of himself, though Mr. Dorset, sure of an impropriety yet unsure what it was, seemed merely confused. Jenny accepted the laughter as a compliment and cleared her throat.

> *A great confusion there was!*
> *And the ship heaved and rolled!*
> *As a bee will have its buzz,*
> *A ship will have its fall!*

"Ho! Brava, poetess!" cried Mr. Dorset in quite some fit.

"Preposterous!" said Mr. Smythe.

"And more then?" asked Mr. Dorset. "The third quatrain for us then?"

"No more," said Jenny, jumping off the box. She ran across the docks and disappeared around a corner, where, fortunately, Mrs. Dorset, the children, and Mrs. Wilson were trying to extricate the McNew twins from a fight.

By now, except for those who earned their daily bread from the sea and were no longer taking any account of the festivities, all had departed. The bounty thrust up by *The Pearl* had been hauled away. The only ones left were myself, Mr. Dorset, and Mr. Smythe, the latter of whom sat with his face in his hands and softly but earnestly cursed everyone he could think of.

Mr. Dorset, sensing that this victory was too great for a worthy foe, patted Mr. Smythe on the back as he passed, a human gesture that touched me deeply, though Smythe barely acknowledged it. We walked along, saying nothing, but I must admit each of us was in fine fettle. Mr. Dorset was besieged by the Muse on the way back to Longacre, and so it was no surprise to any of us when he disappeared into his study and wrote and composed "The Sinking of *The Pearl*," which he unfortunately had performed in Town several weeks later. I should like to think that this composition threw a cold light on his talent and would have dissuaded him from inflicting further disgrace to the Muse, but Heaven has her fine moments of high humor, and in all the Dorset family, such moments were of a rich harvest.

Dedicated to Miff Jenny Dorfet

Engraved by Prioleau and Sons, Charles Town
aetat. 1762

Sinking of the Pearl

Compofed by Mr. Adam Dorfet

Allegro con mare

'Twas on a bleak and stor -my day, the
'Twas quite a sight upon up - on the sea, 'Twas
The *Pearl* went down in - to the dark, she

mi- gh- t- y *Pearl* went down! The
tra – gic for that host! No
ma- de three ful – some sounds! And

thun – ders had their mer – ry way be-
o – ther ves- sel sprung a leak, for
so the mak- er of that barque be

fo- re of - all Charles- Town! Or may-
mi -les a - long the coast! And
be - - ter - off with hounds! The

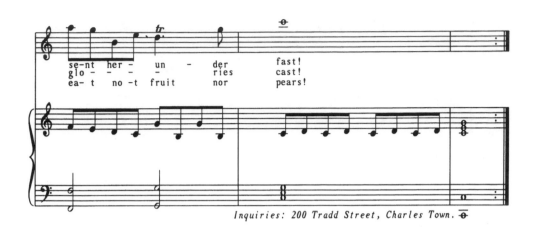

se-nt　her –　un –　der　　fast!
glo – – –　 – ries　　cast!
ea- t　no -t　fruit　nor　pears!

Inquiries: 200 Tradd Street, Charles Town.

BOOK III.

— 1. —

IN WHICH THE AUTHOR APOLOGIZES FOR HIS POOR SKILLS AND IN
WHICH WE MOVE FORWARD IN OUR HISTORY TO THE TIME WHEN
JENNY DORSET HAS TURNED FOURTEEN YEARS OF AGE. HOW THE SAD
DEATH OF MRS. WILSON CHANGES OLD BOB'S LIFE.

God granted me, for my patience and loyalty, a long life. Perhaps that is
a just reward, and I am certainly unsuited to challenge the plans of the
Almighty. Still, I wonder at the urge to put down this History, for I can
think of no one less suited for the task. My meager talents (though perhaps of a higher order than Mr. Dorset's) are strained, for I forget dates
and faces as easily as I forget last week's weather. And having no interest
in searching records of the late Province or the new State of South Carolina for facts, I have written as I recall the world, rather than perhaps as
it really was. But as any man will admit, facts are the least certain of all
our philosophies. One year's faith is another year's fraud. And so I continue this History with confidence that if no worse job might be carried
off, perhaps no better one would be offered, either.

With that consolation, let us resume our story.

By the year 1767, our arguments with the French had faded with the
end of the war. We had repaid the Cherokees for their loyalty by reduc-
ing them to a ragged and impoverished people. They would later fight
with the British in our Revolution, and, for that, we punished them even
more. The one characteristic of the strong I have always noted is that they
despise and humiliate the weak, and, in that wise, South Carolina was no
different from any province or country. Power breeds stupidity, and stupidity in the affairs of state is the birthright of every man born henceforth, and, I might add, for a long time past.

In that year of relative peace, Jenny Dorset had turned fourteen years of age, and no Dryden or Pope could describe her beauty. Her hair, yellow when she was a child, was now a golden color, rich with the very light of sunshine, and her skin was burnished from that light, not as ladies would have it, for they prized pale complexions above all, but lovely anyway. Her cheeks were high, and her deep blue eyes often alive with mischief or the sheer excitement of being alive. In polite company, her mother, Lydia Foxe Dorset, admitted the girl was lively. "Waugh!" her father would cry. "And controlled as easily as a wild horse in a beehive!" She loved beautiful clothes and soiled or tore them so often Mr. Dorset swore he'd never buy her another gown. Then he would see her in a silk dress at St. Michael's, radiant and full of the hope he had long ago lost, and tears would stream down his craggy face, and he would lean to me in a choked whisper and say she was the most beautiful girl in this world. I would not have argued, even had she been the ugliest hag in America. But she was, indeed, the most beautiful girl in that world. No one, not men, women, boys, or girls, could take their eyes off her when she entered a room, and she knew it well. But if she were beautiful, she was also strong, could ride a horse as well as most men, and was taught to be a fine shot, not by any of her brothers, who disapproved, but by Tom McNew. He seemed to be in love with her, but she scorned him as she did most young men, and their shooting lessons finally ended when she became his superior with all weapons.

She learned to play the spinet quite well and had a pleasant soprano voice. Her tutors found her adept at Latin though less so at Greek, and only her inborn stubbornness kept her from a full education. Her manners were altogether elegant, and she knew many poems by rote, if not by heart. And yet behind the polish, she had never lost her streak of wildness, which Mrs. Dorset always attributed to her husband's side of the family. Abel, for instance, was seventeen in 1767, and he was already planning to become a clergyman, to his mother's great pleasure and his father's confusion. No Dorset had been a clergyman, and, though Mr. Dorset's periods of piety were still as variable as the weather, he was unsure this was the proper career for his eldest son, upon whom he was counting to inherit Longacre. Because of this misfortune, Mr. Dorset had to invest his hopes in Isaac, the middle son, who was by then sixteen and simply dull. Matthew, the penultimate child at fifteen, spent all his time in animal husbandry and was considered hopeless as the future squire of Longacre.

Without doubt, Jenny was the center of all attentions, and she had gained her full figure by then, often uncommon in girls of fourteen, but a pleasure to the eye when it occurs.

It happened in the early spring of 1767 that Mrs. Wilson, who ran the household staff, became ill, and it was soon clear that she would not recover. Though Mr. Dorset spent lavish amounts on physicians, they could do nothing, and she soon took to her bed, from which it was obvious she would never rise. I regretted it, because she had been good to me, though some of the others swore they would not miss the tartness of her tongue.

Mrs. Wilson slowly grew worse, and one morning I went with Molly McNew to check on her and, to our amazement, found her out of bed on the floor, making as if to scrub the planking. She looked up at us sternly.

"Bubble," said Mrs. Wilson, and with that she expired.

"Bubble?" cried Mr. Dorset later after we had buried Mrs. Wilson in the funerary ground on the east side of Longacre. "Bubble, Hawthorne? What in Heaven's name could she have meant by that?"

"Probably nothing, sir," I said.

"Or perhaps a great mystery," said Jenny. It was after supper, and the family was in the parlor where Jenny played on the spinet.

"She was a simple woman, and God would not entrust a great mystery to such a person," said Abel loftily. "Only those with great learning and great faith are given such messages from God."

"And I suppose you've received messages from God," said Jenny, hitting a C-major chord for emphasis.

"Very nearly daily," said Abel.

"An old woman at Taper's place can read the future in the entrails of a chicken," said Matthew helpfully.

"Waugh, you will make me sick, boy!" cried Mr. Dorset, clutching his stomach.

"That is blasphemy," said Abel softly. "You should ask for forgiveness, brother."

"Stick it in your hat," said Matthew.

"Now, I will not have this," said Mrs. Dorset. "Adam, see that this is stopped."

Mr. Dorset was scratching his chin and looking quite perplexed. Jenny hit another chord, then another. Mrs. Dorset cleared her throat as if to catch her husband's attention, but she may as well have been trying to catch the wind.

"Bubble?" said Mr. Dorset. "Bubble? Something of the sea perhaps, or the air, or perhaps of the breath as it rises from the body or the soap for scrubbing floors. No, that is too easy, by God!" Abel tented his fingers under his chin in rebuke of his father's impiety. "It must be a great mystery or a message from beyond the Veil. Who could be sending us such a message and what would it mean?"

"Perhaps Alexander," I blurted. I cannot say why I said such a thing, for I certainly did not think it true. But a good servant has a way of diverting attention from difficulties, and I suppose I was turning the conversation from the family to something far more distant. Mr. Dorset's face grew bright.

"Alexander?" he said. "Think of it! That poor woman the vessel of such a message."

No one there save Mr. Dorset thought about it, and, as was his wont, he thought about it all the time.

Because our household staff needed another person, Mrs. Dorset quickly hired a fine-boned woman named Miss Ellen Goodloe, a Scotswoman of little humor who was also a superlative cook and much better organized than Mrs. Wilson had ever been. She was short and thin, with her gray hair pulled back in a severe style, perhaps about fifty years of age and always in motion. I liked her very well and she was fair to me, though uncompromising. The McNew twins did everything they could to thwart her, and soon she was engaged in a great struggle with them that was less like open war than like the moving of pieces on a gaming board. But of all the staff, one was affected most immediately.

Old Bob fell madly in love with the woman.

At first, it was no more than stolen glances and approving smiles. Then we all noticed that his manner of dress, heretofore eccentric and often disordered, became elegant. He took proper care in shaving, as he had not done in years. He shined the buckles of his shoes. His hearing even seemed to improve, as well as his balance with trays and the like. He purchased a new powdered wig and took great care to groom it each evening upon its stand in his bedroom. He agreed with each thing Ellen Goodloe said or did, and his feelings were hurt far less easily than before. He seemed years younger. All noticed it but Mr. Dorset, who had ensconced himself in his library writing a dramatic play with music on the life of Alexander.

One pleasant evening, when I was alone on the grounds, sipping the nectar of the sunset, I was startled to find Jenny behind me. She was dressed in a blue gown with white lace, and her hair had been brushed until it shone. The sun, lingering in the topiary, cast a loving glance over her features.

"Hawthorne, tell me, what on earth has gotten into Old Bob?" she asked. Her face was serious, so I felt I should tell her straight.

"Why, Old Bob is in love with Miss Ellen Goodloe, I believe," I said.

For a moment, Jenny looked at me as if I had lost my reason, then her features gathered a faraway look and she took my arm.

"Love," she said. "Everyone knows that love is for the young and not for the old. You must be wrong about this."

"Love is not merely for the young," I said. We had pursued conversations of such intimacy often, and so she seemed as if she were my own daughter. "Love takes each of us unaware, with as much surprise as a bird flushed by a dog."

"None of my father's dogs ever flushed a bird in his life," she said.

"They are ill-trained," I said. "But if they lack the desire, they are born with the capacity, and all men and women share that capacity to love. Even someone like Old Bob."

"My mother and father do not share that capacity," she said, looking down.

"Certainly they do," I said loyally. "Just as we do not know what transpires on the dark side of the moon, so we cannot say what occurs between man and wife. But the test is in their steadfastness and tenderness."

She clearly did not believe my preaching, and perhaps I did not entirely believe it myself, having seen by then much misery inflicted by married people on each other. Still, I felt an obligation to speak to her of life as it should be, not as it often is.

"When shall I fall in love, Hawthorne?" she asked.

"No one can know," I said. The sun had gone down now behind the topiary, and the fantastic shapes of animals trimmed into those hedges seemed to come alive by their very silhouettes. Birds that had sung all day gave way to their nightly compatriots, and bats banked, idly picking off insects. "It could be a sudden moment, like a storm. Or it could be a quiet afternoon when you find that the person you thought only your friend has suddenly become the object of your adoration."

"And so Miss Goodloe is the object of Old Bob's adoration?" she asked. The idea filled me with such mirth that I had to stifle a laugh, lest I confuse Jenny in my instructions.

"It appears to be true," I said. "But the truth is an elusive commodity, and I have not myself spoken to Old Bob of this. If he be happy, then perhaps it is enough that he knows the cause of it, even if we do not."

"I wish to be happy," she said. She looked at me quite intensely, and I could not think of a thing to say to her, for I had assumed she *was* happy. The harder I tried to think of some homily or helpful advice, the thicker my tongue became, until I found I could only smile. She smiled back at me, curtseyed prettily, and walked rapidly back up the lawn toward the house, leaving me alone with the dying sun. I was sure I had failed her and perhaps betrayed Old Bob, and so I felt downcast. I was determined to make amends. Naturally, I became the fulcrum of even greater confusion.

— 2. —

MR. DORSET'S LETTER TO MR. SMYTHE, AND HIS REPLY IN RETURN.
OLD BOB DECLARES HIS INTENTIONS TO ELLEN GOODLOE WITH
UNFORTUNATE RESULTS. JENNY THROWS THE DORSET HOUSEHOLD INTO
AN UPROAR BY BECOMING OVERLY FRIENDLY WITH RODERIGO SMARTT,
OF THE SMYTHE HOUSEHOLD. ABEL'S FIRST SERMON.

Longacre
May 11, 1767

My Dear Friend Smythe,

I regret that such a long period of time has passed since your invitation to the launching of your ship, The Pearl. *It is rare that such an enterprise offers amusement of such a high level, and I am grateful that you provided it.*

If your mastery of the sea be less than godlike, your perseverance is wholly to be admired, and I am sure that one day you, or your heirs, will find a way to construct a vessel worthy of the tall seas or perhaps the docks in Town.

I hope that your Shakespearean children fare well and that only Fortinbras lives up to his name. From what we hear, that is unlikely; however, hope drives us all on, whether we attempt to launch a new idea or a new ship.

Greetings, &tc.,
Adam Dorset

To which the ill-tempered Mr. Smythe replied in kind:

Foxhaven
May 12, 1767

Sir,

A workman is judged by the quality of his work. If there is shame in my shipping, it evolves to those unspeakable men who designed and built these things. Of my personal works, everyone in the Province knows that I am fair, honest, and intelligent.

You, on the other hand, are an utter fool. If a fool keep closed in his own house, he destroys only himself and those around him. However, when a fool goes so far as to print evidence of his stupidity in the Gazette, *he subjects everyone to that foolishness.*

I am very sorry that you feel compelled to strut your shortcomings in such a manner. (And, from rumors among certain women in Town, your shortcomings are legion.)

> *Your humble serv't, &tc.,*
> *Charles Smythe*

And so the brief truce after the sinking of the ship was ended, and once again Mr. Smythe and Mr. Dorset spent much time devising further insults.

In the meantime, the more Old Bob adored Ellen Goodloe, the more questions Jenny asked of me concerning love and its meanings. I did the best I could, but in truth a man knows little of such things, and I urged her to ask her mother, which elicited a most unladylike laugh from Jenny.

As I have said, I am a self-educated man, and one evening, I relaxed in the kitchen with a travel book concerning the Alps, which I had always desired to see. It was some hours after the evening meal, and everyone had retired. My wife and I had tucked our children in, and I had come back to the kitchen, restoked the fire, and read placidly while drawing on some of Mr. Dorset's fine tobacco, which he generously shared with me. It was raining pleasantly, and the dripping from the eaves gave me a deep calm. I was reading about a daring rescue from the summit of Mont Blanc, when I heard someone walking very slowly in behind me. Leaving my finger in the book, I turned to see a rain-soaked Old Bob standing near the door, smiling somewhat oddly, and dripping everywhere.

"Bob, what on earth are you doing here on such a foul evening?" I asked. "Here, come warm yourself by the fire."

"Yes," he said absently. "The fire."

He tottered over and held out his hands to the flames and rubbed them together and then looked at me knowingly. I helped him out of his coat, which I laid on the table to dry. I poured us each a glass of red wine. I thought I might wait for him to speak, as waiting is my finest virtue, but after a quarter of an hour it was clear that Old Bob was so locked in thought he could not possibly speak without prompting.

"Bob, is there a reason you came here?" I asked.

"Oh! Bother that!" he said. "Of course there's a reason." He went quiet again.

"And what was that reason, Bob?" I inquired calmly.

"For instruction, Mr. Hawthorne," he said.

"Instruction?" I asked. "In what could I possibly instruct you? I am a man who has learned from books, it is true, but, as I have never had a master, I fail to see how I could be one."

"I need to know what I should, um, say, as it were to, um—," he said, nodding, as if I would understand his meaning from the gesture. I did not, of course.

"You need to know what?" I asked, becoming exasperated.

"Oh, you know, what to say, in the meaning of, um, well, that institution, which is noblest among men and its proper wordings and procedures and so forth," he said.

"Bob, you have lost me entirely," I admitted. I tapped out my pipe and refilled it. He stood and took two paces and turned and smiled at me fearfully, as a trapped man will smile when he knows all hope is gone.

"I wish to ask Miss Goodloe to marry me, but I do not know how!" he said. Though not entirely surprised, I was startled by the tone of his voice and his insistence. "What do I say to her, and how should I say it?"

The rain suddenly came down harder, as if urging me to get on with it, to tell him about things of which I knew very little. And yet he needed some answer, so I determined to make something up as well as I could.

"In all things a man should be toward a woman kind and generous and strong. He must provide for her, love her, and take care of her and their children." (Here I choked myself back.) "If they be of childbearing age."

"Oh," said Old Bob.

"He must understand a woman's moods and give way for them accordingly. He must demand little and beg for much. He must comfort her, listen to her, and find what solace exists in this world with her. That and a hundred things more are required of a husband."

"But how shall I ask her?" he said.

"Is she aware in any way of your intentions?" I asked.

"None but my demeanor toward her," he said.

"Then it must be done delicately," I said. "Let me think here a moment." A short time before, I had been dreaming of the Alps, and now here I was contriving marital advice for Old Bob. I now see that it was one of the swiftest descents in my life. I thought for some time, and I reasoned that it must be brief, because Bob could remember nothing of any length. Realizing how long couplets stay in the mind, I decided to compose one I could teach him, and finally it came to me.

"Ah, you have something," Bob said.

"A ditty actually," I said, "but something that you can remember. Remember this now:

> *I ask thy hand and heart upon my life,*
> *That you might be my darling wife.*

"Ah," said Old Bob, quite pleased. "It is a masterpiece, Henry. A masterpiece!"

I had him repeat it many times, and finally he was able to say it completely through without making a mistake. I had to stop him from thanking me more, for I feared he could have spent half the night doing so. I helped put his wet coat back on, and he shook my hand vigorously once more before he went out into the rain. I stood in the doorway and watched as he turned right and walked about a hundred yards into the darkness toward the Smythe plantation before realizing his error and turning around. When he came back past, he ignored me completely. I could hear him muttering my couplet under his breath, desperately trying to remember it.

The next day, we were in the kitchen, preparing the midday meal. Bob had obviously not spoken to Ellen Goodloe, and he was so visibly nervous that his old, vague manner seemed to have reappeared, yet worse. He dropped a platter. He poured wine into a glass until it ran over on the table. He talked to himself.

"For God's sake, Bob!" scolded Miss Goodloe. "Are you daft?"

"Thank you ma'am," said Old Bob. "I will." She looked at him first with anger then with sadness and finally with something approaching pity. Then she muttered something about all of God's creatures under her breath and went about her work. I took the silverware to the table, and Bob followed me, tugging at my sleeve with a panic.

"Shall I say it now?" he asked. "Is now the time?"

I wanted to tell him that he should delay, but I could not bring myself to stop his chance at affection, though I doubted he would find it. And so I said yes.

"Go to her, Bob," I said, "and make your declaration."

"Then I shall," he said. He stood up straight, and I helped him neaten his clothes, which were askew a bit. I could do nothing about the spilled wine on his cuffs. He turned and walked out of the house and back to the kitchen.

I should like to say at this point that I left them alone and let Nature take its course, but in fact I waited only a moment before I followed him out the door. I am not by nature a man who listens to others' conversations, but, since I was putting words in Old Bob's mouth, so to speak, I felt I had the right — or at least that was how I justified it.

I positioned myself just outside a window of the kitchen, and, as luck would have it, Ellen Goodloe was alone when Old Bob went inside. I could not have heard him more clearly if I had been in the room beside him. At first he cleared his throat, and then was silent. I was afraid he would become speechless as he had the night before.

"Don't just stand there, then," said Miss Goodloe. "Be helping with the meal."

"Miss Goodloe, I have come to speak to you of my prevention," he said boldly. I put my hand over my face and shivered.

"I beg your pardon?" she said. Her voice had an edge of concern. He cleared his throat and tried again.

"Miss Goodloe, I have come to speak to you of my attentions," he said.

"*Intentions!*" I hissed from my spot near the window. Aghast, I clamped my hand over my mouth.

"What was that?" asked Miss Goodloe.

"A bird, perhaps," said Old Bob. He then laughed inappropriately, a high-pitched kind of giggle that trailed away as the bubbles of wine do.

"A bird?" she said. "Indeed!"

"Now I must speak with you in earnest," he said. I heard a slight creak of the floorboards from inside.

"Bob, for Heaven's sake, get off your knees," said Miss Goodloe.

"Please listen now to my inventions," said Old Bob, his voice quivering yet sincere. I held my breath and closed my eyes.

"I ask thy heart and life upon my head, that you might be my, uh . . ."

I should have known he could not even remember a simple couplet, and now he was struggling with something to rhyme with *head*, a word that had not ended the first line anyway. I almost heard her amazement, though she said nothing. Bob tried again.

"I ask thy head and life upon my heart," he said slowly, "that you and me might never, uh, part?"

"Have you lost your mind?" she almost shouted. "If you have lost your mind, you are not any good to me in the kitchen."

"I assure you of my sincerity," pleaded Old Bob.

"Get out of here and go to the table," she said, more with regret than anger. "You're of no help to me here."

"Yes'm," said Old Bob. I heard him trying to get up from his knees. There was then a tremendous crash, and I came around the corner and up into the kitchen in time to see Miss Goodloe attempting to help Bob up from the floor. I did the service, and he looked at me sadly and then disappeared out the door.

"Did he fall?" I asked innocently.

"I fear he did," said Miss Goodloe.

A few days later, I was in the sitting room with Mr. Dorset, awaiting his pleasure. He was in a dreary mood because he could find no rhyme for *orange*. I urged him to find another word, and suggested *apple*, but he would have nothing of it. He was struggling with the word when we both, at the same time, saw an amazing sight on the lawn through the large windows: Jenny Dorset laughing and talking to Roderigo Smartt, one of the twins from the house of Smythe.

"Waugh!" cried Mr. Dorset. "Hawthorne, tell me that my eyes deceive me!"

"Sir, I can say nothing," I said.

"Can that be mine own flesh consorting with a b—t—d from Fox-haven?" he said. Just then, Jenny began to move back and forth slightly as women do when they tease a man, and her smile was of such radiance that her intentions toward Roderigo could have had no other meaning.

"I believe not," I lied. "Innocent merriments, no doubt."

"Innocent?" he cried, his voice rising. *"Innocent!?"*

"Surely you make too much of this, sir," I said.

"Get my cane, Hawthorne!" he shouted. "In God's name I'll make the b—t—d pay with his life! I'll not have a man who doesn't know a father even smiling at my Jenny!"

I could not seem to move toward the fireplace against which his cane leaned, so he retrieved it himself, swearing all the while. I followed him outside, though I had to run to keep up. Even before we reached them, Jenny's smile grew broader, as if by provoking her father the pleasures of the match were greater. For his part, Roderigo stiffened his back. He was a swarthy lad, about Jenny's age, with a nose too large on the end, somewhat like that of Matthew Dorset. His put his hands behind his back and stood his ground, which was admirable, since by then Mr. Dorset was brandishing his stick like a sword and speaking under his breath of b—t—ds and God and justice, three subjects which do not always go together. For her part, Jenny did not move to Roderigo's side or appear ready to defend him. She merely watched as one might a street minstrel or a Punch and Judy show, ready to laugh and be entertained but in no wise greatly involved.

"Jenny, get in the house," Mr. Dorset said.

"I believe I shall stay out for a time," she said. "The air is mild and will do my health good."

"Into the house with you, girl!" he said, face turning slightly red.

"You make the biggest fuss over such little things," she said.

Sensing that he was getting nowhere with his daughter, Mr. Dorset turned his attentions and his wrath to Roderigo Smartt. He began to slap his open palm with the stick, waiting for any good reason to brandish it across the back of the young man.

"Why should I not beat you within an inch of your life?" said Mr. Dorset, making it clear with his narrowing eyes that he clearly wished to do exactly that.

"I have done nothing wrong," he protested. "I am here by the invitation of that lovely creature, who has become my friend." He nodded at Jenny, who returned his confession with a quizzical look, as if she had no idea of what he spoke.

"I do not care if God Almighty Himself invited you, I will thrash you if you do not leave at once," he said. Roderigo stood his ground, and Mr. Dorset's face turned crimson.

"I should not take that if it were me," Jenny said to Roderigo. "I should fight anyone who sullied my good name."

"You would?" said Roderigo, his voice sounding weak and silly.

"He wouldn't fight, for a coward never stands for anyone, even himself," said Mr. Dorset. "Now, be gone with you, boy, before I carry you home to the Honorable Smythe in a manure cart."

"See here," said Roderigo.

"Look at this," said Jenny. "My own father too timid to chase someone off his own land." Both Mr. Dorset and Roderigo looked at Jenny, entirely confused now about who should do what. As for Jenny, she was having a grand time, and, while I disapproved, I could not help but admire her cleverness.

"D—n whoever would say that!" said Mr. Dorset.

"But you invited me," said Roderigo.

"I did?" said Jenny.

"I have never been timid in my life," said Mr. Dorset. "God help you, Smartt, for saying such a thing."

"I didn't," he said meekly. "Jenny did."

Mr. Dorset looked at Jenny and then at Roderigo and then at me, so confused now by the scheme of things that he was reduced to being mute. He sighed heavily and rubbed the space between his eyes and shook his head.

"Be off with you, then," said Mr. Dorset.

"Only as Jenny wishes, as she invited me," said Roderigo.

"Oh look!" cried Jenny, suddenly running away. "A butterfly!" She disappeared down the hill and around the house, leaving Mr. Dorset and Roderigo Smartt looking at each other with very foolish expressions. At exactly the same instant, they each shrugged, and Roderigo turned to walk to Foxhaven and Mr. Dorset headed back inside, shaking his head. Just outside the door, he stopped and turned to me.

"Hawthorne," he said. "May I ask you something?"

"Are women worth the cost?" he asked.

"Undoubtedly," I said.

"God save us, then," he said.

That same week, Abel Dorset, now seventeen years old, decided that he should practice for his future profession by preaching a sermon in the large dining room at Longacre. All week long, his piety was impressive, as he fasted, moaned, and prayed out loud nearly night and day. Mr. Dorset, who had recently left that bliss of the spirit to which he was often prone, could only shake his head, though Jenny found it quite amusing. Mrs. Dorset seemed pleased and urged her son to preach on the sin of adultery, but since Abel hardly knew what it meant, he decided to preach on the evil of spirits.

Now it just so happened that the Saturday night before, Mr. Dorset and several of his hunting friends were up all night outside the house, telling stories and drinking, so that when the appointed time came for Abel's sermon, Mr. Dorset was lying on the grass snoring peacefully with one of his dogs. Knowing that Mrs. Dorset would make his life miserable for days (as well she ought), I tried to awaken the Master.

"Waugh! Leave me sleep!" he muttered thickly. His dog rolled over and stretched, sighed and didn't move, either.

"Sir, it's Sunday, and your son is to make his first sermon in the house," I said. "In little more than an hour. Perhaps you should come clean up."

"I am clean," he said, then he started to snore again.

"You have slept in the grass," I insisted. "You must rise now and come with me."

I tugged at him, and he pulled back and finally sat up, pieces of grass sticking to his wildly disarrayed hair and a look of profound confusion on his face. He asked me where everyone had gone, and I told him it was morning, and he looked around.

"Aye, God, if it isn't," he said, then promptly fell back over again. I pulled him aright, and then shook him a little. The dog got up and walked about ten feet and fell over and with a brief groan.

"You must get up, Mr. Dorset," I said. "Abel is right now preparing his sermon, and Mrs. Dorset will be vexed if you do not come for it."

"Mrs. Dorset was born vexed," he said. He opened and closed his eyes several times until the light did not bother him, then he looked around and grabbed his head and made a pitiful sound. "Has a horse kicked my head, Hawthorne? Do you see any wounds?"

"You've drunk too much, sir," I said.

"Oh," he said. "It feels exactly as if a horse had kicked me in the head. Perhaps I should lie down until it passes."

I assured him that he need not rest now, and I pulled him to a standing position, where he wobbled for a moment and then belched heartily. I told him that I was needed in the kitchen and that he should go henceforth to the house and clean himself before his son preached. He nodded, then stumbled to the topiary and remained there quite sick as I went back around to the kitchen.

Mr. Dorset did not come to the breakfast, and his wife took it in the high-minded way she always did, not mentioning his absence. Abel was not present, either, as he was fasting, but the other two boys were, and Matthew ate very much like a pig at trough, his manners repulsing everyone except Jenny, who found him very funny.

Half an hour after breakfast, Mr. Dorset had still not come into the house, and I found him and the dog asleep behind a shrubbery, snoring happily. Leaving pleasantries aside, I walked up to him and kicked him in the backside. He jumped up, as did the dog, and looked around and

asked God to d—n the person who had kicked him. When he saw it was
me, he asked my forgiveness then cursed me again.

"Sir, your son is to preach now," I said.

"Right," he said. He got up and wobbled toward the house, holding
on to my arm to be steadied. We came inside just as Abel, looking pale
and thin, was standing before the fireplace, his choice of a pulpit.
Matthew laughed impolitely when he saw his father, and Jenny smiled as
well. Isaac had no expression on his face, and Mrs. Dorset was stricken.
Abel held a scented handkerchief to his nose to keep out the unpleasing
aroma that Mr. Dorset brought with him. A few of the others from the
house were in the corners watching.

"Late for church, eh?" said Mr. Dorset, then he laughed as well. Matthew
could not stop giggling. Mr. Dorset fell into the open chair next to his wife,
belched once more, and nodded to her, as if the show could now begin. She
refused to catch his eye, and I could hardly blame her for that.

Abel looked at the ceiling as if God were up there and waited until his
father had settled into the chair. He seemed supremely nervous, and tented his fingers in a gesture of prayer while he tried to form his words.

"Now when Joseph led the children of Israel out of their bondage, he
was an old man, and a goodly, I mean godly, one," stuttered Abel.

"What? Joseph?" said Mr. Dorset. "Joseph who?"

"Let him alone," said Mrs. Dorset unhappily. Mr. Dorset shrugged
and slumped a little in his chair. Abel, sensing he had said something
wrong, continued in a great panic.

"Now Joseph had been a prince of India and part of the king's stable,"
said Abel. "Table, the king's table." Matthew brayed like a mule. Abel
flushed but continued. "And when he had been for forty years in the land
of Midian, God spoke to him from a burning bush and said . . ." Abel
seemed entirely stumped as to what God's message might have been, and
the more he tried to remember, the farther it moved from his mind.

"I ask thy head and hand upon my wife," Old Bob blurted from the
corner, trying to cheer Abel up.

"And God said, and God said, 'Get thee behind me, for you stand on
solid ground!'" said Abel.

"What the devil?" said Mr. Dorset. "Is this about the commandments
or about Alexander? I am gravely confused."

"By your own tongue," said Mrs. Dorset angrily. "Let the boy continue."

Abel shuffled around, and it was clear now that he could remember none of the sermon that he had so carefully memorized. I suspected that his fasting had harmed his memory. After a time of staring, Abel held up his right hand in imitation of certain preachers that he had seen.

"Let us pray," he said.

He began to pray, speaking fervently of all the sins that came to mind, including sloth, thievery, murder, and several others, but instead of speaking against them, he merely listed them, as if he had compiled a catalog and forgotten quite why. Halfway through the prayer, Mr. Dorset began to snore loudly in his chair, and, with disgust, Abel ended what he had not really started, and everyone arose and went about their jobs. Abel fled in tears. For his part, Mr. Dorset was content to lie peacefully in his chair, oblivious to God, sin, and everything else.

Some days passed, and Abel, instead of trying again to preach, became morose and sullen, and refused to speak to his father. Mrs. Dorset also refused to speak to her husband. Isaac spoke to no one. Matthew spoke to everyone, and Jenny Dorset was still asking me questions about the quality of love.

One day she asked me to walk outside with her to the enclosure which held her father's riotous hounds, and I did so, it being the middle of the afternoon and a time of no particular duties. The dogs were, as usual, leaping, digging, howling, trying to escape.

"Does God intend us one love or many?" she asked seriously.

"I believe it is His will to wed once for life," I said.

"What if you wed the wrong person?" she asked. She picked up a stick and threw it into the pen, and four or five dogs began to fight over it, making a terrible noise.

"That is why you must choose wisely," I said.

"Or choose not at all," she said.

"It is a great pity to be unmarried, for you miss many of the joys of this life," I said. Just then, there was a shriek from upstairs in the house directed at Mr. Dorset from his wife, followed by a list of his failures. We could hear no particular response.

"I do not know, Hawthorne," she said. She began to twirl about, her long skirt billowing on the gentle air. "Perhaps God is wiser than we give Him credit for being. Perhaps He means life to be a great banquet, where we taste each dish as it is laid before us, knowing we never have to settle on the one or the other. Perhaps God intends us to spend our lives at that table."

"I cannot say I know what God intends except as the Bible directs," I admitted. "And each man can read in the Bible what he wishes."

— 3. —
Jenny falls in love, or something like it, with several men in succession. Mr. Dorset and Mr. Smythe fight a duel. Its unfortunate consequences.

Jenny Dorset, thereafter, began to show that flirtatious behavior that God apparently gave to women who hope to ensnare a lover or a husband. Being but fourteen, her constant attentions to her toilette and her manners was amusing, but it upset her mother greatly, for Lydia Foxe Dorset, like all mothers, was afraid her daughter might one day make the great mistake of marrying as she had. Marriage, I have noted, is a great prize for most men and women until they attain it, and which point it loses much of its luster and becomes like an anchor. While it weighs one down, however, it does (most often) keep one in port and away from the worst storms. Or at least that is how I see it. So much for philosophy.

Jenny's continuing demand for fine clothing exasperated her father and mother, but Mr. Dorset seemed unable to say no. She would ask for some fine silk dress she'd seen in Charles Town, and Mr. Dorset would grow red and ask passersby if he appeared to be made of money. When many said he did indeed, that made him even angrier, but, in the end, he could refuse Jenny nothing, and the coach on the way back to Longacre would have two or three more expensive dresses.

Many times, when I was outside in idle moments, I would peer through the windows of the house, not as a voyeur but simply examining the world, to see Mrs. Dorset in earnest conversation with Jenny, who seemed to be far away or smiling mischievously. As I have said, when God set Jenny on her course, it was irretrievable, and Mrs. Dorset might as well have tried to shift the course of a hurricane.

From time to time, Roderigo Smartt would show up outside, and Jenny would come out to see him, tease him sufficiently to ensure his return, then run in the house and leave him. Finally, confused and exhausted, he would creep back to Foxhaven. After several such incidents, he finally came much less, and I was relieved, for he was hardly the kind of man I would approve for Jenny.

About the time of Roderigo's last attempt to court Jenny, Mr. and Mrs. Dorset received for dinner the new minister of a church that had sprung up not far away, as churches were wont to do in those days. His name was Rev. Bartheleme Morton, an angular fellow with a prominent nose and teeth yellowed from constant pipe smoking. He wore a black suit with sleeves and legs far too short, and his politeness was such that he tried to offend no one with his manner or remarks. This ensured, of course, that his manners seemed overdone, even in that period when the Colonies tried to outdo each other in courtliness. I am glad that since our independence such falsities have given way to a rougher sort of truth. Reverend Morton and Mr. Dorset enjoyed talking of theology, of which at that point Rev. Morton had an excess and Mr. Dorset very little at all.

Jenny often sat with them, and, on more than one occasion, I saw her smiling beguilingly at the reverend. He always returned her attention with the most embarrassing gallantry, and he bowed deeply to her when he left each time. Mr. Dorset, wrapped in his own thoughts as usual, barely noticed that Jenny was encouraging Reverend Morton's attentions while mocking him at the same time. Nor did Mr. Dorset seem to notice that he began to come around more regularly and to interlace his conversations about Sin and the Devil with allusions to the Book of Esther and to other volumes dedicated to the art of love.

In the meanwhile, Old Bob had not given up on Ellen Goodloe and took every opportunity to rehearse his misbegotten couplet, which he could never properly memorize. His attentions to Miss Goodloe continued to baffle her, but, as his conduct was exemplary and his manner mild, she could hardly scold him for finding her attractive. And so, in a sense, love filled the house, and I might say here that Mr. and Mrs. Dorset did love each other, though with the kind of love that spends most of its time on the boundaries of other emotions.

One fine day in early summer, Rev. Bartheleme Morton came to the house when Mr. Dorset had gone to Town to conduct some business (what kind of business I felt sure that I knew, but my loyalty bound me to silence). Reverend Morton had recently broken a finger on his right hand while trying to dislodge a large stone from his garden, and the offending digit was wrapped in cloth and projected from his hand in a strange manner. When he came into the parlor and bowed deeply, Jenny took one look at his hand and burst into laughter.

"What on earth have you done to that finger?" she asked gaily.

"I've broken it, actually, Miss Dorset, while preparing my garden," he said. "I hope it does not offend you." She began to laugh again.

"Almost nothing offends me," she said. "Come in. My father is in Town, but I will be glad to speak with you."

"You will?" he said eagerly.

"Gladly," said Jenny.

I withdrew into the hall, for I had a suspicion that Jenny might take advantage of the situation to confuse the reverend, and I must say I did not entirely trust the man, either. In those days, I felt somehow compelled to help protect Jenny from the men she was chasing, which I now realize was the most foolhardy thing I've done in this long life. Still, all men, whether they claim piety or not, are not exempt from Human Nature, and I could understand if the man found Jenny attractive. Normally, young girls would not receive anyone without an adult present, but Jenny was in no wise normal.

"Now then, Miss Dorset, have you been saying your prayers?" asked Reverend Morton as they settled in their chairs.

"Virtually all the time," she said. "I prayed for our hogs."

"Pr . . . You *what?*" he asked.

"Prayed for our hogs, Mr. Morton," she said. "That they might be tender and fat, and that they might nourish us so we will grow strong. Do you think I look strong?"

"Without doubt," he blurted. "I mean, God has well taken care of you, and I suppose He looks out for your hogs as well. God cares for everything on His Earth, child."

"Does he care for alligators?" she asked.

"Alligators?" he said.

"Why would God create an alligator," she said, "or the French, for that matter? Why would He create either one?"

"Why, Miss Dorset, I cannot say why God created anything, but, as He did, we must take all men and creatures as parts of God's kingdom," he said.

"What about pirates?" she asked. "And Indians?"

"I cannot say about pirates," he said thoughtfully but agitated. "Indians, however, have no souls, and so whence they arose I cannot say."

"Does an alligator have a soul?" she asked. "If God makes an alligator, surely He gives it a soul."

"Only we were given souls, child, that we might be redeemed," he said very slowly. "God must have had a good reason to create an alligator or He would not have done so."

"You have very kind eyes," said Jenny. The reverend was silent for a moment.

"Dear girl," he said in a manner not suited to his profession.

"So do dogs have kind eyes," she said, "and skunks. Why would God give kind eyes to a dog, Reverend Morton?" I leaned against the wall and closed my eyes and realized that I could no longer bear Jenny's teasing. Not long after, I saw the Reverend Morton riding away shaking his head, something Roderigo Smartt would have well understood.

Some time thereabouts, though I am unsure of the precise month, Mr. Dorset took it into his head to have a new survey undertaken of his property lines. Why he did this I do not know, but he took great interest in the surveyor and his instruments, riding out each day along with his wayward pack of hounds to see the work. After several days, he came into the house in triumph and announced that Longacre's boundaries should be three feet farther west onto Mr. Smythe's land. As the common boundary extended several miles, he calculated that the three extra feet added several acres and he could not wait to inform Mr. Smythe.

"Please make nothing of this," said his wife at table. "The enmity between you both makes me ill."

"Indeed," said Abel loftily. "God loves those who give cheerfully."

"Cheerfully?" cried Mr. Dorset. "Waugh! I'll not let that scoundrel allow his hogs and cattle to roam on what is mine." He brought his fist down upon the table and upset his wine, splashing it into his lap. I brought him a cloth, and he cleaned up while he continued his tirade. "The man has no scruples in taking everything he can from me, and so I shall inform him tomorrow of my intentions to take back my land."

"Well done!" said Jenny.

"I would like a beet," said Matthew, looking at no one in particular.

And so the next day, Mr. Dorset rode in great triumph to Foxhaven and told Mr. Smythe of the change in boundaries, and, so the story goes, Mr. Smythe, still upset over his ship's failure, became enraged, slapped Mr. Dorset upon the face, and invited him to a duel.

When our house found out about the impending fight, which was to be undertaken with pistols, a great excitement ensued. Mrs. Dorset became wild with anger and fear and fainted. We took her to her bedroom, where she lay without speaking for the entire week before the appointed time. Abel prayed almost incessantly. Isaac ran away and sent word that he was living with a poor family not unlike the Groats, who lived nearby, and shot at anyone who came near their house. He shortly returned. Matthew continued his studies in animal husbandry.

Only Jenny seemed excited by the duel, and spent time watching as her father practiced outside the house. The sound of gunfire became so regular that I did not flinch when I heard it. I did watch Mr. Dorset as he practiced shooting at a straw man he had pressed another servant to build, and I never once saw him hit the creature, though he did put a hole in a shed once, and grazed one of his dogs that had escaped and was sleeping in the topiary.

One evening, Mr. Dorset asked me if I would be his second, and I declined, saying that I must be alive for my family. I did not tell him that I was afraid, for that would have been unmanly, and I did not want to appear disloyal, but I had no intention of being shot by Mr. Smythe for three feet of land.

"I'll do it, sir," said Old Bob, who was clearly trying to impress Miss Goodloe.

"Brave Bob!" he cried, taking another draught of his wine. Mr. Dorset's face then became somewhat cloudy. "Can you shoot a gun? I cannot think that I've ever seen you with a piece in your hand."

"I can," he said eagerly. Meanwhile, the tray in his hand, which held several dishes of pie, was starting to dip in the front, and, before I could right it, he dropped its entire contents onto the floor. Without stopping his conversation, Mr. Dorset opened the door, and the hound, who was recuperating from his wounds, ran into the house and began to eat the pie from the floor. Mrs. Dorset, who at that moment had roused herself from her terrors, came into the room, took one look at the dog, which was noisily eating from the floor, and made a strangled sound. She turned and fled back up the stairs.

"Lyddie? Eh? Ah, then. Women, Bob," he said. "Do you understand a woman?"

"Can't say as I do," said Old Bob, looking at the dog and scratching his head.

And so, Old Bob became Mr. Dorset's second, while Mr. Smythe's eldest son, Hamlet, seconded his father. The duel was to be fought in the disputed land, for some reason I never understood. I went along quite unhappily, in case I needed to bring back Mr. Dorset's body, for I was sure he could never hit Mr. Smythe. Unfortunately, Mr. Dorset had chosen the evening before the duel to brag about his prowess in all things, and while doing so took too much wine, and so on the morning of the duel was very sick and unsteady on his feet.

"Hawthorne, how do I look?" he asked. His hair was disheveled, his shirt stained, and his skin quite colorless.

"In perfect shape," I said. He sighed.

"What a pity for the world if I am slain," he said mournfully. "I have not finished my odes yet."

"A great pity for the world," I said.

For his part, Mr. Smythe looked refreshed and strong and very angry in that cold and focused way that frightens even brave men. Mr. Dorset, to his good luck, was too sick to notice, and so was not terribly concerned. They drew straws for the first shot, as was the custom, and Mr. Dorset thought long and hard before drawing the short straw, meaning that Mr. Smythe had first shot. Had she been there (she was not allowed), Jenny would, I'm sure, have made no particular comment.

"Waugh," said Mr. Dorset quietly. "A great pity for the world."

They took their paces, and Mr. Smythe calmly raised his gun and aimed it at Mr. Dorset, who began to sing softly under his breath. I thought that Mr. Smythe would take some time to adjust his sights, but instead, he fired right off. Just as he squeezed the trigger, however, Mr. Dorset emitted an enormous belch, and so, when the bullet knocked him sideways by entering and then leaving his left shoulder, Mr. Dorset straightened himself and laughed.

"You have failed!" he cried in triumph. His arm began to bleed.

"Sir," I said.

"Silence!" he shouted, "for now I have my shot!"

He raised his gun and began to wave it unsteadily back and forth. He shouted at Mr. Smythe to be still, then fell to the ground. When his hand struck the earth, however, his pistol discharged, and the ball by some chance struck Mr. Smythe in the leg. As I came to the assistance of Mr. Dorset, Mr. Smythe fell and clutched his leg as Hamlet Smythe put his hands upon his head and began to scream "Murder!" over and over until his father told him to keep quiet or he would reload and shoot him, too. Hamlet's screams trailed off into a mad sort of thunking sound and he came to his father's aid. Mr. Dorset, becoming somewhat delirious from the loss of blood, sat up and saw Mr. Smythe rolling about and holding his leg.

"I have slain the villain," he said weakly. "Though I did not mean to."

"It is you who are slain," replied Mr. Smythe, sitting up in Hamlet's arms. Mr. Dorset then felt the pain in his shoulder and saw the blood and touched it.

"So I am," he said. "And you are slain as well?"

"So I am," said Mr. Smythe.

"Murder!" screamed Hamlet, and he began to cry, whereupon Mr. Smythe hit him with the back of his hand. I could tell that Mr. Dorset's wound was not mortal, and, upon checking Mr. Smythe, I found that though his leg muscle had been hit, the wound was not mortal, either, though both men would need healing. I tied off their wounds as well as I could. All the while, Mr. Dorset had begun work on his ode regarding the duel, taking out time only to be sick for a minute or so. For his part, Mr. Smythe kept looking sadly at his leg and lamenting that it would now have to come off, though I certainly knew better. Hamlet was useless. He cowered by a tree and kept asking his father if he were dead yet, and it was only with all my strength that I prevented Mr. Smythe from reloading his piece and aiming for his son.

"Now we shall have to call you Pegleg Smythe," said Mr. Dorset. "Hawthorne, what in the name of God rhymes with *Pegleg*?"

"I demand satisfaction once more!" shouted Mr. Smythe.

"Both of you cease this nonsense!" I said. Of course, I had no right to say such a thing to either of them, but they both obeyed as if they were children and I their parent. Mr. Smythe instructed Hamlet to take him back to Foxhaven, and Mr. Dorset kept trying to find something that rhymed with Pegleg. "It would be far better if we took you both to one place so that a surgeon could see you at the same time."

"I'll burn in H–ll first," said Mr. Smythe, whereupon he passed out.

"H–ll, bell, well, sell?" said Mr. Dorset. "I shall sleep now."

Soon, both men were snoring, and so I told Hamlet we should go to Longacre, since, according to the survey, we were three feet closer to it. I realize that this made no sense whatever, but in his addled state, Hamlet agreed, and so we tied the men across their horses and led them back to Longacre. When Mrs. Dorset from her bedroom window saw us, she began to scream and make terrible noises. Jenny, Old Bob, Miss Goodloe, and various others came running out, and I assured them that the men were not seriously wounded. I sent Jenny up to tell her mother and comfort her, and for once Jenny did well, and soon Mrs. Dorset was helping unload her husband. We took both men into the parlor and laid them on the floor and covered them with blankets while I sent a man named Cormier into town for the surgeon.

The complications from bringing Mr. Smythe to Longacre were not long in coming. He awoke to find Abel Dorset praying fervently over him, while outside the window Abel's brother Matthew was making pig sounds with amazing accuracy. Mr. Smythe's wound was clean and no longer bleeding, but he was in pain and rolled around a bit, frightening

Hamlet so badly the boy ran from the house howling.

"Get my horse," said Mr. Smythe.

"You are wounded and we have sent for the surgeon," said Mrs. Dorset. Surprised to hear a woman's voice, Mr. Smythe turned and saw her.

"Lyddie?" he said. "Is that you?"

You can well imagine the shock I felt on hearing such an endearment, and it was only then that I understood that years before, Mr. Smythe had known Mrs. Dorset much better than any of us suspected. She was extremely embarrassed, and he sensed he had done something wrong. It all happened in the blink of an eye, and only I understood, as Mr. Dorset still lay snoring and Abel prayed with increasing ardor for the souls about to enter Heaven.

"Be quiet and still now, Mr. Smythe," she said. "We have sent for the surgeon. I shall send Hamlet to inform Mrs. Smythe and your house."

"Aye, God, to have come to this pass," he said miserably. Suddenly, Mr. Dorset sat straight up. He looked over and saw Mr. Smythe.

"Upon my word, Pegleg Smythe," he said sweetly. Mr. Smythe, taking offense, crawled to Mr. Dorset and swung at him, but his leg pained him so that he cried out and doubled down toward the offending member. Just then Molly McNew came in and saw the two men and began to laugh. At the same time, Matthew Dorset leaned in the open window and began to bray like a donkey.

This latest confusion for some reason struck Abel as Biblically inspired, and so he began to pray fervently and loudly while Old Bob and I moved between the men and instructed them to stay apart. Order finally being restored, we determined to move them to a room upstairs that was empty and had two beds. Thus it came to pass that the two men in the Province whose enmity was unequaled by any others were required to live for a week in the same room.

The surgeon came and attended their wounds and cautioned them to remain immobile until the healing had well begun. We did not tell him how the wounds had taken place, instead vaguely hinting that the men had been hunting and mistaken each other for game. The Smythe family came regularly to visit their invalid, who was rough and unpleasant with them. Roderigo Smartt also came, and Jenny dallied with him on the grass long enough to capture his entire attention before abandoning him for a bout of knitting, at which she was not at all proficient.

I attended the men and so saw as much of their behavior as anyone. Mr. Dorset spent much of his time propped upon his pillows writing his ode upon the duel and exclaiming whenever he found a proper rhyme, though he never could match *Pegleg*. For his part, Mr. Smythe attended to business papers that his sons brought him and never ceased complaining about the food, the heat, or his roommate.

"Were my aim better, I would be dining at home on pheasant," said Mr. Smythe one day.

"Were my aim better, you would be dining on clouds in Heaven," rejoined Mr. Dorset.

"You have no aim," said Mr. Smythe. "That you hit me at all was an accident."

"An accident?" said Mr. Dorset, his voice rising. "An accident? Do you know to whom you speak?"

That question set Mr. Smythe to laughing so hard that his wound reopened, and I had to change his dressings twice before the blood was stanched. Far from being bothered by the incident, Mr. Dorset found a place to include it in his ode, though he altered it to have happened during a call of Nature.

The day finally came when we could, by the surgeon's leave, allow Mr. Smythe to go home, and Tom Smartt and Mr. Smythe's sons came to fetch him. I had not seen his boys in some time and was shocked at how thin and ill young Fortinbras appeared. We all saw the Smythes toward their property, though the Master of Foxhaven groaned with every jolt of the horse, and he told Mr. Dorset in vulgar terms what he might do with his ode. That only set Mr. Dorset to laughing, and he warned his erstwhile roommate not to pause anywhere on the three feet of land he now considered part of Longacre.

"Send that poem to the *Gazette*!" Mr. Smythe shouted over his shoulder. "So that the world can see again how stupid you be."

"Send your next ship to the Indies!" shouted Mr. Dorset right back. "With that foresight, it might reach Virginia before it sinks!"

I said nothing, of course, about Mr. Smythe addressing Mrs. Dorset as "Lyddie." But I could not help but wonder that the men disliked each other, and I wondered what the families would have been like without that ancient war between them. It might have made a difference with Abel, perhaps allowing him less piety. Maybe Matthew would have been less simple.

Jenny Dorset, however, was made to be what she was, and nothing in this world could have changed that.

— 4. —

A SCENE WITH JENNY DORSET IN CHARLES TOWN, IN WHICH SHE
ESCAPES ME AND TURNS UP IN A SORRY STATE IN A PUBLIC HOUSE.

Such was the confidence of Mr. Dorset in me that later that summer he
asked me to take Jenny to Town to meet a certain teacher of music and
dance. This man, named Nathan Potts, had acquired a certain reputation
among the very wealthy for teaching their daughters little but keeping
them occupied, which was a major preoccupation among the wealthy. As
Mr. Dorset was wealthy, though not as much as those in Town, he wished
Jenny similarly to be taught little but kept occupied. And so he asked me
on a morning that he felt ill if I would keep the appointed time with
Jenny to meet this Potts. I, of course, agreed, and we set off for Town in the
finest carriage Mr. Dorset owned, as I wished to reinforce the impression
that Mr. Dorset was so wealthy that he would spend money foolishly.
(That, I have found, is the main mark of the truly wealthy — the urge to
spend vast amounts of money on useless things.)

On the trip, Jenny sang and cried out at strange birds or clouds, and
seemed unable to sit still, though she made known her disgust, as she
already had a teacher of music and felt dancing was for idiots, though she
danced well enough already.

"What do you think of Roderigo Smartt, Hawthorne?" she asked
coyly, twirling her long golden hair upon her finger.

"I rarely do," I confessed.

"I often do," she said.

Then she began singing again, this time going through "Victory at
Longacre," with all the verses. I was grateful when she finally ended.

Mr. Potts was in Tradd Street, on the second floor of a building infested with lawyers. We ascended steps on the outside of the building and
came in under his shingle to find a well-kept young woman sitting in a
chair watching Mr. Potts teach her daughter dance steps. I was so astonished by the sight of Mr. Potts that I fear I made a small exclamation.

"D—n my eyes, a giant," said Jenny. The woman on the chair looked
in disgust at Jenny and her breach of all manners. But I only glanced at
her, for Mr. Potts, indeed, was a giant, some six and a half feet tall. But
his movements were delicate, and his voice light, presenting an altogether incongruous picture so that I smiled. Mr. Potts appeared not to have
heard Jenny, which was fortunate.

The room was large and well appointed, with a rug, fine tables, an ornate harpsichord and a piano. The vases on the table cost more than Mr. Dorset paid me in a full year. Several other chairs were about, and so Jenny and I sat. Her mouth did not close as she watched the giant step lightly. I reached over and pushed up her chin, and she cut her eyes at me once and smiled. We were simply sitting when a great shouting broke out downstairs. Mr. Potts and his pupil stopped, and he reached up with his great long arm and rubbed the space between his eyes.

"Forgive the noises," he said wearily. "The clients of these lawyers are low men. I shall be moving to new rooms soon."

"We would be grateful for that," said the pupil's mother.

"What is so bad about it?" blurted Jenny.

"I beg your pardon, Miss?" he said. He squinted his eyes and looked at us. "Do I know you?"

"Miss Jenny Dorset from Longacre," I said. "Her father has spoken to you, I believe."

"Ah yes," he said. His eyes brightened. "Mr. Dorset. And you?"

"Hawthorne, servant to the family," I said, standing and bowing.

"Hawthorne," he said.

"What's so bad about it?" asked Jenny once more. The din downstairs had become nearly intolerable, and the vases shook on the table from the sounds of an apparent fight. Mr. Potts moved quickly to the most threatened vase and swept it up and wrapped it in his arms.

"Villains and thieves," he said. His pupil stared at him with no expression. I glanced at her mother who had no expression, either.

"All lawyers are villains and thieves?" asked Jenny.

"I meant their *clients*," Mr. Potts said dryly.

"I see," said Jenny. "Have you never hired a lawyer?"

"I have, for some people see no necessity in discharging their debts," he said.

"Then which are you, a villain or a thief?" asked Jenny sweetly. I saw Mr. Potts's face go red, and I saw that the situation was, as usual around Jenny Dorset, in danger of spinning out of control.

"Miss Dorset teases a great deal," I explained, clearing my throat several times. "You should not find her too serious."

Mr. Potts was very confused and upset, but he composed himself, smiled slightly, bowed, and turned back to his pupil. Jenny reacted as if nothing had happened whatever, and merely yawned in a most unladylike way. For his part, the teacher began once more to go over steps for what I realized was the minuet, but the girl could not master the motions, no matter how hard she tried.

Jenny leaned over to me and whispered that she would like to go outside for a breath of air, as the day was warm, and I merely nodded, thinking she would be back shortly. It was only after fifteen minutes when Mr. Potts ended his lesson with the indifferent girl that I realized I should check on Jenny. When I opened the door and looked out, she was nowhere to be seen.

I have at times felt foolish in my life, but none that I can recall matched that morning in Charles Town. I had been trusted with my Master's precious daughter, and she had escaped me. I ran down the stairs by twos and into the street, which was bustling with trade. Sailors, merchants, men and families passing through, slaves being taken to market, and even a few Indians were about, but Jenny was not. I thought I might stand and call her name aloud, but I could not bring myself to admit to the passing people that I was missing a fourteen-year-old girl whom I was in charge of protecting.

I was sure that she must have wandered into a nearby mercantile shop or a stationers, but I searched every nearby store and she was not to be found. By this time, I had convinced myself of the worst horrors imaginable, that Jenny had been taken by one of the thieves and villains who were visiting the lawyers or, perhaps, by one of the lawyers himself, as I trusted none who practiced that art. I moved entirely down the street and came up the other, and it was clear by then that she was not nearby. My heart began to beat rapidly, and the most terrible pictures came into my mind before I realized that it was far more likely that Jenny had wandered off on her own.

That was a small comfort but the only one I could grasp as I began to check into the shops on the next block. What might she have gone looking for? A piece of ribbon? A book? Unless she had money hidden somewhere on her person, she could buy nothing, but I did not discount the idea on that account, for Jenny Dorset could talk a bee out of its honey. In each shop, I saw no sign of her but finally realized I must start to ask if she had been about. No one had seen such a girl, and most shopkeepers were alarmed and a bit disgusted with me, assuming rightly that I had lost her.

I was standing in the street looking confused, I am sure, when who should suddenly be at my side but the Weasel, who had helped me search for Jenny the one time she *had* been taken. I fancied that time had done little to me in the intervening years, but Weasel had grown old and bent, his hair, unwigged, turned gray and stringy. He clapped me on the back and smiled, and I could see he had but one tooth left in his head and he smelt strongly of the rumhouse.

"Hawthorne," he said. "Look at us!"

"Look at you," I said sadly. He did, though I had not meant him to take me literally.

"I see a poor old man in need of a guinea," he said.

"Weasel, look, I have no time to indulge beggars," I said angrily. "I am in charge of Miss Jenny Dorset, and she has fled from me."

"That girl," he said, narrowing his eyes and rubbing his chin. Across the street, a man fell off his horse and stayed in the dusty street. After a moment he got up, staggered three steps, and fell again, then began to sing. "She is prone to being lost?"

"Somewhat," I said. "Have you seen such a girl, fourteen years of age, with golden hair and a blue dress?"

"No," he said, shaking his head. Then his face brightened. "Aye, I think I have, Hawthorne. Would you have a shilling then for a drink?"

"Where?" I cried. I took his shoulders and shook him a little. "For God's sake, man, tell me where she might be!"

"Let me see," he said. "God's truth, I think she might be in the tavern. Such a girl was in the tavern singing something about the French and being toasted by several men."

"A tavern!" I said. "Take me to her at once!"

"I could do that," he said, "but I am very thirsty and do not know if I can make it that far."

"For God's sake, man, take me, and I'll buy you a bottle of rum!" I said, shaking him again. The man across the street sang until his breath gave out, and he then groaned and fell upon his face.

"I could take two bottles, as I am very thirsty," he said, so I agreed, and we were off toward the tavern. I felt I would be lucky to retrieve Jenny and return to find our carriage still at the dance master's shop. Someone surely would have designs on it, either a thief, a villain, or a lawyer.

The Weasel unsteadily led me through a tour of the seamiest areas of Town down near the docks. He stopped several times, as if figuring his course, then proceeded slowly to a tavern called the White Horse Inn. From the outside, it was nothing more than a doorway in a wall with a shingle from which the paint was flaking away. Inside, it was low and smoky, as most taverns were, and it took a moment for my eyes to adjust. A number of sailors were already talking loudly and were quite drunk, arguing over the virtues of various mast riggings. Several women of doubtful virtue sat with them, squealing occasionally when one of the men pinched various sensitive parts of their bodies.

I did not see Jenny. The Weasel scratched his head.

"Is that she yonder with them men?" he asked. I sighed and shook my head.

"Ah!" he said, trying to snap his fingers and not quite succeeding. "I think I do remember the place where I saw her. But I am very thirsty."

"I do not have time to buy you a drink," I said. "When you find Jenny, I shall reward you."

He looked so forlorn and small and old that in spite of myself I bought him a mug of rum, during which he told me about his mother, who was the kindest and wisest woman who ever lived, his brother, an evil man if one ever lived, and his wife.

"Your wife?" I said. "You are married?"

"Still in the eyes of God, Hawthorne," he said. "Married her twenty-two years ago this September. But she left me and went off with another man."

"How long ago did she leave you?" I inquired. He scratched his head.

"Twenty-one years ago," he said, "or a bit more than that."

I dragged him out of the White Horse Inn, and we went to several more, at which he feigned forgetfulness and thirst, so an hour later he was reeling and of no use to me anymore. I propped him against a wall near the sea, where he at least had something to watch, as the ships were constantly loading and unloading their goods. He began to speak of his wife, at first cursing her, then weeping because she was gone, then finally cursing her again while laughing. He eventually fell asleep.

I felt foolish beyond words for having followed him around, and very worried and unhappy about Jenny. I walked around the corner and went into the first tavern I saw, which was a rough place called the Black Cat. At first, I could see nothing at all, for it was shuttered like most of the taverns, and its lamps were so low that all manner of ill behavior could take place in its dank corners. As my eyes adjusted, I heard a burst of laughter and saw, to my consternation, that Jenny Dorset sat with an enormous group of men and women near the wall, all of whom were laughing, smoking, and drinking. Jenny, I regret to say, held a pipe in one hand and a mug of rum in the other and was clearly the center of all their attentions. I walked close to them without trying to attract attention.

"And so I said to him that I would not give him the satisfaction, even if he were the King of France," she said. The men laughed heartily, as did their wenches. I was at odds with how I should extricate Jenny from this, but I knew that if Mr. Dorset found out what had transpired, he certainly would dismiss me, leaving my family with no means of surviving. While Jenny found nothing at all strange about the situation, it was very nearly mortal for me.

"The King of France!" one of the men cried.

"Hawthorne?" Jenny suddenly said. She squinted. "Is that you?"

I had the strongest feeling that I should flee or at least back into a darker corner, but there was no escaping Jenny. Everyone suddenly turned and looked at me with expressions ranging from suspicion to hostility. I knew, though, that I must stand my place and say what I must.

"Miss Dorset, we must leave now," I said.

The men began to shout their disapproval, and one man threw his broken, half-lit pipe in my direction, but, due to his state of drunkenness, I was able to dodge it easily.

"Hawthorne, pull up a chair and sit with us," she said. I could tell from her words that she indeed had been enjoying the bottles with them, for her words were slurred and connected poorly. I knew that simple intercessions on my part would probably not move her, and so I decided I must take a different course. I would lie.

"I regret to tell you that I have received word that your home is on fire," I said. The men laughed, as did Jenny, then her face fell, she placed her hand upon her chest, and she made an inarticulate sound. She stood, knocking over her chair, and handed her pipe and mug to the wench next to her, who, far from being moved by such news, poured the rum down her throat as if it were water.

"My home is on fire," she muttered. She came toward me unsteadily, and I led her outside where she had to lean against the tavern wall to steady herself. "Is any of it left, then?"

"All of it, I believe," I said.

"How nice," she said, and she passed out into my arms.

I fanned her and got her some water from a nearby public well, and she finally woke up, staggered into an alley, and was sick, and then sat for a time against the wall as I guarded her, skin sallow, eyes closed tightly. Finally, I said gently to her we must get back to the buggy and thence out to Longacre.

"And if nothing is left of it?" she asked.

"I believe all is saved," I answered.

"Oh," said Jenny Dorset.

It took us three quarters of an hour to get back to the dance master's rooms. In front of the building, a lawyer or a villain was roaring with outrage over some no-doubt petty affair. The dance master himself, looking even taller and more delicate, stood on the landing of the stairs and peered down upon us.

"Miss Dorset has taken ill," I shouted up. "I regret that your schedule has been inconvenienced."

"Will I see you again?" he called lightly.

"Is that the King of France?" Jenny asked me softly.

Fortunately, our horse and rig were still where I had left them, and I drove away as quickly as I could, stopping by a friend's modest lodging, where his wife cleaned Jenny with discretion and made her ready for the journey back to Longacre. As we left, she seemed much better, and the effects of drink were wearing off from her when she suddenly yawned and lay down upon the seat, where she remained until I awakened her less than a mile from home.

"Look, Hawthorne!" she cried. "It stands yet! The fire has not consumed it after all!"

"God is good," I said.

She looked at me and began to laugh too loud, which I did not take as a particularly good sign. Once inside, she went straight to her room, where she slept until the next day. She was ill for some time thereafter, and I thought she might have taken a lesson from it.

As is usual regarding Jenny Dorset, I was to be surprised.

— 5. —

THE SAD DEATH OF FORTINBRAS SMYTHE AND THE
SUBSEQUENT DISAPPEARANCE OF MATTHEW DORSET.
THE UNEXPECTED FRIENDSHIP BETWEEN JENNY AND
DESDEMONA SMARTT OF THE SMYTHE HOUSEHOLD.

As I have recounted, Fortinbras Smythe looked very poorly when he came to visit his father at Longacre after the duel. We came to find that there was good reason. The boy, only thirteen years old, had contracted a wasting disorder of a serious kind, and neither the surgeons nor other physicians in Town could do a thing about it. Mr. Smythe, in great panic, sent for Virginia's best physician, paying him a large sum, but the man could not say what was wrong with Fortinbras, either, except that it was a disorder of the blood and of a grave nature. As the summer faded into a lovely autumn, we kept hearing reports that Fortinbras was fading away and had lost much of his weight, and that Mr. Smythe and his wife, Mrs. Ophelia Van Dyke Smythe, were in despair. Mrs. Dorset spent a great deal of time at Foxhaven, comforting Mrs. Smythe and praying with her. In our house, Abel Dorset was moved to fast, though it lasted only for a day before he consumed a duck. Isaac was unmoved as always and businesslike, while young Matthew rarely came in from his studies of animal husbandry.

For her part, Jenny Dorset was consumed with curiosity about the event of death. She had seen it before in the odd uncle or cousin, but never had she seen her own life in that reflected light as she did then. She asked me many questions about how it came about and how it felt, and how long it would take to ascend to Heaven or descend to Hell, and I answered as well as I could, but she seemed doubtful of what I said, which hardly surprised me. I told her that should young Fortinbras perish, he would surely rise to Heaven because he was but a child, and God would not allow a child to burn in the fires of Hell.

"Can you feel your soul being pulled up to Heaven, then?" she asked. I was waiting on her at a table her father had caused to be erected in the garden near the topiary. It was morning. Birds sang, and the sky, even in autumn, was warm and clear.

"No one knows," I said. "That is the great mystery of life."

"If no one knows, how can we so confidently attest to it?" she asked.

"Because it is the Word of God from the Bible," I said.

"God knows how to write, then?" she asked, twirling a strand of her hair.

"The Bible was written by men divinely inspired," I replied.

"Then who now is divinely inspired?" she asked.

"I could not say," I admitted.

"Is my father divinely inspired in his verse?" she asked. I had no idea how to respond, for if anyone inspired Mr. Dorset in his verse, it was Bacchus, if such a personage existed then or ever had.

"That is not for us to say," I said.

She laughed at me, knowing that, as always, her teasing had hit the mark. I was no scholar, though I read the house Bible when I had time, which was rarely. Abel often read aloud, however, and Matthew sometimes picked out passages about the beasts of the field with which to amuse himself.

In early October, we heard that Fortinbras Smythe had died the evening before. I was sad, for I had my own children, and looked at them through the certain knowledge that I had brought them into this world only to leave it far too early. All from our house went to Foxhaven for the obsequies, and Mr. and Mrs. Smythe were fairly shattered. At the grave's edge, next to the site of a stillborn infant, the Smythe family wept openly, as did Mr. Dorset, and I felt a deep sadness for that loss.

The minister from St. Michael's droned for a time, and my attention wandered from him to the beauty of the day. The sky was high and deep blue, and a fresh wind from the Northwest made the crowns of the trees dip, almost in the time of some long-forgotten song. And I thought, This is a day to take leave from this Earth to go with God, and I was no longer sad.

For her part, Jenny Dorset looked alive and curious, drinking in the scene as if it were a painting, calculating every angle and move, smiling, frowning, then smiling once more. Old Bob and Ellen Goodloe stood beside each other, or, rather, Bob stood next to her. She kept edging a step away from him, and he kept following, until they had moved halfway around the site. She finally looked at him sternly, held up one finger as a mother does to a child, and then took another two steps. Bob was bereft but held his ground.

When the preacher said his final "amen," Mr. Smythe surprised all of us by emitting a deep howl of grief then turning and holding fast to his wife. Not to be outdone, Mr. Dorset then emitted a groaning cry and turned to hold Mrs. Dorset. Old Bob then began to weep and reached out for Ellen Goodloe, but she immediately moved next to Tom McNew, who, it appeared, had been drinking, and Old Bob ceased his public grieving.

Roderigo Smartt, in the meantime, had been slowly making his way around the crowd (which included many from neighboring estates and a number from Town) and finally stopped just behind Jenny Dorset, who was rocking on her shoes and did not appear to be grieving. I saw the calculation on Roderigo's face, and, to my astonishment, he let out a moan and began to make terrible sounds and threw himself into Jenny's arms. At first, Jenny was so surprised that she patted him on the back, but then her expression changed to one of devilish delight, and she put her right leg behind his left and pushed him. Roderigo fell hard on his backside. In the general run of moaning, hardly anyone noticed. Roderigo got up and was about to leave when Jenny reached out and lightly touched his hand.

He shook his head and moved away, carrying that great confusion men always do about women. Jenny moved about and found herself next to Desdemona Smartt, whom in fact she favored somewhat. They seemed friendly and walked off, speaking in low tones, about what I did not know.

Finally, they lowered poor Fortinbras into the grave and covered him, and the general weeping finally slowed to a stop as we all moved back toward the house, where a great meal had been prepared for the mourners. It was only when we turned that I saw Matthew Dorset had not attended the services, but instead was lying in the grass playing with a black dog.

By the time we got inside, the moaning had stopped, and the men had ceased clinging to their women, except for Old Bob, who emitted an occasional yelp and tried to hang upon Ellen Goodloe. She kept thrusting her elbow into his ribs, however, and he soon stopped his attentions with a great sigh.

Mr. Dorset patted Mr. Smythe upon the back and made his way through the crowd to get some food and drink and then came to me.

"Have you ever seen such a vulgar display in your life, Hawthorne?" he asked. I was too surprised to speak for a moment.

"I found it touching, sir," I said.

"I'd sooner be touched by a saber than be buried among such a commotion," he said, gnawing on the leg of a turkey. "When God takes me by the hand, I want merriment and drunkenness and wenches." He turned suddenly and looked me in the eyes. "Hawthorne, promise me there will be wenches."

"I promise," I said, "but surely that will be decades hence."

"I could gather an ode from this, though," he said, ignoring me and waving his drumstick in the air. "I could make it a kind of comic poem with Smythe as the butt of it all."

"That would perhaps be in bad taste, sir," I said. His eyes became wide and bright.

"You've convinced me, Hawthorne!" he said. "I will do it!" He drained his glass, handed me his plate, and wandered off, audibly seeking rhymes for *Smythe*, and I could only hope that he would allow poor Fortinbras to rest in peace before he disrupted the civility at Foxhaven once more.

Jenny came up a few moments later as I watched the reaction of people to the grief of the Smythe family. Most were pleasant enough, though many seemed to have come for the food instead of the obsequies. I was watching a fellow named Selby Fox eat with urgently bad manners when Jenny approached me, dragging Desdemona Smartt with her.

"Hawthorne, what a coincidence!" she exclaimed. "Desdemona here shares many interests with me and agrees that the French are vile and wasteful villains. She also plays the spinet and dislikes Milton and understands the male species ever so well." Before I could say a thing, the girls, looking even more alike than they had outside, left my presence arm in arm and went outside.

When we finally prepared to leave, we quit the house and gathered the clan — all but Matthew Dorset, who was nowhere to be found. Mr.

Dorset was quite amused at first and sent Isaac to look in the stables or the cow pens, but Isaac returned to report that his brother could not be found, and Mr. Dorset became angry and uttered several curses which embarrassed his wife. We all spread and looked for Matthew, but he was clearly neither in the house nor on the grounds.

"He is probably home," said Mr. Dorset, shaking his head.

But he was not at Longacre, and as the day waned and he still had not come back, everyone was agitated, for Matthew, though not the most intelligent boy in the world (nor in the house, for that matter) had never taken it upon himself to disappear in such a manner. The evening passed nervously as Mr. Dorset convinced himself that the boy was simply spending an evening in the fields, which he himself had done.

But when the morning came, Matthew was nowhere to be seen, and the family was taken with an agitation that extended even to Old Bob, who wrung his hands and kept saying, "God keep the boy," until Mr. Dorset begged him to cease. His feelings hurt again, Old Bob hid, lonely in the topiary, until I went and fetched him at midmorning with a soothing word. In the meantime, Jenny Dorset and Molly McNew got into a terrible argument to which only I was privy. I had steered Old Bob inside to his duties and was standing outside marveling at what a strange life God had given me, when Molly and Jenny, who were standing beneath a large tree at the edge of the yard, began to speak loudly to each other. I thought they would fight, which would have caused a terrible consternation, but Jenny stalked off, leaving Molly speaking to herself and waving her arms.

Late in the morning, Mr. Dorset organized a group of men to search for Matthew. This group included a number of neighbors as well as Mr. Smythe and his son Hamlet. Jenny wanted to go, but her father forbade it. She flew into a rage and stormed into the house. I sat upon my horse patiently as the group finally assembled to listen to Mr. Dorset's speech.

"Look in the forests and the fields, men!" he shouted, as if on a great military campaign. "Look in swamp and in trees and anywhere a boy might be hid!" He raised himself in his saddle and turned to his dog keeper and raised his arm as Hannibal must have when crossing the Alps. "Ho, the hounds!"

The dog keeper opened the gate, and the yelping, barking, howling dogs ran straight past us and disappeared into the fields and woods, all except a three-legged dog which ran straight into the house and evoked a scream from one of the women. Mr. Dorset put his left hand over his face while still holding the reins of his horse.

"That is the most useless pack of animals in creation," he said. "Hawthorne, remind me to fire the dog keeper."

"Sir," I said.

He had told me to do the same thing at least a dozen times over the years, but I never did such a thing, of course, and Mr. Dorset always forgot his order within an hour or so. We rode off around the house, where four or five of the dogs were fighting over a bone one had uncovered. None paid us the least attention. As always, I stayed close to Mr. Dorset, lest he need assistance, which he often did when riding. (He also relied on me to supply details of his adventures when he was writing his odes. His lines about the Indian country adventure, which went on for many pages, were filled with things that never happened, but I did not divulge that to anyone and even confirmed them as true to anyone who asked.)

We rode deep into the woods, stopping at times to call Matthew's name. The other men scattered. One of the dogs would occasionally come by, and Mr. Dorset made fruitless efforts to get its attention. The dogs paid heed to no man, however, and went their way. The pack would only come back home when tired and hungry, which took sometimes more than a day.

"Where would that boy be?" asked Mr. Dorset. "And why would he have run away?"

"People do things for many reasons," I said, "or for no reason."

"Wise Hawthorne," he said.

Unfortunately, though we searched much of the day, neither we nor the other men saw a thing of Matthew, and by sunset Mr. Dorset was in despair, and his wife was upstairs weeping copiously. For her part, Jenny was as bright and inquisitive as always and seemed unaware that a grave dilemma had struck the family. Mr. Dorset and I sat in the chairs near the topiary at dusk, and Jenny stood nearby, singing and going through dance steps she had not learned on our visit to Charles Town. (Of course, I delicately lied about our adventure, though it was distasteful.) We were sitting there, exhausted, when one of the dogs appeared before us, carrying in its mouth what was quite clearly a human skull without its jaw. Mr. Dorset inhaled sharply and pointed to the dog.

"An omen appeareth!" he said in a hoarse whisper. Jenny giggled. Mr. Dorset leapt for the dog, which began to growl to protect its prize. Mr. Dorset had decided that he must have the skull, and so he moved more quickly than I had ever seen him and put his hands on the crown of the skull, but the dog would not relinquish his bone. An awful struggle ensued. Mr. Dorset cursed and was dragged backward by the dog, which was heavy and strong, and he cursed it with language improper for his daughter to hear. Jenny, rather than being offended, was thrown into delight, and she cheered lustily, I am sorry to say, for the dog.

A few other dogs appeared and also cheered for their fellow creature. By this time, Mr. Dorset was covered in grass and dirt. Two or three of the other dogs, unable to contain their excitement, leapt into the battle on the side of the dog, and finally they broke the skull free from Mr. Dorset. They went about twenty yards and fell into a terrible fight, finally tearing the skull to pieces. Mr. Dorset sat up breathing hard.

"Waugh," he said softly. "To end up as the plaything of a beast. It is the worst desecration I have ever seen."

"You should have held fast," said Jenny. She danced and twirled off around the house, bored by the way the fight turned out.

Though we looked for several days, along with many of the men in those parts, we found nothing of Matthew Dorset. I even looked in Town, building by building, but that hunt was nearly disastrous, and I later found my employer quite drunk in a tavern and lying in the arms of a woman with less than her full complement of teeth. Meanwhile, Jenny and Desdemona Smartt had become nearly inseparable, despite the disapproval by Mr. and Mrs. Dorset of their daughter associating with the servant class. I had to admit it was good for Jenny to have a confidante, and, since I was of that selfsame servant class, I was cheered by the implications it gave to all of us. For his part, Roderigo Smartt followed his twin sister over from Foxhaven to Longacre on several occasions, and Jenny teased and tormented him as always. Despite her behavior, he seemed unable to leave, as a moth cannot leave a flame. He somehow managed to keep from being burned, which is more than I can say for others of the men Jenny was to know during her life.

After two weeks, we had all but given up hope of ever seeing Matthew again. Mr. Dorset had convinced himself that his youngest son had been kidnapped by slave catchers and taken to England, where he would spend his life as a servant in bondage. Mr. Dorset wrote several hundred lines of an ode on that subject but had no inspiration, he told me. Despite the absence of the Muse, he continued on for about two thousand lines anyway, and insisted on reading them one evening after dinner. Everyone, including, I regret to say, myself, went to sleep in their chairs. I was the first to awake some time later, and Mr. Dorset, if he had noticed, did not seem to mind.

God the following day accomplished the task of taking Diana Seton, the elderly woman who worked for the Smythes, home to Heaven. I attended the rites on the Dorsets' behalf and helped lower the coffin into its grave. As we covered it, a mockingbird sang beautifully, and I felt in the presence of something strange and holy.

Two or three days later, we were all busy with our jobs. Mrs. Dorset had not come down for a time by then, so struck with grief that she could not bear the daily intercourse with anyone. I was standing outside the kitchen, helping Ellen Goodloe take some bread from the ovens, when I looked up and saw, to my astonishment, Matthew Dorset standing not ten feet away looking calm and yet somehow removed. Ellen saw him at the same time and said, "Bless my soul," just as Old Bob walked up. We were staring, and Bob followed our eyes.

"Oh that this boy were poor Matthew," said Bob.

"It *is* Matthew," I said. Bob leaned forward and peered ahead.

"So it is," he said. "I am sent for a bottle of wine by the Master." Ellen Goodloe hissed at Old Bob, and he, thinking she was giving some kind of lover's signal, fluttered his fingers at her lightly and smiled broadly. I walked slowly to Matthew, unsure what I should say. The boy looked reasonably well, though he was dirty.

"Matthew, are you all right, boy?" I asked. He looked around as if the surroundings were vaguely familiar. The look upon his face was like that of a prophet having found the end of his journey on the earth. Just then, Matthew's brother Abel came outside holding his Bible, and when he saw his brother was home, he began to shout and thank God aloud with such fervent airs that soon the entire family had come down. Oddly enough, however, Matthew had nothing to say, no matter how many questions were asked of him. He merely looked off in the distance and pointed at something no one could see. The family nurtured him and fed him, but even after several days, the boy would not speak. In his rush to thank God, Mr. Dorset slipped deeply into one of his periods of piety, and soon he was spending hours every day in prayer. He banished wine and rum from the house, which made his wife quite happy, and he regularly begged God to allow Matthew to speak once more. Strangely enough, as Mr. Dorset's piety increased, Abel's religion began to slip away. He and Tom McNew got into a terrible fight, and Mr. Dorset was about to dismiss Tom until he found, from several witnesses, that Abel had started the battle.

"Then d—n you to H–ll!" cried Abel in tears. He ran off but stayed away only until supper, when he came home bitterly. Jenny did not mind that her brother Matthew had lost his voice. She approved of anything that disrupted the daily routine of the house. But it bothered Abel fiercely, and, as if to make up for his brother's silence, he began to sulk quite a lot. He read the *Gazette* faithfully and then acted as if the news in its columns had somehow come to him from private intelligences. The more he spoke, the more everyone ignored him.

For his part, Old Bob finally gave up on courting Ellen Goodloe, which meant, of course, that she began to pay attention to him. Bob asked me to try and explain women to him, but I said that I could not. After having watched Jenny since her infancy, I was sure that I understood them less and less each year.

That year of 1767 faded into 1768, and thence into 1769, and all through it, the family suffered reversals and gains. Matthew finally began to speak again, but he would tell no one where he had been, what he had done, or what he might have seen. He was entirely changed and no longer spent time with the livestock. Abel lost his piety permanently. Mr. Dorset, as always, lost his piety temporarily.

Jenny Dorset grew more beautiful each day. And more adventurous.

— 6. —

COMMENTS ON THE PRECEDING EVENTS FROM JENNY DORSET'S
JOURNAL, ALONG WITH A MERCIFULLY BRIEF EXCERPT FROM
MR. DORSET'S ODE "THE VANISHMENT OF MATTHEW."

TUESDAY — *My word, what an amazing journey for my brother Matthew, who has returned after more than a fortnight's absence. Now, he is completely changed and none for the better, I fear. I asked my Mr. Hawthorne of this change, and he was unable to satisfy me. Abel, too, has changed and no longer wishes to become a clergyman. Thanks be to God! Too much religion makes a man weak and unattractive, just as does too much ardor. I am the more restless after trying to talk with Matthew, who merely sits and stares and no longer cares for his animals. He seems to be very distant. My mother had been unwell. Old Bob's suit after Miss Goodloe saddens me greatly, for he means well. I cannot let a day pass without thinking of my dear Desdemona, who seems to have the same thoughts I do about everything. Roderigo is worthless, but I tease him anyway. I cannot bear either Tom McNew or his insufferable sister. I wonder about Fortinbras Smythe, and if his soul has indeed gone to God. I believe Miss Diana Seton's soul has gone to God. Nothing has yet been settled about the land my father claims from Mr. Smythe. Such foolishness only men could dream, and I do believe my father cares nothing for the land but instead cares only for leaping about and beating his breast. I have found that most men are that way. Such is the way of the male, and I care for it as much as I care not for it. Mother says suffering is the lot of woman because Eve stole the apple from the Garden. I do not wish to suffer. When I am hungry, I shall eat.*

THE VANISHMENT OF MATTHEW
An Ode by A. Dorset, Esq.

One day my son hath disappeared into the mighty wood
Where he mingled with the oaken voices and hath no good.
The tyger, the alligator, and the very small and fierce ram
Doth not know who this son of Dorset surely am.

Matthew was a natural and uprageous boy for all,
He spent his life and thoughts within an animal stall.
And when he saw the wanderings of the hare and hound,
He left himself where he could not half be found.

He saw the skies at night with their stars abright,
He never saw such a faint yet instructive light.
He held his heart aloft from beasts who hug and tear
And managed to survive the thickened snake and bear.

He saw the wretched footsteps of the bootless French
Without the comfort of a bottle or a goodly wench.
He saw the boar, the cow, and all without a coat.
It is miraculous that he did not also find a Groat.

— 7. —

A CLOSING COMMENT OR TWO ON THE WORLD AS IT WAS THEN AND THE PLACE OF THE DORSET FAMILY IT IN, ALONG WITH A DESCRIPTION OF JENNY AT THE VERGE OF YOUNG WOMANHOOD.

No man can know the span of his years, and so we were unaware that those days were the greatest measure of happiness we would find. Though our house was in a constant state of turmoil due to the lively intentions of Mr. Dorset and his wayward sons and his even more wayward daughter, happiness abounded. The war with the French had ended, and prosperity had come to those who had large plantations as did Mr. Dorset. As his wealth increased so, unfortunately, did Mr. Dorset's leisure, which gave him time for more composition and writing, to which he in due time would add painting, which I am bound to report exhibited as much talent as either of the preceding arts.

Matthew was entirely changed by the experience of his disappearance, the cause and effect of which we were not to know for several years. Isaac was morose and businesslike as always, and it was clear that he would be the one who would inherit and run Longacre after his parents were gone. Abel's piety was variable as the weather, and in that he was surely his father's son. Early the next year Mr. Smythe launched a vessel which finally floated but was stolen by pirates on a run to Antigua. Mr. Dorset immediately wrote an ode about it which the *Gazette*, whose standards seemed to be improving, refused to publish.

As she grew, Jenny Dorset only increased in beauty. Her face, when she smiled, outshone Phoebus, and though she gained in grace, she retained that delight in all things which made her so attractive to Roderigo Smartt and nearly a dozen other boys both in Town and country. Jenny finally did regain her manners enough to take dancing lessons, though not from the towering dance master, who had been seriously wounded by a lawyer when he complained about noise. Instead, Jenny took lessons from one Dolan, who was short, stout, and womanly, and of whom Jenny never ceased making fun.

Jenny's wanderings were tempered by her sense, if only for a time. She would go to Foxhaven to see Desdemona Smartt, and I or Old Bob would accompany her. Once, she and Desdemona escaped and walked in the fields for several hours alone, which I did not report to the Dorsets. I lightly scolded Jenny, though it was not my place to do so, and she burst into that laugh of pure delight.

"Dear Hawthorne!" she cried. "You have more worries than my mother!"

As it turned out, Jenny had need of someone to worry about her. But she could no more be controlled than the sun or the moon.

BOOK IV.

— 1. —

PRELIMINARY COMMENTS ON THE STATE OF THE WORLD AND
THE FAMILY AS THE WAR WITH BRITAIN BEGINS TO NEAR, ALONG WITH
AN UNFORTUNATE EPISODE AT THE HORSE RACES IN WHICH
MR. DORSET CREATES A FUROR WITH HIS BEHAVIOR.

Happiness, like the weather, is variable. One day of sun and warmth may be followed by a storm which blows away the best-built homes. I do not subscribe to the pieties of the Puritans that all life is made for sorrow and that our only happiness is in the next world. Indeed, it is the birthright of those from Charles Town (or, more rightly now, Charleston) to enjoy life with all its variety and failings. I am certain that piety has its place, and our Town has long had many houses of worship, but in those years it had far more taverns and trollops than priests and pardon. We have enjoyed horse races, dances, singing, and all the arts, and many men accomplished them as well as masters in Europe, though others (such as Mr. Dorset) brought standards sadly low. Yet each brought to the task an enthusiasm for living that very nearly overcame their deficiencies. Each laughed and loved and perished without fear of life or even of the next day. Only two streets were paved in town then, and fevers often assailed us, but we lived on, merry with the rising of each day and assured that some adventure would make up for the hours of boredom.

I must hasten to say that this life was indeed the life of the monied, for a poor man always struggles for food and means. But there were so many with money then, so many who in the mechanic arts or in indigo and rice became rich in a lifetime, that the numbers of those who enjoyed this life were large. And even those of the second level in wealth enjoyed their rum and lived generally as if life were a grand game. The poor (which as the Bible notes will always be with us) suffered and starved without much notice from those above them, and worst of all were the slaves, who were mere chattel and used either kindly or ill depending on the temperament of their masters. For his part, Mr. Dorset used his slaves very well indeed, attending reasonably to their comfort, though not as well as I should have liked. As I was, and am, of the servant class with no riches, though then attached to a house of great wealth, I lived a comfortable life, taken almost as an equal by Mr. Dorset and his family, and thus I have been honored by that gesture. Other slaves in Carolina, however, were beaten, starved, or killed outright, and I have always felt that slavery held nothing but ill for us.

In such a time, men like Adam Dorset flourished, of course. They gambled and drank, wenched and caroused, attended balls and races, pretended toward literature and music, even attempted art. They traveled and fought, laughed at the worries of the world, and in general made certain that by the time God called them home, little would have been untasted at the great banquet table of this world.

Such a time was perfect for the creation of certain men and women who embodied that age, who brought its flaws and fantasies to their highest level of art. Mr. Dorset was near the top of that group, and indeed sometimes was king of it. But it was left to his daughter, Jenny, to rise alone upon the throne of pleasure and take the life she inherited to its logical conclusions, beyond which lay only anarchy.

I should, I am sure, disapprove of that life and beg the gentle Reader to return to the sanctities of New England and fall upon his knees and beg God to forgive such nonsense. But in truth, I felt the intoxication of those days as keenly as anyone, and even today, old, bent, and alone, I would travel back in time if only God let our days go both ways. As He does not, I must be content to journey in memory only.

As I said early in this History, most of the planters outside Town in the marshy areas suitable for rice and indigo normally moved into Town in the summers to gather the sea breezes and avoid the stifling heat of the interior lands. Mr. Dorset, as was his stubborn wont, did not do that, for he wished to keep a close eye on his holdings, and as a result the family suffered for it. Finally in 1770, his wife prevailed upon him to build a house in Town, and by then Mr. Dorset was so wealthy that the project gave him something else to do. With his usual enthusiasm, he threw himself into the planning and execution of a marvelous house in Ansonborough, which was just north of Town and contained houses of the most wealthy. In fact, he managed to select a site not far from the Town house Mr. Charles Smythe had built several years before.

The Dorset house was truly magnificent, outshining any other located nearby, and it rose quickly, for Mr. Dorset outbid everyone else for the services of the best carpenters in Town and paid them well to work very nearly day and night. By the summer of 1770, the house was ready to occupy, and the family made a pleasant caravan in moving that June to Town to gather the cool breezes and the society which they all enjoyed (all but Isaac) after being so long isolated at Longacre.

The servants were not sorry to leave Longacre, either, and our new quarters were lavish beyond imagining. We all felt that we were somehow above our fellows at other houses. Mr. Dorset christened the new house Stratford, after the town in which Mr. William Shakespeare was born, and never was a less apt name appended to a home in that Town, for, without doubt, Mr. Dorset was no Shakespeare, except perhaps in desire. I can modestly say, however, that desire, while admirable, cannot replace talent, and of that quality my Master unfortunately had little.

Mrs. Dorset, heretofore languid and unhappy at Longacre, blossomed once more at Stratford, attending balls, musicals, and the theatre, to which she dragged her unwilling husband. Of course I was not invited to any of these occasions, and so I can only imagine what transpired (though Mr. Dorset often confided in me as well); more often than not, they would arrive home early with Mrs. Dorset quite agitated and Mr. Dorset talking loudly about the stupidity of a certain actor or the beauty of a singer's voice and face. Though I admired his persistence and desire, Mr. Dorset must have been an impossible husband, and I wish to erect a monument of these words to his wife, who suffered greatly not from any deliberate mistreatment but from Mr. Dorset simply being himself.

With everything so much closer, I took advantage of the bookshops and the lending Library, for which Charles Town had become somewhat famous. The *Gazette* from time to time published a list of those books that were overdue for return (though not the names of the offenders, for that would have been indelicate), and from that list I gained the names of many books I would subsequently read. I also went out frequently to taverns with Mr. Dorset, because he would sometimes not be in a condition to return home alone. As always, my Master threw himself into arguments, singing, laughter, and even the declamation of his odes, which were the subject of attention because the patrons of the taverns knew no better than to think them fine. Mr. Dorset was delighted, for he had an audience that was uncritical, though it often ignored him after a few minutes of his latest poem. No matter. Mr. Dorset kept right on reciting amid the din and drinking, until finally no one but myself paid him the least attention. He would go on for perhaps a quarter of an hour, then sit down, take a gulp of rum, and say, with great delight, "Now that went splendidly, eh Hawthorne?" And of course I would praise his verse, his recitation technique, and his place among the great men of literature.

Buoyed by my praise, Mr. Dorset took up painting, making one room of Stratford into his studio, where he turned out a great many canvases of such profound poverty of technique and ideas that they sold steadily to men and women wishing to use them for merriment at parties and such. If Mr. Dorset ever heard the final destination of his works, he did not seem to mind.

While Mr. Dorset dutifully went with his wife to parties, balls, and the theatre, she went also with him to the horse races. Our magnificent track was one of the glories of the age, and the wealthy people from Town, trying as always to imitate their peers in England, made great parties to the races, gambling on winners, eating well, and drinking as much as they could hold and still remaining awake for the runnings. Matthew Dorset, so odd since his disappearance, came somewhat alive at the races, while Abel, whose piety was fast fading, seemed out of control, screaming for his bet and then becoming very angry and pale when he ultimately lost. Isaac never went, I need not say, for he found the races a foolish waste of time. Jenny never missed a race that her father attended, and she screamed, shouted, danced, and flirted her way through the several races that normally made up a day.

Now Mr. Smythe, it seemed, had bought a fine horse named Prince George and had it trained for racing, and this horse won over and over until the *Gazette*, in a not-unusual flourish, christened the stallion "king of the track." This article, of course, threw Mr. Dorset into a fury.

"King of the track?" he cried one evening at table. "King of the track? I have seen that nag, and a sorrier bag of bones never walked the street."

"He's won twelve races already," said Mrs. Dorset. "What else would you call him?"

"A mud-encrusted quadruped, unfit to be eaten by dogs!" thundered Mr. Dorset.

"Please, dear," said Mrs. Dorset, looking ill and putting her hand to her mouth.

"By my leave, it is true," he said. "What honor is there to win when there is no competitor worthy of the name? What if Alexander had not had to cross the Alps? How great, then, would his name be?"

"Hannibal," said Mrs. Dorset.

"Eh?" said Mr. Dorset.

"Then you should have a horse for our house, so that it might show Mr. Smythe's horse which is truly king of the track," said Jenny sweetly.

"By God!" he said, striking the table with his fist and upsetting his wine, which I quickly cleaned up and replaced.

"We spend too much time at that place already," said Mrs. Dorset. "I am missing half the important functions in this town."

"My horse to put Smythe's in its place! A wonderful idea!" he said. He thereupon launched into a speech about the place of the horse in history, about wars and epic journeys and horses of the powerful and famous. He ended by standing and shouting, "A horse! A horse! My kingdom for a horse!" By then only I and Jenny remained in the room, the others having taken their leave without regret.

And so Mr. Dorset bought a horse and a groom to train him for the race course, and I would like to be able to set forth in this History that Alexander (for that was his name) blazed across the pages of equine history. Alas, this groom, one Phileas Bobbs, was no better trainer than the man who handled Mr. Dorset's dogs. Blind as always to faults in things he loved, Mr. Dorset watched the progress of the horse with great anticipation and boasting. He began to speak in the alehouses of a magnificent horse that would soon embark on a career that would make thousands of pounds. I must admit that Alexander had a fine head and a sturdy body, but the instincts for victory, which must be inbred and cannot be taught, seemed entirely absent. The horse, when not being run, would stand beneath a tree in his pen, looking as if he did not have a thought in his head (as Matthew often did, in fact). It ran hard but lost its attention easily, and tended to whinny and buck at the slightest fright.

Early that autumn, one of the great races of the season was set at the track, and for days it was all any man talked about, even Old Bob, who had been reading the *Gazette* and gotten it into his head that a horse named Oliver would take the prize. He determined to place a bet upon Oliver with the pitiful amount of money he had, though I begged him not to do so.

"You could lose it all, Bob," I argued. "Besides, it is disloyal. If you must wager, you should put it on Alexander, for doing anything else would wound Mr. Dorset."

"I have also spoken to Miss Goodloe about accompanying me to the race," Bob said, not listening to a word I said. I sighed.

"And what did she say?" I asked.

"Nothing," he said, with a quizzical look upon his face. "What do you suppose a woman means by her silence? Does that mean yes or no?"

"It can mean either," I explained. "You must stay persistent and ask her until she gives you an answer."

"What, what, uh, what if she never answers me, then?" he asked.

"Then she will mean to say *no* to you," I said.

"Then why cannot she simply say no?" he asked.

"No is too final, just as yes is," I said. "By saying nothing, she cannot be said either to accept or reject you, and that is perhaps better than being rejected outright."

"I see," said Bob, but he clearly did not, and when the day came, he bet on the wrong horse anyway.

As the day approached, Mr. Dorset decided to visit the Smythe house to announce Mr. Smythe's impending bad fortune, and he asked me to accompany him. As always, I was glad to do so, even though I had seen Mr. Smythe's Prince George run, and Alexander could in no wise keep up with him. I tried to broach the subject with my Master, but he would hear nothing of it, convincing himself day by day that soon he would be wealthy and famous.

"After his victory, I shall write my crowning ode," he said as we rode along. "I shall gain fame in horseflesh and in verse at the same time."

"That would be a wonder to behold," I said cautiously.

"Good Hawthorne!" he cried, which was more credit than I deserved.

The Smythe town house was not as large as Mr. Dorset's, but it was more elegant and better thought out, with graceful lines, a long walkway leading to the door, and a surplus of lovely gardens around it. We tied our horses and walked to the front door, only to find Mr. Smythe standing in one of the gardens with his hands behind his back, dressed in finery and looking quite stately and even thoughtful. His wounds had healed as had Mr. Dorset's, but the wound of the three feet of property was still raw, as Mr. Dorset pressed his claim in Town, and Mr. Smythe fought it. I had no idea which claim was right, but as always I supported Mr. Dorset.

Mr. Smythe had aged somewhat more than my Master. His grief had lined his face, but he still had the same caprice, the same whims of nature that caused him to compete with any and all who came his way. In a way, he had grown more distinguished through the years, still slender and tall. Mr. Dorset, on the other hand, had grown slightly corpulent and even more hearty, though once in a period of piety he fasted for several hours, until he smelled a goose baking. Now Mr. Smythe turned and looked at us with that civility which men of that class always affected to possess, whether they did or not.

"Dorset," said Mr. Smythe formally. "I welcome you to the garden. As you can see, the flowers are still in bloom and ripe. The air is alive with it." He looked proudly at the garden, with which he had had, I knew, nothing whatever to do. (That was another mark of a gentleman — laying claim to anything he owned, even if his hands had never touched it.)

"Reeks a bit, actually," said Mr. Dorset, passing his thick finger under his nose. Mr. Smythe's color rose slightly, but he only bowed and smiled grimly.

"The aroma of the rose is unavailable to them who only smell dung," said Mr. Smythe. Mr. Dorset, sensing a joust, smiled approvingly, as he was now on familiar territory, even though it clearly belonged to Mr. Smythe.

"Be that as it may," said Mr. Dorset, waving away the whole issue of gardens. "I have not come to speak of your rough hedges and dead flowers."

"Your visit has a purpose then!" said Mr. Smythe. "I must inform the *Gazette*, for this may be the first time any visit from you had one at all!" Mr. Smythe looked triumphant, though his powdered wig was slightly askew from the vigor of the point he was making.

"Amusing, amusing," said Mr. Dorset without rancor. "I have merely come to tell you that your Prince George will lose the stakes Saturday to the greatest horse on this continent or any other, the mighty Alexander, scourge of horseflesh and champion for the ages."

Mr. Smythe at first began to smile wryly, as if an amusing joke had been told, one not vastly funny or dull. Then his expression changed, and he gave way to a sudden snuffling burst of laughter, which grew in strength as a hurricane does, until Mr. Smythe fell to his knees and thence to his side, holding his midsection and laughing so genuinely and with such enthusiasm that I laughed as well in spite of myself. Mr. Dorset was completely baffled.

"Hawthorne, what in God's name is wrong with the man?" he asked. "Is he having a fit of apoplexy or something similar?" I tried to speak but had to cease, as my voice was trembling with laughter as well. I quickly brought myself under control, though Mr. Smythe made no effort whatever.

"He is saying without speaking that your Alexander is not the match of his Prince George, I believe, sir," I said.

"Waugh!" exclaimed Mr. Dorset. "Smythe! You villain! What do you know of my horse, as he has been trained in secret?" Mr. Smythe rose from the earth, brushed himself off and arighted his wig, and looked at Mr. Dorset with a face that trembled from barely suppressed laughter.

"Nothing is secret to any man who wishes to know of it in Charles Town," said Mr. Smythe. "And I have received intelligences of your Alexander." He tried to speak again but then fell into another laughing fit.

"You insult me, sir!" cried Mr. Dorset. "I will have my revenge at the course!"

At this, Mr. Smythe became incapacitated once again with laughter, and Mr. Dorset took his leave angrily and I followed him. As we went back to our horses, I saw, standing on the steps in front of the house, Iago Smythe, who was glaring at us with suspicion. He then went to attend his father, who simply could not stop laughing and was by then coughing and sputtering as well.

Mr. Dorset quickly set about making a series of wagers on Alexander that I knew were bound to fail but which I certainly could not advise against, as it was not my place to do so. When Jenny asked me directly if Alexander would vanquish the mighty Prince George, I could only say that it was in God's hands. She smiled as she often did, to hide the mischief in her eyes, and twirled away.

The races were certainly famous affairs in those days. The pleasures of the Town folk were genuine and quite uninhibited by the sober thoughts of people in the Provinces to the north. Where *they* would groan all day for the comfort of Death and Heaven, people in Charles Town would cry aloud for the joy of life. I cannot believe that Boston could have possibly been the birthplace of someone like Jenny Dorset or her father, for that matter.

And so on the appointed day, I drove the family to the track, hoping for some amusement if nothing else. Mr. Dorset was so certain of his victory that he had begun his ode on "The Vanquishment of Prince George" and recited part of it to us as the horse bore us steadily toward the track. For my part, I believed that our carriage horse had a better chance than poor Alexander, who, in the few times I had seen him run, was positively annoyed by the act of obedience. In that, perhaps he was his Master's horse just as Jenny was clearly her father's daughter.

The track was gaily decorated, and many people had come to see the race between the King of the Track and Mr. Dorset's Alexander. During the course of the day, many races were held, and though some of the crowd stayed sober and attentive, most of it drank, shouted, argued, fought, and generally paid attention only when bets were high and a race was interesting. It was less a sporting event than a social one, and so Mrs. Dorset had dressed finely, as had Jenny. Abel and Matthew went with us, but Isaac stayed behind, saying the races were a pleasure he would just as soon forego. Mr. Dorset, who had long since given up on trying to educate his children, much less direct their behavior, merely shrugged.

"By God, Hawthorne, I feel the luck with me today!" he boomed from behind me as I drove the carriage.

"That is fortunate, sir," I said.

"Will we eat Alexander if he loses?" asked Jenny.

"What? What? My word, such a strange girl!" Mr. Dorset said.

"Jenny, please," begged Mrs. Dorset. "Do not provoke your father."

"Eat the mighty Alexander!" cried Mr. Dorset, banging his cane on the floor of the carriage. "I would just as soon eat my own children!"

"You could eat Isaac, for no one would notice," said Jenny. Matthew, who was more sober since his "vanishment," began to laugh as he did in the old days, almost mule-like. I smiled in spite of myself.

"Eh?" said Mr. Dorset.

Jenny did not answer with words, but merely with a laugh that echoed her brother's, and soon Mr. Dorset was lost in one of his reveries, speaking under his breath and then making an inarticulate exclamation.

Word had spread of the great challenge to the King of the Track, and the track was very crowded when we arrived. Men exchanged bets beneath nearby trees, and sometimes an argument or a fight would break out, but overall it was a civil occasion, and many of the best families in Town attended for the diversion. The men came to exchange words about business and pleasure, and the women tried to outdo each other in their finery. Mrs. Dorset dressed modestly as was her wont, but Jenny was resplendent in a dress of dark red silk, and as they left the carriage heads turned toward her. She knew it, and she repaid each ardent gaze with a brief nod of her head and an excited smile, stepping so lightly that I half expected her to burst into flight any moment. Her mother looked at the spectacle with great unhappiness, while Mr. Dorset was oblivious, as always, to anything except what brewed in his own head. Men smiled and bowed as Jenny passed, and she clearly basked in the attention.

The horses were stabled at one end of the track, and soon we made our way to an area where chairs were set up by the track's owners for the more wealthy who might be expected to bring a horse or a great amount of money to waste on wagering. Mr. Dorset could hardly sit still, and Matthew drifted away down toward the stables without saying a word.

"Where is the boy going?" asked Mrs. Dorset.

"Eh, Lydia? What boy?" asked Mr. Dorset, eyes toward the track. She did not try to explain, for it would no doubt have occasioned a speech. I stood nearby to wait on the family, but I did not sit, for that would have violated all the rules of etiquette. Many servants waited upon their families, and I felt happy to be in that position and in no wise was offended.

The first few races were so one-sided that even the most ardent lovers of horseflesh muttered that the competition was terrible and they should have stayed home. One very fat woman, a Ravenel, I believe, kept exclaiming about the heat and waving a decorated fan. She had just said something about some fabric she had seen when she sighed, then groaned and fell to the ground with a heavy sound. Her servants and family attended her, and Jenny leaped from her seat and came close to watch, with unwavering gaze, the small drama of waking the poor woman up from her faint. The woman must have done this often, because a black servant uncorked a small bottle, whose noxious fumes quickly came over us, then waved it under her nose, until the woman coughed twice and then gagged and began to wave her arms.

"Am I dead, then?" she asked no one in particular.

"No, Granny," said a grown woman who looked not at all sad, though somewhat irritated. "You are still alive."

"Then d—n me," she said very loud, and a few nearby men began to laugh. Their women, however, scolded them with their eyes, and the servants and family helped the old woman away from the track and to some shade where she might recover.

"Did she really wish to die, Hawthorne?" Jenny asked me.

"Some do reach that stage where death is a healing balm and not an end to be feared," I said. "We should all be granted such a confidence in eternity."

"I will never reach that stage," she said with a small shudder. "I have hardly seen a thing of this life." She began to shake her head violently. "I intend to see it all. Do you understand?"

"Ma'am," I said, lowering my eyes. She was very serious for a moment and then began to smile beautifully.

"Ma'am," she said shaking her head. "Really, Hawthorne. You act as if you were less than my second father." She turned and went back to her chair, but I was deeply touched and somewhat perplexed, as most of the advice I had given Jenny over the years had been modest and contained very little more than the common sense imparted to me by my mother. I was thinking over these things and remembering my dear mother, who had passed away a few years before, when Mr. Dorset leapt from his seat and began to point and shout.

"Smythe is here, the villain!" he shouted, pointing toward the assembly of carriages. "Come, Hawthorne, let's have a bit of sport."

"Please don't," begged Mrs. Dorset. "For Heaven's sake, let us have one day without this incessant quarreling."

"Bah," said Mr. Dorset. "Do you think I contest Smythe merely for sport? Do you think I vex him just for the pleasure of seeing him squirm? Do you think I will see that much pleasure from Alexander thrashing his Prince George?"

"Yes," said Mrs. Dorset, her mouth in a thin, sharp line.

"Precisely," said Mr. Dorset absently as he set off toward his rival. Jenny hurried herself along with us, smiling mischievously and glancing at me to see whose side I might be on. I was careful not to disclose that emotion, for a good servant does not appear to take sides; he listens, generally agrees with all that is said, and then silently obeys, though making allowances for small changes that will subtly shift things away from contention. Still, as Jenny glanced at me and smiled that radiant smile, as she stuck her tongue in the side of her mouth and giggled as we followed her striding father across the grounds and past merrymakers, she could not have doubted by my expression that I was her secret conspirator in the pleasures of battle.

Mr. and Mrs. Smythe were both there, along with Iago but not Hamlet. Serving them were the Smartt twins, and Jenny gave a small yelp of delight when she saw Desdemona, not having spoken with her in some time. For his part, Roderigo Smartt looked at Jenny as she came toward them with mouth open, eyes focused only on the angelic sight before him. Jenny blinked several times at him and smiled, then veered away just as he was smiling back, to embrace Desdemona and leave poor Roderigo bereft of her attentions once more.

"Smythe!" cried Mr. Dorset. Mrs. Smythe, upon seeing us, rolled her eyes and then closed them and gave such an expression of regret, very nearly of despair, that I felt sorry indeed for the woman. "Come to see your reign ended? Splendid of you to exhibit such sportsmanship."

"I have come to see your indecencies exhibited in public rather than in the country," said Mr. Smythe. "This will do more than any of your odious odes ever could."

"Odious odes?" said Mr. Dorset. He turned to me and put his hands over his mouth. "That is not bad, Hawthorne. Remind to write that later."

"Sir," I nodded.

"I have such confidence that I have wagered on Prince George the sum of five hundred guineas," said Mr. Smythe triumphantly. That was an enormous sum of money for anyone in those days, and of course we could not be sure Mr. Smythe had done so, but the challenge was such that Mr. Dorset could not let it go unanswered. I saw the blood very nearly drain from Mr. Dorset's face. He had not wagered even half that, and I knew it.

"Five hundred guineas?" he said, affecting a small laugh. A few steps away, Jenny and Desdemona, sharing an intimacy, burst into laughter. "But a pittance to a man who has wagered one thousand."

Mr. Smythe looked at him long and hard and then at me, but I showed no emotion to disclose that my Master was once more making up fabulous stories to cover himself. Finally, Mr. Smythe smiled thinly, convinced that his rival was lying, and he regained his good humor and began to walk toward the crowds at the edge of the track. As we walked, a race took place that prompted the crowd into a brief burst of excitement. Jenny caught up with us, and tugged on my sleeve and pulled me aside from Mr. Dorset, who was waving his arms and speaking loudly about Alexander and how he was the horse for the ages, Etc.

"Hawthorne, guess what Desdemona has given me," she said breathlessly. "Come on now, guess!"

"I could not guess," I said, watching Mr. Dorset closely, for I did want him to think me slack in my duties.

"Look!" she exclaimed. And with that she brought from behind her back a lovely piece of ribbon of a gay yellow hue. She waved it in the air, where it caught the sun and the breeze and looked very pretty. She, who had dozens of fine dresses, hats, and pairs of shoes, seemed transported by that simple piece of ribbon.

"A ribbon," I said.

"A ribbon from Desdemona!" she cried. "A gift from my best friend!" Before I could compliment the slender ribbon to make Jenny feel as if her emotions over the gift were entirely warranted, she twirled away, waving the ribbon in the air before stopping suddenly and tying it in her hair. Men and women halted in their steps to watch her. She moved with a natural grace no dancing teacher could impart, and her sheer beauty and happiness lit her from the inside like a pine-knot torch. In spite of myself, I watched with them, only reluctantly leaving to catch up with Mr. Dorset when I heard him pointing and bellowing that the great Alexander was now to become the new King of the Track.

Fate does not decree that rivals always be near each other, or so I have read, but Mr. Dorset collected rivals as a dog collects fleas, and so by the time I got to his side, he had aroused the enmity of a number of people who had already placed bets on Prince George, with whom they had won several times before lately.

"Bah!" cried Mr. Dorset. "Fools! Do you not know that a new day has dawned for the track here? Do you not know that the scurvy Smythe shall no longer hold court with that swaybacked nag?"

Now Mr. Smythe was standing nearby, listening to Mr. Dorset's tirade, and, instead of reacting with his customary bile, he simply stood serenely and smiled, and his wife sat in a chair their servants had brought. His supporters were all shouting and standing near Mr. Smythe and looking back at Mr. Dorset, who, for all his faults, was wealthy enough to have convinced a number of people to place large sums on Alexander, though none had seen him run.

As we were standing, the crowd burst into applause and hissing, as the two horses and their riders came to the starting line. Mr. Dorset began to leap about and flail his arms, showing an embarrassing excess of excitement to which I was accustomed but which caught many there somewhat by surprise. I found Jenny at my side watching her father with quiet delight. She clearly took pleasure in excess, though at that point in her life, her excesses were mild compared to what she achieved later. (I shall not disappoint the Reader by withholding those exploits, no matter how much grief it may cause me.)

"Do you think Alexander may actually win?" she asked me.

"Only if Prince George were to run straight for Philadelphia," I said absently. She punched me in the shoulder and began to laugh in a most unladylike way before she drifted away, her yellow ribbon shining in the sun.

I came beside Mr. Dorset as the horses came to post. Prince George was a black stallion, with a high head, great discipline, and a fiery look in his eye. I had to agree that he was the most magnificent animal I had ever seen in my life. He stood at post staring at the track as if it were a great obstacle to be overcome. Alexander, on the other hand, could not stop from prancing around in smaller and smaller circles, snorting and hoofing up the dirt of the track and nearly throwing our jockey. Mr. Dorset took that as a sign of spirit and shouted even louder. Finally Alexander was bucking and whirling so fast our jockey fell off and had to be lifted back on. It took three men to calm Alexander enough to get him at post.

Finally, the starter was ready to begin the race. By this time, Mr. Dorset was snapping his fingers, which I knew as a secret sign to get him a small bottle of rum that he often needed when excited. I had it on my person and passed it to him, and he emptied it in one long draft and then handed it back.

"Now, by the Gods, a new King of the Track!" said Mr. Dorset. And with that, the starter fired his pistol and the race began. Prince George was suddenly off amid the screaming and waving of the crowd, and, to my surprise, Alexander was right behind him, catching him and passing him before the first turn. Mr. Dorset screamed until his voice was merely a hoarse croak. He turned once and shook me. Jenny screamed and leaped up and down, something no *lady* had ever done at the track, though many *women* had and did.

"Run, George!" cried Mr. Smythe, waving his fists and not looking worried. As they rounded the first turn of the track, however, an amazing thing happened. Instead of continuing down that stretch, Alexander suddenly bolted off the track and came running straight across the inside of the track, where many people stood watching, and right back toward us.

"Waugh!" cried Mr. Dorset. "Not this way! Not this way!"

The crowd parted, as the waters did before Moses in the Red Sea. Prince George never once faltered in going on his appointed course, but Alexander was now bucking and running from side to side, throwing off our rider, where he landed on a very fat wench who at first was outraged and then apparently somewhat pleased. When Alexander got back to the track, he sensed that he must do something, and in his small brain realized that his job was to run, so he began to dash on the hard surface, but backward around the track, passing Prince George as he came around the last turn and then crossed the finish line. As Prince George won, Alexander was heading backward around the track. People were screaming with laughter, though those closest to Alexander were simply screaming.

Mr. Smythe ran to Prince George and patted him briefly before his rider walked the horse around the track to cool him down and assert that his reign still endured. Alexander, meanwhile, got to the end of the track in his backward running and then continued off it until he got to a grassy area, where he paused to eat. Mr. Dorset, sensing that he had been betrayed by his handlers, began to charge the rider, who was limping from his fall, hitting him with his hat and calling him the most unimaginably foul names. The more proper men and women of the crowd were appalled, but most found Mr. Dorset's outburst amusing beyond words. By the time he had ceased harrying the rider, groom, and trainer, Mr. Dorset's energy was spent and the rum had taken hold of his senses. He came uneasily back toward us, muttering under his breath and waving his arms. Jenny looked at him as one looks at an act of Nature, with respect, certainly, but also with amazement and considerable interest.

"I have been betrayed," Mr. Dorset said. "I shall release them all and make sure they never work in this Province again. Hawthorne, make sure I forbid them to work in this Province again."

"Sir," I said, nodding once.

In a few moments, as we were heading back for the carriage, Mr. Smythe came by, as I knew he would, and looked at Mr. Dorset with amusement, then told him that he was sorry that the race had not been more productive for him and that he would let his Prince George run against Alexander again at any time.

"I have been betrayed," said Mr. Dorset quietly. "I shall see them all hanged." And with that, he fell headlong into the grass, having imbibed both from rum and excitement more than his own Nature would allow. Mrs. Dorset, of course, was scandalized beyond words and rushed into the carriage as Mr. Smythe and I picked up my Master and carried him to it. All the while, Mr. Dorset was coming in and out of his senses and sleep, muttering about Hannibal, Mr. George Handel, and various torments he planned to inflict upon the handlers of his horse.

Jenny was gay and sang all the way home, having enjoyed herself immensely, though she did take some time in saying goodbye to her dear Desdemona Smartt and also spent a moment tormenting an admiring young man who paid her a compliment.

When we got to the house, Old Bob came out and helped me bring Mr. Dorset inside. He was snoring peacefully by then, but I knew that when he awakened he would be unpleasant. Later that same day, Jenny found me in the backyard of the house, where I was standing and thinking about Longacre, to which we would repair in a few weeks. I did miss it, as our quarters there were the only real home I had ever possessed. The sky was threatening, and rumblings of thunder could be heard. Black clouds boiled up from the sea south, and I was enjoying and also fearing the coming storm.

"Jenny, you should be inside," I said, pointing to the sky. She laughed, still wearing her ribbon, and looked at me as if I had lost my mind.

"But isn't it wonderful, Hawthorne?" she said. "Isn't a storm wonderful?"

She practiced a few dance steps. Soon, I knew, Mr. Dorset would be in need of my services as he often did when coming around from drink. His wife, in those periods, would have nothing whatever to do with him, which I found understandable, as he often felt terrible and lashed out at the world.

"A storm is a fine thing when one can watch it from the safety of the house," I said.

"I don't want to be safe," she said. "I want to be in danger. Does that make me an evil person? Does it? Oh, how I love this!" The thunder suddenly grew louder, and a strong wind announcing the presence of the storm lifted her hair and blew it around her face. Just then, the groom and handler came into the yard heading toward the barn with Alexander, whom they had been chasing around the area of the track for some time in an effort to catch him. The horse did have enough sense to know that danger was about and led them straight into the shelter of the barn.

"I should ask you to come inside," I said.

"I cannot get enough of this feeling!" she cried. She danced and shouted and sang and would have embraced the lightning if she could. I should have taken her by the arm and escorted her inside, but merely watching her was so amazing that I forgot my own safety and hers until it finally began to rain heavily, and we both dashed for the house.

I should have taken her confession of excitement more seriously that afternoon of the race, for soon she would make us all understand just how serious she was about her pleasures.

— 2. —

JENNY RUNS AWAY AGAIN FROM THE HOUSE IN TOWN AND APPEARS TO
HIRE A PASSAGE TO THE INDIES. MR. DORSET, OLD BOB, AND I GO
AFTER HER ON A POOR SHIP AND EXPERIENCE MANY ADVENTURES.

Only a few days thereafter, I was asked to summon Jenny to dinner. Ellen Goodloe had roasted several fragrant hens, along with bread and several other fine dishes. Mr. Dorset had been somewhat sullen since his humiliation at the track, but he had of late been writing an ode concerning his betrayal and his revenge in murdering the handlers of the horse. (Of course, he did no such thing. In fact, he did not even dismiss them. But, as it sounded more dramatic, he gave himself that license that all poets do to change the truth as suits them.) I looked for Jenny in the yard and about the house and grounds, but in no wise could I find her. As I thought about it, I realized I had not seen her since early morning, and I began to have that queer sensation which precedes unpleasant discoveries.

I went back into the house from my search and announced that Jenny did not appear to be in the house or on the grounds. Mrs. Dorset went upstairs and searched and came down looking ill and frantic and holding a folded sheet of paper.

"This was in her room," she said. "I cannot bear to read it."

"Eh?" said Mr. Dorset. "Let me read that, Lyddie."

He took the paper, unfolded it, and read to himself and then uttered a curse that I will not press upon the Reader.

"Waugh! Villain! Pirate! Oh, infamy!" he shouted, waving the letter. Mrs. Dorset, not even knowing the contents, began to cry. Abel, who had come into the room, demanded to know what the problem was, and when

Mr. Dorset would only keep ranting and cursing, Abel briefly reverted to his previous habits and fell to his knees in loud prayer. Isaac and Matthew, who were coming for the meal, looked at the scene before them with concern, though Isaac never showed much emotion.

"What on earth has happened?" asked Isaac. I wanted to know myself, but in truth I had already guessed.

"Oh ye heavens!" cried Mr. Dorset. "Ye thundering Gods of the clouds and the sea! The world shall fall to its knees when I avenge this thievery!"

"What, oh what?" said Mrs. Dorset.

"Antonio has taken her to the Indies!" he cried, waving the paper.

"Who is Antonio?" asked his wife.

He suddenly looked perplexed and stopped his demonstrations.

"D—d if I know," he said thoughtfully. Then, as the magnitude of the situation began to enter his brain, his eyes grew wide, his hands started to tremble and his face was contorted with rage. I have seen the look before in men whose quarrel is about to break into a fight, and that moment is not unlike dogs, whose necks bristle when the enemy is near. The change which came over Mr. Dorset was startling, One moment he was puzzled, and the next moment he was apparently ready to kill someone without a last name.

"I'm hungry," said Matthew.

"Antonio!" screamed Mr. Dorset, his voice breaking. "She has left for the Indies with Antonio! Oh, the dread Antonio will wish that he had never provoked this scandal with a child, for I will shoot him dead, as God is my witness!"

Mrs. Dorset began to weep and look unsteady, and so I helped her to a chair and fanned her. The situation was indeed alarming, but, knowing Mr. Dorset's proficiency with a pistol, I did not for a moment feel that Antonio's life was in danger. Back and forth Mr. Dorset strode, reading and rereading the letter, which he handed to me so that both hands would be free for gesturing. I scanned the brief note, and it did not say much more than he had read, except that this Antonio had sworn to take care of her during a visit to the Indies, where she planned to seek adventure and perhaps pirates.

"Pirates?" I said aloud, quite unintentionally.

"Pirates, aye!" Mr. Dorset shouted. "And too I will slay the pirates and all their filthy comrades! I shall slay every man between here and the Indies! I shall . . ." His rage suddenly subsided, as a storm at sea will when the cloud has passed, and he turned to me and his wife while scratching his chin. "Which Indie might it be, eh Hawthorne?"

And so for the second time, we prepared a trip to look for Jenny, though in this case, we had much less idea where she might be. In preparation for the trip, Mr. Dorset asked me and Old Bob to scour the docks and shipworks to ask about Jenny and see if we could ascertain which ship she might have gone on. The first thing I did, of course, was to check the shipping records in the *Gazette*, and there had been only one ship that week headed for the Indies, *The Dove,* out of Bristol, going to Antigua. Bob and I went to the docks and asked around about *The Dove,* and the men who had unloaded her of a cargo of rum freely spoke of their work only after I'd given each a shilling. None seemed to remember a thing, taking their money to the nearest tavern thereafter for a mug of what they'd brought. One man, however, hung back and looked at me as if he might have information. He said his name was Aguillar, and he spoke with a French accent, which annoyed me almost as much as the speech of a lawyer. This Aguillar was a thick-set man with little hair and muscles so large that I assumed he had worked on the docks most of his life. Great tufts of hair sprouted from his ears and nose, and the color of his skin was red-brown. One of his eyes kept in its place like a sun around which planets revolve, while the other moved back and forth. He smiled solicitously, showing one tooth surrounded by a mass of crumbling red gum. In all, he presented an ugly picture.

"I believe I might be able to help you, governor," he said, spitting words from his toothless head.

"You're the governor?" said Old Bob, whose hearing had once again gone bad after his rebuff from Ellen Goodloe. "Mr. Hawthorne, did he say you're the governor?"

"No, Bob," I whispered, "he called me 'governor.'"

"You're the new governor?" cried Bob. "I had no idea!" He grabbed my hand and began to shake it before I could break it away. I thought of trying to explain it, but I did not have the luxury of time, so I held up my hand to show Bob that he should be quiet, which he did, though with a look of admiration on his face that complimented him.

"How might you be able to help me?" I asked. Aguillar looked around and swallowed hard, then smiled again.

"Them men don't know nothing," he said. "They only load the cargo. Now, I helps with the passengers and getting their things and so forth, governor. I'm in a better position to know them what goes out and boards the ships. Even go with them and help them up into it. Now, *The Dove*, that was a ship I worked."

"And did you see this girl I described to you all?" I asked impatiently.

"I may have," he said, scratching the brushy tufts trying to escape from his right ear. "For a guinea, I might remember."

"A guinea!" I cried. "That's ridiculous."

"You cannot speak that way to the governor!" said Bob, shaking his finger in the man's face. "He could have you hanged." I glared at Bob, and he backed up admiringly.

"A guinea it is, though," he said. "Sir, I'm a poor man, and this will allow me to feed my family."

"To feed yourself rum," I said. In truth, Mr. Dorset had given me sufficient money to bribe anyone who wandered the docks, but out of a sense of duty, I wanted to make him earn the money. Aguillar looked at me as if I had an angle he could not quite get.

"It is for me family," he said doubtfully, licking his lips. He could almost taste the rum.

"Then tell me what color the girl's hair was, and I shall see if you deserve your guinea," I said sagely. This tactic, as so often in war, caught the enemy utterly by surprise, and his jaw dropped. He looked around helplessly, and for a moment I almost felt sorry for the man, for in lying once he had bound himself to lie further, and from that web many are inextricably caught. He brightened suddenly and confidently.

"It was black, gov," he said. "Black as the night, it was. Like the wings of a raven." I looked at him and shook my head. He was crestfallen.

"No?" he said weakly. "A redhead?"

We turned and walked away after listening to the man guess brown and white before turning and going in the opposite direction. We stopped a great number of men and asked them the same questions, but none had seen Jenny, and none others had the boldness, the poverty, or the thirst to attempt a lie for a few shillings. The day was passing, and Bob and I had found little or nothing, and I was very discouraged. He kept asking me why I was still serving the Dorsets if I had become the new governor, and I tried once to explain myself and then gave up, for Bob had found in that idea a solace that I no longer wished to take from him. And, in truth, the thought of being wealthy and powerful briefly seduced me, and in my mind I thought of what it would be like to be someone like Mr. Dorset or one of the Ravenels or Bulls. I realized that day, however, that each man is born to his trade, and if mine was in service, there were worse lives, and since then I have neither desired nor dreamed of wealth and power and am pleased that in my long life neither came my way, for they do not bring happiness or even allay misery. Besides, I lived as if I *had* wealth because of the fine feelings, though sometimes wayward, of the Dorset family.

The next day, expecting little more, we went back out again to ask questions. Mr. Dorset was speaking with all his peers about Jenny and this "Antonio," whoever he might be. It pained Mr. Dorset greatly to speak of such things, because in Charles Town that was felt to reflect on Jenny's breeding, which, of course, reflected on Mr. and Mrs. Dorset. Mr. Dorset, however, kept the letter secret, and only implied that Jenny might have gone with him for a shopping tour of the Indies, which was a falsehood in fact, though not in heart.

On that same day, Old Bob and I found a large man helping load passengers on a long boat to go out in the bay to a ship bound for Liverpool. This man had the look of kindness and decency in his eyes, and so when he was finished helping a lady dressed all in black enter the boat, I approached him. We spoke briefly, with Bob watching for breaches of etiquette that might have been directed toward myself, the governor.

"Sure, I took her out to *The Dove* myself," he said, wiping his hands on his oily trousers.

"Yes," I said mildly, though quite excited. "And whom was she with?"

"I couldn't say," he said. "She was talking to a very old fellow, though. White-haired. Looked like he could have been somebody important. Can't say."

I took out my purse, pulled open the string, and offered the man a guinea, which he took with a brief bow. There was general celebration at the Dorset house, for at least we believed that she had, in fact, gone toward Antigua. The only problem was that this was in the early autumn, the season for storms in the tropics. Mrs. Dorset wept for relief, while Jenny's brothers all said they were going to avenge her. Isaac said coldly that he would cut the rascal's throat from ear to ear and then drink his blood. Mrs. Dorset, on hearing such, fled to her room with her handkerchief over her mouth. Ellen Goodloe scolded Isaac so severely that he was ashamed and left the room and never brought up going again. Abel said that whatever happened was God's will, though he did not appear to quite believe it. Matthew said he would come if his father asked him to, and Mr. Dorset merely said no quietly, and Matthew, relieved, went outside. That left, as before, myself and Old Bob.

"Men, this shall be a great adventure of revenge and possibly murther," said Mr. Dorset in a stage whisper, looking out the window with his hands behind his back. "I am normally a mild man, but in this case I shall go with the intention of killing Antonio with my own hands or my own pistol."

"Well spoke!" cried Old Bob.

"Stuff and nonsense," said Ellen Goodloe. "Fetch her back and paddle her, I say."

I repeated what I had already told Mr. Dorset, that Jenny was reported to have been speaking with an old man, so we could not be sure with whom she had departed.

"Twenty or a hundred, I shall slay him, and you may mark it!" he cried, whirling and pointing at me.

"Do not raise your voice to the governor," said Bob.

By checking the shipping logs, we found that another suitable ship was leaving for Antigua later that day, and so we did what was expedient: we managed passage on a ship which was unsuitable in every detail. In the meantime, however, I had an unexpected conversation with Mrs. Dorset, which greatly increased my affection for her.

I realize that in this History I have not shed as much light on Mrs. Dorset as I have on certain other players in the drama. The Reader should know that I have done this not from failure of duties but because she was generally so quiet that she stood back from everything, rarely offering an opinion or a comment. And yet without her in those early years, I believe Mr. Dorset, in his wildness and with his headstrong manner, would have wound up losing his fortunes and perhaps his life as well. If he was a ship loose upon the sea in a wind, she was the ballast, ever steady, uncomplaining, and faithful. While he wenched and drank, she stayed home and taught herself the Italian language so she could better understand opera. While he fought duels and wrote his odes, she did her best to instill in their children the values of rectitude and honor. Unfortunately, blood cannot be overcome, and though the Foxe side of the family had its points, the children clearly inherited most of Mr. Dorset's flaws, as well as not a few of his virtues. About all that could be truthfully said was that Jenny was most her father's child, and for that many gave thanks, some were sorrowful, and others were simply appalled. Still, Mrs. Dorset was a fine, strong woman who was a pleasure to serve, and I memorialize her here and wish that once again I might hear her summon me to her side.

I digress. As we were making preparations to leave, and still wondering who this Antonio might be (for we had had no luck in our journeys around town in discovering it), Mrs. Dorset sent Ellen Goodloe after me. The house was quiet for once, as Mr. Dorset was out looking for rope. I was unsure why, but you did not dare question him lest you wanted to receive a lecture on the history and uses of whatever he sought, usually with a hint of truth and a raft of fancy. I was in our quarters smoking my pipe and reading a book about London, when Ellen said the mistress would see me in the house. I did not ask why or what for, as that was not my place. When you serve, you question as little as possible and obey as nearly as you can.

She was in the drawing room sitting quite still in a chair and looking thin and somewhat ill. I had rarely shared a personal conversation with her because she was not in the habit of doing so with the servants as Mr. Dorset was. I do not think this was due to any distaste for it on her part. She simply held her feelings to herself and offended almost no one if she could avoid it. Mr. Dorset offended very nearly everyone and saw nothing wrong with it.

"Hawthorne," she said. "Come sit here by me."

"Ma'am," I nodded, and I sat in a chair next to her. The room was unnaturally quiet. The boys were gone, to where I could not say, and, with Mr. Dorset shopping for rope, we were more or less alone.

"I want to ask you if you think that my daughter is still alive," she said very softly. Instead of calling Jenny's name, her use of "my daughter" wrenched me in every way, for of all the people I knew, she cared most for that bond of family. She had a natural grace and dignity in bearing Mr. Dorset, much more than some women would have.

"Certainly she is alive," I said. "She has a streak of independence that she will grow out of, I am certain. You need not worry. We will find her."

"Her reputation is ruined," she said.

"Quite the contrary," I said modestly. "We have spread the word that this Antonio, whoever he might be, lured her with promises. I have seen men in Town swear to beat the vile beast if he ever sets foot in Town again."

"And what did you say to them?" she asked. She dabbed the corner of her eye with a handkerchief of Brussels lace.

"I told them it was an outrage," I said. It was a small untruth, but one well meant and without malice. "I would die to protect the honor of this house." She looked at me queerly. I certainly had never thought such a thing, much less said it aloud, and I was startled at my own boldness.

"I believe you would," she said, looking at me carefully. "But in my heart I know that Jenny is like him." She said the last word with a twist of her mouth, as if she were tasting a sour apple, but then her features relaxed into something like pleasure. She clearly loved Mr. Dorset and found him impossible, as nearly everyone did.

"There are worse things than to be like him," I said, looking down. I immediately worried that I had gone too far.

"Oh, please forgive me," she said. "He is a good and kind man most of the time, but he cannot restrain his enthusiasms for life. Keeping up with him is like riding a mad horse, and it has worn me out."

I noticed for the first time how worn she did look, and I felt a fear that perhaps she might be ill and was hiding it from us all. She would be the kind to do so, for the last thing she might do would be to burden any-one with her care.

"He wears *everyone* out," I confirmed. She laughed lightly and waved her hand as if to dismiss me and the conversation, so I bowed politely and left.

Mr. Dorset arrived not long thereafter and sought me out. He pro-ceeded to say that the rope sellers in Town were vile and impossible, and he would see every one of them put into the streets. I did not ask why, and then he told me: all had attempted to charge him the same extor-tionate price for rope.

"If they were all charging the same price, would not one think that is the proper current price of rope?" I asked. He suddenly dropped his tirade, looked puzzled, and rubbed his chin.

"By G–d I hadn't considered it," he said. He then turned away, mut-tering. I only later found out that he was looking for rope to cast over the ship in case Jenny be found adrift in the Indies, an image I am sure he got from reading poetry.

I said my goodbyes to my family, and my wife was very cross with me but understood that this was part of my service. Finally she kissed me, and I felt better for that. Old Bob packed his trunk and then, in front of me and several others of the house staff, attempted to repeat his couplet (on bended knees) to Ellen Goodloe, but of course he ruined it hopelessly again, and all the while Ellen was hissing for him to stop and shouting, "Get up, you old fool!" but he kept at it until it was clear he could in no way remember the rhyme. Disconsolate, he got up with my help. Ellen turned and disappeared, huffing, into another room.

"Should, I say, should I take her demeanor as a sign of affection?" he asked. I wanted to tell him the truth, as I find lying painful, but, as I had already told a small untruth to Mrs. Dorset, I felt I could seek God's forgiveness under the same plea.

"I believe in small ways she has an affection for you, though of a kind," I said. "All women must show equally their displeasure and their affection, lest men believe they mean too much of one or the other." As soon as I said it, I realized it meant nothing at all, but Bob took it as sage advice, brightened and straightened his coat, and patted me on the back.

"And all done by your fine rhyme!" he said, puffing out his chest. "You have served me well!"

He went off whistling, and I could only marvel at his deep goodness and complete lack of displeasure. He was made for life's small pleasures as was I, and, in that sense, he and I were alike. I only hoped that when I was old as he was, that I would have a fraction more of my mind with which to serve my Master.

And so on that same day, which was, I believe in early September, Mr. Dorset, Old Bob, and I set sail for Antigua aboard *The White Oak*. Nothing untoward happened as we were taken out to the ship from the docks. It was a fine day, with a strong wind and high blue skies with only a trace of feathery clouds. Mr. Dorset stood in the prow of the boat as if posing for a statue, to the general amusement of the rough men transporting us. Old Bob lay in the bottom of the boat, his stomach in his mouth. He groaned pitifully and said he was dying, but no one believed him, including the Writer of this History.

We boarded with our trunks without incident to find that the ship we had seen only from a distance was one of the foulest tubs ever to dock in Charles Town, slightly listing to port and full of rotten timbers and terrible smells. For his part, Mr. Dorset might have been entering the epic he was to write about the journey. He was expansive, waved his arms, smacked his chest with his fists, and inhaled the fetid air as if it bore the aroma of honeysuckle or nectar.

"Antigua!" he cried, strolling back and forth. The crew looked at him with the slack-mouth appearance of those too dull even to recognize amusement when they saw it. Most were extremely dirty and stupid, but I was not unhappy for it, because their actions indicated that they at least knew how to make a ship ready for sail.

"The Indies," I added with a smile.

"Antigua!" shouted Mr. Dorset. "Where I shall rescue my darling Jenny from the hands of foul An . . ."

He never finished the sentence, however, as he fell into a hatch and disappeared from sight. Old Bob did not notice, for he was by then hanging over the side of the ship being sick, but I ran to the hatch and peered down into the gloom, but I could see nothing.

"Sir?" I asked. "Are you injured?"

A moment passed, then another, and I repeated my question with alarm.

"Peace, Hawthorne," a small voice said. "I have been undone by villains."

I climbed down the ladder and found him lying in a puddle of foul water. Men were moving crates of materials around him, but none moved to help him or even see if he were injured. It took my eyes a moment to adjust to the dimness, but when they did, I saw that Mr. Dorset was sitting up and rubbing the back of his head.

"A hundred guineas to find the man who pushed me!" he exclaimed. Then he uttered a few curses and held the back of his head. None of the nearby men paid him the least attention.

"You fell into a hatch, sir," I said cautiously. He struggled to get up but was still unbalanced and so merely looked around as he continued to touch his small wound. I examined it, and it bled only slightly, though it seemed to be swelling somewhat.

"Then I must give you a hundred guineas, Hawthorne," he said. "For you found the person who led me into the hatch, and it was myself."

"We drown madmen on this ship," said a thick-bodied sailor with a scowl.

"Then I shall let you know if I see any," Mr. Dorset said. "Come, Hawthorne, let's check out the mizzenmast."

And so we climbed back up into the light, and I realized then why I had never been a sailor, not even taking into account my family history of being on less than proper terms with the sea. The dark, tomb-like enclosure below was not to my liking, and the stench of men and materials, of old boards, and dead rats was overpowering. Still, there was a magnificence as we weighed anchor and got under sail beneath those blue skies, a hint of adventure and regret, for though most men are inarticulate before such majesties, they know in their hearts when the high moments of life are in their grasp. So, as I saw the sails go up and catch the strong wind, as I watched the men scurrying to their places and shouting and receiving commands, I knew that I would never again feel the simple joy of that moment. For the sailors it was simply relentlessly hard work, but, for a servant such as myself or a man of wealth like Mr. Dorset, it was a miracle to feel the ship begin to move slowly away from land in that wind then gain speed and head off into the direction of the sunrise.

Old Bob, unfortunately, was feeling none of the glory, for he had just finished being sick when he wandered back over to us. I had never seen him appear so old or fragile, and I reached to steady him by the arm. His skin appeared to have turned a shade of green. He looked around at the busy men and felt the steady rise and fall of the ship then shook his head.

"I think I will go back to Town," he said.

"Back to Town, sir?" a voice said.

We all turned to see the captain of the ship, a hard, oily man named Pinson. I had made passage for us, but I had not seen Pinson. Still, I knew who he was right away because of his manner and the fact that one of his ears was missing. I had heard that a wench in Martinique had bitten it off, but you hear these stories in Town, and I paid it little attention. I introduced Mr. Dorset to the captain, and they shook hands.

"You're bleeding there, gov," said Captain Pinson.

"*He's* the new governor," said Bob, pointing to me. I shook my head, but it did no good.

"You ain't the governor," Captain Pinson said blackly. "I don't know much, but I ain't being fooled by that."

"Hawthorne is the *governor*?" said Mr. Dorset.

"No, sir," I said.

"He is," said Old Bob insistently. "And he could order this vessel around to let me off or send it to France if he wished!"

"France!" cried Mr. Dorset. "God Himself could not make me sail for France. I would drown myself first like an unwanted cur!"

"Nobody's not going to France," said Captain Pinson, looking at all of us as if we were mad. "And I'll ask you to keep to yourselves and not bother with the crew. This is a merchant vessel, and I took you because I needed the money only. You will be treated no differently from the men, and you will not spread such G—d—d lies. Do you understand me?"

"You cannot speak that way to the governor," said Old Bob, whereupon he got sick upon the captain's shoes. The captain uttered a string of curses while trying to dance away the evidence of Bob's seasickness. He then raised his finger and spoke through clenched teeth.

"See that you stay out of my way, or I'll have you all flogged," he said. He turned and stormed away, and I patted Old Bob on the back to assure him that he was not so sick. Mr. Dorset seemed furious and ready to garrote the captain for making such unseemly remarks, but he realized, as I did, that he was powerless here and that his standing in society and his wealth made no difference to Captain Pinson, who was king, lord, and master of this ship and would indeed serve justice as and when he saw fit.

"There goes Town," said Old Bob, pointing toward the disappearing shore.

All that day, we plowed the waters south and east as a farmer plows his field, and I stood and watched the unfolding whitecaps with great interest, trying withal to overcome my sincere fear of the sea and of drowning. I wondered if the spirits of the drowned, such as my father's, stayed in the ocean rather than ascending to Heaven or descending to Hell, but I knew that it was unknowable, like so many things in this life. I decided to concentrate on what I could see and hear and touch and smell, and it was indeed a dazzling array that spread itself before us, a feast for the senses. Mr. Dorset retired below to sleep, for his head had begun to hurt from his mishap. Old Bob stayed near me, but he, too, was of a reflective temperament and did not attempt to introduce me to anyone as the governor, for which I was grateful. In all, that first day passed pleasantly upon the sea, and I tried to think of what we might say to Jenny when we found her and if we might indeed be interfering with her happiness, young as she was.

As evening neared and the ship was smoothly sailing, Captain Pinson came by scowling at us.

"There's biscuit and water," he said. He narrowed his eyes at me to see how I might receive his news.

"I thank you for that hospitality," I said with a brief bow.

"Biscuit and water?" said Bob, more to himself than anyone else. "What a sorry feast for such a famous man."

"Fame will do no one any good here," said Captain Pinson bitterly. "I am the governor of this ship, aye the god of it, and any man who don't like it can swim back."

Bob wheeled and looked forlornly back toward the direction from which we had come, but now there was only water, endless stretches of it, and when we both looked back at Captain Pinson, he was smiling as if he had achieved some victory over us. His lip curled, and he nodded.

"Biscuit and water sounds good to me, sir," said Bob. I nodded just as Mr. Dorset came walking up rubbing the back of his head.

"By G–d, we're the only passengers on this wreck of a tub!" he exclaimed. "There's nothing below but sailors and rats. We might as well be sailing with a raft of lawyers! Some man offered me biscuit, Hawthorne, biscuit with mold and half gnawed by a rat or his brother. I declare I nearly retched on the fellow's boots. Now, captain, where shall table be set?"

I truly thought Captain Pinson would hit Mr. Dorset. He looked at us and clenched and unclenched his fists in a gesture of defiance, then shook his head and spun and walked off.

"Whales!" cried Old Bob. Mr. Dorset forgot the insult almost immediately, and we turned but saw nothing but the reasonably calm sea stretching into a glorious sunset.

"Whale? Whale?" said Mr. Dorset. "Where, Bob?"

"Mayhap it was but a shadow," said Bob.

Unfortunately that was not the only shadow we chased on what turned into a sorry adventure indeed.

— 3. —

AN EVENING OF LIGHT PLEASURES ON THE DECK TURNS INTO
A DEADLY ARGUMENT, AND THE MEN SEE IT AS AN OMEN.

After we had eaten our bread and water (which in truth nourished me and tasted quite good), the night came about us, with stars too numerable to count in a thousand lifetimes. I marveled at the way God had painted that great canvas and thought intensely for a time about my life and how I had come to live it as I had. For the first time, I wondered what else I might have done if I were a man of wealth and independence, but, of course, in a sense I was a man of wealth, for Mr. Dorset treated me far more like a brother than a servant. For someone humbly born as myself, I could scarcely have come to a better pass. I silently thanked God for allowing me the pleasures of my life, only half noticing that as I watched the stars they began to be obscured in a blanket of clouds.

"Rum now!" cried a one-eyed man who had earlier lit all the torches on the deck. As he spoke, another man began to play a mouth harp, and the men came from below decks and from their posts for the relaxation of a drink after a hard day. I found by speaking with a man named Tib-

ble that these sorts of men would not work without rum and that it was
generally distributed in the evening when the course was well set after a
day of hard sailing. As our voyage that day had been clear and smooth,
the men were in a particularly good humor, and many began to sing and
dance with each other, as if one were the man and the other a woman.
The sight, rather than being disturbing as the Reader might expect, was
rather quaint and even touching, for these men were accustomed to this
kind of life upon the sea and had all (from the stories passing around)
spent their manhood while in Town anyway.

We took rum with the men and joined in their clapping and singing,
even Old Bob, who could not clap in time and was always off. Mr. Dorset
threw himself into the event with his usual enthusiasm, and indeed the
only one who did not seem to be having a pleasant time was Captain Pinson, who watched the event from the foredeck, scowling and shaking his
head. I assumed he did not drink, which to me meant that he wanted to
stay clear-headed either to command or to maintain his anger.

"Now, men," said Mr. Dorset after three quarters of an hour of drinking and dancing, "a real man's song." I felt myself wishing that he might
not sing one of his own compositions when he suddenly began, in a loud
and painfully off-key voice, "Victory at Longacre." I was begging that it
might mercifully be over quickly when I saw that the men had gone silent
with admiration and respect. When Mr. Dorset finished the final verse,
the men burst into applause and hurrahs, and Mr. Dorset was so utterly
suffused with his glory that I was touched by the men's kindness. Never
again would he have that kind of audience, and I believe he sensed it, so
he sang more and more, until finally he sang too much, and the men
began to sing other songs, forcing him to stop. For a moment he seemed
disconsolate, but the pleasures of singing and dancing were too great for
him to remain that way for long, and soon he was clapping and sharing
the songs that others sang.

The dancing seemed at its height, almost a frenzy, when one of the
men stopped and shouted a loud curse at another. Everything quieted,
including the dancing, singing, and drinking. The two men looked at
each other fiercely, and I knew that they were as ready to explode as if
someone had held a match to a fuse.

"You are nothing but a b—t—d!" shouted the first man, who was tall
and had a very scarred face. The other man was shorter but with broad,
strong shoulders and a thick body which appeared to be all muscle. The

other men began to back away.

"And you ain't nothing but dead," said the second man. He suddenly withdrew a knife from his tunic, and the other men backed away from the two and shouted at them to stop, but by then the first man had taken out a knife as well and they circled for the fight. I glanced at Captain Pinson, and he did not move or order the men to stop fighting. In truth, a grim smile seemed to crease his face, as if he somehow expected, even encouraged, this kind of fight. We were all speechless, even Mr. Dorset, which was something entirely unexpected.

They began to lunge at each other and make slashes. I had heard of such fights in Town before, even witnessed one in my youth, and most often someone was cut or perhaps beaten but rarely did one of the combatants lose his life. But it was clear from the outset that these men intended to fight past the simple letting of blood, and it was clear that this argument had been going on for some time. Was it over a woman? Did it extend long into the past with one being a bully and the other forced to act as his toady? I could not guess, but the expressions on their faces showed to one and all that this was not merely a fight; it was a bitter hatred and one that finally must be settled.

The men all seemed to be on the side of one man, whom they called Foxe. He was the taller one with the scarred face, and he appeared bitter and angry, but sometimes I could see a moment of fear as well, and I understood that he was likely the one who had been made sport of and mentally tortured by the short, thick fellow, who seemed already victorious by his taunts and obvious hatred.

I kept looking at the captain, thinking he would order the men to break it up before blood was spilled, but he did nothing of the sort, instead, holding his position and staring at the war as if he wished he were in the midst of it. I had heard that on the sea, each captain was a law unto himself, though more often in recent years felons were brought back to port for trial and judgment. We often read, however, of summary executions at sea, and I could not but wonder if either man could possibly win in such a fight.

Foxe moved to his left and was still moving that way when the short one (who from the shouting I realized was named Sanchez, though he did not look much like a Spaniard) charged him and slashed a gaping wound in his shoulder, through his tunic, and into the muscle. Foxe cried aloud, as did Old Bob, who was holding on to my sleeve and jumping back and forth with groans and grunts. Sanchez began laugh and taunt Foxe, speaking in a rapid mixture of Spanish, Italian, English, and perhaps Portuguese. His demeanor was so much like an animal's that I saw his upturned nose as a snout and felt as if a hog were there before me. I cannot describe the hatred I suddenly felt for Sanchez and was even thinking of how I might intercede when an astonishing thing happened.

Sanchez was so immersed in his apparent victory that he turned his back to Foxe for only a second or so, laughing and taunting the other men, waving his arms and screaming. I understood now that Sanchez was quite drunk, and spittle flew from his mouth as he continued to scream. Foxe, seeing his opening, did not hesitate. He ran the seven paces that had opened between them and with a tremendous groan and shout buried his knife to the hilt in the neck of Sanchez. I thought Foxe would take the knife out and perhaps stab Sanchez again, but instead, he simply backed away and looked at the knife, which protruded obscenely from the other man's neck, almost obscured now in a fountain of gushing, bright red blood.

The swiftness and boldness of the move, as well as the horror of the sight, made the men gasp and give way. Sanchez seemed completely bewildered by what had occurred and dropped his knife and stumbled around in what appeared to be a kind of dance. He touched his neck, made a terrible grimace of pain and fell to his knees. He tried with all his might to remove the knife, but it must have been lodged in bone, and we saw that the power of Death was much the stronger now and held Sanchez firmly and forever in His grip. For myself, it was by far the most terrifying thing I had ever seen, and even those hardened sailors went silent and white at the hideous spectre of death before them. Sanchez began to kick and squirm on his side, whimpering, and saying *madre, madre* over and over. Where only a few moments before I had felt nothing but hatred, I now felt pity for him, and the sudden wrenching of those emotions nearly broke us all. Men became sick over the side of the ship. Another cried aloud to God to forgive someone, though I could not make out whom. In the meantime, Foxe, who had been losing vast amounts of blood from his wound, sat down, and then lay down, saying nothing at all. I watched in horror as he seemed to be looking up at the stars. His heartbeat was visibly slowing at his neck, and blood from both men now ran to a large pool at middeck where it mingled and then fell

away as the ship gently swayed in the mild seas. I was watching Foxe
when he seemed to give a great groan and then a shudder. The pulsing in
his neck stopped, and his eyes were on the heavens forever. Sanchez, still
not believing what had happened, struggled to his feet.

"When do we arrive?" he said in a ghastly whisper. Then suddenly his
mouth was filled with blood that he began to spout as he turned, the
knife still buried in his neck. He gagged and coughed, then stooped and
in a throaty whisper said, "I hear it." Then he simply fell forward without a motion to break his fall and landed with a dull thud upon the deck,
dead. The men were all too shocked to move for a time, and Mr. Dorset
looked gravely upon the dead men, not even whispering to me of how he
might turn the event into an ode. Old Bob still held my sleeve in a tight
ball, and I might have loosened his fingers under other circumstances,
but now I, too, could neither move nor speak.

We stood that way for perhaps three-quarters of a minute, and it was
surely the longest minute of my life. No one seemed to be breathing. The
sea suddenly seemed to be heaving us around a bit, though the sails had
been taken in for the night. Finally, the sailors began the distasteful task
of looking at the men, and, finding them both dead, looked up to the
captain as children will look to their fathers to see what they might do
next. I assumed there might be a burial service of some kind or perhaps
their bodies might be greased and bound, that we might return to
Charles Town to put them ashore for burial.

"Throw them over the side," said Captain Pinson. He turned away
and walked to the prow and into the gloom past the light of the torches,
and I was surprised by his coldness, though the men were not. Without
ceremony, without so much as a word of consolation or grace, they took
Sanchez and Foxe and hurled them over the side of the ship where, by
morning, they would have served as a meal to the monsters of the deep,
no different from any other. The fishes would not know that this feast
once lived, and breathed, and talked, and that thought saddened me
immensely, for it showed to me that a man's life does not extend past his
time and that his influence, which can be vast in his best days, disappears
with his heartbeat. The men washed the blood from the deck before it
had a chance to dry, and within half an hour after the violent end of the
fight, there was no evidence that the battle had taken place or that two
men named Sanchez and Foxe had been on the ship.

Even before we retired, the men were muttering among themselves of bad luck and omens, and I could only shake my head at such suspicions and wonder what a man's mind must become when spent day and night upon the restless sea. I felt I was superior to them and that they were as primitive as men from a cave. I found out only the next day that I should have paid attention to their cries, for, as I have been many times in this life, I was surprised beyond what mere words can describe.

— 4. —

A VIOLENT STORM AWAKENS US JUST BEFORE DAWN, AND, AFTER A TERRIBLE STRUGGLE, THE SHIP AND MOST OF ITS MEN ARE LOST. OUR FIGHT TO SURVIVE UPON EMPTY RUM BARRELS AND OTHER DEBRIS.

The accommodations below decks were cramped and foul, but I was so exhausted that as soon as we lay down, the steady rocking of the ship and the silence of other exhausted men pulled me toward sleep. Old Bob and Mr. Dorset slept nearby, and soon I was lulled away by peace, and was careless of any worry, though I continued to brood upon the violence I had seen.

I must tell the Reader at this point that I do not believe in omens or any other fanciful notions that presage calamity. I am one who comes to belief hard and leaves it just as reluctantly, and during my life I have heard men cry out in fear when they believed something evil was about. And though I do believe evil spreads like a wind among men, I do not believe that God sends messages to alert us of it. For those who believe differently, I beg your pardon.

The men on the ship certainly did believe in omens, however, and when we were awakened by a violent rocking and by a man hailing the crew from a hatch, many of them groaned and began to say they knew evil was about. I did not know exactly what was transpiring until I realized the ship was rolling in a most alarming manner and thunder surrounded us. Men lit torches. I could see water seeping in around the boards, certainly not enough to make the vessel founder but enough to worry me nonetheless. Mr. Dorset sat bolt upright and cried "Ho, Hannibal!" in a very loud voice.

"Sir, we have encountered a storm," I reported, trying not to fall upon Old Bob, who was sitting up and rubbing his head.

"By my leave, I thought I was crossing the Alps," said Mr. Dorset, puzzled.

As everyone was climbing up the ladders to the deck, it seemed proper that we should do so, for I had heard stories of men trapped in their quarters as ships foundered, and that entombment frightened me much more than simply drowning. When we got topside, we saw that the most violent storm imaginable was upon us, and waves crashed over the decks with a great noise and fury. The sails had been hauled in the evening before, as I said, but the ship seemed out of control anyway. Captain Pinson stood on the fo'c'sle screaming and waving his arms, and the men did the best they might to obey him. Suddenly, however, a great wave hit the ship and slammed it sidewise, and the captain tumbled over the port side of the ship and into the sea.

"Man overboard!" they cried, but I knew it was hopeless. They went and peered into the gloom, but the wind was so violent, the sea so dark except in the strokes of lightning, that within half a minute the crew had given up any hope of finding Captain Pinson. By now, all the men, including myself, Bob, and Mr. Dorset were very frightened indeed, and I could only look into the sky and ask that if my time had come that Jesus would take me by the hand. I could not but think of my father, who had died in the sea, though much less heroically, and I wondered if I would see him if I passed to Glory that night.

The blow became harder and more violent, though I did not think it could do so. Men abandoned their posts and lashed themselves to the masts, crying aloud and praying. Two men trying to gather a rope washed over the side. I grabbed my Master around the waist and pulled him back from the middle of the ship toward the captain's topside quarters, also getting a grip on Old Bob's soaked shirt. Poor Bob was terrified beyond doing much but mumbling a prayer, but Mr. Dorset was entirely in his element.

"It is a shipwreck!" he screamed. "I shall be the poet of shipwrecks! Hawthorne, it will be my greatness!"

He was wild with enthusiasm and did not appear to have an ounce of fear in his bones, which I admired and which, in truth, calmed me somewhat. He was shouting about Shelley (which did not encourage me at all) when the main mast came crashing to the deck, hitting two men who were still hard upon their duty. I rushed to them, holding my balance as well as I could, and saw immediately that one had suffered a broken back and was dead, and the other was grievously wounded. Several men and I tried to remove the mast, but it soon became clear that if we stayed exposed on the deck, the lot of us would be swept into the sea. Reluctantly, I rejoined Mr. Dorset and Old Bob, trying not to despair at the terrible groans and cries of the injured man.

I prayed silently for my children and wife and for the Dorset family, and was doing so when it seemed the storm began to subside. At first, I could hardly believe it, but, after perhaps ten minutes, it was clear that the waves were receding and the thunder and lightning had moved off to our west. A few cheers rang out. The ship was still heaving, but not so badly, and several of us rushed to the fallen mainmast but could not lift it, so we had to roll it off the stricken sailor, and in the process injured him mortally. All were in agony over the terrible luck, but at least they knew they were alive, and so spirits began to rise once again. The subcommander of the vessel had taken charge, one Hill, and he was so undone by the events that he stood admidships and gave all manner of ludicrous orders. The men, however, knew what to do, and soon the deck had been secured and the sailors began to speak with each other in a consoling way.

We were starting to feel as if we had enjoyed victory over the sea, when we all noticed, at the same time, it seemed, that the ship was listing heavily to port. For a moment, the men looked at each other and then at their feet, as if something might be wrong there, but, as the moment passed, it was clear that the ship was turning on its side.

"God help us!" cried Hill. "Oh God help us!"

Upon hearing his cowardly cry and seeing the ship list farther and farther, the men also began to scream and cry to God to save them. I grabbed on to a fixed object of some kind (I am unsure at this remove what it might have been), and then noticed that the ship seemed to have settled a bit and was no longer turning over quite so rapidly. Even though the storm had moved off, it was night, the ship was clearly going to founder, and we all realized that Death likely had found us there in the warm waters of the sea. I thought fondly once more of my wife and children, and of the Dorsets and particularly Jenny, of course. This voyage had been a noble one and was certainly not in vain, and though I regretted having to leave the world under such circumstances, I made peace with God as I could and awaited our fate.

The men were absorbed in their madness. They cursed Captain Pinson, though the sinking was certainly none of his fault, cursed God, cursed each other, cured the bad luck of the two men killing each other. Indeed, I myself had never seen fortune change so quickly. One moment we were dancing and singing, and the next men were dead, the ship was sinking, and the night was black as ebony. I looked at my companions and was pleased to see that both were taking the calamity with equanimity, even Mr. Dorset, who rather seemed to be enjoying himself. Old Bob was saddened, but he knew that Death calls us all, and though he clearly had rather it not be that evening, he was not screaming as the men were, having lived a long and reasonably happy life.

"Lost at sea," said Mr. Dorset shaking his head. "Such a thing, Hawthorne, to be lost at sea. Will they write odes about me?"

"Certainly, sir," I said. "Being lost at sea is a noble passing."

"They will needs appoint a new governor," said Old Bob sadly, looking at me.

"There are many men stupid enough to be a governor," I said, and Mr. Dorset laughed.

"Well spoken!" he said.

Just then, the ship lurched and began to turn slowly but inexorably, with starboard down and port now thrust up into the black air. The last of the torches fell off the ship and into the sea swells with a hiss, and we were enveloped by blackness. As my last duty, I reached out for Mr. Dorset so that I might serve him as long as I could, and I was touched to find that Old Bob had done the same thing. The rest of the masts began to break, and everything not nailed to the deck rolled along with screaming men into the heaving ocean. Those ill-fated sailors screamed to God, begging Him and cursing Him, cried out for their mothers or lovers, and exhibited the terror that the situation surely warranted. For myself, I felt only a brief sadness and prepared to meet God, which I believed would be my recompense for a life cleanly lived. I closed my eyes tightly and thought of the City of Heaven, and the golden streets. I thought of my Scots forebears and hoped that I would go with them to a shining corner of that realm.

"I have you, sir!" I shouted.

"And I," said Old Bob.

"What a loss," said Mr. Dorset, and though I suspect he was speaking of himself and his odes, I fancied he might also have been speaking of me, and I took courage from the bare statement, whatever he intended.

Now the ship was entirely sidewise and began to slide prow first into the sea, and there was no holding on to it any longer. I wanted to say something, utter some valedictory statement of thanks for having served

Mr. Dorset, but before I could say a word, we all fell into the sea and went under. As we bobbed back to the surface, we held together. I had the ability to swim quite strongly from my youth, and Mr. Dorset swam, but Old Bob did not, and so we held him to us and treadled in the water and darkness as well as we could. I was kicking and wondering if sharks might be about when my hand hit a spar that was floating, and I curled my arm around it and held on, shouting to Mr. Dorset and Bob to grab as well. When all three of us had hold of it, I feared it would go under, but it held us up. Though I wished none of the crew ill, I silently prayed that no more would find our roost and sink us. I could not say how many, if any, found a piece of wood upon which to hold, but within five minutes the sound of men screaming had faded into the darkness, and the only sound was the sloshing of the sea and the rumble of distant thunder. Below us, the ship apparently discharged a great volume of air and cargo, and that rush from below was as peculiar a sensation as I ever felt. Though I could not see what was before us, I felt barrels and pieces of wood floating in the seas, which seemed to be calming down now from the storm.

"Sir, are you here?" I asked, though from the sounds I knew he was.

"Aye, Hawthorne, a miracle," he said.

"My shoe hath fallen into the deep with monsters," said Old Bob. Despite the calamity, I began to laugh, and so did Mr. Dorset. Just then, there occurred one of those rare miracles in life that one cannot forget. I had certainly not thought that we were delivered from death, though perhaps spared for a brief time. In that blackness, death would be no more than a sleep and a falling. I was looking at the heavens and thinking of God when I saw that the clouds were passing away and that before us was a brilliant full moon that cast the most beautiful light upon us that I could imagine. I had never properly thought of the distance between light and darkness, taking each for granted in its course, but on that night, I can say, as the ancients might, that I *adored* the light from the moon and the courage it gave me.

"Moon!" cried Mr. Dorset, nearly in ecstasy. "We have a moon, Hawthorne."

"Moon?" said Old Bob. I could see my companions quite well now, and though we looked far the worse for the experience, we still held to our human appearances, and the courage it gave me was inestimable. "It is a moon, one of sorts anyway."

I laughed again, and we saw then that the sea around us was full of debris from the wreck, and I set about gathering what drifted past in hopes that it might help us fashion some kind of raft on which to survive. As it turned out, empty rum barrels were plentiful, as well as other pieces of the ship, and soon I had captured a large section of what appeared to be the deck, which had apparently broken apart as the ship foundered. But the task before me was great, and so I threw my strength into getting up on to the piece of wood. As I got aboard it, I felt an exaltation out of proportion to our dilemma, for I somehow knew that I would not drown, at least not that night, and had been spared the fate of my father.

"Sir, give me your hand," I said to Mr. Dorset, and he did so without question, leaving his small anchor, and at no time did his trust in me shine more brilliantly. After I had him up with me, and it appeared the boards would hold us easily, we reached for Old Bob.

"Let go and come to us, Bob!" I shouted.

"I believe I shall drown now," he said in a voice that was expectant and mournful at the same time, and, with that, he let go of the piece of wood and slid under the water. Without thinking at all, and surely with no notions of heroism, I dove into the water where Bob had disappeared and felt of him immediately, dragging him back to the surface and into the moonlight. He was coughing and gagging, but he was alive, and Mr. Dorset all but fell into the sea himself in helping me get Bob on to our raft, where he heaved and wheezed for a moment before sitting up abruptly, noting that he was yet alive and thanking me.

"God, look at it," said Mr. Dorset with a shudder, and in the glow we could see debris everywhere and hear the slowly fading voices of screaming men as they prayed and cried for salvation. Within ten minutes we had all drifted so far apart that we no longer heard a sound but the sloshing of the water over the edge of our small craft. The waves had even dispersed all the flotsam from the wreck, and so we were entirely alone, far out into the sea. Our initial exhilaration at saving ourselves settled into a quiet knowledge that though we might see morning once more, we certainly would never see our families again. For a time, the three of us were silent as we recovered from the exertion of the ordeal, and I thought in that time of what would happen if another storm came our way.

"I believe I have gathered a barnacle," said Old Bob, pulling up his trouser leg.

"A barnacle? What? Barnacle?" said Mr. Dorset.

Just then, Old Bob leaped up and fell across the boards very nearly in my lap and began to shake and shout in a manner not unlike that of a madman, and I felt a chill go through me. He screamed that a barnacle was in his pantaloons, and though I did not know what he meant, I assumed something was there, and so (with great difficulty as it was soaked) pulled back his trouser leg and saw a small crab trying desperately to get away from its unwanted prison. Mr. Dorset, who was leaning close and looking on with the interest of a scientist, began to laugh.

"Crab," he said. "Bob has gathered a crab for breakfast."

If he had not said that, I would have tossed the tiny creature over-board, but indeed it was a thing I had not considered. I plucked it off Bob's leg, and it was no bigger than a crown, not even a mouthful, and I felt sad for it, but not sad enough to throw it overboard.

"How shall we keep it?" I asked stupidly.

"Crab?" said Old Bob. He leaned down and peered at it closely with his bad eyesight. "I could of sworn barnacle. Into my bag, crab." He took it and put it into the small purse which was still tied to his trousers. Soon, we forgot about the crab and sat and looked at the moon, which emitted the most beautiful light I had ever seen in my life. The seas, which had been roiling only an hour before, now settled almost into a calm, and the rocking was no more violent that a mother's hand on a cradle.

"I wonder if that fiend Smythe was responsible for the ship," mused Mr. Dorset. "I can think of no one else who would commission such a foul tub."

"I think it was British registry," I said.

"Ah, then nothing which floats is ever safe," said Mr. Dorset. I felt there might have been philosophical import in the words, but I was so tired, and the sea so gentle, that I closed my eyes and drifted in and out of a desultory conversation that went on for a time. I drowsed while Old Bob launched into a long and rambling speech about the ocean and the monsters which were able to devour humans whole. (He spoke with interest and not with fear, and so the words, which should have aroused my concern, were merely interesting.) Mr. Dorset then launched into a speech on the history of shipwrecks, particularly focusing on the defeat of Spain's *Armada* in 1588, complete with information that I felt certain he was inventing as he went along, though I dared not call him on it.

Finally, though, the conversation drifted away, and we all fell into a sound sleep, and I cannot say that sleep ever again took quite so deeply as it did that night. I awoke only once sometime later, when the night was still upon us, and the sky had entirely cleared and the moon set, and so I saw thousands upon thousands of stars spread across God's canvas with such glory and majesty that it took my breath to imagine how intricate and noble their construction was. Although I felt certain that we would not survive above a few days without food or water, I was glad at least to be in the company of Mr. Dorset and Old Bob and reasonably safe from drowning. It was better, I thought, to die on the raft than in the deep.

I fell asleep with the dome of Heaven overhead and a kind of resigned calmness in my heart.

— 5. —

OUR RAFT HOLDS US WELL, BUT GREAT WHALES OR SHARKS
BEGIN TO SWIM AROUND US, ENCOURAGING MR. DORSET BRIEFLY
BACK INTO A PERIOD OF PIETY. HOW OLD BOB SAVES US FROM
HUNGER IN A MOST UNUSUAL WAY.

I was the first to awake as the sun broke up from the East, sitting just beyond the edge of the vast and empty ocean. I rose up and looked around and saw nothing but water in every direction, though the swells were exceedingly light, and the sky perfectly cloudless. The smell of the ocean and all its salt was overpoweringly strong, but I did not mind it and was glad to be distanced from the wreck. I could not guess how far away we had drifted or if any of the other men had found a way, if briefly, to save themselves. I was cheered by one sight, a number of birds who had flown that far from land out into the ocean in search of fish to eat.

Our raft was solid beneath us and in no way threatened to break apart. Mr. Dorset and Old Bob slept gently, though Bob did snore in a most appalling way. A pleasant breeze blew us in a direction I took to be north-west, which would have been back toward Town, but no breeze shy of a hurricane could possibly have taken us all that way ere we drowned. I was oddly unmoved by the prospect of death, for God had spared us once already, and I could not guess why. Perhaps it was His intention to spare us entirely. (Now, I believe one of the reasons God saved me, at any rate, was so that I might bear witness to the extraordinary lives of the Dorset family, particularly Jenny, though I cannot know that entirely until I meet my

Maker face to face.) I was sitting up admiring the slow rising of the sun when Mr. Dorset popped up like a puppet at a Punch and Judy show.

"By God, Hawthorne, I dreamt that I was shipwrecked," he said. "What a horrible nightmare." He rubbed his eyes and made to stand up and then fell, due to our raft's lack of stability. He looked around. His face relaxed into a pose of understanding. "Ah, then it is an adventure."

"I'm afraid so, sir," I said. "But at least we are alive. That is more, I'm afraid, than I can say for the rest of the crew."

"Was it because they vexed God?" he mused, not speaking directly to me. "Or perhaps the ship sank itself. Have you ever heard of such a thing?" He scratched his chin. "Think of that, Hawthorne. Mayhap the timbers from which the ship was hewn had a memory and decided that they no longer wanted to serve as a ship, just as a man will rebel against servitude in slavery. What a thought. I daresay I am the first man ever to have it. Eh?"

"I daresay," I said.

Old Bob, hearing Mr. Dorset's discourse, sat upright abruptly and looked around us at the sea and then back at us.

"Mr. Dorset and the governor as well," he said. "God hath a manner in his salvations." I smiled at Bob's continued confusion, though Mr. Dorset merely looked at Bob the way most people looked at him, with an admixture of pity and affection.

"Bob, are you well?" I asked. He touched his chest and legs, felt of his head. Of course Mr. Dorset and Bob had lost their wigs in the wreck, and now looked more natural, which in Mr. Dorset's case flattered him, though I cannot say it did the same thing for Bob.

"I believe I am entirely here," he said. "I dreamt that a dog had gnawed my foot away and then told me that it tasted foul."

"What?" said Mr. Dorset. "A dog which spoke? I believe there is meaning in that. What might it be? That we have treated animals poorly? No, that cannot be it. Perhaps God had assumed the shape of a dog and was speaking in riddles. In the Old Testament, God often spoke in riddles, as did the men. I believe in riddles. Hawthorne, did I ever tell you about the riddle that the old woman spoke to me when I was a boy?"

"No, sir," I admitted.

"D—d if I can remember it," he said thoughtfully. He turned to Bob. "What exactly did the dog say?"

"That I was too tough for it to eat," said Bob. "I cannot remember a thing beyond that, I s'pose."

"Too tough to eat," said Mr. Dorset. "Then it is about nourishment." He sighed heavily and looked around. "I fear that rather than being a touch of the fantastic, it was a touch of the fatal fortunes we have found upon this ocean."

"One must keep hope, sir," I said.

Just as I spoke those words, the water seemed to be filled with swiftly moving shadows just beneath the surface, and, without speaking, we all moved toward the center of our raft and peered suspiciously at the shadows and the occasional fin that broke the surface. At first, there were only a few, then perhaps five or six, and then myriads, as the sea seemed to boil with the monsters, who were probably as hungry as we were.

"Sharks?" said Mr. Dorset. "I believe they are sharks or whales."

"Sharks perhaps," I said, straining to get a better observation. "I do not believe it is whales, as I have seen their bones and they are larger."

"Infant whales?" said Old Bob. "Perhaps to swallow babes instead of Jonahs?"

"By Jove what a thought," said Mr. Dorset. "Bob, I daresay you are the first man ever to entertain such a thought, and I congratulate you for it."

"Thank'e, sir," Bob said, pleased.

As the sea creatures kept circling us, they began to fight with each other, until the sea began to turn crimson with blood. As one died, the others seemed to go quite mad, until the fight was of amazing proportions and the splashing wet us. The commotion rocked our raft so fiercely that for a moment we felt we should be dashed into the sea, but finally we drifted away from the battle, and they were so engulfed with the fight that they forgot completely, and soon we sat on a flat sea, saved for a time at least from serving as breakfast for the sharks or whales, whichever they might have been.

The sun came up then, and suddenly we were very hot, since there was no breeze. I was thirsty and hungry, but, as there was nothing to be done about it, we tried to distract ourselves as best we could by scanning the horizon for vessels and talking about why Jenny would have run away to the Indies with Antonio.

"For love, perhaps?" I suggested modestly.

"I think not love," said Mr. Dorset. "A man does foolish things for love's sake, even marries, which is the last thing one might do for love. The female of our species does not run away for love but lies in a lair like a spider awaiting a mate. And besides, Jenny is but fourteen years, and too young to wed."

"Juliet was but thirteen, as I recall," I said.

"D——d if she wasn't," said Mr. Dorset, amazed at the thought. "But in the ancient times, that may have been more in custom than it is now."

"Perhaps it is simply her nature?" suggested Old Bob. I realized that the conversation, had it been overheard by Mrs. Dorset, would have driven her mad, but Mr. Dorset engaged in it as always, as if the observations were independent of any real persons.

"Nature?" said Mr. Dorset. "Each of us is bound to our nature. I am bound by the Muse to be one of America's great poets, am I not, Hawthorne?"

"Certainly," I said.

"Just as it is Bob's nature to be long-lived and yours to serve," he said, drumming his fingers on his chin. "So perhaps it is Jenny's nature to roam and wander, whether with an Antonio or anyone else. We need not put an evil reading upon this, eh Hawthorne?"

"Indeed not, sir," I replied.

"Perhaps she is like Ulysses and in search of treasure or truth," he said, gaining excitement. "Perhaps it is her nature by the dint of blood to seek the great truths of this earth and then speak them to all of us!"

"Or perhaps she is a slut," offered Old Bob. Mr. Dorset and I both went silent, and though I thought I might intercede to soften Bob's horrible breech of manners, nothing came to my mind.

"Slut?" said Mr. Dorset, his voice rising. "Slut?"

"Saint," I blurted out. "He said saint." I looked very hard at Bob and narrowed my eyes, and fortunately he gave me a signal that he understood his foolishness and merely nodded.

"Oh, saint, ah yes then," said Mr. Dorset. "Well spoken, Bob. *Mrs. Collier* is a slut." We both looked at Mr. Dorset, having no idea who Mrs. Collier might be, but he did not seem to mind that he had divulged a private matter, and I merely let it drop.

For a time, we enjoyed the silence and the sun, but soon the heat began to press upon us so that we knew full well that our situation was hopeless and that though we had the option of choosing the manner of our deaths, we had few other choices left in this life. I watched Mr. Dorset as he began to brood. Bob spent perhaps an hour staring at the flap of his boot, which had come loose from the water. For myself, I merely prayed and thought of Heaven, and begged God to give my wife and children peace of mind for my loss.

I was thinking of the streets of Heaven when Mr. Dorset suddenly uttered a great cry of sorrow and rose to his knees and tented his fingers beneath his chin and began to make such awful sounds that Bob moved close to me in fright. I will not in this History attempt to recreate his words, for they came so swiftly and were directed at so many aspects of his life, for all of which he sincerely repented, that it all tumbled together in a speech such as no man ever uttered or heard. I was somewhat fascinated, but Bob was clearly frightened, and I threw him a conciliatory glance. On and on it went, with Mr. Dorset pledging his life against being saved from the wreck. He would even become a priest if that were God's will, if only we might be saved so that he could see his wife and children again.

"Though perhaps not Isaac so much," he interjected.

I cannot say precisely how long he spoke, but it must have been more than an hour, and finally his words began to seep into my head without meaning, and I became so sleepy that I nearly nodded off. That would have been impolite, however, so I pinched myself (quite literally) and did my best to keep paying attention. Finally, I noticed a pause in Mr. Dorset's soliloquy, and looked up in time to see him looked puzzled and hear his stomach rumble.

"I could eat a horse," said Mr. Dorset. Then, "By G–d, Hawthorne, remind me when we return to have a feast made of Alexander. That is the most worthless horseflesh that ever set foot on a racetrack in Carolina."

"Eat horseflesh?" said Old Bob. "The idea makes my stomach revolt."

"We may only eat again in our memories anyway," said Mr. Dorset sadly. He suddenly pounded his fist on the raft. "But I would, by the heavens, eat that worthless animal and leave his bones to whiten in the sun. He cost me a great deal of money! There is no honor is owning something so wild and without conscience."

Strangely, I thought not of the dishonored Alexander but of Mr. Dorset's daughter, who had not a little in common with the horse.

After that, all of us began to think about food, for we were beginning to be very hungry. Worse, without water, our tongues felt parched, and I could believe that we surely would not last upon the sea like that for more than a few days before one misfortune or another overtook us. I thought about it for a long time and decided that I could do no more for my family or for myself, and so I would do the job for which I had been born, and serve Mr. Dorset as well as I might until the end.

We sat silently for another hour, looking at the horizon and seeing nothing. The heat was unpleasant by midmorning, and I knew that in the afternoon it would be merciless, but I tried not to think of it, instead recounting in my mind the books of the Bible. I was baffled after Deuteronomy, however, and began thinking of things which calmed me, when there was a great splash, and a huge fish leapt in the air over our raft. Even though he was the eldest by many years, Old Bob uttered a cry, reached up, and caught the fish and pulled it into his lap, making tiny cries.

"By G–d!" cried Mr. Dorset. "A feast from the heavens!"

The fish was determined to regain the water, but Old Bob and I (for I had entered the capture with him) were equally determined that he not. Finally, I wrested the flapping creature from Bob, grasped its tail, and hit its head upon the boards with such force that it was killed immediately. We began to rejoice, and Mr. Dorset, certain that God had responded to his entreaties, thanked the Almighty for perhaps two seconds before beginning to study the fish and see how we might approach eating it. The creature was about two feet long, and rather pink in color, with large scales and a very plump belly.

"Noah survived by being inside a fish," said Mr. Dorset suddenly. "We shall survive by the fish being inside us. Hah! Oh, Hawthorne! Remind me to include that in my epic of this adventure!"

"Sir," I said with a nod. (I hoped that he would never write about it, but in that I was disappointed.)

We examined the fish for some time before deciding that we should attempt to pull its scales off, and so I set about trying, but they held so firmly that nothing would dislodge them. We felt we might scrape them away on the edge of the raft, but we were afraid of dropping it back into the sea. Finally, Mr. Dorset, working himself into a state of great frustration, took the fish in his hands and bit it violently on the side, ripping through scales, flesh, bone, and blood. The sight was barbaric and yet somehow heroic, for it allowed us to pierce the shell of the creature, as it were, and thereafter we passed it around and ate from the saving flesh. Bob had a difficult time for his teeth were bad, but he managed, and though the flesh was rank and sour, it was food, and we picked it clean until nothing was left but the head and the bones.

"Aye, a feast for a king," said Mr. Dorset, uttering an immodest belch. He paused and sighed. "Except that now I thirst."

That comment, which I had promised myself I would not utter, made us miserable, and though our stomachs were reasonably well fed, the lack of water was beginning to be painful. Soon after our feast, we lay, one by one, upon the boards and rested. I awoke only once in midafternoon, to find the heat painful and the sea gaining swells, though not in such volume to capsize us. No matter which direction one looked, it was the same, utterly and endlessly the same, and for a time I despaired, but then I thought of God, and my comfort returned. I lay back down and slept soundly until we all awoke and found that the sun was setting.

"Over Charles Town," said Mr. Dorset, rubbing the sleep from his eyes. "It sits on my Town, Hawthorne."

And indeed it did, and I could almost see or smell the things I had theretofore found unpleasant. I vowed that if I were returned to it, I would never again take it for granted.

— 6. —

WE ARE SAVED IN THE NIGHT, AND MR. DORSET CELEBRATES BY OVERINDULGING IN SPIRITS AND FALLING OVERBOARD.

We spoke only a little that evening as the sun went down into the ocean and the stars came out. I thought not much about death and tried to ask after Mr. Dorset's comfort, but he was sullen, and so I left him alone. Bob's stomach bothered him from our feast of raw fish, and I tried to distract him with stories of my youth. Finally the sun was gone, and with it the terrible heat, but if we lost that heat we also lost our brightest light, and I cannot say which was the better or the worse, but I supposed there was a lesson in it.

I was the last to fall asleep, gazing at the moon and stars and thinking of my life. I dreamt that I was a boy again, and I felt strong and agile as I no longer was. I was jumping from one branch to another in a tree when I fell. I awoke, thrashing my arms about trying not to be injured when I hit ground. I realized once again that I was not upon solid ground, however, and the swells had become decidedly stronger in the night. Old Bob had one arm hanging off our meager craft into the sea, and I pulled it back for him. I was about to try to sleep once more (for I felt the craft might founder that night, and I assumed that drowning while half asleep might not be unpleasant) when I saw some distance at port what appeared to be a dragon.

I have heard of men's madness at sea from one reason or another, and I was convinced I had lost my reason. I felt I must keep it to myself, but though I be mad, I could not take my eyes from the dragon, which appeared to be coming right toward us. I was not pleased at the thought of being eaten, though I did not really believe in such monsters. Yet there it was before me, its small red eyes and other yellow lights along its back like diamonds.

Mr. Dorset sat up. The light from the moon was bright, so we could see reasonably well.

"Sea's getting rough, eh?" he asked with a dry voice.

"Yes," I said. I cleared my throat. "And I believe we have been discovered by a dragon of sorts, sir." He looked around.

"Dragon? Dragon? Eh?" he said. "By G–d if it isn't, Hawthorne! If we are not eaten, I might have an ode in this."

"Wait," I said, suddenly realizing that it was no dragon. The lights were moving toward us but very, very slowly, almost regally. Old Bob sat up at that point and asked if he might bring tea to Mrs. Dorset. "Sir, it's a ship." I should have shouted the words, screamed them, in fact, but I could only speak them in a normal voice due to my lack of confidence in the vision.

"A ship!" he cried.

The enormity of the sight suddenly hit us all, and I began to shout as did Mr. Dorset and Bob, shouting as no men ever shouted, screaming in fact until we were hoarse. The sounds of our voices had the desired effect, for we heard other human voices — among the sweetest sounds ever I heard — and so we drifted right alongside the ship, which appeared to be making north-northwest, a fine brigantine under full sail, probably because the wind had been so weak during the day, and it was behind its schedule. There was a great shouting on board the ship as the men lowered a rope ladder. I grabbed it, and our vessel (which had saved our lives and which I had come to feel fond of) moved right along with the ship. Climbing up the ladder was unspeakably difficult for Old Bob, but Mr. Dorset and I came up it two rungs at a time, and I could only watch a bit sadly as our raft disappeared into the darkness.

If the Reader be skeptical at such a rescue, I can only say that in this History I have put nothing that is not true, and it happened exactly as I have described it. I have often read fanciful accounts of such things that were clearly the inventions of fanciful minds, but what happened to us was only the truth, and I shall leave God to judge my words when I am called before Him.

There was general jubilation and astonishment on board the brig, which was called *The Hawk* and was on the run from Jamaica to Charles

Town, bringing passengers, most of whom were below decks asleep, and cargo of various types. The captain, a kindly man named Turpenfield, asked after our comfort, and they brought us water and food. The men crowded around us to listen to our story, but, as Bob and I were in service, we would say nothing, which was proper anyway, since Mr. Dorset was beyond excitement in recounting the tale. He did not really begin to speak until we had eaten and they had brought us rum.

"The seas had taken on a great storm," he said, spreading his arms wide, "and the captain, a cruel man, had two men murdered before us for being in a fight." This was utterly untrue, of course, but, as there were surely no other men to counter Mr. Dorset, I let him speak his peace. "The captain himself threw their bodies into the sea, and the men kept crying that God would avenge these murders, and then the lightning began to strike and the thunder to crash! Boom! Booooooooom!" Mr. Dorset here waved his arms and drained his glass, and one of the crew refilled it immediately.

"The ship began to toss and to turn," said Mr. Dorset, "and fires broke out from the torches! One man became lit and flamed like a pine knot and threw himself into the sea where he perished with an evil hiss!"

"He did?" said Old Bob. I nudged Bob and bade him be silent.

"And then the storm came to us so violently that all the masts crashed onto the deck, and a spar came down right through the heart of the evil captain!" Captain Turpenfield placed his hand on his chest and looked stricken. "The men cried out, and some fell to their knees and begged God for forgiveness, but the die had been cast! The seas rose, and with them a horrible dragon with eyes like fire!"

"A dragon!" cried the men. Several crossed themselves, and one fell to his knees and began to pray aloud in what seemed Spanish or perhaps Portuguese.

"And there was a terrible crack, and the ship began to split apart, and it started to list to port heavily, and the men cried to God for salvation!" said Mr. Dorset. He finished his rum and it was immediately refilled yet again. By now, Mr. Dorset was in his natural element, perspiring heavily but having a marvelous time. "But God had already decided what was to happen! The captain cried aloud to God!"

"I thought the captain was killed by a spar," said a man nearby.

"D—d if he wasn't," said Mr. Dorset, momentarily distracted. "Anyway, the ship began to sink and men fell crying into the sea, and suddenly we were thrown overboard! The ship groaned and indeed seemed to sing its death song as the dragon hissed and ate men to the right and to the left! And the storm! The terrible intensity of the storm!"

By then, his audience was in a state of abject terror from the story, and many seemed so upset they began to wander away, not wanting to hear it anymore. I was not frightened at all, of course, since I knew that virtually all of it was untrue.

"And then the ship began to go down, and we were tossed into the sea!" shouted Mr. Dorset, whereupon he twisted himself and attempted to imitate what had happened, then fell over the ship's rail and down into the water. I was so tired that I could only move to the rail to watch. Fortunately two brave and intrepid sailors leapt into the sea for Mr. Dorset and, with help from the rest of the crew, managed to rescue him just as the ship had slowed nearly to a stop because of a failing wind. Mr. Dorset gasped and choked and looked so unlike himself that I pitied him and helped him to a resting place below decks, where I fell into the deepest sleep that I can remember. When I awoke, sunlight was coming through a hatchway to the deck. Mr. Dorset and Old Bob yet slept, so I quietly came aboveboard and saw, to my astonishment, that we were within sight of Charles Town. I am a man who rarely displays his emotions, but on that day I walked away from the crew members, who were very busy, and stood at the rail and wept. I found it a suitable purgative, though the thought that Jenny was still lost to Antonio sobered me with the knowledge that we must do it all again.

I had dried my brief tears and was looking at the ships at anchor in the harbor when Old Bob appeared beside me, rubbing his eyes, then stretching.

"Bless me, it's a city," he said, narrowing his eyes. "Is it London?"

"Bob, it is home," I said. "Charles Town."

"Are we in the North or in the Indies?" Bob asked. "Have they moved Charles Town to Bermuda, eh, governor?" He cupped his ear and awaited the answer.

"Charles Town has not moved," I said quietly so as not to bring attention to us. "This ship was sailing from the Indies back to Charles Town."

"Um," he nodded. Then, "Are you the governor of this island as well?"

There was no use in trying to explain it all to Bob, who held fast to most of his senses but sometimes became confused and disoriented as many old people will. I merely nodded to him, and he smiled, pleased. He would find out soon enough where he was. Just then, Mr. Dorset bounded onto the deck (there is no other word which can describe it), full of great joy, and excitement, and after our misadventures of the past few days, I must admit it was pleasant to see him back to himself, even if that self was a challenge with which to deal.

"Home!" he cried. He grabbed my shoulders and shook me, then did the same to Bob, who smiled strangely and seemed to be without bones at all, flowing as some sea creature might when shaken after its capture. "Hawthorne, we have come back as no other man might from such a disaster at sea! Imagine the joy! Imagine the men in the streets acclaiming us! Imagine the odes I shall wrench from this experience!"

"Imagine going back for your daughter, sir," I said quietly and respectfully.

"Who?" he said. "Oh, Jenny. Indeed. Well, perhaps she is in good hands with this Antonio, Hawthorne. God is good, no?"

"Sir," I said.

With that, Mr. Dorset began to sing "Victory at Longacre," to the merriment of the more cultured passengers, who knew at once that if Mr. Dorset lacked talent in his singing, he had even less in his art of composition. I pretended great approval and threw to them an impression of one who knew music well and might be well satisfied.

Needless to say, there were no men in the street acclaiming us in Charles Town, and no one to praise our exploits, at least not immediately. The fate of our ship had not been known, but not one of the crewmen was from Charles Town, and no passengers were on it save us, so while a few personages were pleased that we had survived, neither the ship nor the crew was mourned, though it gave the *Gazette* something to write about.

— 7. —

WE DISCOVER THAT WE HAVE MADE AN EGREGIOUS ERROR IN
SEARCHING FOR JENNY. MR. SMYTHE COMES BY TO MAKE SPORT
OF MR. DORSET. WE MOVE BACK TO LONGACRE.

The house was pleased at our return, and Mrs. Dorset, looking frail, was sorry to find of our misfortune at sea. But, as they had not known of it, they had the emotions of loss and recovery hard on one another, thereby blunting both, to Mr. Dorset's great sadness. We had been home for perhaps five minutes and were in the sitting room when, to our astonishment, Jenny Dorset walked in, holding a book.

I cannot describe the joy I felt, and yet I was so confused that I could not find the proper words. Old Bob had gone to his quarters, but Jenny's father looked at her and smiled as if her appearence were nothing unusual at all.

"Jenny, we are saved!" he cried. "Give thanks that we have been saved from the sea!"

"I heard from Old Bob," she said, "as he was on his way to his quarters. I am sorry for your troubles." She curtseyed.

"Troubles!" he cried. "Troubles, eh? Waugh, what troubles, child? I would go to the ends of the earth to fetch you back." He seemed well pleased with the speech and looked at me and smiled. Then a most puzzled looked crossed his face, and he leapt to his feet and rushed to Jenny and embraced her and glanced at his wife, who shrugged.

"You are rescued from Antonio?" I asked as politely as I might.

"Oh, that," she said. She twirled about and looked down at her dress and seemed pleased with the effect it caused. "I shouldn't have done so, but it was a fancy, Father, as you have fancies in your epics and such. I merely went to see a friend and decided to spent the night. I meant the letter rather as a joke." Mrs. Dorset looked as if she were afraid her husband might strike Jenny. I was too amazed to speak, and it is a tribute to the wiles of Woman and the beauty of Jenny that I felt no anger toward her at all, only relief that we would not have to set out again upon the sea. (Indeed, that trip was the last I was ever to make on the sea, and I can say with all sincerity that I am pleased for that.)

"What?" said Mr. Dorset, as it was apparently all he could think to say. Jenny repeated her statement, and Mr. Dorset placed his hand over his eyes to try and comprehend what she was saying.

"We asked everyone in Town if they had seen you," he said.

"You didn't ask all," said Mrs. Dorset with a rare flash of anger (and, I might add, insight). "You were too angry to search properly as you should."

"And this Antonio?" said Mr. Dorset.

"He is but a dream, much as the kind you make," she said. "But a pleasant dream for all, and I only wish he was as real to me as he was to you. And I must say again that I am sorry for your troubles." With that, she came and kissed him on his unshaven cheek and went back through the house and outside. Mr. Dorset sank into a chair.

"Hawthorne, sherry if you might," he said.

"He has only just escaped being drowned," said Mrs. Dorset. "I'll get your sherry."

"My pleasure to serve and to be home," I said with a bow, and she let me do my service. I wish I had the power to describe the feelings that were written on her face in swift succession: anger, forgiveness, affection, fear, pain, resignation, and then affection again. She sat in a chair next to her husband and reached out and touched his matted and foul hair, and I left them alone for a quarter of an hour before I returned with sherry for both of them.

We ate well, bathed ourselves, and slept that night and most of the next day, and when I was shaved and had my powdered wig back on along with my livery, I felt so much better that it was an elation of a kind. Matthew Dorset was genuinely glad to have us back, and talked in such a friendly way toward us that I felt much better for his chances at a happy life. (Discretion bids me omit here the great joy given to me by my own wife.) Isaac shook my hand once, as if he were trying to shake ashes off a fireplace poker. Abel did not even bother to notice our return, except to look upon his father with disdain and disgust.

I had only one chance to speak with Jenny alone, which came outside on the third day of our return. I saw her approaching me and stopped and waited for her. It was surely not my place, but I was determined to ask her why she had performed such a deed.

"I know," she said as she stopped by me. "How on earth could I have nearly caused such a terrible thing to happen." She looked genuinely puzzled. "I cannot say, Hawthorne, except that it must be tempered in the blood." That was the one answer which I could not gainsay, and when I smiled helplessly, she knew that, as always, she had said the right thing and escaped censure once more.

The day after that, however, I was cleaning in the sitting room and beginning to prepare for our move back to Longacre. The room was quiet, and I was about the kind of work I enjoyed most, restoring order and cleanliness to the room after an evening in which Mr. Dorset had been drinking rum and telling invented stories to willing listeners from Town. (We had shared fame of a kind, because Mr. Dorset had gone to Peter Timothy at the *Gazette* and told him of our voyage and rescue. Mr. Dorset's version of the story resembled the truth as a crumb resembles a cake, and when the whole story was printed on the front page of the paper, I was startled to find that we had been pursued by sea monsters and that Old Bob had saved us by fetching an octopus from the brine. Mr. Dorset told an amazing story of how he had removed the creature from Bob's face and dashed its brains out after a fierce struggle, where-upon we feasted on the tentacles. He also said that once we had been approached by pirates who had shot at us, but we had escaped by shout-ing that we had plague and wanted to come on board for water. I could not say from where such fancies arose, but as Mr. Dorset told the tales the evening before to his drinking friends from Town, they grew in mag-nitude, and no one questioned him at all. The last thing I recall Mr. Dorset asserting was that a man had fallen from our rescue ship from too much drink and he, Mr. Dorset himself, had leapt into the black sea and saved him.) Anyway, I was cleaning up the room and humming to myself when there was a sharp rap on the front door, as if from the head of a cane. I set down the glasses that I was picking up and went to the door and found, standing before me, Mr. Charles Smythe, looking fresh and fancy in blue silks and a new and fashionable wig.

"Mr. Smythe," I said, bowing at the waist.

"Hawthorne," he said, "is the fool of the house at home?"

"And who might that be, sir?" I asked. He was also carrying a cane with an ivory head of a delicate design, and he looked fit and prosperous, as he no doubt intended. Just as I was trying to formulate a reply that would insult neither our guest nor Mr. Dorset, Jenny arrived with a swish of silk.

"Who might that *be*?" said Mr. Smythe with a laugh.

"Tea, sir?" said Old Bob, who had silently crept into the short hallway behind me, giving me a start.

"Believe I shall," he said, and he breezed past me into the house. Jenny looked at Mr. Smythe with a kind of delighted anticipation.

"I will show him to the sitting room," said Jenny.

"Tea, sir?" said Old Bob. He cupped his hand to his ear awaiting a response which had already been given, so I steered Bob away from our guest and told him again that Mr. Smythe would have tea, and Bob wan-dered off to reveal the news to Ellen Goodloe. For myself, I ascended the stairs and went to Mr. Dorset's room and knocked on the door gently. (I was so bold only because Mrs. Dorset had gone shopping for a hat, so I knew I would not disturb any of their intimacies.) There was no response, so I knocked again, and again I heard nothing, so I opened the door and saw Mr. Dorset lying on the floor with one of his dogs, snoring so loud it sounded like a saw on a pine knot. The dog was pleased to see me, but Mr. Dorset did not move, though his lips seemed to be speaking soundless words. I was about to rouse him when he said "Waugh!" very loud and sat straight up.

"Sir," I said, clearing my throat, "you have a guest." The dog got up and slowly walked past me into the hallway.

"Was I in the belly of a whale, Hawthorne?" he said. "Have I been rescued by God to speak truths to which no man has ever been privileged before?"

"I fear not, sir," I said, "on all accounts."

"Fine, fine," he said, rubbing his disarrayed hair. "My head, I believe, is about to explode." He grasped his face and fell over on the edge of the bed and groaned and made altogether a spectacle of himself.

"Sir, I have never heard of man's head exploding of its own," I said.

"Oh, what a sight," he said, shuddering. "You must pick up the pieces before Lyddie sees them."

I assured him that his head would not explode, and only with great difficulty did I get him cleaned at the basin enough to dress properly and put on a wig. His skin was mottled and his nose red, but at least he was presentable. Altogether, the dressing took perhaps half of an hour, and so I knew our company must be getting impatient, though with Jenny amusing him, he might choose never to leave.

"You are ready, sir," I said, standing back and looking at him. He was very shaky and held on to the bedpost and held the back of his head for a moment.

"Who is the guest?" he sighed finally.

"Did I not say?" I said. "It is Mr. Charles Smythe, sir."

"Smythe?" he roared. "Smythe?! That blockhead?" I tried to calm him, but he was vexed with me for not speaking earlier of who was downstairs.

"Sir, he might hear you," I cautioned, "and that would be bad manners."

"D—n manners!" he cried. He began to get worked up when he suddenly sat upon the edge of the bed and looked quite ill, finally arising without anger only after a few moments of concentrated effort not to be sick. I escorted him down the stairs. Perhaps I should have merely told Mr. Smythe that my Master was indisposed, but somehow I must have thought the bracing company of a worthy foe might help bring Mr. Dorset back to his senses. As we came down the stairs, we heard the nasal whine of Mr. Smythe's laughter, followed by the bell-like peal of Jenny's own mirth. I was struck by the beauty of her voice as well as the rudeness of Mr. Smythe's. At the sound, however, Mr. Dorset, who heretofore had been walking like a superannuated man, regained his strength and stride and moved past me down the stairs two at a time.

We came into the parlor to see Mr. Smythe and Jenny leaning close, sharing something in a very soft voice, and while I was nothing more than surprised, Mr. Dorset's face (or the part thereof not suffering from the aftereffects of rum) turned red.

"Smythe," Mr. Dorset said. "Is there a holiday at the gaol?"

"No," Mr. Smythe said, standing and extending his hand. "Is there one at the madhouse?"

"What do you mean speaking with my daughter without permission?" said Mr. Dorset.

"I gave him my permission," said Jenny. "Besides, you were upstairs suffering from rum."

"Waugh! A falsehood from my own daughter!" said Mr. Dorset. He then belched loudly and struggled to a chair and sat. Just then, Old Bob came tottering into the room and approached Mr. Smythe with a broad smile.

"Tea, sir?" he asked. Jenny began to laugh in an uncontrollable and most unladylike manner. Mr. Smythe nodded yet again, then Old Bob stood before Mr. Dorset and asked the same question.

"Aye, with a touch of Jamaica," he said in what he thought was a whisper. Bob looked perplexed and then went on his way, repeating the desires of the gentlemen as he had the couplet I had composed for his ill-fated courting of Ellen Goodloe. Having sent Bob on his way, Mr. Smythe came down to business, which, as I suspected, was to make sport of his rival both for our search and its unpleasant conclusion.

"So, I have merely come, Dorset, to say that I am pleased that you managed to escape the ravages of the sea," said Mr. Smythe. Mr. Dorset squinted his eyes, wondering how Mr. Smythe meant it, and finally decided (wrongly, of course) that Mr. Smythe's interest was from genuine compassion.

"Ah, then you have heard of my great adventures," said Mr. Dorset. He tried to right himself in the chair, but he kept sliding somewhat forward, which had the effect of twisting and tightening his clothes while putting his wig askew.

"More than is decent," said Mr. Smythe. "Were you really attacked by sea monsters and pirates?"

"Did you not read the *Gazette*?" said Mr. Dorset.

"I read the *Gazette*, but it will print both the truth and lies, leaving men of intelligence to select which is which," said Mr. Smythe, a statement I thought very well put.

"Have you not heard of my fame, then, from men around Town?" asked Mr. Dorset, his voice rising and wig heading farther askew.

"I have heard stories as one does," said Mr. Smythe, waving the air with his hand. I glanced at Jenny, and she was smiling broadly, obviously enjoying the combat, which so far Mr. Smythe was winning, to his great pleasure.

"Then you say I have not spoken the truth?" Mr. Dorset said.

"I say that in your mouth the truth is changeable, like the wind," said Mr. Smythe. At that point, Mr. Dorset sat up to engage his foe when my Master emitted an enormous fart, which act left his daughter helpless with laughter, and Mr. Smythe wiping his eyes as well.

"Waugh, insulted in my own house," Mr. Dorset said, then he grasped his head from the pain and settled back into his seat. He stared very hard at Mr. Smythe, who was trying to bring himself under control. (Jenny made no such pretense and was beating the arms of her chair as she still laughed.)

"You were speaking, I believe, of the wind," said Mr. Smythe. Jenny shrieked and fell on the floor in a shocking manner, tears running down her face, laughing soundlessly. I admit that I had to shade my face with my hand as well, for often laughter is as contagious as a fever, and I felt myself fast succumbing.

"I challenge you to a duel!" cried Mr. Dorset. "Or I shall beat you to death with my own hands, you monster!"

At that point, Old Bob wandered back into the sitting room carrying nothing and approached Mr. Smythe and bowed deeply.

"Tea, sir?" he asked politely. A groan followed by "no, no more" came from Jenny on the floor. Mr. Dorset merely stared at the scene before him and sighed and gave up. I rarely saw him acquiesce that easily, but he was out of strength, and his body, ruined with rum from the evening before, was in no shape to fight any battles. Mr. Smythe nodded, and Old Bob smiled politely and bowed again and left the room.

"I think I shall pass on your offer for a duel," said Mr. Smythe. "But I thank you for the gesture."

"Indeed," said Mr. Dorset. "Your family. They are well?"

And after that, in a somewhat civilized manner, they spoke for some time of normal life and its consequences, and Jenny, finally recovering, became bored and left us. I was touched by the fact that the men seemed to share an affection, though most often it exhibited itself in great anger or challenges of a ridiculous sort. But as Homer (I believe) says, "Great men need great enemies," and if neither Mr. Dorset nor Mr. Smythe was a great man, each believed he was, and perhaps that is all that matters.

Old Bob never showed back up with tea, and when he left, Mr. Smythe once more insulted Mr. Dorset, who returned the favor. I later found Bob asleep in a chair in the kitchen, where Ellen Goodloe was watching over him with what I took to be tenderness.

And so we began that week to pack our belongings for the trip back to Longacre, which I had missed. Town was amusing but too busy for my tastes, and I would be glad to return to the country and the plantation.

Longacre was a pleasure to behold, though the topiary had grown somewhat wild and no longer resembled the various beasts that Mr. Dorset intended. The house was reasonably clean (some of the slaves had been charged with that task and did a good job). In my presence, Isaac Dorset severely scolded a slave for some minor infraction, and I realized that no matter how loyal I was, I could not bear Isaac, for he had taken none of the good qualities of either his father or his mother.

Autumn came, not the kind of seasonal change I have read about in the words of the Poets, but a subtle changing of the sky and the trees, along with hints that cooler weather was not far beyond. The breezes made sleeping in the evening more than tolerable, and, with the pleasures of being home, having our families intact, and the ending of that miserably hot summer, I believed that finally God had smiled upon us and brought us safe through another kind of voyage, this one on the oceans of earthly life. I should have known, however, that we cannot see beyond the skyline for a good reason, for if we see too far in this life, we will only find grief at the end.

— 8. —

MRS. LYDIA FOXE DORSET BECOMES VERY ILL AND SUCCUMBS.
THE EFFECT THAT HER PASSING HAS ON JENNY,
MR. DORSET, AND THE REST OF THE HOUSE.

As I have said, Mrs. Dorset was not well that summer and often seemed at the point of being frail, but she never spoke of her health in my presence, and indeed carried on with the servants as if nothing were wrong. I only realized one morning how ill she was when she had a coughing fit at the breakfast table and put a napkin to her mouth and brought it away bright with blood. Mr. Dorset was terribly upset, though Mrs. Dorset tried to calm him. He carried her upstairs to her bed anyway and summoned physicians from Charles Town, all of whom could do nothing and believed that she had a grave illness of the lungs and perhaps other organs of the body. One evening I was sitting at the table in the dining room playing whist with Jenny when Mr. Dorset walked in, unshaven, looking terrible. Jenny saw him and began to cry, rushing to him as he sank helplessly into a chair by the fire.

"She is fading away from us, my child, and nothing in my power can stop it," said Mr. Dorset. He groaned and put his hands over his eyes, and Jenny knelt at his feet and tenderly laid her face against his knee and wept. "Why is God doing this to my Lyddie?"

I had borne the misfortune with fortitude, as that was part of my job as a house servant, but when he spoke thus of her name, calling her by that familiar form, it very nearly broke my heart as well, and it was all I could do to maintain my composure. Mr. Dorset's tears flowed as he stared into the fire and stroked his daughter's hair, looking alternately between the flames and his daughter's face.

"She will soon be in Heaven?" asked Jenny.

"Aye, with the Heavenly Host and our Lord Jesus," said Mr. Dorset. Matthew came in about then, as well as Isaac and Abel, and when they saw their father so worn by grief and Jenny prostrate from it, they assumed their mother had already passed to God and began to weep as well.

"She is yet alive but fading," I said softly. If it was meant to comfort them, my comment only made their grief somehow worse, and Mr. Dorset bade them follow him upstairs to tell her goodbye. I stood in a corner lost in my own feelings. Jenny came to me, and touched my elbow and motioned for me to follow them. We took candles and ascended the stairs into her room, which was lighted only by a single candle and the fire, which was burning low and quietly. The room was chill, so I put another piece of wood upon the fire, and the room grew brighter, though not much warmer.

Mrs. Dorset lay piled in her blankets, skin drawn taut over her face. She had no color at all and trembled without control. Her eyes could see the children and her husband, however, and she took her wasted arms from beneath the covers and held them open. The children and Mr. Dorset lay with her on the bed, crying aloud, and a look of saintliness came over Mrs. Dorset's face. (I know that such a look is not to be found in most people in their lives or at death, and I cannot explain it, except to say that she looked as if her family held one hand and our Great God the other.) I stood by the fire, watching the scene before me and thinking of how brief our lives are and how little we mind how we spend them until it is too late. Mrs. Dorset had done her best to hold on to her husband, but it was like riding a wild mare.

The family waited for her to speak, and she struggled to do so, whispering something none of us could quite catch. She tried it again, clearing her throat, but once more we could not make it out, though it seemed to start with the letter W. She suddenly exhaled heavily and turned halfway to look toward her husband, and her spirit left her body and ascended into Heaven as we watched. At first, we could not quite believe the sight, but soon it was clear that she had left from among the living, and the grieving began in earnest.

The children were deeply affected, but none moreso than Jenny, who seemed confused at first, unaccepting, and finally so overcome by emotion that she uttered a terrible cry and fell upon the bed with her mother and squeezed the blanket into her hands in tight knots. Sensing the intimacy of the moment, I took my leave, but not before I caught a glimpse of Mr. Dorset's face, which was somehow almost childlike in its horror and loss, completely unguarded and sad beyond description.

The next few days were grievous, of course. The family had no graveyard, so we created one in a spot of high ground about a hundred yards from the house. That place had been cleared of trees and was open to the sun and sky, a kind of hummock that rose a few feet above the flat expanses of swampy land in lower South Carolina. Because Mr. Dorset was incapable of giving many orders concerning the funeral, I took charge myself, securing a minister and sending messages to everyone we knew of the upcoming obsequies.

The house was utterly sunk in gloom. An undertaker from Town came and prepared Mrs. Dorset and laid her out in the parlor in a very fine coffin he brought with him. The family sat with her all that next night, trying to speak of her with kindness and good cheer, but, from time to time, one of the children or Mr. Dorset would burst into unbidden tears, and soon all were weeping as well. I guarded my emotions with the family but gave vent to them in the privacy of my quarters and was comforted by my own sweet wife and children.

It may be indelicate, but I must mention in this History another worrisome facet of the event. Those of us in service had no idea what might become of us because of this death, and there was a general unease, even among the slaves, that somehow the event might split us apart. So we doubly had cause to mourn.

The day of the funeral was cool and clear in the middle of October. I could not believe how many horses and carriages arrived from the areas outlying us and from Town itself. Dozens of people attended, including all the Smythes, of course, who were genuinely upset. Mr. Smythe even embraced his rival and both wept, a sight that touched me deeply. There were Bulls and Ravenels and men and women of other great families. All the servants of the Dorset house as well as the slaves (which was not at all usual) were permitted to attend, and the silence as the minister droned, the men all holding their tricorn hats at the knees, and the wind ruffling their wigs, was a sight to behold.

As we stood near the grave, I watched their faces, the members of this great family called Dorset, and each one's character was written on his or her face. Mr. Dorset's grief was overpowering, as were most of his emotions. He could not take his eyes from the coffin, and he simply wept and shook his head steadily throughout the service. Abel Dorset looked bereft but somehow removed, as if his mind were elsewhere. Isaac for the most part was entirely in control and looked with what I took to be contempt at the crowd around him. Matthew was pitiful, his eyes and nose flowing without stopping, while his sister held his hand and tried to comfort him.

As for Jenny, she had the look she always did: emotional, surely, but also curious about the event and her own reaction to it, and with eyes that took in the scene as a painter might, before rendering it on canvas.

The service was mercifully brief, and Ellen Goodloe had prepared a fine meal for the mourners at the house, though only perhaps twenty or so remained for it, the others shaking Mr. Dorset's hand before disappearing on their horses or in carriages back to their own lives, which continued. (That, I have learned, is one of the graces of obsequies, to give the living courage to continue without the dead. Since I have lived to such a great age, I have seen all go before me, and each time I have learned that lesson even more strongly.)

Jenny, being the woman of the house now, took her role seriously as host, and we worked splendidly together in supervising the meal and making sure that the guests were fed. One man named Finch drank altogether too much, and became drunk and morose and had to be escorted away under the ferocious gaze of his wife, a woman who did not appear to have smiled in several decades. Mr. Dorset tried to speak with everyone who remained, but he finally removed himself upstairs in his grief, and I did not have to make excuses, as everyone clearly understood his absence.

Finally, late in the day, everyone had gone, and we had cleaned table and cleaned the dishes and secured them in the cabinet. I straightened the house, which, as I have said, was pleasurable to me, particularly in that part of the day when everyone was gone to his own interests. The parlor seemed empty and cold without the steadying presence of Mrs. Dorset, who had died in only her fortieth year. I was cleaning a few crumbs from the floor near the fireplace, in which I had built a fine blaze, when Jenny came in and fell into a chair and stared into the flames.

"I cannot believe she is gone from the Earth," said Jenny, without grief but with disbelief withal.

"No one you love ever leaves the Earth as long as we who live remember them," I said. "It is for us who live to keep alive the memory of those who pass before us."

I had not meant it to sound touching, and in truth it was something I had heard many times over and certainly was nothing I invented, for I was not bright enough to do so. And yet I will modestly say that in that quiet room, it sounded entirely right, and there are few moments in life when we feel as if we have said the correct thing at the appropriate time. Jenny stared at me for a long moment, and I returned her gaze. Never had I seen a young woman who was more beautiful, for her face was suffused with a peculiar mix of admiration, sadness, pity, strength, and pleasure. Her large blue eyes filled with tears that I thought might never fall, until they gave the impression of being behind a curtain of pure and beautiful water that buoyed them up. I knew then that I would never see again in this life a person more touched and touching, more self-assured and yet vulnerable at the same instance. I was moved and felt sure that her mother, looking down on us from Heaven, was moved as well.

"Thank you for that," she finally said, and a large perfect tear came from each eye and rolled down her cheeks, catching the light from the fire and lying there, perfect as pearls on her skin. I must admit I felt at that moment protective of her as if I were another father, one whose role it was to stand back and watch and yet who might be allowed the pleasure of pride in her grace and courage anyway.

"It is an old saying," I admitted. "One I have heard many times over."

"And never spoken better," she said.

In the coming years, when Jenny grew up and decided that life was to be drunk whole like spirits from a bottle, I would remember that night and believe that no matter how far she might travel in this life, she would recall that moment in my company. And many years later, she would bring it back up in one of the most agonizing moments of my existence. But that was much later, and, in between, there was much happiness (and much sorrow) left for the Dorset family.

— 9. —

JENNY SCANDALIZES HERSELF BY BECOMING A SINGER IN TOWN AT A
HOUSE WHOSE REPUTATION IS NOT SUITED TO HER CLASS.

Mrs. Dorset's death had a powerful effect on the house. Jenny, heretofore constrained by her mother's noble and steady presence, turned more toward her natural bent, which was from Mr. Dorset, of course. Though he was inconsolable for days after the services, Jenny immediately set about living life as if it might leave her any moment. She asked me hundreds of questions I could not answer, about butterflies, slavery, the music of Mr. Handel, rum, women of ill repute (which I refused even to discuss with her), and the strong feelings in the Colonies that were developing against the British. I should say here that many in the planter class, by virtue of their wealth and emulation of the English way of life, at first supported the Crown, even when King George's mad orders infuriated everyone. Charles Town, however, was a bed of serious malcontent, and I must admit, I held no love for King or Britain and was swept along as many others were with the idea that we might form our own country. I admired the Sons of Liberty greatly. For her part, Jenny developed a refined and elegant hatred for the Crown as strong as anything she had ever held against the French, and often asked me what might happen if war came.

About her musical talent, there was no doubt. She was the heir to that talent that Mr. Dorset thought was his but clearly wasn't. Jenny played the spinet and harpsichord very well indeed, and her ability at the dance had increased so that she could have given lessons to the giant who lived above the lawyers. She also practiced her singing with a master from Italy whom Mr. Dorset had hired sometime before. And so she practiced the musical arts with talent only God Himself could have inspired.

In the days following the death of Mrs. Dorset, the house was a chill and gloomy place. No room seemed warm enough, and Mr. Dorset was so forlorn that I worried about him. He would come down in the morning, spend perhaps an hour looking over his accounts, then spend the remainder of the day in front of the fire, staring at the coals and moving so little that only his eyes indicated he still possessed life. I have often noticed that the quiet men and women are the ones who keep this world afloat, so to speak, while those of great spirit and volume keep the voyage so amusing that we do not think about its final destination. Mr. Dorset and Jenny were clearly of the latter type, and it was painful to us all to witness our Master's misery at his awful loss.

During that autumn, I spent a great deal of time attending to Mr. Dorset, because he was so low that I worried for his health. Old Bob was unwell and not able to handle his share of the duties, though Ellen Goodloe attended to him in such a kind and gentle manner that I was touched. It therefore fell to Tom McNew to take Jenny into Town when she desired. (This History being sincere and entire, the Reader will, I hope, not be offended if I remind him once more that Tom and his twin sister Molly were of our house, while the twins Desdemona and Roderigo Smartt were of the Smythe house.) Tom had grown into a fine but sometimes wild young man, a good, hard worker with the house but always on the edge of trouble. His red hair and wide-spaced blue eyes made him look exotic (or rather somewhat like the Smythes), but he noticed nothing save the next adventure in his path. Only his fierce loyalty to the Dorsets and his obvious fear of Isaac Dorset, who treated everyone the same — poorly — kept him in check. None of us thought much about Jenny's frequent trips into Town, for I had spoken with Tom and allowed I would thrash him (or worse) if anything happened to Jenny.

Day after day, as the winter rains descended on the Province, I attended to Mr. Dorset, who sat at the fire and stared, a cloak about his slumping shoulders, making him look much older than his years. He wrote no poetry or music, did not go hunting with his friends, and made no grand speeches of delight or defiance. In short, he ceased to be the man to whom I had pledged my loyalty and my life, and I missed the former man, as he missed his departed wife. Finally, I decided, though it was not my place, to speak to him. November had come, and the day was cool and raining, and no one on the plantation was doing a thing but keeping inside and trying to stay warm, the slaves in their modest huts and the servants in their quarters. I had made sure that the fires in each room of the house were stoked and fed, but even with candles lit, the house was dark and quiet.

Mr. Dorset sat in his chair, staring at the flames. I sat down in a chair opposite him and enjoyed the quiet crackling of the fire while glancing at him to see if his demeanor might give me the opportunity to speak. I was not sure what I might say, for I did not prepare remarks like Old Bob did with his ill-fated couplet, speaking instead slowly and at the moment. I was trying at least to gather my thoughts when Mr. Dorset broke the deep silence and startled me.

"I wish to be buried as close to Lyddie as possible," he said.

"Sir," I said with a nod. He was quiet again then. "But that will be some years hence, and life can change us in many ways over a span of years."

"It will be very soon, Hawthorne," he said. "For I cannot live without her."

"Sir, may I speak?" I asked. He took his eyes from the flames and for the first time looked at me, then nodded gravely. "I have seen loss myself. We have each seen it. Mr. Smythe has lost his poor Fortinbras and Miss Diana Seton, and our staff here has lost Mrs. Wilson. Life is not without loss and must anyway be borne, for that is the mercy that God grants us: to witness for the lost good ones."

"I want only to die," he said. "And sooner than later will suffice."

"Sir, you must not put yourself in the ground with those who have passed before," I said. "I say this with utmost respect, but life is to be lived, and when death finds us, we must embrace it as an old friend. But we cannot cross that boundary until God wills it, and I think those who are most full of life make its passage bearable for those who have never learned to do more than whisper against the darkness."

God must have guided my words, for they appeared to have a sudden and profound effect on Mr. Dorset. He sat up straight and stared at me, and then into the fire, and, following that, looked for the first time in days around the room, as if seeing it for the first time. A light seemed to open behind his eyes, and then close, and finally open once more and for good. He stroked his face, ruffled his cuff, made expressions of doubt and then pleasure. His features seemed to register the possibilities of life as a young man's do. When he looked finally up at me, I saw the man I had served for so many years returned from his approach to the grave, and the pleasure it gave me was powerful indeed.

"Winter is a good time to write an epic of the sea," he said to himself. "Would it in your mind be improper if I cast myself as the hero, Hawthorne?"

"It would be not only proper but true," I said. "May I send to Town for more paper and ink, sir?" He stood and began to walk about, hands behind him.

"You may," he said. "And new strings for my spinet. Summon out that fool Italian and have him replace the strings."

"Which fool Italian might that be?" I asked.

"Any of them will suffice," he said. He suddenly stopped and turned to me. "Great God! I am going to write a book, entire, of my adventures, Hawthorne! Get me dozens of quills! Get me paper by the pound! I shall write of sea monsters and red Indians and duels and Frenchmen! And I shall write of King George, the scurvy madman! Say it, Hawthorne!" He came and took me by the shoulders and shook me strongly. "Say that King George is a scurvy madman."

"Sir, I would rather not," I admitted. Just then, a much improved and even well-groomed Old Bob entered the room, wearing new white gloves and an even newer wig. Ellen Goodloe's attentions were clearly done lovingly, and I was so glad to see Bob up and about that I was about to curse the King as Mr. Dorset instructed. Instead, my Master rushed to Bob and stood triumphant in front of him.

"Feeling better, sir?" asked Bob in his best imitation English accent.

"Say it, Bob!" he cried. "Say it with me!"

"Beg pardon?" said Bob, cupping his ear with the gloved hand.

"Say King George is a scurvy madman!" cried Mr. Dorset. Bob nodded and bowed low.

"King John is a curvy madam," said Old Bob with a broad smile. Mr. Dorset, instead of repeating his sentence, stopped, began to laugh soundlessly, then started to shake all over, finally falling on the floor laughing until the tears came, pounding the pine boards with his fists and howling so greatly that much of the house peeked into the room, including Jenny, who was puzzled but delighted.

"What in the world is going on?" she asked. Bob cleared his throat obligingly.

"King John is a curvy madam," he repeated. Jenny wanted to laugh, but she seemed to think it was some kind of code. On hearing it again, however, Mr. Dorset became entirely helpless with laughter, and finally I could not suppress it myself. If I live to be a hundred years old, I shall never forget how that laughter brought the house back to life. Soon thereafter, Mr. Dorset was himself again, writing terrible poetry and music, painting bad pictures, and not caring a bit that his talent was not up to his industry.

The rain was followed by a series of sunny and glorious days, and it seemed that God had given life back to us after taking it from Mrs. Dorset. We all were grateful, but we could not have foreseen how strangely things would turn in the coming years for all of us, and particularly for Jenny Dorset.

As I have said, she began increasingly to visit Town, most often in the company of Tom McNew. I was not afraid for Jenny in his company, for though Tom was rather stupid he was no fool, and he knew that any improprieties toward Jenny would probably bring for him the end of a noose. Still, Tom was known to have a drink betimes, and on one occasion he came home with wine on his breath and on his clothes, and I managed to remove him from the house and chastise him severely before Mr. Dorset realized Tom's state.

"It wasn't nothing so wrong, Mr. Hawthorne," Tom replied.

"If anything happened to Jenny during your drunkenness, you should pay the piper, Tom," I said sternly. "Are you not staying with her as she shops or whatever?"

He sighed heavily and looked around as a guilty man does, his tongue probing the corners of his cheek for a word or perhaps the truth. Finally he shook his head and looked down.

"Ain't no keeping up with that girl, Mr. Hawthorne," he said. "Might as well try to put a hat on a hurricane."

"Then what is she doing on these trips to Town?" I demanded.

"I could not say," he said, trying but failing to whisper. "She goes a different direction every time I put her out on Tradd Street, she does. I've tried to follow her to see what she does, but she shouts at me in the most awful way and shakes her finger and says she will have me and Molly dismissed if I follow her farther. She tells me to wait at a certain place, a different one each time, and it's a tavern most often, where there is nothing to do but enjoy meself to a portion of wine or rum, but not enough to unmanage my senses, Mr. Hawthorne. I ain't an irresponsive sort, but if I follow her wouldn't make not a shilling's difference. She's not in my control no more than no one else's."

Though I should have reported Tom to Mr. Dorset, I knew in my heart that Tom was telling the truth, because he was not inventive enough to make up such a lie, and also because it sounded precisely like Jenny. And so I made up my mind to follow them the next time they went into Town, which happened to be early the following week, by then the first week of December. That morning, Mr. Dorset was in his element, enjoying himself in the library, shouting out rhymes and humming possible songs. Old Bob and Ellen Goodloe were cleaning away the breakfast dishes and looking very pleased with each other, which cheered me greatly. When Tom and Jenny left in the carriage, I got my horse and followed some distance behind. The day was cool but not cold, with the sun lazily hiding behind a thin sheet of gray clouds, enough to emit its warmth but not enough to spill its full light — an altogether pleasant effect.

The road was muddy from rains of the days before, but I went slowly enough for my stockings to remain clean and for my wig to stay put on my head. I never let the carriage out of my sight, though I was at their back, and they never turned around to see from where they came. (Tom could not, as he was driving, and Jenny did not because it was not her nature to look back either in distance or in time, because she was far too pleased with the road ahead to worry about what she had passed before.)

Once in Town, I tied my horse some distance away near Gordon & Co., a mercantile establishment. Tom McNew parked the carriage in the next block near the Red Lantern, a tavern which most often played host to neither the worst nor the best of men in Town. As they got out, Tom appeared to be speaking directly to Jenny, but, just as he had said, she waved her finger at him and then walked off down the street. He shrugged and went into the Red Lantern, where I knew he would stay for several hours. By then, it was early in the afternoon, and the streets were not busy, as many people napped during that time of the day, even in the winter, when the air was pleasantly cool. It was a habit from the heat of the summer which carried over. Still, there were men, women, and children about in small numbers, and I could only remark to myself how the Town had grown over the past twenty years.

I followed Jenny at a discreet distance, worrying about her all the time, for evil men did come to Town at times, and then there was a murder or robbery or assault upon a woman, though usually one of poor reputation. A woman alone was a most uncommon sight, though not as unusual as it would have been in Boston, where the men considered women to be marble statues that must be worshipped and ignored, as I have read. In Charles Town, the women were often as full of life as the men, but most still did not go alone on the streets unless they wished to be approached by men, which would have been disgraceful for someone of Jenny's breeding. Anyway, I followed her down several streets and saw finally that she had gone into the Hart House, an establishment which advertised its presence with a large deer's head over the front door, or at least a carving thereof. It was not exactly a tavern or quite a shop but had elements of both, and because of its expense and fine merchandise, neither sailors nor wenches often went there. Neither did Charles Town's finest families visit the Hart House, and so I was relieved and yet baffled at the same time. I waited until I was sure Jenny was not coming back out, and I went to the front door and entered.

Though I was born to service, I can, in my manner, affect the appearance of a man of wealth, because I have always paid good attention to my appearance. The Hart House (which I now entered) was hung with pleasing chandeliers, against which candle flames threw a pleasing light around the corners of the room. The shutters were opened to the daylight, and so the room had a pleasing sense of order to it, as men and women ate, drank, and engaged in intense but well-modulated conversations. A man played the harpsichord with a delicate touch to add a sense of delight to the diners. Nearby, three men were engaged in a low but intense conversation about the British and what must be done to end their arrogance. I stood at the entranceway of the room and looked around but did not see Jenny anywhere and was beginning to fear her entry had been a ruse to escape anyone who might have been following her.

I seated myself near the harpsichordist and ordered coffee, because entering an establishment and not ordering something would have been bad manners indeed. Imagine my astonishment when I saw that the man seated at the keyboard was none other than the giant dance master. Everyone in the room ignored the poor man, who played well but not especially so. As he played, his feet danced in a kind of small foursquare step, and I felt a pity for him and thought that his freakish nature had always removed him from the approval of men. My coffee arrived, and it was excellent. Two men seated quite near me began to prod each other in anticipation of something, and one said to the other words about someone luscious and ripe as a May apple. I did not have time to think much on this information when to my shock Jenny Dorset appeared beside the giant keyboard player wearing a red dress cut so low that her natural endowments were displayed and yet concealed at the same time, a trick of the dressmaker's art which never ceases to annoy and yet draw men. I could barely think what to do, and so I gathered my coffee from the table and went to the back of the room, which had suddenly gone silent. I leaned against a post to obscure myself from Jenny. An old man with a beard stood near me.

"It's Miss De La Hoya," he said, his voice showing the imprecision of drinking.

"Miss De La Hoya?" I said.

"Spanish," he nodded. "Something of a tart, I'd say." He then began to laugh, but the laugh soon turned into a violent cough, and someone showed him to the street as the room became very still. The Giant began to play, and Jenny unfolded a red fan and waved it in her face and started to sway a bit. As the music came to a proper cadence, Jenny began to sing, and though I knew she was musically inclined, nothing could have prepared me for the beauty of her voice and the way it filled that room. Everyone there was transfixed. She sang a familiar old song called "The Boy of Devon," and, as it was a sad tune, it melted everyone's heart who had lost someone, and of course I thought of Mrs. Dorset. Before Jenny had finished, I was deep in thought myself, and the thunderous applause so startled me that I spilled a few drops of my coffee on the floor.

Another man came close to me, this one an older man obviously of some wealth.

"She's Italian," he said. "Signora Cametti from Padua, God save that sweet face."

"Padua," I said.

Jenny accepted the applause and adoration as if she had been born for it, her face lit from the inside with such pleasure that I regretted that her behavior was intolerable for someone of her birth and that I could in no way allow it to go unreported. She sang three more songs, each more meltingly beautiful than the last, and I was forced to admit that I had never heard anything quite so marvelous in my life, and my decision to report what she had been doing flagged as the music continued. Jenny even sang "Victory at Longacre," which she heavily accented so it came out *Veectory at Lonkacre*, to the delight of the crowd, which genially still hated the French as much as they now disliked the British.

As Jenny was preparing for another song, the bearded man who had been drinking came back in the door staggering and shouting about soldiers and King George and Heaven only knows what else. He came to the middle of the room, where one man cried at him to be quiet so the German countess might continue her songs. Then another man accused the first man of defending King George. A third man stood and said the King was mad and only a fool would defend him, and suddenly men were throwing mugs of ale, fighting viciously, and breaking glass. Above it, I heard a woman's high-pitched scream, and was astonished as I rushed for Jenny to see that it was the Giant who was wailing. Most of the women, though backing out of the way, appeared to be enjoying themselves inordinately.

The employees of the tavern tried to break up the battle but were drawn into it themselves, and soon glasses and bottles flew around the room as I dashed to the front and stood before Jenny.

"Hawthorne!" she cried. "What on earth are you doing here?"

"I've come to help you out," I said.

"Not yet," she said, and her eyes glowed with anticipation as she grabbed a nearby bottle and broke it over the head of a man who was battling right near her. She whooped and threw herself into the fight. Most of the women present had run for the doors, but Jenny waded into the battle and began to punch men in the stomach, and scream insensibly about the English and the French and even (I believe) about the Irish. One man turned to her and smiled politely, and she hit him so perfectly on the chin that he fell over. The giant dance master was trying to wade through the battle, continuing his high-pitched screaming, arms over his head. I suppose he thought that by doing so, he would be able to escape unmolested. He nearly did so, until at the door someone hit him in the back with a chair, and he uttered a dull groan and fell with a resounding crash. Jenny by now was having a wonderful time, swinging and screaming and hitting anyone who came near her. Though one man tried without success to pin her arms, none would dare strike her, as it was against everything they had known all their lives. (In a more rude tavern, the kind Mr. Dorset often visited, there would have been no hesitation to fight with women, for they were among the fiercest competitors there, and many a sailor took wounds to his grave from a Charles Town woman of that class.)

I glanced around the room, and all were fighting but enjoying it, and soon the battle began to slow as it will, whether on the field or near the harpsichord. Only Jenny kept it up with the same passion, by now shouting uncouth oaths that embarrassed me. One man, who had been dispatched by another to the floor, reached up when Jenny passed and ripped her red dress, tearing a long piece of it away and exposing her undergarments. By this time, I had regained my senses, and I rushed for Jenny and spun her around. She took a swing at me, which I was able to duck. Her face was flushed from the exertion, and she was breathing very hard, and though her hair was loosened from its ribbons and hung around her face, she was more lovely than any Reader of this History can imagine.

"Hawthorne!" she cried. She covered her mouth, and seemed ashamed yet not overly so. She looked around the room in a panic, probably for her father. "What on earth *are* you doing here?"

"I was following you to find what you were doing in Town," I said. A man with a bottle lunged at me, and I backed up and tripped him and he fell to the floor with an awful grunt and lay there.

"You were following me?" she said.

"Tom McNew was to have taken care of you, and he did not," I said. "He revealed to me that he did not know where you went or what you did, and I was worried for you." I was having to shout a bit at Jenny, and a drunken man whose clothing was askew came up to me and got so close I could smell the stench of rum on his breath.

"You cannot talk to Mademoiselle Camembert in that manner!" he said. He took an ineffectual punch at me, and I put my knee in his stomach, and he fell and then crawled to a corner where he became violently ill. Jenny giggled.

"Why should I have that stupid Tom when you are here to take care of me?" she said in a coy way. "I should never have need of anyone but you, Hawthorne."

"Then may we leave this place before your reputation is further soiled?" I said.

"Reputation?" she said with genuine disbelief that I had such a concern. Before she could resist further, I took her by the arm and escorted her to the door, stealing, I regret to say, a coat which lay upon the floor, which I put over the ripped part of her dress, lest her modesty be compromised on the street. As we left the Hart House, the carving of the buck over the door fell just as we passed and shattered his antlers. One battle had removed itself to the street, but the men were speaking in very civil and even friendly, intimate terms as they continued to swing at each other. I urged Jenny down the street in a great hurry, not looking back to see if the owners of the Hart House had summoned the militia.

"The *Gazette* will have a fine time with this," I said more to myself than anyone else. "I only hope they do not know of your real name, for it would hurt your father's feelings terribly."

Jenny stopped and looked at me in the cool breeze of the day and began to laugh and laugh, in fact laughing so hard that she had to lean against a chandler's business to steady herself. I was perplexed, and tried to encourage her to come along, then I finally asked her what in the world was so amusing.

"My father knows of this," she said. "Dear, Hawthorne! *He* is the one who said I should do it! He said no one should hide his candle under a bushel, and that life was for him who takes it, and that reputation be d—d."

I had heard such sentiments so often from Mr. Dorset, at least before his wife's death, that I knew instantly that she was telling the truth and that I had been overly solicitous to no effect. How could I forget that the rules by which society governed itself in Charles Town did not apply to the Dorset family? I could only sigh and take her arm as we headed back for the carriage. Tom was in a nearby tavern, too drunk to aid himself, and so Jenny and I helped him into the back of the carriage, not even bothering to cover her torn dress as we did so. I felt at least as if I had done my duty and could not know that this adventure would be mild by Jenny's later standards. All the way home Jenny sang, Tom McNew snored, and I was left once again to marvel at the variety of creatures that God had put upon His Earth.

— 10. —

THE FAMILY SUFFERS A FURTHER BLOW WHEN
ABEL DORSET IS IMPRISONED FOR ASSAULTING A PORTRAIT PAINTER
WHO ACCURATELY DEPICTS HIM.

Abel Dorset, by that winter, was twenty years old, and no matter how much I loyally tried, I could not see in him any of his father's qualities, for good or bad. Abel had dabbled in writing and painting, but he found them distasteful, though he assumed by doing so he was an expert now in both. Isaac, a year younger, rarely did anything which might honor or dishonor to his name, instead assuming many duties in running the plantation and remaining aloof from all. The third son, Matthew, had never regained his former intimacy with animal husbandry, and though he might have days when he was pleasant, he for the most part was quiet and dreamy. I could not guess of what he dreamt.

And so it happened that Abel took it into his head to hire a fine portrait painter from Town named Pinkworthy to come to Longacre and paint him. Why Abel thought himself worthy of such an honor escapes me, for though Mr. Dorset had had Mrs. Dorset so memorialized some years before, he had never commissioned his own portrait. He did attempt to paint himself once, but the work looked more like certain fanciful pictures from *The Odyssey* than from any brush I knew.

This Pinkworthy was a gruff and unpleasant man, about my height but with one eye which had gone milky and a left hand which trembled constantly. Despite those infirmities, his work was delicate and skilled, and he fetched high prices. Mr. Dorset must still have been grieving when he approved the portrait, for its expense was one we certainly did not need to bear. Mr. Pinkworthy came to Longacre, where he settled in for sketches and then for the painting, staying several weeks with us. I never saw the man smile, nor did I see him without his pipe clenched between his teeth, burning foul-smelling tobacco. He sometimes would stand back from the work, which he forbade anyone to look upon, snarl at it, and then launch himself, with very tiny and fine strokes, back into the work. I found the stench of paints and the various solutions he used noxious, but it was not my place to say so, and because it was winter, the house was closed and the vapors had no place to escape.

Jenny found the process hilarious. After the brawl at the Hart House, she decided that her singing career should be in eclipse at least for a time, and so she spent her days trying ineffectually to take her mother's place as the lady of the house, a role which Ellen Goodloe also helped fill, much to Old Bob's approval and admiration. Mr. Pinkworthy did not approve of anyone watching him work, and so we had to come in and out of the parlor only when necessary, so that he would not glare and growl at us. Each day when he finished, Mr. Pinkworthy would gently place a cloth over the painting to keep out dust, though we also suspected that it was to keep us from seeing it. Abel's opinion of himself grew in proportion to the amount of canvas covered, and soon he was holding forth at dinner as if the act of having his portrait struck somehow made him a great man.

"Perhaps we shall exhibit it in the Masonic Hall," Abel said one evening.

"I was thinking of Mr. Allen's fish market," said Jenny. Matthew began to laugh as a donkey brays, and Abel took it with lofty disdain.

"Allen's fish market?" said Mr. Dorset from his place at the end of the table. "What on earth might rhyme with fish market, Jenny dear?"

"Dish fart," said Matthew, and then it was Jenny's turn to howl with laughter. Abel and Isaac merely stared at the proceedings. Mr. Dorset pounded the table with delight, belched, and toasted his youngest son with his wine glass.

"The tact of this family leaves me speechless," said Abel.

"Would that it did," said Jenny.

"Anyway, the day it is exhibited in Town is the day I shall rightly be considered a gentleman of honor," said Abel.

"Or a fishmonger," said Matthew.

The day finally came two weeks before Christmas when Mr. Pinkworthy said with some unpleasantness that the work was completed and that he would unveil it that evening. The house took upon itself an air of gaiety, and we all dressed in our finest clothing for the event, though I was worried that something might go wrong. As usual, something did, almost from the time we were seated for the unveiling. Abel had dressed so imperially that he looked rather foolish, though he did not know it. Powder from his wig had fallen into his eyebrows, making him look older than Old Bob, and one of his silk shirt cuffs was stained with what appeared to be wine. As we came into the room, Jenny touched me in the side with her elbow and nodded toward Abel with a smile, and I saw all. Abel, to make the occasion grander, had hired a consort of viols from Town, and as we entered they played pleasant tunes. I had raised the fire to great heights, and the room was very nice. With the sound of viols, the crackling fire, the light cast from chandeliers, everything might have been perfect for any other family.

The family sat in their chairs, with Abel at the front, a break with tradition that honored Mr. Dorset's manners, if not his sense. Mr. Pinkworthy stood by the fireplace, drinking what was obviously not his first glass of wine, scowling as always, and looking impatient. The portrait was before us on its stand with the cloth over it. Though we had all been curious, none of us had taken even a quick look over the past few weeks, for Abel had warned us it was bad luck to see an unfinished portrait and would bring calamity to the house.

"Well, we shouldn't want that, now, should we?" said Mr. Dorset drolly.

We awaited the unveiling, but Mr. Pinkworthy seemed in no particular hurry, and after a time Abel turned to the family and said, "Ah, the wait makes the excitement greater, as the chase makes the hunt more pleasing."

"Well spoken," said Mr. Dorset.

"You've never hunted in your life," said Isaac.

"That is untrue," said Abel, clearly embarrassed that his inexperience had been unveiled in front of Mr. Pinkworthy. "I have been hunting."

"You've never hunted," said Isaac. "You wouldn't know a hound from a hare."

"This is a calumny," said Abel bitterly toward Mr. Pinkworthy, who merely shrugged and emptied his glass. "I have ridden to the hounds as often as any man." The tone of desperation in his voice gave him away, and I felt almost sorry for the young man.

"You have hunted as much as I have failed in my duty to Longacre," said Isaac.

"Then he has hunted a great deal," suggested Jenny. "How kind of you to give Abel such a compliment on this special night." Isaac turned to his sister and flared at her, face turning red, but he said nothing.

"Here, here," said Mr. Dorset. "No reason for such talk, boys, now is there, Matthew?"

"What?" said Matthew. "Did someone speak my name?"

Jenny began to laugh, and I realized how foolish, even pointless, the viols sounded next to the music of her mirth.

"On with it now, Pinkworm," said Mr. Dorset. Jenny was beside herself now, and I touched my finger to my lips lightly and discreetly while looking at her, and she regained control.

"Pinkworthy, sir," the artist said grimly. At this point, Old Bob came into the room carrying a tray with nothing upon it, but before he could interrupt the proceedings further, I caught him by the arm and told him to go back to the kitchen to get something for the tray. He seemed surprised that nothing was on it, and asked me where it might be, and I merely repeated my order. He bowed so deeply that if anything had been on it, the contents would have been spilled on the floor.

"Ah, whatever," said Mr. Dorset. "Hawthorne, is Bob going for wine? I have had a magnificent day working on my poetry and am ready for a libation."

"Yes, sir," I lied.

"Ah, good then," said Mr. Dorset. "Please proceed, Pinkman."

The artist walked to the painting, and grabbed the corner of the cover and was about to pull it back, when Abel leapt from his chair and shouted for him to wait.

"We must have majestic music now more than ever," said Abel. "If you please." He nodded toward the consort, and, after speaking among themselves for a moment, they began to play a martial tune which did not at all suit the occasion, in my mind, but Abel seemed well pleased. He reseated himself and waited for the great unveiling. Without any statement or speech (a chance Mr. Dorset would *never* have let pass), Mr. Pinkworthy threw back the covering to reveal the most astonishingly fine portrait I had ever seen, the deep, rich colors almost leaping from the surface, and Abel rendered in such lifelike detail I could have sworn that his face had been transported there by some trick of sorcery.

Mr. Dorset began to applaud, and then so did the rest of the family except for Isaac, and, curiously, Abel, who leaned forward in his seat and seemed to grow wild with confusion and anger.

"This is madness!" cried Abel. The music stopped, and so did the applause. The room was utterly silent but for the noises from the fire. "You have insulted me!" Abel stood and was so furious his hands trembled. He turned to his father. "Look what he has done!" Mr. Dorset leaned forward to do as he had been asked.

"Fair likeness, I'd say," he blurted. "Well, much more than that. An excellent likeness, Pinky!"

"An excellent likeness!" cried Abel. "It is an abomination! He has deliberately insulted me! No one can treat a Dorset in that manner!"

"Oh, grow up, Abel, it's precisely the way you look," said Jenny. "Not a mole more nor one less."

"I would be ruined by that face!" he cried, pointing at the picture, which indeed looked precisely like him. "I shall not pay a shilling for it, and I will see it destroyed before anyone else sees it!"

Just then, Old Bob came back into the room, carrying his empty tray and looking pleasantly lost. When he saw the portrait, he gasped, dropped the tray to the floor with a terrible crash, and then approached the painting as if with reverence. He leaned forward to inspect it.

"Seems familiar somehow," said Old Bob. Jenny began to laugh, which raised Abel's ire even higher. Unable to bear it, Abel leapt to his feet and

began to wave his arms and scream curses. His face was near purple with
rage, and Bob gathered his tray and ran from the room, certain that Abel
was angry at him. For a moment, it seemed that Abel would spend his
anger, but then, to our great surprise, he rushed at Mr. Pinkworthy.

Human nature cannot be explained away in simple terms. On occasion, the mildest men become monsters, and men who have heretofore
been monstrous can weep like a child. The world bends us to its circumstances, and all we can do is watch the grand comedy unfold and try to
maintain our dignity and our position. Abel, who had never been greatly happy for reasons I cannot say, now exploded in wrath that was so far
beyond what the situation demanded that I could only guess that it had
been building for years and now finally gave way in him, as water after a
storm makes a dam give way. Abel stopped for a moment, let his arms
hang, and then he raised them and rushed at Mr. Pinkworthy, who was
now ready for the blow and looked quite fierce and furious himself.

"Abel!" cried Mr. Dorset. "See here!" Jenny's smile quickly faded, and
she stood, knocking over her chair. I knew that I must intercede, but
somehow I felt frozen to my spot, perhaps disbelieving what had happened so quickly. Mr. Dorset and Matthew likewise stood up, but none
of us quite had the will to move until Abel was roaring and upon Mr.
Pinkworthy. I can only say that Abel seemed to have been consumed with
madness, for his rage and manner of fighting, complete with screaming,
shouting, and cursing in the most foul way, were startling, even to Jenny,
who enjoyed a good start. Mr. Pinkworthy fought back with all his
strength, which was considerable, but it was soon clear that Abel had the
better of him, and finally I rushed into the battle, as did Mr. Dorset. The
entire scene had taken no more than a few seconds, but I was ashamed
that we had let it go on for that long.

Mr. Pinkworthy lay on the floor with blood coming from his mouth, and
Jenny ran for help and cloths with which to stanch the bleeding. Abel was
screaming and cursing still, for he wanted to get at the painting and destroy
it with his bare hands. Up close to it, I could see that the likeness was not
only accurate, it displayed an extraordinary talent and had captured Abel as
I thought no artist might. Mr. Dorset and I could scarcely hold Abel down,
and finally I looked at Mr. Dorset and raised my eyebrows, and he knew
instantly that I was asking permission to deal with the situation, and he merely nodded. And so I did what was unspeakable, even unthinkable: I hit Abel
Dorset on the chin and knocked him out. The room was utterly chaotic, and

soon filled with servants, including Ellen Goodloe, who with Jenny and a few others began to care for Mr. Pinkworthy.

The artist, as it turned out, was badly injured, but not so much that he could not ride to Town the next morning and summon the constable. During that night, we had tied Abel to his bed, and twice when he awoke (I stayed by to attend him) his rage was as great as it had been, and if the bonds had not been secure, he would have, I believe, gone to kill Mr. Pinkworthy. Finally, however, he awoke toward morning and began to weep inconsolably and ask over and over, "What have I done?" I loosened his bonds, and he cried himself to sleep, and I felt utterly exhausted and sorry for him.

When he finally fell into a deep sleep, I went to the parlor and got the portrait and secreted it, so that it would cause no further pain. For most of that next day, Abel slept, and the family spoke about what should be done but came to no conclusions because they somehow felt as if it had not happened, as if it were so fantastic it defied belief. They finally had to look squarely at it the following day, however, when a troop of militia came and arrested Abel on a charge of assault, of which we all knew he was guilty. Abel himself had spent all the anger he seemed to possess, and went along with no emotion but sadness. Isaac Dorset was sure it marked the end of the house, and he began to add accounts furiously in hopes that somehow the Dorsets would not be ruined. Matthew went to the horses and dogs and did not reappear for the remainder of the day. Jenny stayed with me, asking me questions about the nature of life, which as usual I answered as if I knew, which in fact I did not.

A few days after that, Abel Dorset was brought to the bar for trial, and he offered no real defense whatever, and, as we were required to show the portrait, the jury was able to see that the likeness was splendid. Fortunately, the *Gazette* felt that someone of Abel Dorset's stature should not be spread across its pages, but Charles Town was not so big that everyone did not know it anyway. Abel was found guilty of assault and sentenced to two years' imprisonment in the gaol. He had no words or emotions as he was escorted away, and neither did anyone from the Dorset family, all of whom appeared with regret to think the sentence was fair.

"This world is too various for my tastes, Hawthorne," Mr. Dorset said to me after his son had been taken away. "I should prefer a quiet time to write verse and think." He sighed heavily. "But for now, let us drink to Abel's health and hope that after his sentence he is a better and finer man."

"Little chance of that," said Isaac coldly.

None of us could know that Abel would redeem himself in the Colonies' Revolution and become a great man, but that is the nature of Time, that we cannot guess what will arise next.

— 11. —

THE MARRIAGE OF OLD BOB AND ELLEN GOODLOE,
AND THE SADLY SHORT LENGTH OF THEIR NUPTIALS,
ALONG WITH PART OF MR. DORSET'S POEM ON THE OCCASION
AND A SECTION FROM JENNY DORSET'S DIARY.

For some time, as the reader knows, Old Bob had been pursuing Ellen Goodloe, still trying to say his couplet and still getting it wrong on every occasion. For a long while, she rebuffed him, but sometime that fall, before we had moved back out to Longacre, her affections began to turn in response to his considerate and gentlemanly attentions. By that winter, when Abel was imprisoned, they had become quite close, and she and Bob often spent time in the kitchen attending to the dishes at length and speaking and laughing with their heads close. The sight was touching to me, for it reaffirmed that love knows no boundaries, either age or circumstance. I was therefore very pleased and not entirely surprised when one evening they announced that they were to be wed. The family had eaten and was in the parlor, Mr. Dorset smoking his pipe and reading a book.

"Wed?" said Mr. Dorset. "Wed? Bless me, a happy occasion! We need a happy occasion at Longacre!"

Jenny seemed amused and yet overwhelmed with happiness for them. Isaac hardly looked up from his book, but Matthew began to applaud. Ellen Goodloe smiled as if she were a young woman, and Bob bowed deeply and then had to be helped back up by myself and his betrothed. The announcement did indeed bring joy and light back into a sad and quiet house, and Mr. Dorset and Jenny threw themselves into preparations for the wedding as if it were a royal occasion. Jenny in particular had great fun planning music and decorations, and Bob and Ellen were made to feel as if *they* were Dorsets. Such attentions are only part of why living with and working for the Dorsets was a fine place to spend one's life, and yet another reason why I was inclined to report this History.

The day finally arrived in late January when the weather was cold and drear, with a steady rain falling. The house was warm and cheerful, however, and Jenny had decorated it with garlands and the family's best porcelain. I assigned myself to help Old Bob dress, and I never in all the years I knew him saw him so frightened and yet so cheerful at the same time. It took some time to get him into a suit of clothes that Ellen had altered from one owned previously. It consisted of a dark green waistcoat and matching trousers with white silk stockings and a ruffled blouse that Ellen had ironed until it was quite stiff. Bob's wig was powdered and then shaken off so that none of the dust would soil his fine clothing.

Mr. Dorset had brought Rev. Thomas Boles to Longacre for the occasion, a genial subminister at St. Michael's, where he rarely was allowed to perform weddings or much of anything else. As far as I could tell, this Boles was in charge of begging for money, though he sometimes sang rather well. He was very short and fat, with red cheeks that drooped down over his collar and one eye which seemed somewhat independent of the other. He also had a particularly bad limp, for one leg was perhaps two inches shorter than the other. Whether this was from some injury or a misfortune of birth I did not know, but when he walked, his step was heavily steered to his left and shorter leg, as if he were a sailor just off a ship after a storm.

Mr. Dorset was kind enough to invite not only all the service staff but a number of his friends from the area, including the Smythes, who, having nothing else to do in January, arrived in a grand new brougham that bore a large S on the doors. Though the driver was soaked, Mr. and Mrs. Smythe, along with Hamlet and Iago, arrived dry. They were dressed so finely they put everyone else to shame, and that was clearly the idea behind it, which Mr. Dorset noticed right away.

"Waugh! Look at the fop and his whore," Mr. Dorset said as we peered through the parlor window watching guests arrive. "And their bastards as well. I believe we may see some merrymaking yet."

"Sir, it is the occasion for Bob and Ellen," I said modestly. "Perhaps we might allow the battle to be moderate and tempered today."

"Perhaps," he said. Then, as he turned away, "Or perhaps not. Some things are not in my control."

And with that, he welcomed his foe as if he were the King of France, complete with solicitations and commiseration. In his turn, Mr. Smythe spoke softly of Mrs. Dorset and clasped Mr. Dorset's arms and then patted him on the back. Mr. Dorset left the room briefly, and as I took his cloak, I heard Mr. Smythe say to his wife, "See how overdecorated this pigsty is? No one has worse taste than Dorset."

Reverend Boles was hopping around the room, meeting people and drinking punch which was not to have been consumed before the service. It had been liberally stoked with rum, and already Reverend Boles' jowls were turning pinker by the minute, and his laugh was too loud. He was certainly enjoying the attention that a subminister never received, and with it came an overestimation of his capacity for company and punch.

Soon, Jenny began to play the spinet, and she had progressed so far in her studies that her playing was like an angel playing upon a harp. Along with her dazzling beauty, she entirely took the attention away from the wedding. If she had sung, I believe no one would have recalled the occasion at all, but finally she stopped and watched as Old Bob and Ellen Goodloe came into the room for their nuptials.

Bob's wig was already askew, and Ellen stopped briefly to right it, but she only managed to turn it so Bob's ear was partially covered, which was unfortunate, since he was almost deaf anyway. Ellen wore a blue gown, and though her age was in no wise covered by the womanly art of cosmetics, she looked quite nice, and I felt a deep pleasure, as I am sure the others did as well. The room was so filled with men and women that it was quite warm, and so I opened a window to allow air to blow in and cool us.

"Now, now, let us come together, Christian men and women, for the servey," said Reverend Boles.

"Survey?" said Mr. Dorset, who stood not far from me. "Did he say survey?"

I knew that Reverend Boles meant "service," and I saw instantly that he was too intoxicated to perform the event. He kept shifting back and forth from his long to his short leg, and I saw Matthew Dorset beginning to imitate him, as if it were a new dance step to be coveted.

"In the name of the Lord Jesus Christ, amen," said Reverend Boles.

"Amen," said the group.

As the Reader knows, the Church has a regular service for weddings, and all of us had seen it enough to know the words well, if not entirely by heart. And so I was startled to hear that Reverend Boles immediately deviated both from tradition and Church law in his enthusiasm for being given such a sacred task, instead of merely singing or raising pounds for St. Michael's.

"Now, I should like to speak of the wedding feast at Canna that our Lord attended," said Reverend Boles.

"A meddling beast?" said Old Bob, cupping his ear and looking confused.

"Wedding feast!" shouted Ellen in his ear.

"I'll serve, then," said Old Bob, and he turned and began to head for his accustomed station, and would no doubt have gone outside to the kitchen if we had not turned him around and pointed him back toward Ellen, who, rather than being distraught, seemed amused and loving toward him. For his part, Reverend Boles appeared confused and was not sure what to say next.

"Where was I, then?" he asked.

"You were going to begin the service proper," said Mr. Smythe.

"*Mais oui,*" said Mr. Dorset, trying to show his erudition to the crowd.

"May we *what?*" said Reverend Boles. By now, it was clear that he had badly overestimated his ability to hold his punch, and he shifted back and forth from leg to leg so much that I was afraid he would plunge headlong into the fire at any moment. At the same time, I was startled to hear, from the front of the house, Mr. Dorset's pack of hounds, which someone had released.

"*Proceed,*" said Mr. Dorset.

"Indeed," said Reverend Boles.

"Ah, there's a perfect rhyme," said Mr. Dorset. "That is an omen of good luck."

The Reverend Boles by now looked quite ill, and began to mumble the service as rapidly as he could, forgetting all about the wedding feast at Canna, which was just as well, as the room was so hot, even with the windows opened to the rain and cold, that the guests were beginning to perspire freely. As the service proceeded I opened the front door a bit, and the air seemed to circulate more properly, which was a blessing, for Reverend Boles soon became lost in the liturgy, and it was clear to all involved that he had entirely forgotten the wedding service and was wandering in circles, desperately hoping that he might recall the words. Finally, hopeless and embarrassed, Reverend Boles put his Bible under his arm and rubbed his face and began simply to ask Bob and Ellen if they agreed to take each other in wedlock, and if they knew that this was a Holy State. Ellen said that she knew it was.

"A snake, did he say?" asked Bob. Mr. Smythe, to whom Bob seemed to direct the question, became convulsed with laughter, which he tried to withhold as mannerly as he could, but without success. I looked around the room for Jenny, and my eye found her leaning against the wall, shaking silently and beating a doorjamb with her small fist.

"A holy state!" cried Reverend Boles. "A holy state! Holy state! Marriage is a . . ." He then stopped. "Oh what the h—l."

The crowd gasped, but Mr. Dorset enjoyed the breach of propriety enormously, as did Jenny. Finally, Reverend Boles pronounced the vows, which Bob and Ellen repeated without incident, and he reported them husband and wife according to the holy laws of the Church. Just as Bob was leaning to kiss his bride, a most astonishing thing happened. A large and very wet hare appeared in the room and ran through the crowd, which parted as it hopped around. As I saw it, I had a shiver of knowledge and ran for the door, entirely too late, for after I had taken two steps, the entire madly barking host of wayward hounds came storming into the house and straight into the parlor, as if they had been trained to do so for the marriage.

"Waugh! *Canus marriagus est!*" cried Mr. Dorset. Those were the only intelligible words, for the women began to scream as the men tried without success to herd the dogs out. The poor hare took refuge at first under a chair and then it ran directly under Mrs. Ophelia Van Dyke Smythe's long and fine dress. She shrieked. As Mrs. Smythe tried to move away from the hare, it clung to her feet and beneath her dress, and the hounds bayed and leaped at her as her husband tried valiantly to keep them away, kicking and shouting. Unable to contain herself, Jenny leapt into the middle of the fight, falling to the floor and lifting Mrs. Smythe's dress so that her undergarments were exposed briefly, to the surprise of the women and delight of the men. Ellen Goodloe was very angry at having her nuptials thus interrupted, but Old Bob merely tried to herd the hounds outside as was his duty in such situations.

Jenny came up shortly, holding the trembling rabbit and kicking the dogs, which were yapping and barking around her. The ones who could not get closest bayed intolerably, and the poor hare held to Jenny as a small baby might to its mother. Jenny swore in a way that dishonored her, but I knew nothing could change that girl or her course in life. At least she did not try to present herself as other than she was.

"Get the thing to the kitchen!" shouted her father. "We shall have it for dinner!"

"I shall die first!" cried Jenny, and she ran upstairs. It was only with the heaviest exertion that Mr. Smythe and I, along with a few others, turned the rout and managed to get the dogs out of the parlor and into the yards, from whence they immediately ran into the woods, carrying their terrible racket and stench with them.

Mrs. Smythe cried and heaved a bit, not because she was hurt but because she was humiliated, and I did not blame her husband for coming to her defense.

"D—n you, Dorset, your dogs are an abomination!" shouted Mr. Smythe.

"I know," said Mr. Dorset with a broad grin. "Magnificent, eh?"

And so the wedding of Old Bob and Ellen Goodloe was the event which finally brought the house entirely out of mourning, for it was, like other things, so gone terribly awry that it was entirely as Mr. Dorset would have liked. Unfortunately, God in His wisdom had another idea about how the event should play out, and though I cannot question His plan or His magnificence, I have always regretted the necessity (if it be such) of what transpired next.

Old Bob was truly in bliss through the coldest part of the winter, and he and Ellen Goodloe were inseparable, working in the kitchen, at table, and walking on the estate. Often, she would straighten his wig or gently clean something from his lapels before they served, and I never saw a more pleasing sight than those two old people so much in love. Jenny also approved and spoke of them fondly and admired their affection. (She had tried to keep the hare as a pet, but when it became too unruly or when she became bored with it, as the case may be, she turned it over to one of the servants, and Mr. Dorset ate it with a bottle of Portuguese wine.) Soon, however, the grippe and catarrh began to claim dozens of victims in Town, and it was only a matter of time before those dread diseases made it to the plantations. While yellow fever was a summer illness, pneumonia visited us when the rains came.

Now Ellen Goodloe was a strong woman with an iron will and a sturdy body, so we were all quite surprised when she was the first of the house to come down with a coughing disorder, which, despite attentions from the best physicians in Town (at Mr. Dorset's expense, of course), grew worse as the days progressed, so bad in fact that she was unable to work and took to her bed. Bob was in desperate condition, attending to her tenderly and alternately asking me if I thought she would be well and praying beside her bed on his knees. On more than one occasion, I had to help Bob up from the floor where he had knelt, for his legs would not lift him on their own. We attended to Ellen as well as we might, but in the end, God had His plan, and we could only watch, wait, and make her as comfortable as possible.

In late January, she seemed strikingly better one day, and we all rejoiced. She sat up in bed and gave orders to the sub-cook, and each of us came in to see her in bed, which though indelicate was not really improper, as she was old and heavily clothed beneath her covers to prevent a chill. The next day, however, she awoke in a delirium, and during the day it was clear that she was sinking toward death. I recall that a heavy rain fell, and the temperature was so cold that some of the slaves felt a snow might come, though it never did. Old Bob was at first inconsolable, but as the day waned, he seemed to accept that his wife was dying, and she suffered so that I do believe he prayed that God would take her, which He finally did just before six in the evening.

Our house was thus thrown again into deep mourning, and Bob took it badly. Despite support from Jenny and myself, Bob was too miserable to do much as we prepared yet another grave at Longacre. The world seemed smaller without Ellen Goodloe, for she brought order with her, and the Dorset household needed order brought to it, as it had little from Nature with which to deal.

The funeral was on a cloudy, wind-swept day, with a threat of rain never far away. Matthew, Isaac, and I, along with Mr. Dorset, Tom McNew, and Ellen Goodloe's brother, Thomas, from Town, were pallbearers. We laid her to rest in the soft cold earth, and on the way back to the house, Old Bob wept like a child, wrenching us all, but especially Jenny, who was dissolved in tears, not for Ellen, whom she had never known that well, but for Bob, who was always so vulnerable in his too human failings that we protected him from the world as well as we might. Later that day, I visited Bob in the quarters he had shared with his wife. He sat on the edge of the bed looking at his hands, without a fire lit or a candle for light against the dreary day. I built a fire for him, and the small room warmed, though it took half an hour to do so, then I lit the candles in the inexpensive candle holders that were common at Longacre. The room was warmer and brighter but no more cheerful.

"I cannot go on living," said Old Bob. "For she was my life, Henry. I spent all these years in search of someone, and now after three-month she is taken from me. What kind of God would punish me so for being a faithful servant to Him and to my family here? What kind of God would do that?"

"Faith is a delicate commodity, old friend," I said. "I often find mine tested, as when my child was stillborn a few years back."

"Seems I recall that," said Bob.

"We can never know in this life what events mean or what might happen next, and so I suppose that is why we must live as if each dawn were our last on this earth," I said. "We must listen for what is real and true and praise it. There is no need to live afraid of the world as so many do, for if there is consolation afterward, God surely meant there to be consolation here as well."

Bob stopped looking at his hands and scanned the room.

"Everything is changed, even how these walls look upon me," he rasped. "If God has mercy, He will take me to my Ellen and give me the consolation of Death."

"We cannot question the plans of the Almighty," I said. "We must simply endure and go on."

"We must endure any pain?" he asked.

"We must," I said. "Mr. Dorset has lost his wife to Death and his son to gaol all at the same time," I said. "And he endures."

"That's true," said Bob. "And you have lost that child."

"I have," I said. "And Jenny has lost a mother. And Mr. Smythe has lost his son Fortinbras and his good servant Diana Seton. Each of us in turn must love this life, for I believe that is what God intends. And when it is over, we stand before Him as humble servants, king and commoner alike. The difference is that you shall be better prepared, for your life has been in service, just as was your wife's."

Bob brightened and turned toward me.

"Upon my word, Henry, that is a thing I have never thought about," he said. "We who serve will also be servants unto God in Heaven, and what would God have more need of than a good and faithful servant?"

"He would have more need of nothing," I said. Bob got up and threw another log on the fire, and wiped his hands carelessly on his coat. He looked around the room and smiled a bit.

"What time is the Master's dinner, then?" he asked. And with that, he let go of the worst part of his grief, the kind that wrenches and tears, and though in his quiet moments I could see him lost in thought and with soft regrets for his loss, he never again wept so deeply, that I saw, or felt sorry for himself. I will not flatter myself that my words healed Bob, for the art of healing begins within, as all men find out sooner or later if they are to survive. But in some manner I turned him away from grief, and for that skill I can claim no native talent but only that God directed my words.

Besides Old Bob, no one in the family was more stricken than Jenny. She never lived in the shallows of her emotions but in the deep water, where one might rise to see the sun or moon or sink for hours to the sea floor. In that, she was like her father, of course, though moreso. And I believe her brothers would have been more like him, if they were not restrained by convention, which they saw everywhere but in their own house. Abel was not a bad young man, only one who wished to have his father's power and failed to find it (at that time anyway). Isaac was more at home with figures and business, which were concrete and kept away the emotions that kept the house lively. Matthew felt those emotions keenly but could not keep them balanced and so was reduced to occasional mild outbursts. Jenny Dorset, however, felt no restraints either on her passions or her grief, and that made her quite attractive to men and women, for they saw in her what they might be if they could simply let go of what restrained them.

Jenny spoke to me only once about Ellen Goodloe, and said that she was sad that Old Bob had lost his wife. I was therefore most surprised when I found an entry in her diary that bespoke much deeper feelings than I suspected.

February 12, 1772

Miss Goodloe dead! Oh this world is sometime a wretched place! I cannot think of her now but I also think of the grave and its narrow sides and know that we all must fall into that pit. I cannot understand how people settle themselves into a life in which nothing transpires. I cannot bear it. Isaac has been a beast about Miss Goodloe's passing and Matthew will not talk of it yet seems affected all the same. I must see my friend Desdemona Smartt and ask how one should feel in the presence of such a thing. I know that for my own mother I felt terribly bad. But it is almost worse, for I knew that my Father would go on with his life, and I am unsure that Old Bob may with his. I have never seen one so crushed by the weight of grief. My Mr. Hawthorne has comforted me, but I walk in the countryside on sunny days and I think how life should be, and I do not see it spent in labour or toil only. I believe that one should rise and live so that Death, in his admiration, delays his harvest until he cannot avoid it any more. We have been once to see poor Abel in jail, and he is hard and does not repent his thrashing of Mr. Pinkworthy. There was a scandal, of course, but Father has chosen to rise above it and ignore those who have questioned our house. Molly and Tom McNew are animals. I wish some days that I understood more of this world, and on others, I wish only to live and fear nothing.

If Jenny was transparent in her diaries, her father was equally forthright in his poetry. He came to me one morning with bleary eyes and inkstained fingers, his clothes unkempt and a smile on his unshaven face.

"Henry, I have made a most astonishing discovery!" he cried. Isaac walked through the room, took one look at his father, and made a face of grave distaste and disappeared up the stairs.

"Really, sir," I said. "And what might that be?" He rubbed the hair back from his forehead, smearing it with the fresh ink that covered his hands.

"I have found something entirely new in verse!" he said. "It came to me in the middle of the night like a phantom. I believe it shall mark my entry into the sacred halls of English verse!" (I must tell the Reader that by "English" he did not mean the language but the country of England, a goal that always loomed for him as Jerusalem does for a pilgrim. He felt that once his verse was well known in England, that country would so delight in his presence that he would arrive a hero in London. All this, despite the dark feelings already rising in the Colonies against England.)

"How wonderful," I said. "Might you explain it to me, sir?"

"It is the echo, the sound of words coming back as off a great precipice, so that each line is increased in its majesty and is placed squarely in Nature."

"Echo verse," I said. "That is something of which I have never heard, sir."

"Of course you haven't heard of it!" he cried joyously. "It was a gift to me in the night from the Muse. Oh, I am beloved of her who inspires men to great heights of thought!" Without meaning any disrespect to my Master, I can say that no more unfortunate, untrue, or impossible sentence ever escaped the man's lips.

"We cannot question why we are the vessels of inspiration," I said.

"Most true," he said. He looked at me expectantly, and I knew my next lines, as if we were in a play at the Orpheum. He wanted me to ask him to read some of the verse from his great discovery, but we were interrupted by Jenny, who came into the room in a storm, face flushed with anger. She came to her father and stamped her foot so hard a vase on a small table toppled and would have shattered had I not been standing nearby and able to catch it.

"What is it, my dear?" asked Mr. Dorset. She looked at her father's disarray, the ink on his fingers and his face, his clothes, the sheaf of poetry in his stained fingers, and also, I think, saw the open honesty, the lack of guile, the genuine love he held for her, and the worry she had caused him to feel. She looked at him and snorted out a small laugh, then looked at me, and though I tried to betray no mirth, she saw perhaps the barest twinkle in my eye, and she smiled in spite of herself.

"The stallion you bought as friend to my mare has betrayed her and serviced another of the herd," she said.

Mr. Dorset at first was amazed at the words, then decided to say something that would be fatherly and wise, for he nodded in a knowing way.

"Then perhaps it is love," he said.

"Love!" Jenny fairly exploded. "They are horses, not human beings."

"And who knows but that horses cannot love," he said. "Who knows that pigs may not love, that worms or snakes may not love? Because we do not speak their language does not mean that in their privacies they do not speak of love."

"This is madness," said Jenny, looking at me for confirmation and receiving none.

"Certainly not," said her father. "Do you not see the dogs fight to the death in their anger? Have you not heard of a bear chasing a man? If they feel such anger, why should they not feel love as well?"

"Is this your answer to the question, that the stallion has fallen in love with another mare besides mine?" she asked.

"Love, or perhaps another of its kindred emotions," Mr. Dorset said. "I shall speak to Mr. Cleghorn." Cleghorn was the overseer of the animals, a slovenly man with an erratic temper who was rather good at working animals except for the pack of hounds, which remained wild and disobedient.

"What is that?" asked Jenny, pointing to the papers in his hand.

"Ah, my dear, it is the great poetic discovery of the age, which shall make me famous in England," he said. "They shall honor me when I arrive in London."

"The English are bloody fools," she said.

"You judge them too quickly for the actions of Parliament," he said.

"Perhaps we should reserve judgment until more transpires or at least until they have had a chance for my arrival."

"Tory," she said. And she turned and walked out of the room. Mr. Dorset looked at me with astonishment.

"Why would she have said that?" he asked. "I fear the absence of her mother is allowing her to grow a bit wild."

I wanted to reply that it was not the absence of her mother that affected her but the presence of her father, but we in service learn in our youth to think clearly and speak as little as possible, for in that we appear to agree with ideas that no man could find agreeable at all. And so I merely looked inquisitive, as if I wanted to hear more. He took that as a sign to begin reading, but before he could, there was a tremendous crash in the hallway, and both of us ran to the scene to find poor Old Bob lying on the floor amid the debris of a tray, which had been carrying tea.

"I seem to have found that slick spot yet again," he said helplessly. The dark tea ran the length of the boards toward the back of the house.

"Bob, are you hurt?" I asked. He touched his arms and legs and said he did not believe so. His wig, however, was twisted over his eye and, as it had recently been powdered, the dust from it covered his face and clothing.

"Sir, I am sorry that I have spoilt the tea," he said. "I shall fetch another tray."

"Blast tea, Bob," said Mr. Dorset. "Are you well?"

Bob looked at Mr. Dorset's disarray and then asked his Master the same question. Mr. Dorset replied that he was, and so we helped Bob up just as Molly McNew came into the house and saw Bob, then looked at us as if she had tried to stop him and failed.

"Who requested tea?" I asked.

"I believe it was Mrs. Dorset," he said. He looked at Molly and then back at me for some understanding or confirmation, but all I felt was a terrible sadness at his predicament.

"Oh mercy," said Mr. Dorset. "God help my Lyddie."

"Bob," I said gently, "Mrs. Dorset has passed away. You remember. Who else might have asked for tea?"

A great cloud seemed to arrive over Bob's features, and I put my hand on his shoulder as Molly began to clean up the tea.

"I suppose it was no one then," he said. "What on earth was I thinking, Mr. Hawthorne, that I brought tea to someone passed away?"

"Do not worry, old fellow," said Mr. Dorset, "for I still speak to her myself as if she were still alive. It is very hard to let go of those you love, so hard that they seem very real for the longest time after you know you shall never see them again this side of Heaven."

"I suppose I am mistaken," Bob said. He tried to right his wig and only placed himself in further disarray. Molly placed the tray to one side and took Bob by the arm after giving me a meaningful look, then escorted him out the back of the main house and toward his quarters. The hallway was suddenly very quiet, and Mr. Dorset's features seemed lost in the shadows.

"That was a very fine thing you said to Bob," I said, "if you will forgive my saying so."

"How hard it is to be lost," he said.

"Now, to your verse," I said. "I should very much like to hear this echo effect of which you have spoken with such enthusiasm."

"I may speak of it later," he said, "but for now, I cannot bring myself to think of anything but my Lydia."

He handed me the sheaves and went outside to attend his mourning, and though I was somewhat mournful myself at that time, Mr. Dorset's poem was so ill-conceived and structured, so genuine and so lengthy that I felt better almost instantly. I shall not try the Reader's patience by reporting the entire poem, which was called simply *Ellen Goodloe*, for it went on for some forty pages and virtually all of it was untrue, just as were Mr. Dorset's stories of our sojourns among the Indians and during our wreck at sea. I cannot say if Mr. Dorset really thought them true, for he was usually an honest man, but I believe he saw truth as merely another part of a story that had no more nor less import than excitement and adventures. Jenny, as we have already seen, shared that trait. I shall, however, report the first few quatrains so the Reader can gauge for himself Mr. Dorset's great discovery of the poetic echo.

ELLEN GOODLOE

She came to Longacre in the years of our plenty
(our plenty)
She was a young girl but two and twenty.
(and twenty)
Her name was not Peggy or Ann or Louise
(Louise)
And in service, the woman took all her ease.
(her ease)

Like Mary Magdalene who served Mother Mary
(Mother Mary)
Her movements were like those of a little fairy.
(little fairy)
She was in no wise unpleasant or thin
(or thin!)
And she had this thing that grew on her chin.
(on her chin)

From those few lines I believe the Reader can judge that as the years passed, Mr. Dorset's Muse had not abandoned him, to our great misfortune, and I cannot guess which Muse he followed, unless it was the Muse of Humor. Yet so strongly did Mr. Dorset believe in that Muse that he was happy and did not care what anyone might say of his works, which is a quality that we all should desire.

— 12. —

HOW THE BATTLE BETWEEN MR. CHARLES SMYTHE AND
MR. ADAM DORSET ONCE AGAIN HEATS UP, ALONG WITH A FIGHT
BETWEEN MATTHEW DORSET AND IAGO SMYTHE. JENNY DORSET'S
REACTION TO THE AFOREMENTIONED, WHICH ASTONISHES EVERYONE.

For the remainder of that winter, to our great relief, Mr. Dorset let go of his literary and musical labors and worked as a plantation owner once more, studying the steady rise of indigo and ordering even more planted, along with our continuing harvest of rice. He also invested in a ship called *The Endeavor*, which would make shipments less expensive and make him even wealthier. Though so many of Mr. Dorset's plans were stillborn, he did know how to make the plantation run, and his wealth increased steadily, even dramatically, in the coming years.

The season from winter through spring was the social time in Town, and Mr. Dorset attended several balls and joined the Tuesday Night Club, but he did not need to be rescued from any of these events. The death of his wife appeared to have tempered him somewhat, but I found that his nature, while subdued that winter, reasserted itself in the spring, and I cannot say that I was sorry for it.

That spring, with the crops growing splendidly and *The Endeavor* plowing the seas, Mr. Dorset finally decided to cease his agricultural labors and pay a visit to Mr. Charles Smythe at Foxhaven. Why he decided to do so remains a mystery to me, and even moreso why Matthew Dorset decided to accompany him. I believe now that for Mr. Dorset and Mr. Smythe, each was like an itch which must be scratched, and which, after a long time, is missed if it is not present. Jenny was in Town that day, accompanied by Tom McNew, who was under my strictest orders not to let her out of his sight but to allow her some leeway in her actions, as doing otherwise was nigh impossible.

I went along to Foxhaven as Mr. Dorset's bodyservant, and it was on one of those days when Carolina seems a paradise granted by God, with gentle breezes, a warmth that feels like a kiss upon the skin, and a sky so blue and bright it dazzles all the senses. Matthew and Mr. Dorset rode their horses side by side, and I hung behind them, despite Mr. Dorset's entreaties that I come alongside him. I never felt comfortable being beyond my state in life, and Mr. Dorset knew it and finally let it lie. Matthew also asked me to ride beside him, but I only smiled and shook my head. Neither Abel nor Isaac ever asked me to ride alongside them. Jenny rode her horse only rarely, but I stayed with her out of fear for her safety and because she would not ride unless I was with her.

And so we crossed the countryside, including the disputed three feet of property (which were still in dispute, the lawsuit having become a fond game between the men that neither was inclined to give up). We finally arrived at Foxhaven, which was alive with activity, with slaves working the rice and indigo, along with servants in the house garden, which was coming along nicely.

Mr. Smythe was standing near the house peering at a shrubbery and shouting at a cowed servant who seemed to have done something wrong. Alongside Mr. Smythe was his son Iago, who at the time was about twenty-one years of age and seemed to have assumed the qualities of his namesake. While Mr. Smythe was dressed properly and comfortably, his son was in silks and finery and stood too tall and had on his face a look entirely of contempt for everything around him. Matthew was a year younger than Iago and the contrast could not have been more striking, for Matthew was at his ease and open and unhurried. He seemed to be everything that Iago was not, without much intelligence, to be sure, but still with a kindness and calmness that was attractive in a young man. I often thought that if Jenny had possessed some of those qualities her life might have turned out differently.

"Look at him befouling the gardener," said Mr. Dorset. "Bah! What a thing to do in the presence of his son, as it were." Then, with his hand to his mouth, Mr. Dorset said, "Not that the son amounts to much."

As we rode up, Mr. Smythe turned as he saw us and his expression was one a painter might have captured, for his face showed he felt amusement, exasperation, scheming, disgust, and, I believe, not a small amount of pleasure, as if he were engaged in a game of chess and felt the winning move was within his reach.

"Dorset," said Mr. Smythe, "have you come to learn how a proper grounds should look?"

"I have indeed come to learn," said Mr. Dorset. "I wish to find out how you make such a lovely piece of ground into such a wreck." We swung down from our horses, and several servants came and took them to tie up. Mr. Dorset and Mr. Smythe shook hands as they always did, and Matthew offered his hand to Iago, who took it lightly, as if smelling something unpleasant, and, after shaking it once, dropped it with overly polite disdain.

"Would you like a toddy?" asked Mr. Smythe, "or have you reached your limit of spirits for the day already?"

"I have no limit on spirits," said Mr. Dorset, "though I understand your inability in that regard and honor it by declining your polite offer."

"Then may I offer you fresh water to clean your face, as it seems some days since you have had time to do so," said Mr. Smythe.

"Judging by your own person, I should say that fresh water is somewhat lacking at this plantation, and I would not want to deplete you of what little remains," said Mr. Dorset.

"You cannot address my father in that manner!" cried Iago.

"Certainly he may," said Mr. Smythe. "Mind your manners, boy. If those at Longacre have no couth, that does not mean we should catch the same disorder."

"I have more couth that the entire household of Foxhaven combined," said Mr. Dorset. "Don't I, Hawthorne?"

"As you say, sir," I said with a nod.

"A servant to insult me?" cried Iago. "I shall not stand for this! Father, have them thrown off the land, including the three feet which remains ours to this day!"

"Why would it matter if you had another three feet," said Matthew mildly. "You would make ill use of it as you do the rest of your acreage."

"Father, have them thrown off our land!" shouted Iago.

"He was not speaking to me," said Mr. Smythe, by now quite interested in the chess moves among the four men. Both he and Mr. Dorset had the same expression.

"Mind your manners," said Mr. Dorset to his son.

"What manners?" said Iago.

"Apologize to my father this instant!" cried Matthew.

"Father, throw them off the land!" said Iago.

"They are our guests," said Mr. Smythe. "Why should I?"

"Well said, Smythe," said Mr. Dorset.

"At your service," said Mr. Smythe.

"This is madness!" screamed Iago. "This insult is intolerable, and even if my father will not stand up against it, I shall!"

"Mind your manners!" said Mr. Smythe.

"What manners?" said Matthew.

At this point, Mr. Smythe turned to Mr. Dorset in amazement and asked if this might perhaps be some musical form in which the conversation proceeded, and Mr. Dorset, face alight, averred that it certainly might be just such a thing. They both seemed pleased by the discovery, but Iago was by then in a rage that could not be withheld.

"Tell us where you went when you disappeared," said Iago with blunt sarcasm. "Was it to the bosom of some whore in town so that you might purchase what your nature would not allow you to receive free?"

"Waugh!" cried Matthew. "You speak as if you are expert in the subject."

"I am not expert in the subject!" said Iago. "I only know that weak men have weak minds and weak hearts and that other parts of them as well must be weak!"

"You speak as if you are expert in the subject," said Matthew.

"Well spoken," said Mr. Dorset.

"D—d if it wasn't," said Mr. Smythe. He and Mr. Dorset looked at each other with complete agreement, even pleasure, that the mantle of their battle had been assumed by the new generation and might continue after they were gone.

"You are siding with a Dorset?" screamed Iago. "My own father?"

"I am siding entirely with you," said Mr. Smythe.

"Well spoken," said Mr. Dorset.

"Sir," said Mr. Smythe. By now, I was so bemused by the sight that I wished it could go on for some time, as I saw that the continuing war had as much affection as anger and that when nothing else might do, men would create their own quarrels, even in sport.

"As I am siding with Matthew," said Mr. Dorset.

"I am befuddled!" cried Iago.

"Should that come as a surprise to any of us?" asked Matthew.

Whereupon, Iago hit Matthew on the face with his fist, knocking him to the ground. With the reaction a bear might have to defend its cub, Mr. Dorset without a moment's thought spun Iago around by his shoulder and hit him in the stomach so hard that Iago turned white and fell to his knees, spitting and gasping. In turn, Mr. Smythe then grabbed Mr. Dorset by the arm and hit him square on the jaw and knocked him flat. Not to see that my Master was treated so ill, I caught Mr. Smythe when he was turning away in satisfaction from the scene and struck him a fierce blow on the cheek, which knocked him down and over Mr. Dorset.

"Strike me, you villain!" cried Mr. Dorset.

"Strike my son, you monster!" cried Mr. Smythe.

"Strike me!" shouted Matthew to Iago.

"Strike me!" screamed Iago to Mr. Dorset. Mr. Smythe began to say something but then became confused about whom he should insult and so began to fight with Mr. Dorset on the ground as Matthew and Iago did. I stood back and watched, wondering what consequences might befall me for hitting a wealthy planter, though I really didn't fear for my position because Mr. Smythe would not want to upset the delicate balance between the households. On the ground, the men fought like tygers, not as sport but to hurt the opponent and render him incapable of continuing. All the while, all four men cursed and insulted each other, stood and fell, fought and rolled.

I was looking at the sight with astonishment when Roderigo Smartt came around the house holding a spade with which I presumed he had been gardening. He uttered a gasp and ran to the side of Mr. Smythe and raised the spade over his head. Knowing this could mean a dangerous injury, I fell to my knees and grasped Mr. Dorset by his ankles and pulled him away just as Roderigo came down with his spade, hitting Mr. Smythe flat on top of his head. Mr. Smythe gave a short, deep groan, turned his head as his eyes rolled into his head, and passed out on the grass.

"Oh dear," said Roderigo. He ran off around the house. Iago, who had been occupied with his own battle, saw Mr. Dorset scrambling to his feet and Mr. Smythe lying on the grass without moving.

"Fiend!" Iago screamed.

"Fiend?" said Mr. Dorset.

"Villain," said Mr. Smythe, sitting up weakly and then falling back down.

While they untangled the skeins of the argument, I fetched our horses and brought them around and urged Matthew and Mr. Dorset to mount, which they did, though without their best balance.

"This is war, then, between our houses!" cried Iago.

"You are a fine lad," said Mr. Dorset, whereupon he fell off his horse and landed quite hard on his shoulder.

"I shall kill you!" cried Iago. "I shall kill all your family!"

"Was I struck with a spade?" asked Mr. Smythe from his prone position.

"I shall avenge you, Father!" said Iago.

"I hear birds apace," said Mr. Smythe.

I finally got Mr. Dorset back on his horse, and we rode back to Longacre. When we came home, Jenny wanted to hear details of the battle, and Isaac said it was bad for business and left for Town upset with the entire affair.

After she heard of the battle, Jenny began to redden and stood over her father, who was lying in his bed and holding a wet cloth to his face.

"Why do you fight?" she asked.

"What else should I do?" said Mr. Dorset.

"I am leaving, then, for Barbados," she said.

"Waugh," said Mr. Dorset quietly.

She ran from the room, and I went after her and found her downstairs crying. When I asked why, she could not say. She cried for the entire day, and no matter how much Mr. Dorset or I tried to comfort her, she would not stop. Finally, toward evening, she ceased her weeping and seemed quite well again. I wanted to ask her for what she had been weeping, but I did not, though I believed it was that her mother was no longer at Longacre to tell her father how foolish he was.

I should not need say that Iago Smythe did not avenge his father, nor did the battle continue quite so hot for a time, though Mr. Dorset and Mr. Smythe insulted each other in private and in public whenever the occasion arose.

— 13. —

A FEW FINAL COMMENTS CONCERNING EVENTS THAT WERE TO FOLLOW,
ALONG WITH JENNY'S VOW, WHICH PLEASED HER FATHER AND LATER LED
HER INTO NEW ADVENTURES DURING OUR WAR WITH THE BRITISH.

As I said at the beginning of this book of our History, happiness is variable, and during these years we found it proved to us each and every day.
The deaths of Mrs. Dorset, Ellen Goodloe, and Fortinbras Smythe had
changed the world for us. Mr. Dorset, Old Bob, and I had nearly
drowned while going to fetch Jenny from a man who did not exist. And
the family, which should have been scandalized by Jenny's adventures in
Town, did not mind at all (except for Isaac). The imprisonment of Abel
Dorset for assaulting Mr. Pinkworthy the artist had been a terrible pain
for my Master, but he bore it well, and we became ever more wealthy.
And if Mr. Dorset was poor at selecting horseflesh for the races, he was
at least keen in selecting his servants, a boast for which I humbly beg the
Reader's pardon.

Still, above all that, one inevitable force kept pressing upon us in the
Colonies, an anger over unjust taxation policies and a general feeling that
it was time for us to sever our ties with England. In Charles Town, there
was much sympathy for the British, and it took quite some time for the
men to come entirely around to the side of those who wished us free, but
that all changed permanently when the British army invaded Town in
1780 and stayed for two years.

By 1774, the intensity of that argument was getting as hot as a blacksmith's fire. In that year, Mr. Dorset was a ripe fifty-four years of age and
came to be pursued by several women in Town with strange consequences, which I shall report in the next volume of this History. By then
Abel was released from jail and immediately threw himself not into farm-
ing but into the works of the Virginians and their desire for freedom.
Isaac was entirely against a war and fought it with his words and actions
so that later, when we were under siege, he was briefly detained and then
despised until people forgot about it some years later.

I felt that Old Bob would go downhill rapidly after the death of his
wife, but, in truth, something occurred which gave him a kind of second
life, and he was to be with us for several more years, during which time
his presence was a comfort.

Jenny Dorset, meanwhile, went her own way, becoming quite the most beautiful young woman in Charles Town. In that year of 1774, she turned twenty-one years of age and should have been looking for a husband, and Heaven knows that many men paid her court, but she ended by frightening them all away with her independence and plain manner of seeking merriment. To some, her laugh was coarse. To others, she had too many opinions. And some, while enchanted by her presence, found they could live neither with her nor away from her, and so were condemned to live like the wretches in the First Circle of Hell in the *Divina Commedia*.

We might have expected Mr. Dorset and his sons to become involved with our Revolution, but it was less expected that Jenny would play a role that helped us undermine the rule of the hated British.

For myself, I can only say that I continued to serve the house as well as I knew how and that in those years, while sorrow was mixed with happiness, on the whole it was a good life, and it possessed a gentility and lack of care that none of us shall ever seen again, except perhaps in the next life.

The world changes and all of us are left behind in one way or another, but if we live in memory, we outstay the time that God has given us, and, in that sense, the Dorsets, while not achieving immortality, have at least left pleasant memories, and men could certainly do worse.

BOOK V.

— 1. —

A FEW COMMENTS ON THE ISSUES FACING US DURING THE YEARS IN QUESTION, ALONG WITH THE REACTION OF THE DORSET FAMILY TO THEM, PARTICULARLY FROM JENNY.

It would take a far brighter man than I to speak of the events which led up to our late war with England. Still, if this History of the Dorset family is to be complete, I must point out how the events changed the Dorsets, particularly Jenny. As we have seen, even from her girlhood, Jenny was charged with the will to react strongly to public events. During the war with the French and their Indians, she was full of sentiments against all things French. She was sincere, even though she was a child and could not judge issues for herself and was merely echoing what she heard from her father. When she grew up, however, she was able to make sense for herself of the events which unfolded, and she became as angry toward the British as any Son of Liberty.

It took Mr. Dorset much longer than his daughter, however, to come to the realization that the issues with the Mother Country could only be resolved through war. The troubles went back years, but they got worse only in 1767 when, in force of Acts of Parliament, the English seized three of our ships, the *Active*, the *Wambaw*, and the *Brought Island Packet*, the latter two belonging to Mr. Henry Laurens. In retaliation, the citizens forced the Collector of the Customs, Daniel Moore, to leave Town.

Then our Province formed a Plan of Regulation and with it brought forth a Congress of Regulators, which fought the following July with Provincial Authorities at Mars Bluff on the Pee Dee River. The Stamp Act was enacted and then repealed. The country northward in South Carolina, which many called the Back Country, began to fill with citizens who grew tobacco as a crop. By 1774, when the Continental Congress met for the first time, the die was cast, as Shakespeare would have it, and the following year, the first shots were fired at Lexington and Concord.

The Stamp Act, of course, occasioned great speeches from Mr. Dorset, usually to himself, though once or twice in Town at gatherings of those most offended, the wealthy planters. During one such speech he was eloquent and direct, leading several in the crowd to ask him to stand for public office. His second speech, before which he had consumed a great quantity of beer, undid any effect of his first, as his logic was faulty, his allusions incorrect, and a point entirely missing. He had been speaking for nearly three quarters of an hour when someone threw an overripe tomato, which hit him in the face. He thought it was a shot fired by British sympathizers, and when he saw the red all over his clothing, he was certain that he was mortally wounded and that he was a martyr. He was very displeased when he understood the situation from the laughter of the crowd.

But that was early in 1776 when Mr. Dorset spoke, and this book of our History will deal only with the year 1774, when Jenny Dorset was twenty-one years old. By that year, Abel Dorset had been released from prison and had moved into Town, where he was very much involved in the Sons of Liberty. It was the year that Matthew Dorset surprised us all with a decision which was based on his strange disappearance of several years before. And it was the year that two widows in Town began their own war, with Mr. Dorset as the unwilling prize.

In the summer of 1774, if I recall correctly, there was a General Meeting of the People, at which delegates to the Continental Congress were elected. The Town and indeed the Province were in quite a state, and I would like to say that the excitement was confined to men of wealth, but, in truth, history had changed course, and few spoke of anything else but the events unfolding before us. If before, Charles Town had been a city with few morals and overly inclined to the bottle and wenching, now it was a city with a purpose, though, I must report, still with few morals and inclined to the bottle and wenching.

Matthew seemed entirely indifferent to the world changing around him, while Isaac was concerned only with the plantation, our shipments down the Cooper River toward Town, and how much money we were losing due to British policy. We rarely saw Abel. Mr. Dorset was consumed with an oratorio he was composing called *Saul, King of Greece*, at which his sense of art was no stronger than his knowledge of history. Old Bob's health was never entirely restored after the death of his wife, but if his heart was broken, his body managed to keep working, and in 1774 he was a ripe seventy-seven years of age. Mr. Dorset and his continual nemesis, Mr. Charles Smythe, were well into their fifties, and in that year I turned forty-nine myself.

I do not remember the month, but it was in 1774 that Jenny came walking rapidly into the parlor one morning as I was dusting and making all things right after an episode the evening before, during which Mr. Dorset and a number of his hunting friends had become quite ill with rum while talking not of the Crown but of their adventures. Hardly a man there believed Mr. Dorset's stories, which was only fair since he had invented them all. But as Mr. Pope has noted, "*[A] lie which shall not die can, in the mind of its fomenter, become the truth, and from thence he cannot tell the difference.*" Jenny was furious when she entered the room wearing a beautiful blue dress, her yellow hair set off with a ribbon of blue fabric. She held a closed fan in her hand and was hitting her other hand with it in the manner men will do with a riding crop to reinforce a point.

"It will not do!" she cried. "It simply will not do!"

"Pardon?" I said.

"I have thought about this insolence from the Crown, Hawthorne, and about how they insult us, and I have decided that it will not do," she said. "Are we cattle that we should let them herd us around with their Acts and seizures? Are we so weak that we cannot stand for ourselves and say that this is entirely without reason and shall not be tolerated?"

"It should be a terrible fight," I said, sweeping up hair from the dogs, several of which had also attended the gathering the evening before.

"And one which must be made!" she cried. At that, her father, undone by rum and a lack of sleep, came running down the stairs in his nightgown, hair standing up all over his head, looking more like a spectre than a man. Jenny, who on other occasions would have laughed, was so worked up over the Crown that she looked at her father, shook her head, and turned away.

"What is the matter?" asked Mr. Dorset. Then he suddenly shouted to Our Lord to help him, and he put both hands on his head and leaned against a wall, knocking off a picture of a hunting scene. (The Reader may be interested to know that the house still possessed Mr. Pinkworthy's portrait of Abel, but it was stored away in case the son ever returned and became angered by it again.)

"The Crown is mad, and we are doing nothing to gainsay it!" shouted
Jenny, whirling about to him and pointing with her fan.

"Please lower your voice, dear," said Mr. Dorset. "I feel an ague coming on."

"I have thought about it, and it is intolerable!" she cried, stamping her
foot. "It is entirely intolerable, and I shall do something about it! I shall
raise arms against the Crown, and shoot the first one who puts his scurvy
face near mine."

"Hawthorne, is that treason?" Mr. Dorset asked, still leaning against
the wall.

"I believe so, sir," I said.

"Very well, then, very well," he said, waving and then heading slowly
back upstairs, groaning with every step. If Mr. Dorset was disinterested
then and unwell, Jenny's passion had only begun to blaze, and she railed
for nearly an hour against the British, the House of Lords, indifferent
planters in Carolina, and all punitive Acts which had caused us all grief.
I kept cleaning but stayed facing her so that she would see my interest,
which was far more in her beauty and fire than in her arguments, which
were, after all, standard fare for many a street-corner orator in Town,
some of which Jenny had heard during her frequent visits.

"I cannot bear this and so will act," she said finally.

"What will you do?" I asked. She walked around the room waving her
fan and thinking. I saw through the open windows the horse of Mr.
Dorset's failed glory at the track escaping from its cursing handler and
trotting off down the road. I righted the last of the vases and hung the
hunting picture again in its proper place. Jenny turned to me.

"The Daughters of Liberty!" she cried.

"The Daughters of Liberty?" I said.

"I shall form the Daughters of Liberty and no man shall dare tell us
what we might not do in defense of our home!" she shouted, hand raised.
(I should say here that if anyone in the house should have been exercised
by the villainies of the British, it should have been Mr. Dorset, for the
continual friction had meant the export business for rice and indigo had
gone up and down severely. If it had not been for Mrs. Dorset's early
insistence that Longacre be unencumbered with debt, then I could not
say where we should have been then. As it was, Jenny's anger was from
principle, not business, and so I could only admire her, as her father was
to do in the coming years.)

"I would be careful, at any rate," I said.

She lowered her hand and stared straight at me and said, with an arch smile, "I do not know what is meant by careful." In that, she was at least honest.

— 2. —

MR. DORSET HIRES A NEW HOUSEKEEPER TO REPLACE ELLEN GOODLOE.
WE ALL REGRET IT, BUT MR. DORSET REFUSES TO RENEGE ON
A PROMISE OF EMPLOYMENT UNTIL HE HAS NO CHOICE.

As the Reader will remember, Mr. Dorset had very fine housekeepers in Mrs. Wilson and Ellen Goodloe, and so after a time, during which none of us could bear to think of Ellen and did not wish to sully her memory by hiring a replacement, Mr. Dorset set about to hire one. We interviewed several, including a free black woman who impressed me and Jenny greatly with her letters of reference, her intelligence, and her ingenuity in answering Mr. Dorset's questions, which sometimes had as much to do with classical scholarship as housekeeping. There was only one candidate that Jenny, Old Bob, and I agreed must not be hired, and we were so certain that Mr. Dorset would not take her that we laughed when she was gone and did not counsel against her. And so imagine our frustration and surprise when he hired that selfsame woman, Miss Annie Mackle. She was so tiny that she might have come from a fanciful tale that children are told at bedtime, and she wore what might have been a frown had it been more pleasant. Instead, it was a scowl, which sometimes turned into a fierce hag-like look.

Miss Mackle had never married and so hated that institution with all her heart. She also hated Negroes, Mr. Christopher Gadsden (whose fame the Reader well knows), the idea of independence from England, and just about everything else. She walked so quickly it was something like a trot, and during her tours of the house, she shrieked at the staff with such unpleasantness that everyone avoided her whenever possible. Old Bob could even hear her well in his deafness, and the sound of her voice made him flee the house whenever she entered.

Miss Mackle had a large wen on her nose, small crooked hands, bad teeth, and hair which grew only in small tufts. She took care to hide it under a stern bonnet, however. She also disliked all animals and tried without success to have the dogs all shot as a nuisance to the plantation. In short order, she had disrupted Longacre to the point that we could hardly function. She deferred to Mr. Dorset and his sons (but for Abel, who was in Town), but she constantly tried to tell Jenny how to act and live, assuming that since the young woman no longer had a mother, she was in need of proper counsel. At first, Jenny found her amusing, but as the weeks passed, even Jenny became extremely annoyed by Miss Mackle's constant advice that she never marry and have nothing whatever to do with men. (If there was ever a woman on whom that advice had no effect, it was Jenny Dorset.) Once, she reduced Old Bob to tears for not properly serving tea to Mr. Dorset and the subminister who had married Bob and Ellen Goodloe. The subminister had no real friends or duties in Town, and thought that by closely allying himself with Mr. Dorset he might grow in stature. Mr. Dorset enjoyed these conversations, for he loved to talk philosophy, a subject about which neither man knew a whittle. Still, men will talk at length about what they do not know, and so I could gainsay neither man the pleasure of the act.

One evening, Bob had brought tea for the men. Mr. Dorset was holding forth on the meanings in *The Odyssey* and had just proclaimed that the Cyclops had three eyes because Mr. Homer had meant him to be all-seeing.

"I believe he had four eyes, did he not, eh?" said the subminister.

Just then, Old Bob came stumbling into the room looking at the cups of tea on the tray, and then dumped the entire contents onto the floor, beneath the baleful glance of Miss Mackle at the door. Mr. Dorset and the subminister helped us pick up the mess without stopping their conversation about *The Odyssey*, and I thought little about it until we got to the door and Miss Mackle stood there trembling with rage.

"I will see you in the kitchen!" she said angrily. "Now!"

"Ma'am," said Old Bob, head down. I followed at a distance, and we left the house and went out to the kitchen through a warm rain. I felt terrible for Bob, and it was a mistake that could happen to anyone, but Miss Mackle stomped through the mud toward the kitchen with severe purpose, and I hung outside the window beneath the eaves as I had done when Bob was trying to repeat his couplet to Ellen Goodloe. Miss Mackle scolded Bob severely, as if he had been a small child and had thrown a cat down a well. Bob kept saying "yes'm" over and over, and it near broke my heart to see the old fellow reduced in such a manner. I was startled presently to find Jenny standing quite near me, looking puzzled. I put my finger to my lips and shook my head to indicate that what was transpiring inside was beyond necessity. The bawling out continued, and the more it did, the angrier Jenny became, and she might have stormed inside had I not gently cautioned her that it might be best at this point to let Miss Mackle's anger spend itself. Finally, Bob came out of the kitchen looking bereft and heading for his quarters.

"I shall fix this," said Jenny. And she stormed back into the house. I could not have imagined what she had in mind.

Now it seems that Mr. Dorset had placed a small rug from Asia at the entrance to his library, a rug no more than two feet square but rather pleasant, with a large peacock or some such fowl upon it. Late the following night, Jenny, with my collusion, went to the spot by the light of a single candle and removed the rug. We polished the spot beneath it with oils until it shone. Even though she did not divulge her plan to me, it was obvious enough, and the next morning when she announced that she wished to play the harpsichord for the house that evening, I was not surprised. My job was to make sure that the rug was in place and did not move as I escorted people into the library. Matthew came, as did the McNew twins (though Tom protested), a few of the other house servants, and of course Mr. Dorset. He had labored all day with his Muse and apparently with Bacchus, and so he was in fine spirits, though somewhat loud, when the event was to begin at eight in the evening.

Jenny had dressed in one of her finest gowns, dyed with family indigo, which was of very high quality indeed. The room was bright, the windows let in a brisk breeze, and in all measure it was pleasing. I had stood at the door with my foot on one corner of the rug to make sure that it did not move, though it fairly floated on the pine boards because of the polishing Jenny and I had affected. Everyone was seated before Jenny made her appearance to light applause started by her father, who appeared ready for a diversion from his grand labors of the day.

"Do you know any music by Dorset?" he cried, laughing and nodding. She smiled beautifully at him but said nothing, which was discreet. Matthew didn't understand who Dorset was and kept asking until his father pointed to his own breast and grinned. Matthew laughed, then looked puzzled and shrugged. Old Bob stood in the corner with the other house servants, who normally did not sit at such gatherings, though I was often invited to do so. He still looked fragile and broken to me, and I was more certain than ever that our ruse was proper.

I was still by the door with my foot on the edge of the rug when Jenny sat, raised her hands, and then stopped. She turned on the seat and looked straight at the servants.

"Miss Mackle, is there punch ready?" she said. Miss Mackle curtseyed grimly.

"Yes, Miss, but it is for after the playing of your little pieces, I'm sure," she said.

"I wish a glass of punch before I begin, as my throat is dry," said Jenny.

"Punch!" said Mr. Dorset. "My throat is dry as well. The labors of the poet are great labors indeed and are never done." Miss Mackle smiled unhappily and turned and snapped her fingers at poor Bob, who bowed low.

"Miss Mackle, I'd prefer if *you* went for the punch," said Jenny. The woman was so startled and upset that her face, which normally had the color of cold ashes, began to glow red with pale splotches that made her appearance, already unpleasant, nearly hideous.

"Me, Miss?" she said. "That is not properly my work here."

"Are you denying my request?" asked Jenny. Mr. Dorset turned and looked at Miss Mackle and dreamily awaited her reply.

"I am denying you nothing, child," said Miss Mackle. "It just seems to me that . . ."

"Must I repeat what I wish?" said Jenny, a little louder.

"Yes," said Mr. Dorset. "Must she?"

"No ma'am," said Miss Mackle darkly. "I understand entirely." Of course, she didn't understand entirely at all, and when Jenny stopped and demanded six glasses of punch be brought on a tray, Miss Mackle curtseyed again, then glared at everyone in the room, none more so than Old Bob, who was wringing his hands and unsure what to do next.

In the few minutes that Miss Mackle was gone, Jenny decided to start anyway, and played so sublimely that Mr. Dorset was transported with joy, and I felt the effects myself. Matthew played with a rock he had brought. Isaac was not in the room, having declined the invitation so he could look over ledgers once again, for he was sure that some unnamed villain was cheating Longacre. Soon, I heard Miss Mackle coming in the back door, and I left my position by the rug and entered the room to await developments.

I looked at Jenny, and her face was flushed with anticipation. We both heard Miss Mackle about to enter the room, and Jenny took a breath and waited. As it turned out, we did not have to wait long, for Miss Mackle came walking quickly down the hall muttering to herself. She got to the rug, and our plan worked so amazingly well that for a moment I could hardly believe it.

She came over the threshold, looking irritated and a bit vile, even, for she did not think it was her station to do such work at that moment. When she stepped on the rug in her haste, it seemed to rise and float, so slick was the spot beneath it. The punch flew into the air and when the cups landed they all shattered and their contents sprayed around the room, dousing Matthew and splattering substantially on Mr. Dorset. For a moment there was nothing but silence. I glanced at my co-conspirator, and though I felt sorry at a glance for Miss Mackle, that feeling lasted only a moment as Jenny began to howl with laughter. Soon Matthew began to laugh as well, and Mr. Dorset. For in her disarray, Miss Mackle lay on the floor with her knees up and her dress raised so high that her pantaloons were exposed to the room.

At first, she was too disordered to know what had happened, but by the time I came to offer her my arm, she had regained her unpleasant temperament and growled at me and waved me away. Old Bob then came over and bowed.

"Quite a mess, eh, Miss Grackle?" he said. His demeanor showed that he meant no harm; on the contrary, he was trying to be helpful, but his words had the unintended effect of throwing the room into complete disorder, as the rest of the house staff began to titter and then to laugh heartily at Miss Mackle's predicament.

"Who was the fool put that d——d rug in the door?" she cried as she stood up, dripping wet and shaking with anger. Tom McNew's head lowered itself to catch a final glimpse of the amazing pantaloons, and Miss Mackle took it as an improper expression of ardor and shook her fist at him, which caused him to back up a step. The room at that point went suddenly quiet except for Jenny, who continued to laugh behind her hand. Miss Mackle fumed and began to pick up the mess.

"Just a minute there, Miss Grackle," said Mr. Dorset.

"It's Mackle, sir," she said angrily, blowing a piece of hair from her face.

"Whatever," he said. "You asked who placed that rug on the threshold."

"No," said Jenny. "She asked who was the *fool* who put the *d——d* rug in the door."

"Stop picking up this minute," said Mr. Dorset, without raising his voice or seeming angry at all. Miss Mackle stood up straight, her hair ruined, punch running all over the floor. She dripped and scowled and looked around the room, perhaps thinking she had been gulled, which was true, though I would never admit it. "Now as to the rug, it is an expensive piece from Asia that Mrs. Dorset became fond of and which I purchased at a great price in Boston. It has been there for these twelve years, and now you seem to have spilled punch on it and insulted me."

Jenny looked triumphantly at me, but I betrayed no emotions.

"I meant no insult," she said between clenched teeth. "But if I fell, then others might as well, including your honor."

"No one has ever fallen over that rug, not even you, eh, Bob?" asked Mr. Dorset.

"Not over that rug, no sir," he said. "Though I fell down the steps once."

"I believe you did mean me insult, Grackle," said Mr. Dorset. "And this being my own house, I should do something about it." He put his fingers on his chin and drummed them there while deep in thought. The room remained entirely quiet. Jenny waited. Miss Mackle dripped and looked around the room to see if anyone was laughing at her. Finally, Mr. Dorset looked at me and beckoned me to come to him. He then motioned that I should lean down to hear his whispering.

"Sir?" I asked.

"What do you think I should do, Hawthorne?" he asked. "I prefer not to lose face with the staff or my children."

"You might dismiss her from your service?" I suggested gently.

"Oh ho!" he said, clapping his hands. He stood then, with his hands behind his back and looked at Miss Mackle, lifting his head and acting as the head of the house. "Look here, Grackle."

"What?" she said bitterly, sensing her fate had already been decided.

"I am certainly not angry that you have spilled punch, for even the best of us can slip and make a mistake," said Mr. Dorset. "But in each of us is a manner of conduct that speaks of what is inside us, and that manner is best observed under duress. When Hawthorne, Old Bob, and I were ship-wrecked and threatened by flesh-eating creatures, we found out of what we were made, and it was a bracing experience. I had not known I possessed such heroism, but I now recognize that I had set my limits too low."

"Here, here," I said.

"Where?" said Old Bob cupping his ear and looking around the room.

"You, I believe, Grackle, have set your limits too high, for you do think of yourself more able to run a household than Nature had endowed you," he said. "I believe now that I have made a mistake in elevating you to that position in our staff. Therefore, with the wisdom shared to me by the

Muse, I would like to offer you a position as subkeeper of our hounds rather than director of the household. I believe that is fair and just and will allow you employment, though at a lower fee, of course."

"Solomon could have done no wiser," said Jenny.

"When hogs fly to the moon," said Miss Mackle, her voice rising to a shriek. "Because some fool placed a rug in the doorway, I have ruined my clothing and been humiliated. And I will not stand for it! Do you hear me?! I will not stand for it!"

With that, she turned to walk out of the room and once again hit the polished spot, this time without its rug but slick all the same, and her feet flew from beneath her, and she landed hard on her backside. Then she screamed.

"She will not stand for it," said Mr. Dorset.

"Appears she will stand for nothing," said Old Bob. The household staff, which was now laughing without restraint, was clearly overjoyed at Miss Mackle's downfall, as it were, and now no one came to her defense or tried to pick her up. Jenny came over and stood beside me as Miss Mackle finally righted herself, turned in her notice angrily to Mr. Dorset, and waited outside for one of the servants to drive her to Town.

"*Sic semper tyrannis*," Jenny whispered in my ear, and for a moment I thought she was speaking of the British, but I realized anon that she was merely speaking of the unlamented Miss Mackle, who never again set foot on Longacre. Later, we heard, she became attached to a family in Town but was soon thereafter drowned in the harbor while seeing a charge off to London.

— 3. —

JENNY STARTS THE DAUGHTERS OF LIBERTY AND ASKS THAT I GO WITH
HER TO THE MEETINGS AS HER ESCORT, AS IF SHE NEEDED ONE.

About the time that Miss Mackle departed from our house, Jenny began to make plans for the group she would call the Daughters of Liberty. This was patterned after the Sons of Liberty, as I have said, and it was to be a secret group that could bind the women of the Province into a society which might help find ways to seek our freedom from increasingly unfair taxation and Acts of Parliament. Mr. Dorset did not know about the group, for he was far too busy writing a history of our trip to the Cherokees going after Jenny some years before. Isaac, her brother, found out one evening when he overheard Jenny speaking of it to me, and he was enraged.

"I shall report it to Father at once," he said imperially.

"You shall do no such thing!" said Jenny. We were in the hallway downstairs, and through the doors in Mr. Dorset's library, we could hear him singing and trying out rhymes. Isaac was as cold as something from the sea depths, erect and proper. Jenny took her brother's arm and shook it hard.

"I certainly shall," he said. "This talk of separation from England is nothing but treason, and I will not have it heard in this house. Is that clear?"

"You do not order me on what I may do!" she said softly but urgently. "I have the license of my own life, and if you wish to spend yours in the counting house, please go right ahead, but I am bound for larger issues."

"You are bound for children and a kitchen," he said with bitter condescension. "You do nothing to contribute to Longacre, and you never have. You have no talents other than music, and you may as well end up like father, raving and pretending that he is a poet." Isaac spat out the last word with great venom.

"You are the one with no talents!" said Jenny, punching him in the stomach with her finger. "And no conscience, either. How do you think this will play out? What do you think will happen if we do not place our own liberty beyond the altar of tyranny?"

"Hold your tongue," said Isaac. "You know nothing of what you speak, as you are but a female. During the times trade has been interrupted, we have suffered losses, not that I would expect you to know or Father to care. I have been left to run this place, as one brother has suffered prison and the other can do nothing but walk in the fields. Mother is gone, and father is deluded. So do not pretend to tell me how I should run Longacre or my life!"

He was breathing very hard. The two of them were toe to toe, and quite angry. Jenny pushed her hair back from her face and curtseyed.

"And do not pretend to tell me how I should run mine," she said. "At least I may bear children. You are too busy to sire anything but a temper."

"I shall tell father if you push forward with this mad idea," he said. "And I shall be watching." With that, he walked back through the house and upstairs, and Jenny and I stood in the hallway and looked at each other for a moment.

"Perhaps it is something about which to worry," I said cautiously. "Treason is nothing to be taken lightly."

"Nor is tyranny," said Jenny. And at that moment, the Daughters of

Liberty was born at Longacre, and I knew that nothing in this world could stop it but Jenny's death or imprisonment.

From the beginning, I was a conspirator, because Jenny trusted my discretion and common sense. She also enlisted her dear friend Desdemona Smartt from the Smythe house, who, even though a servant, was given wide range because of that friendship. Jenny decided from the outset that the group must have a regular but discreet place to meet, and at first she was baffled over where to put it. Neither Longacre nor Foxhaven was possible, and so she was momentarily concerned that it might not happen at all. Finally, however, she recalled that her father had purchased a building on the northern end of Charles Town for the holding of ships' stocks, following his purchase of interest in shipping after his wife's death. The building was normally locked and used only to remove stores as needed, but Jenny, convinced it might be right for her group, ordered me to accompany her on an overnight trip to Town, along with Molly McNew for propriety's sake. We would spend the night at the house in Town. The story Jenny put for her father was that she wished to shop and needed my services to help her carry parcels. Isaac glanced at us suspiciously as we left in the carriage, but I knew that Jenny was determined.

That evening, comfortably settled at Stratford, Jenny told Molly McNew that she wished to go out to a dance being held at Timm's Tavern, a house frequented by the social class. (Indeed, there was a dance that evening, for we had consulted the *Gazette* about it.) Molly, thinking nothing about it, simply nodded, and we were off, not in the carriage, but on foot. We walked rapidly north, looking all around for anyone who might be watching us.

The night was very black, with no moon or stars and a hint of rain. Lights from within houses spilled out only a few feet, and so as we walked, she held my arm to make sure she did not get far from me. I held the lantern, which I felt certainly had more than enough fuel for our walk. I did not tell her, but I had secreted a pistol in my trousers, for as always many ships were in port, and unpleasant characters abounded. We were not far from the building when an amazing sight accosted us: a large dog ran into the street howling in fear and pain, being chased by a cat, whose fur and tail were fully expanded, as cats will do in a battle. The cat would not forgo its chase, and the two went straight down the street until they disappeared from sight.

We came finally to the site, and around it were only a few buildings that were also locked and black, and so both the danger and the excitement of the journey were paramount.

"It is removed and reasonably safe," I said. "Perhaps we might go back now."

"I want to see inside," she said.

"It is locked," I said.

"So?" she said, and she walked steadfastly right up to the building as I followed her. By this time, a wind had arisen and lightning was flashing not far in the distance to the southwest, perhaps between Charles Town and Edisto Island. By the lantern light, I could see that Jenny's jaw was set and firm and that she would not leave before her purpose was served. The large front doors of the building were secured with a massive lock, and so we walked around until we found a window that we could reach. It, too, was securely locked, but Jenny solved that by finding a rock and throwing it through the glass, shattering it with a great crash.

"Please!" I said. But no one was around, and Jenny merely came to me and took the lantern, indicating that I was to go first through the window. After pushing my arm through the place where the pane had been, I was able to disarm the lock which held it in place and raise the window enough so that I could climb inside. Jenny handed me the lantern through the window. Unlike Mr. Dorset's personal world, the inside of the building was well ordered, with each implement and rope in its place, and in the center was a large space that was used for maneuvering the cargo around.

"I am coming in," said Jenny. She began to climb in the window (the Reader will recall that from earliest girlhood she could scale trees, Etc.), and I helped her, worried that she might tear her dress or injure some part of her body. But she came through without complaint and soon stood beside me in the quiet room.

"It seems as if it might serve," I said cautiously.

"It is perfect," she pronounced. "On this spot I will form the Daughters of Liberty, and we shall fight the scurvy British until they bow down before us!" At that point, a large rat came running out of a corner and, confused by the lantern light, came running straight for us. Jenny, to my shock, screamed as loud as I had ever heard and got behind me. Her shout so unnerved me that I was torn between fighting off the huge rodent and trying to get away from the scene. (Even though her father owned the building, explanations would be impossibly complicated, and my involvement would be suspect.) Finally, though, with the beast just at me, I had no choice, and so I kicked the rat as one might a ball, and it sailed across the room out of the lantern light, where it hit some stores and then scurried off.

"Are you all right?" I asked Jenny. She shivered.

"God is my witness, the sight of a rat will make me ill," she said. "I would be pleased if all rats were drowned in the sea."

"There would be many rats if you chose to meet here," I cautioned. She straightened herself and took a deep breath.

"Then we must take care that they not bother us," she said. And with that, she climbed back through the window and into the darkness. We made our way back to the house, and she awoke the next day so pleased that she went to several stores and bought hats and clothing.

She called the storage building Liberty House, and soon thereafter, she began to supervise meetings which were held every fortnight, and within a few months, perhaps ten or twelve women would come to every meeting. My role was to stay in the background and sometimes to look out the windows to make sure that no one was coming near. Since Liberty House was not far from many houses in the newer section of Town, Jenny had no trouble collecting a group of young women who could divert attention from their husbands or parents and walk the short distance to a meeting. The meetings were held by the light of a single lantern. Desdemona Smartt came to some meetings, but not many, for she was of the service and had less reason to be roaming about.

Watching Jenny Dorset lead the arguments of the Daughters was an amazing sight, to be sure. She would talk forcefully about taxation and about the fact that the Crown was using the Colonies to pay for its wars without allowing us representation in the Crown's work. The women were easily angered (though I believe some of this was directed toward their husbands personally and probably well deserved) and listened to Jenny with rapt attention. They made plans soon to begin a campaign of works to undermine the authority of the Crown in subtle ways — not speaking and writing as the Sons of Liberty did — but insidiously and slowly. Jenny soon had the Daughters ready to do whatever was necessary to help in the fight.

For her part, Jenny did nothing subtly and soon was haranguing her father about the British. He was somewhat sympathetic but far more interested in his poetry and history. Isaac watched with disdain and looked for evidence that Jenny was doing something treasonous, but she was able to mix so many trips to Town with her meetings that keeping track of her was not practical, so Isaac could only grimly watch and wonder.

The Daughters of Liberty would not reach its full fruition until we were occupied by the British Army in 1780, and before then, Jenny had more adventures. Her help, though entirely unknown until this History, was important in throwing off the yoke of oppression, and each Reader should thank her at this remove.

— 4. —

Mr. Dorset is pursued by two widows from Town, and each begins to covet the possible prize in a most undignified manner.

That summer, when the crops were growing well and the heat of the interior was unbearable, we made our annual journey back to our house in Town, from which it was easier for Jenny to meet with the Daughters, and from which Mr. Dorset began a round of parties and clubs that brought him fully back to life from the disaster of his wife's death.

Now a wealthy planter in Charles Town without a wife was a grand catch, and so certain women immediately set their sights on Mr. Dorset as a possible husband. Some were entirely unsuitable, of course, but Mr. Dorset, with the lack of foresight and discrimination that often led him into troubles, could not tell the fine women from those ill-suited, and this led him into all manner of adventures. Mr. Dorset had married his beloved Lydia early in life and so he had had no experience (outside of his regrettable wenching) with other women for many years and had entirely forgotten the rituals of courtship. Sometimes at church that summer, women would approach him with pleasing smiles or predatory glances, and though I hung back and never spoke to him, it was clear he could not tell the difference. He had a way of seeming to expect the attentions of women yet not quite knowing what to do with them.

I will not pretend to say that I understand the female sex, but I do believe that some who have lost a husband through death are often sad for the rest of their lives and others seem relieved of a beastly burden and go about life with a gaiety that is attractive. And so it was that Mr. Dorset succumbed to the pursuit of two particular women, whom I will now describe.

Mrs. Sally Hill was about forty years old and had lived in Charles Town her entire life. Her husband, one Oliver Hill, was a merchant who had amassed something of a fortune only to lose it in bad investments. He had been working night and day trying to recoup his losses when he was felled by a stroke of apoplexy. He had left her with only a modest house and a daughter who was sent away to England as a rest from the rigors of her father's death. That daughter, one Pamela, stayed in London never to return, which left Mrs. Hill with only a modest amount to live upon. She was tall and rather attractive, but about the time that she began to pursue my Master, her mind was beginning to unloose itself from the hinges of sanity. She was therefore erratic, loud, and full of pronouncements that made little sense. Needless to say, Mr. Dorset found these qualities quite appealing.

The other woman was Mrs. Leila Roe. She was somewhere on the far side of fifty and had lost her husband, James Roe, two years before when he had taken a knife in the ribs following a brawl on the waterfront over another woman. Mrs. Roe was singularly unattractive, with a fat lower lip and a thin upper one, which gave her the appearance of having a perpetual pout. Also, she had an unpleasant habit of clearing her throat, even when nothing needed clearing, often to the point of hawking, though not spitting. She rarely smiled and never laughed. She seemed always to be smelling something slightly unpleasant. But she had one quality which attracted Mr. Dorset greatly, and that was her perpetual piety. It had been some time since Mr. Dorset had gone through one of his religious periods, but he was always on the verge of doing so, and he enjoyed speaking to Mrs. Roe, who seemed to have memorized the entire Bible and would not hesitate to condemn everyone for one sin or another. As I have said, something in Mr. Dorset's nature was prone to enjoy condemnation, and, as Mrs. Roe seemed to dislike and condemn everything, Mr. Dorset mistook her bitter demeanor for a certain kind of purity of purpose that he desired.

And so he was pursued that summer by Sally Hill and Leila Roe, and his utter lack of discrimination led him into great miseries on account of both. As it was by no means common that a man might see two women at once, Mr. Dorset hid the truth of one from the other as he began to see them regularly and encourage their visits. (I would not like to give the impression that Mr. Dorset was making a decision on which one to bestow his faithfulness, as he often visited houses of poor reputation, from which I had to

collect him.) Still, my Master had a feeling for propriety, and so he would
see one when it was sure that the other would not know of it.

I would not dare advise him regarding this matter, of course, and Jenny
refused to do so, for she found it very funny, and she was involved with
the Daughters. (She was also beginning a serious career of amours herself,
about which I knew nothing at the time.) And so he went his way, like a
ship which floated well but somehow always missed its port.

"So, what do you think of Mrs. Roe, Hawthorne?" Mr. Dorset said
one evening as he prepared to host a visit from her.

"She is most unusual," I said.

"Indeed she is," he said. "She is the most godly of women. That is why
the Almighty caused her sorry husband to be murdered. If she had been less,
God might have spared the man. No great loss, I am sure. God is good."

"God is good," I said.

"How do I look?" he asked. He looked, in fact, rather ridiculous, over-
dressed and perfumed, with black shoes which had golden buckles. He
also wore a decorative sword, and his wig was poorly powdered. But he
thought he looked wonderful, and so I told him so. "But of course! Now,
as to the meal, is it properly done?"

"Yes, sir," I said.

"Good. Now, as she does not approve of drink in her presence, I
believe I shall have a sip before she arrives," he said. And so we went
down the stairs and into the dining room, where I poured him a glass of
Madeira, which he quaffed in two throws. He held the glass out to me
and I refilled it, and he did the same.

"So, Hawthorne, why do you think it is that my Jenny has waited so
long to wed?" he asked. "She is more than twenty-one years, and the most
beautiful girl in Charles Town. I cannot make sense of her reluctance,
though I do not wish to let her go."

"Perhaps she has found no man who is quite as grand as her father," I
said.

"Brave Hawthorne!" he said. "Well spoken! I shall drink to it!" And so
he did, and the passion with which he finished off the next glass of wine
rather alarmed me. "I must say that I am a rather hard standard to rise
to. A man of wealth, taste, and talent, a man whose name is known all
over the Province if not the country? A man of adventure and experience,
who has in his own right been heroic? What more might a worthy
woman such as Mrs. Roe want?"

"I have no idea," I admitted.

"A man who drinks his wine as he has drunk his life! Refill me!" he said. And so I did, three times more, until he had consumed a bottle and a half in the span of half an hour, the effects of which were soon all too apparent. His words became thick and his movements unsteady, and I only dissuaded him from another glass with difficulty. He went into the parlor and sat in a chair.

"Shall I bring you the Bible, supposing Mrs. Roe might wish to discuss some part of it?" I asked.

"Ah, she might wish to query me on Ephesianaties," he said, and then he belched with such volume that the room fairly shook. "Or Matthew or Mink or one of the others."

I left the room to fetch his Bible just as Old Bob came in wearing a smile, a single glove, and unmatched shoes. He had also forgotten to put his wig on, yet had somehow managed to powder his head, so that he resembled what some might consider a spectre. He was entirely unaware of the picture he presented, and bowed low before me, shaking powder on the floor.

"Has Mrs. Rue arrived for her visit, Henry?" he asked.

"Roe," I said.

"Row?" he said. "Has she come by boat?"

"Her *name* is Roe," I said carefully, sensing that the evening was headed for disaster. "And remember that she is pious and will permit nothing foul to intrude upon her visit."

"Fowl?" he said. "I believe we are preparing a pig."

"A pig?" I said. "I ordered that we have fish."

"Would she want fish, having come here by boat?" he asked. "Perhaps we might bake some pigeons instead."

"She did not come by *boat*, Bob," I said. Mr. Dorset began to sing one of his compositions, called "The Death of the Irish Washerwoman," which was meant to be sad but which was in fact quite amusing. "She is coming by carriage."

"Mrs. Rue is coming by carriage over water?" he said. "Quite amazing, Henry. I shall see that she is well fed with lamb to calm her stomach from the voyage."

"Just check the kitchen," I said. I left him hurriedly to fetch the Bible, which was in its place on the stand next to Mr. Dorset's bed, along with two empty wine bottles, a pistol, and a piece of red cloth which appeared to have come from a garment peculiar to women. When I came back downstairs, Mr. Dorset was at the sideboard draining another glass of wine and singing "A Guinea for Your Troubles, A Pence for Your Smile," one of the worst songs he had ever composed, and that is saying quite a bit. (The song was never printed, and the writing of it was lost, so I cannot give the Reader an idea of how poor it was, though I wish I might.)

"Sir, have you not had enough to drink?" I said.

"Can one have enough?" he asked. "My temperament does not admit such, Hawflown."

"*Hawthorne*," I said modestly.

"Haw," he said. "A slap of the tingue. Please admit my forgivelies."

At that point, the heavy door-knocker sounded, and Mr. Dorset hurriedly finished his glass, pouring part of it on his shirt. I brushed my Master off as well as I might and hurried to the door and opened it to Mrs. Roe, who was dressed in black and trying to look pleasant, though that emotion seemed a great chore to her. I asked her to come in and welcomed her. Mr. Dorset had seated himself in the parlor, where I took her. When we came in, I could see that he was gripping the arms of his chair fiercely, as if to prevent it from flying around the room with him.

"Sir, Mrs. Roe," I said.

"Mr. Dorset," she said, eyes fluttering and lips pulled back in what I suppose she called a smile. "How wonderful to see you this evening, and how kind of you to invite me for dinner."

"Ah, Mrs. Raw, how kind of you to receive my invitation," he said. He stood unsteadily and walked to us, one eye halfway closing from time to time. "I hope you have brought interesting biblical questions for us to discuss."

"Mr. Dorset," she tittered, ignoring his appalling mispronunciation of her name. "Indeed we might. I was thinking of the Book of Matthew."

"He has written a book?" said Mr. Dorset quite loudly. "The boy can't even breed hogs properly. Imagine him to have written a book!" At this, Mrs. Roe looked at me for explanation, but I merely smiled, and left the room to help with the dinner.

By the time we had everything on the table, Mrs. Roe had divined the situation, and had grown quite concerned, though she was trying hard not to show it. Piety is one thing, but a widowed man of wealth is quite another, and she was trying to balance her disgust with her desires, and the compromise made her very uncomfortable. Mr. Dorset, needless to say, was having a grand time and saw no problem in the least, except that he was looking at me hopefully for spirits, which I refused to bring or allow him leave to pursue in private. Mr. Dorset's manners at table were frightful, and he ate with his hands and bellowed out words, spitting food over his plate and the table, as he recited an unconnected story about the British (which, to his credit, he was hating more and more in those days), a giant turtle which had been netted earlier in the week, and the Stamp Act. Mrs. Roe did not seem to care about any of it, and so looked as if he were the most intelligent man on earth, though at great cost to her honesty.

Old Bob came in with more food on a platter.

"Duck?" he said. Mr. Dorset, who had lately been pursued by one Rupert, whose wife Mr. Dorset had spoken to in an intimate manner in a tavern, cried out and went under the table.

"Mr. Dorset?" said Mrs. Roe.

"Duck!" he cried from under the table.

"Or is it goose?" asked Old Bob. I had sent him off to be straightened up, but it had done little good, and now he stood, platter tilted, his head still powdered, and his stockings mismatched. At that point, when it appeared little else could go wrong, the front door opened, and Jenny Dorset came in and glanced into the dining room and saw her father crouching beneath the edge of the table, Old Bob dumping crumbs of duck on the floor, and Mrs. Roe looking with horror at the entire proceedings. Bob turned to Jenny and bowed, dumping the entire contents of the platter on the floor.

"Pea hen?" said Old Bob to her hopefully.

"Jenny, girl, duck!" cried her father.

"Whatever for?" she said. She looked around the room, and, seeing no threat other than Old Bob, began to smile.

"Well, I can't say," said her father. "Bob, what threat causes us to duck?"

"He meant he was *serving* duck," I explained, trying to help him up. He retook his seat, and belched once more. Mrs. Roe appeared positively ill. I helped Bob pick up the shards of meat as he muttered his apologies, and Jenny came into the room and looked things over with her usual keen eye. She had met Mr. Roe before and did not like her and therefore found no reason to leave the situation as it was.

"*Serving* duck," said Mr. Dorset. "Hah. The joke is on me, then, Mrs. Roe. Would you like some more peas or beer?"

"Beer?" she said coldly. "You offer me beer, Mr. Dorset?"

"Or punch," he said. "Rum punch with lemons and sugar. We make so it would flap your skirts."

"What!?" she cried.

"Pardon," he said. "Flip your wig."

"I do not *drink*, Adam Dorset, as you obviously do," she said. "Ungodly men drink and godly men abstain. I had hoped that you were the *latter* and not the *former*." He looked perplexed by her allusion.

"Say again?" he said.

"I shall get the ladder," said Old Bob, dropping the plate and exiting. Jenny came in and sat at table to watch, and I did not bother trying to prevent her, as I picked up what was left of the duck.

"Well, I do not drink to drink," said Mr. Dorset. "Only drunkards drink to drink." He thought for a moment. "That's correct, I think, only drunkards drink to drink."

"Are you less than a drunkard, then?" asked Mrs. Roe hotly. Jenny watched each intently but said nothing.

"Madam, I do not drink to drink," he said. "I drink to *think*. It is something of a burthen to be weighed with such artistic talent, but we must carry what God gives us. It is a matter of balance." With that, he fell sideways out of his chair and onto the floor near the duck. Jenny did not move a muscle, as I tried to help her father up. He wiped himself off somewhat and tried to push me away as superfluous.

"Really!" said Mrs. Roe. Why she did not take her leave at that moment I cannot say, unless she thought she might marry the man, acquire his estate, and then reform him. Women sadly misunderstand that while the first two are possible, even likely, the third never happens, though they continue to believe it may.

"Enchanted," said Mr. Dorset, and he took one step forward and collapsed in Mrs. Roe's lap and then fell on the floor, unconscious. Mrs. Roe stood and stepped over him and looked at the sight before her with such a pallor that she put her hand to her mouth and gagged. Jenny came around the table and looked down at her father, who had begun to snore and sing simultaneously, which was quite a trick.

"Do something," entreated Mrs. Roe.

"Why should I?" said Jenny defensively. Through the open window I heard a crash and saw Old Bob, helplessly tangled in a small ladder. I cried out to ask if he was all right.

"Fine, governor," he said, trying to stand and falling again. "I should be there momentarily."

"Help him to bed," Mrs. Roe said with a shiver. Mr. Dorset burst into wild laughter while never opening his eyes, then immediately began to snore again.

"He sleeps on the floor often," said Jenny. "When he does not sleep in the topiary."

"Topiary!" cried Mrs. Roe. "God forgive him!" She looked up at the ceiling as if God were there and might forgive us all. Old Bob stood again with the ladder and rammed it through two panes of glass, sending sparkling slivers all over the room. I gave up and sat at the table.

"You, servant!" Mrs. Roe said to me angrily. "What kind of animal are you to let your master fall into such degradation in front of a lady."

"I don't know," I said. "I shall deal with it *if* and *when* a lady is present." Jenny began to scream with laughter finally, and Mrs. Roe pulled herself to her full height and stormed into the hall and out the front door, where she ran into Bob and his ladder and took a bit of a tumble on the grass. I thought of helping her, but decided I would not bother. By that time, Mr. Dorset had ceased his twitching and was entirely asleep. I got a cushion and put it under his head while I cleaned up the duck and the glass.

Jenny helped me, and soon the dining room was clean except for the unconscious Mr. Dorset, on whom I spread a light blanket later in the evening. He did not awaken until sometime the next morning, when he came tottering toward me, looking deranged and begging me to shoot him.

"Shoot you, sir?" I said.

"I cannot bear the pain in my head," he said in a hoarse whisper. "This is my last wish, that you get my pistol and shoot me."

"Shall I help you to your bed?" I asked.

"That is a suitable alternative, I suppose," he said.

Incredibly, Mrs. Roe did not cease her flirtations with Mr. Dorset, reasoning quite rightly that a man is not like a woman and must be attended to as a beast of the field and sometimes indulged in his lapses and bad manners. Mr. Dorset, however, was ashamed to see her since she was so pious, and he was too often impious, and so their meetings were reserved for occasional balls or dances, wherein I understand Mr. Dorset spent more time talking to male friends than attending his escort.

Mrs. Sally Hill was another matter entirely. Unlike Mrs. Roe, she had no delusions about either the male sex or Mr. Dorset in particular. She, in fact, found his waywardness charming, his poetry magnificent, and his musical compositions beyond reproach. I do not for a moment think she actually liked Mr. Dorset's creations, but her tact was such that she could not merely praise them but managed to give the impression that Mr. Dorset was one of the key artistic figures of the age. Unfortunately, although she was pleased with Mr. Dorset in most matters, she was among the most superficial of women, with almost no opinions on anything, including the British, about whom everyone had an opinion. At first, Mr. Dorset was charmed by her constant praise and her ability to put up with his odd moods, but after a time, it was clear that she began to bore him, and so she began to work twice as hard at capturing the prize that seemed within her grasp. And so it was that there occurred an incident which turned Mrs. Hill finally away from Mr. Dorset.

They were walking in the garden of Stratford, her arm in his, looking at the sunset and speaking softly. We had taken on a new indentured servant named Hamm, who worked in the gardens, and had four years to serve before his freedom. This Hamm was the kind of person Mr. Dorset routinely hired, extremely superannuated, forgetful, and pleasant, withal good at his trade. He was a good companion for Old Bob, though I believe this Hamm was even older. I never knew quite why Hamm at his age was still indentured, and I did not ask, but it mattered little. Within a few months, he died in his sleep. Hamm, anyhow, was working nearby and being pursued by a bee, which he kept swatting away with small curses. At that same time, two of Mr. Dorset's hounds had somehow escaped and were digging up a fragrant bush with all their might.

"Mr. Dorset, your dogs are ruining that fragrant bush," Mrs. Hill said with a small twitter.

"So they are," said Mr. Dorset. "Bah, dogs! Away!" He waved at them, and they went to the other side of the bush and began to dig even more ferociously. "Dogs. What can one do with a dog which will not be restrained or take training, eh?"

"Oh," said Mrs. Hill. "This is so true and quite amusing." She laughed politely. (I was standing near the house, close enough to be called for service, though I believe Mr. Dorset had placed me there as a buffer against the widow.)

"D—n!" cried Hamm, swatting at the bee. He looked up to see Mrs. Hill and Mr. Dorset, and bowed and begged their pardon.

"Not at all, old fellow," said Mr. Dorset.

"Not at all," said Mrs. Hill with a curtsey and a broad smile.

"'Twas a bee after me, ma'am," said Hamm.

"Waugh!" cried Mr. Dorset. "That could serve as the first line of a poem fit for Mr. Dryden, or even a song. ''Twas a Bee After Me.' Thanks be to you, Hamm."

At that point, the bee, which had been hunting this Hamm, found its mark and stung him, causing a string of the most unimaginable curse words, at which Mrs. Hill finally seemed shocked and angry. Mr. Dorset, of course, was neither, and he laughed and slapped his leg and turned to see his escort's face, which had grown cold.

"What, sir, is so amusing?" she asked.

"The bee has had Hamm for dinner," said Mr. Dorset, whereupon he began to laugh indecently, almost braying as Matthew once did. In fact, I laughed myself, while Hamm continued to dance from his wound and curse everything he could imagine, including, finally, God, which was too much for Mrs. Hill. At the same time, the dogs, sensing the merriment, came running over toward us, only to begin a fight that ended with one mounting the other for an impromptu mating, at which Mr. Dorset laughed even harder. Mrs. Hill walked out of the garden, into the house, and thence to her carriage. I escorted her and tried to make apologies, but she would not speak to me, and at that point she ceased her pursuit of Mr. Dorset.

My Master finally came in the house wiping the tears from his eyes and looking about for his companion.

"Where is Mrs. Hill?" he asked. "Is she indisposed?"

"She has left, sir," I said. "I believe she was offended."

"Very well," he said. "Very well. I shall have rum and a quill, Hawthorne."

"Sir," I said, bowing.

— 5. —

JENNY AND THE DAUGHTERS OF LIBERTY DEAL WITH AN INTEMPERATE
BRITISH SOLDIER NAMED HUFF, AN EVENT NEVER REVEALED
BEFORE THE PUBLICATION OF THIS HISTORY, ETC.

The dead are safe in their small cocoons, unworried about their past lives and unconcerned about a future. God has already punished or rewarded them, and I believe He casts a merciful eye on the sum of a man's life and anoints his flight to Heaven with charity. It is not in my way of thinking that a person who means well shall descend to Hell, and, therefore, I believe that what I am about to reveal for the first time has had no bearing on the departed souls of those who conceived and planned it. And, as we are no longer under British law, nothing is to be done about those who survive.

There was in Town a soldier named Huff, a minor legate from London whose position involved reporting on violations of import tax rules. Since the Stamp Act had been stricken, the Townshend Acts had aroused hatred in the Colonies, and further anger was abuilding, so that any official involved with these Acts was the subject of constant vilification. This Huff was a loud braggart, who felt safe from harm due to his official position, and therefore took every public opportunity to mock the desires of those who wished for freedom. He was particularly critical of Mr. Gadsden and Mr. Rutledge, and other men who forcefully stated their position. Night after night, he would hold forth in one of Charles Town's many taverns, surrounded by a small group of soldiers who were very loyal to him and protected him against harm.

I recall one particular night when this Huff was speaking loudly in a small tavern called the Hedgehog. His uniform was soiled and pulled open, and he grew louder with every sentence. He was a short man, and, as with many men of minor stature, he felt it necessary to pull himself higher in men's eyes. He was not corpulent but stocky, and he had red hair and a freckled face that was usually flushed with drink. He also had blazing green eyes that he used to great advantage to stare down opponents. Word was about that he also considered himself quite the ladies' man, and that he had cuckolded a man and then laughed in his face, surrounded by his escort. Anyway, Huff was speaking from his table and holding a mug of rum. I had come to the Hedgehog by myself for a smoke and a mug of beer and to escape Stratford for a time. It was a Tuesday evening, when I was normally given time off, and my wife understood that it was helpful to me.

"Independence," said Huff in his high voice. He spat out the word impudently, and the men around him laughed heartily. "I understand that now the Colonies believe they can survive without England. Do you, men, believe that the Colonies can survive without a tit to suck?"

"No!" they roared, raising their glasses. The others in the low and smoky room glowered, and a few muttered oaths, but Huff was protected, and he knew it.

"I would like to see the day that a rude group of provincials could ever so much as eat and drink for a single day without the benevolence of England," said Huff. "They would starve and then fight among themselves until they were on their knees begging us to return and take care of their pitiful affairs. They should have thanked us for the Stamp Act, but instead they act as barbarians and pretend that we have committed some offense against them. How very sad and how very stupid!"

When I went back home that evening, Jenny was in the parlor playing the harpsichord. She was by herself, and I bowed to her as I passed, and then stopped for a reason I shall not know. She asked what I had on my mind. I relit my pipe and sat in a chair across from her. She turned on the stool and waited. I then reported what Huff had said at the tavern, and Jenny's ire grew until her face was red and she was walking around the room in a ferment.

"This shall not pass!" she said.

"He believes it shall, and he has men to protect him," I said.

"No man is ever entirely safe," she said. She was thinking as she stood next to the candles on the mantel, pulling at her chin and formulating a plan. "Tomorrow night I shall need the warehouse for the Daughters. Do you think you might distract my father sufficiently for me to leave?"

"I doubt that is a problem," I said.

"Then do so, and I shall meet at nine o'clock," she said. "I intend to deal with this Huff in my own way."

And so on the next afternoon, when Mr. Dorset had ceased working on an oratorio he was calling *Saul, Highwayman of Tarsus,* I told him that there was an amusing show playing at the Orpheum and that, after his mighty labors, he might be able to do with a spot of levity. He agreed, and about sunset rode off. I knew from experience that he would laugh uproariously at the show, then retire to a tavern, coming home only very late and in poor shape.

The Daughters of Liberty did indeed meet that night at Liberty House (Mr. Dorset's warehouse) and came up with a plan to deal with this Huff. I remained outside as a watchman, while inside seven young women gathered and spoke in low voices of how they might go forth on the issue. I was reasonably certain that Jenny had a plan already. The meeting lasted perhaps three-quarters of an hour, and the women came out, and left, mostly walking back to their houses, though one rode a horse.

"Was everything satisfactory?" I asked when Jenny joined me.

"Not for Mr. Huff," she said.

I felt bad somehow that my report to Jenny had been the instigation for this act, and yet I hated the man's arrogance so that he seemed to represent our oppressors, and I felt in my heart no pity or remorse for what might befall him, and, knowing Jenny Dorset, I assumed the man was in mortal danger.

I finally learned a few days later of their plan and was so startled that for a time I simply stared at Jenny. She had confided in me that she and another of the Daughters, Miss Sally Theobald, were to decorate themselves as bawds to entice Huff from a tavern and then deal with him.

"This is madness," I said. "Surely you cannot be serious in this."

"Oh, I am serious," she said, walking around the room with no purpose but only to diffuse her anger. "And it shall work."

"But what about Huff's retinue?" I said. "They shall follow him to make sure he is not harmed."

"He will tell them to stay where they are," said Jenny. "He will not risk having his pleasures ruined."

"Jenny, this is madness, and you must not do it," I insisted.

"I shall," she said, and I knew that it was useless to argue further. Jenny forbade me from coming to the tavern that night. I was once again assigned the task of diverting Mr. Dorset and her brothers, which was easy enough. Mr. Dorset went to a play, and Isaac was at dinner with a man who might help the Dorsets in terms of shipping. Matthew was at church, for reasons which I will explain later in this book. The other servants were sent from the house, including myself, though I hid and waited until it was mid-evening and saw Jenny come out of the house. Had I not known of her plans and not known it was her, I should never have recognized her. She wore a dress that she must have bought second-hand in a shop, for it was scandalous, red, and cut low. She also wore a blackened wig.

I followed her to the Hedgehog, though at a distance. (I had told her where Huff did his drinking.) She met Miss Sally Theobald at the entrance. Miss Theobald was several years younger than Jenny and just as full of spirit. She had disguised herself as well, and I would not have recognized her, either. They went in, and I followed after perhaps five minutes. When I got into the tavern, I saw they had already approached the table where Huff and three of his men were loudly holding forth, I believe, on the price of coffee. Huff had already been drinking for some time. The men had moved from their previous positions so that Jenny sat on one side of Huff and Sally on the other. I hid my face as well as I could and sat in the corner and lit my pipe and took a beer while anxiously awaiting what might happen.

I could not hear the conversation exactly, though sometimes Huff would boom out about England, rum, or the Stamp Act. Jenny and Sally laughed with him, and Jenny kept refilling his glass from a bottle on the table before him, and he kept drinking so that soon, he was singing and laughing to the disgust of the others in the tavern.

After perhaps half an hour, Jenny began to whisper in Huff's ear, and, finally, he straightened himself as well as he might and leaned down and said something to one of the men, who nodded. Jenny and Sally got up with Huff and led him out the door. He was laughing but very unsteady on his feet, and though people seemed glad to see him go, no one made to follow. I waited about a minute and left myself and saw them on the side of the street before me, about a hundred yards hence. I followed at that distance but was careful to stay concealed. The women were holding Huff up. After a few more steps, they urged him into one of the dozens of dank alleys that crossed that part of Town, and I hurried to catch up to see what transpired.

It seems this alley opened into a small area of land upon which there were a few cows and a well. Though the Council had tried repeatedly to keep livestock from the streets, some men ignored the rules and the beasts often ran free. There was little light in the alley from a few windows, but I could see clearly enough to know they had walked to the well and were standing beside it. I suddenly had a thrill of terror and understood what was about to happen.

Huff leaned against the well and laughed heartily at something when suddenly Jenny and Sally looked at each other and pushed Huff backward into the well. I cannot explain the feeling in my heart, for I thought at worst that Jenny might steal the fellow's money. It was at that moment that I understood what our Revolution might be about. Huff made a kind of cry or shriek, then began to call for help, but soon his voice faded, and he was gone. Jenny and Sally came walking quickly out of the alley, so I dashed across the street and hid myself, still not quite believing that they had killed the man. I silently asked God to forgive Jenny, but I felt perhaps that justice in the Court of Heaven might conclude only that an evil man had perished and that it was all to the good. Drained of emotion, I went back home.

Later, I found Jenny quite happily playing the harpsichord as if nothing had happened at all. There was an investigation, of course, and the officials sought, without much ardor, to find the two "notorious bawds," as the *Gazette* had it, but, after a brief period, Huff was left to rot in the well, in which, if anyone wishes to disinter him now, he still rests.

6

BACK AT LONGACRE, MR. DORSET AND MR. CHARLES SMYTHE
DECIDE ON A GENTLEMANLY GAME OF BOWLS TO SETTLE
THE DISPUTED THREE FEET OF PROPERTY.

The frequent outpourings of sentiment against the Crown meant that
business was some years very good and some years very bad. Isaac, however, managed to keep the Dorset fortunes on an even keel, a chore that
Mr. Dorset entirely trusted now to his son, for he was spending all his
efforts in courting both the women of Town and his Muse. I cannot say
with certainty which Muse he attended, but most of the women were not
of his class and their liaisons rarely lasted more than a few hours. This
gave Mr. Dorset more time on his hands than was good for him, and he
spent the rest of it hunting, riding, and, I regret to say, drinking. Jenny
more or less became a constant companion, and rode with him, shot as
well as most men, and still managed to work quietly against Britain, just
as her brother Abel did, though he now lived in Town and no longer with
the family. More of Matthew later.

One evening, while into his third bottle of French wine, Mr. Dorset
came running out to the kitchen looking the worse for wine.

"Hawthorne, I am a genius," he said, short of breath.

"That is not news to me, sir," I said.

"Certainly, certainly," he said, happily waving away my confession. "I
have decided on how to get the three feet which that fool Smythe owes
me without having to continue the suit in court."

"Really," I said. I was finished and walked outside with him. The
evening was hot and still and full of flying bugs, the kind which was common much of the year. There was a pleasant breeze, however, and I lit my
pipe to listen to Mr. Dorset.

"Yes, yes," he said. "I shall challenge Smythe to a duel."

"Sir, if memory serves, you have been on this road previously without
pleasing results for either of you," I said.

"No, no, no," he said. He walked around in small circles. "I mean a
duel at bowls! The one sport in which I have no peer! And I will challenge that the winner gets a full *six feet* of the other's property for the
entire length of the line! It is genius! He cannot refuse the offer because
of his lack of honor and his greed. Congratulate me, Hawthorne!"

"Congratulations," I said.

"How kind of you to congratulate me," he said.

"Not at all," I said.

Old Bob, who had been growing more decrepit, at that point came limping rather badly past us heading in the direction of the house. I stopped him and inquired after his foot, and he said that something was in his boot.

"Then why do you not remove it, Bob?" asked Mr. Dorset.

"Then I would not be able to walk as well," he said.

"Waugh, you walk poorly now," said Mr. Dorset.

"That is true enough," said Bob, and he sat on the earth and began to tug at the boot, which would not move.

"I am to increase the holdings of Longacre," said Mr. Dorset to Bob.

"Then it would be, I should say, *Longeracre*," said Bob, pausing to admire his own words.

"Longeracre!" cried Mr. Dorset. "Brave Bob! Oh, this is a grand evening! I shall send the challenge yet once again to the fool in the morning! Hawthorne, will you bear it for me?"

"With pleasure," I said.

Bob finally got his boot off, and we took it back into the kitchen and dumped the contents on the table and found a small stone, a clump of hay, a shilling, and a fork.

"A fork?" said Mr. Dorset. "An omen, perhaps?"

"Bob, how on earth did a fork get in your boot?" I asked.

"I could not say, governor," he admitted. "Perhaps the foot itself became hungry."

"Feet cannot eat," I said, softly touching Bob's shoulder.

"Who knows but what happens in the world of fancy?" said Mr. Dorset. "In fancy a foot might eat just as a pig may fly!"

Bob looked at me for an explanation of Mr. Dorset's words, but I merely shrugged, deciding that the effort to explain the phrase to Bob would not be worth the effort. We helped Bob replace the boot, and, as he complained about the other, we removed it and found a button and a small rock.

The next morning, I saddled my horse and rode to Foxhaven. Mr. Smythe was not outside, but his son Hamlet was, shouting angrily at one of their overseers regarding the conduct of slaves. Hamlet said that everyone knew that the slaves were little more than animals and that he should beat them if they were insolent. He said that an insurrection in Carolina would wipe all Christian people from the face of the Earth. Hamlet worked himself into such a state that his face was nearly crimson, and his eyes seemed to push out from his face. It was as disgraceful a display by a man of property as I had ever seen, and I felt badly for the overseer and even worse for the slaves. All the time that Hamlet Smythe was chastising the overseer, he did not look at me or speak to me, even though I stood patiently not ten feet away. Hamlet, in fact, acted as if I had not arrived and did not exist. Such an outburst by Mr. Dorset against his overseers or slaves was unthinkable, and I was silently glad that I was not in service to the Smythes. Finally, Hamlet (who was by that time twenty-five years old and had married not long before) acknowledged my presence with a small nod and made a minor motion that I should approach him. He did not move from his spot.

"Sir, I am Hawthorne from Longacre," I said, "and I bear a message for your father."

"I know who you are," he said impatiently. "Please deliver yourself of it to me, and I shall give it to my father."

"I have instructions to deliver it directly to your father," I said.

"Nothing but ill has come to Foxhaven from your employer," he said coldly. "My father still has a bad time with his wound from that mad duel. I shall on no account deliver a message to him from that Dorset. You are dismissed."

He turned and began to walk away just as Mr. Smythe himself came from the house, and, seeing me, came, shook my hand, and warmly welcomed me to Foxhaven. Hamlet came rushing back to the scene to intervene.

"It is Hawthorne from Longacre," said Mr. Smythe warmly.

"He bears a message from that madman, and I told him to be gone from our land," said Hamlet.

"Nonsense," said Mr. Smythe. "You have a message? Come inside and refresh yourself."

"No honor at all," said Hamlet bitterly, and he stormed away and disappeared around the house. Mr. Smythe stared at his son for a time, shook his head, and invited me once more inside where he served me a glass of wine and offered me a pipe, which I declined. He sat back in the magnificent surroundings of his library and asked me politely what sort of message Mr. Dorset sent.

"He wishes to challenge you again regarding the disputed three feet of land," I said. "But this time, he wishes to increase the stake to six feet, and the one who loses forfeits the six feet along the entire property line."

"Another duel?" said Mr. Smythe, sighing heavily and sinking into his chair.

"Yes, but a duel not of guns," I said. "He wishes to challenge you at bowls."

The room was silent for a moment as Mr. Smythe stared at me, then slowly his face turned into a wry smile, and he shook his head in disbelief as he lit his pipe. He puffed away until the smoke encircled his head and lazily rose to the ornate ceiling.

"Bowls," he said. "Is Dorset losing his senses?"

"No more than I have noticed before," I said. Mr. Smythe, disarmed, laughed heartily, and shook his head.

"I accept his challenge for the six feet," said Mr. Smythe. "Please convey to him that I await the time and place, and will attend him with my second."

"That will please him greatly," I said.

I rode home with the news, and Mr. Dorset was so delighted he attempted to deliver himself of an ode upon the spot regarding the event, but eventually he became stumped on a rhyme, and I was mercifully allowed to leave him and go about my duties. That evening, Jenny found me dusting and asked if it were true that her father and Mr. Smythe were to have a duel at bowls.

"I shall not believe it until I hear it from you," she said.

"Regrettably, that information is correct," I said.

"And in a time of such ferment," she said. "In a time when the British are such villains. Can he not see that his diversions are wasting efforts that might better be directed against the Crown?"

"As always, I believe that he is following a path chosen for him, rather than one he chose," I said. "Perhaps that is true for each of us."

"Perhaps it is," she said.

The contest itself was held on a sunny day at Longacre, to which Mr. Dorset was also referring as Longeracre. The area for bowls had been groomed beautifully and the topiary was reshaped. The grounds were altogether beautiful, and the day was fine as well. Isaac Dorset, of course, was outraged by the event. Matthew was pleased and readied a chair near the site of the duel, where he sat for a full hour ahead of time, doing nothing but sitting and waiting.

I must now address a circumstance about which I warned the Reader much earlier in this History, and though this matter is indelicate, I cannot but mention it here briefly if Truth is to be served. As I said, each of us must follow the path upon which he is set, and though I believe that bad men can change and that good men can turn to evil, our path is generally set and we can deviate from it only a small amount. So it was that Jenny Dorset had become, as a young woman, determined to enjoy love as she found it, somewhat as a man will. Her life by that time had become a tangle of assignations, lies, and joys in which I was her assigned conspirator. Distasteful as it was to me, I knew that I could not stop it, and she knew that I would not betray her trust. And so she embarked on a remarkable career of amours, so that in only a few years her reputation was destroyed, which brought great sadness to Longacre. For her part, Jenny never once contemplated that she was doing anything wrong. She believed that it was her right to enjoy life as much as her father did, and she seemed bent to prove that her mother's quiet life and early death were nothing she wished to repeat. I will report fully on the entanglements of Jenny's adventures in love in the next book of this History, when it is more appropriate.

The event of the challenge was known about, and so a number of people who lived within a few miles came to Longacre. The household staff had to prepare drink and food, and I must say that we made a very good job of it. Mr. Dorset selected Matthew as his second, and Matthew did not know this until the appointed time, and he was so touched by the honor that he burst into tears and had to be comforted by his sister. Earlier that morning, Mr. Dorset had spent his time firing guns to true their sights and was never pleased. He grazed one of his dogs who was sleeping in a hedge, and the poor animal came charging from the spot where it was resting and bit my Master on the leg so severely that I had to dress the wound. (Mr. Dorset, forgiving as always, held the offensive animal in his lap while I placed a bandage on his wound, and the dog squirmed, licked, and emitted such noxious vapors that I had to open the house as soon as it had been put back out.)

I was amazed that during the morning, Mr. Dorset did not drink a drop of spirits, though Jenny did, in the most extraordinary way. She had asked me to fetch her a bottle of wine, and she sat on the stool of her harpsichord with her glass, which I kept refilling until the bottle's contents were gone. All the while, she delivered herself of a speech on her hatred for England and the King and filigreed it with various indecent reports of two men in Town with whom she was sharing a liaison. I begged her not to reveal such personal affairs to me, but she persisted, and then sent me for another bottle of wine, which I retrieved in good order and opened for her.

"Why does six feet of land matter so much to them?" Jenny asked.

"The land does not matter," I said. "It is the competition."

"Men are fools," she said, draining another glass.

"Often that is true," I said, "and more often than in your sex. But foolishness is not a thing limited to one group or another, and those who are most often sensible can be the worst fools."

"That is the most foolish thing you have ever said to me," she said. "Your judgment is impaired." With that she belched very loudly and began to laugh.

"I have said many foolish things in my life," I admitted. "But I have never done anything so foolish as fight a duel over a few feet of disputed land."

"Oh, I have done many things worse than that," she said. I thought of Huff but kept my mouth closed and my expression calm for fear of giving it away. "And I probably shall do even worserer." She paused thoughtfully. "Is that a word?"

"I do not believe so," I said.

I went outside where the tournament or duel was about to begin. Someone other than I had set up the bowls on a nice green part of the lawn, and Mr. Dorset was involved in some sort of exercises to give himself strength, while Mr. Smythe watched with amusement. I came to Mr. Dorset's side and asked if he needed anything.

"Only a surveyor to mark my new land!" he cried. "For there is no way the fool Smythe will win in this contest. Does he not know I am a hero of the oceans? That I am the poet of the age? Bah, what a fool he makes of himself!"

"You are all that and more," I said.

"I am!" he said. He repeated the exercises he had been going through. "Now I shall lift myself on that tree to strengthen my arms." He walked quickly to a lovely oak which had low-hanging limbs covered with the moss peculiar to Carolina. He stood beneath the limb, leapt up to it, and pulled his body up to the limb and nearly touched it with his chin when his hands slipped and he fell off backward and hit his head on the ground with an awful sound. Several people came running over to see if they could help, but Mr. Dorset had lost his senses and looked as if he had fallen into a deep sleep. A few of the men brought water to splash on his face, and it took him an alarmingly long time to wake up, and when he did, he seemed bewildered and did not know where (or who) he was. His head was bleeding but a little, and we stanched the flow without great effort. Matthew wept when he saw the small amount of blood on his father's head and had to be helped away. Just as we were getting Mr. Dorset to his feet, Mr. Smythe came over and saw his rival and asked him if he was all right.

"Right as rain," said Mr. Dorset. "Will someone dress me for the ball?"

We all looked at him with fear and some amusement, I regret to say. Jenny came up at that point, weaving scandalously from her drinking and looking impossibly beautiful, with the sun catching her golden hair and making it seem to glow from within. Her face was blushed from the wine, and she smiled at her father, not knowing he had been injured. At once, all the men turned from Mr. Dorset to attend Jenny, and if they had been holding him, I believe they would have dropped him to the ground to look at her.

"Well, well, what has happened to the old patriarch," Jenny said, belching loudly. The men, of course, found it charming, so dazzled were they by her inestimable beauty. I explained that he was attempting to exercise on a tree limb and had fallen and hit his head on a rock. Mr. Dorset, standing beside me, smiled in a distracted sort of way, as a benign village fool might, with no thoughts in his head at all.

"Miss, are you going to the dance?" Mr. Dorset said. He then began to totter, and I caught him before he fell and helped him sit on the earth. Mr. Smythe sat with him and looked into his eyes, then glanced at me and shook his head. "The Earth seems to be dancing beneath me. Is it a modern thing to have the Earth dance instead of our feet?"

"Be calm, and you will feel better shortly," I said.

But he did not, instead growing more confused as the minutes passed, though in such a way that you would have thought he was perfectly fine had you not known what was happening about him. He was simply in another part of his life, as if Time had skipped him forward or backward. He was convinced a ball would be held soon, that he was at Raper's Tavern in Town, that the French Army was not far away, that the Cherokee Indians were coming for dinner, and that Jenny was his dead wife, Lydia Foxe Dorset. The last part was quite poignant to everyone but Jenny, who insisted that she was not her mother but someone called the Avenging Angel and would in her time deal with all who wronged her or the Province. One of the men offered to bring her punch, and she instead said she would accompany him to the bowl, and she left us.

"I too am the Avenging Angler," said Mr. Dorset, sounding very sleepy. "Bring to me my rod, and I shall catch a sea monster."

"See a monster?" said Old Bob, cupping his ear. I had no idea he was about, but there he was, his coat misbuttoned so that he was entirely askew, making him look rather deformed. "Is there a monster on the grounds?"

"Rather," said one of the men, and the others laughed and went in the direction Jenny had gone, back toward the punch bowl. Mr. Smythe shook his head, flipped a shilling he held, and drifted back toward the site of the competition. Bob and I helped Mr. Dorset up from the position where he had been sitting. Mr. Dorset extended his hand to Bob and introduced himself as Hannibal and asked if Bob wanted to see his elephants.

"Yes," said Bob, "though I do not wish to see a monster." He looked about himself warily.

"Are the Alps nearby?" asked Mr. Dorset. "I shall scale them and be famous, and then I will go and live with the Indians."

"An elk?" said Old Bob. "I don't believe an elk is here. Perhaps they are afraid of your elephants."

"We need to get him back to the house," I whispered to Bob, "for he has hit his head and his senses are changed."

Bob helped me, and we took Mr. Dorset back the several paces to the site of the bowls, where Jenny was waving a fan and was surrounded by a large number of men, whose wives sat nearby and scowled at them fiercely. By the time we got Mr. Dorset back, he was convinced that he was a king, though of which country he could not remember. Bob suggested that perhaps it was England and then requested of me, as governor, to clarify the matter. I did not respond, for it would only have entangled me further, as a fly is tangled in a spider's web. I gave Mr. Dorset a glass of punch, and he drank it off too quickly. I explained that he was Mr. Adam Dorset and that he had challenged Mr. Charles Smythe to a game of bowls with six feet of the property line at stake. He did not believe me, and called me Hector and asked if the Carthaginians might be approaching. I assured him they were not, and then he accused me of being a spy for the Spartans and ordered me martyred. A moment later, he rescinded that command and anointed me King of the Turks and told me to take my troops into Ireland and await his orders. Jenny, meanwhile, threw the entire company into riotous disorder by pulling one Thomas Coll to her and kissing him passionately. Mrs. Coll, who brooked no foolishness, came to her husband, hit him violently with her parasol, and demanded to be taken home. The other wives, sensing a breach in the battle lines, came and rescued their husbands from a similar fate, though each cast lingering glances backward at Jenny. Old Bob disappeared. Matthew stood helplessly by the bowling green, looking terribly disappointed at the failure of his role as second in the duel. With everyone soon gone but the Smythes, the affair could not have turned out worse, and none of our food was eaten and would be spoiled soon in the heat.

Mr. Dorset sat in a chair and drank his punch and looked about his estate with his head high and his senses entirely deranged.

"Bring me a wench, Hector," he said. "I have need of one."

I sighed and tried to think of something to say. Mr. Smythe saved me by walking up and reporting that when a man who issues a challenge is unable to stand for it, he shall forfeit what is in dispute. I knew that this was true and said so. I suggested that he might try himself to speak with Mr. Dorset one last time, and he agreed.

"Shall you give me satisfaction in this matter?" he said to my Master. Jenny was talking to Hamlet Smythe across the way, and he seemed so smitten that his mouth was permanently open.

"I shall allot you two elephants to clear your swamp," said Mr. Dorset loftily. "More than that and I cannot defend myself from the Tartans."

"The Tartans?" said Mr. Smythe.

"They are fierce," insisted Mr. Dorset. He added absently, "Though well dressed."

Mr. Smythe looked at me, and I told him, as I was bound to do by my honor, that I would advise Mr. Dorset of his failure in the duel when his senses returned, and I would see that the suit in court was dropped and that the property was transferred.

"Whatever," said Mr. Smythe, and with that, he mounted and left, though not without a problem with Hamlet, who was deeply loathe to leave Jenny.

— 7. —

OLD BOB BECOMES DESPERATELY ILL AND ORDERS A GRAVE DUG.
DESDEMONA SMARTT MOVES IN WITH US AT LONGACRE,
WHILE MOLLY MCNEW GOES TO FOXHAVEN.

Not long after the ill-fated duel of bowls, Old Bob began to say, by way of apology, that he was not feeling well. More and more, I would find the old fellow in his bed, trying to speak about Ellen Goodloe and then dissolving into the most heartbreaking tears imaginable. He spoke of his youth, and it was hard for me even to imagine that he had ever *been* a youth. Day after day, he would attend to some of his duties then wander off. We would find him sitting in the library touching the keys of the harpsichord without making the quills pluck, or in his quarters lying on the bed and staring at the ceiling. Alarmed, I informed Mr. Dorset that I believed Old Bob was ill. Mr. Dorset then summoned Dr. Paquin from Town, and he came and examined Old Bob for us.

"Well?" said Mr. Dorset anxiously when Dr. Paquin had come up from Bob's quarters to the house. "What can you say is wrong with Bob?"

Dr. Paquin was somewhat old himself, and he settled into a chair by the fire and sighed heavily.

"I believe your friend is mortally ill," he said slowly. I could not bear to hear the words, and Mr. Dorset gasped and put his hand on his chest.

"From what ailment?" said Mr. Dorset. "Should we quarantine the house?"

"There is no quarantine from this disease," said Dr. Paquin, taking off his glasses and rubbing them with his shirtwaist. "And we all shall catch it in due time if we live but long enough. It is called old age, and Bob has entered its last confines, I fear."

"But he has *always* been old!" said Mr. Dorset emphatically. "He was old thirty years ago and has changed little since then. Has he, Hawthorne?"

"He seems more fragile now, sir, I believe," I said. Dr. Paquin stood and put his hand on Mr. Dorset's shoulder to comfort him.

"Adam, I see death every day, and it comes to those young and old alike," said the doctor. "As you know too well, worthy souls in their prime are summoned to God, and often when that summons is strong enough, there is nothing that I or anyone else can do to prevent that sad departure. As the Bible says, there is a time to live and a time to die, and I fear this is Bob's time."

"Is he in pain?" I asked.

"Only the pain of impending departure from those he loves well," said the doctor. "And that is a very bad pain indeed, but it is one about which I can do nothing."

We were saddened by the news, particularly Jenny, who had suffered the loss of her mother and now faced the loss of her old servant and friend. For myself, I determined to make Bob as comfortable as possible. He still tried to get up each day, but it was difficult for him, and he could not properly address his livery, so I would help him dress and adjust his clothing. About a week after the doctor's visit, Old Bob took me aside and ordered that a grave be dug for him, for he was certain that he would perish within a fortnight. I told him that I felt he would not, but he was so insistent that I had two of the slaves dig a grave beneath an oak tree not far from Mrs. Dorset's resting place, and next to the stone we had fashioned for Ellen Goodloe. I took Bob to it, for he wanted to see where he would lie. The day was very cool, with a pleasant wind blowing after a day of rain. The earth was wet and moved beneath us like a sponge. I held Bob's arm as we walked, and he did exult in the beauty of the day and the high blue sky. We arrived at the spot, and I saw immediately that the rain had washed some of the soil back into the hole. Keeping it clean until Bob passed away would be a chore indeed.

"There I shall lie?" he asked. Birds sang, and the clouds danced by on the breeze above the treetops.

"There you shall lie," I said. "At peace for eternity."

He knelt with great difficulty and looked into the hole and then stood and touched Ellen Goodloe's stone. Tears filled his eyes and spilled down his thin cheeks.

"I shall be with my Ellen, and we will serve at the gates of Paradise," he said simply. I was deeply moved, and helped him back toward the house and then to his quarters and to bed. From his appearance that afternoon, I was sure that he would survive no more than a few days at most or perhaps a week or two if he rallied. But the days passed, and he did not seem to be any worse, and in fact his hearing and memory improved with each day. I was astonished but convinced myself that it was as a lull before a storm, a last gathering of strength before a collapse.

Each day, Bob would walk out to the grave and stand for a few minutes and look around, then walk back and help with the chores around the house, saying little. That walk began to change his color remarkably, and he kept at it every day, even during the rain, though I admonished him it was bad for his health. As it happened, I was entirely wrong, and Bob's weakness turned to strength, and his closeness to death began to fade. At first, Bob did not quite believe that he was better, and he was loathe to believe it entirely.

"Then I am not to be with Ellen yet?" he asked one day. We stood beside his grave, which had almost entirely washed back in and was then no more than a depression in the dark soil.

"It appears not, as God wishes," I said.

"Well then," he said, and he turned and walked back toward the house, and the subject of his demise did not come up again for some time.

As I have said, Jenny and Desdemona Smartt had become such close friends that they spent as much time together as Desdemona's duties at Foxhaven would permit. And though the twins were each not ready to lose a sibling, Mr. Dorset and Mr. Smythe finally worked out an exchange, whereby Molly McNew would leave her brother, Tom, at Longacre (or *Shortacre*, as Jenny was now wont to call it) and go to live with and serve Mr. Smythe at Foxhaven. Desdemona would leave her brother, Roderigo, and come to live with us at Longacre. Jenny was delighted beyond measure, and Tom McNew, who was drinking and wenching his way through the Province when not on duty, did not mind losing his sister for the nonce. Likewise, Roderigo Smartt was too busy chasing the servant girls at Foxhaven to mind his sister's move.

Though Desdemona was required to work at our house under my supervision, she and Jenny spent so much time together (which I could not gainsay, of course) that Des (as Jenny called her) seemed more like another child of Mr. Dorset's than a servant. Some other members of the staff chafed at this intimacy, but Mr. Dorset was pleased that Jenny had companionship. From reports I heard, Molly McNew got on splendidly with Mr. Smythe, and so the exchange worked well. Soon, Jenny had involved Desdemona deeply with the Daughters of Liberty, and all manner of conspiracies were about, including late-night meetings in the library by the light of a single candle. I cannot say what they discussed, but once, being unable to sleep and walking around the house, I saw through the window that they were gesturing and speaking with urgency, and, knowing Jenny, I understood immediately what it was about.

And so, as we drifted toward war, Mr. Dorset was still without a wife, Jenny had no husband, and Longacre had six feet less property along its cojoined line with Foxhaven. Mr. Dorset was finally disinterested in property lines anyway, and the plantation still produced fantastic amounts of rice and indigo so that his leisure was secure, and he could pursue his Muse. He took up painting again, and immediately struck a self-portrait which looked rather like a peasant with a dull, stupid expression on his face. I praised the work, or course, and Isaac, in horror, said it should be thrown in the fire before anyone in Town saw it. Matthew asked if it were a representation of God.

— 8. —

MATTHEW DORSET SURPRISES US BY ANNOUNCING THAT
HE WILL STUDY TO BE A CLERGYMAN, AND HIS FATHER ARRANGES FOR
HIS EDUCATION TO TAKE PLACE IN BOSTON.

Matthew had been more and more dreamy and less certain of himself
during those days just before the war, and he finally stopped his interests
in animal husbandry altogether. One evening at table, he asked if he
could speak. Isaac had been fretting aloud about the cost of a shipment
of implements, and Mr. Dorset had been asking if anyone had seen his
name in the *Gazette* lately.

"Speak?" said Mr. Dorset. "Of what? My glass, Hawthorne." I refilled
his glass, which he drained immediately and sat back to listen.

"For God's sake, Matthew, you cannot make a speech," said Isaac dis-
dainfully. "Sit down and eat your pork."

Jenny was eating very little, for she had been in Town all day conspiring
about something which I did not wish to know and was clearly preoccupied.

"I wish to announce to the family that I have decided to enter the ministry," he said. "That is why I disappeared that time, for God in His wisdom was calling me to be His servant."

"Sit down and quit making a fool of yourself," said Isaac, eating his own
food with the poor manners common to the Dorsets. (Isaac was already
rather portly and would become enormously fat in the ensuing years.)

"Let him speak," said Jenny.

"Certainly, speak of this," said Mr. Dorset, suddenly excited and interested. "Would you be of the Church of England or perhaps a Presbyterian?"

"I wish to be a priest of the Catholic Church," said Matthew.

"Waugh!" cried Mr. Dorset. "A Papist? My flesh and blood bound to
Rome?"

"Let him speak," said Jenny.

"This is madness," said Isaac. He looked at me unhappily. "My glass is
empty, Hawthorne. Do something about it." I refilled his glass.

"Go ahead then," said Mr. Dorset.

And so Matthew did, presenting the most theologically confused picture of his calling to the ministry that I have ever heard.

"When I ran away from here, as you recall, it was because God had
asked me to do so," he began.

"I'm glad He did not ask you to dance on one leg in the Council

House," said Isaac, and he began to laugh and shake, but no one else saw the humor.

"God asked me to come away for a time because He wanted to speak to me, as He had always spoken to me through the animals," said Matthew.

"Through the animals?" said Mr. Dorset. "Did he say that God speaks in the mouth of animals? Hah! Fancy that, Jenny, to hear a pig speak and know it is the voice of God." Mr. Dorset did not mean it unkindly at all, but Isaac roared with laughter, and Jenny hid a modest smile with her hand.

"I meant that I *felt* God when I was with the animals," said Matthew. "And I began to understand that if God created the Heavens and the Earth, as it is read in the Bible, He created the worms and the pigs and such, and He must have given them reason, though we do not understand it."

"Blasphemy," said Isaac gaily as he speared a slice of pork.

"And so I thought it my duty to understand what God meant in the words of these animals, and so I listened to them and found that I could translate their languages into ours," said Matthew. Mr. Dorset gave a worried glance to Jenny. "And through them, God spoke to me, and He said that I should become a priest and spread the word of the animals as Sir Francis of Asinni did."

"*St.* Francis of *Assisi*," said Jenny quietly. She was looking at Matthew now with love and sadness. Mr. Dorset was consumed with interest, and Isaac had stopped listening entirely.

"Yes, him too," said Matthew. "And God said that I should become a priest, and I ran away and I mocked Him!" Matthew began to weep. "I mocked Him, and when I came back, I was very sad because I did not believe the voice. But now I know it is true, that animals have thoughts and feelings and may speak to me if I but listen. And in their pain they are full of love and happiness, and I could not bear it, but then I could, and I said I would spread this word around the country. And so, Father, I ask that you send me to school to study for the priesthood."

"You should go about teaching that pigs may speak?" asked Mr. Dorset.

"Wine?" said Isaac impatiently, and I refilled his glass.

"I shall," said Matthew.

"All right then," said Mr. Dorset.

And just like that, Matthew was packed and bound for school in

Boston where he was to study for the priesthood. We received letters from time to time regarding his progress, but finally the mail stopped during the war, and it was only much later that we found he had been removed from the school and had become a farmer in the state of New Hampshire. He did not come home again.

With Matthew's departure, and Abel living on his own in Town and making money now as a purveyor of shipping goods, only Jenny and Isaac were left home with Mr. Dorset, and the family, once full, was slowly slipping away. Fortunately, Mr. Dorset was too busy with his rhymes to notice, Isaac was too irritated with his overseers, and Jenny had embarked on the career of her own personal war against the British (not to mention her amours). Still, we could see time passing us, and we who were servants worried that the family would fade entirely, and then we would be lost.

— 9. —

THIS HISTORY MOVES INTO THE YEAR 1775, AND THE ANGER WITH
ENGLAND FLARES INTO WAR. JENNY MAKES A DECISION
THAT AFFECTS MY LIFE.

We are forever hoping that the world will not change and that we may live out our days in the happiness we may have experienced in youth (if we are lucky). The world *does* change, however, and how we deal with it marks us deeply. The bitterness toward England had risen and fallen and then risen again in those years. Revolution could well have broken out after the Stamp Act, and might have but for its repeal. The Townshend Acts as well brought a great outcry from the merchants, and sentiment began that irretrievable march toward war that, once started, cannot be turned around.

In those years, Charles Town became greatly enlarged due to the successes of commerce. Many new wharfs were built, along with markets, public wells, and drainage systems. The Customs House was completed in 1770. By the time of our narrative in late 1774, the Town had seen days when more than eight hundred vessels would enter and leave our waters each year. In all, the times were very good indeed for business, which meant it was good for those of us who serve, as well.

Mr. Dorset's Stratford remained in very good condition because of a small staff that worked there, but, increasingly, Mr. Dorset remained at Longacre and confined his forays into Town to periods of only a few days,

depending on which tavern or whose arms he collapsed in. He frequently attended Mr. David Douglas's comedians, who had become wildly
popular in Charles Town during the early seventies. The troupe had built
a brick theatre in Church Street, and I particularly remember the season
of 1773 as being quite brilliant.

In June of the year 1774, however, the Crown closed the port of Boston
in retaliation for the dumping of tea into the harbor six months before,
and all the provinces were thrown into the most fervent anger. In South
Carolina, Mr. Gadsden was the one who, more than anyone, was enraged,
and he convened a meeting that summer to consider steps that Carolina
must take in the face of the King's insolence. By October, the Continental Congress itself had resolved that all Americans — for that is what we
now considered ourselves — must not partake in public frivolities in order
to demonstrate the seriousness of our response. Mr. Douglas's comedians,
even with a new theatre, had no choice but to cancel their season.

About all this, the Reader can have no doubt about the reaction of
Jenny Dorset. She was every day inflamed more, giving speeches to anyone in the house who would listen, and I was reminded of her childhood
when she spoke about the French in the same way. By November of
1774, Jenny had made a decision that would affect my family and my life
in a way I could not then imagine.

"I shall move into Town permanently," she said one evening at table.

"Here it comes again," said Isaac.

"Why would you do that, dear?" asked Mr. Dorset.

"For reasons of my own, being of age and able," she said forthrightly.

"You have been of age to marry, and look how you have handled that,"
said Isaac.

"I have handled it from my own free will," said Jenny angrily. "We are
born with that free will, all of us, even though some do not choose to
exercise it. And you are not wed, either."

"Say something new," said Isaac.

"Where do you get such notions?" said Mr. Dorset.

"From my friends in Town," she said. "It is in the air, Isaac, even if you
do not choose to reckon it."

"The only thing in the air is the stench of treason," he said. "Gadsden should be hanged. We will face losses of unimaginable magnitude
from this."

"Think of more than Longacre!" shouted Jenny. "Can you not see what is happening? That we are now slaves to England and will be made more so if we do not act?"

"Well spoken," said Mr. Dorset, who clearly agreed.

"Bah," said Isaac. "The only slaves are from Africa and are for sale to the right bidder."

"The very attitude that will drive you away once we have defeated England in war," said Jenny. Isaac began to smile knowingly, shook his head, and laughed.

"These friends of yours have given you more education than you can understand," he said. "You should remind them of your sex and its incapacity to retain more than one thought at a time."

Jenny, who should have exploded in wrath, merely took a deep breath and shook her head. She turned back to her father and repeated that she was to move into Town, and said — to my amazement — that she wished to retain my services along with that of my wife there. Of course, I could say nothing, but, in truth, Isaac's coldness and demands, and Mr. Dorset's vacant states made the proposition immediately attractive to me.

"And how do you feel about this, Hawthorne?" asked Mr. Dorset.

"I am pleased to serve as I am directed," I said. "I am particularly pleased to serve your daughter, as she has been kind to me."

"Well then," said Mr. Dorset.

"We cannot spare him," said Isaac loftily. "Neither Hawthorne nor his wife shall move with Jenny. She will return here in short order anyway."

"I shall not," she said. "And when this is over, you may be driven from the Province like a dog into the wilderness if you do not see what has happened."

"She has lost her reason," said Isaac. "Hawthorne? My glass is empty." I refilled it and glanced at Mr. Dorset, and I believe he knew from that small incident how I felt.

"I agree," he said. "My daughter, you may move into Town, and Hawthorne and his wife may accompany you. That is the least I can do for you."

"That is madness," said Isaac. "And you have overruled me in the presence of a servant." At that, Mr. Dorset rose to his feet, his face red with anger. He walked with his glass around the table and threw his wine into his son's face. Isaac stood, trembling with rage, but he could not speak back to his father, and finally, on the verge of tears, bowed curtly and left the room. Jenny went to her father and hugged him, and they both wept in the most touching way, and then he kissed her on the cheek and wished her his best.

"I shall be honored," I said when their intimate moment had passed. "And I have one favor to ask."

"Anything," said Mr. Dorset.

"May we take Old Bob with us?" I said. "He is growing more feeble by the day, and I believe I can take care of him best in that way."

"With all my heart, take Bob with you," said Mr. Dorset.

My wife was pleased with the assignment, for Town was exciting, whereas Longacre was increasingly an unpleasant place. Instead of the silence and the acres of indigo and rice, Town meant tinsmiths, tobacconists, gunsmiths, coachmakers, tanners, chandlers, blacksmiths, and much more. It meant a library and our fine natural history museum, which had been founded two years earlier. It also meant being at the living heart of the insurrection, which, of course, was Jenny's reason for moving into Town in the first place. Though public amusements had been banned, the work of taverns went on without stop in the dark alleys, and though the *Gazette* railed against the continued presence of "notorious bawds and strumpets," that old profession continued as well.

At this point in my life, I was fifty years old. Our daughters had grown, married, and moved off on their own. My wife and I thus moved alone into that new world, and she was happy indeed. (As I have said to the Reader before, I do not wish to place my family in this History and so have protected them in this manner. The Reader must not believe, however, that I was not devoted to them, for I was through all my years.)

Jenny was the matriarch of Stratford, and she ran it with surprising efficiency, giving orders for meals and for the upkeep of the grounds. Because Town was expanding around us so rapidly, she ordered the stables behind our house pulled down and made into a garden spot. She also hired the cabinetmaker Thomas Elfe to construct an oak sideboard, which was the most beautiful piece of furniture I had ever seen.

The use of the warehouse for the meetings of the Daughters of Liberty was now unnecessary, as Jenny ran her own household. And since I was head of her household staff and knew well about her activities, there was no reason to hide any of it from me. Though I worried about it all and continued to bear the guilt of knowing of the death of the soldier Huff, I protected Jenny in all ways. Her brother Abel, who had grown into a fiery young man of twenty-five, stopped by for dinners at times, and he and Jenny were consumed with details about the latest outrages or about rumors which swept the city like flames. I was pleased at how the refiner's fire of gaol had tempered Abel rather than charred him. He cut a dashing figure, and his heroism in the war turned out to be just as grand in life as his father's was imaginary. Isaac never came at all, and the only times I saw him were accidentally in Town, when he refused to recognize me in the street and went about his imperious way, supporting the Crown in all things. He seemed to put on fat by the day, and soon was shockingly corpulent, which he appeared to take as a sign of affluence. I heard little from Mr. Charles Smythe except that he was very much in favor of separation from Britain and so were his sons, Hamlet and Iago.

Old Bob continued to live, though in such a way that it was sad to see him try to move through every day. In that year he was seventy-eight years old, having been born into a different world and survived to see everything change and fade from his grasp. I was as patient with him as I knew how, but he was of little use around the house, for his memory was of such length that he could not be entrusted with the simplest instructions. I knew that God must have a reason for keeping Bob so long past his appointed time, but I could not see what it might be.

Jenny and Desdemona Smartt were inseparable, and Des became a full partner in the workings of the Daughters of Liberty, even though she was not of the class of those women. By sheer force of personality, she rose above it and became with Jenny among the most outspoken leaders of the group and of women who opposed the Crown.

We had no more serious outbreaks of smallpox, but there were still scarlet fever, measles, dysentery, and diphtheria with which to deal. Edmund Egan, a brewer, became famous for his beer, and John Cleaton was reputed to be the best blacksmith in the Colonies.

In a very short time, however, the fox hunts and cockfights and other amusements would come to an end. The taverns for gentlemen would be the scenes not for pleasures but for speeches and shouting. And the world as we had known it was to change with what seemed to be startling swiftness.

Jenny Dorset's career was to blossom in that fertile ground, and soon she would be more famous (and in ways her father was to find startling) than I could imagine. The world, whether we wished it to or not, was about to change forever.

BOOK VI.

— 1. —

IN WHICH WE SPEAK OF JENNY DORSET'S NEW LIFE AS A WOMAN LIVING ON HER OWN, ALONG WITH A DESCRIPTION OF HOW THIS BOOK WILL PROCEED.

I never had doubts that Jenny would flourish living alone in Town, but I was amazed withal at how much she enjoyed it. It was by no means unusual that a woman live by herself, but most were of a different class than Jenny, or, if of that class, had family living with them. In that heady atmosphere of taverns, sedition, and love, Jenny was in her natural element. She still worked against Britain with the utmost discretion, however, and her open warfare would not come until November of 1775, when Charles Town finally felt the first fire from the British in a war we thought might never end.

Our house became the center of what husbands and fathers thought to be women's parties. The men were glad to have the women gone for a time, and the women did not reveal their true purpose, the husbanding (so to speak) of a plan of many small actions against the enemy. They wrote letters to the *Gazette* in the name of British officials making preposterous claims of vilification against the Colonies. The women somehow managed to confuse British shipping agents' logs, so that even untaxed goods arrived at the wrong docks or were delivered to incorrect addresses. And they brought to the attention of the Sons of Liberty what they learned from British officers about their disposition of affairs. All this helped to undermine the British, and drew to Jenny the admiration from men such as Mr. Gadsden, who, for a while, did not identify her or her actions.

At the same time, Jenny embarked on a remarkable career in the art of love, for which I was both sorry and envious. I will not say that Jenny was not bound by conscience or the Church, for in those arts I cannot say how firm her faith was. I do know that she simply followed her instincts as her father did, and for that I can only assume that it was part of God's plan. I have overheard, in these late years, stories about Jenny Dorset in taverns, some of which are undoubtedly true and others of which are so fanciful that they must be an invention of men who never shared her pleasures but wished they had. Jenny never expressed to me any regret for her actions nor did she seem to feel any. She believed in her right as a free-born woman to allow herself expression in whatever form took her fancy. No woman of her breeding would now admit to such adventures, though some must surely share them.

I must admit that in my heart I desired Jenny as well (for it was nearly impossible not to), but along with that desire was a stronger urge to protect her and to remember her as a child, and those conflicting feelings seemed to cancel the other out, and I was left with friendship. She valued it from me as much as I valued it from her, and I can say before God that never in my marriage did I forsake my vows to my wife. In that, I can attest that I may have been one of the few men in Charles Town who did not.

I spoke much earlier in this History of Jenny Dorset's diaries and of her letters. I have made spare use of them so far, because they reveal intimacies which I felt should be reserved to Jenny as a child and young woman. In her full maturity, however, Jenny surely knew what she was about, and so I feel I can present them as the words of a mature woman. As they also shed light upon the character of Jenny and others, I believe they help to tell this History in a way I cannot, being of a limited education and known for no style. So I will take the liberty in this Book to use the words directly from Jenny's pen to explain how she felt in those days. The journal entries speak for themselves, for they are Jenny's record for her own accounting. The letters, however, require a modest amount of explanation.

When we lived at Longacre, Jenny sometimes wrote to Desdemona at Foxhaven or to friends in Town. Only when we moved to Town for good did Jenny understand the true value and joy of writing, and thereafter she was a writer of great proliferation, writing to patriots in the North, to friends in Town, to the Daughters of Liberty, and to Desdemona Smartt, when they were not together.

She also wrote letters to her lovers, and was forever correcting and rewriting them until she was sure they sounded correct. She saved all her first and second attempts, and so I have been able to read for myself the intimate details of her loves. I will spare the gentle Reader passages of the greatest passion and intimacy, but I can only say that without using some of them, this History would be dishonest, and I believe God wants honesty above all.

In the coming years, we had great tribulations and great joys. There was insurmountable pleasure and unbearable sadness. There was a trial and an execution. And there was growing alarm as the British, by the spring of 1776, mounted an invasion against us. Life, however, is not the delineation of great events, but the small daily acts of love and anger and hope and despair. While I shall use as guideposts the events of the world, I hope to tell the History of the Dorsets and not of our new state, as there are ample stories about the latter and none but what I know of the former.

— 2. —

BEING A LETTER FROM JENNY DORSET TO MR. JEDEDIAH BEARDEN, DISCLOSING THE INTIMACY OF THEIR RELATIONSHIP, ALONG WITH NEWS OF HER FAMILY AND THE CURRENT STATE OF AFFAIRS IN CHARLES TOWN. AND ANOTHER LETTER WHICH CASTS DOUBT ON HER RELATIONSHIP WITH MR. BEARDEN.

March 18, 1775
My dear Mr. Bearden,

My darling, did you think I would not respond to the four letters you have so kindly sent me? How you wrong me, sir! I pledge that you alone are utmost in my thoughts and my heart, and I can only share with you my delight in the memory of that _____ which you performed with such ardor. You are surely my darling and cannot be displaced in my affections, so rest at ease, sir.

I cannot but think of the delegates of our new government as much more than rogues, but at least we have the satisfaction of working now together against the British. (It is only with utmost effort that I even write the word!) My family continue to be deeply divided over the issue, with my father leaning now strongly toward our cause, while Isaac, my corpulent brother, continues to support the Crown. I fear he carves his own tombstone. The works of Abel Dorset you of course know, and, despite his sentence to gaol, I believe he now is on the track to greatness (or gaol again, if he not heed his conscience).

You fret unwisely for my steadfastness. I share my affections with no other man and never can, because none has your princely devotion to me or your wisdom. I find your manners exquisite, your clothing impeccable, and your compliments flattering. I beg you, however, to speak to me no more of marriage at present, for I am not of that mind as I have told you, and even the most admirable persistence in this regard will not arouse me to act.

Mr. Elfe is constructing for me the finest sideboard in town, decorated with sheaves of rice and our crescent moon. I can scarcely wait to see it!

Our flowers are in bloom in the garden, and my Mr. Hawthorne says that spring is like the resurrection of Christ's body. I see it in much less lofty glories, but I find them anyway.

My friend Selena told me yesterday that a soldier named De Vaugh was at a tavern on Tradd Street bragging of the brilliance of the British army. What imperious nonsense! The British army has nothing but failure ahead of them.

I have heard that a monster was washed ashore on Edisto Island, some hideous beast with two heads and many arms. I wrote to the Gazette and suggested that it be named King George IV, but Mr. Timothy did not find the letter amusing enough to publish.

> *Ever yours,*
> *Jenny Dorset*

March 18, 1775
My dear Mr. Thomas,

My darling, did you think I would not respond to the several letters you have so kindly sent me? How you wrong me, sir! I pledge that you alone are utmost in my thoughts and heart, and I can share only with you the delight in the memory of our latest assignation!

Yesterday I said in the presence of Bob, our very old servant, that I feared an attack by the British, and he misheard me, and, supposing there was actually an attack under way, he retrieved a gun from the house and went into the yard and fired off a shot which hit a tree and was deflected into the street, where it grazed a passing rider's horse apparently on the rump. The horse reared back and only with the greatest difficulty managed to fall so no bones were broken. Bob, believing the man was a British soldier, began to shout that he had defeated the man in legal combat and was due a boon from the King. The rider picked himself up, however, and when Bob went to inspect the body, it was gone. Mr. Hawthorne was the one who discovered what had happened. He promptly locked the guns away from Bob.

I need not say that you are the only one in my affections, and that I will always be yours, &tc. I really must close now, as I have many pleasant chores to do as mistress of this house. I hope that you recover your health soon.

Ever yours,
Jenny Dorset

— 3. —

MR. DORSET SHOCKS US ALL BY REMARRYING.
THE DREADFUL CONSEQUENCES OF HIS SELECTION,
AND HOW MR. DORSET SOLVES THEM.

I have spoken of how some women pursued Mr. Dorset and how those women fared against the unsteadiness of Mr. Dorset's character. In his life, there was only a Heaven or Hell and never a Purgatory, and so in all his decisions, he might be expected to be sound and wise or, on the contrary, spectacularly wrong. We have seen that he made a manifold mistake in hiring Miss Mackle to head his household staff after the death of Ellen Goodloe. And we have seen that he rarely knew in art what was good and what was less than good. In his frequent meetings with women, some were very fine and others unashamedly miserable. It was therefore cause for great alarm when one day a man named Mahlon, who was a field worker, arrived in Town with a letter from Mr. Dorset to Jenny that he was to be wed at Longacre on the following Sunday to a penniless woman named in his letter only as Miss Tonning.

"He could not have known her long enough to wed!" cried Jenny. "What on earth goes in men's minds that they make such sudden decisions about love?"

"I cannot say," I admitted. We were in the parlor, having packed some of Jenny's belongings for the trip out to Longacre. "Perhaps she is kindly and loving and in her your father sees a helpmeet for the coming years."

Jenny stopped her pacing and looked at me with such scorn that I could not continue to speak in that manner and so merely let the matter drop. I could only tell myself that this Miss Tonning could not possibly be as bad as many of the women Mr. Dorset had seen in recent months. I even managed to convince myself of her looks as I drove Jenny out in the carriage. I saw a young woman with light brown hair, kindly eyes, and a shy but frequent smile. She would look on Mr. Dorset with the greatest admiration and love.

Unfortunately, she in no way resembled that pleasant picture. She was nearly six feet tall, very heavy, and seemed to have been carved from stone, so set was her face against any pleasant looks at all. She was at the house when we arrived, helping to plan the wedding, and she began our relationship by cordially growling that our shoes were muddy and must be removed. She then told me I could not come in the house through the front door as I was a servant.

Jenny started to speak back, but I touched her arm gently and shook my head. She still looked extremely angry as I went around the house to the kitchen. When I got there, some of the other servants were huddled near the fireplace as if planning an insurrection, and their feelings were not short of that. Tom McNew came to me and shook my hand and then said Mr. Dorset had lost his senses entirely.

"This woman he intends to wed Sunday is mannish and mean, and she has already given notice that the household staff are to be used also in the fields!" said Tom.

"Perhaps he sees in her a love that is not seen by others," I suggested. The others laughed and mocked me, which I probably deserved.

"She is a d—d bear!" said Tom. The others begged him to lower his voice, and he did so, repeating the same sentence and adding that she was also vile and ugly.

"Talk some sense into him, Henry," said a woman named Sarah Hazel. She had been around for years and worked hard but was so devoid of personality that she at times seemed to vanish into the cabinetry. "He is lost in a world he made up. It's a fate foretold."

The others agreed and then cautioned each other to lower their voices. At that point we heard the sound of singing and looked up to see, through the open door, Old Bob holding a chicken and singing to it as he passed. For a moment, everyone forgot the war inside the house and stared beyond comprehension at the sight. Tom McNew returned us to our mission.

"Sarah is right, Henry," said Tom. "Speak with Mr. Dorset, or we are lost."

"I shall inquire after his health and mind," I said. "But cautiously."

And so I found myself a courier of yet another message to Adam Dorset, a mission I wished had not been thrust upon me. I went into the house and found that many of the furnishings had been rearranged to no purpose. The harpsichord had been simply turned halfway around. Paintings were moved to different rooms. The offensive portrait of Abel Dorset had even been hung in the stairwell, and chairs had been moved from one room to another. An entirely new set of vases had been installed, and their color and shape matched nothing else in the house at all. It was like visiting Longacre in a dream, where the night rearranges materials at its whim.

Miss Tonning came through the house once in her long dress, with its hem imperially sweeping along the floor, holding a small book in which she seemed to be taking accounts of something. She stopped and looked me over and then moved silently up the stairs, passing Mr. Dorset on the landing. He was running excitedly downstairs, dressed in finery as I had never seen him before, with a blue coat, a dazzling white shirt, and highly polished shoes. He seemed excited and yet somehow not himself.

"Henry!" he said when he saw me. "What a happy day is awaiting me on Sunday! Come into the library with me!"

I greeted him and followed behind. He bade me sit in a chair next to him, which I did. He sat very straight and smiled at me, crossing his legs at the ankles and seeming far more composed and ordered than I had ever seen him. That alone was enough to make me suspicious. There were no inkstains on his fingers, no ideas bursting from his head, no exuberant shouting.

"Have you met my intended?" he asked.

"I have, sir," I admitted cautiously.

"Is she not the very Venus for whom I have searched since the passing of Lydia?" he said. He wanted to me to agree with him so much that I nearly did before honesty overcame me.

"She is most unusual," I said. "May I get you a glass of wine?"

"No," he said softly. "I have sworn never again to touch a drop of spirits. It was a requirement from my dearest Miss Tonning for our nuptials, and I have had no trouble in obeying it. I am a changed man, as you can see."

"All of this comes suddenly to me," I said. "How long have you known Miss Tonning?"

"Nearly an entire month," he said. "She is the fairest woman in Carolina, and it is only by the grace of God that I have been permitted to ask her as my wife. No one can say that my heart is not now in the sound control of a fine woman."

"Have you gone mad?" asked Jenny Dorset from the doorway. Mr. Dorset stood and embraced his daughter as if he had not heard what she said. She repeated it.

"Mad?" he said. "Why on earth would you say such a thing, my dear?" They came in and sat. I stood out of deference and moved to the edge of the fireplace. "Have you seen my beloved?"

"I have seen an ill-tempered sow in the house ordering people around as if she were their mistress," she said.

"Lower your voice," he said, trying to smile. "Now what would make you say such a thing about Miss Tonning?"

"How did you know it was about Miss Tonning?" said Jenny. "What has happened to you that you would wed such a monster?"

"You speak as if you have been drinking, my dear," cautioned her father. "Please take better control of your emotions. A quiet, controlled person is what, above all, I admire."

"She has bewitched you," said Jenny. "We should hire someone to cast out spirits."

"Bewitched me with her steadfastness and her honor," he said. "I am unworthy of such love."

"She is unworthy of *you*," said Jenny. Just then, Isaac Dorset, stout and imperious, swayed into the room and said good day to his sister, ignoring me entirely. Jenny told him that their father had lost his reason in his preparations to marry Miss Tonning.

"In a fortnight, he will be shouting that someone bewitched him and that he was wrongly taken by her into marriage," said Isaac.

"A fortnight!" cried Jenny. "He said it not one minute ago." It was most peculiar to see them so discussing their father while he was there in front of them. Mr. Dorset seemed interested but took no offense, which added to the strangeness of the scene.

"I cannot say what has happened to him, but it is tragic for all of us," said Isaac. "And most tragic for Longacre, now that I have turned around the sad state into which it had fallen."

"Nonsense," said Jenny. "You could not turn around a child's mare."

"How dare you confront me with such nonsense," said Isaac. "This plantation continues to thrive only because of my firm hand and my course against the nonsense that you and your friends are spouting against the Crown. Your lack of honor will come back to you, dear sister, and when it does, I wish you Godspeed."

"And your lack of honor will come back to you at the end of a rope!" shouted Jenny. As their argument had become loud, Miss Tonning came into the room and demanded to know what in the world was causing such a problem in her house.

"It isn't your house, yet!" said Jenny. "And my brother is a fool!"

"My sister is mad," said Isaac, barely controlling his rage. "You should forgive her manners, but I will ask you not to speak of *your* house until it is so in fact."

"You cannot speak to me this way!" screamed Miss Tonning. "Adam, tell him he cannot speak this way to the mistress of Longacre."

"You cannot speak this way to the mistress of Longacre?" he said doubtfully.

"You are unruly children who must learn their place," said Miss Tonning, and, with that, she went to Isaac and began to mercilessly twist his left ear and criticize him in a voice so loud and harsh that the pen full of Mr. Dorset's hunting dogs began to howl and shriek and fight among themselves. Isaac tried to slap her hand away, but she kept wrenching his ear as Jenny began to laugh. Miss Tonning, seeing Jenny's mirth, went to her as if to twist her ear, but Jenny held up her fists as a man would and with her eyes welcomed the coming fight. Miss Tonning, startled that she would be so threatened, appealed to her husband-to-be, but he appeared to be thinking of something else entirely, perhaps verse or music. Miss Tonning finally gave Jenny a tongue-lashing and then turned on Isaac and did the same to him.

"Hawthorne, our father is mad," said Jenny as Miss Tonning left. "Please try to talk to him." She left the room, and so did Isaac, muttering to himself and staring at his sister with disgust. Mr. Dorset and I were alone, and he was humming and looking out the window, rocking back and forth on his heels. I went to his side and looked out the window with him.

"Sir, I mean no disrespect," I said, "but in nature there are things meant for each other, parts that live in perfect harmony. Each must have its mate and its time under Heaven. There are also those who cannot by nature do the same, such as the lion and lamb. Should they lie together, the lion would surely devour the lamb, just as a cat would eat a rat."

"I see," said Mr. Dorset.

"Sometimes, however, we put our trust in the wrong persons, for reasons we cannot immediately see," I continued. "We become like the trusting lamb who lies beside the lion and is then eaten. You see my point, sir?"

"Indeed I do," he said. "Jenny and Isaac are both like those lions, as I am, and together we are too many great animals for one house. Keen insight, Hawthorne. I shall hold it to me."

I bowed and left, for I realized that only time could now heal Mr. Dorset. I went outside and found Old Bob walking around in small circles and talking to himself, which made me sad.

The wedding on that Sunday was such a lavish affair that I knew Miss

Tonning had ordered up a huge amount of Mr. Dorset's funds to pay for it. There were garlands and new silver, decorations with gilt, a band of instruments, pipers, cooks hired from Town, a group of singers, and finally a guest list that included half the Low Country. My work began far before dawn, though the wedding was not to begin until half past two that afternoon. Jenny was in a fine outrage all morning, trying to undo all that Miss Tonning had ordered, which was a mighty lot. I will say for her that, if nothing else, Miss Tonning was thorough. She came out to the kitchen once, tasted a broth, and threw the spoon across the room while shouting that it was too salted and that the fool who cooked it should mind after his job.

The staff was in an uproar. They kept asking if this could be true and what would happen after the wedding, when the bride is most often less pleasant than before. I could not say, but the entire affair seemed unreal, and so I determined to speak to Mr. Dorset. I found him in his library, alone for once, reading a volume of poetry. Miss Tonning had wrought one miracle, that is, in Mr. Dorset's appearance. Rather than the ink-stained fellow with boundless enthusiasm, he was now very neatly dressed and seemed very restrained.

"Hawthorne," he said with a smile, "congratulate me, for it is my wedding day."

"My congratulations to you, sir," I said. The library was the only room where servants and slaves were not busily working, and it seemed an island of repose amid a storm.

"How kind of you to say so," he said. "Please sit next to me." I did so, and for a moment I composed my thoughts.

"Sir, may I be so bold as to offer you some advice?" I said.

"Of course you may," he said. "Have we not known each other all these years now as friends, Henry?" It was one of the few times he had ever called me by my Christian name, and it made what I had to say far more difficult.

"Yes, we have," I said. "Sir, this is not easy for me to say, but all of us are quite worried on account of this marriage. We fear that it will make Longacre a place in which we can no longer work."

"Why would they feel this way?" he asked without rancor.

"It is your bride-to-be," I said slowly, looking around. "She tolerates no pleasantness and seems offended by everything. She does not seem worthy of you, sir."

"Worthy of me?" he said. "It is I who am not worthy of her! She is kind and generous and as you have seen beautiful as a woman can be."

"She is?" I blurted.

Just then, someone dropped a tray in the room across the hall, and Miss Tonning's relentless screech, like a pig headed for the slaughter, floated above it all, eliciting mumbled apologies from the offending servant. I looked at Mr. Dorset as if to say, "See how even now she confirms my point?" but he looked only puzzled.

"Certainly she is," he said.

Feeling I could do no more, I went back outside to attend the kitchen and found Jenny on the lawn where the duel of bowls was to have taken place. She was pacing back and forth, holding a parasol to shield the sun. When she saw me, she came rushing over.

"I am thinking of having the strumpet killed!" she cried, her face red with anger. "She called me Maid Jenny! Can you imagine that monstrous thing as my stepmother, Hawthorne? I will not stand for it, I will not!"

"I fear your father is set upon it," I said. Desdemona Smartt came up, looking so much like Jenny that the sight was dazzling — two beautiful young women struck by sun and their emotions.

"Then we shall have to kill the strumpet!" shouted Jenny.

"Please, I beg you to lower your voice," I said.

"I have inquired around, and she is notoriously unwelcomed in Town, for she treats everyone in shops and so forth as her inferior," said Desdemona. "I can only think your father has been taken by a spell or a witch."

"Then how shall we kill the strumpet?" Jenny said. I thought of the soldier Huff, who had been buried unwept and whose murderers were not known to anyone but myself.

"Jenny, listen to me!" I said. I did not realize for a moment that I had stamped my foot to gain her attention and was now holding her arms to her side to stop her pacing. She calmed and looked at me just as Old Bob came tottering over holding a fork in one hand and a cat in the other. "You cannot change what someone is like. Your father has had these various moods all his life, and nothing will change things until he comes back to himself. You must allow him to be who he is and have faith in the powers of restoration, if not love."

"I have fetched this pig for table, but it seems to have grown a great hair along its back," said Bob. Jenny tittered, and turned her umbrella down to cover herself and Des. Once covered, they laughed so hard that their plans to murder Miss Tonning seemed less likely, and, for once, I was grateful to Bob. I told him gently that the creature he held was a cat, and he, surprised, took a closer look and admitted that it was.

"Are we eating cat, then?" he asked. Jenny swung the umbrella back and took the bewildered animal from Bob.

"Poor puss," she said. "We should not eat you, though Miss Tonning might. You stay away from her as you would a dog."

"A dog?" said Old Bob, peering closer. "I thought the fabric of their hair was coarser." With that, he took his fork and walked back toward the kitchen.

The wedding was to take place early in the afternoon, and I was surprised to see the subminister from St. Michael's return to Longacre to perform the ceremony. I heard that he had been demoted to a sub-subminister now and had very little to do, so he was in his glory. Late in the morning, the guests began to arrive. There were Ruperts, Bulls, Rutledges, Garfields, Ravenels, Sternes, and several dozen other families of note, all dressed in their finery, the women exulting in it and the men chafing at it. They wore powdered wigs, polished swords, and exotic perfumes I assumed came from the Orient. They came with their servants to attend them, tried to outdo each other in courtliness, and in general acted as if the world were perfect for them.

"Look at the swine," Jenny whispered to me as the ceremony got under way on the lawn not far from the topiary. "Little wonder they are in favor of the Crown. All that strutting pride and assurance."

"You are most observant," I whispered back to her.

"This is a foul day," she said. She drifted away to stand with Desdemona.

Needless to say, the entire Smythe clan was present, including the imperious Hamlet, who looked around him with a superior sneer, shaking his head at the food, the entertainment, the grounds, and everything else. Mr. Smythe himself also delivered himself of some fine insults to Mr. Dorset, who returned them cheerfully. At least between them the world was clear enough, a contest that, though at times was unpleasant, most of the time had an affectionate edge. It was my understanding that none of the men or women assembled for the marriage had ever seen the bride-to-be, and I do not know what they expected, but they clearly did not expect the woman who emerged from the house, wearing a plain dress which hung down like a curtain, and a frightful frown. She shielded her eyes from the sun with her hand and looked around for Mr. Dorset.

"Come and escort me," she said.

"Yes, my dear," he said obediently.

The crowd gasped when it got a good look at her. Miss Tonning, unlike the other women, had used none of the cosmetic arts to change her looks, instead seeming to dare anyone to mention her plainness. Before Mr. Dorset could arrive at her side, one of the hounds came galloping up to her from a long run, foaming at its mouth and looking tired and happy. She rewarded its attentions by a violent kick, which caught the poor animal in the hindquarters and sent it crying off around the front of the house. Men and women began to whisper to each other. Jenny and Desdemona came back to my side, and Jenny whispered.

"Do something," she said. "Shoot her. Do something."

"Be quiet now," I said. "It's in the hands of God."

Perhaps God's blessings were about, but you could not have guessed it from the long faces of the crowd. The sub-sub-minister, not caring if Mr. Dorset were about to marry an ape, came rushing over and smiled with such genuine pleasure that I felt sorry for the poor man. I looked around at the crowd, which had gone silent. Everyone had been astonished when Mr. Dorset had chosen not to marry in the church itself, but that was nothing compared to the surprise of seeing this wretched, heavy, unhappy woman ready to take Mr. Dorset in marriage.

I kept having the feeling that something would intrude, some calamity such as Old Bob wandering into the middle of things, but he kept his place as did everyone but Jenny, who could not stop pacing. But no such thing happened, and the ceremony was over in less that half an hour, and the band began to play, and all came up to congratulate Mr. Dorset and his wife. She never one time smiled through this, though she seemed to try, and curtseyed as well as she might, though for a woman of her weight, there was always a chance she might fall.

As I worked through that afternoon, most of those present were appalled by the demeanor of the new Mrs. Dorset and could not stop whispering of how ugly she was and mean as well. The rest of the afternoon faded past without incident, and the next morning, my wife and I took Jenny, Des, and Bob back to Stratford, but not before Mrs. Dorset (though it pains me even at this remove to describe her thus) had shouted at us for several imagined violations of her procedures in the house.

"He has gone mad," said Jenny simply. "And once a person is mad, he will never come back to his senses."

"Fences?" said Old Bob.

The next morning, in the heavenly silence of Stratford, there was the sound of a door slamming and rapid footsteps. Jenny was still asleep, and so I was baffled as to whom it might be. I came into the parlor to find Mr. Dorset sitting in a chair, his legs sprawled out before him, his hand over his eyes.

"Sir?" I inquired. "What are you doing here? Are you all right?"

"What have I done?" he cried. "She is monstrous!" He stood and looked around as if seeking something important.

"May I bring you something?" I asked.

"A bottle," he said. "And no glass."

He drank half of the contents of a bottle of French wine and sank back into his chair.

"What on earth has happened?" I asked.

"I was preparing last evening for, well, how shall I say this, Hawthorne — intimate acts?" he began. "And I had begun to undress myself, when she began to scream at me that the very thought of me in that fashion gave her a catarrh. She began to call me names I could not imagine she knew, and then she took an implement from the fireplace and chased me into the library, where I fell over a chair and sustained this bump upon my head." He pointed to his forehead, but I saw nothing that seemed very serious.

"She hit you?" I asked. He exhaled and shivered.

"I did not give her the opportunity!" he said. "I leapt through a window and saddled my horse and left." He took another long drink from the bottle. "And she is *ugly*! She is so malformed and ugly! Hawthorne, what came over me? Had I sipped some brew through which all senses fled from me?"

"We all lose our reason at times," I said carefully.

"Then I must have lost mine," he said sadly. "She came into the yard and waved the implement around her head and said to me that I was not welcome back in the house as long as I had such impure thoughts. She said I must undergo a mortification of the flesh. Then she started shouting it over and was so loud that the dogs became upset and howled piteously and then fell into a great fight with each other. What can I do? Now what can I do?"

"I am sure Jenny would not mind you staying here," I said.

"I most certainly would!" she said coming around the corner from the hall, where she had apparently been listening to her father. "It was not madness that seized you. It was your blindness to the world and its truths! You have for all these years never looked at the world, instead believing your misbegotten fancies and your verses. Now you want to plead that your eyes have been opened? This is my house now by right, and I will not have you here, much as I love you, deterring me from my purpose." I knew what Jenny meant — her meetings with the Daughters of Liberty — but Mr. Dorset seemed baffled and then broken, and so he took another sip of the wine.

"Then I am cast adrift on this sea," he said sadly. "I will pass into history without a tear shed or a memorial given. It will be as if I never existed."

"You are bringing me to tears," said Jenny with biting wit. "Please stop before I am unable to continue."

"Should I go back, then?" he said. "Back to that creature who has inhabited my house?"

"You are a man," said Jenny. "You own Longacre. Do as you will."

"But now she owns it by half as my wife," he said, nearly becoming sick over the final word in the sentence.

"You should have seen what she was," said Jenny. "And I do not wish you here now explaining your multiple failures to me."

Mr. Dorset retrieved his hat and walked toward the door, finishing the wine and handing me the bottle. He was utterly broken in spirit, and moved slowly, like an old man or an old horse, not caring in which direction he went. He turned back to Jenny and waited for her to change her mind, but she was in no mood to do so, and he merely bade us goodbye and rode slowly farther toward Town.

It was only two days later that I learned — to my great astonishment — that Mr. Dorset had moved into Mr. Charles Smythe's town house, with his compliments! Reports reached us from Longacre that the new Mrs. Dorset was such a monster that slaves were begging to be sold. I would like to say a word here in Mr. Dorset's defense, but nothing comes to my mind.

— 4. —

A LETTER FROM A SUITOR FOR JENNY DORSET,
A CERTAIN MR. THOMAS HILLFORTH, AND HER REPLY.

Charles Town
April 15

My dear Miss Dorset,

As we have known each other this year now, I would like finally to press my suit and make formal what we both know is in my heart. When I first met you I had despaired of finding for myself a companion suitable to my taste and education, and I dared not think that, if I might, she could ever be as beautiful as you. For you are like the sun which hath an appointed fixture with night and yet lingers above the horizon for the sheer glory of the day. You are like the rose, when, upon opening and damp with dew, is perfect yet grows even more beautiful as it dries and opens further. As you know, I am a man of no small means, and though salting fish may perhaps be unseemly to you, I have found wealth in it, and I am now independent in my means and well suited on that account.

And therefore, humbly in the eyes of God and trusting in the strength of our friendship, I now ask that you become my wife. Please do not keep me waiting but post your answer at first opportunity to me.

Yours,
Thomas Hillforth, Esq.
Merchant, &tc.

To which Jenny Dorset replied:

April 15

Dear Mr. Hillforth,
Thank you for your posting, which your servant so kindly left here this morning. I admire your handwriting and your way with a sentence.
Have you heard the terrible and insolent news that the Crown is sending more troops here to enforce their illegal policies? I cannot bear the thought of them here to force us to be pigs with them in that trough called England! It is worse than wallowing in the filth called France!
The weather is lovely, is it not? We have a fine garden growing, though some insect is eating our tender plants and we have not yet been able to dispatch the beasts.
Perhaps we might have rum together sometime, as I have found it a pleasure to have a man's company when I submit to the pleasures of the bottle. I only wish I could remember the man's name afterward!
I hope you fare well on this pleasant day.

Yours sincerely,
Jenny Dorset

— 5. —

Old Bob passes into History, and we lay him to rest beside his beloved Ellen Goodloe at Longacre. The new Mrs. Dorset is unpleasant in the extreme, and Jenny makes a plan.

About that same time, it was clear that Old Bob's health was declining rapidly and that soon he would join his ancestors in Heaven. Jenny hired several of the best physicians in Town, but the dilemma was expressed best by one James Rideaux: *That which nature has brought forth at some time must she take back, and nothing upon this Earth may stop it.* So hearing that, we decided to make Bob as comfortable as we could. After a day abed, he could no longer walk or move, and his voice had dwindled to a hoarse whisper. I sat by his bed, encouraging him to take water, but he finally surrendered against that need as well.

It was a morning in early May when he passed away. The flowers were in their great blossoming, and despite our fears of war, the world was soft, damp, and fragrant (if you did not go too far into Town, where there was a fetid stench which hung over the alleys like a pall). Bob lay propped in his bed, and his breathing was uneven and slow. He looked as old as anything which had ever lived, and I knew that soon his aging and his pains would be gone.

"Henry," he said. I sat next to him and leaned close. I had summoned Jenny, who was present and in tears, as well as my wife, who was likewise affected.

"I am here, Bob," I said. "What is it, old fellow?"

"I have been visited by a tall man with spectacles and no teeth," he said very slowly. "He waved an implement at me and told me to make sounds like a horse. Do you think I should do so?"

"Whatever you will," I said.

"Is this death?" he asked, not at all afraid. Jenny cried aloud.

"Yes," I said. "You are approaching what we must all accomplish sooner or later. I will pray for your soul."

"Fluuppp," he said. "Is that how a horse speaks? Fllllupppppp!"

He tried to make the sound again, and his eyes closed and then opened once more, and he smiled broadly, looking around the room and seeing nothing. Just then, Mr. Dorset arrived, for I had sent after him a servant like myself with the news.

"Is he dead, then?" asked Mr. Dorset.

"I am dead," said Old Bob, nodding. "Would you like a pudding?"

And with that, he exhaled long and slow, and his eyes did not close or his mouth, and Old Bob had died. Jenny ran from the room, and my wife went with her and comforted her. Mr. Dorset and I looked at Bob, and I closed his eyes.

"I cannot remember a time when he was not with me," said Mr. Dorset. I thought he might fall to his knees in prayer. "I believe I feel an ode coming upon me. Make arrangements, would you, Hawthorne?"

"Sir," I said with a nod. He left, and Old Bob and I were alone. The window was open and birds' songs came in like flutes. The day was in its way perfect, and I sat and held Old Bob's thin, bony hand for perhaps a quarter of an hour before I was convinced that his soul had left his body and was flying up toward Heaven.

Jenny decided that Old Bob should be buried at Longacre next to Ellen Goodloe in the grave we had dug for him the year before, and so we called the burial preparator and had him make Bob's body ready for burial. We put it in a fine coffin and drove sadly out toward Longacre, with myself and my wife and Jenny in the brougham, and Mr. Dorset and his son Abel following on horseback. We had sent word ahead that Bob had died and that we were bringing him home for burial, and we therefore supposed that the new Mrs. Dorset would be at least sympathetic to the situation, but we were wrong. Though she allowed us inside for a few moments to refresh ourselves, she gave me an order to scrub floors, which Jenny immediately countermanded with a shout and the stamp of her foot. Mr. Dorset hid behind me, whispering how terrible his wife was. The staff was deeply saddened, and one by one came by outside to see Old Bob's coffin as we bore it soon thereafter to the resting place beside Ellen Goodloe.

Mr. Dorset's wife did not come to the obsequies, instead choosing to stay in the house and complain bitterly about how we had brought mud and dust on our feet and spoiled the parlor. We got to the grave site and took the coffin down from the wagon and set it on the ground. I looked up to wipe my brow and was startled to see a line of men and women, both white and Negro, coming up the slope toward our family burying ground. I felt a pride and only wished I could have said to Bob in his life: *See how they come, friend? Thou hast done thy service well, and now they honor thee.*

Mr. Dorset had tried to get a minister, but the sub-sub-minister of St. Michael's had been dismissed sometime before in an incident involving a washerwoman and her baby. The *Gazette* never printed anything about it, but all knew it anyway. The disgraced clergyman went to the Indies, we heard, where he reportedly tried to convert a tribe of savages. I do not know of his success, but I never again heard his name spoken, and no word of him came back.

Mr. Dorset therefore asked me, as Bob's lifelong friend, if I might say a few words. I rarely spoke aloud in such situations, being more inclined to watch and listen, but I could not forego the request, as I owed both to my employer and my friend. I waited until all the mourners had arrived at the grave site, and there must have been nearly fifty, which would have pleased Bob greatly. I did not commence my few remarks until the silence had quite overwhelmed us.

"We come today to bid farewell to our friend Robert Burke, aged seventy-eight," I said, "and to lay him beside his beloved wife, Ellen." Jenny cried aloud, and Desdemona Smartt comforted her by holding her shoulders. Abel Dorset leaned pensively against a tree, and his father glanced suspiciously into the grave, which had been dug out properly. "We knew him variously as Bob or Old Bob, and he brought delight into our hearts. He was a good man and decent, and he always did his best to serve well. I can think of no better epitaph for someone of this class than *he served well.* He lived long, asked little of us, and brought us hope and cheer. He is now at the throne of God with his Maker and with his wife, and I can only say that in my heart I am not sorry that he has been allowed to leave this earthly body behind, even though all of us shall miss him. He was for many of us like a brother, and uncle, or a father."

Mr. Dorset began to weep, and Jenny left Desdemona and went to him and they embraced. Abel looked as if he wanted to join them more than anything, but he withheld his emotions and stood by the tree and looked down. I read a few verses from the Bible, including the Twenty-Third Psalm, and then we took the ropes and lowered Bob into the earth. Several of the slaves with shovels covered him up, and soon the grave was finished. Jenny had cut a flower from the garden at Stratford that morning before we left and put it in her hair. She knelt and placed it on the grave and turned and walked back toward the house with her father. The rest of the company, except for Abel and myself, followed them. Bob was dead and nothing more was to be done. I stood by the grave in silence for a time before I noticed that Abel was still there.

He pushed himself off the tree and came to me, glancing down at the grave and then back at me.

"Do you know," he began, and then he fell silent. He cleared his throat and stood straight with his hands behind his back. "Do you know how much you have meant to this family?" His voice was hoarse and confined. "Do you know how much you have meant to me in my life?"

"Myself, sir?" I said.

"I am proud that you are my friend," he said, and he clasped my arms, turned on his boot heels, and walked quickly after the others. I was dumbstruck, and, to this day, no one has ever said a finer thing to me or made me feel as if this life of service had been less than wonderful.

I said my farewells to Old Bob, remembering his various mishaps and mistakes, and wishing more than anything that he would be around that evening to make more. I was surprised that Mr. Charles Smythe did not come, but I found out why in short order, and it was to be terrible news for our neighbor as well.

I got back to the house just in time to see Jenny and her stepmother engaged in a violent screaming match, during the course of which the stout Mrs. Dorset grew steadily uglier while Jenny grew steadily more beautiful. Abel and Mr. Dorset got on their horses and fled, riding back toward Town, and it was only with all my urging that I got Jenny from the house, and we joined my wife in the brougham for the ride back.

"She is a vile beast who should have been drowned at birth!" Jenny cried. "I cannot live with that monster in my house. Help me think of something, Hawthorne!"

"I am sure something proper will come to you," I said.

"I daresay it will," she said.

I could not think then of her warfare with the British or the woman who was lately Miss Tonning. I could only suffer my loss of Bob in silence as we made the trip back to Town, where the house would be much quieter.

After that, I quietly ordered a sandstone marker for Bob, which merely said *Robert Burke, servant* and the dates *1696–1775*, and I drove out one day when it was finished and set it into the ground myself. I believe that I shall see him soon in Heaven, and I wonder if he has been made young again by grace or whether he will be old for eternity. Either way, I look forward with gratitude to seeing him once more.

— 6. —

A SECTION FROM THE DIARY OF JENNY DORSET
CONCERNING OLD BOB'S DEATH AND HER BATTLE WITH
MISS TONNING, ALONG WITH INTIMATE DETAILS WHICH THE MORE
DELICATE READER MIGHT DO WELL TO PASS OVER.

May 1, 1775

We laid Bob, the old servant, to rest amidst the grove of trees next to his wife and not far from my mother's grave. It was a very sad occasion and yet somehow refreshing, for it gave me a sense of life and how to live it yet once again. I wish to be laid near the same spot, and I hope that the sun is bringing his warmth in a cool season but mildly, for I do not wish the rot to begin too rapidly. Regarding Miss Tonning (I refuse to call her by any other name), I believe she will have to be driven from Longacre like cattle from a field, though I do not yet have an idea of how to do so. She is too large to push down a well and too canny to fall for many other tricks, but I shall find some way in which to deal with her, and when I do, she will never want to speak the word Longacre again.

Mr. _____ believes that because I have laid with him that he should now marry me and relieve me of the sin, the burden of guilt, &tc. I have tried to dispel these notions, but he persists in thinking that he has ruined me and that should a child result my reputation would be ruined, not to mention his. Strangely enough, I received a similar dispatch from Sr. _____, who is heading back for Seville and wanted me to come with him so that I could live with him on his estate. He swears with all his heart that his wife would not mind, as long as I did not appear in the hacienda too often! Where men gather these notions, I cannot say, but they cannot believe that a woman might wish to enjoy what men do, for they have been taught that none but evil women can enjoy these pleasures. With men so foolish and rash, it is a wonder their kind has lasted long enough to keep the world peopled with children.

I will answer both men that they are kind and thoughtful, but that in this life I go my own way without fear and that I have no need of their succor to survive. They will be sad and relieved and remember me with fondness in their old age.

7

THE UNEXPECTED ARRIVAL AT STRATFORD OF AN AUNT OF WHOM
I HAD NEVER HEARD, AND HOW SHE CHANGES THE RELATIONS THERE.

Not long after Old Bob died, an event entirely unexpected occurred at our
house. We had no need of replacing Bob, as he had not been able to do
much for a long time anyway. Mr. Dorset came over from time to time
from the Smythe house, where he still resided, and visited with his daughter. Sometimes in a tavern, I would be sitting in a quiet corner enjoying my
pipe when he might come roaring in with a woman not of his class and
laugh, recite poetry, and in general pay court to a woman with whom court
was usually paid in shillings rather than in words. He seemed to enjoy himself, however, free from the mad mistress of Longacre. We heard from Longacre that Isaac and Miss Tonning had been involved in furious battles over
the house and that he was slowly giving way to rages over the situation. He
even went so far as to hire a lawyer to see if the marriage might be declared
illegal, but nothing could be done, and the lawyer demanded a fee so
absurd that Isaac hit him, and might have drawn prison time had this particular lawyer not been adjudged by one and all as eminently and repeatedly hittable. As for Abel, he was becoming more and more known in Town
for his fiery speeches against the British, and I had to admit that the young
man had turned out far different than I might have expected. We heard
nothing from Matthew, studying for the ministry in Boston.

Early that summer, Charles Town was in a ferment, reacting to continual news that the British were to arrive with troops, that we were in mortal danger, Etc., but nothing happened directly. Then one steaming hot
morning, when the sea breeze seemed to die and leave us swarmed with
mosquitoes and other biting bugs, there was a knock upon the door which
I answered. There stood before me a tiny woman with tiny feet and a black
dress which seemed to make noises even as she stood still. She carried a
parasol and had something of a mustache and beard, though her hair was
not yet entirely gray. Her eyes were nearly shut against the sun, and she
was wet from the intensity of the heat. She smiled and curtseyed, showing
teeth that were quite crooked yet well maintained. She had placed a beauty spot on her left cheekbone, but it had slid from the dampness of the air
down her face and was now hanging on the hair from her beard.

"Madam?" I said. "Who may I say is calling?"

"Is Miss Jenny Dorset home?" she said in a low but very pleasant voice.

She smiled, and it contained something so genuine, with such a lack of guile, that I liked her instantly and found the mobile beauty spot almost charming.

"Yes, she is," I said. I was about to ask again who she might be when Jenny passed behind me and stopped and took a few steps toward me.

"Auntie Sally?" she said. Jenny came so close behind me that I could feel her breathing on my neck. "Auntie Sally!"

"My word, Jenny!" the woman said. "Look at you!"

They embraced, and Jenny told me that the woman was indeed her aunt, the widow of her father's youngest brother, Isham, who had moved early in life from Charles Town to Williamsburg and died young from a fever. Auntie Sally had early in Jenny's life made a long visit to Longacre, but, for a reason I could not recall, I had been gone at the time. She had borne but one child who died soon after birth, and when her husband died, she had remained in Williamsburg for many years.

She told Jenny she had come to visit, being newly arrived in Town and having heard by letter from Mr. Dorset of his daughter's place of residence. They had much to catch up on, and I left them in the parlor talking excitedly about the old days, when Jenny was a child. (I confess once more that in the comings and goings of Longacre in those earlier days of ferment I could not recall Mrs. Isham Dorset at all, and, from the look of her, I think I would have remembered.)

I brought tea for what I thought was to be a polite visit and found to my amazement that Aunt Sally had brought all her bags with her, a porter being outside with a wagon now bringing them in. Their number and variety were staggering, and their condition ranged from pristine to wretched and tied up with rough rope.

"Auntie Sally has come to live with us," said Jenny excitedly. The old woman twitched her mustache and smiled, then uttered the most alarming laugh I had ever heard from a person, like the hoot of some bird from the swamps collapsing from mirth. I had never heard anything like it, and I was so astonished that I simply held the tray and did not move to pour tea for them. Aunt Sally's beauty spot by now was hanging from one whisker, from where it refused to fall, though it fluttered each time she laughed, which seemed now to come in gusts like the wind before a storm.

"I am very pleased," I said finally.

"That's four shillings, ma'am," said the porter, who was leaning against the wall, chewing on the inside of his cheek and looking around at the elaborate furnishings of the house with disdain.

"Jenny, dear, can you pay this tradesman?" said Aunt Sally. "I am down to my last coin, and I wanted to save it for good luck." Jenny smiled at her aunt and nodded to me. She had given me control of a small household fund for such things, which I kept in an alcove in the hall in a small porcelain bowl. I gathered the shillings and paid the man and escorted him out the door, where he turned and looked at me.

"Say, sport, is that an old lady or an old gent'lman in a dress?" he said.

"A lady of some standing," I said. "Who does not condescend to deal with such as you directly."

"Don't she then," said the man. He went to his wagon and I came back inside just as Jenny was watching with amusement as Aunt Sally held a small vase nearly to her nose and tried to read the maker's mark on the bottom. When Aunt Sally began to set it back down, she missed the table and it shattered, which amazingly set off another round of laughter from the woman. Jenny, caring little for such material possessions, laughed along with her. By now, the traveling beauty spot had moved from her whiskers to her dress and was hanging off an intimate part of her body in a most conspicuous way.

"My, the table has moved," said Aunt Sally, and, from her squint, I deduced instantly that the old woman was very nearly blind but would not admit it nor would she condescend to spectacles.

"It moves often," said Jenny.

"Well, perhaps that is why it has legs," said Aunt Sally. Jenny began to laugh with complete disregard for her manners, more like a girl than a woman, and I must admit it was attractive on her. Given the signal that her destruction was no disaster, Aunt Sally began to cry and hoot again with her own laughter.

"Perhaps that is why it has legs," said Jenny. I poured them tea, and Aunt Sally could barely see the cup. Jenny and I were both watching the beauty spot for further mischief on its part, and indeed it took only a short time to occur. Aunt Sally was talking about her voyage down from Williamsburg and how it had been quite rough. As she held the teacup in its saucer, the beauty spot became dislodged from her person and fell straight into the tea. Jenny gasped and looked at me, but before either of us could say a thing, Aunt Sally took a large drink of the tea, and, upon swallowing, looked down into the cup.

"Might have been strained better," she said. At this, Jenny lost control entirely and got up and excused herself for a moment and went down the hall where she could hardly catch her breath. I tried not to laugh, but it was nigh impossible. If Aunt Sally knew that we were making fun of her, she did not let on, but she kept looking in the cup.

And so Mrs. Sally Dorset moved in with us, and Jenny seemed very pleased to have the company, even though, as each day passed, we found that she was even more blind than we had imagined, and was constantly running into walls and spilling things. And yet she took our minds away from the loss of Old Bob in a way that was, I think now, quite touching, and perhaps ordered from God who knew our loss. Mr. Dorset, when he found out that his sister-in-law was living with us, came to visit, but he stayed only three-quarters of an hour before he fled to a tavern.

The old woman had nothing whatever to do, and, since public amusements in Town had been banned, she could do little but sew clothing, at which she was so bad that even a sock was beyond her, being enormous on one end and so small on the other that even a child could not wear it. Once she told me that we might have the hog in the street for dinner.

"I beg your pardon?" I said.

"The hog in the street," she answered. "I believe it is fattened. See for yourself." I went to the window and looked out to see a large vagrant dog which was leaning against our gate asleep with its tongue hanging out because it was hot.

"I shall attend to it," I said.

She was pleased and went back to sewing upon a dress for Jenny, which she subsequently finished, but which was higher on one side by about two feet. After Jenny modeled it, and Mrs. Dorset had seen her error, she set about making it right, but only managed to make it even worse misshapen, after which she tried to turn it into curtains, an attempt which also failed.

— 8. —

THE SAD DEATH OF MRS. OPHELIA VAN DYKE SMYTHE,
AND HOW THAT EVENT REARRANGES OUR NARRATIVE IN A WAY
WHICH COULD NOT HAVE BEEN EXPECTED.

That spring of 1775 was beautiful, as I have said, with mild breezes and blossoming flowers. Our fight against the British had not taken full hold yet, and our house in Town once again seemed a family, though a strange one, it is true, with the arrival of Aunt Sally. The old woman for a time even kept Jenny from her amours and her meetings with the Daughters of Liberty, but soon everything was back as it was ordained, and Jenny was spending her nights God knows where, and Aunt Sally's blindness was such that she was constantly walking into doors and furniture. It appeared for a time that we might spend a year with no departures from the living for Heaven in our circle, but then we received the word that Mrs. Smythe was mortally ill with a disorder of the heart or lungs.

"I must go to him," Mr. Dorset said at table one night. Since it would be easier for us to keep vigil from the closeness of Longacre, we packed and moved back to the country to await the death of Mrs. Smythe. Mr. Dorset's wife (a term I used only in the legal sense) had entirely rearranged the furniture, putting the fine pieces in storage, replacing them with the most ill-assorted and poorly constructed chairs and tables imaginable. Where Jenny's harpsichord once stood was now a large throne of sorts that had no connection with anything else in the room.

"Would that it were the seat of Henry VIII," Mr. Dorset whispered to me as we came into the room. Jenny was furious that her keyboard had been moved. (She had a spinet in Town but had not yet moved the family's harpsichord because, as she said, it "lived" at Longacre.)

""Would that it were a *gallows*," said Jenny. Isaac Dorset came into the room, and the change that had come over him was so astonishing that we barely recognized him. He had gained even more weight, and his eyes were dark circles from which no light seemed to emanate. In the interim he had been married, and his wife, who was as colorless as winter, did not appear. (We had attended the wedding, but, as it does not directly affect this History, it may await telling in another volume, should God give me strength to do so.)

"You look ill," said Mr. Dorset. "Have you had a catarrh?"

"I have had your wife until she is making me mad," said Isaac. "Could you not see to take her into Town with you?"

"God save me!" cried Mr. Dorset. "I would be dead in days."

"She is possessed by Satan and his legions," said Isaac, and then he began to laugh in a most shocking manner. "She is an agent of the darkness."

"Speak to me of something I do not know," said Mr. Dorset.

At that point, we heard footsteps, and suddenly that enormous Miss Tonning, wearing a scowl and a black dress, appeared in the doorway and looked over us with a frightful glance that seemed to grow more furious by the second.

"Your feet have not been cleaned!" she cried. "Your hands are filthy! You may not be allowed into the streets of Heaven with filthy hands!"

We were dumbstruck except for Jenny, who coolly said, "What have you done with my harpsichord?"

"You would lay those soiled fingers on such a thing?" said Miss Tonning.

"What have you done with it, you swollen sow?" said Jenny. There was a moment of silence, following which an explosion occurred with such force that I thought a keg of black powder might have been ignited.

"Punish her!" Miss Tonning screamed at her husband. When Mr. Dorset seemed baffled and startled, and did nothing, Miss Tonning gasped. "Punish her and be done with her blasphemy, Mr. Dorset! I am your wife and I demand it!"

"Don't say that word," said Mr. Dorset weakly. "I become ill when I hear that word."

"Punish her!" cried Miss Tonning. And with that, she took matters into her own hands, not by punishing Jenny but by rushing to Mr. Dorset and hitting him in the stomach with her fist. He cried aloud and fell to his knees, because Miss Tonning was as tall as he and a stone heavier. She told him again to punish Jenny, and he reacted, coughing and spitting, by rushing from the house. For a moment, it appeared she would punish Jenny herself, but Jenny fled as well, and Miss Tonning's shouts chased her out the front door. I was so consumed by the spectacle that I did not realize I was now the only one in the room with the swollen sow, as Jenny had put it. (Aptly, I thought, except that the idea of Miss Tonning as a sow about to give birth made me quite ill for the thought of it.)

"I shall attend them," I said stupidly.

"You shall attend *me*," she said with icy reserve. She carried her bulk toward me, as a ship cutting through waters, glaring with a victorious gleam, because I was now the final challenge left in her path to crush. "You shall do what I wish, when I wish it. You are a servant, despite how my husband has treated you, and I swear before God that I will remind you of your place. You are not above washerwomen and field hands or even the slaves, for that matter. I am the woman of this house, and if I ask you to do my bidding in any manner, you will bow, admit my authority, and do as I bid. Is that entirely clear?"

"Entirely," I said.

"Very good," she said bitterly. She began to shake a thick finger at me. "Then cut down all those hedges in the shapes of animals. They are the sign of the devil."

"I will not," I said. Her face reddened.

"You will do as I say!" she shouted. "You said that I was entirely clear."

"You were entirely clear," I said. "And clarity has its uses. However, I do not work for you and never shall, for you are rude, insensitive, loud, and, if I may add it, uncommonly ugly." For a moment, she was simply stunned beyond words, and in truth I was speechless myself due to the loss of my self-possession. I had never in my life spoken thus to a superior, but I knew as soon as I uttered the words that I meant them, and that I was willing to suffer the consequences, though I was modestly certain there would be none.

"You are dismissed and your family, too!" she screamed, standing quite close. "I hope you all starve like animals or drown in the sea!"

"You cannot dismiss me, as I work for Jenny Dorset," I said calmly. "And if I did work for you, you would not have to dismiss me, either, as I would have long ago hanged myself."

"I will kill you with my bare hands," she said with a frosty precision, and she came toward me. I backed up and up, but she was still heading toward me with her hands out and a look in her eyes like a large cat prepared for the kill. Heeding the wisdom of my Master's action, I fled, but she was faster than her weight might imply, and she cut me off before I could reach the front door, and then began to chase me throughout the house, first upstairs and then down again, throwing at me vases or whatever she happened to encounter along the way and presume was appropriate to hurl my way. She screamed and called me the most vile names imaginable, which I no doubt deserved, but though she was large, I was agile, and I managed to stay ahead of her until I got out the door where I presumed she would not come. Jenny and her father were standing near a tree, and when they saw me come out the door with Miss Tonning in pursuit, they ran away into the woods, leaving me to fend for myself.

In that manner, we ran around the house thrice, and all the while Miss Tonning shouted at me to stop and called me rude names. Finally, her weight and the length of her dress captured her before she captured me, and she tripped, rolled on the grass, and sat up gagging and choking for lack of breath. She then uttered the most horrifying scream I have ever encountered, and burst into tears. I rejoined Mr. Dorset and Jenny at the front of the house.

"I have insulted your wife," I said before Mr. Dorset could say anything.

"Thank God for it," he said. "Let's get away to Foxhaven before she gathers her strength again.

"Courageous Hawthorne," said Jenny, and she hugged me. This was not the response I had expected, but it was gratifying nonetheless.

We gathered ourselves together, and Mr. Dorset, Jenny, Desdemona, and I rode over to the Smythes', which house was in extreme mourning. If Mr. Dorset reviled his current wife, Mr. Smythe had adored his as much as the late and lamented Fortinbras. We found him in the parlor with his sons Hamlet and Iago, and all were sitting quietly, weeping inconsolably. It tore at my heart to see them this way, for I remembered how our house was such a sad place when Mrs. Lydia Foxe Dorset had died. Mr. Smythe surprised us all by standing and coming to Mr. Dorset and hugging him like a lost brother and sobbing. Mr. Dorset held his rival and patted him upon the back, while Hamlet and Iago merely stared into the distance with tears flowing down their eyes. When Mr. Smythe finally stepped back, he looked at Mr. Dorset and shook his head.

"My life is over," he said. "She was my life."

"Yes," said Mr. Dorset simply. "I know that she was." Jenny went to the young men and pulled a chair to them, and comforted them, which they received more warmly than I might have expected. I retired from the room to let them air their grief in private.

The service itself was simple and with great nobility, and more than one hundred men and women attended, and I was particularly struck with the genuine grief which Mr. Smythe could not withhold, and I knew that he was in agony at having lost his life's helpmeet. When it was over, Mr. Dorset helped lower the coffin into the grave next to that of Fortinbras, and now both men shared the bond of having outlived their wives, an occurrence that no man expects. I could only hope that Mr. Smythe's future was better planned than Mr. Dorset's had been.

After the funeral, we went back to Stratford, of course, each of us lost in thought about his own mortality, and I had a sudden and shocking fear that my own wife might die before me. Jenny was as solemn and silent as I had seen her in months, and I could only hope that we would have no more shocks very soon.

In this, however, I was wrong. As I have said, Mr. Dorset had been living at Mr. Smythe's house in Town, and now he was unsure what he should do or to where he might move. Jenny had him for supper one evening not long after Mrs. Smythe's funeral, and he was still considering what he might do.

"I will on no occasion move back to Longacre," he said, draining a glass of punch. "Until something might be done about that woman who lives there."

"I think we should carry her to the Cherokee Country and leave her alone," Jenny said.

"She would drive them all into the sea," said Mr. Dorset mournfully. "They would not be able to stand against her."

"We must have a plan to get her to leave," said Jenny.

"I cannot worry about that now," said Mr. Dorset. "Great things are aborning, daughter, and you know them as well as I do. I have had conversations with your brother Abel, and I am now convinced that we must at all costs throw off the yoke of England before it breaks our necks."

"Yes!" cried Jenny. "And it must be done soon! We must stand together in this matter. I cannot bear the thought that these swine will tell us how to live and then tax us for the privilege."

"Well spoken," said Mr. Dorset. "But I cannot see where I might live, for now Smythe will surely need his Town house as a retreat from the familiarities of Foxhaven."

"Then you must move in here with me," said Jenny with some finality.

"Out of the question," said Mr. Dorset. "This is your home now and I will not encroach upon it."

"Mightn't you live, then, with Abel?" said Jenny. Aunt Sally, who had been at table but had excused herself temporarily, came back into the room, bumping into tables and chairs and then the sideboard because of her poor vision. She sat heavily in her chair and attempted to set the candle on the table but missed it by more than an arm's length. It fell to the floor, spilling tallow and spluttering out. Jenny and her father looked at the mishap and then shrugged.

"Now, how about some excellent conversation?" said Aunt Sally. Her head barely came past the edge of the table, and she seemed like an ancient child in her size and demeanor. I cleaned up the tallow from the floor with a cloth and righted the candle in its holder and placed it some distance away.

No solution came to Mr. Dorset for some time thereafter, until one day Jenny came in from God alone knows where and announced to me the startling news that Mr. Smythe had moved from Foxhaven into the Town house and invited Mr. Dorset to share the quarters with him. After years of bickering, duels, challenges, and the like, this turn was amazing indeed, but I knew whence it came. If adversaries, they were at least familiar ones, and their lives had become like wild country without a map, a place they might have traveled before but now could not quite place. The pleasant landmarks of marriage had escaped them, and now they were testing waters in which they had not sailed since their youths.

Jenny continued her career as a patriot and as a woman who was indiscriminate with her affection, and though entries in her journal make clear what was happening at least with her affairs of the heart, I will omit them at this point in our History for the sake of delicacy. Suffice it to say that she was active, and that the men who shared her pleasures were no doubt honored in a way they would never be again.

We would soon be thrown into a war by which Charles Town would be changed forever, and the British would in fact lay siege to the Town and occupy us for the better part of two very difficult years. During that period, Jenny Dorset rose to greatness, but that is later in this History, and so we shall proceed as events happened.

— 9. —

The trial and execution of one Thomas Jeremiah,
and how it brings the Dorset family together,
excepting Isaac, who refuses to involve himself.

Charles Town was in a constant uproar that spring of 1775, and thus it was natural among all the powder that someone would, with malice or unwittingly, set off a conflagration. The actor in the drama was, I am sure to this day, innocent of any part whatever in mischief, but that did not matter. When men are prepared to fight, they will attack almost any target, including the wrong ones, which is why war can be wrong while moral. Such a lesson goes so far against our understanding of right and evil that a wiser man than I might sometime explain it.

There was a free black named Thomas Jeremiah who was accused of arranging a slave rebellion. I had known Jeremiah (or "Jerry," as he was often called) from visiting his blacksmith shop, and I found him to be honest, forthright, and hardworking — precisely the kind of Negro that men pretended to admire while secretly fearing. For years, the most wealthy men, who ran all the business and government of the Province, had feared such a rebellion, for there were more slaves, I believe, than white men. Even the rumor of an uprising was enough to call militia out to roam the streets in search of possible conspirators, or make the Council pass grave resolutions threatening actions against all blacks, slave or not, if a rebellion occurred. It was only by threat and edict that they maintained their fears, though I always believed that such a fight was most unlikely because the Negroes knew that it could not last long.

Mr. Dorset and Abel knew Thomas Jeremiah very well and liked him enormously, giving him a great deal of business over the years, and though she had only met him once, Jenny was convinced of the man's honesty. So it came as a surprise when he was arrested and charged with inciting treasonous behavior among the Negroes in mid-summer 1775.

"This is madness," said Mr. Dorset one evening as he and Mr. Smythe had joined us for supper at our house. The weather was hot beyond bearing and the breeze from the ocean had flagged, so I posted two servants at the table to fan the family as they ate. "Thomas Jeremiah would not work against this society for he owes it too much. His livelihood, his life, his business. He has nothing whatever to gain."

"Well spoken," said Mr. Smythe. "What people fear is the Crown, but they must have some enemy besides shadows to fight."

"*Blast* shadows!" said Mr. Dorset. "I do not know what this Town is becoming when an innocent man can be imprisoned for an offense he did not commit. For two years I came to the defense of the Crown because I could not believe they could possibly be so mad as to provoke the Colonies, but now we are provoked, and that provocation shall not be withdrawn. But in our anger, will we strike out at any rumor with an iron rod!"

"We shall break into the gaol and free him," said Jenny. "I will see to it."

"You will see to nothing," said Abel, pointing at her with his fork. "He is guarded by thirty men, and the trial is to begin on the eleventh of August. No man could break him away, and certainly no woman."

"What?" said Jenny angrily.

"Even one as skilled as you," said Abel, mollifying his sister but not changing his opinion.

"And what does one make of these other Negroes, Sambo and Jemmy, who have forsworn that Thomas Jeremiah is guilty of the act?" asked Mr. Smythe. "Why would they wish him convicted if it not be true? What would they gain?"

"Their lives, Charles!" said Mr. Dorset. "They must surely have been threatened to lie so that someone would pay for the rumors."

"That is precisely it," said Abel. "They wish to sacrifice Jerry so that the British will fear the strength of their retribution."

"All madness," said Jenny. "It shall not stand. Justice will prevail at the trial."

Justice, however, has been said to be blind, and when the trial came on August 11, she was blind more to truth than evil. Sambo and Jemmy, the slaves who said that Jeremiah had tried to foment an insurrection, so testified at the trial, and the jury summarily found him guilty and sentenced him to be hanged and burned to ashes one week hence. Mr. Dorset, Abel, Jenny, and Mr. Smythe, though joined in their opinion by many fine citizens, had to face a startling turn of events, however. The day after the sentencing, the Province's royal Governor Campbell announced that he felt certain that Thomas Jeremiah was innocent and that he planned to do everything he might to reverse the jury's verdict. That action, though well intentioned, certainly sealed Thomas Jeremiah's fate, because the Town erupted into something near a riot, feeling that once again the Crown was attempting to run its business — and in the serious business of trial by jury.

By evening, a mob had assembled in Town, which was airless and brutally hot, and the weather only seemed to fan the flames of their discontent. Mr. Dorset, Abel, and Mr. Smythe had gone off on their own, for what business I did not know, so Jenny begged me to accompany her into the maw of the mob.

"Certainly not," I said. "You must not risk yourself. Men there have been drinking." Just then, several shots were fired into the air, and we could hear the sound of shouting not far from the house.

"I shall go," she said, "and you may come or not as you wish." She disappeared upstairs and came down half an hour later wearing trousers and a shirt of her father's. She looked in no way like a man but at least would be able to move about more freely than in the dresses normally worn in those years.

"You are determined to do this?" I asked.

"Here," she said, and she handed me a pistol while putting one into the band of her trousers. "If you must, shoot someone and I shall lie for you. I expect you to do the same for me." Before I could answer, she swept out the door, and I ran after her as she walked toward the torches and guns of the mob. I cannot say I had ever seen a thing like it, for the anger was directed equally against the Crown and against Thomas Jeremiah, who was now, they seemed assured, the evil man behind a coming revolution of slaves that might destroy what they had spent their lives building. It escaped them entirely that their success was built upon the backs of slaves, or perhaps they simply did not care, but the allegiances of the men in the streets were confused by fear, never the best of bedmates.

Jenny walked straight into the edge of the crowd, and I reached her side just as a British soldier had the misfortune to burst from a tavern, drunk and staring at the men as if he could not quite understand what might be aborning.

"There is one!" a fellow cried, and the shout that went up, I daresay, must have been heard from the Cooper to the Ashley rivers on either side of Charles Town. "Seize him!"

"My God," said Jenny with disgust. The mob rushed at the soldier and took him, though he kicked fiercely and looked wild in the torchlight. They carried him down the street, and I was certain they would kill him, which would bring out the army, and a battle might break out. Jenny walked so rapidly with the men that I could scarcely keep up with her. I was wrong that no women would be there, but most were the worst kinds of trollops and bawds, who were more afraid of losing their customers than of being shot. I felt ashamed for Jenny to be in that company, but I could do little about it.

When we reached a corner several blocks away, the soldier was tied to a stake and tarred. He cried out in pain as the hot, black, smoking substance was wiped over his clothing and his body. It appeared the man was cooking, so fierce was the smoke that arose. Before the tar had a moment to cool, two men threw buckets of feathers over him, which stuck all over his body, leaving the man gagging and coughing fiercely. A great cry went up against interference by the Crown, and then the mob began to parade the poor man around Town, stopping before every house of known sympathizers with the British, shouting for them to come out and see what would happen to them if they interfered with the Colonies' right to freedom. The crowd moved, and I ran after it and was surprised to find Jenny sitting on a doorstep weeping bitterly. Soon, all we could hear was the fading sound of the mob.

"What does it mean that innocent men are attacked instead of the guilty?" she asked. "No one hates the Crown more than I, but Governor Campbell was only doing right. Instead of attacking him, we attack Jerry. And instead of attacking *him,* we attack a poor drunk and tar him."

"We must not try to understand the mind of such a group," I said. "Shall we go home now?" I paused and looked at her in the moonlight where she wept steadily. "Shall we go now, my dear, dear Jenny?" She stood, and I put my arm around her, and we walked through the streets where a few men were shooting guns at the edge of the mob. When we got home, the house was quiet. I later learned that Mr. Dorset, Abel, and Mr. Smythe were making plans that evening which had nothing to do with Thomas Jeremiah, but which would have much to do with events of a later date.

Following the riot (for that is what it was), Governor Campbell found it impossible to intervene more for Jeremiah. There was a deep division, however, about Jeremiah's guilt, and cooler heads among the patriots questioned if the trial had been fair. The slaves Sambo and Jemmy came forward and confessed that their testimony had been coerced by threats and that indeed Thomas Jeremiah had nothing whatever to do with any impending slave revolt. Still, the peace in Town was fragile, and Jenny was deeply torn by her loyalties and saw for the first time that the issues of war and peace are not so clear-cut as she had imagined.

The week passed with no reversal of the verdict, and on August 18, Thomas Jeremiah, professing his innocence, was taken out, hanged, and burned. Jenny was thrown into profoundest mourning over the event, but it only hardened feelings between the colonists and the British. Through all that summer, the tensions between them was rising to a pitch which could not be stopped, and even the most ardent foes of the Crown were stunned when Governor Campbell fled Town in early September and reached the HMS *Tamar*, a warship in the harbor.

We learned only from the *Gazette* that Abel Dorset had become the assistant to Col. William Moultrie and had been with him when he took Fort Johnson along our coast on the fifteenth of September. For a time, Jenny seemed so overwhelmed by circumstances that she could do nothing but sit for long hours in the house and stare from the windows. But finally she reasserted herself and declared that henceforth the Daughters of Liberty must fight, even if she had to forfeit her life.

— 10. —

THE PROVINCIAL CONGRESS MEETS IN CHARLES TOWN,
AND HULKS ARE SCUTTLED IN THE MOUTH OF THE COOPER RIVER.
THE BRITISH OPEN FIRE FROM THEIR SHIPS, AND WAR COMES TO US.

Early that November, the Second Provincial Congress for South Carolina opened in Charles Town, and sentiments were high for a dramatic passage away from England. Jenny met frequently with the Daughters and (as her diary makes clear) with a number of gentlemen in their quarters. At the same time the Continental Congress met in Philadelphia to plan a response to the British.

Our private life continued apace as well. Aunt Sally broke her nose by walking into a wall, and it caused her some discomfort for days, as she lay in bed with a plaster across it. I became very ill late that October and despaired for a time before I resumed my health. And Mr. Dorset continued to live with Mr. Smythe, though not always on the most cordial terms. A supper at that time caused Mr. Dorset great embarrassment later on.

Jenny was invited and went happily because a guest was none other than Mr. William Henry Drayton, president of the Provincial Congress, who was relying on such men as Dorsets and Smythes to help fund the events which were unfolding. Because Jenny did not wish to leave Aunt Sally at home, we took her as well. I had no need to attend table as Mr. Smythe's servants took care of that duty in fine manner, but Jenny wanted me to come anyway, so I stood in a corner and awaited her. The dining room of Mr. Smythe's town house was magnificent, an extravagant setting with a chandelier and furnishings by Mr. Thomas Elfe himself. The rich lustre of the wood, the bright candlelight, the polish of the silver, and the proper dress of the men and women all painted a marvelous picture of wealth and propriety. And though Mr. Drayton spoke with quiet conviction about what the Congress must do, he could not take his eyes off Jenny, who was dressed in a gray silk gown that seemed to shimmer in the light. At one point, the man entirely lost track of himself when Jenny leaned over to pick her napkin up from the floor.

"What is this?" Aunt Sally blurted just as Mr. Smythe was working himself into a fine fit over Governor Campbell's desertion from Town. She held up the leg from a chicken which had been prepared with spices.

"Chicken," said Jenny.

"A chicken?" said Aunt Sally. "I am eating a poor chicken?"

"If he had been wealthy, he should never have been slaughtered!" cried Mr. Dorset, whereupon he began to laugh in a most horrible way. Mr. Smythe frowned and glanced at Mr. Drayton to make sure that Mr. Dorset's manners had not offended him. "Or perhaps he would not have been invited to our table if he were not wealthy!"

Jenny, accustomed to her father, glanced at me with little expression and shook her head. Aunt Sally tried to place the chicken leg back on her plate, but, seeing little of it, she dropped it on the table, where it lay, to the horror of Mr. Smythe, who was trying greatly to impress the President of the Congress. Mr. Dorset congratulated himself by emptying his glass and then belching very loudly and praising both the cook and the vintner, whoever they might be.

"For God's sake, Dorset, control yourself," said Mr. Smythe.

"And what is this?" asked Aunt Sally, peering at a forkful of peas.

"They are peas," said Mr. Dorset. Then he blurted, "We should all wish for peas, lest war undo us, eh, Jenny?" His daughter smiled wryly and shook her head, and I felt the familiar edge of events beginning to go out of control.

"Please forgive Dorset, your honor," said Mr. Smythe to Mr. Drayton. "He is sometimes a great fool and cannot tell right from wrong."

"There is no problem," said Mr. Drayton with impeccable manners. "I have seen worse from Mr. Gadsden himself."

"You see, Smythe?" cried Mr. Dorset triumphantly. "He has seen worse from Mr. Gadsden himself, so you should not bother yourself over such trivial things. You are often a trivial person and should keep your eye on the horizon, not on your stomach."

"Oh G–d," said Jenny, in anticipation of what was to follow.

"I beg your pardon, sir!" cried Mr. Smythe. "You may not speak that way to me in my own house!" He stood halfway up and threw his glass of wine in Mr. Dorset's face. Mr. Dorset then stood and threw his plate of food onto Mr. Smythe. Aunt Sally, trying withal to act properly, took her last piece of chicken and hurled it at Mr. Drayton, who leapt to his feet as well. Jenny, by now enjoying herself enormously, threw her glass of wine at her father to complete the circle of the table.

"Pig!" cried Mr. Dorset to his housemate.

"Ass!" cried Mr. Smythe back. And suddenly, they leapt upon each other and began fighting fiercely, neither gaining much of an advantage, though landing blows to the face and head. Aunt Sally, watching with great interest and thinking that it was her turn to do something, poured the entire contents of her plate on the men. Mr. Drayton, no doubt, had never seen *this* of Mr. Gadsden, so he stood and bowed, which neither of the men saw, of course, and took his leave. Jenny, to my surprise, also walked out the door. I ran after her and saw her moving steadily down the street toward the heart of Town, unaccompanied and unafraid. I felt an urge to go after her, to protect her as I had for years, but she was far beyond that now, and my attendance upon her was not possible when she did not want my service. Thinking I might do something to stop the fight, I went back inside, where the men, drenched with wine and covered with food, had nearly exhausted themselves in their wrestle upon the floor. Aunt Sally, however, peered at them as she stood nearby, and encouraged the fight, which she seemed to believe was between an Indian and a Frenchman.

"Swing, Pierre!" she cried, making the motion of a punch herself. "Take care of Si-Wa-Can-No!"

"Speak to me thus in my own home," said Mr. Smythe, gathering enough strength to slap Mr. Dorset on the jaw.

"It is my home, too, by your invitation!" said Mr. Dorset, and he slapped back, though ineffectually. Inspired by a pause in the action, Aunt Sally scuttled over to Mr. Dorset and kicked him in the ribs with her sharply pointed shoes. He cried in pain and clutched his stomach, and so Mr. Smythe tried to attend his wound just as Aunt Sally kicked *him* in the cheek.

"Woman, are you mad?" cried Mr. Smythe. I pulled Aunt Sally away with great effort, finding to my surprise that the old woman had amazing strength. She squinted her eyes at him and shook her finger.

"Only at your audacity, Pierre!" she said. I whispered into her ear that in fact the gentlemen on the floor were Mr. Dorset and Mr. Smythe, whereupon she merely smiled, curtseyed, and sat back down at table and looked at her plate. "Where is my lamb? Has someone eaten it?"

Mr. Smythe and Mr. Dorset picked each other up, got a bottle of wine and retired to the parlor, agreeing that their meeting with Mr. Drayton had not gone particularly well. Each took the blame for the incident, and they were apologizing and drinking when I escorted Aunt Sally home. She bid me good evening and called me Eduardo, then said something in Spanish which I could not understand and took her leave. Exhausted, I sat in the parlor and looked around the room, wondering if other families resembled the Dorsets in any way at all. I went to our quarters and spoke with my wife and told her of the disaster, and she was neither surprised nor moved by it.

The next morning, I began my service as always by arranging Jenny's meal with the cook and then serving it promptly at nine, when Jenny normally took her breakfast. By small signs, I could always tell that she had come in from her late-night visits — a shawl, footprints from the mud, a half-empty glass of wine on the table. But this morning, none of those signs was present, and so after a time, I began to worry about Jenny and finally decided to go out for a walk in hopes that I might see some sign of her.

Charles Town had changed so much since my boyhood when we arrived on the ship from England that I would have scarcely taken it for the same town. Then, it was quiet and properly ordered, though with taverns, it is true, but with attention only toward commerce and survival. In the years since, Charles Town had blossomed with art and leisure, as well as bawds and hundreds of sailors, and the businesses of all kind to attend them. There were dancing masters and artists, coopers and chandlers, lawyers (I regret to say), and saddlers. We had fine cabinet-makers, blacksmiths, and even a few statesmen, though of a low order. And we had slaves, thousands of them imported from Africa to work the fields, and who in their misery stained us all.

The streets that day were full of mud from a shower the evening before, and, as it was November, the air had a mild chill about it and the skies threatened rain again. I passed a man beating a donkey, which refused to move and was bleating piteously. A woman, seeing the mistreatment, ran from her house with a gun and threatened to kill the man lest he stop. He did so. I saw two men lying in the mud snoring, obviously sailors and obviously drunken. The wind came strongly from the sea, and I could smell the combined odors of animal waste, mud, salty air, and humanity.

I had no idea where to go, but for a reason I cannot explain, I felt that Jenny was in trouble, a state which was uncommon to none of the Dorsets. I walked through the streets, hearing streetcorner orators crying against the Crown, seeing wives confront their whining and repentant husbands, watching many lovely, beautiful, and self-assured young girls heading for a shopping trip or to a lesson from a music master. I stood on a corner and watched it all, realizing only after a time that I truly enjoyed that fine drama which unfolded every day in this most unreined of American cities. I was staring at a man carrying a sack far too heavy for his shoulders when someone tapped me on the arm, and I turned. It was John Black, a man I had known from time to time since my youth, a servant for the Ravenels. He was in a terrible condition, covered with mud, smelling very unclean. He was unshaven, and his eyes could not quite focus on me or anything else. The thin sun seemed to bother him greatly.

"Henry, me boy, pleasant to see you this day," he said.

"John, what on earth has happened to you?" I asked.

"I was up all night attending to the frolic with the soldiers," he said. "Where might ye have been, Henry?"

"Frolics?" I said. "What frolics? Have not public amusements been banned by the Continental Congress?" John Black laughed and slapped his leg.

"Not *them* kind of frolics, governor," he said. I briefly and wistfully thought of Old Bob. "The frolics attending to harrying a sorry bunch of Englishers back onto the boats from when they cometh."

"Soldiers?" I asked.

"Aye, and a worse bunch of sots you never seen in your life," he said. "We drank 'em into oblivion at Raper's Tavern and then tarred 'em like chickens." He paused to laugh miserably, which was a terrible sight. "Then we gave 'em two choices, to ship out or get thrown in the bay. Which choice do you think they accepted?"

"The one I should have, I suspect," I said.

"Right as rain, Henry," said John Black. "And there was even women to chase the fools. Several women in Town calling themselves the Dames of Liberation or something of the kind joined in the frolic as well."

"The Daughters of Liberty?" I said cautiously.

"Mayhap, it might have been that," he admitted.

"Does Mr. Ravenel know your whereabouts?" I asked.

"Don't nobody," he said proudly. "Not even me wife. A fine frolic!"

I left him walking unsteadily down the street singing a song of recent composition which spoke badly (and without craft) of how hated England was. I briefly shuddered at the thought that it might have been composed by Mr. Dorset. From what John Black had said, I was sure that Jenny and her friends had been involved with the tarring of the evening before. I could only guess now what Mr. William Henry Drayton thought of the Dorset clan as a whole or the Smythes, for that matter, following the catastrophe of the evening before. If it became public knowledge that Jenny Dorset was involved in such matters, the family's name, or what was left of it, would suffer further outrages.

I walked along the streets, remembering back to the time when the Weasel and I had looked for Jenny years before. I remembered the day Mr. Dorset, Old Bob, and I left Charles Town for the Indies to search for Jenny, when all the while she had not left Town. I missed those days with all their confusion, but as I walked, I realized that confusion was the normal state of the Dorsets, and as long as one was alive and had me to their service, my life should never sink into boredom. Abel was becoming more and more important as a patriot, while his brother Isaac was becoming fatter and more defensive of the Crown. Matthew was in the North, attempting to become a clergyman, from which we have already seen, he was never to ascend (or descend, depending upon one's point of view). And strangest of all, Mr. Dorset and Mr. Smythe lived together in

Town and sought some purpose following the demise of their wives.

I thought of the best way to look for Jenny, but inquiring after her was fraught with too many indelicacies, as it had always been, so I merely went up one street and down another, looking keenly into all the corners and glancing at open windows. In them one could see the small dramas of life, not unlike scenes from Mr. Shakespeare's plays. In one, a shrill woman cursed her husband and said he consorted with vile women. In another, a woman and man, embraced each other and simply stood in the light, catching the wind on the second storey. In front of a cobbler's shop, two men argued with great civility over which owed the other for a meal. A man chased a dog with a gun, but the dog was far faster, and the man in no condition for the event. He was left to curse and fire his gun into the air.

I went into several taverns, which, even that early in the morning, had their regular amount of besotted customers, many of them sailors who had not slept, some townsfolk who began each day with a drink to steady them for the rigors of facing the city before them. In none did I see Jenny or even a trace of her. I passed men whom I knew casually, and bowed to them and spoke softly if they were my superiors, and merely spoke pleasantly if they were not. After an hour, I felt that the search was futile, but I still could not rid myself of the feeling that Jenny was troubled. I was near the Cooper River side of Town when I saw, running at the end of an alley, the object of my search. Jenny Dorset, wearing men's trousers, rushed past, followed closely by a man who was stumbling and shouting that he intended to kiss her. He said more, but they disappeared before I could hear them. I ran as rapidly down the street as I could to see if I could meet them at the next intersection, but by the time I did so, they were passing, so I kept running and stayed parallel with them, as it were, until, finally, Jenny turned and ran straight for me. I could not quite believe my luck or quite understand that I was now bound by honor to place myself in danger.

I waited until Jenny passed, and then, just as the man reached me, I stepped out from the corner and hit him in the face as hard as I could. He immediately fell to his seat, said something unintelligible, and tumbled over. Jenny stopped when she saw me, breathing hard. I knew Jenny for her entire life, and never before or after did she look quite as beautiful as she did that morning, which is saying quite a lot.

"Hawthorne?" she said. "Is that you?"

"I have stopped him cold, it seems," I said, trying to shake the pain from my hand. "Are you hurt?"

"Hurt?" she said. "We were at play." She came and knelt beside the man and turned him over and looked at him, then stood and shrugged. "All pleasantries must come to their appointed end."

"Pleasantries, Miss?" I said, still not entirely breathing well. "Then that chase was by design?"

"As all chases are," she said, "by one party or the other or by God."

"I am sorry then," I said. "I was worried for you, and so I came to look."

"You *do* take care of me, do you not, Hawthorne?" she said, smiling as only Jenny could, her face catching the now-risen sun. I bowed modestly and returned her smile as much as was polite. "Dear Hawthorne, you always take care of me. For that, God shall smile upon you and give you rest." She came to me and hugged me, and such a confusion of feelings came over me that I could scarcely lift my arms, but I did, and just then, as if a signal from Providence or a warning from the Nether regions, cannon began to fire.

"Is it war?" I said, looking about.

"Not yet," said Jenny. "Come with me. The scuttling's begun."

She took my hand, and we walked through the streets east toward the Cooper River, passing washerwomen hanging out clothing, dogs sleeping in the street, proper men off for their shops kissing wives or daughters goodbye for the day. We passed a tired old mare standing at post for her master and switching flies away with her tail. We saw others coming from their houses and heading the same direction to see what might be happening. Men bore arms. Women stood in second-storey windows and looked out with fright. Jenny, of course, was excited and in a great hurry, for she was attracted to excitement as a moth is to a flame.

"What scuttling?" I finally managed to say.

"Mr. Drayton's ordered it," she said. "All the taverns were full of the news last night." I thought of what she said and decided not to pursue where she might have been.

"For what purpose?" I asked.

"Scuttling old ships in the mouth of the river so that the British cannot come up and attack us from that side," she said. "Governor Campbell has said that if the ships are scuttled, he will open fire on us."

I stopped running beside Jenny and turned her to me.

"Who has told you this?" I asked. "How have you come to find out such things?"

"Mr. Drayton told me," she said. "Sometime earlier this morning." She began to run again, and, trying withal not to think of that scene, I came alongside of her. There were at least two British warships in the harbor. One was the *Tamar*, to which Governor Campbell had fled, and the other was the *Cherokee*, and both had the guns to throw a scare into Town, though hardly enough to break us. The one hope was that Colonel Moultrie had been at Fort Johnson since the middle of September with the able help of Mr. Dorset's eldest son.

We came finally to the river, and dozens, nay, hundreds of people were there watching as the old ships were scuttled. The people were cheering and waving their fists in defiance, and I must admit that I was swept into the excitement myself and wished that we might turn our guns upon the warships in the harbor.

"They shall never take us now!" cried a bent old man waving a pistol.

Jenny took my hand so we would not be separated in the crowd, and we were walking rapidly south when we ran suddenly and without preparation into Messrs. Dorset and Smythe, who looked tired but somehow exalted.

"Jenny, girl!" cried Mr. Dorset. "This is no place for a lady."

"As it is no place for a poet," she said.

"Hawthorne, have you brought her to see the scuttling?" he asked.

"He has come to find me, for I was out during the night doing as no lady should," said Jenny defiantly.

"Ah, he has done you a service, then," said Mr. Dorset, brightening.

"They will never dare fire on us," said Mr. Smythe. "Never."

Just then we heard a hollow thunder of cannon fire from a different direction entirely from the scuttling, and the crowd suddenly grew quiet, but no shells landed near us. Everyone looked at each other as if perhaps they had misheard the sound. Several more shots followed, however, and suddenly the explosion of fused shells began, one landing not a quarter-mile from us. I took Jenny's arm and held it. Women began to scream from the crowd and nearby houses. Everyone fled as more shells came, one setting fire to a fine house, from which a woman came out in flames. Without hesitating, Mr. Smythe ran to her and threw her down to the street and clapped out the flames at the cost of burning himself slightly. The woman was hurt, but not mortally. By this time, the sound of gunfire from the British ships was steady, and everyone began to run north to escape the range of the guns.

The scene, which a few moments before was one of supreme confidence, turned into complete chaos, with people running and holding but a few possessions and dogs barking. Mr. Dorset and Mr. Smythe ran alongside us, but soon we were separated by perhaps a hundred yards, and I knew that I must hold to Jenny at all costs. Though we were pushed hard by the men and women, nothing could induce me to let go her hand. It took us quite a while to get back to the house, from which all day I saw men running to and fro and listened with concern to rumors that an invasion was near. For her part, Jenny went to bed and slept the entire day.

By the following morning, a caravan of people fleeing inland began to take shape, and it seemed that any moment British troops would come into Town from the ships in the harbor. While many women and children were sent away, the men began to erect defenses, and in the next week, with Jenny's permission, I did what I could to help. I told Jenny she should return to Longacre immediately, and she refused, saying she had rather face a British gun than Miss Tonning. Of course that was probably true, but inevitably, Jenny Dorset wanted to be where events were unfolding, not at Longacre. And so we began our lives in the state of war which would last for the next seven years.

— 11. —

A MIRACLE OCCURS AT CHRISTMAS, FOR WHICH EVERY ONE OF
THE FAMILY IS GRATEFUL.

Though we could stay away from Longacre for most of the time, even Jenny wanted to be there for Christmas, and so with reluctance, we all moved back out to the country for the celebration, which in the Dorset family was normally an occasion either for quiet piety or drunken parties, during which items might be broken or lost. The idea of seeing Miss Tonning was unpleasant, but Jenny decided that we would chance it, for even Abel had sent word that he would arrive back at Longacre on the twenty third. Aunt Sally had been worried about the British, and kept watch from a window, and every man, woman, or dog she saw was a soldier, she would exclaim. Once, a stray mule appeared at our door, and she screamed and said an Irishman was present.

In truth, the threat of invasion (which that winter did not occur) had brought out doubts among many of the people in Town. What had been a struggle for freedom from improper taxation now became simply a struggle for freedom — a complete break with England. Messrs. Rutledge and Laurens were against it, fearing that our economy could not bear the weight of a permanent separation. Mr. Drayton and Mr. Gadsden, of course, were loudest in defense of an entire break, and their voices carried much weight in the Province. Because the weather was poor, however, no invasion occurred, and it was unclear when one might. And so we left the house in Town and rode to Longacre on a cool but sunny day just before Christmas. Aunt Sally was pleased at the change of housing for a time, and exclaimed during our ride about a hideous alligator crossing the road. I did not try to explain that in fact it was a pig.

We arrived at Longacre to find that it had grown somewhat shabby in our absence, with the topiary so overgrown that the animal shapes were hardly recognizable. Likewise, the grass was unkempt, and I felt a sorrow that the place where I had spent so much of my service was not doing well. Inside of the house was even worse, looking as if it had been decorated by someone determined to exhibit the worst taste imaginable, with garish red buntings hung around the ceilings, and Mr. Dorset's heavy chairs replaced with ones so fragile they seemed to be for looking at only. The house was rather cold, for the fires were improperly laid, and dust covered everything.

"My God, what has happened here?" said Jenny.

"Is this an inn?" asked Aunt Sally.

"This is an abomination," said Jenny. Just then, Isaac Dorset walked in with his colorless wife, looking impossibly fat and sour. Jenny loyally went to him and kissed him on the cheek, but he drew back slightly, as if unsure how to deal with such affection. Isaac's wife tried without success to smile and then withdrew to one side, where she wrung her hands and looked miserable.

"Good tidings to you, sister," said Isaac formally.

"And to you," she said. "What on earth has happened here?"

"If you had been home, you would have known," he said. "We are not doing well, of course, thank you for inquiring. Our trade had dropped by two-thirds, and I have had to sell ten of the slaves to let us live in the manner a Dorset should. And yet everything I do is crossed by that woman. I thought to poison her before the New Year."

"You recall Aunt Sally?" said Jenny. Isaac looked at her for a long moment as Aunt Sally tittered.

"I cannot say that I do," he said coldly. Aunt Sally, undaunted by his lapse of memory, extended her hand, and he kissed it, making a face.

"You must be the new Mrs. Dorset," said Aunt Sally. Isaac stared at her for a time and then shook his head.

"Is Father here yet?" asked Jenny.

"He has sent word that he is coming with the criminal of the family," said portly Isaac.

"For G–d's sake, Isaac, Abel has become an important man working with Mr. Drayton," said Jenny. "Everyone has long forgotten his offense against Mr. Pinkworthy." Isaac smiled blandly.

"You know that woman has hung the offensive portrait here," he said. "When Abel sees it, he may go mad. As if that were not a common family trait."

"He is changed," insisted Jenny. "Hawthorne, has not Abel changed?"

"As you say," I said softly.

The front door swung back to let in a chill along with Abel and Mr. Dorset. Abel looked entirely dashing and strong, wearing a modest suit of clothes, while Mr. Dorset was somewhat disheveled, with wine-stained cuffs that, to me at least, indicated that he had fortified himself in anticipation of returning to Longacre for the Yuletide.

"Happy Christmas," said Abel cautiously. Jenny hugged her brother, and Isaac shook his hand cautiously, as if unsure if he were a dog who might bite.

"Is the beast lurking about?" whispered Mr. Dorset, standing somewhat behind Abel. Aunt Sally came boldly up to Abel and said he must be the new lady of the house, Etc., which led to an exasperated curse from Isaac and a muffled laugh from Abel. I found myself wishing only that Matthew, ensconced in the rigors of New England, and Lydia Foxe Dorset were about. My wife had gone directly to the kitchen upon arrival, but I know she also felt as I did that she wished our daughters were with us as well. Such homecomings are wistful occasions at best, with memories of when we were younger, and, we always seem to believe, happier.

"She is upstairs dressing, I fear," said Isaac. He introduced his wife, who seemed by her lack of speech and general reticence to be quite invisible. "She is mad, of course. I had thought to kill her before the New Year."

"Could it be done without discovery?" asked Mr. Dorset, coming briefly to life.

"Now *you* are acting mad," said Abel. "Whatever mistake you have made, she *is* your wife." Mr. Dorset put his hands over his ears and began to walk nervously around the room.

"I beg of you not to say that word in regard to Miss Tonning," he said. "That she is any man's wife is a misfortune. That she is mine is a tragedy.

I think I shall go and see my hounds. If they cannot hunt or retrieve, at least I do not question their loyalty."

A door slammed upstairs, followed by a shout that seemed not quite monstrous and not quite human. Mr. Dorset leapt behind Isaac, who was the fattest one in the room by many stone. In fact, we all moved away from our positions as if forming a skirmish line, and soon the sound of great weight descending the stairs along with a cascade of mutterings came to us, so that rather than flee the house, we seemed to be paralyzed, as when a bear appears suddenly in the forest and leaves one no option but to freeze like a deer in hopes that the danger will pass.

She got to the bottom of the stairs and, seeing, through the open door, that we were all huddled against her in the parlor, she came heavily into the room, wearing a shocking red dress and a fierce scowl. Mr. Dorset made a kind of squeaking sound, and I do believe that if the family had fowling pieces, they would have shot the woman on sight. Aunt Sally, being unable to see much past her nose, tottered out into the room and curtseyed. The floor was so highly polished that one leg suddenly slid outward, leaving her in an awkward position from which it took her a moment to recover, while Miss Tonning's expression turned from sour to furious.

"You must be the new Mrs. Dorset," said Aunt Sally. Mr. Dorset groaned and whimpered. Jenny, after looking at the dress, began to snigger, as I knew she would, and Isaac hushed her, knowing far more than we about the massive Miss Tonning. Indeed, in the weeks since we had seen her, she seemed to have grown enormously, and the dress only served to underscore her most unfortunate features (though which of her features was *fortunate* I cannot say).

"Happy Christmas?" Mr. Dorset said, his voice unnaturally high.

"Happiness is for the next world, you fool," said Miss Tonning, whose pious sentiment was so at odds with her dress that a chill descended on us. "Well, I see all of you have come, as if this were still your house."

"I told you," said Isaac softly.

"Happy Christmas?" said Mr. Dorset in a vanishingly small voice. Aunt Sally had somehow gotten turned around and stood in front of the rotund Isaac and curtseyed again and asked if he might be the new Mrs. Dorset. Everyone kept their eyes on Miss Tonning.

"God will crush you for your infidelity," said Miss Tonning.

"He will?" squeaked Mr. Dorset.

"What is worse?" said Jenny boldly, stepping forward. "Infidelity or rage?"

"Trollop!" cried Miss Tonning, pointing at Jenny. "You are unfit to set foot in my house!"

"See here," said Abel, defending his sister. "She is as pure a woman who ever lived." Jenny cleared her throat and looked at me doubtfully but said nothing. "You must apologize this moment."

"How dare you speak to me like this in my house!" she screamed. "I shall have you driven into the woods and shot by the hunters!"

"What is worse?" asked Jenny. "A full life or one stillborn?" Aunt Sally walked up to Jenny, smiled and asked if she were the new Mrs. Dorset.

"Stillborn?" screamed Miss Tonning, her voice rising at the end. "Stillborn? You dare to ask a question of a woman abandoned by her husband? Who has left her for Town in the height of her power and passion?" Mr. Dorset gagged, and for a moment I thought he might puke upon a chair. The idea of Miss Tonning in the throes of passion made me somewhat ill as well.

"Shall we dine?" said Isaac desperately. His wife had gone into a corner and stood quite still with her hands folded, her eyes unseeing.

"Abandoned!" cried Miss Tonning. "Abandoned!" She stepped forward, and we all backed up a step, except for Aunt Sally, who was over speaking to Isaac's wife to inquire if she were the new Mrs. Dorset, Etc. Miss Tonning, sensing a victory near, lumbered to the fireplace and took an implement and began to brandish it like a short sword. At first, she merely waved it as one might wave a riding crop, but soon she began to make thrusts and jabs, which scattered the family about the room and out into the hall. In her madness, Miss Tonning began to break vases and to hit furniture with great fury, all the while screaming and uttering oaths inappropriate at any time, much less at Christmas. She was advancing toward us when she suddenly stopped, and a quizzical look came over her face. She dropped the poker and looked back and forth as if not able to see what was before her. Her hand rose to her breast, which she touched tentatively, as if testing it. She then looked back up, and her face was quite red, though not quite so red as her dress. She wished to say something, but the words would not come out. Then, without warning, she fell with a crash to the floor.

No one in the room moved to her defense or to see what was wrong until, after nearly half a minute, I walked to her, knelt, and with great exertion turned her over to see that her eyes were open and that she was quite dead. Though shocking, it seemed to send a pulse of exhilaration through the room. Finally, Mr. Dorset crept forward and leaned down a bit.

"Is it dead?" he asked.

"I fear so," I said.

Not yet sure, Mr. Dorset poked the body with his foot and then stepped back cautiously. Doing it again and seeing that indeed his wife was dead, he turned to his children, who were startled but now smiling.

"It is a miracle from God," said Mr. Dorset. "A miracle for the Yule. Hawthorne, bring us a bottle! Nay, several bottles, for I'm of a mind to celebrate the season and my wife's passing!"

"Should we not take care of making plans for a funeral first?" I said, standing. Miss Tonning was staring at us as we spoke. Her mouth had slowly opened and stayed that way, giving a ghastly appearance.

"Let's put an apple in that maw and roast her for dinner," said Jenny.

"My heavens," said Abel.

"We should bury it," said Mr. Dorset. "And better it was done quickly before some evil magic might bring it back to life. G–d, what a thought!" He shuddered.

And so we did, building the most flimsy coffin imaginable before noon that day, one that might fit her girth. It took six of us with ropes to carry the coffin out to the burying ground. We had taken her near Mrs. Lydia Dorset's grave, but Mr. Dorset came walking up with a full glass of wine and told us to move Miss Tonning some distance away, which we did. Earlier, we had instructed a few servants to dig a grave, and they did so, but I could tell at a glimpse that it was too narrow for us to lower Miss Tonning's width into the earth, and I said so.

"Set it upon the grave, and I shall dance upon it, and maybe it might fall," said Mr. Dorset, a shocking statement but one which was shared by all present. I explained that blasphemy in the presence of the dead might indeed be unforgivable, whereupon Jenny fell into one of her fits of laughter and grabbed the glass from her father and poured its contents down her throat. He wished her good health, and she belched heartily. The family went back to the house while I oversaw the redigging of the grave to an appropriate width, and it was so large that one of the men present asked if we might not include in the hole a horse which had died during the night. Rather than wait the family's return to lower Miss Tonning, I took the opportunity to have her lowered, which we did with great difficulty, and I must admit that even then I was somewhat afraid a loud knocking and a shriek might come from within the box. She was dead, however, from a stroke of apoplexy, I assumed, and somehow I regretted that she was of

such a temperament that everyone liked her better dead than alive. All this
digging and lowering had taken the better part of an hour, so when I went
to fetch the family, I was drenched in sweat. We had not covered the coffin because it was Mr. Dorset's right to throw the first handful of dirt upon
her. When I got to the house, I found Isaac hastily taking down many of
Miss Tonning's more eccentric decorations. Abel had already taken down
his portrait painted from life by Mr. Pinkworthy and thrown it on the floor
where it lay. Jenny lay on a sofa by the fire in the library reading a book and
drinking, while her father, making occasional exclamations of pleasure, was
at the desk, writing furiously. Isaac and Abel both refused to come back for
the obsequies, citing the cold, damp weather and the fact that they hated
Miss Tonning and would be committing a sin to pretend they were sorry
regarding her demise. Jenny would not have missed it, and neither would
Mr. Dorset, who seemed happier than I had seen him in some time. Just as
we were ready to return for a few words at graveside, Aunt Sally appeared
wearing an enormous tricorn she had apparently found upstairs. It was so
large that it hung down over her ears and her eyes were barely visible.

"I am ready for the service," she said. She walked to me and asked me
if I was sorry that my wife had expired so near to Christmas, and before
I could say anything, Mr. Dorset roared that God was good.

"Yes, He is that," said Jenny laconically. "Else why would He keep having to right my father's mistakes?"

"Well spoken," said Mr. Dorset.

A few of us walked back up to the grave, Mr. Dorset carrying a piece
of paper on which he had written some verse but had not blotted the
paper so that the words drizzled a bit down the page. We arrived at the
site to find it actually very nice, though at the edge of the forest and far
enough away from the others that she might have had no relation to
them at all. We stood around the grave, looking down at it, and all I
could think was that Miss Tonning was lying inside with her scowl and
that red dress. Mr. Dorset and Jenny both had been drinking, and so neither was very steady, and I positioned myself between them.

"I am cold," said Jenny. "Shall we get this over with?" Aunt Sally
began to sing, in a voice so devoid of talent that I instinctively clamped
my ears shut, a ballad about a young woman taken in death very young,
the kind of song you heard late at night in taverns. Jenny grabbed her
arm and shook her quite hard, and Aunt Sally, whose tricorn had slid
entirely over her eyes now (not that it bothered her vision), abruptly

quit. That seemed the signal to Mr. Dorset to clear his throat and lift the sheet of paper. Here is the poem, which I have in my possession still, which he read over his wife's grave:

The Death of Miss Tonning

Upon the yule, death brought us no mourning
For the one that he took was none but Miss Tonning.
I made a mistake when I took her in marriage,
Thank God we had no need of an infant's carriage.

Miss Tonning was shrill, a lady was not,
Her tongue was a furnace, her temper was hot.
She sailed through Longacre, a tempest of wrath
No virtues I saw did she ever quite hath.

Now she is dead, the saints bless us all
The angels or something did finally call.
I pledge to my God that if she is up there
My soul shall go elsewhere, in fire or in air.

Now farewell, farewell, to the porcine Miss Tonning
The feast is near ready so we must be running.
Never again, for the rest of my life
Will I take one a woman who might be a wife.

For Time hath all merriment planned in His heart
From Lyddies and Tonnings to strumpets and tarts.
And we cannot see what's for us on that road,
So live as to lighten your heart and your load.

Farewell, and goodbye, to a woman who's sailed
To whom as a husband I tried and I failed.
But some are more happy in rage than in bed,
And some are more useful when quite safely dead.

Aunt Sally burst into appreciative applause, but I said nothing, and Jenny laughed. Then, as a final and perfect tribute to his wife, Mr. Dorset slipped and fell headlong into the grave on top of the coffin. He began to shriek and insist that Miss Tonning was in league with the D'vil and was trying to take him with her to H–ll. I helped him out, and he kicked what dirt he could into the hole and left, quite shaken by the experience. He and Jenny took Aunt Sally back to the house, and I was left to cover the body, which was an exertion greater than I might have imagined. When finished three-quarters of an hour later, I said a few words over the grave, threw the shovel down, and walked back to the house. It was full of pleasure and joy, not to mention punch and wine.

We had a pleasant Yule, during which all the servants sang and thanked God for the miracle of Miss Tonning's demise. After that, Mr. Dorset made elaborate plans to return to Longacre, but each time he did, something in Town seemed to contravene his desires, and, it truth, the happenings in Town were so full of adventure and danger that he could no more have left it than a cat might leave a mouse.

By early in 1776, many of the women and children (and some of the men) had fled from Charles Town to the backcountry, fearing an invasion from the Crown, but, for the time, most of the fighting was confined to the North. However, the throwing up of breastworks around the Town continued, and men drilled constantly in the streets to be prepared for the oncoming battle. I thought to join such a regiment myself, but I could not run the house, serve Jenny Dorset, and keep her father out of trouble if I were to be marching in the streets with a gun (though I handled a piece quite well in those days). As for Mr. Dorset, he and Mr. Charles Smythe continued to live together and with their combined personal wealth managed to raise their own company of volunteers, who, I regret to say, would not distinguish themselves in the war. In fact, Mr. Gadsden once said in Council that the Palmetto Volunteers (for that is the name which the men took for their corps) "were as likely to kill a British soldier as a flea was a dog," which to my thinking was unkind and entirely accurate.

As for Jenny Dorset, she was rather alone, for the Daughters of Liberty showed that they were not ready to fight for what they believed in, and most of the members had fled Town. As the Reader of this History must know by now, Jenny would not have moved away from danger and indeed was drawn to it, for that was her nature, and no woman or man can entirely escape that nature, even if they wish to, which Jenny Dorset did not.

— 12. —

IN MAY, THE BATTLE FOR CHARLES TOWN BEGINS AS THE BRITISH
ATTACK SULLIVAN'S ISLAND, AND JENNY DORSET BECOMES A SOLDIER.

After Charles Town was shelled by the *Tamar* and the *Cherokee* in
November of 1775, the war, as I have said, shifted to the North, which
gave time for us to erect more defenses and for women, children, and the
aged to leave. By the spring of 1776, there were few women in Town
besides those plying that most ancient of trades, and Jenny Dorset. I had
sent my own wife back to Longacre along with the rest of the female servants, and I tried to send Desdemona back to Foxhaven, but she refused
to leave Jenny. Aunt Sally likewise claimed that she would die in Town
rather than in the country because she did not like the new Mrs. Dorset.
Mr. Dorset and Mr. Smythe threw themselves into the conflict with their
Palmetto Volunteers, gaining for themselves names that neither had
much before to be proud of. (Two of the ships that Mr. Drayton had
caused to be scuttled in the Cooper River had once belonged to Mr.
Smythe, but had continually sprung so many leaks that causing them to
founder required only a few shots.)

That May, it was clear that the British were being reinforced with ships
in the harbor, and a panic swept through Charles Town like a conflagration. The word arrived one evening when Mr. Dorset and Mr. Smythe
were dining at Jenny's house on the very meager fare that I could manage,
largely vegetables from the house garden. Since the autumn before, few
ships had arrived or left, and we were by then largely on our own devices.

Mr. Dorset and Mr. Smythe were having a heated argument about the
play *Hamlet,* and Mr. Dorset was saying that Hamlet was visited by the
ghost of his dead uncle. Mr. Smythe said rightly that the ghost was of
Hamlet's father, and the men were starting another of their frightful arguments when there was a rap on the door. I answered it, taking along a
candle because by orders of the Council, few lights were lit to keep the
Town dark and safer from cannon fire in the harbor. I had seen the man
at the door before, but he looked quite afraid and asked to see Mr. Dorset
if he be home. I let the man in, and he came and bowed and said he had
a message from Mr. Drayton that the invasion was imminent, and that
volunteers were needed to reinforce the works on Sullivan's Island, which
was just to the north of Town and the place most likely where the British
would arrive.

"Let the monsters come!" cried Jenny. "The English are nothing but vile rogues and deserve their fate at our hands!"

"I shall come immediately," said Mr. Dorset. Mr. Smythe said the same.

"I will be along after I have put on a hat," said Aunt Sally.

"I will be there as well," said Jenny with a coldness that brought me great worry.

"Hawthorne, take Jenny and Aunt Sally to Longacre and await instructions there," said Mr. Dorset. He then turned to the courier. "Tell me, good man, in *Hamlet,* is the ghost that visits Hamlet that of his uncle or his father?"

"Ghost, sir?" said the man. "There is a ghost about?" He looked into the house with great suspicion.

"Never mind," said Mr. Smythe.

"I shall not leave on any account for Longacre," said Jenny. "Nothing you could do short of binding and gagging me could make me depart."

"Bind her and gag her," said Mr. Dorset. The courier seemed utterly bewildered, a state common to most strangers when first visiting any of the Dorsets.

"Certainly not," I said. "She is of age to make her own decisions." I had never spoken thus to Mr. Dorset, but the situation and the futility of disagreeing with Jenny seemed to call for it.

"Sir, your presence is needed forthwith," said the courier. Mr. Dorset sighed, looked at his daughter, and shook his head. "Adm. Sir Peter Parker is, we believe, ready to attack us within forty-eight hours, and we must react now."

"I do not know where you learned such nonsense," said Mr. Dorset. "Hawthorne, in any case, look after her, will you? Can you promise me that?"

"I always have, sir," I said.

That, of course, was going to be nearly impossible. As soon as the men left, Jenny ran upstairs and put on her men's clothing and came running back down and told me that we would now walk to the harbor and see for ourselves what was transpiring. I said that it was dangerous and in any event we could not leave Aunt Sally alone, and we certainly could not take her with us.

"No gentleman would dare hurt a blind old lady," said Jenny. And with that, she fled out the door, leaving me either to stay or to follow, never doubting which action I would take in her defense. The night was warm, and the moon was half filled, and the lack of lights gave the Town a strange appearance. I could only hope that if Jenny decided to become a soldier she would not join the Palmetto Volunteers, for I had no confidence in their ability to survive even a modest engagement.

If the northern part of Town was quiet, we encountered more and more action as we walked south, so that the lack of light where we lived finally seemed pointless. Men continued to throw up barricades in the street and shouted instructions. Jenny was excited beyond measure and looked like a young man with her golden hair folded up in the tricorn hat which Aunt Sally sometimes wore. When we got far down town, we went to the Cooper River side, where crowds of men were razing buildings so that our cannon could have a wider range of fire. As the men worked by torchlight, their bodies glistening with sweat, I must say that I had never seen a thing quite like it in my life.

As we stood watching them work, Jenny took my arm, uttered a small cry, and began to sag. I caught her as she began to fall, and gently set her on the ground, where she lay in a faint. I ran to a nearby public well and drew enough water to bring and put upon her face. She was starting to rouse when I came back, and after I held her and put water on her temples and bade her be still for a time, she sat up and said she was recovered and that we should be heading for the river's edge to see what might transpire in the battle. Charles Town, having been constantly swept by plagues of one kind or another throughout my life, sometimes left everyone, even men, in a fright, and for a moment I was worried that Jenny could have small pox or perhaps yellow fever. Those were more common when the heat was at its worst, however, not in the month of June, so I hoped that perhaps the ague, whatever its origin, would pass. At any rate, she seemed fine in a moment, and we pressed forward toward the river, where men were running like mad, shouting and drilling, razing structures, and re-directing their cannon, none of which had yet been fired.

"To the boats, men, for Sullivan's Island!" cried a man I did not recognize. He cut a heroic figure in the cloaked darkness. "The attack will commence soon!"

"How do they know that?" asked Jenny.

"The way men know all things," I said. "Someone told to say nothing could not bear the weight of his silence."

A group of men came by me, heading for the boats, and for a moment

I felt the urge of patriotism so keenly that, despite my fifty years, I thought I might join them in the defense of our Town. I was watching the caravan of men when Jenny grabbed my arm.

"To the boats, men!" she cried.

"What?" I managed to say.

She began to run, and I could hardly keep up with her as she ran, all the while holding on to her tricorn hat so that her hair (which was pinned anyway) might not be visible to the men. I tried to speak to her and tell her to stop, but she insisted on the flight. I was certain that when we reached the river, someone would laugh and push her aside, but to my astonishment she strode right into an oared boat, walked across the boards, and sat next to an oarsman, who was under orders to leave as soon as the boat was filled. I could not let her go alone, nor, I felt, could I expose her trickery, so I stumbled along and sat next to her.

"Are you mad?" I whispered.

"Yes," she whispered fiercely. "And a glorious madness it be to defend our lives against the scurvy Brits!"

I was consumed with a feeling that this was somehow not occurring, but a moment later we were pushed off, and the oarsmen began to row us across the broad mouth of the Cooper River and north toward Sullivan's Island. A number of similar boats were in the dark water, and from one I heard a voice that sounded suspiciously like Mr. Dorset's, and with a fleeting shudder I wondered if we had somehow stumbled into the midst of the Palmetto Volunteers, an event which would bring fear even to seasoned soldiers, much less to an old man and a young woman. We were separated soon, however, by distance and by repeated hushings of superior officers (I assumed), so that before long, we were gliding on the water — a feeling which I never hoped to enjoy again. The stars and a brief moon, somewhat illuminated the scene, and in the harbor, lights played on some ships, so it was neither entirely dark nor entirely silent.

Halfway across or so, Jenny took my hand. I say this now with no disrespect to my late wife, but though she obviously wished some fatherly comfort, I felt exalted as a man in a way which I cannot describe, and I wished that I had been thirty years younger. For a moment, I almost felt as if she had chosen me among all men, but it was only a fancy of the mind, the kind which preyed on Mr. Dorset constantly, and I was careful not to take it for more than it was meant. I could understand, though, how those men with which Jenny had shared intimacies were never quite the same.

I seemed to half doze in the glory of the night and the movement of the water past us and us across that selfsame water, and I somehow hoped the trip might go on forever. But such moments of pleasure are but glimpses of Heaven, and soon they must end, as ours did when we finally arrived safely sometime later on the south end of Sullivan's Island. Men on the shore pulled us about, and soon we were all scrambling on to the sand. From torchlight, I could see that most men had weapons, and I suddenly realized that I had nothing with which to defend myself, nor did Jenny Dorset, either.

"To the left, men!" cried someone.

"Stay with me," I said to Jenny, but I let go her hand, for, in the light, the men would have thought us mad and perhaps have shot us — two men holding hands in the prelude to battle!

"I will," she said back.

It did not take us long to get to the fortification, which was getting higher by the moment. I guessed it might be fifteen or eighteen feet high, built with stacks of palmetto logs, which, as the Reader must be aware, are of a spongy wood which can absorb a shock without breaking. Soon, I recognized someone I hoped we would not see — Mr. Adam Dorset. I cautioned Jenny, who uttered a word not fit to be printed in this History. Mr. Dorset was trying to rally his Volunteers, but they moved in all directions like ants stirred from their hill. I was particularly reminded of his hounds, and I realized that the Truth follows a man like his shadow and neither can ever be escaped. The night was quite amazing, as men kept bringing up new palmetto logs, which were added until the structure was near twenty feet high and quite a good fortification. I still worried that neither Jenny nor I had guns, but we would have to serve as we could. She worked alongside me as a man would, lifting part of the logs and passing them to men up ladders. I was worried that her hat would fall away and reveal her sex or that she would faint again, but neither happened, and so the night passed on, until sometime before dawn, we lay down and slept, careful to stay away from Mr. Dorset and Mr. Smythe, whom by then we had also seen. When I was starting my sleep, which was not hard despite the noise and the light, I saw Abel Dorset there as well, giving orders which men took as if they were Scripture, and I knew finally that he had found his office in life.

The next day, which was June 28, as I recall, the morning was quiet, with our usual sea breeze, and the frantic work of the night before had clearly succeeded in strengthening the fort. Jenny had the problem of her toilet, which we solved by my standing watch while she went into a grove of trees from which she emerged unseen. When she came alongside me, she seemed unsteady again, and so I held on to her until the feeling passed.

"We should hire a boat back," I said. "You are ill."

"I am as well as any man here," she said.

"You are not a man," I said.

"I am strong as many and reckless as all!" she cried. "Besides, the rumors are likely false about an attack. No scurvy British would dare open fire on us."

Just then, the cannon from either the *Tamar* or the *Cherokee* boomed in the harbor, and a ball went over us, landed not far from where Jenny had been, and exploded. She looked at me and shrugged, then we both ran for the relative safety of the fort. By then the gunners were beginning to get their range on both sides. Our cannon, mounted some days before along the wall, which had already been completed on the sea side, fired back, and soon men were shouting and smoke drifting over us. We were not on the wall, of course, so we could not see what transpired, but the men at the cannon called out that the ships were unmoored and moving. The parapets were filled with men, and I turned in time to see Mr. Dorset shouting at his men, who were trying to drill and making a foul mess of it, some going one direction and some another. Mr. Smythe, watching, shook his head, and got his gun and went to the parapets to watch the cannonade.

Our flag was a palmetto tree on a blue field, and it flew proudly over us as the war was brought to Sullivan's Island. The men called that there was no shelling of Charles Town itself, but that the British seemed to be heading for Breech Inlet to our north. That would mean that the ships would pound us with cannon fire head-on and the troops would at low tide walk across Breech Inlet to attack us from the flank. It was a clever plan, and I could only hope that God might intercede somehow on our behalf.

The firing from Sir Peter Parker's frigates was now hot upon us and began to land inside the fort and to hit the walls. Almost immediately, the Palmetto Volunteers scattered, many of them running away to corners, where they screamed to God for mercy, while Mr. Dorset stormed around shouting and calling out orders which were entirely ineffectual. A shell landed inside the fort and exploded, killing two nearby men instantly, leaving them lying in parts, their entrails spilling out like a hog's at slaughter time. The sight sickened me, but it only fortified Jenny, who was trying against my advice and restraint to climb a ladder and get up where she could see the fight. Soon, another shot landed within the fort and exploded, taking off the leg of a man, who crawled about screaming, despite attentions from a friend, until he shuddered and died. By now, most of the men were huddled against the front wall where they were protected by the logs, which absorbed the fire with excellent results.

"They are almost to Breech Inlet!" cried a man from the wall.

"Steady boys!" shouted Abel Dorset. "The tide is against them."

I could not believe they would try to cross the Inlet against the tide, but I suppose, knowing the British fancy for order without question, Sir Henry Clinton (for it was his men who were landing, we found out later) may have miscalculated, and no one had the courage to countermand him. From calls above, we also knew that three frigates were now moving toward our south slightly, so that the Regulars and the ship-fire could catch us in a pincers from which we might not escape. Only a few more men died in the next hour, largely from one cannon burst that hit a gun emplacement on the wall. Jenny huddled next to me and was standing there, when her father was suddenly near us.

"Hawthorne!" he cried, coming to me. Jenny turned away and tried to hide her face. "Brave Hawthorne, to fight for this cause!"

"Sir," I said. "How do your Volunteers fare?"

"Brave and true!" he cried. A group of them nearby began to pray and whine as a shell landed about a hundred yards away. "Where is your gun?"

"I have lost the piece in the confusion," I said.

"I should lend you mine, but something seems to be in the barrel, and I cannot dislodge it," he admitted. He stepped up, took a glance at Jenny, then whispered to me, "Aye, some of these boys are too wet behind the ears to be in combat with men of our standing."

"Sir," I said.

Since the Palmetto Volunteers seemed ready to disengage from the battle from poor training and cowardice, Mr. Dorset fled to them with Mr. Smythe, and attempted to restore them to order while I took Jenny by the arm and escorted her to the other side of the wall.

"So what if he should know?" she said. "What of it? What will they do, escort me to a boat and send me back to Town in the midst of the fight? I am here to fight for the honor of South Carolina!" She turned, then suddenly turned very pale, tottered toward me, and fainted into my arms. I thought to call for medical help, but then her secret would be divulged, and I did not want someone ripping open her blouse and revealing to all her ample natural assets. We had but little fresh water in kegs, and I fetched her some, wiped her face, and put a little in her mouth, which brought her back from the faint and choked her at the same time. She coughed and spluttered and fought me with such strength that I had to hold her tight and soothe her with words so she would know where she might be.

As it turned out, her awakening coincided with heavy fire which began to be directed more accurately at us from the ships in the harbor, and one ball killed two men and blew our flag down from the parapet. For a time, the men cowered and looked at each other. In the smoke and noise I tried to see Abel but could not, and the soldiers appeared to lose hope. Then, in an act since memorialized in our History, Sgt. William Jasper, at risk to his life, gallantly replaced the colors, thrust his arm high into the air in an act which seemed both one of defiance and honor, and shouted for the men to rally. I cannot say how magnificent the sight was and how the men, stunned by his bravery, rallied back to the fight. Jenny was too insensible to see much of it, but I could not help but be swept up in the grandeur of the gesture.

"What is wrong with me?" Jenny asked finally.

"You must have one of the fevers," I said. "I fear for you. We must get you back to Longacre without delay."

"That is not possible," she said. "Let me die here in the glory of it all."

"I will not let you die at all," I said. "I will care for you if it means death myself."

She looked at me with a brief smile, sat up, and leaned forward as if to embrace me, from which I shrunk for obvious reasons. She said she felt much better then, and I helped her up just as a shout began to go up from the men — at first incredulous, then certain — that the frigates were stuck in the sand off the island and could not move. Some believed it untrue, but soon it was clear enough that the ships were not moving and could not maneuver to fire. Our men redirected our guns and simply began to blow the ships' decks to pieces. The British would not be able to move until they could disengage themselves from the sand. At almost the same time, runners came from the north saying that the British soldiers who had debarked at Breech Inlet thinking to walk across it and attack us, had soon gotten over their heads in the depth and turned back. The entire British plan was falling to pieces before us, and the mood within the fort changed in the space of half an hour from despair to jubilation.

The fire from the British ships almost entirely ceased, because they were out of position to be of much harm to us, and therefore our fire became even more heavy toward them. It was at that moment that I decided that I would take Jenny from the fort to one of the many boats on the south end of the island and see if I could row her back across the Cooper River to Charles Town.

"I shall not leave my comrades!" she said.

"You are ill, and you will leave them or I will carry you out," I said calmly. "I care more for your life than I care for this battle."

She looked at me skeptically at first, but when it was clear to her that I indeed was firm in my resolve, she appeared quite touched by my solicitations, and merely nodded. Also, she was feeling ill once more, though not enough to faint. Without request, we let ourselves from the fortification and walked in the trees back toward the boats, listening with growing pleasure to the fire from the fort and the lack of it from the ships. We saw one direct hit amidships on the *Cherokee* that must have killed a number of men. Jenny bore the walk well, and soon we came to the cluster of boats, which were largely unattended, everyone having fled for the fort when the battle began. I found one toothless man sitting in a small boat sipping from a bottle and watching the battle as one might watch a display of fireworks.

"Gaw, what a sight," he said. "We be blowing them from the water, eh governor?"

"I would like to hire you to take us across the river to Town," I said.

"In the middle of the battle?" he said in his wet, high-pitched voice. "Are ye touched?"

"I shall pay you two guineas," I said.

"I'm ready when you boys is," he said.

The boat was leaky, but the man rowed with vigor, singing all the while and stopping between songs to curse the British. Jenny stared at the fight with clear pleasure, for the British ships, being grounded, could not fire at the fort, while the Colonials could hardly miss with their cannon. Only the distance prevented a complete slaughter of the British on the ships, for many shots went awry and landed harmlessly in the water.

When we were about halfway across, the sea breeze coming up the river suddenly intensified, and Jenny's tricorn hat was lifted off her head before she could grab it, and her golden hair came cascading down around her shoulders. We were facing the rower, who was watching the fight and cackling. When he looked back at us, his mouth went slack.

"Bless me, a woman," he said.

"And a better shot than you will ever be," she said.

"Bless me, a woman," the man said again. He kept at his labor, but could find nothing else to say, though for the rest of the trip across he did not look at the fight but only at Jenny Dorset. We landed finally, and the man followed us to the house, having to work with us around barricades and palmetto-log walls among the cheering of men who could easily tell what was happening. We got to the house, and Jenny paid the man from her purse, and he touched his forehead with two fingers and blessed himself again and noted that Jenny was a woman. I thought she might throw something at him, but he moved away, flipping his coins and whistling.

I bade Jenny lie down and I went to look for a doctor, which I thought would be difficult, even though Sullivan's Island and not Charles Town was under siege. I crawled over barricades, saw trollops standing at their leisure smoking pipes and drinking from mugs, heard wild rumors shouted, became drenched in sweat. I could scarcely get to one of the physicians' offices, but when I managed, he was gone, perhaps to Sullivan's Island. I wandered the streets, worrying that I could find no one to attend Jenny, when I suddenly ran (quite literally) into Dr. Arthur Williams, who was walking rapidly away from one particularly large barricade.

"Dr. Williams, sir," I said, bowing. "I have the necessity to ask you to attend the daughter of Mr. Adam Dorset of Longacre, who is ill."

"Dorset?" he said. "The fool who writes those miserable poems in the *Gazette*?"

"That very one," I said. "His daughter is here in Town and ill."

"What in the name of G–d is she doing here?" he asked. Dr. Williams was of medium height and a dark complexion and was wearing brown trousers and a white shirt that seemed to have bloodstains on the sleeves. "This is no place for a woman!"

"No, sir, but she is here and ill and I must ask that you come see her," I said.

"Very well," he said. "I cannot understand why the delicate daughters of a wealthy planter would be left in such danger."

"It was a matter of circumstances," I said. I then told him who I was, and he did not seem impressed. He followed me back to the house and told Jenny to go upstairs with him to her bedroom from the couch where she had lain. Time passed very slowly, and the distant roar of cannon fire continued. I wondered if the British troops had indeed failed to cross Breech Inlet or if they had disengaged their ships from the sand. We were alone in the house, everyone else having fled to Longacre, from the look of things. Aunt Sally had left a note, but, with her eyesight, the script looked like nothing I had ever seen. I was trying to decipher a sentence which seemed to read, "We have growed four lank amens," when Dr. Williams came down the stairs finally, sleeves rolled up high, looking very tired.

"Is it yellow fever?" I asked. "Can she be moved to the country?"

"She can be moved to the country, but it is not yellow fever," he said.

"Not small pox?" I said, alarmed.

"No, it is another disease, and a dread one in a time like this," he said. "Miss Dorset is expecting a child."

"I'm d—d!" I cried. The doctor, who had seen it many times from the look on his face, merely shrugged and repeated his assertion. "Are you certain?"

"She is not married?" he asked.

"Certainly she is married!" I said.

"She told me with equal volume that she was not and would never consent to be married," said Dr. Williams. I could only say *really* as he bade me good day and walked out the door and down the street. I felt entirely crushed, from sadness for the family and for Jenny, but also, I supposed, for myself, for I had somehow made Jenny into a chaste creature in my mind, despite the opposite clearly being true. I sat down and stared at the hot, quiet room, not knowing what to say or how I felt. I thought back to the lovely child playing in the yard at Longacre those years before, and I wished somehow I could bodily transport myself back there.

"You have heard the news, I gather," said Jenny, coming down into the room wearing a nightgown and looking very tired.

"I have heard it," I said. "And I cannot say what is in my heart."

"I was thinking just now that I have two hearts in me," she said. "Does not one with such an advantage deserve compassion and love?" She began to weep. I went to her and held her amid a great confusion of feelings, not quite knowing if I felt compassion for her or love. After a few moments of sorrow over her predicament, she stood back from me and dried her tears, and nodded, back once again in control of the situation.

"We will care for you and never leave you alone in this," I said.

"We should go to Longacre now," she said.

She walked away from me and looked out the window at the street. I stood by awaiting her orders and wondering what might be going through her head. I thought that she must have known of her condition and simply not believed it. That was another Dorset trait, to believe at will what was untrue and disbelieve that which was irrefutable.

"I will prepare for it," I said. She turned to me.

"I shall be confined there," she said. "And I shall not keep the child."

— 13. —

THE BRITISH WITHDRAW IN DEFEAT AS JENNY AWAITS THE BIRTH OF HER CHILD. THE DISBANDING OF THE PALMETTO VOLUNTEERS AND MR. DORSET'S RETURN TO LONGACRE. THE NEWS OF OUR INDEPENDENCE.

So often in battle or in life, a victory which appears close suddenly fades into the shock of defeat, but in the case of the attack on Sullivan's Island, the British loss was entire. A number of Sir Henry Clinton's troops drowned while trying to cross Breech Inlet, and the rest turned back, soaked and exhausted. The frigates finally were swept off the sand at high tide after taking a terrible battering, and within a few days the entire British army had fled to the North, where the promise of victory must have seemed greater. Charles Town, though still vigilant, was swept with the sounds of church bells and benedictions, as we were at Longacre (though without church bells). Jenny, on hearing of the British retreat, went out and fired a gun into the air and whooped about like an Indian, despite our warnings of her condition.

Unfortunately for Mr. Smythe and Mr. Dorset, the Palmetto Volunteers were charged with being cowardly under fire and ordered not to appear henceforth at any engagement. Mr. Smythe blamed Mr. Dorset for the debacle, while Mr. Dorset blamed Mr. Smythe, and soon they had engaged in a great fight on Queen Street in full view of Mr. Drayton. Neither won the fight, but it brought their disagreement back to where it had been sometime before, and I did not doubt that another duel might have been in the offing. As for the Palmetto Volunteers, they went as a group to a tavern, got exceedingly drunk, and managed to break tables, chairs, Etc., and many spent the remainder of the summer in gaol.

On the fifth of August — glorious day! — we received the word from Philadelphia that we had declared our independence from England, and I felt such a joy that I could not describe it. Isaac Dorset thought the entire idea mad and was certain the new states would crawl back to England after they had been whipped in the war. This comment caused a furious rebuttal from Jenny, and Desdemona had to take her outside and calm her, lest the child be harmed.

Mr. Dorset arrived back at Longacre, full of stories of his bravery and of his troops, not knowing that word of the Volunteers' demise had reached us first. He ordered a fine dinner to celebrate his arrival, and so we set about it, making a feast of hog and vegetables from the house garden. It was at dinner that evening when Jenny's secret came out.

"By God, we whipped them," said Mr. Dorset. "I already have an epic in mind to write, having myself had a great hand in the defeat on Sullivan's Island. Oh, Jenny girl, you should have been there and seen me high on the parapet, directing fire against the British! They grew closer and closer in their frigates, and though they maneuvered back and forth, they could not escape the righteous wrath of our fire!"

"I heard they were grounded on sandbars," said Jenny.

"Eh?" said Mr. Dorset.

"I heard the ships were grounded on sandbars and that their troops nearly drowned trying to cross Breech Inlet against the tide," she said.

"Eh?" said Mr. Dorset.

"And we heard that the Palmetto Volunteers destroyed a tavern and were ordered disbanded for their refusal to fight," said Jenny.

"Waugh!" cried Mr. Dorset. "Who passes such calumnies? I shall tear him apart with my hands!"

"Perhaps I was misinformed," said Jenny with a smile, turning as she often did in a different direction in an instant. "I am sure your version is the correct one. After all, you were there."

"I *was* there!" he said. "As was Hawthorne!" He looked at me and suddenly realized that I was in a position to know the truth, and so launched immediately into a long discussion of rice cultivation and the need to revise the sonnet form. Isaac's small and timid wife looked only at her plate as her enormous husband sighed and shook his head during his father's discourse. As with many of Mr. Dorset's speeches, it began in one place, ended in another, and accomplished nothing in between. Aunt Sally, who was of course at table, looked toward Mr. Dorset as if he were the most brilliant man on earth, making guttural sounds of agreement every half minute or so. I could see that Jenny's patience was eroding by the moment, and her father's essay had suddenly veered to crabs in all their varieties.

"I should not doubt that somewhere in the depths of the ocean there is a crab the size of a ship, waiting to drag it down with its great pincers," said Mr. Dorset.

"I am expecting a child," said Jenny quietly.

"A child," said Mr. Dorset, nodding at her. "And perhaps even that is not the greatest crab. Imagine one as large as ten ships lashed together! Imagine . . . What did you say?"

"I am expecting a child," said Jenny more forcefully.

"Disgrace," said Isaac. "We are finally ruined. First Abel, then Matthew, and now this. We are ruined. It is over."

"A child?" said Mr. Dorset. "You are expecting a child?" His face, which had been full of bluster, softened suddenly, displaying disbelief, regret, sadness, sorrow, and perhaps even understanding. An entire tableau of the world's emotions played over him. Jenny looked firmly at him, showing neither regret nor tears.

"Yes," she said. "It shall be born in December, and I will not keep it. I will see that it receives fine care and a good home, but I will not keep it." Isaac's wife excused herself and left the table, holding her napkin to her mouth.

"We are disgraced," said Isaac, punctuating the assertion by eating even more aggressively.

"Jenny, why have you done this?" Mr. Dorset asked. "What could you gain by such intimacies outside the bonds of marriage? I cannot believe this has happened."

"My life is my own, and I will do with it as I please," she said. "You may love me or not for that, but I will not allow the fine people of South Carolina to tell me how I should live my life, any more than you will allow the British to tell you how to run yours."

Mr. Dorset walked to the window and looked out. Rain had begun to fall during one of our many storms, and from the window he could see that the grounds of Longacre no longer looked as they had during the plantation's height. Though the wilderness was still being held away from the house, it seemed to be coming closer. He finally turned around and looked at his daughter with tears streaming down his face, and merely opened his arms to her. She came from her chair and ran to him, and they both wept. Isaac properly left the room, and I escorted Aunt Sally from it, to allow Mr. Dorset and Jenny privacy in their intimate moment.

After that, Jenny's condition was just another part of life at Longacre, and even Isaac quit saying we were ruined and went about business, which indeed got dramatically better after the British troops left for the northern states. Not only were we not ruined, we began to prosper once again, so much that Mr. Dorset became interested in business, and he and Isaac saw great gains in our income for the next four years. Abel came once, for he had heard in Town of his sister's condition (which was a scandal there, of course). He was kind and solicitous, almost gallant, and when he left Jenny confided in me that Abel was now the man her father only thought himself to be. She did not love one the more or the other the less for it, however. Nor did she reveal the father of her child, if indeed she knew it. I, myself, believe she could not have known, but in this I may have been mistaken, and later, as the Reader will see, a number of men claimed the honor. If Jenny did know, however, it was a secret she never divulged.

— 14. —

JENNY'S CONFINEMENT ARRIVES. AUNT SALLY COMPLICATES MATTERS
BY BECOMING LOST. HAMLET SMYTHE OFFERS TO MARRY JENNY, AN
OFFER WHICH SHE DECLINES IN A MOST UNLADYLIKE MANNER.

That autumn, we were again at war with the Cherokees, who had allied themselves quite naturally with the British, for they had maintained such a friendship for many years. The Cherokees' defeat was preordained, not from God, as I believe, but by the fact of better armaments. Messrs. Middleton, Rutledge, Lynch, and Heyward signed the declaration of our freedom in Philadelphia and thus became even greater men than their wealth would purchase. As the enemy had withdrawn to the North, we were free to trade, and once again Charles Town became a great port city, and the wealth of men like Mr. Dorset and Mr. Smythe soared, though neither took a wife again. Mr. Dorset did not because of his unfortunate experience with Miss Tonning, and Mr. Smythe did not because of Mr. Dorset's unfortunate experience with Miss Tonning. Also, they were not on good terms because of the great failure of the Palmetto Volunteers at Fort Moultrie (which it was now called), where the men from up-country under Mr. William Thompson saved the day.

These are but details of the world, alas, and, as we know, History is not the great movements of armies or armadas, but the daily routine of life, those who leave for another life, and those who enter this one to see what might come next. The life in Jenny grew so great that we thought it might be twins, though the doctor, who came once or twice, said he felt it was not.

"Then it must be a monstrous big boy," said Mr. Dorset one evening at table.

"You shall make me ill," said Jenny, who felt none too well as it was. November was nearly over, and the cool breezes felt delicious after another suffocatingly hot summer. "It has been so long since you have seen a child born that you forget the shape of its mother entirely."

"Untrue!" he said. "I recall your dear mother's condition at all the births." He paused to chew on a slice of mutton. "I cannot remember mine, however. I wonder why that is?"

"Because you were drunk, no doubt," said Jenny.

"No doubt," said Mr. Dorset, not offended. "Women do not know it, but birth is as much an ordeal for the father as the mother. That, I believe, has been proven scientifically, has it not, Hawthorne?"

"I do not know of such things," I said.

"I wish to talk about something else," said Jenny. "I worry about Matthew. Should Isaac not travel north to see after him?"

"Are you mad?" said Isaac. "The war is there. For all we know, Matthew has moved to the West or to Italy. Perhaps he is now a cardinal or another of the assistants to the Papists. Were it not for father's occasional madness regarding religion, Matthew would never have moved away in search of something which will do him no good. All that exists here is success or failure, and there is only one manner in which it can be measured: money. Hawthorne, is there more gravy?"

"I regret to say not," I said.

"We never have enough gravy in this house," said Isaac. "Do we, dear?" His wife, trying very hard to say nothing, merely smiled and made a brief noise of apparent assent.

"Gravy?" said Mr. Dorset. "Waugh. That we should be reduced to speaking of gravy when I feel another song aborning."

Jenny stood suddenly, groaned with great urgency, and clasped her stomach. I rushed for her, and she turned and held to me, her face pale and sweating, despite the cool weather and the open windows. Her father asked if it were time for the child to come, and Isaac said certainly not, for it was not due for another two weeks or more. Jenny, now in agony but angry as well, picked up her fork and threw it at Isaac. Its blunt end bounced off his cheek, and Isaac made a great deal of it, giving a speech and asking his wife if he were not insulted. Mr. Dorset and I took Jenny up to her bedroom, where she lay on the sheets and screamed, cursing all men, the British, the French, Etc., then a series of men in Town, some of whose names were familiar, and some of whom were not. Mr. Dorset ran around the room not knowing what to do, so I instructed him to make the fire, as the room was cold. I went for the old midwife who had attended Jenny's mother and had delivered Jenny and the others. By now, she was ancient and forgetful, but she came immediately from her quarters with the slaves, passing Aunt Sally in the hallway, who still could see nothing and had little idea what was transpiring.

I led her up the stairs, holding the candle before us, and when we came into the room, Mr. Dorset had managed to set his coat on fire and could not seem to get it off. Jenny, holding her stomach, was trying to help him take the flaming garment off.

"I am afire!" cried Mr. Dorset.

"Child, get you into bed," said Lizzie, the midwife. "These mans will douche the fires." Jenny ignored her, and the old woman dragged her back to the bed with surprising strength, while I removed Mr. Dorset's coat and threw it into the fireplace, where it promptly blazed and disappeared.

"I'm burning up!" cried Jenny, now gasping for air as well. "Put out the fire!"

"All mans must now be gone," said Lizzie. "Boil me up a water and bring to me cloths. This child is to be born."

"Open the window!" cried Jenny. Lizzie did as she said, and a gust of cool, damp wind came in. Jenny began to take off her clothes, so I escorted her father out and went to the kitchen and brought water to boil. As I was bringing the kettle back to the house, I heard Jenny scream and utter a blasphemy that could be clearly heard. My wife heard and joined me with the cloths, and together we went back upstairs in the main house and handed them in to Lizzie. My wife asked if she might help, but Lizzie pushed us out as Jenny, now clothed only in a gown, screamed and cursed and threw the pitcher from the bedside against the fireplace, where it shattered.

"This may take a time," said Lizzie.

Mr. Dorset was running back and forth in the hallway, wanting to see his daughter but afraid, like most men, of the event itself. He asked what he should do then, and, knowing it could be some hours, I suggested, for reasons I cannot say, that we release the dogs and hunt for a coon.

"Coon?" he said. "To the hunt now?"

"To get out of the way here and to occupy yourself," I said. "Hands well occupied leave heads devoid of worry."

"Ah, is that from my writings?" he cried. "Tell me that is from my writings!"

"It is from your writings," I said. In fact, I had read it some years before in the *Gazette* as an example of the paucity of serious thought in the Colonies.

"Brave Hawthorne!" he cried. "To the hounds!"

Just then, the bedroom door burst open, and Jenny appeared before us, face contorted with pain, hair askew. She screamed, bent over, then straightened up.

"May all men suffer the pains of h—l!" she cried. Lizzie took her by the arm and pulled her back into the bedroom, where she continued to scream and thrash about. My wife touched my arm and went into the room to help.

"Let's to the hounds," said Mr. Dorset. "They will be a comfort."

Back downstairs, Isaac was still at table, complaining about the lack of gravy and urging his wife to agree with everything he said, which she did. We got two guns from the rack, along with power and ball and two lanterns and went out to the dogs, who were already roused by Jenny's screaming. As we crossed the lawn, Jenny cursed men, babies, soldiers, ships, and Lizzie. When we came to the dogs' enclosure, I suggested that we might arouse the keeper of the hounds to go with us to keep them in order, if such a thing was possible, but Mr. Dorset said that he was himself a master of hounds and could lead them straight to the hunt.

"Sir," I said. All the dogs were by the gate, which Mr. Dorset flung open with a grand gesture while shouting, "Ho, the hounds!"

Most of the dogs ran straight for the house and entered into it. Mr. Dorset rebuked the hounds for their behavior, and we both set out at a run to chase them out. When we came inside, about ten of the dogs were up to the table in the dining room, knocking over plates and eating all the food, despite a furious swatting from Isaac. His wife, who was terrified of dogs, stood on the sideboard with her skirts up, screaming soundlessly.

"Get down! Get off me!" cried Isaac. He swatted at one of the dogs with a mutton bone, and the animal latched on to it and, because Isaac refused to let it go, pulled him to the floor and began to make terrible threatening sounds. Another scream from upstairs came down, but it did not sound like Jenny, so I ran up there to find the door open and three dogs on the bed with Jenny, who was wincing in pain but laughing as well, while Lizzie had the fireplace implement and was beating on the dogs without effect. My wife was kicking ineffectually at a dog who seemed to be playing with the hem of her skirts. It took me nearly five minutes to throw all the dogs out, against Jenny's wishes. We finally got them all out of doors, or, rather, they left when the last of the food was gone. One knocked over a bottle of wine and proceeded to lap up its contents.

"Are you to the hunt with us?" Mr. Dorset asked Isaac, who looked upon the carnage in the dining room with utter disgust.

"Are you quite mad?" he asked his father.

"I suppose you are not," said Mr. Dorset. We retrieved our guns and went out the door. The hounds had gone off in three streams into the woods, barking and howling, and within a moment were all gone but for the distant baying and fighting sounds. Mr. Dorset and I stood at the edge of the yard and looked back at the house, realizing we had forgotten the lanterns and could only see by a small slice of moon which rose on us in her minor glory.

"We perhaps would not succeed in hunting without the dogs," I said.

"Nor would we succeed *with* them," he said sadly. "Is it a wonder that men move to Town and never come back? Say, would you mind retrieving our pipes and some tobacco?"

"With pleasure," I said. He sat in the grass as I went for the pipes and the fine tobacco he kept in a large bowl in his study. I was free to take from it as I wished, though I rarely did. Now it was a pleasure to join him for such a smoke. The house was still in ruins, and when I came in, Isaac shouted at me that I must immediately attend to his person. I said I was under order from Mr. Dorset and that I meant no disrespect.

"I remember when we were the finest family in the lowlands," said Isaac.

I took the pipes and tobacco back out to Mr. Dorset, who sat and was gazing at the stars. It was a brilliantly clear night by then, though, as I have said, rather cool. We lit our pipes and sat and looked at the sky, the silence punctuated only by Jenny's occasional screams.

"Do you believe that Jenny has done wrong?" he asked.

"She has done as her nature dictates," I said, enjoying the rich tobacco. "Can a person do else?"

"Her nature is to ignore the rules of society in her own fashion," he said.

"I believe that is so," I replied.

"Is that such a bad thing?" he mused. "She could be a murderess or a thief or a bawd, but instead she merely chooses to live apart from the rules created by man for the convenience of community. She does not fit into that community, does she? Since she was a child, she has always gone on her own and never been untrue to herself for the convenience of some overblown pompous fool in Charles Town. I should think that God would look on such devotion kindly. I would think that God in His wisdom might balance the fate of her bastard against the honesty of her life."

"I should think that, too, sir," I said. "Well put."

"No man or woman can account for their birthright," he said. "We are not put to choose our forebears just as we cannot finally account for our children. We must do our best to honor both and then let life take them as it may. If Matthew wishes to become a priest, then we must let him do so. If Isaac plans to grow fat and fret over accounts, he must do so. And if Abel had to strike Mr. Pinkworthy and spend time in gaol, he must do that as well. And if Jenny's pleasures have brought us this child, at least I am not barren as a grandfather. I wish my Lyddie were here to see this child, ever if it is a bastard."

"I have learned not to try and purchase the world with my deeds," I said. "Or I know that I shall ultimately fail. I can only serve as well as I might and hope that in some small measure that service has been pleasing to man and God."

"It hath been pleasing to man," he said, touching my arm. Soon, Mr. Dorset felt drowsy and lay in the grass and went to sleep, the first time in my memory he had ever done so while sober. I went into the house where Jenny was still screaming piteously, fetched a blanket, and brought it back out to cover Mr. Dorset. I then came inside, stoked the fires a bit, sat on the couch in the library, and fell into a sound sleep which was not disturbed until I felt someone shaking my arm. I awoke to see my wife standing over me. I noticed immediately that the fire was low and the room cold, and I was ashamed that I had failed to keep it aflame.

"What is it?" I asked.

"Jenny has given birth," she said. "She is well, and the child."

"What is it, then?" I asked.

"A fine daughter," said my wife. "And certainly with her mother's features. Would you like to come and see before we fetch it to the wet nurse?"

"I would," I said.

My wife handed me the lantern, and we went up the stairs and into the room, where Jenny lay, her hair wet with sweat, and a smile of exaltation upon her face. In her arms she cradled a child who neither wept nor stirred, instead looking with wide eyes around the room. The midwife was standing by the fire smoking a pipe and staring at the flames, which crackled merrily.

"Hawthorne, it is a girl," Jenny said. "Come see."

Through the window, I could see the faint light of dawn and in my mind I joined the images of that new day and the newborn child, and I realized that each day is a beginning in which we may face life anew if we but learn how. I came close and leaned down and looked into the child's face as it looked back at me. The resemblance to its mother was startling, for her features were fair and lovely, and her eyes the same shade of blue. I could not from the child's face guess who its father might be, but if she had been in a room with a hundred babies, I should have picked her out instantly as the daughter of Jenny Dorset.

"She is very beautiful," I said.

"I know she is," said Jenny. "And I shall not keep her."

"She is tired and must think this over," said my wife. "We must take the child to the nurse and let her mother sleep."

"I have thought it over," said Jenny mildly, looking down at the child, "and I shall not keep her. I will love her all my life, but she is not mine to bring properly into the world, so she must do that in a family which shall love her."

"Love is as shifting as sand," I reminded her softly. "Therefore trust no one with it but yourself."

"Dear Hawthorne," she said. "More maxims? No, I trust to do what is right in my heart."

The midwife, Lizzie, emptied her pipe and came for the child, which she wrapped up thrice and took from the house and to the wet nurse. My wife bade me good night and retired to our quarters, and I went to see if Mr. Dorset were still asleep in the grass. The morning was breaking by then, delicious and bright, with a wind from the Northwest, from whence the cool breezes born in the North sweep down in the late autumn and winter. Mr. Dorset still lay beneath his blanket, and close to him were two or three hounds, stretched to their length. A few other dogs were lying about the yard, all asleep except for one which was sitting still as a monument and looking over the new day at Longacre. When I came close, the dogs near Mr. Dorset stirred and sat up, yawning and stretching. One promptly fell back over and landed on Mr. Dorset's stomach. He sat straight up and cried that the British had come into the fort.

"And their hounds!" he cried. "Their hounds!" The dog which had attached itself to Mr. Dorset seemed loathe to leave but finally did stand up and wag its tail.

"Good morning, sir," I said.

"Hawthorne? Are you the master of the British hounds?" he asked, then fell into a coughing fit which could only be stopped by standing. When he finally looked around and saw that he was at home, he sighed in relief and tried to shake the dream from his head. He then looked at me directly and inquired about his daughter by simply stating her name.

"She is fine, and the child," I said.

"The child?" he said. "What sex does it possess?"

"It is a girl who looks very like her mother," I said.

"Bless it then," he said, "and God help it."

We walked back into the house, and I shortly presented him with a pot of fine coffee, which he drank before going into his library and closing the door. Aunt Sally came downstairs just then, feeling her way along the wall and seeming to be in danger of falling at any moment. She sang and whispered to herself. She had gone to bed long before the child had arrived, and now seemed to have forgotten it entirely, as she bid me welcome to the day and asked if she smelled coffee. I told her she did and that I should be glad to get her a cup.

"And get one for Jenny as well," she said upon reaching the bottom of the stairs. "She has much labor left to go, no doubt, and I do not think it would do the child any harm."

"The child is born," I said. "It is a girl, and it and Jenny fare well."

"Farewell," said Aunt Sally. She walked away and might have left the house entirely if she had not opened the door to the library where Mr. Dorset stood looking out the window. I tried to apologize, but Mr. Dorset said it was fine, and he told Aunt Sally good day and asked what she thought of his becoming a grandfather during the night.

"You are a grandfather?" she said. She turned and looked at me. "Why did you not reveal this to me, servant?"

"It escaped my mind," I said.

"Then if you are a grandfather, Adam, I am a . . . I am a what?" she asked.

"You are a witness," said Mr. Dorset. "And more, you are a witness to the life of this house, how it has come new upon us. I think on it, and when I do, I cannot help thinking of the life that we have lost as well. I cannot help it. I cannot."

I took Aunt Sally by the arm and guided her out, and we left the Master of Longacre to his thoughts.

— 15. —

A SECTION OF LETTERS, ALONG WITH EXCERPTS FROM JENNY DORSET'S DIARY, PROMISED MUCH EARLIER BY THE AUTHOR AND INTERRUPTED BY THE PROGRESS OF OUR NARRATIVE AND BY THE AUTHOR'S LACK OF ART IN THESE MATTERS.

Longacre
December 15, 1776

Dear Desdemona,

I hope that your visit with your brother at Foxhaven has been gratifying, but I miss you terribly, as I have no one with whom to speak my feelings. The child is beautiful, and I have held her with great curiosity. When she does not get what she wants (as if she quite knew), she throws the most amazing fits that you have ever seen, full of arm-waving and screams. When she has grown large enough in a few weeks, I have arranged to have her given to a family which I cannot name. Not even my father knows.

I hear almost nothing from the war in the North, having been cut off from friends since my confinement. I do not believe the British have designs on the South any time soon, but one can never be sure.

Was the weather today not full of charm and warmth for this time of year? And when are you returning to Longacre?

Yours,
Jenny

Longacre
December 15, 1776

Mr. Hazlett,

Your presumption that you are the father of my child is amusing to me, for I can assure you that Nature in her wisdom did not give you such gifts as to cause this kind of event to transpire. Your noble offer to "put me up in a small house near Jacksborough, though without a servant," is an insult that I will not tolerate.

You were not at Fort Moultrie, despite your assertion that you were, and I suspect you were cowering in your basement with full knowledge of what a fool you were making of yourself. Our brief liaison was unpleasant, and you are ignoble, ignorant, and rather ugly.

Regards &tc.,
Jenny Dorset

DECEMBER 19, 1776 — *This journal is my only hope now, and I wish that I could live my life in the world instead of on its bound pages! The child is beautiful, but I must give her up. She will not remember me or ever know who I was, a thought which gives me pause, but only slightly. Perhaps the story of her birth will come to her when she is grown, and she will forgive me for my Nature and for hiding her bastardy from her. Or perhaps _____ will tell her in good time, revealing that her true mother was a woman of great passions and a foolish heart, and one who above all hated tyranny in all its forms. I cannot but wish this burden would pass from me, but, as it will not, I can do nothing but live with my decision. My father has been wonderful and has forgotten there is any ill-thought attached to such a birth, though Isaac fears it has hurt his chances for political fortune, as if he had any. He is so fat that he has caused a servant to resew his clothing three times this year already. We do not see Abel, as he is engaged in the work of patriotism. And my poor Matthew — where are you now? I cannot see my simple and gentle brother made a soldier or priest. I miss my mother in the worst way this morning.*

DECEMBER 25, 1776 — *And so we spend another Christmas at Longacre, this one rather sad, however. Mr. Hawthorne and his wife decorated the house gaily, and he attempted to draw me out of my sadness, but soon the girl must leave me, and though it cannot be any other way, the very idea tears at my heart. We sang old songs today, and my father as usual drank himself into great excitement and happiness, then went to sleep, from which he could not be roused. I took a walk on the grounds, and the sky was somewhat clouded, but it did not rain, and the earth smelled good and felt pleasant and familiar beneath my feet.*

Longacre
December 27, 1776

  Dear Mr. Prioloux,
   How insolent, of you, sir! I do not know why you overrate your abilities thus or why you would make your laughable assertion regarding the paternity of my child, but I assure you that this matter is none of your concern and that you were in no wise involved.
   Please cease all further communications with me.

Sincerely, &tc.,
Jenny Dorset (Miss)

DECEMBER 31, 1776 — *The year gone! And such a one it was, with victories and defeat like all years. Thank the heavens at least that Desdemona is back from Foxhaven so that I have her company to rely on, else I would have no one to speak to but this journal or Mr. Hawthorne. I fear for my father's health and wish he would take a wife, but that seems impossible after his hideous mistake with Miss Tonning (how I hate even to write the name of that vile creature!). Oh that I could somehow keep my child, but it cannot be. I have come to love her, but I know that if I love her truly I must let her go, for she would grow to be wild at Longacre or in Town and must needs be raised by a family calmer and more in control of its passions. What genuine sadness I feel! But my work is hardly begun, and so I must sacrifice what is necessary to do it. Farewell, beloved child! I weep over you!*

— 16. —

IN WHICH WE COME TO THE END OF BOOK SIX OF THIS HISTORY AND
PREPARE FOR THE SEVENTH AND FINAL BOOK, WHICH THE AUTHOR
HOPES WILL BE BETTER CRAFTED.

And so Jenny Dorset, in secret and in the middle of the night, left Longacre the first week in January 1777 and took her child away, arriving home at dawn without her. No one was more bereft than Mr. Dorset, but he did not question the wisdom of the act. Aunt Sally was sure the child was still about but that she could not see it. Jenny played her harpsichord, wept, and walked the grounds for several days before she was better.

Her friend Desdemona kept her company. Molly McNew sometimes walked with them, but she was not like either so much that they appreciated her company. Molly's brother, Tom, on the other hand, enjoyed being at Foxhaven greatly. Isaac Dorset took advantage of the holiday to eat more than I had ever seen a man consume and thereby grew fatter almost beneath our eyes.

Mr. Dorset was very quiet in those days, and though he and Mr. Smythe exchanged mocking letters, Mr. Dorset's heart was not in it, and indeed I must admit here that I wrote several of the letters for Mr. Dorset at his request.

That year of 1777 and indeed the one following it made little effect on us as to the war, for it all was being waged in the North. It was not until late 1779, in fact, that the British finally decided to open a campaign in the South, and for two miserable years they took over Charles Town and occupied it as a conquering army. During that time, Jenny Dorset ceased her amorous wandering and saw only one gentleman. She also gained fame in the most unlikely manner, and achieved a revenge for which she is still remembered.

I thank the Reader for his (or her) patience in reading this History, and promise that the next book shall be the final one, in which the story comes to its inevitable conclusion.

BOOK VII.

— 1. —

IN WHICH TWO YEARS ARE SPED BY WITH A HASTE WHICH NO MAN
WOULD WISH, SO THAT WE MAY ARRIVE AT A TIME WHEN
THE BRITISH ATTACK CHARLES TOWN.

The world changes around mere men to remind them that life is eternal
only in Heaven and not upon this Earth. Or at least that is my thinking,
for if the affairs of men never changed, we could not sense what messages
the Almighty has for us. Being a man without requisite book learning
myself, I cannot say what all those years might mean, but I know that
Jenny Dorset came into her glory not through the domestic arts but
through war. Perhaps it was a happenstance of her childhood or the blood
of the Dorsets, but it was also the time itself which helped conspire in the
character of Jenny. She could never have been a housewife, though I
believe motherhood to be the most fearfully difficult job upon this Earth.
Nor could Jenny have been a society matron, arranging porcelain and
attending parties to exchange scandalous stories. She could only have
been who she was, and for that I am thankful, for in this life or any other,
I will not see her like again.

Following the failed attack of the *Tamar* and the *Cherokee* upon
Charles Town in June of 1776, we entered a period of relative calm, as I
have said, when the rich grew richer and the poor often went hungry. The
fear of a mob even turned Mr. Christopher Gadsden, that most fiery of
orators, into a conservative believing in the need of government. No men
were more riotous than the enlisted soldiers, who were largely a drunken,
disorderly group who seemed always on the verge of mutinies, and who
suffered so many courts martial that such proceedings ceased to be novel
in the least. Despite attempts by the Council, little could be done to control

the wild drinking and wenching of the men, and Town seemed more full of lewd women than ever, painted without even taste, much less art. (I am sorry to say that Mr. Dorset's pleasure in such company went on unabated.) There were constant worries of a slave insurrection, but after the hanging of Thomas Jeremiah, slaves were on their guard even about the talk of freedom from Britain. We received reports of the war in the North, and we believed all news of American victories and none of British successes and never really knew which was the truth or really cared, so long as the shooting was far away. Inflation was a source of worry to those who lived by margins, but to people of the Smythe and Dorset class, it was merely a nuisance. Life continued as it had for decades in the dark, ill-smelling alleys on the Cooper River.

In January of 1778, a fire of catastrophic proportions destroyed more than two hundred houses, the Library, and our Natural History Museum, though it did not reach us. Someone asserted that it must have been started by British sympathizers, and two convenient loyalists were found and hanged, which satisfied revenge but not justice. More than a few people felt God would visit punishment upon us for such an act.

It seemed that by early 1779, we had suffered that revenge, when the British, who had already captured Savannah and Georgia in its entirety, threatened Charles Town. By that May, the Redcoats, though not reaching Charles Town, began to plunder plantations, take slaves, and kill animals wholesale for rations. Fortunately, they were not able to reach Longacre or Foxhaven before an army of Colonials under Gen. Benjamin Lincoln arrived to harry them away. Still, we knew that the forces of the British, secured in Savannah, were by then a serious threat which could no longer be ignored.

I tried without success to locate Jenny Dorset's daughter in those two years, and indeed that search became with me an obsession which I could not let go. Most of the women and children had returned to Town after the threat of the *Tamar* and *Cherokee* in 1776 had come to naught, but by late 1779, they were again leaving for the up-country, which in truth was not safe, either. Still, as Charles Town sits upon a peninsula from which escape is impossible if invested at once from land and sea, the men sent their families away, and I knew that at least for then my search was futile.

Though the Palmetto Volunteers were no longer in defense of the state, Mr. Dorset and Mr. Smythe were making plans, spending vast amounts of money for defenses, Etc., much to the anger and horror of

Isaac Dorset, who had firmly announced his support of the Crown in public. Mr. Smythe was luckier in his sons, in that Hamlet and Iago had both become officers with the state militia. Neither was exceptionally brave or cowardly, intelligent or stupid, which made them fine middle-level soldiers. Abel Dorset continued in his capacity as a model soldier, however, and was much admired throughout South Carolina for his heroism during the attack in 1776. We heard nothing from Matthew.

Jenny, Desdemona Smartt, and I, along with my wife, who had not been well, went to Longacre for Christmas in 1779, and the house and grounds were in terrible condition. The house, once white and magnificent, had lost much of its paint, which was no longer obtainable, and, rather than maintain the tangle of topiary, Isaac had ordered it all cut down, an act which I regretted but which seemed not unreasonable. It seemed that Isaac's wife was barren, and so they had conceived no children, which only increased the sour disposition of Isaac toward the world, for it was clear that he would have no children to leave, while Jenny, who had no husband, would. If Abel Dorset had a sweetheart, we never knew of it.

By then, the furniture was getting old and that which had broken was nailed crudely back together or braced with hewn pieces of palmetto planking. The vases which in the course of daily life had been broken over the years had not been replaced, so that the entire house seemed empty and sad. Unknown to Mr. Dorset, Isaac had been selling off slaves so that he could try to reinvest in money-making schemes that always came to nothing. By that Christmas, only about ten slaves remained and five servants, not enough to run a plantation. The rice wetlands had grown back over, and the fields for the cattle were putting up small trees that in time would turn the place back into forest. The disputed three feet along the common property line of Foxhaven and Longacre was lost in a tangle of brambles, which, I suppose, was a lesson of some kind.

Aunt Sally had moved to Longacre, where she had become no blinder. Tom McNew had finally decided to stay permanently at Foxhaven with his twin sister, Molly, and Roderigo Smartt likewise had left Foxhaven to move in with Isaac and his wife. Roderigo's sister, Desdemona, lived with us in Town, still Jenny's closest friend and confidante. Of all the children who had once roamed the fields and woods in that country, only Isaac Dorset was left in his place, and he was so fat by then that he could scarcely roam from one room to another, much less in field and wood.

Like soldiers trapped in a prison, Mr. Dorset's hunting dogs had constructed a tunnel beneath their fence in the summer of 1779 and taken off for a trip from which they never returned. Only one dog remained, which was blind and sedentary, lived in the house, and was given to flatulence and bouts of attacking invisible enemies.

"Men like Gadsden have thrown us into a time from which we may never recover," said Isaac as we ate our Christmas dinner. "You hear the dispatches as well as I do, and you know that the British troops will be here within a few weeks. Those who have defied the Crown will suffer, as will even those patriots who have defended it."

"Patriots!" cried Jenny Dorset. "A patriot does not defend tyranny, Isaac. When will you learn that?"

"I saw a cat with five legs at Mr. Manigault's on Tuesday last," said Mr. Dorset. "I should wonder if it isn't the fastest of its kind ever born." Isaac looked at Jenny as if in pity for their father, then ate from the potatoes saved during the fall.

"My," said Isaac's wife, who seemed to be trying to learn to speak in the company of others.

"A patriot is one who defends his country," said Isaac. "And this mob of drunkards and treasonous fools does not make a country, dear sister. They make only misery for themselves and for all of us when we are rightly punished by the King. Men such as myself will endure it, but the stench of having family in that mob will stay with us for years to come."

"Stench?" said Aunt Sally. "My word, what *is* that?"

The dog was lying on a rug near the fire sleeping, and he was suspect, but no one else had the lack of tact to say anything. Jenny began to laugh, however, and Mr. Dorset started to sing "Victory at Longacre." Isaac took the lapse as proving his point for some reason, and looked with disdain and superiority at the proceedings.

Afterward, Mr. Dorset and I took a tour of the grounds, which proved philosophical for him. We walked to his wife's grave, and he wept theatrically as he recalled their finer moments and spoke in general as if she were a saint rather than flesh. The day was pleasant and clouded, and a fresh breeze lifted the trees.

"Hawthorne, what if each breeze is a ghost who is roaming about where it once lived and trying to impart its message to the living?" he asked. "What if that ghost only comes when it sees a person it has known in life? What should one say to such a thing?"

"The Scriptures do not to my knowledge speak of ghosts returning from the dead," I reminded him. "I believe that the disposition of souls is clear enough."

"Yes, yes, but what if, on occasion, they were allowed to roam from Heaven with the intent of taking messages or warning to their loved ones still below?" he asked. "Would it perhaps be a warning that a family's life is destined in total to send its purveyor to the Nether Regions?" He suddenly gasped his chest and took a few steps from me and turned.

"Sir, are you ill?" I asked.

"I will be punished for my iniquities," he said hoarsely. "God has sent his legions to warn me of my sinful life!"

"We have all sinned and fallen short of the glory of God," I said.

"I have fallen *far* short, have I not, Hawthorne?" he said. He begged me for an answer which I was unwilling to present him.

"So have we all," I said. "It is Christmas, and I would not weary myself with such thoughts. Be of good cheer and praise God in the highest."

"I do so," he said, looking around, now appearing entirely frightened. "But does God praise me? What shall He do to me for what I have allowed this family to become?"

"God knows all," I said, touching his shoulder. "He knew before you were born that your family would turn thus, so why could He hold that against you? Besides, everyone knows that it is in no wise a man's guilt if his sons go bad. Sometimes the things simply occur."

"He knew of me before I was born," said Mr. Dorset. "Of course. But, oh, I am in agony for my mistakes." He ran back to me and clasped my shoulders and held them firmly. "Hawthorne, tell me I will burn in H—l. Please tell me I shall burn forever in H—l's fires!"

"Sir, please get a grip on yourself," I said. "What would Miss Tonning have thought?" Without meaning to, we had strayed near her unmarked grave, though both of us knew precisely where it was. He looked down and stepped lightly away, as if he might be standing directly on the offensive earth.

"She would have wished me madness on Christmas Day," he said. His eyes opened as if he had been given a Great Answer. "Waugh! It is *she* who haunts me! Away, wretch! Fly back hence to the fire from whence you have arisen!" He threw his arms outward grandly and then began walking back toward the house, and, on the way, he said that he believed he would partake in a glass or two of wine in honor of his victory over Ghost

Tonning. He could not wait to tell the others of his battle and its conclusion, but Isaac was asleep on a sofa, and Jenny was in the backyard giving a speech regarding the British to several servant children, who,
though uncomprehending, seemed inspired by her presence.

— 2. —

IN THE EARLY SPRING OF 1780, THE BRITISH TROOPS ARRIVE
NOT FAR FROM CHARLES TOWN, HAVING WORKED THEIR WAY UP
FROM SAVANNAH. PANIC FILLS THE STREETS, AND
EXCITEMENT FILLS JENNY DORSET.

By March, it was clear that we were in dire trouble in Charles Town, for
our troops had been unable to keep the British in their camps in Georgia. We had reliable reports that they were approaching from the South,
from the North, and from the sea as well. Commerce from the Indies had
stopped entirely, and the poor were destitute, and the rest of us were
often hungry. I pleaded with Jenny to leave Town, for I fully intended to
fight for my home, but she said that she would sooner hang than leave,
and I knew that it was so.

She and Desdemona were the last of the Daughters of Liberty, and
they entirely abandoned the practice of wearing skirts and wore trousers
only, and cut their hair short to resemble men, binding themselves as well
to hide their female forms. As a young *man*, Jenny was still the most
beautiful woman in the state, and nothing she could do might hide that.
The chaos of the times was such, however, that she passed unnoticed
among the hundreds of young boys who thought the fight was somehow
a great adventure in which they had been invited to participate. Those
who had seen more were less sanguine.

I should not give the Reader the idea that all in Town were in favor of
revolution, for many were still against it. The loyalists included many
good men who felt that the talk of independence, though already
achieved on paper, was sheer madness and would be reversed shortly.
These men (like Isaac) would not let ideas come before commerce. Mr.
Dorset and Jenny, however, never in their lives let commerce come before
an idea. Abel had the passion for public action that his father lacked and
the fire of his sister as well. As such, he had become an outspoken supporter of the revolutionists. At the same time, he and his sister mended
years of estrangement and became once again quite close.

By March of 1780, the British had virtually cut off Charles Town by sea and land. Mr. Peter Timothy of the *Gazette* had climbed the steeple of St. Michael's and looked south toward Edisto Island and seen the campfires of thousands of soldiers. At the same time, the British began to come from the North so that we were isolated in our peninsula. I begged Jenny to leave and go to Longacre, which, we heard, was not being molested since Isaac was a fervent supporter of the Crown. (Foxhaven, in the meantime, defended by neither Mr. Smythe nor his sons, who were at war, was looted and some of the outbuildings burned before a gentleman officer forbade any further depredations.) We cut a deep trench the width of the Town and allowed it to fill with water while throwing up abatis, but in truth all we had done was cut off any possible escape from the British, who had more cannons, more shells, and more time. We would be bombarded and starved. We became desperate.

Desperation, however, worked on us in many ways. Some despaired and fled to the churches. Some despaired and fled to the ale houses or to women of pleasure. And others worked night and day to meet the battle and to survive as they might upon what was left. To them, death was preferable to subjection. No one was more excited (or excitable) than Jenny Dorset, who schemed, acted as a courier, practiced her skills with pistols and guns, and in general entered whole into the life of a soldier for freedom. She was, indeed, one of the few women of her class left in Town, along with Desdemona. I had sent my wife to Longacre, where I knew she would not be harmed, and I missed her terribly. Before the troops encircled us, I managed to get a few letters to her by friends who still came and went from Town. Soon, such communication was impossible, however, and I could only guess what her health was.

— 3. —

IN WHICH WE COME TO THE SAD DEATH OF ABEL DORSET AND JENNY'S
REVENGE ON THE MAN WHO KILLED HIM.

Abel had grown into a brilliantly handsome young man of thirty years, with dark hair, sharp blue eyes, and fair features that reminded me entirely of his beautiful mother. He seemed so different from the callous young man who had thrashed Mr. Pinkworthy that I could only assume that in him a miracle had been wrought. Many predicted for him a fine future in the new state, possibly as governor. Mr. Dorset was proud of his son and took every opportunity when he visited us to inquire of his exploits or to report them if he had heard before us.

Abel came by our house one evening in early March when the British were approaching. He rode up on his fine white horse, dismounted, and tied it to the hitching post in front of the house, where Jenny and I stood, talking with an old man named Thomas Flynt, who thought an attack from the French was to take place shortly. This Flynt, a boyhood friend of Mr. Dorset, had aged far worse than he, and was toothless and what seemed very nearly boneless. He moved as if he were a tentacled thing in the sea, and I could not see how he remained upright, though he did by an ungainly series of gestures, countergestures, and lunges for pillars and posts. Mr. Flynt had one eye which had gone milky, and he kept rubbing it to see if the sight could be restored.

"Abel, what is the hurry?" asked Jenny. "It is come?"

"Soon," he said. "We heard they are to bombard us from the sea and from the land. They mean to blow us from here and squeeze us until we beg them to enter and save us."

"I will die first!" cried Jenny.

"Dead soldiers are of no help," said Abel. "May we sit? I am thirsty."

"Come in the house," said Jenny.

"Certainly," said Flynt, who then walked into the fence and fell over it. Abel helped him up and gently suggested that perhaps he might go back to his house to await developments. Flynt agreed and walked off down the dusty street. We went inside, and I brought one of our last bottles of wine, along with two glasses. Jenny immediately ordered me to fetch a third glass, for which I was honored and grateful. We sat in the parlor, listening to the increasing sounds of men running and shouting outside.

"I beg you to leave here, sister," said Abel. "I know it shall do no good, but I wish you to go to Longacre."

"I will suffer death ten times over before I abandon you or this cause," she said fiercely. "Do not tell me such foolishness again."

"I have done my duty by you as a brother, at least," he said. "You should know that we may hold out here for a week, no more. If we are not relieved, the British will blow us to pieces here until we surrender."

"Surrender?" said Jenny.

"Slaughter or starvation are not choices but deaths," he said. "Better we lost once in a small way that entirely in a large one."

Jenny took this intelligence angrily but could say nothing back, as she knew that Abel was well connected with all the leaders of the state and that he would be in a position to know if we could survive the coming assault. After a few more moments of idle chatter, Abel got up, kissed his sister on the cheek and bade her take care.

"And you as well, for we need you," she said. Then, "And *I* need you." He smiled at her, bowed gallantly, and was gone. Jenny finished her wine and retired for the evening, while I stood in the street and wondered what had brought us to such a pass that we were at war with the very country which had given us birth. I thought perhaps nations move as men do. They grow, love their parents, reject them, embrace them once again, then die. The idea filled me with such a melancholy that I still felt it keenly when I went to bed.

I was up early the following day, and it was not much past dawn when there was a sharp rap on the door. I opened it and saw Mr. William Henry Drayton, looking exhausted. He held his hat in his hand.

"Smith, is it?" he asked me.

"Hawthorne, Mr. Drayton," I said.

"Surely," he said. "Is Miss Dorset arisen yet?"

"I am certain not," I said. "Would you like to come in?" He nodded, and I allowed him to enter the parlor, where I had not lit a fire, though it was not very cool for March. I lit the candles and lamps and then came back to him with a sense of dread that I could not contain.

"I do not quite know how to convey this message," he said. He looked terribly careworn, and, instead of addressing me, looked at his hands. "But Miss Dorset's brother Abel was murdered last evening."

"Murdered!" I said. I sat down in a chair and looked at the patterns the new sunlight threw on the floor from the windows. "By whom? How can this be?"

"We had met at Mr. Timothy's regarding our plans, and when we left just after midnight, we all went our ways, and we heard a gunshot," he said. "We rushed with guns to the direction from whence it came and found Abel shot through the heart. He was killed instantly." Mr. Drayton seemed shaky. "We have his body at Mr. Timothy's, as I could not bear to bring it here in the night."

"My God, what have we become," I said idly. "And you found no one who might have killed him?"

"We are already out looking this morning, but the man got away under the cloak of night," he said. As he spoke, I saw Jenny coming into the room, her hair tangled from sleep. She wore a night robe and slippers and seemed to be shivering. She said that she heard voices and spoke to Mr. Drayton and curtseyed. He stood and kissed her hand and gestured for her to sit, which she did. He then told her of the disaster, and Jenny nodded, began to tremble mightily, but did not cry.

"Bring him to me," she said. "I shall bury him here."

"Madam," he said. "It is a great loss for us all. He was a fine man. He was a patriot."

I paid a man named Punt, who lived wherever his money ran out for rum, to go over to Mr. Smythe's and inform Mr. Dorset of his son's death, which he did ably. Jenny dressed and came back down and sat in a chair by the small fire I made and stared at it, still trembling and not crying. I tried to comfort her, but she might have been made of stone. Mr. Dorset arrived not more than an hour later and wept as they brought his son's body into the house in a coffin already supplied free by an undertaker in Town. Jenny looked at her brother and did not weep. We sent word to Isaac, but we could not await his arrival to bury Abel. Mr. Smythe soon came as well and wept with Mr. Dorset, but still Jenny refused to cry. Mr. Smythe, Mr. Dorset, and I dug the grave in the backyard, making it very deep so that it would not be molested. All the while, Mr. Dorset sang sad Irish tunes, ones I had not heard since my boyhood, and I was seized with a terrible sadness for Abel, for Mr. Dorset, for Jenny — for us all.

We lowered the coffin in the grave, and as father, Mr. Dorset had the privilege of throwing the first shovel of dirt upon his eldest son, and the chore nearly broke his heart, but he managed. Mr. Smythe, perhaps remembering poor Fortinbras, said nothing was so bad as losing a child, and then he began to sing along with Mr. Dorset, and they stood arm-in-arm over the grave as the day, lovely and full of spring life, rose around us.

"Now rest the soul of Abel Dorset," said Mr. Dorset. "He was his mother's first and his father's joy. Take him into your bosom, O Lord, and bring him peace."

Jenny finally wept for her brother, tears mixed with a fierce anger, and she knelt and pressed her face into the sandy soil as if to leave her impression on Abel one last time. She stood with sand still clinging to her cheek, which her father brushed away as we all walked back into the house for a drink. That very day, Jenny began to make inquiries around Town regarding her brother, as I did and as her father and Mr. Smythe did as well. Though most men were engaged in building barricades and fortifications, and most women were gone except for bawds and various old maids who refused to leave, many stopped to answer questions from us.

It was soon clear that we were having no luck whatever in attempting to uncover Abel's murderer and might not have if not for a chance conversation Mr. Dorset had with a woman of the streets. Jenny, Mr. Dorset, and I were walking down Queen Street when the woman, who was painted and unafraid of the impending invasion, recognized my Master and hailed him in a loud voice. Mr. Dorset looked stricken.

"I know her, child, from trying to save her from her wicked ways," he said desperately to Jenny, who did not believe any of it but pretended to.

"Of course," said Jenny.

"You ain't been around in a bit," the woman said as she approached Mr. Dorset. "Run out of money or time?"

"Take care of thy vices and answer a question for me, whore," said Mr. Dorset, raising his hand in an ecclesiastical manner.

"Who is the old fellow and the baby face?" the woman asked, looking at me and Jenny. I felt Jenny stiffen, but I held her arm and cautioned her with my eyes not to say anything quite yet.

"No bother about them," said Mr. Dorset. "I am trying to find who killed Captain Dorset. Might you know anything about it?"

"Poor Captain Dorset," she said. "I might know something about it. Men do talk at the most inopportune times."

"What do you know?" said Jenny harshly.

"Men do talk," said the woman, fanning herself and smiling to show crooked teeth. "They talk about their adventures. About sea creatures and Indians and . . ."

"Never mind that now, woman!" said Mr. Dorset desperately. "What do you know?"

The woman, of course, was accustomed to being paid for everything, and, business being poor because of the men's preparations for war, she asked for a pound, which Mr. Dorset gave her.

"I'd ask about Major Pinkworthy," she said. "I believe that is the name I heard."

"Pinkworthy!" cried Jenny. "The artist? He drowned!"

"Not the artist," said the woman. "His son. A sour sort if there ever was one. I heard tell that he is the one who done in young Mr. Dorset."

Straightaway, we began to inquire about Pinkworthy the Younger, and we found his lodgings, but no one was there, and signs indicated that he had not been there for a time. He was no doubt with the soldiers, who were working and living along the streets and in their encampments around Town. Exhausted, Mr. Dorset gathered Mr. Smythe and went back to their work with the army, but Jenny Dorset had no intention of giving up until she was avenged.

Each day, she went out among the men to look for Pinkworthy, and each day reports came to us that the British were closer and closer. We did not find the young man for a long time, until one day we heard his name called out as we stood on a corner nearly ready to give it all up. Both of us stood fast to our positions as a corpulent young man with thin hair and an air of undeserved dignity walked over to speak with the man who had summoned him.

"Get him over to me in that alley," said Jenny, pointing east. I nodded but felt a deep worry about what might transpire. When the soldier finished conferring with Pinkworthy, I approached him and asked it he were the Pinkworthy who was son of the artist.

"I am, what of it?" he asked. "Old fools should have long quit Town. It is near too late to leave."

"I have someone who wants to meet you," I said.

"Meet me?" he said. "I have no time for it. Be gone."

"Only a moment, sir," I said.

He shrugged and walked with me toward the alley where Jenny stood, smiling and looking coyly about. Pinkworthy began to smile with interest when he saw Jenny. She turned and walked to its dank end, and Pinkworthy, like a starved dog, followed her, as I did. When we came to the end, which branched off in other directions, she motioned for him to come close.

"You are a fine and strong man," she said in a soft voice. "I have heard something for which I wish to reward you if it be true."

"Reward me?" he said.

"Indeed," she said, running her finger along his cheek. "I have heard that you are the one who killed that dreadful Abel Dorset. Is it true?"

"What if I did?" he said coyly. "He was a fool. He insulted men who were his superiors. That is what I hear."

"But I want to know truly, before I give you a reward," she said, bouncing lightly on her feet. I looked about, having no idea what she had in mind but worrying all the same. Pinkworthy laughed.

"The man insulted my father," he said. "He got what he deserved." I could see that Jenny was in a quandary now, for though he had admitted joy that Abel was dead, he had not quite admitted that he had killed him. I felt a deep rage toward the man, and wanted to thrash him myself, but the situation was equivocal.

"But to have been stabbed like that," I said.

"He was shot," Pinkworthy said. "Get away from us, old man. I will get my reward from this lovely young lady."

"He was stabbed in the throat," said Jenny. "I heard that to be true."

"Then the fool who told you that lied," said Pinkworthy, "because I shot him in the back! He died as cowards deserve!" I could no longer doubt that we had found Abel's murderer, and my blood felt weak and cold inside me. Jenny, however, was triumphant.

"Then it is true," she said softly, coldly. "You are the one who killed my brother."

"I killed him dead and I would . . ." he said. "Your brother?"

"And now he is avenged, you b—t—d!" she cried. With that, she took from the back of her dress a pistol that I did not even know she had brought, lifted it under the man's chin, and fired. Even though I agreed with her revenge, I was shocked by its violence. The top of Pinkworthy's head was blown perhaps ten feet away, and he fell in a heap of smoke and blood. For a moment, I could say nothing, but soon I gathered my senses, and ran for Jenny, bade her drop the gun, and walked around a building and out the other side then down the street.

"All of this because of a misbegotten portrait!" I said more to myself than anyone else.

"Abel is avenged," Jenny said. "There is now work to be done."

— 4. —

IN LATE MARCH OF 1780, THE BRITISH BEGIN THEIR SIEGE OF
CHARLES TOWN, FOLLOWED BY THE BOMBARDMENT, WHICH FORCES US
TO TAKE EVEN MORE DESPERATE ACTION.

As spring blossomed in Charles Town, so did the clarity of our plight. We now could no longer escape, and we were obviously not be relieved. Jenny and Desdemona worked furiously to undermine the works of the sympathizers and had some success. Sometimes, they would be gone from the house for several days and return in a terrible condition. Throughout the month of April, our hunger became worse and worse. Men took to eating dogs and rats, and they openly quarreled about what we should do next — fight or surrender.

In the middle of April, Jenny received a letter from her brother Isaac, who was holding court at Longacre for a number of British officers. He obviously believed himself in a position of power and clearly expected to become more powerful when the British defeated us in the war. Knowing Isaac myself, I had great doubts.

Longacre,
April 16, 1780

Dear Sister,

I would like to beg of you again to return to Longacre, where I have the personal agreement of my friend Colonel Johnson of the Regulars that you will not be hurt or charged with sedition or other crimes. I am afraid that I can no longer protect our Father from his foolishness, and, despite my repeated warnings, our brother Abel received what traitors always receive.

If you will take a dispatch to Thomas at the Queen Street Port on the Cooper River tomorrow night at 8 o'clock, I will receive it safely. Please tell me that you will come both to your senses and to Longacre.

I regret to inform you of the passing of Aunt Sally. She was upstairs, or so a servant tells me, and, seeing a butterfly out the window, thought to reach for it. Though it was more than ten feet from the house, her wretched eyesight made her think it was close, and so she fell from the window and landed on the flagstones below, dashing her head. She was killed instantly. I pray for her soul but cannot regret that she is gone, for she was quite a nuisance.

You must know by now that the Revolution has failed and that all who take part in it will be held accountable for their treason. Please send me word that you will return home. As we are short of help, you could be useful here both to us and to yourself.

Your most concerned brother,
Isaac Dorset, Esq.

Postscriptum: You may bring Hawthorne with you if it seems necessary.

Jenny read the letter and went into a spitting rage, cursing him, threatening to burn down what was left of Longacre. She consigned Isaac to many of the levels of Hell and said that she wished she might send him a bomb instead of a note. She finally wore out her rage and stormed from the house and stopped at our fence long enough to kick it until it became wobbly on its posts.

"I suppose she is not going to Longacre, then," said Desdemona, as we watched Jenny from the parlor window.

"I suppose not," I said.

We had little time to think of Isaac, however, for suddenly, on May 9, the British began a massive bombardment of Town. On hearing the first shells, Jenny and Desdemona ran into the street, as I did, begging them to come back inside and go to the cellar where we might be safe. A shell landed not a hundred yards away and blew apart a barn and a horse inside it. Old men and a few women poured from houses screaming and praying. The smell of smoke began to rise in the air, and the gunners found a range farther south of us toward the heart of Town. Soon, our men began to fire back, but I knew our munitions were limited and would run out long before those of the British did.

"To the barricades!" cried Jenny.

"To the cellar!" I shouted back. For a moment I thought I had succeeded, for Jenny and her friend ran into the house, but it was only to retrieve their rifles and powder and bullet bags. Since I knew I could not hold her against her will, I got my gun as well and joined them in the race for the nearest of the barricades. Just as we arrived, our boys fired a shell that roared not thirty feet over our heads. The sound was deafening, and Desdemona jumped with fright, but Jenny acted as if it were, at most, a dandelion blown over us, whose filaments might fall harmlessly to the ground.

The sound, by the time we got behind the barricade, was even more violent, and shells from the British were exploding all around us. We fired back as we could, but soon our men were withholding fire for lack of powder and ball. I huddled behind the barricade, wondering how we could possibly withstand this assault, but Jenny and Desdemona ran up and down the street, rallying the men, cursing the British in the most foul and colorful terms. Jenny's cheeks took on color, and to me she looked nothing so little as a man, but in the bombardment no one had time to notice. From the trajectory of the shells, I deduced that one battery could see us and was sighting in on our barricade, for one shell would land too far, and the next too short. By increments, however, each shot was coming closer, and, fearing for Jenny's life, I finally leapt to my feet and dragged her down a side street, Desdemona at our heels. Jenny screamed and fought with me and asked me if I had gone mad from the smell of powder (as some men were reported to do in battle). Just as we came between two buildings, we saw, down the street, a shell hit the barricade itself, blowing it to pieces, along with a number of the soldiers and patriots who had manned it.

"My God," said Jenny. One man came running toward us, his arm loose and swinging like a sea creature's flipper, blood on his face and coming from his ears. As he came near, Jenny stepped forward and intercepted him. He collapsed almost immediately. "We need something to tie off his wounds!"

"I will find a cloth," said Desdemona, and she went running off down the street to my great consternation. I knelt with Jenny over the young man — no more than a boy — and saw that he was mortally wounded, bleeding profusely from the arm and chest.

"Sir, I have done my duty," he said, and then he said it again.

"You have done your duty," said Jenny. She took his head in her lap and stroked his temples. He was seized by a great trembling, which ceased after a few moments.

"My mother," he said. "Tell her it is was Tom."

"You will tell her yourself, Tom," said Jenny. It seemed at that moment that this Tom realized that Jenny was female, that she was more beautiful than any angel.

"Will you go with me then?" he asked. "Will you go with me?"

"Yes," she said, repeating as she had done for so many years, her most favorite of words. He then shuddered again and seemed to move up, as if to stand, and began to speak in syllables no man ever before spoke or heard. When he shuddered for a third time, his soul went to God, and Jenny, now covered with poor Tom's blood, began to weep inconsolably.

"This is madness," she said, choking. "That they would kill this boy. It is madness."

"It is nothing less," I said. Just then, Desdemona came running back down the street with a piece of cloth she had obtained from some shop which no doubt was empty from the fear of the shelling. She came to us, flushed from the exertion, breathing hard and flinching at the shells which continued to fall around us.

"I have a piece of fabric," she said.

"He is dead," said Jenny. She cradled him like a child and rocked him, spilling his last blood even more onto her clothing. "They have killed him."

"No," said Desdemona, more of a groan than a word. "No."

Jenny seemed disinclined to let go of the boy, and I finally had to gently pry her arms from him and lay his body down in the street. I leaned down and closed his eyes and suggested that we take his body back to the site of the barricade, where soldiers were gathering the dead and wounded.

"They might take care of him there," I said.

"We will take him with us and bury him at home," she said. "He deserves a patriot's burial."

"But Jenny, we cannot," I protested. "It would be dangerous, and, besides, we should not expose ourselves to further fire."

"He died for this cause, and, if necessary, so shall I," she said. I looked at her for a long while, and in her eyes she was saying, *This is the right thing to do, trust me in this and help me.* Finally, I nodded, and knelt and lifted poor Tom over my shoulders and we began to walk, in the dizzying smoke and under the sound of vast, thunderous cannon fire, north back toward our house. Twice, I had to put the body down to rest, for I was no longer a young man, and my breath was not what it had been those years before. We were not three blocks from the house when we ran immediately into Mr. Dorset and Mr. Smythe, who were running about, shouting at several men who seemed to be somewhat under their command.

"Jenny!" he cried. "What are you doing here? Get to the cellar! Hawthorne? A casualty?"

"A young man dead from a shell," I reported, my breath short and Tom still on my shoulders. "Jenny says we are to bury him at the house."

"Leave him for the others to take care of," said Mr. Smythe. A shell exploded a few blocks away, followed by screaming and shouting. The stench of gunpowder from both sides was now so acrid that it fairly burned the eyes.

"Never," said Jenny. She kissed her father and motioned for me to continue bearing my bloody burden, which I did faithfully. Mr. Dorset came alongside and asked me if he could carry the body, but I declined, as I was already soaked with the boy's blood and did not wish Mr. Dorset to suffer it. Mr. Smythe caught up and took Mr. Dorset by the arm and pulled him back toward the barricades, leaving Jenny and me to bear home the dead young man whose name we did not know. I felt as if we might never achieve our destination, but we finally did so, and I was relieved to see that the house was unmolested by shell fire.

I bore the young man around the house and set him down at the edge of the garden, realizing that I was very unfit for such a job. My arms hurt and my back felt twisted. I had become soaked with blood. But, looking down on the face of the boy, now at peace, now gone to his ancestors, whoever they might be, I felt the exertion had been worthwhile.

Jenny wept.

She knelt and touched the boy's temples and seemed to speak to him as I went for a spade and began to dig in the sand amid the din of shell fire. The job of digging his grave seemed even more work than carrying him back, and once I faltered before regaining my resolve and finishing the job. Jenny and I took the boy and laid him low in the grave. She had fetched a blanket from the house to cover him. This was an improper burial, of course, but, as we had neither coffin nor time before the body would be spoiled, I agreed that we must do as well as we could. Jenny, seeing my exhaustion, took the shovel from me and covered the boy up.

When she got through with the job, we both stood for a time looking at the grave. Desdemona, who had lingered in the street to talk to someone, came up in time to see that the business was over. Jenny wanted to say a few words over the grave, but she faltered as she began to speak and once again dissolved from the soldier she wanted to be, into the beautiful woman that she was. The transformation was astonishing, and she and Desdemona held each other for a moment before going back inside.

The bombardment continued the next day and the day after that, and death and destruction surrounded us. Once a small piece from a shell grazed my arm, giving me an injury, whose vague ghost I carry until this day. I was by now deeply worried about my wife and concerned about what I should do. I had discharged my duties to Jenny Dorset as well as I might, and it was clear that she could take care of herself. Still, by then, only a nighttime trip up the river toward Longacre could take me to my wife, and I was not strong enough for that kind of voyage. I briefly thought of paying someone to take me, as I had paid the man to take

Jenny and me across the Cooper River when she had been expecting her child. But I knew that it was folly to hope that I might arrive there unmolested. And since Isaac Dorset was firmly on the side of the Crown, his protection should have been secure.

The shelling from the British continued on May the tenth, the eleventh, and finally on the twelfth. By then, we were nearly out of powder and ball, were starving, and had no escape, even to the sea. On the night of May 12, we sat in the darkness of the house, not daring even to light a candle. Desdemona had gone upstairs to bed, and Jenny and I sat in the parlor, which was lit only by near and distant fires touched off by the bombardment.

"This is not the life which my father had planned for me, is it, Hawthorne?" Jenny asked quietly.

"I cannot say what he planned."

"Come now, you know he wished me to be a lady."

"Who says that you are not a lady?"

"I am not a lady and will not be one," she said. "I am instable. I cannot be still long enough for anyone to love me. Would that I could." It was the first time in so long that I had heard a softness from her that I was astonished and barely knew what to say.

"You have been loved by all who ever met you," I said. "What could give you the idea that you are unloved?"

"Then it is I who cannot love," she said. "That is even sadder."

"I have always loved you," I said. The words were meant to sound as if her father had spoken, as if they contained a parent's affection and care. I realized as soon as I said them, however, that they came out in an entirely different way. I was shocked myself, and sat in silence, looking at my hands and feeling a great fool.

"And I have always loved you," she said. I looked up at her, confused as to her meaning, as perhaps she was. The moment was so sweet and awkward, that neither of us could speak for a time. I could just make out her face, and it was somehow serene and yet intense. I was sure that she spoke of her love as a daughter for a father, but I could scarcely be sure of it. Even having such feelings was against my marriage vows, and I fought them, but Jenny knew what I meant. I tried to speak, but nothing would come. She stood and came to me in my wretched confusion, touched my cheek gently with her hand, and went up the stairs to bed.

— 5. —

THE SURRENDER OF CHARLES TOWN. A DARK DAY FOR THOSE OF US
WHO HAD CHAMPIONED LIBERTY. ISAAC DORSET COMES INTO
TOWN AS A CONQUERING HERO.

The bombardment lasted for four miserable days, and finally it was clear that we must face honorable surrender or death, and our leaders, to my frank relief, chose the former course. Jenny was outraged, but she often was, and within a day she was scheming how to work against the Crown during our occupation. On May 12, the siege ended, and the British came marching into Charles Town, rank on rank in their red coats, as the patriots withdrew and hid themselves, and the supporters of the Crown — and there were many — came into the streets and cheered. Mr. Dorset and Mr. Smythe suffered a terrible argument over the reasons for the collapse of our defenses, and Mr. Smythe threw my Master out of his house, from which he moved in with Jenny in Town. As soon as it was safe, I journeyed to Longacre and visited with my wife, who was quite healthy. The soldiers had made a miserable mess of the grounds at Longacre, and the beauty and order it once possessed were now gone, replaced by broken bottles, vast amounts of garbage, and patches of raw, sandy earth where once there had been a lovely expanse of grass.

I brought my wife with me back to Town, and once more we were settled, though worried about what would happen to us under the British occupation. On the ride back to Town, my wife asked me if I had heard anything of the whereabouts of Jenny's daughter, and I said I had not, though I had asked around a bit. I wanted to believe that one day I would see the child, for I could not help but believe that the end of the Dorset line was a personal calamity for myself.

One evening as Mr. Dorset and Jenny were sipping wine and speaking in low tones about the world and its disorder, the door was flung open without so much as a knock, and in came the now-massive Isaac Dorset, looking as if he had just been named King. Over the previous year, he had managed to keep food in his belly, while many others could not, and by then he was so fat that his great girth was like a thing he carried with him as a beast of burden, rather than part of his own body. He wore a newly tailored suit, made of blue silk, and his white shirt sleeves were ruffled at the cuff. He had on a huge powdered wig, so large and so curled that he had the odd appearance of having a sheep upon his head. His jowls drooped so low that he seemed like a great, upright, mobile hog.

"Ah, the father and the sister," he said in a lordly way. Right behind him came a small, bent young man with a worshipful stare. "Permit me to enter, as I will soon be an official of the government and may offer you my benevolence."

"Who are you?" said Jenny coldly.

"Now, sister, it does not become you to be a spoiled loser," said Isaac, "for that cause for which you so comically fought is now ended, and the right of the Crown to manage its Colonies is restored. I have been promised a position of power, and from that loft, I will grant you my greatest and most affectionate protection."

"I had rather be eaten by sea monsters," said Jenny.

"Well said," muttered Mr. Dorset.

"Shall I thrash her, Your Highness?" said the small young man. "No one can speak to His Highness in that manner." Isaac held up his hand to the man, who seemed to have some malady of the shoulder, and one of whose eyes was turned outward and staring at nothing in particular. Isaac laughed benignly and shook his head.

"Heaven knows my sister and father have needed thrashing at times in their lives, but, now that they are under my protection, I am sure that they do not need it, and that each of them will give me the respect I have earned but have never had in this family."

"You are mad," said Jenny. "You could not command the respect of a dog in the street, much less two people who are in every way your moral superiors." I thought Isaac would blow into pieces from the rising anger that he only barely managed to control. His face turned purple, and he began to clench and unclench his thick hands, not believing that Jenny and Mr. Dorset had not given him the honor he was due.

"We shall just see, then!" he cried. "I cannot give my mercy and protection to those who do not want it!"

"You have no mercy to give," said Jenny. "Or protection. One day, it will be I who must protect you, and I will do it as I am bound by blood, but for no reason of affection or respect, for you have earned neither."

"Then it is over!" cried Isaac. "You will live to regret this day!"

"I already regret it!" cried Jenny, leaping from her chair and rushing to her brother. The bent young man watched Jenny with absolute adoration and seemed to have forgotten entirely about his mission. "I regret that I am bound to you by blood. I regret that my misery in this life is not one

I could share with even one of three brothers! And look at you, Isaac. To call yourself a leader, even a man, when you have allowed your desire to overcome your sense. You are as large as the whale that swallowed Jonah! But you will not swallow what we have built. Neither you nor the British army nor the entire bloody country!"

"I have tried to offer you my benedictions!" said Isaac. "Now I shall be away, and you may trust in God, for you shall not receive a boon from me!"

He turned, and the young bent man stayed behind to stare with raw admiration at Jenny, and only followed his Master when Isaac grabbed his shirt and jerked him toward the door and then out of it. Jenny resumed her seat, breathing hard and holding firm in her resolve.

"Very good speech," said Mr. Dorset touching his only daughter on the back of her hand. "Not a bad one from Isaac, either. Perhaps oration is in the blood, eh Hawthorne?"

I thought Jenny might be furious, but as she looked at her father, the sublime oddity of his comment, the sweetness with which it was delivered, and the look of genuine pleasure on his face melted her. She began to smirk and then to giggle and finally laughed out loud. The sound of that sweet laughter echoed through the room, or it seemed so to me, for the longest time.

— 6. —

AS THE OCCUPATION BY THE BRITISH TAKES FULL FORCE,
A CALAMITY OCCURS WHICH NONE OF US MIGHT HAVE FORESEEN.

Jenny and Mr. Dorset both wondered if the British would round up patriots and put them in gaol, and, for a time, it was true. But there were so many troops, and so few gaols and impoundments, that the conquerors realized soon that they were better off keeping an eye open for sedition than imprisoning half the Town. The men who had never overthrown their allegiance to the King were treated royally, including Isaac Dorset, though the high post in government which he expected did not materialize. He was named subminister for inventories, a position in which he was largely responsible for counting things. For a time, he pretended that it was a magnificent reward for his steadfastness, but soon he could not disguise his disappointment.

Many of those who had left Town now saw no reason to be in the country and came back, unsure what might happen next. While we could be only bitter at our capture, the lifting of the siege did accomplish one thing: ships once again came in and out of the harbor, and we had food and materials, though not in the abundance that we had before the war began. Jenny, unafraid of any man, went about her business, making plans for the ruin of the British, conspiring, achieving minor victories, and all the time chafing at our captors. She also fell in love (but more about that later).

Now Mr. Dorset, as I have informed the Reader, had moved out of Mr. Smythe's house and moved in with us, for which both Jenny and I were glad. And of course my wife moved back with me from Longacre. In the meantime, in an odd exchange, Desdemona Smartt's brother, Roderigo, moved from Foxhaven to our house in Town, while Molly McNew and her brother, Tom, moved in with Mr. Smythe. As well, Mr. Smythe's sons, Hamlet and Iago, left Foxhaven and moved into Town, leaving the plantation in the care of overseers. Thus we were all once again in the proximity that we were when this History began, except for Matthew Dorset, who was in the North, and Fortinbras Smythe, who was dead. Of course, we had also lost Mrs. Dorset and Mrs. Smythe, along with Old Bob and Abel Dorset. Still, the families retained that familiar shape which they knew so well, and I was pleased to see them all near each other once again. Alas, Roderigo Smartt and Tom and Molly McNew all left the service soon after their arrival and disappeared into the mass of people in Charles Town and thence away from us forever.

Even though our bitterness toward the Crown scaled new heights, for a time there was a calmness in our homes, and life, which, while ignoble, was in no way truly unbearable. That, I suppose, is why God sends couriers from the far parts of the world to remind us of how fragile our hold upon happiness is in this world. For that summer, there was a knock at the door. Mr. Dorset and Jenny were seated at a small table in the parlor playing a game of chess, a game of which Mr. Dorset seemed to know little or nothing, and he kept making impossible moves and being corrected with tenderness and laughter by his daughter. I walked to the door, opened it, and saw before me a ghost. But it was not only a ghost — it was a spectre to chill the heart and bring a man to his knees. For a moment, I said nothing at all, merely stared, felt my eyes go round, and was frozen to the spot, though it was a very hot day.

"Where *is* he?" the woman growled. I said nothing. Standing before me in the doorway holding a cloth bag and wearing an expression of fury and disgust was Miss Tonning. "Is this Mr. Adam Dorset's residence to which I have been directed or not?" I could not speak. "Are you dumb, man? Speak up!"

"Who is calling?" asked Mr. Dorset from the parlor. "Invite our guest into the house, Hawthorne, and bring us a cool drink."

"Come in, please," I said hoarsely. The woman came inside the house and dropped her bags heavily in the hallway and then proceeded in the direction of the voice toward the parlor. I was dumb to prevent it and followed with grave distrust of what might happen next. I came around her and cleared my throat. Mr. Dorset and Jenny were staring hard at the chessboard between them and so did not immediately look up.

"Enter," said Mr. Dorset, waving his hand in a circular motion without glancing up.

"Sir," I said, gulping and closing my eyes, "may I present Miss Tonning."

The sentence caught Mr. Dorset's outreached hand as it rested on the pawn he was about to move. He looked behind him beneath the arm and saw that indeed, Miss Tonning stood in the room, eyes narrowing with what appeared to be pure hate.

"J—s, Joseph, and M—y!" cried Mr. Dorset. He jumped up with the agility of a young boy, overturning the chessboard and scattering pieces to the floor, from which they skittered around the room like an army in retreat. He dashed to the fireplace and held on to the mantel, as if that might give him a measure of stability. Jenny uttered an unprintable oath and stood as well, but, instead of heading into retreat, she came forward, though warily, never taking her eyes off Miss Tonning, whose sour expression now seemed to include a haughty appearance of victory.

"You *are* the scoundrel, then," she said.

"G—d protect me from all phantoms," said Mr. Dorset weakly. "I have tried to be a good man in this life, though I have not always succeeded." His legs seemed weak, and he had to keep locking his knees to keep them straight.

"I am Miss Felicia Tonning, sister of the woman you wed and drove to her grave," she said. She began to walk toward Mr. Dorset, who was forced to leave his handhold on the fireplace and move around the room, holding tight to furniture as he moved. "My sister wrote me of your ill treatment of her, your wenching, your moving into Town, your attempts to compromise her honor."

"She had no honor," said Mr. Dorset in a boy's voice.

"What?!" cried Miss Tonning. By then, I understood what had happened: unknown to us, a family accustomed to twins with the McNews and the Smartts, Miss Tonning had her own twin sister, which must have been a joke from God on the world to see how much we might suffer. The second Miss Tonning looked almost exactly like her sister, though she had less hair and more jowls. If anything, she looked uglier and less pleasant. "You are the one with no honor! You have no concept of the word *honor!*"

"You are her twin, then?" asked Jenny, now backing up as well.

"As if it were not obvious!" cried Miss Tonning. "As if you could not see with your own eyes that which you drove into an early grave!"

"She did not speak of a sister," said Mr. Dorset, picking up a vase and holding it unaccountably to his breast. "I cannot be sure you are not the Phantom Tonning. Hawthorne, should we retrieve a priest?"

"Undoubtedly," I said. Jenny looked at me and smiled briefly.

"You are disloyal, too!" cried Miss Tonning, now pointing her fat finger at me. "My sister wrote me of you, too! You ran away here and left her alone in that wilderness! And if you are the trollop of a daughter, you are disloyal as well!"

Jenny, who had begun to seem amused and interested in the unforeseen proceedings, suddenly became red and stepped up to Miss Tonning and looked her in the eyes. Mr. Dorset retreated to a curtain on the window facing the street and wrapped it around his legs in a manner that made him appear to be a classical statue of some kind. He still held the vase with one hand and the curtain with the other.

"I can only believe that God was asleep on the day that He allowed two such fools to be brought into the world," Jenny said coldly. "One Miss Tonning was twice too many for me."

"Disloyal trollop!" cried Miss Tonning.

"See here," said Mr. Dorset. He took a step forward, became entangled in the curtain, and dropped the vase, shattering it into many pieces. The sound seemed to frighten him, and he retreated to the safety of his wrapping.

"You are an ill-bred, overweight, ghastly ugly monster, and I would rather see you run down like a hog in the street than set foot in my house," said Jenny. There was a brief moment of silence from Miss Tonning, during which Jenny's father whispered, "Fairly done." Miss Tonning then began to smile, as if she had gained an advantage, and she lowered her head like a snake about to strike and showed her teeth (which were in bad condition) to Jenny.

"You both think you will defeat my family," she said. "You killed my sister as I have heard, and then you think to defeat me. I will have half of your money, and I will resort to court, to my fists, to hiring vandals — to anything to see that my sister is avenged."

"Bit dramatic, isn't it?" Mr. Dorset said.

"Bide your time, sir, and you, whore," she said. "You will see me again."

"I would gladly forego the pleasure," said Mr. Dorset, after which he laughed nervously and looked at me doubtfully. Jenny came close, and I thought she was going to strike Miss Tonning, so I took Jenny's arm and pulled her away.

"My sister wrote me of you, and a friend here in Town told me of your desertion of her and her tragic death from pining away for you," she said.

"Waugh!" cried Mr. Dorset. "You misjudge your sister. She could not pine away for anyone or anything. And it was she who drove me out."

"Liar!" cried Miss Tonning. "Fool! I will have my revenge upon you!" Mr. Dorset's rising courage evaporated instantly, and he moved behind me.

"Hawthorne, is it spirit or flesh?" he asked.

"Flesh, sir," I said.

"And an abundance of it, at that," he said.

"I will be back for what is rightfully mine as my sister's heir," she said darkly. "I also understand that you are a traitor to the Crown, so I will do all in my power to make sure that the proper people know of your activities."

"And I will make sure that you are known in Town as the monster you surely are," said Jenny. Miss Tonning's fat face broke into a malicious smile, and, without another word, she turned, gathered her bag, and disappeared out the door and down the street. Mr. Dorset staggered back to his chair and fell into it, looking baffled and exhausted.

"I shall have her killed and dumped down a well," said Jenny, rushing to her father and kneeling before him.

"The breath of the Great Defiler himself is upon me, Jenny, dear," he said. "It is finished."

Jenny pushed herself back from her father and looked at me. I could only shrug and wait for whatever might happen next.

"Annoyed, perhaps," she said. "But finished?"

"Aye, aye, the end of my time draws near," he said. "The ghost Tonning has arrived to escort me to the lower regions. I am doomed."

"Ridiculous," said Jenny, standing. "Father, why you act so dramatically at every turn amazes me." I could not suppress a smile at the words, for she was describing herself perfectly. She looked at me and furrowed her brow. "And what are you looking at?"

"I beg your pardon?" I said.

"He begs my pardon," said Jenny. "This has no point. I am going out."

And so she did. Mr. Dorset, however, moved about the house so slowly one might have thought him Methuselah. He went into the study and asked that I bring him a bottle of port. I did so, along with a glass. He had already taken out a quill and dipped it and was working on a poem, which I later found among his papers. I present it here in its entirety to show that Mr. Dorset, though increased in age and experience, did not increase in art as he grew older (and in 1780, he was sixty years of age).

THE PHANTOM IN THE PARLOR

One day as I was playing chess in the parlor,
A knock upon the door brought forth my glance.
I looked at Phoebe with her sicklied pallor
And threw my fabled strength to chance.

The day was pleasant, in the fair month of May,
When cherubs rub their darling cheeks
Against the pane once and again as if to say,
"Oh sweet tidings from the bird's fair beaks!"

But then I left the fair game so poor
Where I had my opponent fair defeated,
To open up the knocked-on door
Before the knocker must needs repeat it.

And there before me in the threshold
Was a phantom from the world below,
The Phantom Tonning had returned in mold
And black before the driving snow!

"Phantom!" said I, raising my hand,
"Begone with you to nether regions!"
And it replied, raising its thick hand,
"You frighten me, sir! I take my legion!"

And so the witnesses will report,
I saved my hearth and home from pain,
By chasing off from my home port
The Phantom Tonning once again!

I would not report this poem (which Mr. Dorset later that summer set to music) were it not for an extraordinary change in his literary talents somewhat later, regarding which I promise a full report to the patient Reader.

And so the Dorset family that spring suffered the double tragedy of the twin Tonning and the occupation of town by the British. Mr. Dorset seemed to believe that he was being tested by God and went for several months into the most pious period of his life. Jenny Dorset, of course, underwent no such conversion, and soon was back to her old habits of sedition and seduction, both of which seemed to please her greatly.

— 7. —

THE GHOST TONNING FILES A LAWSUIT AGAINST MR. DORSET.
AN EXCERPT FROM THE JOURNAL OF JENNY DORSET REGARDING
ISAAC'S RISE IN PROVINCIAL AFFAIRS THAT SUMMER,
AMONG OTHER THINGS, AND A TRAGEDY BRINGS MESSRS. DORSET
AND SMYTHE BACK TOGETHER ONCE MORE.

If Mr. Dorset thought Miss Tonning's twin sister would leave Town, he was mistaken. In fact, she became so well known in Town that she was soon being actively avoided in the streets. Once I saw Mr. Gadsden cross Tradd Street simply to pass her, and others did likewise. She had taken to imagining slights from everyone who looked at her, and that proved to me, if there had been any doubt, that personality is born in the blood. With Jenny's permission, Mr. Dorset sent Desdemona Smartt to keep an eye on Miss Tonning, and Desdemona reported that she had gone to the den of lawyers who still infested the building where the giant dance master once nearly had the pleasure of teaching Jenny. His dancing school had long since closed, and the man himself had left Town for Europe.

One of the lawyers filed suit for Miss Tonning, claiming that she was entitled to Mr. Dorset's entire estate as the heir of her sister!

"Oh, I suffer for that moment when I thought I loved Miss Tonning!" said Mr. Dorset miserably one day at table. "One moment's indiscretion may lead to a lifetime's misery, Hawthorne. I have no way of climbing out of this misery. I am lost! Oh, I am lost!"

Feeling lost, he went to the Black Cat Tavern, where he found forgetfulness in a bottle and at least for a time absolution for his mistakes.

During this time, the Loyalists and Revolutionaries often assaulted each other, verbally and otherwise, in the streets. Isaac Dorset, with his newfound connections, used his position as subminister for inventories to walk lordly around Town, stopping at tavern after tavern to eat and drink, often many times a day, until he was, by early summer, so fat that he could scarcely walk more than twenty paces without having to stop and sit for a while to regain his breath.

Jenny remained angry at her brother and refused his many offers of giving her his "protection," as if he had any to offer or Jenny Dorset any need of it. I quote from her journal as to how estranged she had become from her brother.

AUGUST 9, 1780 — *Oh, that we are bound even by blood! Isaac came here today with his mouse of a wife and said that he asked my attendance at a meeting where he would be recognized as subminister for inventories! I told him that I had rather be drowned in the bay, and he was so offended that he began to berate me so cruelly that his wife wept at the sight, and he told her to be quiet and stop being so weak! His small power has corrupted him entirely, and I wish that I had never seen him, much less been born to be his sister. Were it not for that very blood, I would devise a way to cause his downfall. Perhaps I may anyway! I have met a man who finds me amusing.*

The last statement I find entirely unexceptional, for every man found Jenny beautiful, amusing, and brilliant.

Now that summer, our cause suffered a terrible loss at the town of Camden, where the British defeated us after a fierce battle. All of us were deeply distressed and worried that our cause was entirely lost. Even worse, at the same time, a fever swept through Charles Town, carrying away, to our horror and shock, the two remaining sons of Mr. Smythe, Hamlet and Iago. Only thirty-one years, Hamlet had showed signs of becoming an important young man, even though his delay in marrying baffled us, and his lack of fight disturbed his father. Hamlet succumbed after four days of the illness, while his brother Iago, who was two years younger, took a week to die in great pain and suffering. Mr. Smythe was beside himself with grief, now having lost his wife and three sons, leaving him alone in this world.

As Hamlet had taken the illness later than his brother, both perished on the same day, and Mr. Smythe had the double funeral take place in St. Michael's with burial in the church grounds. Mr. Dorset laid to rest the enmity with Mr. Smythe, and held hands with him during the service. Jenny, who knew the brothers well, wept without restraint, all the time holding her hand over her mouth to hold in the inevitable groans. During the ministrations, Mr. Smythe kept saying over and over, *My boys, aye God, my boys!*" The words were enough to break a heart of stone. After the burial, Mr. Dorset left us to move back in with his friend in Town, where they stayed for two weeks without contacting us until the terrible events of August 27.

Despite the British victory at Camden, the rulers of the Crown on that day arrested a number of prominent citizens, gathered them in gaol, and sent them to St. Augustine for imprisonment. Among those so defiled were Mr. Dorset and Mr. Smythe, and though we tried to do what we could to have them released (Jenny even going so far as to present herself at the gaol and scream until she was subdued and brought home), it was to no avail, and the men were sent aboard ship south where, it was thought, they could influence the Town less. If the Crown thought it was a fine plan to lessen sedition, it only showed how little they knew of our nature. Instead, it stiffened our resolve so that we believed nothing might ever stop our search for justice.

Jenny felt crushed and thought of various ways to take her revenge, but little presented itself. The final blow was a celebration by the Loyalists in September of the victory the previous month at Camden. Lord Cornwallis himself was in Town, and a victory celebration was set. By means I have never known, Isaac Dorset managed to have himself appointed one of the speakers for the day, during which Lord Cornwallis was to be presented thanks. We had begun to feel quite defeated by then, and Isaac, never the most bearable of men, became entirely insufferable, sending emissaries and invitations to our house. We were still in mourning for the loss of Mr. Dorset, but Isaac seemed to think it was only justice.

"It is unbearable!" cried Jenny at table the night before the event. "That with our father imprisoned he would speak for the captors!"

"Perhaps he has a kind of madness," I said from my position near the door. Jenny and Desdemona Smarrt dined together, and the heat was oppressive as it often is during September.

"Mad enough to be dumped in the sea," said Desdemona.

"Mad enough to be shown his place," said Jenny.

Now, as it happened, we had a vast and lasting storm the night before the presentations to Lord Cornwallis, which many people took as an omen. The next morning dawned clear, but the streets were full of mud, and the fine ladies and men had to take care that they not soil their hose as they walked to the events of the morning. Along the way, patriots stood back and watched the flocking Loyalists with anger and disgust. Though the events of the day were at several places in Town, one stage had been erected in Queen Street, and it was there that many of the speeches took place.

I went alone. Jenny and Desdemona had left much earlier, and I did not know where they went or even if they were coming to the events. I went only to disdain the proceedings, as did many others, and I was careful not to stand near the supporters of the Crown. Several minor speakers droned on for some time before Isaac Dorset was called to speak. He was dressed in a blue silk suit which must have taken many yards of fabric, a ruffled white blouse, and a new powdered wig, which looked insurmountably foolish on him. The stage creaked beneath his weight as he mounted it.

"Oh, my brothers, justice has triumphed!" he said loudly. He was prepared for a magnificent oration (or as magnificent as he could make it, which was little or not at all). "These fools who have brought with them the stench of disloyalty have been dealt with, and we are free to resume the bounty of commerce before the eye of God!"

He paused for the drama of it and absorbed with pleasure the small applause which trickled through the crowd. Just as he was beginning to speak again, a small man suddenly appeared from around a corner and walked straight to Isaac, carrying a cloth bag.

"An honor for the subminister!" the man cried.

"An honor?" said Isaac. "Bring it to me before my speech, then, good man, for honor is due and will find its men in time enough!"

The man dashed up, and, as he did, men and women in the crowd began to make faces of repugnance, and I thought the man smelled foul, as he seemed unwashed. He jumped on the stage and handed the cloth bag to Isaac, who seemed greatly pleased, then fled. Isaac knelt and opened the bag, suddenly sensing that something was amiss. To our surprise (and to my great laughter), a skunk burst forth from its confinement and, turning on its paws, sprayed Isaac well, assuming that he was the enemy which should be attacked. The crowd backed away, and from one and all, there was only laughter and not a wisp of sentiment or sympathy.

"Catch that man and hang him!" cried Isaac, choking from the stench. The skunk ran off, scattering the laughing crowd. Soon, the people began to drift toward other events, and Isaac was left nearly alone sputtering and gagging. He saw me and came rushing toward me, and I backed away in time to see Jenny Dorset at a building's corner, laughing silently. "You, Hawthorne! I demand you go after that fiend at once!"

"He is gone, and I am old," I said, holding my nose. A dog came up and, sensing the smell on Isaac, began to chase him. Isaac lumbered down the street, kicking at the dog and losing his wig, which the dog proceeded to tear into shreds. As he was so fat, Isaac's wind was gone in less than a hundred paces, and the dog came up, sniffed him closely, and then howled and ran off down the street, leaving the stinking Isaac lying in mud. His humiliation complete, Isaac stood and walked down the street cursing and waving his fists at the laughing Loyalists.

Once again, Jenny Dorset had taken her revenge.

Miss Tonning, though pleased at Mr. Dorset's removal from Town, pressed her lawsuit that late summer and early autumn. We had not seen the last of her yet.

— 8. —

THE BATTLE OF KING'S MOUNTAIN IN OCTOBER STUNS US AND SENDS
WORRIES THROUGH OUR BRITISH CAPTORS. ALAS, WE REMAIN IN
BONDAGE FOR SOME TIME TO COME. MR. DORSET AND MR. SMYTHE
ESCAPE FROM THEIR GAOL IN ST. AUGUSTINE AND RETURN.

After the festivities in honor of Lord Cornwallis that August, we despaired of hearing any good news regarding the Revolution. Most of us believed that the war was in doubt if not lost, and it seemed improbable that we would ever have our freedom. For her part, Jenny did whatever she could to thwart the wishes of the Crown, from delivering false orders to certain soldiers, to causing handbills to be printed which listed meetings to hear important news from the occupation force. As these meetings had not been planned, no one in authority appeared, leaving many citizens angry and confused.

Jenny stayed in a rage over her father's arrest and imprisonment. She tried in vain to find out about him, but we knew nothing, and only by constant vigilance did I dissuade her from undertaking a journey to see if he were alive or dead. Isaac, meanwhile, had not quite recovered his dignity from the skunk episode, and he refused to visit us or send any word, much less "protect" us as he had offered. I thought often of how life had taken us from those early happy days at Longacre to a new world and to the loss of the family to which I had attached my life. I was at such a low point in my thinking, when one day a gentleman knocked upon the door and announced that he had a dispatch for a Miss Jenny Dorset.

"I am she," said Jenny, who was behind me in the hall. She took the paper and walked into the parlor, unfolding it and looking at it with great interest. "It is from Matthew!"

"Matthew?!" I said. "A miracle to have come through!" She read it aloud.

Boston
July 25, 1780

My dear sister,
This war is perhaps of God's will or not. I think it is, then some days I believe it is not. Please give the following scrap of verse which I have composed to Father, for I believe he will appreciate how far I have educated myself. Make sure that Father receives it; he can see that I am his heir in literary matters, or you may receive it yourself and convey it to Father so he will know I am his heir in verse affairs. Any of the foregoing will please me.

THE BATTLE FOR AMERICA
A poem by
Matthew Dorset, Esq.

> *The summer day was bright and drear*
> *I saw a large and larger deer.*
> *This deer was white from head to foot.*
> *His toes, except, were colored soot.*
> *This doe had antlers on his head*
> *And hath been fairly fed*
> *To look upon his ample girth*
> *Since he was born or his birth.*

He said this war was good or bad
And aye, I believed what he said.
For it was not a deer but omen
And I loved it as a woman.

I said to the deer I understood
What was wrong or not so good.
The world hath measures weak or strong,
And so I end my sleeping song.

I pray for your safety and wish for you all God's blessings. I am at work
now on a farm where the cows are all for milking.

Your brother,
Matthew Dorset

Jenny looked at me with sorrow, but not disbelief.

"Poor Matthew," she said. She handed me the letter and drifted upstairs to salve the wounds of her brother's one communication since he had left. The letter sounded exactly like Matthew to me, which made me even more reflective about the old days.

It was during such a time that we received news that sent Jenny and much of the Town into an ecstasy: patriots had given the British a sound beating at a place called King's Mountain near the border of North and South Carolina. As the first reports came into Charles Town, I could not credit them, but soon, the word was so widespread and the demeanor of the British soldiers so downcast that we all knew it was true. Though we had been in bondage for months and feared it long before that, the news of our victory was like a tonic to us. Men and women dared to go into the streets to celebrate, for the British could not imprison all of us. Jenny and Desdemona were beside themselves with joy, and I went into the streets with them that October. The British were careful to look over us, but they kept back, for a massacre would have been quite impossible, and they knew it. None of us would any longer stand for it. Still, not knowing which way the wind blew or if we might find ourselves the target of reprisals, we were enthusiastic but polite.

All of us but Jenny Dorset. There was a great gathering in Queen Street, where people were joyous or glum, depending on which side they fell. Redcoats watched it all, armed and seemingly ready, but, we knew, unlikely to fire unless fired upon. By this time, Jenny had let her hair grow back out, and it gleamed golden in the sun that morning as she ran inside of a house and came out on a balcony and began to scream and scream until the crowd began to become quiet and look her way. I stood by Desdemona, who was quiet and lovely, looking all the world like Jenny. I have heard that husbands and wives who grow old together come somewhat to resemble each other, and so it must have been with these friends, though that day was the first time that I had truly noticed it. I also noticed in the crowd Isaac Dorset, whose clothes, even newly tailored and expanded, did not fit his growing and massive girth. The bent young man who attended him seemed confused and sorrowful and stayed close to his benefactor. When Isaac saw Jenny, he put his hand to his face and shook his head.

"Can you not feel it?" cried Jenny. The crowd, which had still been mumbling and moving, slowed to a halt and went completely silent. It would take a true poet, not I (and certainly not one of the Dorsets), to describe the effect Jenny had. Her long golden hair waved on the cool and gentle October breeze. She wore a dark blue silk dress. She raised her fist over her head as her voice dropped to a whisper. "Can you not feel it?" A man near me made a rude comment, and I hushed him with my eyes.

"A new wind is come to Carolina," said Jenny Dorset. The men crowded up to the balcony, though most of the women looked at Jenny with suspicion if not outright hostility. "And on that wind is the breath of freedom! For man was not meant to serve his life in bondage. God did not choose one people to be servants and others to be their masters. He made us all in His image and made us free!"

The crowd began to rise to her. Men nodded and spoke in agreement, and even the Loyalists and the soldiers could not take their eyes from her. Isaac laughed and said something to his assistant, and the small man laughed too loud.

"I tell you that a new wind has come to South Carolina," she continued. "We look upon this Town and upon the waters of the sea, and it is in everything! It is in the mouth of new babies which come to us in these days. It is in the eyes of England, which must know that it cannot outlast us now or win this fight. It is in the eyes of old men and women who think for the first time that they may be free to make their own lives, to be taxed without threat and protected without anything asked in return.

"It is in the fields of Virginia and the towns of the North. It is in the water that runs from the mountains into great rivers that flow to the sea! It is in the very blood that courses through our bodies!"

By this time, Jenny seemed to be only the voice of some higher purpose, and the crowd would, I think, have all jumped into the harbor had she asked any of them to do so. Isaac did his best to stir up some opposition to his sister among the people he stood near, but he was ignored with irritation.

"The world that we inherited from our fathers was a good one," she continued. "And in these rice fields, in the places where we grow cattle and indigo, and even here where we buy and sell and trade, there is a growing sense of freedom. To whom do we owe this world?"

"To the good King George, bless him!" cried Isaac Dorset. The crowd turned to him, startled. Some of the Loyalists in the crowd nodded, though many of them appeared to have smelt something bad (which was understandable, considering their knowledge of Isaac and the skunk). "All you say is monstrous lies. You are but a woman who cannot know the inner workings of government."

"Cannot women know more than fools?" said Jenny. Desdemona grabbed my arm and began to grip it tightly.

"Foolish women know even less than foolish men," Isaac said loudly. "If they know anything at all. You should come down and be ashamed."

"The shame is entirely yours, Isaac Dorset!" she cried. "For you have let down your father and your family and your country. And for what? All for a few coins. Why are you better than Judas Iscariot?"

"How dare you compare me thus?" he cried.

"You have sold yourself for commerce," she said. "You know it, and so does everyone in this crowd!"

Then an astonishing thing occurred. Isaac raised his finger to counter his sister but suddenly seemed struck dumb. He looked for words to make a point, but it seemed as if, finally, the truth of his life had dawned upon him. He was nearly thirty years old but seemed never to have considered who he was or why he did anything. The small, bent man at his side urged him on, looking like a sprite or spirit from fanciful tales, but by now, the silence between Isaac and his sister seemed a living, palpable thing. Before our eyes, Jenny's strength and resolve appeared to grow, while that of Isaac seemed to crumble. He was first to break the stare between himself and his sister, and soon he turned his head to look at the crowd, which was clearly now swayed by Jenny entirely, bought and sold by the power of her voice.

Isaac seemed lost in thought. He blinked, shook his head slightly, then turned and waddled away from the crowd like a man who had failed in everything and knew it. I felt a genuine sadness for him, just as I felt a pleasure in Jenny's rhetoric. I remembered Isaac when he was a young boy, full of promise as they all were at Longacre, when Jenny was but a girl and a wild one at that. Now he had lost the small boon of the British overlords, and no one took him or his word to any purpose. He left utterly defeated and broken.

Later, I told Jenny that her speech had been perhaps one of the greatest in Carolina and that, had she been a man, she might have been elected governor. She looked at me as if I had said something incredibly foolish and went upstairs to her bedroom. The speech and Isaac's humiliation, as well as Matthew's pitiful letter from the North, had their effect on Jenny. She sat in the parlor in the day and read from novels. She played her spinet without any passion, all slow and sad songs, many of her own devising, for she would play by the hour with the same music upon the stand before her. She sent a letter of conciliation to Isaac, but he did not answer, and we heard that he had moved back to Longacre with his wife and removed himself from the post of subminister for inventories.

All during that winter of 1781 and on into the spring, Jenny and Desdemona did little but watch the world from the house, speak in soft voices, and allow the weight of our captivity to bear heavily upon them. My own wife was very ill twice during 1781, and I was so alarmed that I felt I would go mad with grief, but both times she recovered, though with only a small part of her former strength. I had to attend her often, and her pride was wounded, as was my heart.

It was on a mid-summer day in 1781 when a knock came to the front door, and I went to answer it. I opened the door to see before me a face I thought never to look upon again — my Master! He looked small and very old, thin and wasted. His hair had turned nearly white, but it was Adam Dorset all right, and at his side, holding him up, was Mr. Smythe, also thin but somewhat less worn.

"Mr. Dorset!" I cried. "Mr. Smythe! How have you come? Have they released you and the others from gaol?"

"Waugh, would that they had," said Mr. Dorset weakly. "I have

organized the greatest escape known yet to history, and here Smythe
and I stand, free men."

"He is feverish and foolish," said Mr. Smythe. "And poor company on
the road at that."

"Poor company?" said Mr. Dorset. "It was not I who allowed the
chicken to escape, was it? Had you but captured the creature we would
have eaten well, and instead we had to dine on roots, of which I never
hope to taste again. And I hope never to be chased by such thieves and
rogues."

"It was a single old man as starved as we were," said Mr. Smythe to me
as he helped Mr. Dorset inside, and they sat in the parlor. "Dorset has on
the trip lost what was left of his reason."

"Eh?" said Mr. Dorset. "Reason? I will now compose the great poem
of the age, you foul Smythe! My hunger is only from my body, not from
my soul."

"He is mad," said Mr. Smythe. A few of the other servants had come
inside, and though they were momentarily shaken with joy for Mr.
Dorset's return, I sent them for food and wine. Within ten minutes, however, the men were asleep in their chairs, snoring peacefully, and I
thanked God for bringing them back safely. Jenny and Desdemona had
been out, and a quarter of an hour later, I saw them, through the front
windows, returning through the gate and up to the house. I ran outside,
scarcely able to control my happiness.

"A great miracle has occurred," I said.

"What is it?" asked Jenny.

"Your father and Mr. Smythe have returned from their imprisonment
at St. Augustine," I said. "They are inside now."

Jenny carried a parcel, and, upon understanding the meaning of my
words, she dropped it on the ground, and her hands came up to her
mouth. Though she had often been as unyielding and hard as a man, she
could also at times melt into that softness of womanhood, and therein, I
believe, lay much of her charm on the male race.

"He is in there, alive?" she asked.

"And awaiting you with all his heart," I said.

Without stopping to pick up the parcel, she ran up the steps. I gathered it and went out to my quarters without disturbing their privacy, but
as I walked out the back door of the house, I could hear, above the light
wind, the sound of Jenny Dorset crying. The next day, to my great (but

temporary) joy, Mr. Dorset and Jenny decided to move back to Longacre, and Mr. Smythe to his Foxhaven.

— 9. —

OUR LIFE AT LONGACRE. THE FOUL CONDITION OF ISAAC DORSET
REGARDING THE DEPARTURE OF HIS WIFE. MISS TONNING ARRIVES AND
DEMANDS LODGING BUT IS REFUSED. THE BATTLE WHICH ENSUES.

The plantation had somewhat come back under Isaac's direction. I had thought it vanished, but I was wrong. With the port now open once again and trade allowed for the Loyalists in particular, Isaac had sold part of the land, bought new slaves, reopened the rice fields, and begun once again to grow indigo. Still, the once-lovely topiary was gone, the lawn trampled by cattle and horses, and the house itself in poor repair and in need of paint. Yet it was home to us, and my wife, now very ill, rejoiced upon seeing it, as I did. Mr. Dorset, to his credit, did in no wise act as if the house were his, instead deferring to Isaac in most matters. Deference, in fact, is what Isaac most demanded and what he least deserved, but many men are that way, I reasoned, and little can be done about it.

Isaac would barely speak to his sister after the problem in Town, and she made sport of him at every opportunity, for by then he had grown so hugely stout that he could scarcely move without the aid of a walking stick. To stay out of Isaac's way, Mr. Dorset once again assembled a pack of hounds for hunting and set about trying to train them, with much the same results as before. At least the sound of their barking and baying was familiar and somehow reassuring, and though we all knew it was not so, we pretended that in some way we had not aged and that the world of twenty years before was still part of our lives.

One morning, Isaac came almost staggering to table, and sat, holding his head in his hands and making a sound not unlike a dog accidentally stepped upon during a nap.

"Please stop that sound or I shall be ill," said Jenny, tasting her eggs and approving of them.

"My life is concluded!" said Isaac with drama. "The world has turned against me in all its finality. Hawthorne, prepare for me a grave!"

"Of course, sir," I said. "Will you need it before breakfast or after?"

"Disloyal fool!" he said. Jenny laughed, and so did Mr. Dorset. Desdemona came in with freshly brewed coffee and refilled their cups. "My world is over! And as I support us, the world is over for one and all!"

"What on earth has happened?" asked Jenny.

"This," said Isaac. "This." He lay upon the table a single sheet of paper.

"Is it an ode?" asked Mr. Dorset, who had been working on a lengthy poem about his imprisonment at St. Augustine with Mr. Smythe. (Unaccountably, Mr. Dorset had changed the scene of their sojourn to Hanover and their names to Helfrich and Urdel.)

"It is from my wife," said Isaac. "She left me in the night."

Jenny picked it up and read aloud:

Longacre
July 28, 1781

Dear Isaac,

I am gone in the night. Do not try to find me, as you will fail. I regret the necessity of this action. I was sad.

> *Once, but no longer,*
> *Your wife*

"Not a very good letter," said Mr. Dorset. "Poor form. No beginning nor any end. Where on earth would someone learn to write in such a manner?"

"It is not a matter of form!" cried Isaac. "My life's helpmeet has fled!"

"Life's helpmeet?" said Jenny. "She has not spoken a word in the past three years as far as we knew."

"How dare you taunt me in my time of grief!" cried Isaac.

"O grief, o grief, like a . . . Hawthorne, what is grief like?" asked Mr. Dorset.

"Like a thief in the night?" I suggested.

"No, no," said Mr. Dorset, sipping his hot coffee. "More like leaf falling slowly from a limb when the cold winds come from the south."

"Cold winds come from the north," said Jenny.

"Ah, a minor directional error," said Mr. Dorset.

Unable to bear the chatter any more, Isaac bellowed to show the depth of his grief, grabbed the letter, and lumbered out of the dining room.

"I only wonder why it took her so long to leave," said Jenny.

"Point well made, I must say, though it saddens me," said Mr. Dorset. "Sheaf! Quite a good rhyme with grief!"

Isaac for a few days thereafter was more sad than angry. He tried, of course, to find where his wife had gone, assuming she must have been in Town, but no ships registered such a passenger, nor had anyone seen her. In my mind, she was such a slight figure, without character or speech and always overwhelmed by her husband, that she might have moved through Town undetected, like a phantom. It was clear after a few weeks, however, that she was not returning, and that Isaac was alone, had no children, and refused to believe that his own conduct was in any way to blame.

"I do not wish her name to be spoken again in my presence," said Isaac one evening in a lordly way as they ate.

"What *was* her name?" asked Jenny. Isaac glared at his sister and redoubled his efforts at eating.

Not long after the departure of Isaac's wife, Mr. Dorset was walking around the house singing a new composition regarding his imprisonment and escape. It sounded like all his compositions to me, with minor embellishments which made no sense whatever. Jenny had gone into Town to purchase a dress, and Isaac was in the field harrying the overseer and the slaves. By then, even getting out of the house was nearly impossible for the bloated and bloating Isaac, and he leaned heavily on a cane and breathed with great labor even to walk a short distance. His departure for the fields and wetlands that morning was painful to watch.

"I believe I have composed the work that shall make my fame," said Mr. Dorset. "It is about my valiant escape and how I led my men through the horrors of the swamp."

"How *did* you escape?" I asked. "I heard Mr. Smythe say you were allowed to leave."

"Oh, and what a great liar he is!" cried Mr. Dorset. "To allow him to ruin the greatest musical sensation of the age! He is . . . waugh! Hide me!"

He had been looking through the window when he had seen something which frightened him so that he left me and disappeared up the stairs hooting and crying like a child. I ran to the window, half expecting brigands when I saw, coming up the walk, Miss Tonning, who wore a black dress and a look of furious indignation. She appeared more like her twin than did either of the Smartts or the McNews, and, indeed, if anything, she was more fearsome. She came to the door and banged upon it. I looked out to see who might be with her. The carriage and driver

Dedicated to Miff Jenny Dorfet
Engraved by Prioleau and Sons, Charles Town
aetat. 1777
Escape from Captivity
Compofed by Mr. Adam Dorfet

Allegro con escapee

From the pri - son gates ca-me out a
They went through rain, they we-nt through fire
Hel - frich then be - came a - knight, A

sa -ng hi- s vic — t'ry song!
ou-t a - sin — gle sound!
ev'ry sle'ping dog is curled!

Inquiries: 200 Tradd Street, Charles Town.

remained at a distance from the house, and the man fanned himself with his hat, as much from relief, I gathered, as the heat.

"I know you are in there!" she screamed. I went to the door, took a deep breath, and opened it.

"Whom may I say is calling?" I asked.

"Oh, you are the servant who is more friend than servant," she said in a loud voice. "You do not know your place! Where is he?"

"He is not here at the present," I said icily.

"I am not," said a faint echo from upstairs. I tried not to act as if I had heard it, but Miss Tonning clearly had, and she smiled bitterly and injected herself into the foyer. I could only give way and try to keep myself between her and the rest of the house.

"This is mine," she said. "It is all mine. Do you hear me, coward upstairs, this is all mine and I will have it! Servant, take down that ghastly painting! What fool would it be?"

"It is Mr. Dorset's son Abel, a hero to the Revolution, now gone to God," I said firmly. She leaned close to the painting and stood back up and sneered.

"Looks like a Pinkworthy to me," she said. "I despise the man's paintings."

"How dare you speak that way of a great artist?" asked Mr. Dorset, now appearing on the stairs and coming down with anger in his eyes. "My son was a fine man, and you may not come into this house and speak of him in this manner."

"I know nothing of your son, but if he were like you, he was a liar and a thief and should have been killed!" shouted Miss Tonning. I was on the cusp of throwing her out of the house (no matter how difficult it might have been) when Mr. Dorset arrived at my side.

"Get thee hence, foul spirit," said Mr. Dorset. "Or I shall chase thee back to H—l from whence thou camest."

"What?!" she cried. "How dare you speak to me in that manner?"

Mr. Dorset, at this point, became what he had always imagined himself to be: heroic. Miss Tonning picked up a vase and hurled it at him, and he dodged it easily, though it shattered in the foyer. She chased him then into the parlor, where he picked up a fireplace implement and began to fence with her, with very good form, I might add. She tried to parry his thrusts with her fat hand, but she was entirely too slow, and so she backed up to regroup and began to throw other vases, books, lamps, glasses, and cups, each of which Mr. Dorset hit in the air with his rapier, punctuating each stroke with a loud exclamation.

"Oh, stout phantom, I come now for the kill!" he cried. Having nothing else to throw, Miss Tonning began to back toward the door, shouting and crying, threatening and trying to keep the sword away. "Be thee quiet so I may slay thee!"

"You have already slain me!" she cried. "As you did my sister. For this, you shall burn in the fires of H—l for eternity!"

Mr. Dorset, sensing a change in the battle, lowered his implement and stared at Miss Tonning with interest. She turned and ran from the house toward her carriage, crying and making terrible sounds. Mr. Dorset sat in his chair amid the destruction of the war and looked thoughtfully at the room around him.

"Shall I burn in H—l for eternity?" he said.

"You have been, in large, a good man," I said. "God will judge you mercifully, I am sure."

"I do not want to burn in H—l for eternity," he said. "I do not like fire. I fear fire, Hawthorne. When I was a small boy, I saw the Town burning, and since then I have feared the flames. What if God sent the Phantom Tonning as an emissary to correct my ways, lest I fall prey to the fires of H—l? What if He is displeased with my conduct or my truthfulness? What if I were to die after all?"

"Sir, it is the way we all must pass," I said.

"I never considered seriously that I must die," he said. "Or that the possessions of this life must pass and change. And now Matthew is gone to the North, Abel had been slain, and Isaac's wife has left him. I have no grandchildren to carry on. I shall be entirely forgotten."

"There is one child," I said. He looked puzzled at first and then sighed heavily.

"And she, too, is lost to me," he said. "I do not know where she lives or what her future might entail. Friend, I am defeated. I am defeated by life and the changes it has wrought in me and this world. Even Longacre has nearly dissolved because I have attended art more than business. God has sent the Ghost Tonning to prepare me for His absence for eternity! I am consigned to flames!"

He forthright fell to his knees and began to moan and pray in a loud voice, then went entirely prostrate and began to tremble, speaking variously of fire, Satan, the British, and many other things of which I could make little sense. I felt sad for him, but I knew him well enough to know that both his passions and his sorrows, though deep, passed away quickly, as a cloud passes over the face of the sun. After a quarter of an hour of his display, he sat up and asked that I fetch him a bottle of wine, which I did with relief. I poured him a glass, and he thanked me and took the bottle from my hand and poured a long draught down his throat.

"Would you like to be alone, sir?" I asked.

"No," he said. "Will you walk with me?"

"Yes," I said.

I took the filled glass with me and sipped from it. We walked out the front door and into the yard. Everything had changed, and nothing, a feeling of familiarity yet strangeness which often comes over us as we age. We walked around the house to the open field where cattle grazed peacefully under a hot blue sky. The dogs — a new pack purchased by Mr. Dorset — moaned and barked when they saw us, and Mr. Dorset smiled and hailed them with a noble wave of his arm, as if he were a visiting potentate, bestowing a benediction upon them. A strong wind had come, and the trees bent and bowed, their mosses waving. The sight had a certain majesty which I have never forgotten, and I felt as if the Earth were receiving us with honor, knowing that one day its victory would be complete as we lay beneath it.

"I have had a good life," said Mr. Dorset, taking a long draught. "I have seen many things. I cannot say my life has meant much to me since my Lydia went to God. A lack of love makes men do strange things."

"Indeed it does, sir," I said.

"Once I thought that I could earn enough to keep my children and my children's children safe for all their lives," he said. A large white bird sailed over us, wings turning slightly to catch the wind. "But we can do nothing to save those who come after us. We can scarcely help our own children in the end. We cannot protect them from death or give them riches or good sense. We think we can do so much when we truly can do so little. Is that a paradox?"

"I believe you have stated it brilliantly," I said.

"I know this land as my own, but it is not mine," he said. He turned and looked about. "None of this was ever mine. I held it for a day in eternity and loved it well, and soon I must give it back. Hawthorne, may I propose a toast?"

"Sir," I said, bowing at the waist.

"Here is to our lives and our land and our children," he said. "They have given us comfort, and joy and grief and hardship, and still we love them all. That is the truth of this life."

"Here, here," I said softly. I raised my glass and he his bottle, and we touched them briefly and then turned to look at the land of Longacre, drank, and said nothing more for quite some time.

— 10. —

THE DEATH OF MY WIFE, WHICH I TREAT BRIEFLY BECAUSE OF ITS PERSONAL CHARACTER AND THE PAIN IT STILL CAUSES ME.

I have asked the Reader's indulgence in this History regarding details of my personal life, for I regard it as too sacred to violate in its parts. I can only say that my wife and I lived many years together in utmost happiness and that in my eyes she was more beautiful than any other woman I ever saw, including Jenny Dorset, though I recognize that this judgment comes from love and not from Nature.

That summer of 1781 was inconclusive and curious for us all. There were gains in the North and stories of victories by patriots, but we remained in bondage like the Children of Israel. The British, however, had wearied of their role as captors, and Jenny had once more gone about her mission of sedition with great pleasure. Miss Tonning disappeared, and, from shipping records, Mr. Dorset learned she had gone back to the North, from whence we never saw her again. (I wonder now if she still lives, not the most pleasant of thoughts.) Mr. Dorset's momentary fit of piety after the battle with Miss Tonning lasted through part of that same day and then was gone.

My wife had grown more and more ill through the summer, and when autumn came upon us, it was clear that she must die. She was not afraid or unwilling, for she had suffered and looked with anticipation toward seeing her mother and father at God's throne. I was miserable beyond description, however, and did all I could to save her. Mr. Dorset brought several doctors and surgeons from Town for me at his own expense, but they all agreed the case was hopeless and that I should prepare myself for her passing. Her pain was not great, and it seemed as if she were preparing for a long sleep rather than Death.

I nursed her and stayed at her side for the long days and nights of her decline, losing weight and sleep and turning myself in such misery that Jenny came to me one night as I sat alone by the fire in the kitchen smoking my pipe. She came up the stairs and into the kitchen bringing with her a scent of rosewater. The odor reminded me of the summer days when I first met and married my wife, and, quite unaccountably, I began to weep. Jenny came and knelt beside me and held my hand.

"I cannot bear to see her gone," I said.

"She will not be gone," said Jenny. "She will be with you. It is a different presence, but she will listen to you and be with you. I hold my daughter in my arms each night and kiss her and love her and tell her stories of her family."

"It is not the same," I said, regaining my composure.

"Not at first," she said. "Then it is, if you will it, Henry." Her speaking my Christian name was such a surprise that for a moment I did not know of whom she talked. "Hold her tight in your heart, and she will never be gone."

"Dear girl," I said. "Dear Jenny."

Two days later, my wife passed to God, and we laid her to rest near Old Bob and Aunt Sally. Mr. Dorset delivered himself of an eloquent tribute, which I cannot bear to set down here because the words are sacred and remain mine alone. The emptiness of my quarters following her burial was, I thought, beyond bearing, but I slowly began to see the world about me again and realized that if she was gone, I was not, and that I owed God a full life, and that I must live it as well as I might.

That faith in God and in my own life sustained me through the autumn. More was happening, however, which kept us all in thrall: the State of South Carolina was reasserting its right against the Crown. The war was nearing its climax.

— 11. —

JENNY DORSET AND I MOVE BACK INTO TOWN WHERE SHE FINDS LOVE AT LAST. THE SUDDEN REESTABLISHMENT OF THE ARGUMENT BETWEEN MR. DORSET AND MR. SMYTHE.

Just after Christmas that year, Jenny and I moved, along with Desdemona Smartt, back to Stratford. Being amongst the people, both for and against the Crown, was energizing, and soon I managed to put my sorrow away, in a place close to me but not so close that it pained me every day. When we arrived on a cold day near the end of December, Jenny was outraged to find that four or five British soldiers had broken in and were living there and drinking her wine. The soldiers were surly, unclean, and defiant as we came in. They sat by a fire in the parlor, drinking and laughing.

"Who the bloody h—l are you?" said one of the soldiers, who was the tallest and was clearly the best of a sorry lot.

"And who the bloody h—l are *you*?!" cried Jenny. "Get out of my house this instant!"

"Your house?" said the tall man. He had obviously been drinking too much, as had the others, but they only laughed at him.

"My house, and you will leave or I shall kill you," she said. The man looked at his fellows, smiled, then held up his hands in mock horror.

"I should hate to be shot by such a fierce soldier as yourself, ma'am," he said, voice shaking with laughter.

"That's the sport, Tolley!" cried one of the other men, who drained a bottle and broke it on the stones of the fireplace. "Such a fierce soldier as yourself, ma'am!"

Jenny left the room, and I immediately knew that the men had made a serious error in judgment and tried to tell them so.

"Old man, go on out with the girl and leave us alone," said Tolley. "We have requisitioned the house. You can live in our stable if you wish. It is fit for horses, old men, and pretty girls." The men toasted Tolley's slurred sentiment, and, having done all I could, I sat down to watch. In a moment, Jenny came walking back into the room carrying two cocked pistols. The men looked at her, and it seemed as if nothing had ever seemed so amusing.

"She's going to shoot you, Tolley," said one of the men.

"Do you know how to fire a pistol, Miss?" asked Tolley. He leaned down and picked up a bottle and held it at arm's length. "See if you can break this." Jenny raised the pistol in her right hand without so much as a pause and fired it. The ball did not hit the bottle. Instead it went clear through the man's hand. The bottle landed on the floor but did not break.

"Great G–d!" cried one of the other men, going for his rifle, which leaned against the wall.

"I would not do that," I said. Tolley held his hand, which bled profusely, and began to make awful noises. The man paid no attention to me and got his rifle, which by his actions was loaded, and turned to face Jenny. She coolly lifted the pistol in her left hand and pointed it at the man's head.

"What a mess to clean up on the day of my return," she said.

"She's mad!" cried Tolley. "She is mad, I tell you!" He ran out of the house, and the others, gathering their belongings, joined him. Desdemona came into the room from the hall.

"Shall I clean the floor, Miss?" she asked.

"I feel hungry first," said Jenny. She turned, handed me the pistols, and walked from the room with Desdemona.

The soldiers did not return, and neither did they send any others after Jenny. I later saw the soldier Tolley, and his hand had been removed by a surgeon, something that did not cause me the least regret or sorrow.

Soon after this time, Jenny fell in love. Considering her faithlessness to so many men in Charles Town and the birth of her daughter, I should have thought that Jenny would have given up men, but I knew her too well to be surprised. Despite my age, I also felt some regret that Jenny had found a love, for though I was in no wise her lover then or ever, I was able to fancy myself so at odd moments. The man's name was Mr. Thomas Kent, and he was tall and dark haired, with blue eyes and a quiet demeanor. He had distinguished himself at the Battle of Fort Moultrie, and though he had been briefly imprisoned after the occupation began, he was soon released and was at that time living on a plantation some twelve miles up the Ashley River. I do not know where Jenny met him, but it was soon clear that they were seeing a great deal of each other at various places in Town.

About his family I knew little, except that his father was dead, his mother was old and infirm, and he had a single sister who had died many years before of yellow fever. He had earned his fortune in much the same way Mr. Dorset had, but, instead of whiling away his time with verses and music, he had invested well and was wealthy. Jenny had not told me of Thomas Kent until one day I saw them in the street, and she smiled at me and waved. I bowed, and that evening she told me of her love for the man.

"How can you be sure it is love?" I asked. "What is its character that you know it is love?"

"I do *not* know," she admitted. "How does a bee know on which flower to alight? It is a matter of Nature. I have found him, and he has found me. How did you meet your wife?"

"At a dance," I said. "I was too awkward to make the steps, and she saw me and came and taught them to me. She was patient with me, and

I amused her. Had I known how to dance, I should never have met her."

"And what lessons might you draw from that?" she asked.

"It is I who should be teaching you," I said.

"You can still learn things."

"I suppose I can at that," I said. "I suppose I learned that love can take you unawares. That each time in our lives has a significance if we but look for it. Each day, perhaps, even each hour or each minute, something may happen which suddenly and forever changes everything. And this moment is planned not by ourselves, but perhaps by chance or God. And we most often do not know these things have happened until they have been passed for a long time."

"Did you know when you came to work at Longacre that you would spend your life in service to this family?" she asked.

"I suppose I had not thought much of it," I admitted. "A young man does not think of the distance from birth to death. It is more like a dream he is sure will never end."

"But it does end, all the same," said Jenny. "It ends, and when it does, the world goes away with you, even if you rise to the gates of Heaven. And whatever you have missed on this Earth is such a sorrow that regret must follow you for eternity. If the priests do not say it that way, then I believe it is so anyway. I will not have regrets, Hawthorne. And I will look to my life for the hours when this significant thing has come."

"You are far more able, it seems, to teach than I am," I said.

"And you are far more able to learn," she said quietly. "That is why you are wise, and I am wild."

Several nights later, she had Mr. Thomas Kent to dinner, and Desdemona and I, along with several other servants I had hired, prepared a fine meal of duck and breads. I had been able to obtain a rare wine from Portugal, and its fragrance, along with the bread and fowl, filled the dining room. I stayed far enough away to be called but not close enough to hear their intimate talk, but it was clear that they spoke to each other with affection. Their laughter was like music, both in phrase and content, and a deeper calm descended over me than I had felt in months, for I knew that Jenny Dorset was truly happy.

I was sitting in the parlor awaiting any call and reading from a book on natural history when the front door flew open without so much as a knock, and Mr. Dorset stood before me, his clothing in shocking disarray, his hair soaked from the rain, and his arms raised over his head.

"My guns and my hounds, Hawthorne!" he cried. "I will track the villain to H—l if I must! He has dishonored me for the last time!" The laughter stopped in the dining room. I stood and came to Mr. Dorset, and found him unsteady on his feet and smelling strongly of rum and the kind of noxious scent worn by women of poor repute at taverns.

"Sir, what has happened?" I asked. He waved his arms and began to walk around the room, listing to starboard and thence to port, as if tossed in a storm.

"He has stolen my wench!" cried Adam Dorset. "The cad has stolen my wench! I found her first, and Smythe has the spleen to come up and entice her away from me! Waugh! The villain! I shall lay him low in his own shadow!"

Jenny and Thomas Kent appeared in the doorway as Mr. Dorset raised his arms to the heavens and continued his speech, though modifying it for the sake of delicacy.

"What on earth has happened?" asked Jenny. Mr. Dorset, who to my knowledge had not met Mr. Kent, looked at him as an old and intimate friend.

"I have fought the foul Mr. Smythe in Queen Street for the honor of a woman," said Mr. Dorset. "O, the monster! The craven beast! She was my fair lady, and he has stolen her from me by enticing her with wealth! I shall not sleep — nay, the entire state of South Carolina shall not sleep! — until I have my satisfaction with the cruel man! Jenny, girl, fetch my pistols!"

"I shall do no such thing," she said. "Are you drunk?"

"Drunk?" he cried. He took a step away from the chair on which he had hold to show his sobriety and fell into a small table and knocked it over, as well as the vase it held, which hit the floor and shattered. He stood back up and brushed himself off. "Waugh! The carpenter who built this house is a villain! The floor is uneven, and the furniture cannot hold!"

Jenny put her hand over her eyes and shook her head. Mr. Kent looked amused but did not betray it more than was polite.

"You are drunk," said Jenny.

"Well put, daughter," he said. "And as well, I am drunk." He peered at Mr. Kent. "And who might you be? Are you an emissary from Smythe? Nay, are you his second? I have slain him once in a duel and will do so again if I must!"

"I am Thomas Kent," he said. He stepped forward.

"My father," said Jenny.

"What are you doing here?" asked Mr. Dorset as he shook Mr. Kent's hand. "Is he your friend, Hawthorne?"

"I hope so, sir," I said.

"He is my lover," said Jenny. "And the man to whom I will pledge my life." Mr. Kent seemed entirely surprised by Jenny's sudden declaration of love, and he turned to her, touched her cheek, and then kissed her gently on the lips.

"Lover?!" cried Mr. Dorset. "Lover! You have taken advantage of my girl? She is as pristine as the spring, and you have taken advantage of her?"

"Pristine?" said Jenny. Mr. Kent, clearly knowing all, smiled politely and looked at me with one raised eyebrow.

"Is that not the word?" he said. "Ah, never mind then. The girl over whom the demon Smythe and I fought was beautiful but not pristine. There is value in each living creature, eh, Hawthorne?"

"Well spoken, sir," I said.

"Then it is good," he said. Then he fell headlong to the floor, from where he began to snore heartily and did not move. I covered him with a light blanket, and he slept peacefully as Jenny and Mr. Kent went back to their dinner. I knew that after Jenny's declaration of love, he and Jenny would wish to be alone, so I left them, and went outside into the garden and sat on a bench. The rain had stopped, and stars had come out, millions of them, as if poured from God's pitcher into the blackness of eternity to keep us from fright.

If I thought that Mr. Dorset would awaken having forgotten his quarrel with Mr. Smythe, I was wrong. I assisted him in taking a bath in his tub, pouring water I had heated over his head. He spoke something in a language which was not Latin but which might have seemed so to one who did not know the language.

"I have in mind a way to get my fair lady back from the monster Smythe," said Mr. Dorset. "But I will need an assistant in my deed of honor. Are you the man for this job?"

"I am, sir," I said. "But what is it that you plan?"

"Never you mind," he said. "I have devised a brilliant plan, but first we must go to a few shops so that I might buy what I need."

"I will assist you as I might, sir," I said.

As he dressed, Mr. Dorset seemed once again in charge of the world, though his head hurt somewhat, and he demanded coffee and an herbal preparation which sometimes gave him relief from his drinking. He declared himself cured after his breakfast, and we went toward the shops of Town. British soldiers patrolled, but they appeared tired and unhappy, and, as a patriot, I felt the first glimmer that our captors could not endure this much longer.

We first stopped by Mr. Bearden's. He was a printer of some note, and though paper was not abundant, Mr. Dorset paid the price for it to have Mr. Bearden print his long poem regarding our trip to the Indies. The printing was proceeding apace, and Mr. Bearden showed my Master a few pages from the book, discussing the quality of the type but refusing to be drawn into a discussion regarding the quality of the verse. (I read several quatrains and was not surprised at the utter lack of truthfulness or art in the writing, but about their sincerity there is no doubt.) We left finally and visited a wig shop, where Mr. Dorset bought a large and ugly wig of doubtful provenance and seemed very pleased by it. Then we bought a tin of black grease and some second-hand clothing of the Spanish cut, finally stopping at Mr. Blackdales, the bootmaker, and purchased a pair of ready-made boots which came to the middle of the shin and turned outward. Finally, Mr. Dorset purchased a dress saber, which was made to shine and had no strength whatever. Though it appeared menacing, it would break at first swing in a fight. I could not imagine Mr. Dorset's plan.

"I have the bloody scoundrel now," he said as we sipped rum at the Black Cat when our shopping was finished. A group of fiercely sober patriots sat in one corner eyeing a drunken assembly of Loyalists in the other. Between them were two British soldiers speaking longingly of home and of the endless police work in Town which all hated.

"What on earth is it that you will do?" I asked.

"You shall see," he said. "You shall see."

He drained his mug and poured himself another and seemed so pleased that I was pleased myself, though I could not say why.

"Then I will help you as I may," I said.

"Hawthorne, let me ask you something," he said, leaning close. A change came over him. The drunken Loyalists burst into laughter over some amusing story, I supposed. The patriots glowered at them, and the soldiers sipped their drinks wistfully.

"Certainly."

"My children," he said, scratching his chin. "Do you see anything quite unusual about my children?" I was so taken aback by the question that, for a moment, I felt as if I might not answer.

"Unusual?" I said.

"Yes, unusual," he said. "They are not as I had imagined my children to be. When I married Lydia Foxe, we believed that our children would have grace and honor and restraint. Those are not qualities that I would ascribe to them."

"Surely such a discussion is more private than you wish to share with me," I said.

"With you?" he said very quietly. "But you are my brother."

If I had been surprised by his asking my opinion of his children, I was now so deeply touched that tears came to my eyes. I did not have a brother of my own, and though Mr. Dorset was about five years older than I, we had lived our lives together, and that bond felt to me as I supposed a brother's might.

"I am not worthy of that sentiment," I managed to say. He touched my arm.

"You might have done better for a brother, just as my children might have done better for a father," he said. "But we take the lot we draw, do we not? For ill or good? We watch our lives pass us, watch the world change, and in the end we know little more of wisdom than when we started, if somewhat more of history."

"I cannot imagine a greater honor than to have you as my brother," I said. He squeezed my arm and nodded, satisfied with my answer, then drank another mug of rum and waited for my answer as to his children.

"And what might you say of them?"

"Sir, I have found that nothing is what we might suspect," I said. "And I have also found that your children have lived according to their hearts. Sometimes that is good and sometimes it is not. But so it is with each of us."

"What would you have done had you been able?" he asked.

"What would I have done?" I repeated, surprised. "I suppose I haven't thought of it a great deal. I do not live in that world of fancy which you do, for I cannot see beyond what is real before me. I am witness and can chronicle my life, but I do not see beyond into the imaginary world as you do."

"Surely there is a thing you might have done," he said.

"Sometimes in my private moments I think I might have been a merchant," I said. "I could have sold implements for the ships. Though I do not much like the sea, I like those who sail upon it."

"There!" he cried. "Is that not a dream? Is that not living in what does not exist but in your fancy? You wrong yourself, my brother! I will write a sonnet about your dream and present it to you!"

He did not, of course. Instead, he finished his drink, and we left and walked back to Jenny's house, where he put all of his purchases on the table and went upstairs for a nap. I busied myself by straightening the house and dusting it.

Soon enough, however, his plan to seek revenge on Mr. Smythe was clear enough. He would dress as a Moor, attend Mr. Smythe, and claim that the woman in question was his wife. Then he would challenge Mr. Smythe to a duel and thrash him a bit before revealing his true identity.

"That is your entire plan?" said Jenny in disbelief. "It is a fool's errand."

"The fool is Smythe, for he will be made to pay," said Mr. Dorset.

"I cannot understand this," said Thomas Kent. I failed my Master in that regard, for I did not try to explain what was unexplainable.

A few days later, Mr. Dorset announced that he had sent, by way of a man Mr. Smythe did not know, a request to call upon him that evening. I asked under what name he sent his regards.

"As Don Diego Marinelli!" he cried, raising his arm over his head in some kind of gesture I found to represent nothing. "And I will demand honor, and when I have thrashed him, I will reveal myself for that monster and for all the world to see!"

"Will all the world be there?" I asked carefully.

"In a manner of speaking," he said, making a pass at me with a sword which existed only in his fancy. "I shall write of it, Hawthorne. Other men will write of it. There will be dramas and epic poems! There will be songs sung by the men of the sea! There will be . . ." He did not finish the rest of his statement, as he passed me with a thrust, lost his balance, and fell over a chair. I helped him up. "Phantom enemies are often the worst. Waugh, I have banged my elbow."

The appointed day came, and I had determined that I would not accompany Mr. Dorset, for I felt I should not encourage his folly, even though I could not entirely prevent it. I said I planned that evening to smoke my pipe and read what little news we had, as I had lately acquired a copy of the *London Times*, which, though months old, at least had in some measure a picture of that other world we no longer shared.

"Nonsense!" bellowed Mr. Dorset. "You shall come as my brother and stand as my second! You will be witness to the greatest thrashing that fool ever took! It will be his undoing before all men, and he will never again dare cross me!"

"With all due respect, I decline your invitation," I said.

With a less persistent man than Mr. Dorset, that might have been the end of it. Instead, just after eight that evening, we both stood in the parlor of Jenny's house, great wigs piled upon our heads, faces blackened as Moors with the grease. I did not have a Spanish costume as Mr. Dorset did, and I felt we both appeared lower than actors, almost to the level of lawyers.

"Heigh! We go for the battle now!" cried Mr. Dorset, whose excitement had been raised by several cups of punch flavored with a small amount of water and fruit.

"Si," I said.

We crept out of the house, and Mr. Dorset immediately fell over his sword, which hung at his side in a shabby scabbard. He landed in a hedge, and I pulled him out only with a great exertion. The hedge had thorns and so kept possession of Mr. Dorset's wig, which we extracted only with effort and by leaving a number of thorns in the hair. I helped him put it back on, but it looked not unlike he wore the hedge itself. We walked into the street, not carrying a torch or lantern, as Mr. Dorset wanted to arrive in the dark for dramatic purposes.

Once, Mr. Dorset began to sing a Spanish song, though in a combination of English, French, Spanish, Latin, and a tongue I believe known only to himself. A dog in the street came forth to bite him, so my Master ceased with reluctance.

"Everywhere critics abound," he said grandly.

We had little difficulty walking the blocks to Mr. Smythe's house, and when we arrived, I tried to straighten Mr. Dorset as well as I might, but his wig was askew, his grease smeared over the front of his clothing, and his sobriety long gone. He knocked on the door, and Mr. Smythe himself opened it, expecting the company. He looked at us for a long moment and began to shake with silent laughter. He then backed up several steps, fell on the floor, and laughed so loud and hard that it somewhat resembled a bellow.

"Zhou offend me!" cried Mr. Dorset. Mr. Smythe was unable to respond. Mr. Dorset pulled his sword from the scabbard, but only the handle came away, leaving the blade ensconced in its casing.

"Oh help, brigands!" cried Mr. Smythe, by now howling and rolling around on the floor. I put my hand over my eyes, as if to make the scene vanish, but when I removed it, all was the same. Mr. Dorset looked at me and then passed the sword handle to me, and I laid it on a table.

"I have come to slay you for possessing my woman!" Mr. Dorset cried.

"And well I should be slain," said Mr. Smythe, sitting up. "For she took my purse and twelve pounds before she fled into the night."

"I have come to . . . she did what?" said Mr. Dorset. Mr. Smythe repeated his statement, and Mr. Dorset sat on the floor with his friend and tried to understand the dilemma.

"Why is there a hedge upon your head?" asked Mr. Smythe.

"Twelve pounds entirely?" asked Mr. Dorset. "The foul wench."

"And the hedge?" Mr. Smythe pointed to Mr. Dorset's head, and Mr. Dorset removed the wig, sifting powder over his chemise like the fall of snow.

"Briars and thorns," said Mr. Dorset. "Is there a lesson here, Hawthorne?"

"Undoubtedly," I said.

— 12. —

JENNY AND MR. THOMAS KENT ATTEND THE MEETING OF THE
SOUTH CAROLINA LEGISLATURE AT JACKSONBOROUGH ON THE EDISTO
RIVER. I ATTEND NOT AT HER SERVICE BUT AS A PATRIOT. HER SPEECH
AND THE MANNER IN WHICH IT INFLAMES THE MEN.

Late that January of 1782, the threat of the British had shrunken so greatly that only inside Charles Town was there a problem for patriots assembling. And so the great Democrats of the age, including Mr. Gadsden, Mr. Charles Pinckney, and various of the Ravenels, called a meeting of the state's governing body, which was still in power, though without much of it. The meeting was to take place at the small town of Jacksonborough on the Edisto River, perhaps forty miles east of Charles Town.

Mr. Thomas Kent was not a member of the assembly but was friend to many who were, and when he informed Jenny of the meeting, she immediately demanded to be taken. Mr. Kent tried to dissuade her, as this portion of Jenny Dorset's journal attests:

JANUARY 17, 1782 — *Monstrous! That the Legislature should meet and that women should not be there to speak for their sex! Are we not the future of Charles Town? I argued bitterly with Thomas and then wept, not because I wished to, but because it came upon me unwanted. I declared that no one had done more than I in the service of patriotism and that I should be able to enjoy the glory of our coming freedom as well as any man. Finally, Thomas agreed, and he shared in that Sweet Reward which all men desire.*

There also exists in the Dorset Papers an exchange of letters between Jenny and her father regarding the meeting at Jacksonborough. I believe I must have served as the courier for these missives, but time has undone my memory of it.

Monday

Father,
  I will be accompanying Mr. Kent to Jacksonborough for the meeting, and I do not regard your efforts to stop me as seemly. I am saddened by your words that this is not a fight for me, and though I know you mean to protect me, you wrong me. Many women have the fight that many men lack. I cannot say why this should be, yet it is so.
  I beg of you not to argue with me henceforth in this matter. I shall see you at Jacksonborough.

Your faithful
Daughter

Monday

Dear Jenny,
  Waugh! You wrong me to believe I wish you no voice in the world. I wish you only safety, which I doubt the man Kent may provide any more than the fool Smythe might. Should you feel the necessity to make this pilgrimage, please take Hawthorne with you.
  I have composed an air that I believe will make me famous. It is to my own words and deals with the mad Phantom Tonning.

Your loving
Father

Though Mr. Kent was displeased that I accompanied them, I went anyway, and we arrived at the spot on the Edisto not an hour too soon. A great amount of secret travel had been involved for all, and Jenny, Mr. Kent, and I each rode separately, Jenny taking her horse astride like a man. My poor old mount had trouble keeping up with her.

The site of the meeting was pleasant and sunny, though cool, as it was January. I had nothing whatever to do except wait for the meetings. Mr. Dorset came, and, to my surprise, the massively large Isaac arrived. Most of the men were the wealthy and the blessed, not men of my class. I took a long walk near the river, thinking about my life and the world that had changed so greatly since my youth. A great variety of birds called and flew around, and in the water I could see reflections of the trees, drooping down with their mossy hair. I could only think that the world in its variety is a fine thing, and if an alligator eats a rabbit, so much the pity, but it is God's design in all. And if a woman spend her life in a search which comes to nothing, who am I to say if it was a proper or ill-fated journey? And if a man have desire but not talent, is that a failing or a blessing?

I could not speak to all these feelings, but as I walked, I was not sad that my life had brought me the interesting rewards of the Dorset family. In all, I suspect I wandered for several hours along the Edisto before I realized that it was perhaps unsafe to be so far from humanity, and I reversed my course and arrived back at Jacksonborough. The course of speeches was sometimes fiery, often dull. Men of vision spoke of a new country of liberty and a vast design. Small men spoke of worries about the formation of the Legislature, what the garrison in Charles Town might think of all this, and the division of power. Most of those who spoke were the great men of our state, those who had amassed wealth and then chanced to lose it in the defense of liberty. I was proud that I was of a house which had done likewise, though not entirely. In truth, I was thinking of that very issue when Isaac Dorset was announced as the next speaker.

The building at Jacksonborough where we met was too small for the crowd, and I stood in the gallery, meant for slaves but now holding others of my own class who had come to attend their masters. The building was poorly heated and drafty, and around me old women and older men chafed at the conditions and spoke openly of their worries that the Master or Mistress would take a sickness from the place. One man in particular, dressed shabbily and speaking through his nose, kept walking around saying "Time will tell — oh yes — time will tell!" One of his legs was a full three inches shorter than the other, so that his clumping and speaking gave a peculiar rhythm, as if he were beginning a selection of verse yet was unable to continue beyond the first line.

The ponderous Isaac came to the front of the fervent crowd and raised his arms to silence them, although they were already silent.

"Who be that fool?" asked a superannuated old woman next to me.

"I cannot say," I responded.

"Men of the Legislature of South Carolina!" cried Isaac. "Hail and farewell!" There was a confused mumbling. I looked down at the crowd and saw Jenny and Mr. Thomas Kent. Jenny had thrown up her hands and was shaking her head. I looked for Mr. Dorset or Mr. Smythe but failed to locate them. "I say farewell, for this madness in fighting the Crown shall come to nought for you all!"

The men erupted into a whistling and laughing creature, a thing with more than a hundred legs but of one mind and heart.

"No, no!" cried Isaac. "You have forsook the world which built you all!"

"*Forsaken,*" shouted a voice, and the men all laughed heartily.

"You may mock me, but would you mock the world that your children will inherit?" he said. "As for me, I wish my children to live in the arms of the King."

"They could live 'twixt his legs, wouldn't mind me," said the old woman next to me.

"The time of your foolishness is all but over now," said Isaac. "You will look upon a world of such utter confusion, and a world that you made, that it will last not a month before each of you is on your knees begging for the British to return and take you by the hand like children and lead you back out of the darkness into the Promised Land!"

"Bloody traitor!" cried someone below. Mr. Gadsden, however, who knew the family, raised his hand, and the place went silent. By now, Isaac appeared a swollen madman, unable to speak what he wished or control his rage.

"I wish my children to know a world of order!" he spluttered. "A world I have tried to hold together if others have not!"

"You have no children!" cried a woman's voice. Everyone in the audience turned and looked at Jenny Dorset. "And you never will, for you lack what those in this room have: love and courage!"

The men erupted into such a long and sincere applause that the sound chased Isaac from his position at the front of the room, from which he moved through the men, waving them away and pushing their jeers back as if warding off insects that were trying to bite him. As he was chased away, the men turned and looked expectantly at Jenny.

"She is more beautiful than the stars," said the old man next to me. He grasped my arm and squeezed it with such force that I feared he would have a stroke of apoplexy. I gently dislodged his thin fingers and told him Jenny's name, but he did not appear to hear anything I said. Below, the crowd separated, not unlike the Red Sea, and Jenny was urged forward to speak to them, a chance which she was not about to pass on. Mr. Kent accompanied her for a few steps and then was pushed back by the crowd, who did not want to see or hear him. When she came to the front of them, the men became quite silent, and the old fellow next to me almost fell over the balcony. I pulled him back in time, and he did not thank me or see the necessity in it.

"I am Jenny Dorset of Longacre," she began. "Many of you knew my brother Abel and now my brother Isaac who has spoken before you here today." There was a spattering of applause, and I thought how short our memories be! Abel should have been given a thundering ovation, but in death he was receding from us, as all men do, with as much speed as a falling star. "There is a blood in my family, but for my brother Isaac, which flows for liberty. It spurns the boot heel of dominion and asks the freedom to make its own way in a new land.

"Each of us is born with a given place in this world, or so men say. I have never felt that a fact or a necessity. The station we achieve is what we fall toward or rise above. No man is born into slavery, and no man has chains which cannot be broken!"

The men applauded vigorously and seemed to move a step forward toward Jenny.

"Today, you meet to keep faith with the great gift you have bestowed on the people of South Carolina. You meet to tell the foul British that they may hold us for a moment in this life but it cannot stay! They do not have the resolve of a free people in a free land! They believe they can stop us with guns and cannon and soldiers, but they do not know us. They do not know the old men and women who have labored under this tyranny for a lifetime, nor the small children born into it who will watch it wash away!

"And in a sense we cannot blame England for these miseries alone. But there is a time when a servant becomes a slave, and that slavery, so detestable, cannot long be endured before it is risen above! I ask you now to keep faith with the children of South Carolina and give to them your word of honor that never again will we be made to suffer such a fate in this world! I say to you: Long live the sovereign state of South Carolina! Long live liberty!"

She raised her fist and shook it, and the men both below and in our balcony went simply mad. The uproar was deafening. Had Jenny been a man, I believe she would have been acclaimed governor, but as a woman, she had no standing, of course, and, knowing it, she walked out of the room, trailed by Mr. Kent, and went outside. The men, all by then madly in love with her beauty, her fire, and her honor, could not applaud enough, though I suspect much of it was for themselves, for having such a woman in South Carolina. The old man next to me sat down in a chair and wept.

I could understand his feelings. I went down the winding staircase and outside. The day was lovely, and Jenny and Mr. Kent were walking away from the men, who had ceased applauding and were now back to their business. I stood for a long time under an oak tree and thought of many things.

— 13. —

A SAD OCCASION IN CHARLES TOWN IN THE EARLY SPRING.
A FEW PHILOSOPHICAL COMMENTS CONCERNING IT.

The meeting of the Legislature at Jacksonborough was a high-water mark for us during the occupation, yet that hated force did not leave. The battles continued throughout the land, and though news was slow arriving, we could not yet say who might win. Jenny spent more and more time with Mr. Thomas Kent, leaving me a great deal of time alone, which I enjoyed by reading, smoking my pipe, and watching ships in the harbor. I tried to live in the present day and keep my feelings from the past, but an inevitable part of them always turned back, and on those days I was melancholy if not miserable.

After his disgrace at Jacksonborough, Isaac Dorset became even more

the toady for the Crown, and took to wandering the streets with his
small, bent stooge, harrying citizens and giving blustery, ineffective
speeches chastising the citizens for their unfaithfulness. Only a surly overseer was left to grow the rice and indigo at Longacre, which had largely
ceased to exist as a plantation.

One night in early April, the loveliest time in Charles Town, I
went to a tavern for a mug of buttered rum and some conversation.
I often did this, and I had acquired many new friends in just such a
way. I was talking to a cooper named Jeremiah Doe and pleasantly
smoking some fine tobacco when a commotion near the door caught
my attention.

"They have him!" shouted a man. "Come and see!"

The room nearly emptied, to the consternation of the proprietor
and several bawds, who were unhappy at the thought of their income
disappearing.

"Let's have a look, then," said Jeremiah. I nodded, curious myself at
what was happening. We came outside and saw several dozen men with
torches standing in the street surrounding what appeared to be a monster
of some kind. The crowd was laughing at him and taunting him. I saw
the barrels of tar and feathers then, and realized that the man had been
smeared with pitch and had feathers dumped upon him. He waved his
arms and roared.

"Great God in Heaven," I said.

"It's Dorset!" said a man in the crowd. "They got the hog!"

And it was. Isaac was flailing, shouting, roaring. He seemed in pain
from the hot pitch and yet in such a rage that he merely wanted to strike
out at anyone near. The men hooted and laughed. I felt miserable at
Isaac's plight, though he had brought it upon himself. Isaac struggled
against his condition for a moment more and then stopped and gave a
kind of coughing, gagging sound and fell to his knees. He then looked
up, as if searching for someone in the crowd, and fell over on his side and
did not move.

I rushed to him. He coughed once more, blowing feathers from his
mouth. I rolled him over and saw immediately that he was dead. A man
near me dropped his torch and ran. The others suddenly were gone, even
my friend the cooper, leaving me and the dead Isaac Dorset in the street.
A man rode by singing, unaware of what had happened. I sat upon my
knees and looked at the body and felt unable to move. As God would

have it, just then a man came walking up the street, singing with drunken pleasure of an Irish girl who had betrayed him in his youth. It was the father of the deceased, of course.

I stood and held the torch, not knowing what to say. As he got close, Mr. Dorset recognized me and then looked down.

"Hawthorne?" he cried. "My heavens, a passing large duck that you have shot! We shall dine well!"

"Sir," I said. I knelt before the body, and he stood over us.

"Eh?"

"They tarred and feathered him," I said. Suddenly my emotions were whipped raw, as if by a cold wind, and I began to weep. "He was your son, Isaac."

"Isaac?" said Mr. Dorset. He knelt and looked into the bloated face and the still-open eyes. "Dear boy? My Isaac? Wake up, boy." He shook Isaac, but of course he had fallen into that sleep from which none of us will ever return.

"Sir, he is dead," I said.

"Oh, Isaac!" he said in a strangled whisper. "Oh, my son!"

He then threw himself on the body and began to cry, in the process becoming covered with pitch and feathers himself. We stood there in the street for a long time until the shock had somewhat worn off. I left Mr. Dorset with the body and found a wagoner willing to be hired, and we took the body back to the Town house. Jenny and Mr. Kent had returned home and were sitting in the parlor. Her father could say nothing when we entered, and though Jenny laughed at first, I took her aside and told her that Isaac lay outside dead in a wagon.

"Sweet God," she said. She was silent for a moment and then began to cry. Mr. Dorset sat in a chair and looked around the room as if in a daze. Mr. Kent, at my behest, went for the undertaker, who arrived after a time and took Isaac into a back room with our help, to prepare for burial. The undertaker's assistant dug another grave in the backyard past the garden.

Jenny and I were in that garden sometime far after midnight. Mr. Kent had gone home for the night, and Mr. Dorset was asleep in his chair. The undertaker's assistant came from the house carrying a large bucket, from which he dumped a dark liquid into a corner of the yard.

"It is my brother's blood," said Jenny. "Strange that it should pour through us our entire lives and then be cast aside as if it were no more than feed for hogs. We honor ourselves too little in this life."

"A life properly lived has its honors," I said. "If Isaac disagreed often and was often disagreeable, he was constant in devotion to his own self."

"That was his downfall," said Jenny. "To die in such a manner is more than any man deserves. At least he should have disappeared into the wilderness or been swallowed by the sea, lost but somehow alive with the possibilities."

"It is a fate we might all wish," I said. "I will no doubt die in my bed, as God seems to wish that I carry on until great age."

"That for you would be an end to be desired. It is your place, and you have held it with great honor."

"Perhaps I might have wished another place in this world," I said cautiously. "For I might have done great things. Yet I do not think that was so. I was born for service and as a witness. A man could have a worse life."

Jenny was quiet for a time amid the chirping and humming of insects, and I could not stop staring at the place where Isaac's blood had been so unceremoniously dumped. Does not a man's blood deserve words spoken over it as well?

"Mr. Kent has asked me to marry him," she said presently. She sighed heavily. "I have not told him of the child, nor does he know of it. Why was I born for such cruelties?"

She began to cry, and I took her in my arms and comforted her as well as I could, feeling my neck grow damp with her tears, and my feelings regarding Jenny were never so confused or acute, and as I held her, I realized that should I be denied Heaven for some reason, at least I had been in the presence of something celestial and extraordinary.

The next day, along with the new subminister from St. Michael's, a man nearly as fat as Isaac was, we laid Mr. Dorset's second-eldest son to rest. The sky threatened, but it did not rain, and the service was mercifully short, and it took eight strong men to lower the coffin on its ropes into the earth. Jenny threw the first handful of clods onto the box, then turned and went inside. Mr. Dorset held himself erect next to Mr. Smythe, and though tears dripped down his face and chin, he did not break or lose his composure, for which I admired him greatly.

For a long time after that, our house was quiet and sad, and though Mr. Thomas Kent came to visit many times, he and Jenny never seemed to grow any closer, and the subject of their marriage never came up in my presence again.

— 14. —

BY THAT NOVEMBER OF 1782, IT IS CLEAR THAT THE BRITISH ARE
FAILING IN THE WAR AND MUST LEAVE US SOON. THE EXCITEMENT.
JENNY DORSET'S ROLE IN HARRYING THE BRITISH.

Summer passed, and then autumn came, with its cooler breezes and pleasant temperatures. Though Mr. Dorset still owned Longacre, he had closed it entirely as a plantation, and the grounds lay fallow, being taken over again by brush and swamp. He lived with us in Town entirely, and on his one trip returned to say that the house was being used by patriots who had requisitioned it as the home of a traitor. I could not bear to go out to it, and so stayed busy in Town with what entertainments I could find.

Jenny Dorset and her dear friend Desdemona Smartt went everywhere together now, and Mr. Thomas Kent seemed to have accepted his fate as yet another of Jenny's amours, though the closest she ever had to a husband. Often I saw him in the street looking dejected and lost, unsure of what he should do next. For her part, Jenny was so openly involved in sedition that I cannot understand why she was never arrested. The Daughters of Liberty had long since faded into history, and only Jenny was left to post secretly printed handbills against the British, in favor of liberty, and as a warning to Loyalists that they should repent, as it were, before they would regret it. She spoke on streetcorners to enthralled crowds of smiling men and scowling women. British soldiers listened to her with rapt attention. Her golden hair, which seemed thicker and more brilliant than ever, tossed as she spoke, and her eyes flashed. She would shake her fist, and her voice would be suddenly inaudible, rising in less than a minute to a shout. She called Lord Cornwallis unspeakable names in a tavern one evening. Indeed, her demeanor at times seemed unhinged, and I worried that she might lose her reason altogether. I believe, however, she felt the nearing of what she had yearned for since her childhood — liberty. And, that near, she could not rest for a moment to worry if it might arrive on its own accord.

By early December, it was clear that the British were preparing to gather on their ships and leave us to our own future. The news began to spread through Town like a stroke of apoplexy, and the few remaining Loyalists switched their affections, though they would suffer anyway in the coming years.

"Think of it!" cried Jenny one afternoon as she and her father ate their meal. "We shall be one people and not divided! We shall command the world to look upon us through the centuries with awe and respect!"

"There is none," said Mr. Dorset, shaking his head. "I am defeated."

"Sir?" said Jenny.

"There is no word which rhymes with *orange*," he said. "I have been thinking on this for thirty years, and it has ended. Such a word does not exist in our tongue, though perhaps it might in the Indian tongue."

Jenny looked seriously at her father and then began to laugh.

In the next week, the rumors clearly began to turn into fact. The soldiers moved their goods and arms toward the docks on the Cooper River, from whence they could be removed to the ships in the harbor. The people subjected the troops to great scorn and by then openly harried them in the streets. Jenny moved, it seemed, day and night, never resting, never taking the departure of the British for granted. She prodded the reluctant, condemned the Loyalists, shouted unseemly language at every British soldier, none of whom seemed to mind hearing it from her. In fact, many smiled and tipped their hats as she cursed them and were reluctant to leave.

Mr. Kent tried to stay by her side, but even he was unable to survive her relentless energy, and soon he was reduced to watching her from the streetcorners like everyone else, dreaming about what might have been.

By December 12, the departure was clearly near, and though Mr. Dorset came home at night, Jenny and Desdemona did not, and I tried not to guess in what pursuits they were engaged. I myself felt the excitement sweep me along, and I cannot remember a time that was more fraught with both pleasure and danger. I tried to think back over my life, but I was always brought back to the inevitable present, for Time would not allow such wanderings when great events had come upon us.

I could not imagine that this hopeful beginning would end so suddenly for me and bring me a grief which, though I have endured, has never entirely healed.

— 15. —

THE DEPARTURE OF THE BRITISH FROM CHARLES TOWN ON
DECEMBER 14, AND THE UNSPEAKABLE EVENT WHICH
HAPPENED ON THAT SAME DAY.

Two weeks before Christmas, the Town was wild with rumors that the British were leaving the next day, and so all of us stayed out, watching, by torchlight, the garrison moving the last of its materials (and many which belonged to us) to the ships in the harbor. Some patriots broke the windows of stores owned by those who had remained loyal to the Crown. Several men were tarred and feathered. Men and women danced in the street, and taverns were filled until they overflowed with both customers and rum. Once I even danced with a bawd, which was quite unlike me. Though I was not proud later, I was not especially ashamed, either.

There is a tonic in great events and great changes. Even those which are unpleasant raise us to a place we rarely visit, and so it was with the British evacuation. Those who had been no more than bored citizens or even cowards through their lives suddenly saw themselves as heroes. They would tell their grandchildren that they had help chase the British back to England and make a new land free. On the day before, it was obvious to all that the garrison was about to depart, and, in spite of it, Jenny was even more determined in her fight against it. She seemed to believe that a lapse in vigilance would keep the British in Charles Town. I thought her idea absurd, as they had already sent all of their munitions, Etc., to ships in the harbor, and I tried to calm her, but she would not be dissuaded from her excited state. Desdemona Smartt held the same sense of resolve.

"What a grand adventure, however," Jenny said at table on the evening of December 13. I had built pleasant fires in all the rooms, and our house was aglow. With Christmas near, I felt festive and thankful for our deliverance and so was in a fine fettle myself. "Have we not had a fine adventure, Hawthorne?"

"Fine indeed," I said from my station near the cupboard.

"To think what I have seen and done," she said. Desdemona ate with Jenny as she had been doing for several years by then, entirely abandoning her position as a servant for that of a friend. Still, she spoke rarely, and whether this was due to deference or the recognition of her class, I cannot say. "Do you remember when I went with the Groats to the Cherokee Country?"

"Of course," I said. "That was an adventure for your father and myself as well."

"I should not have gone," she said with a laugh. "But I did, and you came for me. I feel as if I never thanked you for rescuing me from myself."

"No thanks are needed for the performance of a duty," I reminded her.

"Just the same, I thank you now for saving me from the Groats," she said. "And I thank you for coming after me when you thought I had gone to the Indies."

"It was my honor," I said. "My goodness."

"What?"

"I thought of our Old Bob just now," I said. "I had not thought of him in some time."

"Dear Bob," she said. "Poor dear Old Bob. What a selfless man he was. I cannot love a selfless man too greatly, for they put whomever is before them in greater stead than themselves."

For a moment, I was caught off guard, for I wondered about whom she spoke, but then she went on to another subject, for which I was both saddened and relieved.

"And do you think they will truly leave, then?" asked Desdemona presently.

"We will, by the grace of God, make sure they leave!" cried Jenny. "We will harry them with insults or stones or whatever we must until the last one is gone! We must never again suffer an Englishman!"

I smiled modestly, and Jenny saw it and inquired after my mirth.

"I was just thinking that you gave the same speech as a small girl against the French," I said. "Some things in this world do not change, no matter how much we think they might."

Jenny smiled and nodded, but soon she was lost in thought about the departure of the garrison the next day, and she and Desdemona went to their separate rooms soon thereafter, leaving me to clean the table in the pleasant glow of the fire, which I drew down until it was only a deep orange glow on the hearth.

The next morning was brisk and clear, and the air fairly crackled with excitement. I arose very early to kindle the fires and help our cook prepare the meal. Jenny and Desdemona came down early, and Jenny, to my surprise, wore a fine gown, a frilled and feminine dress she had not put on in years. Had I guessed, I might have supposed she would wear trousers to make her motion more practical in the streets. Desdemona likewise wore a dress and was almost, though not quite, as beautiful as Jenny.

"Have you seen my father this morning?" asked Jenny.

"He did not return last evening," I said. "I suspect he is performing patriotic duties and preparing for the grand day before us." Jenny looked at me with sweet scorn.

"What a delicate lie you tell," she said.

"I prefer to look upon it as discretion," I said. Jenny Dorset laughed out loud, and the music of her laughter filled the room, and the sound of angels could not have been more uplifting. I felt that morning as if the world were born anew and that nothing could harm us, either in our Town, the State of South Carolina, or the United States of America.

After a light repast, Jenny and Desdemona left the house in great excitement, and soon I followed them. The streets, even early that morning, were absolutely filled with the populace, which were exploding fireworks, singing, dancing, and generally having the celebration of their lives, from one end of Town to the other. Old toothless men danced Irish jigs. Children in their best clothes — and some of this clothing was tattered in the extreme — shouted and played. Men drank, and their wives at their sides forgave them. I had never seen anything like it, nor had any of them there.

The streetcorner speech-makers had their day. A few shops of the Loyalists had been pelted with eggs and rocks, and some of their proprietors insulted, though none was injured. A large flag of South Carolina was raised on a pole over Queen Street.

About mid-morning, the remains of the garrison came out of their quarters and began to march in file down to the docks where they would be taken on boats to their ships and then, we supposed, to Virginia to fight more. I was swept along with the crowd, though I did not hurl anything at the troops, either eggs or insults. In a way I felt sorry for them, having come so far from home for so long and now leaving everything behind. But that minor sadness was overwhelmed by a greater joy.

"Liberty!" cried an old man, falling to his knees. "Liberty!"

I stepped around him and kept going with the crowd. Soon I saw Mr. Dorset and Mr. Smythe, arguing with each other over some point, but cheering the departure of the troops, anyway. Mr. Dorset held over his head in one hand a sheaf of papers, which intrigued me. When the last of the troops passed my position in the street, I moved around to Mr. Dorset to inquire about them.

"The great work of the century!" cried Mr. Dorset. He was flushed and drunk, and paint from some unsavory woman was smeared from mouth to ear on the left side.

"He is useless," said Mr. Smythe. "He has drunk himself silly. He is useless."

"Useless!" cried Mr. Dorset. He hit his friend on the shoulder with the sheaf of papers in an entirely ineffectual way. "Useless! To call the great work of the century useless!"

"On what topic is it written?" I asked.

"It is called *The Flight of the Tyrannists!*" he said. "I have been up all night composing it! God has graced me, Hawthorne!"

"There is no word such as *tyrannist*," said Mr. Smythe, who was not entirely sober, either. "I have told him this, but he refuses to hear it."

"Waugh! A Loyalist *and* a traitor!" cried Mr. Dorset.

"A lover of freedom and poetry!" shouted Mr. Smythe. At that, they began to fight, though with such a lack of energy and skill that few, if any, blows were landed. I shook my head and left them to continue their lifetime quarrel, moving behind the garrison toward the docks on the Cooper River.

I looked, of course, for Jenny and Desdemona, and at first did not see them. Then, from a distance ahead, the sound of a woman shouting came to me, and as I walked I realized who it must be. Finally, I was very nearly running to the spot, where Jenny stood beneath an ancient oak on a wagon bed and was shouting a speech at the retreating troops. A few men had stopped to watch Jenny (including one Redcoat, who was dragged back into line by a superior officer), but by and large, the crowd was more interested in departures than speeches. Jenny, of course, never in her life looked more beautiful, and her lovely dress and her golden hair caught the sun and refused to release it. Instead, the glow seemed to grow around her, so that she was unnaturally bright. As she spoke, even to the few who listened, she seemed to become more and more angry. Perhaps she was thinking of what conflict had done to her brothers Abel and Isaac. She might have had in mind the lost brother, Matthew, who simply faded away into silence. Or she might have considered her own life and its servitude to the enemies of freedom. She had lived her life always in opposition to one thing and then another, whether the French, the British, or custom. And now, her chief nemesis was heading for the harbor.

She climbed down and ran, which was not easy with her skirts, and Desdemona was at her side. We finally came to the boats, which the soldiers boarded to a chorus of song, jeers, and laughter. It was nearly impossible to believe. Not only were they going away, they were leaving us with a gift of freedom. I thought for a moment that I was unsure what I might do with such a thing. My service had been pleasant beyond what I deserved, but I was of the servant class nonetheless. Would that class disappear now, and would we all become equals in the eyes of the law and God? I could not imagine such a thing.

I looked for Jenny and her friend, but did not see them for a time. Mr. Dorset and Mr. Smythe suddenly showed up arm in arm, and behind them for a hundred feet were various sheets of Mr. Dorset's masterpiece. He looked at his hand, and, realizing little was left, he threw it down with less thought than you might give the wrapping of a parcel. If Mr. Dorset suffered from an excess of vanity, he also had by nature a humility which was quite touching.

As the last boat of British troops shoved off into the river, I was startled to see, coming out from a position just upstream, a flat boat being paddled by a single, gray old man, and in the prow, fist up and screaming, Jenny Dorset.

"Look at that!" cried a man next to me. "She is a daughter of liberty!"

I could not quite believe his comment, and it struck me so that I have never forgotten. It may sound theatrical or impossible to the Reader, but I was there that morning, and it was spoken at my side. Jenny indeed seemed to embody something, though more for myself than for anyone else there. She simply could not be still in the presence of this world. I recognized Mr. Thomas Kent not a hundred feet away, and when he saw her, he turned and walked back from the whole spectacle toward the streets behind us.

The boat bearing Jenny and Desdemona could not, of course, keep up with the longboats holding the soldiers, but it was rowed straight out toward them into the broad river anyway. I have often wondered why the old man rowed them out — indeed who he was — and if Jenny paid him well or merely smiled at him when requesting his service. I suppose it does not matter, but I have never ceased to bear the wonder of it in my heart.

Mr. Smythe and Mr. Dorset had turned away from the troops, assuming the spectacle was over, and had walked away, no doubt toward a tavern, all of which did spectacular business that day. I am not sure that anyone on the shore at that time save me ever knew who was in the small boat. One man laughed and said that trollops were trying to collect unpaid fees for their services.

They had gone perhaps a hundred yards offshore when I noticed that the old man seemed to stand up, hunched over like a cruelly malformed creature. He took two steps, and looked down into the boat. He then put his hands on his hips as if something perplexed him, and he took off his hat and set it down. Jenny and Desdemona turned back to see what had happened. The boat began to drift with current toward the bay and thence the sea. I felt my hand rise to let them know I was at their service should something be wrong, but it was a foolish gesture, for they were too far away to see, and there was nothing I could do at that remove anyway.

The stern of the boat suddenly seemed heavy, and the prow was a pivot around which it turned. Jenny and Desdemona came together for a moment and held to each other while the old man wiped the sweat from his brow and made a gesture of defeat and disappointment, though, it seemed to me, not of any grave concern. Then the stern of the boat slipped under the water.

I felt as if the breath had been sucked from my body. The old man jumped into the river and swam a few strokes and then was carried by the river, floating above it, until he simply went under and did not come back up. The bow of the boat lingered above the water for only a moment, but somehow it seemed to last for seconds, minutes, for a lifetime. And then it silently slipped beneath the white lip of the river current.

"Help!" I cried. "Oh, help!"

A few men turned back and came to me, and I pointed out the two women who now seemed suspended at ankle depth in the current, as if they might have risen from some other world.

"After them, men!" cried a man who had a boat tied nearby. It is a fine trait of mankind that someone in danger will be saved if men can but act quickly enough. I leapt into one of three boats which were cast into the river and would not take my eyes off Jenny and Desdemona. I kept crying Jenny's name over and over, begging her somehow to hold on. It seemed to me that she pointed at me, or perhaps it was at Charles Town itself, or past it toward the country and to Longacre. I have told myself that she knew that it was her valedictory moment, and that, like a candle, she had burned herself out. But I take no comfort from that suspicion.

The boat sank suddenly beneath them. The river caught up their large and ornate dresses and seemed to twirl them like flowers in a punch bowl. Jenny and Desdemona held hands above the rushing water for two seconds and then both of them disappeared beneath the water.

"Hurry!" I screamed. "They are in the water!"

The men rowed with all their might, and within three-quarters of a minute we were at the site, but nothing could be seen. Faintly from a distance, I could hear the regimental piper playing a mournful tune on one of the longboats as it headed to the British ships in the bay. The river men expertly steered their craft against the current, and we looked and called, but I knew that Jenny Dorset would not resurface in this life. I kept looking, and we steered downstream, calling and looking, but the current was strong, and I knew that no one could swim against the garments the women wore.

"Believe they're gone, gov," said one of the men in my boat. I was overcome by memory and grief, and sat down with my hands in my lap as we rowed back to shore. I thanked the men and offered to pay them, though all rejected it.

"I shall take care to report it to the authorities," I said.

"And who might that be?" said one man with a laugh. They left, and I went to a large oak tree and sat under it and wept, losing all that precise control I had spent my life attaining. I wanted to leap into the river and swim again to the spot and go down into the flood and reach out for her. But I knew it was a vain gesture and I restrained myself. I thought of my great loss, but, more, I thought of Mr. Dorset, and the necessity of telling him.

I wept for half an hour. Then I stood and made myself proper, took a deep breath, and began to walk back toward the center of Town, where a wild celebration had broken out. Men and women continued to dance in the streets. They fired guns, burned powder bombs, drank, and sang. My feet seemed to have no feeling. I could barely say the name *Jenny Dorset* in my heart without a collapse. I tried to smile as I walked slowly back toward Jenny's house, but I could not, for my heart, and all that was in it, was broken.

I finally dragged myself through the riotous streets and to Jenny's stairs. I came inside and closed the door behind me, only to find Mr. Adam Dorset standing in the parlor singing "Victory at Longacre" at the top of his voice, holding a bottle in one hand. He came to me and embraced me.

"Why so glum now?" he asked. "This is the day of our liberation! Here, share a drink with me from this bottle!" I shook my head, and then, quite uncharacteristically, I did so, sampling a long draught of the rum it held. The spirits braced me but gave me no more courage.

"Sir, you should brace yourself for the greatest of shocks," I said.

"Shocks? Waugh, no shock can defeat the glory of this day!" he said. "I believe I shall take up the art of fresco, for none else but myself could paint the jubilation!"

"Sir, your daughter Jenny has drowned in the Cooper River," I said.

He was caught, rising on his toes, before he could make another point. I wished I had died before I had to tell him of that greatest of losses. His face was suddenly vulnerable, almost childlike, and he begged me with his eyes to tell him it was a bit of mischief. I could not do so, and it took all my powers of restraint to keep from losing my control altogether.

"What did you say?" he whispered. His eyes still hoped he had misheard me, but his heart seemed to know it was true. I sagged for a moment and then pulled myself aright.

"She and Desdemona Smartt have been drowned in the river," I said miserably. "You had gone back, and she hired an old boatman to row them out to harry the departing troops. When a hundred yards from shore, the boat foundered, and all were lost."

"You are mistaken, of course," he said, turning away and nodding. "It was another and another, but not Jenny. She has been in scrapes before, has she not, Hawthorne?" He turned to me as if his argument might reverse the tide of history that had now overwhelmed us.

"She has, sir," I said. "But it is my sad duty to report that there is no doubt of the course of these events. I gathered a number of the men to go out with me into the river in boats and search for them, but they had disappeared beneath the water. She and Desdemona had worn fine gowns and the weight pulled them under. I must express to you my sincere regrets for the loss of such a fine child."

"But she might have resurfaced and then floated to the shore?" he begged. "How can you be sure of this intelligence?"

"Sir, she went under and did not come back up," I said. "I watched for quite a long time and searched for her. The currents are strong and would have taken her away from the land and into the bay."

"Toward the British ships at anchor," he said absently.

"Yes, sir," I said. "I must give to you my most sincere regrets."

"Then she is truly gone," he said, less as a question than as a statement with which he was trying out to discern its truth.

"I regret to say so," I said. "And if I might say, she was the most extraordinary woman I ever knew, and I am certain we shall not look upon her like again in this lifetime."

"Thank you," he said softly. He set the bottle on a table and walked to the window and looked out, standing erect with his hands behind his back. Men and women and children ran in the streets, shouting, hugging, dancing. The world seemed to have risen on the feet of Charles Town.

"Sir, may I attend you, or do you wish to have time for yourself?" I asked.

"I cannot believe she would be gone from this world," he said. "Of all the losses and sorrow a man must suffer in this brief life, to lose such an ornament seems cruel and incalculable. She was the dear love of my life, and I cannot believe that I shall survive that loss very long."

"We survive as we can when those losses overtake us on this road," I said. "We think of them in our wretchedness and then bless the memory and move on. We can only believe that we shall join them in Heaven, for other than that would be unbearable."

"Shall God allow Jenny into Heaven, do you suppose?" he said.

"She is already on those streets," I said. "And they are in celebration that she has finally arrived. God must be in His glory, for He allowed her to be with us for this life, and now He has her at His side for the measure of eternity."

Mr. Dorset sat in a chair, a broken man, and wept. I touched him on the shoulder and was about to leave him alone to his grief, when he called me back from the hall where I had stationed myself.

"The child," he said, brightening slightly. "What of Jenny's daughter? Might we find her, do you think?" I had not considered her daughter that morning — indeed had entirely forgotten about her.

"It would be a journey to be desired," I said. "Perhaps your greatest journey, sir? The one by which your name shall be known for all time?"

"Jenny's name shall endure and my blood as well," he said.

"I have no doubts," I said.

For two days thereafter, we searched the shore, spoke with fishermen, hired men to search for Jenny and Desdemona, but it was to no avail. On the third day, the body of the man who had steered that final course in his wretched boat floated back toward Town on the tide. It was rescued and buried by his family, but of the other two, there was no trace.

"The old man would have come back," said Mr. Dorset glumly. "Old men return to what they have known and loved best. The young are always gone for the adventure of it. Jenny might be in the Indies by now. Do you think?"

We could not leave Jenny's soul unhonored, and so Mr. Dorset arranged for the subminister at St. Michael's to accompany us to Longacre so that a few words might be spoken over the family burial plot. Mr. Smythe, who had comforted my Master in his sorrow, was invited, and he in turn told a few others who had been friends of both men. I had not been to Longacre in some time, and what I saw was like the crushing weight of a heavy stone. Since Isaac's death, the house had been empty, the servants gone, the slaves sold away. British soldiers and then patriots had encamped in it. The once lush grounds had gone entirely wild, and the house was falling into ruin.

"That once was mine," said Mr. Dorset without bitterness. "And look, Hawthorne. The world has come to reclaim it for her own. But I have it stored in my heart, where it shall not pass until *I* do."

The service for Jenny had been set for eleven o'clock on that day, a Tuesday, as I recall, and soon a few carriages and horsemen arrived. We had no way to serve them, of course, and I was somewhat befuddled by what I should do. In the end, I did nothing but stand close to Mr. Dorset. By ten o'clock, something truly astonishing had begun to occur. A long and steady line of mourners began to arrive from all directions: from Town, from the plantations to the east on the Cooper River, from those to the west on the Ashley River. Mr. Dorset looked startled and touched. The subminister seemed to grow taller as he realized his audience was to be far greater than he could have known.

"Can you imagine it?" said Mr. Dorset in wonder. Mr. Smythe was at his side.

"I can imagine it and more," said Mr. Smythe. "She was greatly loved and admired by all."

"She loved many, it is true," said Mr. Dorset doubtfully. "But is that not a fine thing for a woman of culture, my friend? Love hath no season and lays claim only to those who welcome her. And who would not have welcomed my Jenny?"

"Anyone who wished for love or who dreamt of it," said Mr. Smythe.

"Then what is called sin may have its reconciliations in both number and variety," said Mr. Dorset. "That is a comfort to me."

"*There* is your comfort," said Mr. Smythe. He gestured to the road, where a steady line of people was now emerging, dozens of them. Proper men with their sympathetic wives arrived in carriages. Some men arrived with wives still bowed and scowling over memories of the most beautiful woman ever to grace Charles Town. Others, like Mr. Thomas Kent, arrived alone and stayed by themselves, declining the intercourse with others. Mr. Dorset was in his element, speaking to all who had known Jenny, loved her, heard of her exploits. As for myself, I stayed to the side, watching and thinking of Jenny with affection and regret.

The service was held at the family burial ground, which had grown over somewhat. My life and my history were in that ground as much as was Mr. Dorset's. I thought of them all, from Old Bob to Miss Tonning, and, strange to say, I was not morose or melancholy in the least. I felt a reward in having been granted age enough as the bearer of their witness. Most men live until those who have known them are gone. Then they are no more than words upon a stone, the flesh, the laughter, the families, all forgotten. That is as it must be. But a true witness has his values as well, and I believe now that I was spared by God to write this History so that others might know and remember those who were true and real, flesh and bone, and who brought me happiness in this life, and love.

By the time the subminister began his service, more than a hundred people were at the site, and Mr. Dorset was so touched that he wept and tears dripped slowly off his cheeks. Mr. Smythe stood ready at his side to hold him up if need be, but it was unnecessary. Mr. Thomas Kent stood far to one side where he could not hear well, but I knew that it was not necessary that he hear. He was present, and that was enough.

I will not present the message of the subminister in the service, for it was drab, self-important, full of standard pieties, and altogether inappropriate. But I do not believe many people listened to him anyway. More seemed lost in their thoughts about Jenny Dorset. When the minister said his final *amen* and shook hands with Mr. Dorset, I was startled, as were many, to find that it was over.

The crowd left only slowly, the long line standing in the hot sun to shake hands with Mr. Dorset and bear their regrets to him. He seemed to enjoy it, but by midafternoon, he was exhausted. Mr. Smythe hugged him and left as well, and Mr. Dorset and I were alone.

"She was a fine girl, was she not?" Mr. Dorset asked.

"Fine indeed, and I shall miss her more than I can possibly express," I said. "I am sorry for your loss."

"But she was ours for a time, wasn't she?" he said. "That is how I know there is a God above, for even fools receive great gifts. And they lose them as well."

We stood there for a long time in the cool air of December, each lost in his thoughts, before we went back to Town.

— 16. —
A dinner in Town at Mr. Dorset's house, during which
he and Mr. Smythe exchange startling secrets.

In mid-January, during a siege of foul weather, Mr. Dorset invited Mr. Smythe to our house to dine. We prepared an excellent meal, built fine fires, and had at table rare wines, of which they each consumed two full bottles. They talked volubly of the British, and the new freedom that we were about to possess. Would we be ready for it? How would we manage on our own?

"No doubt the new states will need a poet laureate, and I am prepared to nominate myself for that high honor," said Mr. Dorset.

"You *should* nominate yourself, for no one else would," said Mr. Smythe.

"Jealousy does not become you, old friend," said Mr. Dorset, to which Mr. Smythe merely laughed.

"You overrate your virtues as a poet," said Mr. Smythe.

"As you overrate yours as a critic," said Mr. Dorset. "What then shall you offer to be in the new state?"

"I should think king," said Mr. Smythe. Mr. Dorset laughed riotously.

"As if the one who lately ruled us were not mad enough," he said. "Now you wish us to suffer King Smythe? And where would your palace be laid?"

"Somewhere that a nearby fool would not debate the merits of a poor three feet of land," said Mr. Smythe. "And where a jester of a certain age and lack of talent in verse might amuse my subjects."

"Waugh!" cried Mr. Dorset. "Is that an offense?"

"Yes, and what of it?" asked Mr. Smythe. Mr. Dorset drained his glass.

"Nothing, I suppose," he said. "But then you should remarry so that you shall have a queen and more children to inherit your title. In fact, we should both have more children."

"Upon that score, I have a modest confession to make," said Mr. Smythe.

"Confession is good for the soul," said Mr. Dorset.

"You know the twins Molly and Tom McNew, who lived so long at Longacre in your service before they came to mine?"

"Certainly."

"They were my children by a woman whose name I do not wish to speak."

"Blast me into h—l!" cried Mr. Dorset. "And do you know Desdemona and Roderigo Smartt who lived at Foxhaven before they came to live with me?"

"You cannot be serious!" shouted Mr. Smythe.

"They were my children by a woman whose name I do not wish to speak!" cried Mr. Dorset.

I sat from my station near the door into a chair and uttered a curse which I thought was soft enough not to be heard, but I was wrong. Both of the men looked at me and began to laugh. At first, I could hardly make it clear in my mind, but then I understood: Desdemona Smartt was Jenny Dorset's half sister. At first I thought it too amusing to believe, but slowly, I understood that Mr. Dorset on the morning of December 14 had lost two children at a single stroke, even if one was illegitimate. Of course, none of the bastard children could inherit what little the men had to leave them, but the revelation of their parentage seemed somehow correct in the grand plan of God for these two men.

"We have had a fine life and have failed in it, have we not?" said Mr. Smythe.

"Failed?" said Mr. Dorset. "Of course. All men must die, and in that death is failure. But I shall take away no more than I brought to the world. And I must say that I have not wasted this life in idle motion."

"Nor have I," said Mr. Smythe. "May I propose a toast, then?"

"Certainly."

The men stood (though Mr. Dorset unsteadily), and held up their glasses. The wine twinkled in the firelight through the crystal, and, for a moment, I was swept up in the color and friendship of the men.

"To we who have survived," he said. "May we bear witness to the pleasures and the pains of our day henceforth in this new America."

"Indeed," said Mr. Adam Dorset.

They drank, and, in that moment, reached the high point of a friendship (or quarrel) which had lasted for several decades. I was touched and wished that somehow our life could continue with such comfort for years to come.

God, however, in His mercy, does not merely harvest in the autumn as men do, but takes them as He wishes to enter His service. And so the time came all too soon when He looked upon our Town and made yet another decision regarding my life.

— 17. —

A FATEFUL DUEL WHICH NEVER QUITE TAKES PLACE.
THE SORROWFUL OUTCOME.

Charles Town was unsure of itself after the British left, as the war was slowly coming to a close. The drunken revels finally ceased for the most part, and the great men of our Town began to restore order and to put in gaol those who continued to deny that the time for celebration was past. I spent my time keeping house with our small domestic staff and taking long walks in the countryside, during which I contemplated my life and its variety. I wrote letters to my daughters and asked that they come to visit, but the journey was still somewhat dangerous, and they declined, having to attend their children and husbands. I understood, but I wished for more that I was able to receive. I planned to visit one in Williamsburg, but my health was somewhat fragile that spring of 1783, and so I delayed (to my future sorrow).

Mr. Dorset was at loose ends, as the saying goes. He had enough money upon which to live and pay for his servants, but not enough to start a business, for which he cared nothing anyway. He continued to write poetry and music, but taste had improved over the previous years, and no one would any longer print or perform his works. He was not deterred by this, blaming the stupidity of others rather than his own lack of talent. I believe he was correct in that attitude, for it kept his faith in himself and kept him occupied.

I was sitting alone one evening in March in the parlor, smoking my pipe and thinking about my late wife, when the door burst open and four men came in carrying Mr. Dorset, who smelled strongly of wine and gunpowder. I stood and then saw in horror that a bloody bandage was wrapped around his right hand.

"What has happened?" I asked.

"He was going to fight a duel with some man over honor, and his pistol blew up in his hand," said a man I had never seen.

"Honor," said Mr. Dorset, who was very drunk. "It was a matter of honor."

"My God," I said. "Lay him here in this chair. And fetch a doctor."

They left, and I was alone with Mr. Dorset. I pulled the bandage away and was shocked to see that most of his right hand was gone, and out of the wound, his life's blood was pouring. I ripped off my shirt and bound the wound as tightly as I could.

"Hawthorne, it was about honor," he said.

"Whose honor?"

"D—d if I remember," he said after a few moments of silence. "Was that important?"

"No," I said. "If it was about honor, then it was correct."

"I believe I shall expire," he said. "Shall I?"

"No, sir," I said. "You cannot die."

"Friend," he said softly. "Is this not the new adventure? My Lyddie and three of my children are there already. What should I have to fear?"

"You should fear nothing," I said. The binding on his hand could not stanch the blood, and I stood by helplessly and knew that I could do nothing now to save his life. He sang snatches of his compositions, spoke a few lines of poetry of which I was not familiar, and then tried to stand. His strength was waning, however, and he could not.

"I am a South Carolininan, by God!" he said. "Bred to the palmetto and the . . . uh, what else am I bred to?"

"All else," I said. A fear of unsurpassed magnitude came to me, and I began to tremble without control for a moment, and then it subsided, and the fear went out of me, even in the presence of Death.

"All else," he said. "Shall I see my Jenny?"

"You shall," I said.

"Then it is well," he said. "All is well."

With that, he smiled peacefully, rearranged himself as if he were settling for a pleasant sleep, and died. I watched him for a long time, sitting in the silence of the house, and wishing that I had passed away before I saw that noble family pass before me. But God will have His plan fulfilled, and I could not question it. I wept for a few moments and then set about preparing for yet another funeral.

Mr. Smythe was devastated when he heard of the misfortune. I had already arranged for Mr. Dorset's body to be prepared, and it was at the undertaking establishment when Mr. Smythe came running into the house.

"It is true, then?" he asked.

"It is true," I said. Mr. Smythe sat, without knowing it, in the very chair where Mr. Dorset had died. He wept for a time and kept asking if there was any longer a use in living. I brought him a cup of tea, which he drank. He tried to talk to me about my late Master, but his emotions overcame him at every turn. Finally, he was able to bring himself under control somewhat.

"Did you ever know a man more full of life?" he asked.

"I did not," I admitted.

"Or a daughter more beautiful?"

"I did not."

He seemed lost in thought for a moment.

"I believe that I was half in love with her all my life," he said.

"I, too, share those sentiments," I said. I was surprised that I had said something so bold in front of a superior, but it was true, and I knew it.

"We must plan for him the grandest funeral in the history of Charles Town," said Mr. Smythe.

"I quite agree," I said. "But that is beyond my abilities."

"I shall take charge of it," he said.

And so he did. Two days later, St. Michael's resounded with trumpets. I had not known that Mr. Dorset was held in such esteem, for the church was entirely full, and the service moved with a magnificence of which Mr. Dorset would have entirely approved. The minister — not the subminister — presided, and Mr. Smythe, who had worked around the clock, had seen to every detail. As a tribute, a man and wife musical team performed "Victory at Longacre," he playing the spinet and she singing. It did not sound quite as ridiculous as it had those many years ago. Then Mr. Penfield Van Dyke recited part of the long poem about our adventure to the Indies, and though he approached it seriously, the congregation was full of smiles and knowing glances. I must admit that I smiled myself, for it was so fanciful and inventive, though entirely untrue, that it entertained me.

The sermon was very long, self-important, and boring, and I wished for a time that the subminister had been available for the job. But I scarcely listened to it anyway. My mind was far away, thinking of adventures and the faces of those with whom I had spent my life. I found that I was no longer sad regarding Mr. Dorset's passing, indeed was filled with a surpassing calm. I thought of Old Bob and the days when the family was together; of Matthew Dorset spending time in his studies of animal husbandry; of the wild and wayward pack of dogs; of the dispute and duel over three feet of property line; of the duel of bowls on the lawn to which Mr. Dorset never arrived, having struck his head on a limb. My life had lacked nothing, and I had been blessed to be a witness to wonderful things. For what reason should I mourn?

Mr. Smythe arranged for the cortege to go to Longacre for the burial, and the sight of the minister of St. Michael's there blessing the grave was strange to me. Yet it was a new year and a new country, and the final arrival of the great man of the church amused me. In his late years, Mr. Dorset had suffered few bouts of piety, as he had in his youth, but if he had, the presence of the minister would surely have cheered him.

Soon, the service was over, and my Master was comfortably covered next to Lydia Foxe Dorset for his eternal sleep. I shook hands with many important people, and finally only Mr. Smythe and I were left. He asked if I would like to accompany him back to Town.

"No, sir, I believe I shall ride back alone," I said.

"What will you do now?" he asked.

"I shall seek other employment," I said. "The house will now belong to Matthew Dorset, wherever he is."

"I shall see to it that he knows of this," said Mr. Smythe. "Remain at the house, and I will come and see you tomorrow."

"That is most kind, sir," I said. He shook my hand and left.

I found a patch of wildflowers and lay one on each grave, including Miss Tonning's, for which I asked the spirit of Mr. Dorset to forgive me. I walked back to the house where my horse was tied and lazily munching the long grass. The structure had long fallen into ruin, and part of it had been burned, though whether from the hand of Man or Nature I could not say. The front door had fallen away, and part of the ceiling was missing. I walked into it and tried to remember what it had been like thirty years before, when a family had flourished there. Little sign was left as to the world which we inhabited. I was then fifty-eight years of age, and I felt sure that soon I would join my wife in the earth of Longacre.

Of course, I was wrong about that. God had plans for me and so allowed me time to write this History and see the new country grow and flourish. I stood that day in the ruins of the house and felt a kind of exultation, for I knew that God had a reason for my life, as He did for that magnificent family called Dorset.

— 18. —
THE END OF THIS HISTORY. THE TOLL OF THE YEARS, AND THE
PASSING OF MR. SMYTHE. MY DISCOVERY OF A WORK OF ART.
A STARTLING RUMOR WHICH I FEEL INCLINED TO PURSUE.

I was never to work for Mr. Charles Smythe. We talked about it for some days before the idea slipped his mind. He was unhinged, as it were, by the loss of his friend, and with little to occupy his time began to drink to excess. Less than a year later at the age of sixty-two, he died in his sleep.

I had written several times to Matthew Dorset in the North, and I had enlisted, against my inclinations, the help of a lawyer regarding the estate of the Dorset family. Though the lawyer could not rightfully say to whom the house belonged, he said it clearly was not mine. Matthew did not answer repeated missives, and so it was ordered that the house be put up for auction. A certain Quinch, a man in the trades and late from Bristol, bought it.

"It was the home of Jenny Dorset," I said proudly as he sealed the purchase.

"And who might she have been?" he asked.

I cleaned out what I could from the house and moved into rooms in a boarding house on Tradd Street. The situation was not unpleasant, and the landlady was a fine Christian woman who possessed both sense and honor. I soon found employment in service to the Viscount Anthony Clark, a man of a certain age who was constantly involved with intrigues and adventures and had his own share of amours. I worked for him from 1783 until 1791. He was a strange and amazing man, but, as those years do not contribute to this History, I will silently pass them over here.

During that time, I lost both my daughters to illnesses, and for the better part of a year I was inconsolable. They were survived by their husbands and two children each, and though I tried to maintain contact, it was ultimately broken. I knew of these events only by dispatch, and so was deprived of seeing either again. I console myself with memory of them as children, as I do with the memory of my wife.

For some time after Mr. Dorset's death, I was disinclined to look at the papers and belongings which I saved from the auctioneer's gavel. Finally, several years later when I was settled at the Viscount's home, I brought into my lodgings several of the large crates of papers that I had saved and began to go through them. I discovered many letters and Jenny Dorset's journals, along with copies of Mr. Dorset's poems and songs, both those he had caused to be printed and those only in manuscript form. It was while perusing this material that I came across an astonishing discovery.

It was a poem in Mr. Dorset's hand. The paper upon which it had been composed was stained with wine and had a few holes, where burning cinders from his pipe had obviously fallen on it. As I read it, I was shaken, for it showed an art and a sensitivity that I did not believe Mr. Dorset ever possessed.

JENNY DORSET

And so my darling joy hath fled to Heaven's door,
Where God rejoices in His fortune and His time,
To have before Him one whose loss has made us poor,
A girl whose tenderness once alone was mine.

She came into this life when all the day was bright,
When only half my days on pleasant Earth were done.
She brought a luminescence even to the night,
And brought a brighter face unto the brightest sun.

I loved her well and lost her to the endless wave
Of sea that God hath brought upon this sweetened shore.
Had I been the man to reach for her and save,
I should have done it, giving all my life and more.

But now she lives on High where angels fold their wings,
And sorrow has no claim on hearts or sullen time.
And all the host of Heaven in their pleasure sing
For one whose kind and loving heart alone was mine.

I had the poem set into type and properly printed, but it was too sacred to show to anyone, though now I present it here as a final legacy for Mr. Adam Dorset.

That would write FINIS to this History, were it not for an amazing rumor that I heard last evening at the Black Cat Tavern. (Though I am now seventy years of age, I do still enjoy my modest pleasures.) Several men there spoke freely of a woman new to Town, of whom it is said she once had relatives in the vicinity but no longer does. She is perhaps twenty years of age, very beautiful, with blond hair, and a fresh and forward demeanor. She spoke with great urgency about political matters and yet drank and cursed like a sailor. One man who had seen her said no such woman had ever been seen in Charles Town.

I cannot believe more than I can see, but I will be curious enough during my regular morning walk to ask more questions and to seek this new marvel out. Would God have such a humor that He would bring my life to a close in such a way? I can only wish it to be so.

It is a beautiful day, and our new country delights in its liberty. The younger men now take our freedom nearly for granted, but they will learn as they grow. Nature may be frugal or extravagant by turns, and perhaps that is the lesson of these lives which I have chronicled. This Earth will take us back soon enough, and if we have grace and fortune, we may linger enough to see amazing things.

But I shall never again see such a woman as Jenny Dorset. From this enduring distance, she yet holds the secrets of my grateful heart.